D0994374

Jeff Gulvin was born in 1962 and has lived in various parts of the UK, New Zealand and Idaho, USA. He currently lives in Norfolk with his two daughters.

JEFF GULVIN

THE COVENANT

ORION

An Orion paperback

First published in Great Britain in 2000
by Orion
This paperback edition published in 2001
by Orion Books Ltd,
Orion House, 5 Upper St Martin's Lane,
London WC2H 9EA

A CIP catalogue record for this book is available
from the British Library.

ISBN 0 75284 327 3

Printed and bound in Great Britain by
Clays Ltd, St Ives plc

This novel is dedicated to my dad

GLOSSARY

ASAC	assistant special agent in charge	IAD	International Activities Division
ATF	Alcohol, Tobacco and Firearms (Bureau of)	INS	Immigration and Naturalization Service
BLM	Bureau of Land Management	ISA	Intelligence Support Activity
DCI	Director of Central Intelligence	JTTF	joint terrorism task force
DDO	deputy director of operations	NCIC	National Crime Information Center
DGSE	Directoire Générale du Service Extérieur	NSA	National Security Agency
EOD	Explosives Ordnance Disposal	2nd REP	Régiment des Etrangers Parachutistes
FEMA	Federal Emergency Management Agency	SWAT	special weapons and tactics
		TOC	tactical operations center

Prologue

February

Texas sky, purple and black above his head.

Tom Carey squatted on his rucksack, gazing up, straining the muscles in his neck. Beyond the railroad tracks, the land stretched endless and flat to the shadows of mountains far in the distance. The warmth still clung to the ground, though darkness had fallen early. No stars. No moon. The cloud pressed the heat to the earth. South of him was the Rio Grande. This morning he had woken up in a cheap hotel in Del Rio, with last night's beer thumping in his head, and even water was unwelcome in his gut. He had run out of cash: he and Steve in some dive of a *cantina* that rang with Tex-Mex music, where sweat-stained Mexican women danced with one another. A far cry from London. A far cry from anywhere he had ever been. He had woken with the hangover and then tried to get money on his MasterCard from an ATM machine. But it would not work and he could not understand why. Steve got the bus to San Antonio that morning, then on to Dallas for the flight home. Tom had thought about it, but he did not want to go back until he had seen Mardi Gras.

He looked at his watch, the hands illuminated in the darkness. Far in the distance, he heard the mournful lament of the train's horn sounding across the desert. He imagined the clank of the wheels and the straining wood of the boxcars, and a shiver of anticipation ran the length of his spine. He had never jumped a train in his life, and yet here he was, sitting at the peak of the curve where the track circumnavigated the lake. Logic told him the train would be at its slowest at this point; and he had seen the open boxcars many times from a distance. Anything heading east would take him closer to New Orleans and there were only three days until Mardi Gras. Once he hit another big town, he would try his MasterCard again, and if that didn't work, he could phone his mother in England.

Excitement bubbled in his throat as he watched the beam from the headlight cut into the vast expanse of Kinney County nothingness. Highway 90 uncoiled like a rattlesnake to Uvalde, with a few hick towns in between. No-man's-land, that's what it felt like. One hundred years ago this place had still been pretty lawless. Fifty years before that, it was totally lawless. Texas. Mexico. The Alamo. Images of the past clicked through his mind like a movie reel, as the train rolled closer and closer. Most of the afternoon he had sat here, waiting, hoping a train would come by before dark. But then, as the sky purpled above him, he did not care any more. The day had been soundless except for the distant drone of the odd truck on the highway, or an aircraft sweeping in low to Laughlin. When darkness fell, he still sat there, sipping water and listening to the sounds of the desert at night, watching desert squirrels make one last foray for food before heading for the burrow. The train drew closer. He stood up and headed towards the tracks.

His rucksack hung off one shoulder and he felt like some old hobo who had ridden the skids for years, not an awestruck kid from England about to begin his medical degree. He thought of his mother in London and his father in Cape Town, and for a moment he saw the beach from Table Mountain and imagined Christmas, surfing. The train drew closer and he was Lee Marvin, king of the rails, climbing through the Rockies in an open boxcar, with the sky grazed scarlet above his head and a harmonica pressed to his lips.

The locomotive rumbled by at no more than ten miles an hour and he found himself walking, then trotting, as the coal-laden cars passed him first. He hoped they weren't all carrying coal, the ride would be dirty if they were. But the train was long, even by American standards, and pretty soon the coal cars gave way to flatbeds carrying containers and then the boxcars, some open, some with roofs, and most with side doors slid open. He picked a roofed wooden car and ran alongside the track, thinking how foolish it would be to fall now and slip under those wheels and be ground into mincemeat in Texas. He was careful – the loose stones and shale dragging at his feet. Pack in hand, he hoisted it ahead of him, then grabbed the side of the door and jumped. Belly over the lip he dangled for a moment, getting his balance, and then hauled himself up and rolled into the darkness. He sat for a second just getting his bearings. The boxcar was very dark, blacker than the greyed landscape he had come from, and it took him a few moments to adjust his vision. He could smell wood grain and dust and what he thought was sugar beet, but he might have been mistaken. Getting to his feet, he found he could stand OK without holding on to the door. He shuffled his pack into a corner with his foot, then looked to see if he had interrupted any sleeping hobo. He had not and in a way he was disappointed. He had rather hoped he might share his car with some old-timer, some gentleman of the rails. A song suddenly rang in his head. 'He rode the rails since the Great Depression, fifty years out on the skids.' Bruce Springsteen. He had taken his mother to see the great man perform solo at the Brixton Academy, a couple of years previously. From his pack, he took out his Walkman and fitted the tiny headphones into his ears. The land rolled by, featureless in the dark. He sat close to the open side of the car, grateful for the breeze it generated. The wind tugged at his short-cut hair, and he sat and watched the landscape, lunar almost in the darkness. The rhythm of the wheels and the rocking motion of the boxcar carried through his headphones and music was suddenly incongruous with the solitude of the moment.

He woke to Texas sunlight, hot and insistent on his face. He was lying with his head crooked at an awkward angle in the fold of wood that formed the corner of the car. Still alone, nobody else had jumped the train in the night. Again, he was a little crestfallen. He thought he would have bumped into somebody riding the tracks along with him. Maybe the hobos didn't venture this far south. Maybe they had trouble with the border patrol agents he had seen at various locations between here and the big river. Another Springsteen song came to mind and he hummed softly to himself as the car rattled and rocked around him. Outside the sliding wooden door, the world went by as sagebrush and bristled, scrub desert. He took his water from the pack and sipped from it before rescrewing the lid. It was warm, but eased the parched rasp that had developed, with sleep, in his throat.

Morning became afternoon, and he slept in the corner once again and woke as darkness was falling. The first thing he heard were voices. He sat up sharply and fumbled for his pack. Two men faced him. One was sitting directly opposite, looking at him: faded scuffed jeans, leather waistcoat over a yellow T-shirt, and half a beard on his face. His arms and neck were covered with tattoos and his hair was hidden beneath a black bandana. When he opened his mouth to smile, one overlong canine on the left side of his upper jaw dominated his teeth. The second man squatted on his haunches in the open doorway. He was smaller, thinner and younger than the other man. Tattoos protruded in spiders' webs over his elbows from the cut-off sleeves of a denim jacket. He had a drooping handlebar moustache, black and grey with flecks of ginger, and one of his eyes was slightly slanted, so he only half looked out of it. He was rolling a cigarette with one hand and balancing himself with the fisted knuckles of the other. His hair, too, was hidden beneath a black bandana.

'Howdy.' The one with the long tooth smiled at him.

Tom looked back, relaxed and grinned. 'Hello,' he said.

'Where you headed?'

'New Orleans.'

'Mardi Gras?'

'I've never been before.' Tom spoke a little breathlessly, not quite believing he was sharing a boxcar with two ageing hobos covered in tattoos. 'I want to see it before I go home.'

'Where's that?' The man with the tooth reached out and took a newly rolled cigarette from his partner. He plucked a single match from his waistcoat pocket and popped it on his belt buckle, before cupping black-nailed hands to his face.

'England.'

The two hobos looked at one another, then the second man spoke from his perch in the doorway. 'England? Hell, I thought you was from Galveston.'

'Galveston?'

'Sure.' The man gestured to the boy's oriental features. 'I thought all you guys were dug in deep there in shrimp country.'

'No. No. I'm British. From England. My *mother's* from Vietnam.'

Galveston Bay. Another Springsteen song. Tom smiled to himself and the first man cocked his head. 'Guess we missed the joke.'

Tom shook his head.

'Something funny?' The man was staring at him and Tom, suddenly feeling awkward, tried to explain what had gone through his mind. An English kid in America, riding a freight train from the Mexican border to New Orleans for Mardi Gras. Bruce Springsteen songs stuck in his head. It was the stuff of dreams.

'Dreams, huh?' The first man looked at his friend. 'Go figure.' He shifted his position slightly, took a paper-wrapped bottle from his pack and drank. He wiped his mouth, looked over the neck of the bottle at the boy and passed it to his friend. 'What's your name, boy?' he asked.

'Tom.'

'And you're a limey. You're all the way from England.' The boy nodded.

'What you doing in the United States?'

'Just travelling.'

'On your own?'

'I did have a friend with me.'

'Where's he at?' The man from the doorway again.

'He took the bus to San Antonio. He had to get back to England.'

'But not you.' The first man again. 'You wanna see Mardi Gras.'

'If I can get there in time.'

The man took the bottle back, waved it vaguely in the boy's direction, then put it away again. He folded his arms and sucked on his cigarette. 'This here train'll take you all the way if you ride her long enough.'

'Really?' Tom felt a small surge of excitement.

'Oh sure. All the way to New Orleans.' The man showed his tooth again. 'Party town. Mardi Gras. The whole nine yards.'

'How long will it take?' Tom dragged both feet under him and squatted with his back to the wall.

'Oh, you'll be there tomorrow.'

The sun went down and the night was fresher and colder than the previous one. Tom took his fleece jacket from his bag and wrapped himself in it. He was hungry and regretted not spending the few dollars he had left on some bread or something, an *enchilada* maybe, before leaving Del Rio. But he had not, so he would have to go hungry. The two hobos did not have anything, or if they did, they didn't eat it, just smoked and drank from the seemingly bottomless bottle. They appeared friendly enough. Tom laughed and joked with them, told them about England and his plans for the future, while outside, the moon rose full, clear and silver above the desert. When finally he fell asleep, they went through his pack, item by item.

He was dreaming he was lying on the beach in South Africa, watching the women in bikinis play volleyball, nurses from his father's hospital. There was one in particular he liked, with red hair cut short against her scalp.

6

The sand was in his face, irritating his lip, and he woke and rubbed his mouth with the heel of his palm. He could feel hot breath and for a second he wondered where he was. Then the jarring sensation through the floor reminded him – and in the morning he would be in New Orleans for Mardi Gras. But it was not morning. The darkness formed a blanket against the open side of the car and he was looking into the long-toothed hobo's face. His breath stank and there was a coldness in his eyes that reminded Tom of a shark they had caught off Durban.

He scrabbled back, slithering to the wall opposite the open door, his heart rising against his ribs. The thinner one still squatted, almost out of the door and not appearing to hold on to anything, just balanced on the balls of his feet. Long-tooth was watching him, that chill light in his eyes and his head slightly to one side. The cotton bandana was very black and fixed low over his eyes.

'What you doing on my train, gook?' His voice was soft and burred and Tom almost did not hear it.

'What?'

'What you doing in my boxcar?'

Tom was pressing himself against the wooden wall of the car now. He looked from one of them to the other and back again. The skinny one was laughing, somewhere deep in his throat. The wind rushed in from outside and the night was cold and glassy over the desert.

Long-tooth reached behind him, slowly, eyes cold like twin dead weights. And then Tom's own eyes balled as he pulled a revolver from his belt. He snapped open the chamber, gaze not wavering from Tom's, and slipped out three of the shells. He weighed them in the palm of his hand, moved them over one another with his fingers. Then he snapped the gun shut and spun it round by the triggerguard. Tom had been so intent on him that he hadn't noticed the skinny one move away from the door. Now he looked up and saw that a 9mm was pointed at his stomach.

Long-tooth laughed quietly, spun the pistol again and handed it, butt first, to Tom.

'We're gonna play us a little game,' he said softly. 'Trip's long and I'm bored. We got hours till we get to New Orleans.'

Tom just stared at the gun. He could not quite believe this was happening.

'Take the fucking gun.' Long-tooth's voice chipped like shards of glass. Tom flinched as if they had physically struck him. He reached out and took the pistol – it was heavy, much heavier than he would have thought. It occurred to him vaguely that he had never held a gun before. It was cold against his palm. Long-tooth leered at him. The other one sat against the wall with his gun arm resting on his knee. 'Spin the chamber, asshole. Let's see what you got.'

Tom still looked at the gun in his hand, then he felt the point of something sharp pressing against the soft flesh of his thigh. He looked down and saw Long-tooth holding a switchblade. 'You got two choices.' His breath stank of tobacco and stale alcohol. 'Either you spin that chamber, put the pistol to your head and squeeze – or I cut your balls off.' He grinned then, and pressed the knife a little harder.

Tom closed his eyes and squirmed. 'Please,' he whispered. 'Don't make me do this.'

The man shifted his position so he was closer to him. 'OK. Then I cut off your balls, stuff them in your mouth and let my buddy here gut-shoot you. Ever see a man who was gut-shot? Ain't pretty. Takes a long while to die.' He jabbed his thumb at the open doorway. 'We toss you over the side and let the vultures pick your entrails.'

Tom opened his eyes and stared at him, thinking this was a joke, hoping this was only a joke. He thought of his mother in London. His father. But the hobo was not smiling. His eyes were black and cold and he pressed again with the knife. 'Spin the chamber, boy.'

Sweat on his palm, Tom span the chamber. Slowly,

inexorably, he lifted the weapon to his temple and felt the chill of the metal against his flesh. Finger in the trigger-guard, the breath stopped up in his throat. The hobo's dead eyes, the knife and the black 9mm. He applied the faintest pressure on the trigger and his hand shook. 'If it's empty, that's the end of the game. Right?'

'Sure.' The hobo showed his tooth. Tom squeezed and, as he did, tears broke on his cheeks. He held the hobo's glassy stare and a Springsteen song lifted spectral in his head: 'Somebody killed him just to kill.'

Etienne Laforge nosed the white Crown Victoria through the open-fronted freight yard north of Hahnville and caught the security guard in the beam of the headlights. A tall black man with a pistol slung low on his left hip, he flagged the cruiser to a standstill. Laforge looked sideways at Robbins, his partner, and the two deputies got out of the car. Laforge tugged at his belt buckle as was his habit. 'You the guy that called us?' he said to the black man.

'That's right. You all got here real quick.'

'We were in the area, bro. What you got?'

'I got me a white male with his head blowed off, is what I got.'

Laforge cocked his head to one side, reached to his shirt pocket for a toothpick and stuck it in the corner of his mouth. He nodded. 'You wanna show us where he's at.'

'*He's* either in heaven or in hell, Mr Deputy. I can show you where the body's at.'

Robbins stared at him. 'Joke a minute, ain't you.'

'You ever do this job?'

Robbins snorted. 'Do I look like I'm stupid?'

The black man laughed then. 'Jokes is all you got, man. Jokes is all you got.' He shook his head and twisted away on his heel. He signalled over his shoulder, shining his flashlight ahead of him, and picked his way between the empty boxcars and coal carriers to the lines at the far side of the yard. 'Tracks run in back here,' he said. 'Trains come in and unload for road freight to the river.'

'Right on.' Laforge tried to sound enthusiastic.

The guard stopped by an open-sided car and shone his torch inside. He looked back at them and his teeth were very white in the darkness. 'Kinda messy. Hope you boys didn't eat dinner.'

Laforge hated the sight of blood. He always had done. He swallowed, glanced at Robbins, then stepped forward, upending his own torch over his shoulder. The stiff lay against the far wall, a mass of bloodied bone and tissue above his shoulders. Laforge gagged, forced the vomit down and took a handkerchief from his pocket.

'Smelly, huh.' The guard shook his head. 'Awful hot for February. I figure he's been here a coupla days.'

Laforge looked again. He could make out black hair and eye sockets, bloated cups of flesh with the eyeball missing from one. The skull was shattered inwards from one side, and bits of bone, tissue and shrivelled muscle poked at odd angles across what was left of his features. He looked away again. 'Any ID?'

The guard slapped the floor of the car which stood chest height from the ground. 'This is as far as I got, brother. I *know* I don't look stupid.' He laughed again, slapped his thigh and took a cigarette from a pack in his shirt pocket.

Laforge turned to Robbins. 'Better get on to the sheriff, John. We're gonna need homicide dicks down here.'

Joe Kinsella, the chief of deputies, phoned the sheriff at home and told him about the body as soon as the road unit called in. Unlike New Orleans, the crime rate in St Charles Parish was low. They had a large jail above the Hahnville courthouse which was rarely full and the sheriff kept fending off those politicians who wanted to build another. No need, he told them. You elected me sheriff to keep the crime rate down and that's what I'm doing. Half of those who had elected him were developers vying for the contract.

Kinsella was forty-two years old, with short dark hair and a moustache. He was a little chunky round the middle these days. Louisiana born and bred, he had been an FBI agent for five years before coming home to this job when Clements got elected sheriff. Clements was old family Louisiana and Kinsella was old family, but Clements knew next to nothing about law enforcement. He was a damn good lawyer, however, so between them they worked things pretty well. This boxcar thing sounded like a homicide, and Kinsella hadn't had a homicide since the coke whore murders three years previously. He took his jacket from the back of his chair and popped a fingerful of chew under his lip. The road unit had the evidence technicians en route and the doctor had been summoned, but had not arrived as yet. All Kinsella knew was the obvious death determination: gun-shot wounds to the head.

He parked his car next to the cruiser Robbins and Laforge drove. Laforge looked a bit green round the gills. He was a squeamish sonofabitch at the best of times.

Kinsella spat tobacco juice. 'What we got, Etienne?'

'Looks like a homicide, boss. Guy with his head blowed off.'

Kinsella glanced round the freight yard. 'No doc yet, huh?'

Laforge shook his head.

'Who found him?'

'Bull over there.' Laforge pointed with his billy club to where the black guard was sitting smoking on a lump of wood by a blackened open fireplace. Kinsella grunted, nodded and strode over to the crime scene. Robbins had just about finished taping the area off, and Kinsella pushed underneath it and shone his flashlight into the boxcar. Quickly, expertly, he took in the scene. The victim lay on his side, arms smothered beneath him against the back wall of the car. The entry wound was on the right side of his head, a close-quarter shot. Kinsella would put money on the pathologist finding powder burns on the skin. A handgun

11

then. To the side of the head – it was either execution or suicide. He could see no weapon lying around, so that discounted suicide. Carefully, he took an unopened packet of surgical gloves from his pocket and stripped the cellophane off. Laforge was next to him now, shining his torch. The floor area was dusty and Kinsella could make out at least two separate sets of footprints.

'I don't figure he shot himself, do you?' Laforge said in his ear.

'I don't figure anything for sure yet, Etienne. You wanna make detective, you got that to learn already. Figure nothing till you have all the evidence in your possession.' He chewed his lip. 'Alls I can see so far is a close-quarter bullet wound or wounds to the head. Either he did it or somebody else.' He pointed to the scuff marks on the floor. 'Looks like he wasn't alone, though, and I don't see a gun. Do you?'

He turned then and strode over to the security guard, who flipped his cigarette butt into the fireplace and sat with his arms folded, his long legs stretched in front of him.

'Joe Kinsella. Chief of Deputies.' Kinsella offered his hand. The guard shook it and stood up. 'Raymond Floyd Patterson.'

Kinsella raised an eyebrow and Patterson shook his head. 'I know I don't even look like him and I hate the fight game. Figure my daddy either had a sense of humour or ambition, don't you?'

Kinsella smiled. 'You've not touched anything back there?' He jabbed a thumb over his shoulder.

'No, sir.'

'Good.'

'You know who he is yet?'

'No. Can't touch him till the doctor certifies him dead.'

'Oh he *dead* all right. I told your deputies he was dead when I called you up.'

'I know it. The law, though, Raymond. Gotta be a doctor who tells us he's dead.'

The doctor arrived, certified him dead and conducted his

12

preliminary investigation. Then the evidence technicians went to work. They found no ID, driver's licence or social security card. He had no belongings at all and no wallet or money.

Kinsella stood over him and saw a necklace glint at his throat. He thinned his eyes and squatted, then reached with a gloved hand and fished the chain out from the top of the blood-stained shirt. *Medic-Alert*. He twisted the flat piece of silver with the snake embossed on it and lifted one eyebrow. *Thomas Carey. Diabetic*. London and a phone number. 'Oh shit,' Kinsella said. 'We got ourselves a tourist.'

I

June

Harrison stood on the sidewalk and tied his hair into a ponytail. Twenty-five years in the FBI and he still looked like a bum. At this time of year in New Orleans, he figured he ought to finally admit defeat and get his hair cut, but he never seemed to get round to it. He wanted to buy food in the French Market, but Decatur Street hummed with tourists who obviously had not heard about the typical summer temperatures here. He sucked humid air, shimmering in a wave from the river, and stepped into Nu Nus Café. Dewey had basketball on the TV.

'Hey, bro. What's up?'

'Just get me a cold one, Dewey. I know what you're like when you've got the game going.'

Dewey Albert Biggs – big, heavyset, with blond hair and beard – flipped the top off a bottle of Miller. 'Get a little animated, I guess, don't I.' He turned to the small, oriental woman seated at the end of the bar. 'Just excuse me if I make a noise, mam. I won't mean anything by it.'

'Oh, that's all right. Don't mind me.'

Harrison squinted sideways at her as he raised the bottle to his lips. She had an accent, but he couldn't quite place it. He thought it might be British, but there was an edge to it. He caught her eye and smiled. She returned the smile and stirred what looked like a tall glass of iced water with a straw. Harrison looked away. Yeah, British, he thought, with a trace of wherever it was she started out still hanging around. He glanced at her again and caught her face in profile. Black hair, a few strands of silver just beginning to lighten it. Crow's feet at the edge of her eyes. She wore a pair of navy blue shorts and open-toed sandals, and the skin of her legs was rich, dark and smooth. Harrison realised he was staring and looked away suddenly, a glow of perspiration at his neck. He wore a white T-shirt and blue jeans and his habitual, battered cowboy boots. Today had been hot; hotter still cooped up in the police department's surveillance van deep in St Thomas Project. Four hours he had been stuck in there, him and Dave Cimino from the 6th District, dripping pools of sweat and watching gangbangers out on the street.

Harrison hated surveillance in the projects. No matter what kind of vehicle you put out there, the kids were not stupid. Strange vehicles in black neighbourhoods – watching the 'bricks' of one teenage ganglord or another. But surveillance and undercover work was what he did: it had been pretty much the same since he graduated from Quantico. God knows that felt like a long time ago now.

Dewey gave a shout, smashing fist into palm as his team scored again. Harrison glanced sideways at the woman once more and rolled his eyes to the ceiling. There was something engaging about her eyes, something behind the fragility of the smile. She looked away again, obviously not in the mood for conversation. Harrison slid the empty bottle across the bar and Dewey cracked open another. Harrison plucked a Marlboro from the crumpled pack in his jeans' pocket and took a box of matches from the pile on the bar. He popped the match on his thumbnail, a trick he had learned during hours of boredom in Vietnam thirty years ago.

His mind rolled back and age crept up on him. Thirty years and change; Lai Khe base in the Iron Triangle. He scratched the tattoo on his upper arm, a cartoon of a grinning rat standing upright, six-gun in one hand and a whiskey bottle in the other. He remembered lying in a hammock in the hootch, listening to mosquitoes and smoking, just waiting for a bunch of grunts to get pinned down by the VC, who popped up from the tunnels. The call

15

would come and his outfit would saddle up and be choppered in by the Cavalry.

Vietnam: his past, 1st Engineer Battalion Tunnel Rat. He had volunteered to go back for a second tour of duty, after he could not transfer to the Rats the first time. Eli Footer's fault, God rest his beautiful soul. If Eli hadn't got himself all blowed to hell, then Harrison wouldn't have got so pissed off he had to join the most dangerous outfit there was. He thought about it now, crawling underground – just you, your flashlight and your pistol. One on one; warfare pure and simple. He remembered some of the guys: 'Batman' and Rejo and Ray 'the Probe' Martinez. Martinez had been the one who pulled him out after he screwed up the last time he went underground.

Harrison sucked on the cigarette, letting smoke dribble from his nostrils, and glanced at the woman again. She looked Vietnamese; he could tell after having spent so much time out there. She was the reason his mind was running off at all kinds of tangents, after a day frying in the van.

His beeper vibrated against his midriff and he plucked it from his belt. Penny calling from the office. Harrison asked Dewey for the phone and walked to the door that led up to the hotel, so he could use the one on the wall. Now the woman sat face on to him, but her stare was through him, eyes like onyx glass in her head.

'Hey, Matthew. What's up?' he said when Penny answered the phone.

'Just checking with you, buddy. Making sure you didn't cook out there.'

'All but, bro.' Harrison crushed his cigarette in the ashtray.

'Where are you?'

'Decatur. Nu Nus Café. Dewey's watching basketball.'

'Who's Dewey?'

'Bartender.'

'Listen.' Penny's voice grew more serious. 'I just got

back from the range. The team leader asked me if I knew where you were.'

'Mackon, why?'

'I don't know. I told him you were on surveillance for us. I figure he wants to talk to you about something.'

Harrison shrugged. 'Well, I guess he can page me if he wants me bad enough. I'm through for the day, bubba.'

'Yeah. Me too. Time I was outta here.'

'How's that little rug-rat of yours?'

'Keeping us awake at night. Think yourself lucky you live on your own.'

'Yeah, right.' Harrison put down the phone.

Penny was a good agent and they formed one of the sniper observer units for the SWAT team. He was ex-Marine Corps and had done some special forces stuff in his time. He could separate a target's brain stem at two hundred yards with a rifle. Not that he had had to do it. As far as Harrison knew, Penny had never shot anyone, which was probably a good thing. He was just a kid really. His wife had only recently given birth, so the Penny household out in Slidell was turned just about upside down. Slidell. Harrison lit another cigarette and flapped out the match. All the guys from the field office lived out that way, except Cochrane who was St Charles Parish born and raised. Harrison was the only one who lived in New Orleans itself: all but fifty years old and two crummy rooms on Burgundy and Toulouse in the French Quarter. The part that tourists were told to avoid after dark. The ankle holster sweated against the inside of his boot. He finished his beer and ordered a third, and Dewey leaned on his elbows.

'Summer in New Orleans, Johnny Buck,' he said. Then he smiled at the oriental lady. 'We don't get but two temperatures here in the summer, mam. Stop and mildew.'

She laughed then and Dewey poured her some more water. 'About the best thing you can drink in this weather.'

'You don't mind?' Her voice was soft and easy on the ear, the words perfectly formed in her mouth. Harrison looked at her again. She was tiny, even on the stool he would put her at no more than five foot two. She was small-boned and delicate, which belied the strength he could see in her eyes.

'You on vacation, mam?' Harrison asked her.

She sipped iced water through a straw, pursing her lips so the colour faded only to return again when she smiled. 'Not really.' She looked beyond him once more, as if not quite sure of herself, as if not sure she wanted to speak.

She could feel this man's eyes on her, but she looked through him now to the wall, something that she did a lot these days. Everything would crowd in on her and grow tall, even the tiniest, most simple of things would take great shape and weight and stop her right in her tracks. As a doctor she had told herself to expect it – mind wandering, things not making sense. It had been going on for four months now. She looked back at the man and he was still looking at her. Blue-grey eyes set in wrinkled cups of flesh; a lined and seamy face, tanned dark by the sun. Long, gunmetal-coloured hair tied at his collar in a ponytail that hung down his back. He wore no hat and she could see the hair was fuzzing and just beginning to thin at the crown. Normally, she did not like long hair on men, but somehow it seemed to sit well on him.

'I'm sorry,' she said at length. 'That wasn't much of an answer.'

'Mam,' Harrison said. 'If that's the only one you got, it'll do just fine.' He smiled again. 'Are you from England?'

'Yes.'

'Whereabouts?'

'London.'

'Really?' Harrison swivelled round on his stool. 'I know a guy in London.'

'You do?'

'Yeah. He's coming out here, in fact. Next few weeks, I think it's gonna be.'

'What's his name?'

18

Harrison laughed then. 'Mam, from what I hear London's a big place. I don't figure you're gonna know him.'

They both laughed then and Harrison asked her if she wanted anything else to drink. She ordered a glass of white wine.

'And another beer,' Harrison said to Dewey. 'All this heat makes me thirsty.'

'Does it ever cool down?' the woman asked him.

'Only when it rains.'

The woman asked to see a menu and Harrison got one too, and they both ordered the house po-boys. There was something about her, something behind the broken smile. Old instincts pricked at Harrison and he wondered. 'As we're both about to eat,' he said, 'would you like to join me at a table?'

'Thank you. That would be very nice.'

They moved beyond the mirrored partition, leaving Dewey to the third quarter of the game. One of the regulars, a reporter for the *Times Picayune*, came in, saw the basketball and satisfied himself with a beer and a silent stool at the bar.

'My name's Dollar,' Harrison introduced himself. 'John Dollar. But everyone calls me Harrison.'

'Why Harrison?' she asked him.

He thought about that. Harrison had been the name he had picked when he first went undercover for the FBI and somehow it had stuck. He had been deep three times since then and always the same name.

'Just a kinda nickname,' he said.

'John Dollar and they nicknamed you Harrison?' Her eyebrows stalked.

Harrison looked a little awkward. 'Well, that and Johnny Buck. You know – buck – dollar.'

She nodded her head and smiled. 'My name's Jean Carey.'

'From England?'

'Yes.'

'Originally?'

She leaned on a palm, long nails cupping the delicate lines of her face. 'No. I arrived in England as a refugee from Vietnam when I was eighteen.'

'When was that?'

'A long time ago. More years than I care to remember.'

The name Carey rang a bell somewhere in Harrison's head, but he could not remember why. He looked at her again. She wore a wedding ring on her finger.

'So Carey's your married name?'

'Yes.'

'And Jean?'

She smiled. 'Now we're on to nicknames again, I suppose. My real name's Jung Sook, but being a student in England and a Vietnamese boat person to boot, it was easier to pick something the locals would be able to remember.'

'So you chose Jean.'

'The first thing that came into my head.' She laughed again, but he could sense little merriment in her.

'Is this your first time in New Orleans?'

Her face darkened all at once and she laid down her fork on the salad dish. 'No,' she said. 'It's not.'

Four months ago now and it felt as if it were yesterday. She knew that would never change. It would always feel like that. Nothing would get any better. The pain, she hoped, might ease: other people she had spoken to, who had been through similar experiences, told her the pain did ease. But the memory never faded. It remained as fresh as that first night when the telephone had woken her.

It had not actually woken her. That was the following night or the night after perhaps, she could not quite recall the details now. But she remembered waking up at three minutes past two, one night back in February. The curtains were open and the Fulham street outside was quiet and still. The moon was large and full and she could see it above the lights of the city. There was frost on the windows, patterns

20

gathering on the inside even. She was suddenly wide awake, taking in minute details as if she had never been to sleep. Something was wrong. She could feel it. A tremor, the smallest of sensations somewhere deep inside her and all she could see was her mother's aged face. She could hear her mother's voice and, in the distance, gunfire. There was nothing new in gunfire. She had grown up with the rattle of gunfire. M16, AK47: she knew the sounds they made by heart. But this was new gunfire, different gunfire, and she knew that what they had feared had happened, and now it was time to go.

She sat up in bed. Those were distant memories, going back twenty-five years. She had had a life since then. This was a new emotion, but the sentiments were the same. Which was why she knew she was not imagining it, why her bowel suddenly irritated her, yet when she sat on the toilet nothing happened. She went downstairs and set the kettle to boil, but the artificial light and the chilled silence unnerved her, so she switched out the lights and made tea by the glow of the streetlamps. She sat in silence and waited, but nothing happened that night. How could it? With hindsight, nobody knew. Yet she sat there cupping a mug of hot tea, watching the silent phone on the wall. She waited for it to ring, to tell her what, she did not know. But she watched it, waiting until the moon died and the weak sun rose, casting night into wintered day. The phone did not ring and she went to work at the hospital, made her rounds, looked at the yellowed faces of bald-headed children, some dying, some not dying of cancer. That day she took in every detail of her surroundings, saw every face for what it was – a little life desperate not to be snuffed out. She took in the paint on the walls and the patterns and pictures the children had made, and every little bit of everything that made Great Ormond Street what it was. She took in every expression of pain, every hint of silent anguish. She watched parents being brave for their children, and her own pain was acute. She did not know why.

Throughout the day she thought of that other day in Vietnam, when the NVA came swarming across the border and the Americans were pulling out. Then later, when her mother shook her and her sister awake and told them to get dressed, and then very matter of factly that their father had been taken by the North Vietnamese, and that they had to get away. She never saw her father again, and her mother died on that accursed, wretched boat that should have sunk many times, but somehow did not. She and her sister arrived at Thorney Island naval base in England as both orphans and refugees.

The phone did not ring that night, but she did not sleep and in the end she phoned Paul in Cape Town. 'Paul, it's Jean. Look, I'm sorry to disturb you, but I'm worried.' Paul Carey, her ex-husband, whom she had met at medical school, fallen in love with and married. They had split up, though, when their careers clashed. He wanted to take up a post in his native South Africa and she had just been offered a job as a paediatrician at Great Ormond Street Hospital for sick children. Thomas had only been nine, but the separation had been amicable and they had only actually divorced two years ago, when Paul wanted to remarry.

'What's wrong, Jean?'

'I don't know. Have you heard from Tom?'

'Not since a postcard last week. Why?'

'I don't know. I'm worried, that's all.'

'What about?'

'I don't know. Look, it's probably nothing. I'm sorry, Paul.'

He was gentle. He had always been gentle. She missed him then. He told her not to worry, it was just a motherly thing and everything would be fine. Tom was grown up now, a man who could take care of himself, and he would be home, as he had planned, in a few days' time. Jean said, of course he was right, and she put the phone down and went up to bed. She slept only fitfully and late the following afternoon she was summoned to the registrar's office where

22

two policemen were waiting to speak to her. As soon as she saw them, she knew.

Harrison watched her carefully as she told him, tears close but still under control. Jean looked at him then and realised she had just told a perfect stranger everything about her life and what she had just been through.

'You're Tom Carey's mother,' Harrison said quietly. 'I'm sorry for your loss, mam.' He sat back, pushed away his plate and plucked a cigarette from his pocket. 'D'you mind?'

'Not at all.' She tried to smile. 'So you see, this is my second time in New Orleans.' Harrison lit the cigarette and blew smoke from the side of his mouth. 'I thought the name was familiar.' He folded his arms across his chest. Jean was looking at his tattoo. Her first visit had been during Mardi Gras, the streets heaving with drinking, eating, drug-taking, shouting revellers, which made her own silence all the more acute. She had stayed here at the Hotel Provincial because the only thing she knew about New Orleans was the French Quarter, and the sheriff's department at St Charles Parish had come and collected her. The chief of deputies, Joe Kinsella, had driven her over the bridges of Highway 310 to Hahnville and the mortuary, where she had identified the body of her son.

'Boxcar,' Harrison said quietly. 'A security guard found him at the Hahnville freight yard.'

'You remember?' She shook her head. 'That surprises me. The sheriff over there told me that New Orleans had been the murder capital of the US a couple of years ago.'

'New Orleans, yeah. But that was St Charles Parish, mam. Nobody gets killed in St Charles. It's old families, traditional Southern folk. Besides, your boy was a tourist and that makes all the headlines.' Jean looked beyond him then to the bar, where Dewey had switched off the basketball and was playing a blues tape. She paused, listening to the rhythm of the music for a moment, then looked out to the street but did not see any of the faces. Across the road, a lone trumpeter was playing. 'I always liked Bruce Springsteen,' she said absently. 'I saw him at Wembley Stadium in 1987. Tom took me to see him playing solo a couple of years ago.' She looked back at Harrison. 'I'm sorry. I'm rambling.'

Harrison laid a hand over hers and squeezed. 'No you're not. Tell me – why did you come back?'

She sat back, shook her head and made an open-handed gesture. 'I don't know. When I was here last, I took Tom's body home with me. He's buried in London. But I know he didn't kill himself and the sheriff's office says the same. Tom never had a gun, nor access to one, and he had absolutely no reason to take his own life.' She broke off, bit her lip and again tears threatened. 'I had to come back. I don't quite know why. I just can't leave it where it is.' She stopped again and sipped at her drink. 'I just don't know what to do or where to be. I look at all the parents at work, worried sick about their children, and my own child is gone. I can't get my head round it. I think I should be in London, but it's unresolved over here. I don't know.' She sighed. 'In the end, I took a leave of absence from work, rented out my flat and just got on a plane. I flew here, checked into this hotel again, and now I'm here I don't really know why.'

Harrison leaned his elbows on the table. 'Have you spoken to Kinsella again?'

'Not yet. I'm getting a cab out there tomorrow. He doesn't sound very hopeful, though.'

'He wouldn't.' Harrison made a face. 'Jean, your boy was murdered in a boxcar on a freight train. Whoever did it could've been five states away within hours. There was no weapon recovered, no forensics to speak of, not that it would point to anyone, anyway. There're hundreds of fingerprints in a boxcar.'

'What I want to know is why he was in one in the first place.'

Lydia, the waitress, brought them some coffee and Harrison lit another cigarette.

'What time are you seeing Joe?'

'You know him?'

He hesitated, then hunched himself forward. 'Yeah, I know him.' He gave a brief glance around to see who might be listening, then told her he was an FBI agent.

Her eyebrows shot up.

'I know. I look more like a hobo, but that's part of my job.' He shook his head. 'I shouldn't be telling you any of this, but hell, there you go. I know Kinsella pretty well. I've done some stuff with the homicide dicks out there in St Charles. Joe's an ex-Fed and if there's anything he can turn up, he will.' He sat back again. 'Got a pen?'

Jean fished in her handbag and brought out an address book and fountain pen. Harrison gave her his pager number and told her to call him any time she wanted to.

'You never know,' he said. 'I might be able to help.'

'Thank you.'

'Pleasure.' He stood up. 'Jean, I'm really sorry for your loss.' He paused then. 'How long are you gonna be in town?'

'I don't know.'

'How many people d'you know?'

She laughed then. 'You and Dewey.'

Harrison squinted at the bar. 'Well, Dewey's a good guy. He's the only person in town who knows what I really do. Everyone else just thinks I'm a bum. You need anything, you ask Dewey or call me. And be careful. New Orleans can be a really dangerous town.'

She nodded and looked up at him. 'I think I know that already.'

Harrison could not get Jean Carey out of his head, the trouble in her eyes, the terrible churning left in the wake of tragedy. He lay on his bed in his room on Toulouse and Burgundy, listening to a hooker arguing with the cab driver who had just dropped her, and thinking that she ought to just get along the street because he could be one of those cab drivers who rape or murder women if they get pissed off. Jean again in his head, the way she looked, the frailty yet strange depth of strength about her. He slept, and later in the night the wind got up, which brought the temperature down a fraction, and then it poured with rain and the wind blew it into his room. He woke to hear it, but did not close the window and in the morning there were puddles of water on the floor.

Harrison worked with the FBI's special operations group and had been attached to the gang squad, or New Orleans gang task force as it was more formally known, for the past three weeks. The squad was FBI-led, but had people from the New Orleans police department and the Louisiana state police, as well as others like the ATF and Immigration.

In July of 1997, the level of gangbangers, dealing in heroin primarily, in some of the government-funded housing projects like Magnolia, The Caliope and St Thomas, was getting out of hand. People were being murdered left, right and centre and the politicians and the decent project-dwellers were at desperation point. Since then, the gang squad had left its mark, and a number of the really bad boys had been taken off the street.

Recently, they had been focusing on a particularly nasty twenty-two-year-old known as Little Nate. The gang squad reckoned he was behind at least nine unsolved homicides, and perhaps a half-dozen more, and they were trying to get him off the street. He ruled a four-block area of St Thomas – his 'bricks', as these guys liked to call it. Harrison had known little of the street gangs until he came to New Orleans. His undercover history had been with the Mafia and the militia, and the urban jungle was new to him in that sense. The squad had seconded in a real hardcase agent, called Swartz, from Chicago. He was a big guy who had won a football scholarship to college and had been with the Bureau for fifteen years now. Tom Kovalski, the ASAC up at the Washington field office, described him as one of the best street agents going and a really serious hunter. Swartz had taken out a whole chapter of Gangsta Disciples in Chicago. He had been responsible for getting a confidential informant into Little Nate's operation and so far they had made enough controlled buys to get his cellphone number. Swartz and Matt Penny were working the case and they had written the affidavit for a Title 3 wire tap on his phone. Harrison had been drafted in from special ops for surveillance purposes. Harrison had been Penny's partner on the drug squad for a while, and he liked Swartz. Swartz knew Harrison's pedigree, probably the best UCA since Joe Pistone, and there was mutual respect between them.

This morning Harrison was due on surveillance for the second day in a row and had arranged to meet Cimino at the office. They were trying to get a handle on Little Nate's heroin supplier. He had made a couple of phone calls to Dallas, then a number to small-town phone booths dotted around the South-West, but none of them made much sense to the listening FBI agents.

Cimino was sitting in the office Swartz shared with Penny, when Harrison arrived.

'Hey, Linda,' Harrison said to the secretary as he walked past. 'How are ya, baby?'

'Just fine. How are you doing?'

'I'm OK.' Harrison paused. He liked Linda. She was his age, maybe a bit younger – he doubted she was fifty yet – single again and worldly-wise, and had been with the squad since its inception. Mike Hammond, the supervisory agent, knew he could not do without her. Harrison squatted on the edge of her desk. 'I met the mother of that Carey kid last night.'

'Carey kid?'

'Yeah. The English kid. You know, the freight train homicide. The cold case out in St Charles Parish.'

'I didn't know she was in town again.'

Harrison looked beyond her and nodded. 'She's a nice lady. I think she's a bit lost.' He shook his head. 'Hell, hardly surprising.'

Cimino poked his head round Swartz's door. 'Hey, Johnny Buck. Your SWAT team leader wants to talk to you before we head out.'

Harrison got up off Linda's desk. 'So Matt Penny told me. Where's he at?'

'He said to tell you the squad room.'

Harrison took the elevator and paused by the organised crime squad section. Shawn Stone looked up at him. 'Hey, hick,' he said. 'You looking for Gerry?'

Harrison nodded. 'Word sure gets around, don't it.'

Gerry Mackon, the SWAT team leader, worked white-collar crime with Jeff McGee who had recently joined them from Washington, where he had been permanently attached to the Hostage Rescue Team. They were both ex-marines and McGee was about as tough as anyone Harrison had ever come across. His hair was so grunt short it was sharp on top. The two of them were talking when Harrison came in. Mackon looked up at him, but did not smile.

'You looking for me, TL?' Harrison asked him.

'Yeah.' Mackon stood up and adjusted the jacket on the back of his chair. 'I gotta check my car. You wanna walk with me?'

They went up to the parking lot and Harrison could feel the spider's walk between his shoulder blades. This felt like something from school or the academy and he had an idea what was coming.

'How you doing, JB?' Mackon asked him as they climbed the stairs two at a time.

'Fine, Gerry. Just fine.'

'You busy on the gang squad?'

'Always busy, Gerry.'

They went out into the car park, where they could feel the heat blasting across the city after the air-conditioned comfort of the office.

Mackon wiped his brow with a handkerchief. 'Guess you must fry in the back of that van.'

'Fry and broil and roast. Yeah, it's hot in there.'

'Special ops keeps you on your toes though, huh?'

'Gerry.' Harrison plucked a cigarette from his shirt pocket and rolled it between his fingers. 'You wanna get to the point. I'm due in St Thomas Project right now.' He popped a match on his belt buckle.

'Yeah. Sorry. Listen, it's special ops I wanted to talk about.'

'What about it?'

'About how busy they keep you.'

Harrison cocked his head to one side, leaned and spat tobacco juice. 'What's your point, Gerry?'

'Well, John, I figured you might wanna stand down from your SWAT duties for a while.'

Harrison stared at him. 'You trying to tell me something, Gerry?'

'No. I just thought that you were doing too much.'

'You telling me I'm too old or something.' Harrison stood taller and pushed his hair from where it fell across his face. 'I passed my physical same as everyone else.'

'I know, JB. I'm just saying. With you stuck out on spotter duty all the time, we might be one short on a SWAT roll.'

Harrison sucked on the cigarette. 'That's bullshit and you know it. I've been on special ops for six months now and I've never missed a SWAT roll. Fuck, I've never missed a SWAT roll in my life.' He paused then. 'You want McGee, don't you?' Mackon looked evenly back at him. 'Come on, Gerry. Tell it how it is, for Christ's sake. You want McGee, because he's ex-HRT and he's younger than I am.'

'Twelve years younger, Johnny.'

Harrison turned then and leaned on the concrete parapet. 'You should just spit it out, man, instead of shovelling this crap down my throat.'

Mackon moved next to him. 'Look, I'm sorry. I didn't

know how else to put it. I'm not saying you're too old. But Jeff's got more SWAT knowledge on his own than our whole damn team put together. I need him, JB. It's a matter of resource, is all.'

Harrison nodded slowly. 'I know it.' He breathed out heavily. 'If you want me off the team, then I'm off it.' He bit his lip and felt Mackon's hand on his shoulder.

'I'm sorry, buddy. You're one of the best. I know it and you know it. But time comes to us all.'

Mackon left him alone then, and Harrison flipped away the butt of his cigarette and immediately lit another. Whenever he had not been undercover, no matter what field office he was attached to, he had always made the SWAT team. He thinned his eyes and stared across the city and thought back over the past couple of years. After his last undercover job he had been determined to quit altogether, but then there was some unfinished business with Jack Swann, an English police officer who he thought had been responsible for having his cover compromised while watching a militia leader. Harrison had decided to remain in the job just long enough to do something about that. Eventually, he found out it had not been Swann at all and he and the Englishman had become friends. Swann was due here in a week to lecture the joint terrorism task force at the Louisiana State University, at Baton Rouge. Harrison had not quit like he thought he would when everything was sorted out. He had realised that maybe the FBI was all he had. They would forcibly retire him at fifty-seven anyway and he had decided to remain till then.

But all at once he realised that he had nothing now and he would still have nothing in seven years' time, except be seven years older if the cigarettes did not kill him first. He stared at the haze of white and silver buildings that dominated Poydras Street and the business district. He had no family save a sister, who he never saw. He had no wife or child or anything other than this. He thought of Jean Carey and her loss and in a funny kind of way he identified with her. His life: the army, Vietnam, Tunnel Rat, the INS border patrol in New Mexico and then this – the FBI. That was it and he was fifty years old. He flipped away the cigarette and walked back inside. Kirk Fitzpatrick was talking to Charlie Mayer, the special agent in charge. They both looked up.

'Hey, Johnny Buck.'

Harrison ignored Kirkpatrick and looked at Mayer. 'Boss, have you got a minute?'

'Now?'

'If you can do it. Yeah.'

Mayer squinted at him and then nodded. 'Step into my office.'

Harrison followed him into the airy, spacious room on the twenty-second floor. The view was towards downtown and the crescent of river beyond the World Trade Center and the old Jax Brewery. Mayer indicated the leather chesterfield couch and Harrison sat down.

'What's on your mind?'

'Boss, I'm due a whole buncha vacation time and I wanna take it now.'

Mayer furrowed his brow. 'Right now?'

'Yep. Right now.'

'You're working with the gang squad, aren't you?'

Harrison nodded. 'I'm sitting in a cookoven of a van with Dave Cimino. Any fucker can sit in a van. Boss, I need the time, and I really need it now.'

Detective Inspector Jack Swann sat in the Antiterrorist Branch offices on the fifteenth floor of Scotland Yard. He looked at his watch, drumming his fingers on the desk as he listened to the whirr and click of the phone connection in his ear. Then all at once he heard his fiancée's voice. 'Hi, honey. I'm sorry. They must've put you on hold or something.'

'Or something, Cheyenne. God knows how long I've been listening to that music.'

She laughed then and Swann relaxed. But he missed her. She had been back in Washington for only a week and yet it felt like a lifetime. 'Any news on the leg-att's job?'

'Deputy leg-att.'

'Whatever, Chey. Is there any news?'

'Jack, the job is mine. I've just got to complete this assignment for the Washington field office and I'll be back in the UK.'

Swann sighed heavily. 'How long's the assignment?'

'Six weeks tops. Alls I gotta do is break in the new terrorism response co-ordinator for Tom Kovalski. It's no big deal, and I'm in limbo till they post me to London, anyway.'

'Kovalski wants *you* particularly, does he?'

'Yes. Honey, he's been up to his neck ever since Bin Laden hit us in Africa. Not only that, he's still responsible for militia activity, which is on the increase again. He knows I can do the job without him even having to think about it.'

'OK.' Swann held up a palm, as if she was there across the desk from him. He knew better than to argue with her over things like this. Cheyenne was as good an FBI agent as any he had met, notwithstanding his bias. 'It's not a problem, love,' he said. 'I'm flying to Louisiana on Monday, anyway. It should be three weeks, but maybe I can spin it out to a month. We can get together at weekends.'

'Then there's no problem, is there.' That tone of voice again. Not quite admonishment, but something very close. Swann felt suitably chastened.

After she had put the phone down, he sat for a moment and stared at the wall charts. Activity here and there: the Serbian threat was still with them, and with the stalemate over decommissioning weapons in Ulster dragging on and on, there was always a danger of one of the ceasefires breaking down. Word had already come down from MI5 that fresh weapons had been stockpiled at three separate hides in different parts of the country. Swann could feel that familiar tingling sensation deep in the pit of his stomach. The last time the IRA broke a ceasefire they blew up Canary Wharf. He stood up and looked at the Commissioner's commendation plaque on the desk before him. He had received it for shooting Ismael Boese, one of the worst terrorists the world had ever come across. He had meant to take the plaque home, but had not got round to it yet. He had met Cheyenne while working that case jointly with the Americans. They had got together and she now was in line for the deputy legal attaché's post at the US Embassy in London.

Swann had been a sergeant until only two months previously, and then got the surprise of his life when the Commissioner broke all the protocols by promoting him to inspector in the field. Only the third man in the history of the Metropolitan Police ever to hold such an honour. He felt pretty good about it all.

In the corridor he bought bad coffee from the machine and bumped into Christine Harris from Special Branch. 'Hello, Jack. You're not supposed to be here, are you?'

'Next week, Chrissie.'

'The Deep South, eh. What is it – Baton Rouge?'

'Well actually, no. It was, but it's been changed.'

Harris acted as liaison officer between the Antiterrorist Branch and Special Branch and had dealings with the MI5 operatives that worked with them. MI5 and Special Branch did most of the intelligence work to combat the threat of terrorism, and the Antiterrorist Branch got involved when it came to the sharp end of things. Swann had been unofficially approached to join Special Branch on more than one occasion and, with his recent promotion, he was now seriously considering it. He had worked with them for a six-month secondment when the yakuza threat was growing, but had returned to the Antiterrorist Branch after that. He was doing nothing permanently, however, until Cheyenne had her London embassy posting in the bag and he was helping her unpack in his flat. He told Harris that his

33

counter-terrorism lectures had been moved to New Orleans because he had been involved in dealing with a tanker hijack on the Mississippi River the previous year. The FBI headed up the joint task force and it was agreed that New Orleans, with its special logistical problems, would be a good place to run the course. So now he was headed for the FBI field office and he was looking forward to sinking a few beers with Harrison, his old sparring partner.

Back at his desk he set the coffee down and was sifting through some court papers when the phone rang. He picked it up. 'Swann.'

'Congratulations, limey. I heard you got promoted.'

Swann sat back and lifted one foot to the edge of the desk. 'Harrison. I was just thinking about you.'

'All bad, I trust.'

'How could it be any other way?'

'*Touché*, duchess. How's it going over there?'

'Not bad. I'll be over there next week.'

'I know. It's why I'm calling, bubba. I ain't gonna be around, not for the first week or two at least.'

Swann sat upright again. 'Why? What's happened?'

'Nothing's happened, Jack. I got some vacation coming to me, is all. I might be in D.C., though, if you get your butt up there to see Logan.'

'That's what I plan to do.'

'I could always check on her for you.'

'Yeah. Right.'

Harrison's tone quietened then. 'Listen, Jack. I normally wouldn't call you up about my holidays, but when you hit town there's something I want you to do for me.'

'In New Orleans?'

'Yeah. Where you staying?'

'I don't know.'

'Well, there's a lady I want you to look out for. Her name's Jean Carey and she's staying at the Provincial on Chartres Street.'

Swann looked up as Christine Harris opened the door. 'Who's Jean Carey?' he asked Harrison.

'She's an English Vietnamese lady. Her son's a cold-case homicide over with the dicks in St Charles Parish. Joe Kinsella, the chief of deputies, is gonna be attending your stuff on counter-terrorism.' Harrison paused. 'I don't know why I'm calling you up, Jack. I don't even know how long the lady is planning on staying in New Orleans, but she's a little lost. You know what I'm saying?'

'Of course.'

'I figured you were a Brit and she's a Brit, so if you can, try and look out for her. She's got no friends here, and I think she figures she can do something about her son's murder herself. She's gonna get hurt or disappointed.'

Swann frowned. 'Are you *seeing* her or something, John?'

'Naw, nothing like that. I happened to talk to her one night in Nu Nus Café, is all. She's a nice lady, Jack. If you get a chance to speak to Kinsella about the murder, do so, will ya? If she thinks people are concerned, it'll help some, maybe.'

'OK.'

'Gotta run, bro. I'm leaving town this morning. See you when I see you, duchess.'

Harrison hung up and Swann looked over at Christine Harris.

2

Billy Bob Lafitte ran the gun store in Hope Heights, Oregon. He did not just sell guns, but knives, survival gear and fishing rods as well, and a little bit of pawned stuff when the opportunity presented itself. He was a tall man with jet-black hair cut above his ears and a trimmed black beard. His face was burned by the sun. Mid-June and the small coastal town was heaving: every motel room in the place was taken, mainly with 'Californicators' coming up for the surf. Lafitte did very well in the summer, which made up for the lack of custom come wintertime.

He heard the phone ringing out front as he was doing the books and checking the stock ledger in his back office, a chore he did every Monday afternoon. The extension through to his office was switched off and he did not allow anyone to disturb him till after the figures were done. The knock on the frosted glass door made him look up, bunch his eyes and clench a fist on the desk. 'This had better be damn good,' he said as he got up from his chair.

Tommy Brindle stood on the other side of the glass. Lafitte could make out the set of his hat, and the way his shoulders sort of hunched up to his neck. His frown deepened and he opened the door. Brindle's eyes were shining, a mix of fear and excitement. Lafitte looked squarely at him. 'What's up, Tommy?'

Brindle glanced over his shoulder and nodded to the office. Lafitte moved out of his way and closed the door behind them. Brindle was standing at the desk now, clenching and unclenching a fist. 'I've just seen a black Chevy Suburban drive through town real slow.' He pushed out a cheek, with his tongue feeding the chewing tobacco round the inside of his mouth. 'You ain't gonna believe this, Billy Bob. But they stopped for gas.'

Lafitte was busy and irritable. 'What're you on about, Tommy?'

'Three gooks got out. Dark suits all of them. Sunglasses.'

Lafitte stared at him.

'One pumped gas, while the other two snooped around. Real short haircuts, Billy Bob. And I mean grunt short.'

Lafitte leaned against the door for a moment and drew breath audibly through his nostrils. He stared at Brindle, then through him, and then he walked to the window which overlooked the vacant lot they used for additional parking to the side of the gun store. He could see a stretch of Pacific highway, hear the thunder of the surf, whipped high today by the wind. 'You're absolutely positive,' he said, aware of the sweat moistening his palms.

'I saw them with my own two eyes. It weren't no mistake.'

'Three of them.'

'Right.'

'But they're gone now.' Lafitte turned again.

'Yep. Headed on up the coast.'

'OK.' Lafitte sat down again. 'Thanks, Tommy. I'll see you for a beer tonight. I got work to finish right now.'

When Brindle was gone, Lafitte sat in the sudden stillness of the office, oblivious to the sounds of custom from the other side of the door. Three gooks driving a black Suburban. He sat back, looked at his figures, but knew he could not finish them now. A cold sweat had broken out at the base of his neck and he pushed himself away from the desk, grabbed his hat and went out through the store. He spoke to Lorraine, his weekday manager. 'Lorrie, I've got stuff to do at home. Lock up for me, honey. Will you?'

'Sure thing, Billy.'

He fired up the Dodge Ram V8 pick-up truck he always parked out front and swung on to the highway. Behind him in the cab, a Winchester 30/30 hung on two brass hooks. He saw Maplethorpe, one of Riggins's deputies, easing his cruiser along the blacktop, and signalled to him. They pulled up in the middle section of the highway, door to door, and Lafitte rolled down his window. 'D'you know anything about three gooks driving through town in a Chevy Suburban, Map?' Lafitte asked him.

The deputy pushed his flat-brimmed hat higher up his forehead and wiped away sweat. 'No, sir.'

'Tommy Brindle tells me they stopped for gas. Government-looking types.'

'I ain't seen them, Billy Bob.'

'Get a hold of Sheriff Riggins, will you. Ask him to call me up at home.'

'You got it.'

Lafitte gunned the motor and spun the wheel, hauling the heavy truck across two lanes and up Indian Creek Road towards his house, which overlooked the sea from the mountain. That was the wonderful thing about Oregon, the mountain and forest in your backyard and, out front, the carpet of the Pacific rolled to the horizon. Millicent wasn't home, and both the boys were working with the loggers on Pierce Hill. Up there for a week at a time, only coming home to stock up on food at the weekend.

The dogs barked and raced each other out of the barn to meet him, as Lafitte swung down from the cab. A German shepherd called Piper, and Dillon, the Rottweiler/Dobermann cross. Lafitte had wanted to get one of those wolf dogs, but Millie said they were too unpredictable. He had seen one about seven-eighths pure wolf one time; a guy up in Washington owned him. He looked just like a wolf, only his ears were slightly taller and he had that Husky/picturebook quality about his features.

Lafitte ran rough palms over the dogs' heads as they followed him as far as the screen door of the kitchen. They lived outside and knew better than to try and enter the house. Lafitte paused in the kitchen. The windows were open to the screen mesh, but the wind off the sea was dry and the heat seemed to clog up the air. He wiped the back of his neck where the short hairs prickled with sweat, and hunted down a soda from the icebox. In his den, he closed the door and switched on the extendable desk lamp, twisting the bulb round to face his computer screen. He had to wait a few moments to let it boot up and then he went through seven separate security codes to see if anyone had hacked into his system. Only when he was satisfied did he open his private files.

The room was in permanent darkness except for the glow of the lamp. The windows were blacked out with heavy cotton blinds, as this side of the house faced straight up the hill. There were plenty of places for someone to spy from up there, if they had a mind to do so.

He had started the Pacific Coast Militia in 1992 after listening to Louis Beam at Estes Park, Colorado, calling for Leaderless Resistance to defeat state tyranny. Now it was close on a thousand men strong and the FBI would be watching him. Lafitte had come across Beam in Vietnam and had been present as a guest when he took over as Grand Dragon for the Texas Ku Klux Klan.

Right now he had things to check, so he scanned his filing system and then began to print off various sightings from various groups all over the country. He took each sheet of paper, set them before him on the desk, and then took out his glasses and began to read. The first similar sighting had been in December 1997, in a small town thirty miles south of Clarksburg, West Virginia. Two members of the Mountaineer Militia had come across three Orientals in suits, driving a black Crown Victoria with the windows tinted out. They tailed the car as it made a circuit of the city limits, before heading off in the direction of Washington D.C. The following weekend, the farm of one of the same militia leaders was buzzed by a black helicopter. Two weeks after, it was buzzed again. Lafitte read on: numerous accounts, particularly those mentioning helicopters, because that was what he wanted to check. On 15 April of this year, one of the surviving members of the Washington chapter of the Phineas Priesthood circulated the fact that his house was being monitored by video cameras in a black helicopter. It had been three years since Verne Jay Merrell and his buddies had been arrested by the FBI. Lafitte sat back again, the sweat heavy now on his neck. Only last weekend, Millie had told him that an unidentified helicopter made a low-level fly-by, right over the house.

He picked up his cellphone and dialled. He was pretty sure the Feds could not monitor cellphones, though he was damn sure they were listening in to his land line. All that bullshit about affidavits, probable cause and federal judges, before they could set up a wire tap. Everybody knew the FBI did exactly as they pleased and federal judges were in cahoots with them anyway. He sat back, drumming his fingers, and took a pinch of Copenhagen from the tin in his shirt pocket. The phone rang four times, then Reece answered.

'Bob?'

'Yeah.'

'This is Lafitte.'

'How you doing, Billy Bob?' Reece ran the West Montana Minutemen, the oldest and most established people's militia in the country. Not only that, he ran a co-ordination programme of survival training and guerrilla warfare, which took in everyone from the KKK to the Priesthood and right across the board of peoples' militias. Last year at a secret meeting between the main players from all over the country, Reece took it upon himself to carry the phantom-cell concept one stage further. Lafitte had been one of the first to agree: Leaderless Resistance was fine, but every other successful group in the world had strategists and planners, a pillar of central command.

He tweaked aside the blinds on the window and told Reece what had happened. He had already circulated the weekend helicopter movements across the encrypted Inter-net channels. Reece had been right on the phone, telling him

40

and his sons to scour the mountain for hides and lay-up points that a Fed in a gilly suit might be able to use. Both of Lafitte's sons had received paramilitary training at Reece's Montana compound and they had sectioned that hillside like they were Red Berets. Reece was quiet for a moment.

'They just passed through, then.'

'So far.'

'But there were three of them.'

'Yes, sir.'

'One hundred thousand Hong Kong troops on sovereign US soil.' Reece's voice was a murmur. 'They're beginning to pop up everywhere.'

'I thought I oughtta let you know right away, Bob. Just in case. You know what I'm saying.'

'I hear you, brother. Don't worry. Take all the normal precautions and I'll spin it out on the web. The more people that know about it, the better our advantage.'

'Thank you, Bob. Yahweh be praised.'

'Be praised.' Reece hung up the phone.

Lafitte did not sleep well that night and, in the end, he got up so as not to disturb his wife any more than he had done already. He moved through to the kitchen and set the coffeepot on to boil. He had quit smoking two years ago and it was only at times like this that he really missed the habit. Still, Copenhagen under the lip helped some, and so he stuffed a fingerful into his mouth now, sucked and spat, the minted tobacco threads congealing into a ball. He leaned on the sink in the darkness, peered across the yard and thought he saw movement. The hairs climbed the back of his neck and he looked more closely. Maybe his eyes had deceived him because all seemed still again, but his instincts were alive and he told himself not to be so foolish. From the drawer in his den he took a Beretta 9mm handgun and pushed it into his belt. Then he opened the cabinet, pulled out the pump-action Remington shotgun and worked a round into the breech.

No need to use a flashlight: he knew every inch of his

yard, in darkness or snow or the broiled heat of summer. Everything was always put back in its place. The four of them – Millie, himself and the two boys – knew not to shift stuff around. Keeping order was a way of making sure you knew who had been in your yard. The dogs never left the property. Lafitte had taught them to patrol its boundaries without crossing them. It was not fenced all the way round and there was no gate off the dirt road, but Piper and Dillon only went so far and no further.

He stepped outside and could hear nothing but the scratched calling of cicadas. He stood for a moment, the world dipped in a darkness made all the deeper by the swirl of cloud that had massed throughout the evening. It had not rained yet, but the wind had died to a stillness in the air, which hung with electricity. It happened like that up here: the wind off the sea, then the silent stealth of a storm creeping over the mountains. Lafitte scanned the yard. No sign of anybody and no sign of the dogs either. If anyone had been here, the dogs would have let him know. He stepped into the dust a few paces, paused, then quartered the property again, shotgun held loose in one hand, the tip of the barrel only a few inches above the ground. He shifted the Beretta where it dug into his flesh and then moved towards the barn.

The dogs raised their heads as he entered, but they made no move to get up from the lair they had fashioned amid the hay bales he stored for the winter. They ran five horses on the property and winter-feed was always at a premium. Lafitte looked at the dogs and they looked back at him, and still they did not move. Then Piper laid his head on his paws and licked his lips. Dillon just kept on looking at him with his tongue hanging out. Lafitte turned again and looked back across the yard, lighter than the darkness of the barn. Now he flicked on the flashlight, made one lengthy sweep of the yard and flicked it off again. Everything was in its place, he could tell that at a glance; from the trucks and the horse trailer to the pickaxe that leaned against the wall under the window of his den. He frowned and scratched his head, then made a circuit of the trucks and wandered down to the dirt road. For a couple of moments the cloud parted above his head and the moon peeped out, casting the sand at his feet in silver. He saw a set of tyre tracks and every muscle in his body stiffened. He shone the flashlight and confirmed what he already knew. The tracks were fresh and they weren't from either his Dodge or Millie's Jimmy. He paced towards the road and made another sweep with the torch, then he crouched on his haunches and stared at the tracks more closely.

They had not been here when he shut up the house for the night. He made a habit of walking round the property last thing before the sun went down, and these tracks had definitely not been here. They came right up to the driveway and then stopped. The road did not go any further. And yet it did not look as though the driver had turned round. He must have done; there was no other way to get down. Lafitte walked a little way down the hill to where the road widened in a little ridge, which dropped away off the mountain. There were two miles of dirt road, falling over three thousand feet to sea level before you hit any tarmac. He knew what had happened: the driver had rolled the vehicle backwards, running through his own tracks until he got to the turning-point. Then he pulled it round and headed on down. Again Lafitte felt the chill running through him: the tracks were wide and deep-treaded and belonged to a four-wheel-drive.

He walked back up the road with the shotgun held across his chest now, cocked and ready to go. His heart was high, bumping against his ribs, and all manner of thoughts flew back and forth in his head. Paranoia. That's what people called it – the people that didn't believe, or didn't know or didn't want to believe. A black Chevy Suburban is real. A black helicopter making a fly-by is real. These damn tyre tracks were real. And then he stopped. It occurred to him that neither of the dogs had come out to the boundary with him. That was odd. They hadn't even got up. More quickly now, he strode up the driveway to the yard and the big barn. He passed the two trucks from the rear and he was halfway to the barn door when he stopped. He stood for a second, then whirled, flicked on the flashlight and panned it over the windshield of his Dodge. A noise at the house made him turn and then the kitchen light came on. Millie stood framed against the screen door in her nightgown. 'Billy Bob, is that you?'

'Yes, honey. It's me.'

'What's going on? It's three o'clock in the morning.'

Lafitte was staring at the Dodge. The two hooks set either side of the rear window were empty. 'Somebody's taken my 30/30, Millie. Somebody stole my gun.'

They looked down at the dogs, lying with their tongues loose, like old withered flesh, against leathered black lips and white teeth. Their eyes were open but dull, the life gone out of their bodies. Millie stood next to him shivering violently.

'They didn't get up.' Lafitte's voice was a cracked whisper. 'When I came in just now, they didn't get up to meet me. They didn't walk the yard with me like they always do. I never noticed. Head musta been fuddled, I guess.'

His wife squeezed his hand more tightly. 'They were two of the best guard dogs God ever made, Bill. Who could have poisoned them? Who could have snuck up here and done this without us hearing a whimper?'

Lafitte slipped an arm round her shoulders and pulled her more closely towards him. 'Somebody who really knows what they're doing.' He let go of her then. 'Go call the sheriff, honey. Go call up Riggins for me.'

When she was gone, he knelt beside the dogs and ran his fingers over their heads, gently fondling their ears. Tears burned in his forty-eight-year-old eyes and he realised then that he had not shed tears since his mother died five years previously. He bit hard on his lip and fought them now,

44

rocking back on his boot heels. Then he stood up and went back to the truck. The door had been opened with a piece of wire or something. He could make out the series of tiny scratches that had flaked away the paint. His wife came out again and told him that Riggins was on his way. She had spoken to his wife and she was coming out too. Riggins was the county sheriff and a good friend of theirs. He and Lafitte were the same age, both had grown up in Coos Bay and both had fought in South-East Asia.

When he arrived less than fifteen minutes later, Lafitte went out to meet him.

'Greg,' Lafitte said, as Riggins got out of the car. 'They came on to my property and they took away my gun.' He stood with his hands on his hips. 'They had to poison my dogs to do it, but that's exactly what they did.' He spat a stream of dark spittle into the dirt. 'And people say we're paranoid.'

Three days later, Lafitte walked out of his office at the gun store and stopped. An oriental man, in a grey three-button suit, was inspecting a selection of fishing lures. Instinctively, Lafitte looked beyond him to the parking lot, searching for the black Suburban. Then the man looked up and stared at him from behind black, wraparound sunglasses. Lafitte held his gaze and the man looked away, ran his finger over the lures and walked to the counter where the handguns were displayed. Lafitte stood where he was, for a moment unsure how to react. Keep it calm, he told himself. Say nothing. Do nothing. He moved behind the counter and looked down where the man bent, resting both elbows on the counter. Lafitte could see traces of yellow-brown scalp through the gelled prickles of his hair. 'Can I help you?' His voice was stilted, the words chipping unevenly from his tongue.

The man looked up. He was small, like all of them were small, much smaller than Lafitte. He looked into Lafitte's face, though, and his features were smooth as stone and his eyes remained hidden behind the glasses. Slowly, he shook his head. He did not speak, but stood a moment longer, then turned somewhat laconically and wandered out of the store. Lafitte was aware of the pulsing vein at his neck. He picked up the telephone.

'Sheriff Riggins, please,' he said, when the girl answered.

'One moment, sir.'

'Riggins.'

'Greg. This is Billy Bob Lafitte. One of those damn gooks just came in the store.'

Three of them were seated at a round, formica-topped table in the bar area of the Captain's Table. Neal Reardon, the bartender, polished glasses and watched, his back to the liquor bottles and the window, which looked out at the Pacific. The sun was a ball of flames hissing into the sea and the restaurant was packed with diners. Business was good, but Reardon wondered about the three Orientals in their matching suits and matching ties, and their black Suburban parked right out front. He shook his head, set up the glasses and began mixing the margaritas.

The door opened and Lafitte walked in with Tommy Brindle and Maplethorpe, the deputy sheriff out of uniform. They walked past the Orientals' table and took the stools at the bar. Reardon shook up the drinks he was making. 'Be right with you, gentlemen.'

None of them answered him. They settled themselves on the stools, then swivelled right round till their backs were to him. Reardon lifted his eyebrows and stared from under raised lids. He had to look at people with his head tilted slightly back, otherwise he would have a seizure. One car wreck too many. 'Back in a jiffy, gentlemen.' He lifted up the flap in the counter and placed the three brimming margaritas on to a tray, which he carried through to the restaurant. When he came back, the three men were still looking at the Orientals, who ignored them and carried on

46

their conversation in whatever language it was they were speaking.

'Goddamn gooks.' Maplethorpe swung round to face Reardon. 'What you doing letting gooks in here, Neal?'

'They're customers, Map. And this is a free country.' Reardon cracked a genial smile. 'Now, what'll it be?'

'Just give us three beers.'

'Three cold ones coming right up.' Reardon flipped off the tops and slid the beers over to them. Lafitte was staring at one of the Orientals, who stared right back at him.

'Where you from, mister?' Lafitte's voice was deep, a slow rumble in his chest. The man did not answer him. 'I asked you where you were from.'

The Oriental stared for a moment longer, then the three of them got up and one took a wad of bills from his pocket. He peeled off a twenty, waved it at Reardon and laid it down on the table.

'Thank you, sir,' Reardon said. 'You have a good evening.'

The Oriental nodded to him, glanced at Lafitte, and then the three of them walked out of the restaurant. Lafitte slid off his stool and inspected the twenty-dollar bill lying on the table.

Reardon watched him. 'Something wrong with it, Billy Bob?'

Lafitte ignored him and brought the bill back to his stool. He sat down, sipped beer, then turned the bill over in his hand. It was crisp and new, and he looked at it very carefully. Reardon plucked it from his grasp. 'Thank you kindly, sir. Nice to see some people still know how to tip.'

Lafitte stared at him. 'You gonna take that, boy?'

'Billy Bob.' Reardon rested his elbows on the counter. 'I'm nearly as old as you. I've lived here nearly as long as you, and you know what – I'm no longer a boy.'

Lafitte stared at him.

'No, really. It's true,' Reardon went on. 'I got pubic hair and everything.'

'Hey!' Maplethorpe jabbed a finger at him. 'Watch your mouth.'

'Neal,' Lafitte said more quietly. 'Those Chinese men that just left are government agents. You're a wise guy, I know. And you got a big mouth. Why don't you listen up for once in your fool life?'

Reardon cocked his eyebrows. 'I'm all ears.'

Lafitte tapped the back of the twenty where it lay on the counter. 'It ain't printed on these, but see here.' He took out a dollar bill and showed the all-seeing eye to Reardon. 'See that?'

'You mean, right there?' Reardon tapped the bill and shook his head a little sadly. 'Hovering above the pyramid. Don't tell me, the mark of the beast.'

'The Illuminati, Neal. The Devil's mark. The all-seeing eye of the Federal Reserve. The money's worthless. It's just another tool of entrapment.'

'Uh huh.' Reardon lit himself a cigarette. 'So the three beers, right there?' He pointed to the counter. 'You guys gonna pay me in gold?'

Lafitte looked at him for a long moment and then he shook his head. 'You can joke, Neal. You can mock all you like. But I'm gonna tell you something. Those three men that just walked out of here. Two nights ago they were at my house. They drove up the dirt road to the edge of my property. Then they came in, poisoned my dogs and took my 30/30 outta my truck.'

Reardon stared at him for a moment. 'Piper and Dillon are dead?'

Lafitte flapped a hand at the telephone on the wall. 'Phone the veterinarian and ask him. They ate meat laced with strychnine.'

'You're kidding me.'

Lafitte got up from the stool and pushed his empty bottle across the counter. 'Do I look like I'm kidding you?'

When he got home, his wife was making biscuits. 'Sit

down, honey. I've got you a steak all but ready and I'm just gonna cook these up real quick.'

Lafitte kissed her gently. 'We got any of that country gravy left?'

'I made some fresh this morning.'

'You sweetheart.' He laid a palm on her cheek and then told her about the three men in the bar. 'Did you hear from the boys today?'

'No. Should I have?'

He shook his shoulders. 'I guess not.'

Halfway up the hill, a figure in black watched through the kitchen window. No dogs now to disturb him. He saw Lafitte and his wife talking together and then he saw him kiss her, and he smiled behind his ski mask. He squatted, muscles coiled, and scanned the scene through binoculars. Lafitte disappeared, leaving his wife alone to her cooking. The figure set down the binoculars and sat in absolute stillness for a moment, before getting up, black and unseen against the rising darkness of the hill. He placed the binoculars back into the hessian field bag and strapped it over his shoulder. Then he began to pick his way down towards the house.

Lafitte stared at his computer screen and the e-mail from BobCat Reece in Montana. Daniel Pataki, deputy leader of the Missouri Breakmen Militia, and wanted by the FBI for an alleged bank robbery, had been found dead in a motel room near his home in Poplar Bluff, Missouri. Lafitte leaned closer to the screen, eyes widening as he read on. Pataki was twenty-seven years old, a fitness and survival fanatic. Four weeks ago, he reported seeing a black helicopter fly over his position while training in the hills west of his home. His autopsy result stuck out like a Union Jack on the fourth of July. Pataki had died of yellow fever. Yellow fever could only be contracted in the tropics. He had never been east of Kentucky.

Lafitte got up with a jerk and grabbed his jacket. Millie

looked up as he stormed through the kitchen and wrenched open the door. 'What's the matter, darling?'

'It's started, honey. It's begun. They've killed one of our members in Missouri. I've got to see Riggins and call some kinda meeting.'

'Phone.'

'I can't do this on the phone, Millie. They're absolutely everywhere.' He paused to get his breath. 'It's a call to arms. That's what it is.' He stood with one hand on the door. 'D'you know what the worst of it is?'

'What's that, Billy Bob?'

'People don't know. People don't want to know, Millie. Ninety per cent of the people of this country have no idea what is happening.'

She stared after him, watched him cross the yard and climb into the black Dodge. She heard the electronic twist of the key, heard the sudden thundering of the V8 motor, and then he spun the wheel and drove down the drive, not pausing as he hit the dirt road. She never saw him again.

Lafitte drove quickly, too quickly, the wrong gear and not thinking straight. His mind was falling over itself. For years little incidents had gone on, nothing you could nail to the wall, just little bits and pieces here and there. But now this. He thought of Reardon and his fool-glib comments; his little jibes and jokes. How fool would he be when they came to take his guns? The road was steep and the first sharp bend was coming up, with the mountain falling away on the right. Dark again tonight, the smell of more rain and no moon or stars. He eased his foot off the throttle and dabbed at the brake pedal. It went all the way to the floor and his eyes balled in their sockets. The corner came up too fast and he span the wheel, heard the gravel hissing, felt the shudder and thump as the wheels slid over the edge, and then he was careering down the slope with the roof against his head.

Cheyenne Logan, supervisory special agent with the FBI, had a temporary desk in ASAC Tom Kovalski's office, on

4th Street, Washington D.C. She used the circular conference table, had a computer linked to the network and stored
her paper files in a bank box in one corner. Kovalski did not
mind; the office was three times the size of the one he had
had at headquarters, less than ten minutes away. The D.C.
field office was the flagship and it showed. Logan was
breaking in the new terrorism response co-ordinator for the
Washington joint terrorism task force, a function she had
fulfilled for three years when she and Kovalski were
working with the operations unit on Pennsylvania Avenue.
Kovalski had been promoted to assistant special agent in
charge at the field office, and he had been hoping to leave
some of his terrorism responsibilities behind, but that was
not to be. The Bureau liked nothing better than experience
and much of his remit in domestic ops had followed him to
4th Street. On top of that, when Osama Bin Laden bombed
the embassies in Kenya and Tanzania, he had taken charge
of the operation that followed. He looked over at Logan
now, on the phone to his ATF counterpart in California, and
was glad she was back, if only for a while. He had
confidence in Carmen McKensie's ability, but did not have
the time to teach her the ropes himself.

Logan sat at her computer and the ebony sheen of her
forehead furrowed into twin horizontal lines. She wore a red
two-piece suit and low-heeled shoes, and her gun lay in its
shoulder holster across the back of her chair. McKensie was
seated on the couch, sifting through papers. Logan glanced
at her. 'Come over here a minute, will you, Carmen?'

At thirty-five, McKensie was slightly older than Logan
and had been married to an agent in the Bomb Data Center
for three years. Her last posting had been San Diego.

Logan tapped a scarlet-polished fingernail against the
computer screen. 'This just came up on the NCIC. Billy
Bob Lafitte, leader of the Pacific Coast Militia, was killed in
a car wreck in Hope Heights, Oregon.' Kovalski had put
down the phone and was listening from across his desk.
'Did you hear that, Tom? Just came over the wire. Lafitte's

51

dead.' Logan paused. 'The brake lines on his Dodge were cut.' She sat back. 'That's two in a week. Pataki in Missouri and now this guy out west.'

Kovalski got up and came over. 'Were there any other circumstances like we had with Pataki?'

'Well, it wasn't yellow fever, but his brakes were tampered with.' Logan scrolled down the report that had been logged on the National Crime Information Center by a Detective Cameron from the State of Oregon criminal investigation division. 'Two nights previously a Winchester 30/30 rifle was allegedly stolen from the same truck, which was parked in Lafitte's yard. The vehicle was locked and he had two guard dogs.' She paused again. 'They were poisoned with strychnine.'

Kovalski's phone was ringing. Mary, his secretary, put her head round the door. 'Mr Kovalski,' she said. 'That reporter's on the phone again.'

'Which reporter?'

'Carl Smylie. The freelance one. He wants to know if we have a comment about the homicide in Oregon.'

Kovalski rolled his eyes to the ceiling and then he smiled. 'Your call, Carmen.'

McKensie got up. 'It'll be a pleasure.' She picked up the phone and told Smylie that the FBI had no comment to make on the death of Billy Bob Lafitte, which was a state police investigation.

Smylie laughed in her ear. 'Yeah, right. That's what your St Louis office said about Daniel Pataki. Of course, yellow fever is rife in that part of Missouri.' He went on to ask her if she did not think it a little strange that two militia members had turned up dead in as many days, in different parts of the country. 'Pataki was wanted by the FBI,' he said. 'St Louis bank robbery, remember? The word was you couldn't pin it on him.'

'That was not the word, Mr Smylie,' McKensie said. 'The word was he was on the run. We'd issued a UFAP warrant for him. That's *unlawful flight to avoid prosecution*, if you want to print it.'

'Jeeze, I know what it is, lady. But don't you think it's just a bit weird that he wound up dead within a week of you obtaining that warrant?'

'My opinion is irrelevant, sir. The murder investigation is, at this point, a state police matter.' She asked him in future to contact the Office of Public and Congressional Affairs and hung up. 'That guy's gonna be trouble,' she said.

'Carmen,' Kovalski said. 'Carl Smylie is the voice of the militia. He's been trouble for years.'

Logan sat back in her chair and scrolled through the Oregon detective's crime scene report. 'Apparently, Lafitte complained to the local sheriff about being harassed by three oriental men wearing grey suits and driving a Chevy Suburban,' she said. 'He also claimed that his property was buzzed by a black helicopter.'

'Same as Pataki before he went AWOL,' McKensie put in.

'Pataki was a fugitive,' Kovalski said.

'But we didn't chase him in a helicopter.'

'No.' Kovalski shook his head. 'I don't think we did. We only got as far as the UFAP. This guy Lafitte could've seen anything – National Guard chopper, Game and Fisheries. Goddammit, these black helicopters have been the bane of my life for the past five years.'

Logan stood up then and smoothed down her skirt. 'I want to fly out to Oregon, Tom. Show a federal face in Hope Heights. Pataki was a hoodlum, but Lafitte was a respectable businessman and a major player in the patriot movement.'

'Christian Identity follower?'

She made a face. 'I don't know. But I would imagine so. We know he was in Vietnam the same time as Louis Beam, and he's had dealings with the leaders in Idaho. He was vocal at Ruby Ridge and went to the Aryan Nations compound at Hayden Lake when BobCat Reece was guest speaker at their annual congress. Latterly, like the rest of them, he's tried to become more respectable.' She broke off. 'That guy Smylie is right in one way, Tom. There's something weird going on here.'

Kovalski smiled at her. 'The old spider sense tingling, is it?' He made an open-handed gesture. 'Do whatever you got to, Chey. And take Carmen with you. It'd be nice to have my office back for a while.'

They left him then, Logan packing up her laptop and strapping her gun under her jacket. 'Are you planning on it being just the two of us, Cheyenne?' McKensie asked her.

Logan looked back at her. 'Oh, we'll let the Portland office know we're making the trip, but yeah, I figured just you and me, Carmen. Two female Feds in small-town Oregon, right after a militia leader got killed.' She broke off and smiled. 'Should be interesting, particularly with the victim being a white supremacist and me being one of the mud people.'

As Kovalski watched them go, his phone was ringing again. 'ASAC,' he said when he picked it up.

'I've got a Mr Horowitz, Mr Kovalski. He wants to talk to you about "housekeeping".'

Kovalski drew in his brows and hunched over the table. 'Put him through, Mary. And get someone to close my door.' He sat back again, listened to the click, and then a new voice sounded in his ear. 'Mr Kovalski.'

'Mr Horowitz.' Kovalski swivelled round in the chair so he faced the wall. 'What can I do for you?'

'It's what I can do for you.'

'I'm listening.'

'Word comes to me that you may have a fly in your ointment.'

Kovalski sat more upright. 'Go on.'

'I don't know much more.'

'Do we need to meet?'

'I don't think so.'

'That's it? Just a fly in the ointment.'

'*Your* ointment, Mr Kovalski. The only other thing I heard was this fly likes to settle on cherry blossom.'

Kovalski put down the phone and sat quietly for a moment. Horowitz was a source in the Israeli Embassy, one that the CIA did not have their hooks into. Now and again he fed information directly to Kovalski, who knew him from his early days as a spycatcher. He had arrested two Israeli Embassy employees on suspicion of spying and got them both convicted. During the course of that investigation he had come across Horowitz, who had proven to be a very reliable source over the intervening years. Now he was a sort of unofficial asset. What Horowitz said, generally turned out to be right. Ointment was a codeword for Washington D.C. and a fly was going to be trouble.

3

Logan and McKensie flew to Portland, Oregon, where they were met by an agent from the field office, a probationer who was ex-Marine Corps, with muscles bulging in places Logan did not remember other people having. His name was Stroud and he talked incessantly all the way to the field office. 'The word is it's us,' he said. 'The G-men.'

'Orientals in black Suburbans.' Logan leaned her elbow on the back of her seat. 'It sounds like the Hong Kong troops the UN is supposed to have sneaked into the country.'

McKensie was in the back, listening. Stroud glanced in the rearview mirror. 'You guys want some company when you go down there?'

'I don't think so.' Logan looked sideways at him. 'Why, do you think we need it?'

He lifted a palm. 'Hey, only if you want. The boss's got no great desire to get involved. If it is murder, then it's either the sheriff's dicks or state police CID. They're welcome to it.' He unwrapped a sliver of chewing gum and rolled it into a ball. 'But you know what these assholes are like. They're gonna love having you two show up, especially as Lafitte's outfit are Christian Identity and you're . . .' Stroud broke off.

'Black,' Logan finished for him. She pushed back her sleeve. 'And not just a little on the tanned side, either.'

Colour prickled across Stroud's neck and jaw line, flushing into his cheeks. 'Hey, I'm sorry. I didn't mean anything by it.'

'I know you didn't.' Logan patted him on the arm. 'Don't you worry, Stroud. I've been black for a long time now. I can handle the rednecks.'

The special agent in charge of the Portland office briefed them thoroughly on what he knew of Lafitte and his followers, and told them that as far as his office was aware, some of the big names from the militia movement were going to attend the funeral.

'We know BobCat Reece is coming over from Montana and a few from Hayden Lake. There's Paul Hannah from Texas. He's a player too. There'll be representatives from the NRA and Guns of America. The Pacific Coast Militia is planning some kind of rally on the beach down there. Reece is gonna make some kinda speech. Oh, one other thing you might wanna know. Billy Bob Lafitte – or William as everyone is calling him now – was pretty good friends with the congressman up here. John Rayburn, a Republican.'

Logan thanked him and then drove the rental car to the Holiday Inn on the edge of town. First thing in the morning, they drove south for Hope Heights.

'Jesus. Look at all the media.' McKensie pointed through the windshield, as they entered the city limits from the north. Hope Heights: population 1,584.

'We're talking small town,' Logan said. 'One street. Two bars. Maybe a diner somewhere and an Atkinson's supermarket.'

She was right. There was one wide street with a log homes building company on one side of the road and a small industrial estate for logging beyond it. After that, it was stores, a diner and a pool bar on the ocean side of the street. There were more stores on the left, then a motel made up of a mixture of log cabins and modern condominium-style units. TV company vans were parked everywhere – everything from the local stations to NBC and CNN.

Logan sucked at her teeth as she swung off the road and into the turning-area for the motel. 'You know, this is bigger news than I thought it was going to be.' She parked and sat behind the wheel for a moment. 'We're gonna do well to get a room,' she said, and then turned to McKensie.

'You go, Carmen. They don't like black women in this part of the world.'

McKensie grimaced and climbed out of the passenger seat. Logan sat and waited for her, watching the hubbub on the street. It was not warm today, and a vicious wind was blowing in from the west. The only people on the beach were the surfers. The motel looked pretty full and she could see there was a kids' play area and a path that led to the dunes, where a lookout tower, painted red, dominated the horizon. A couple of people walked past the front of the car and Logan smiled at them.

McKensie came back. 'We're in luck,' she said. 'They have one cabin free. It was vacated this morning and, as yet, no one from the media's been in.'

'Great.' Logan looked sideways at her. 'Did you tell them who we were?'

McKensie smiled then. 'Only *after* they rented me the room.'

'Good on you, girlfriend. You're learning this game fast.'

They dumped their stuff in the cabin and Logan checked her gun, taking it out of the holster and breaking it open. She worked the action, slipped a round into the breech and snapped on the safety catch. Then she slid it back into her holster once more.

'We need to be careful,' she said. 'According to the militia, the United States government has drafted in one hundred thousand Hong Kong troops to round them up and take away their guns, and they've just had what they believe to be a government-inspired murder in this town.' She flared her nostrils slightly. 'We're representatives of that government.' She left her suit jacket on the bed and slipped on a raincoat, which gave her more room under the arms. 'Let's go see this Detective Cameron.'

The sheriff's department had set up a mobile incident room in a trailer on the beach. Vehicles were dotted round it: sheriff's department 4 × 4s and state police cruisers. Logan and McKensie drove back up Main Street and parked in front of the diner. People thronged the sidewalks – tourists and media people alike. Cameras were everywhere and Logan could smell the tension in the air. The day was bright and overhead the sky was blue, but the wind was blowing and she had a feeling that a storm was just across the horizon.

The door to the incident room stood open and a deputy in uniform, with Maplethorpe written on his name tag, leant against it, a super-sipper of coffee in one hand. His hat was tipped back and a band of sweat lined his face where the sunburn ended. He glanced at McKensie briefly, then looked Logan up and down.

'What can I do for you?' He addressed McKensie.

Logan smiled and flashed her shield. 'Special Agents Logan and McKensie,' she said. 'We'd like to talk to the detective in charge, please.'

Maplethorpe looked at her for a long moment, then very deliberately he took the shield and studied it. 'F-B-I.' He said it loudly enough for anyone inside the trailer to hear, and within seconds, a portly man with grey, thinning hair filled the doorway. He stared at them, shifting a plug of chewing tobacco from one side of his mouth to the other. His gaze lingered on Logan's very pretty, black face, but it was not lust in his eyes. Ah, Logan thought. We have a militia sympathiser in local law enforcement.

'Sheriff?' she said. 'Agent Logan.' She offered her hand, moving on to the three steps that led up to the doorway. He took her hand, albeit a little reluctantly. 'Riggins. Curry County Sheriff,' he said.

'Nice to meet you, Sheriff.'

He squinted at her, then spoke to McKensie. 'You all from Portland?'

'No. We're from D.C.' Logan answered for her.

'We didn't request an FBI presence. This is a state inquiry.'

'I know, sir. But the circumstances that Detective

59

Cameron logged on the NCIC seem a little on the strange side.'

'You bet your sweet . . .' Riggins broke off and spat tobacco juice into the sand.

Logan smiled at him. 'Can we talk to Detective Cameron?'

Riggins seemed to think long and hard about that and then he stepped aside. 'You better come in,' he said.

Cameron was younger, perhaps thirty, perhaps less, with a certainty that was not arrogance about his features. He stood up and shook hands, then offered them a seat in the cramped surroundings. Riggins leaned in the doorway with his arms folded. 'Feds, huh?' Cameron poured them some coffee. 'If you listen to rumour, you're not the first who've been here.'

'We never listen to rumour,' Logan said.

He gestured through the window. 'Maybe, but other people certainly do. I've never seen so many people in such a small town.' He fished in his wallet for his card. 'I'm with the state police criminal investigation division.' Cameron nodded to Riggins. 'Sheriff Riggins here was a friend of the deceased, so his interest is more than just professional.'

Logan looked over her shoulder. 'Did you know Mr Lafitte very well, Sheriff?'

'As well as I knew anyone. Grew up with the man. We're Oregon born and raised. Only ever moved but one county.'

'So you were pretty close, then?'

'Yes, mam.' Riggins spoke through tight lips, white lines of muscle in his face. 'Billy Bob, I mean William, called me to his place at three o'clock in the morning, two nights before he died. Somebody'd stolen his rifle from where it hung in his truck. Not only that, but they poisoned his dogs.' His face was lined and closed, animosity barely veiled in the ice-blue of his eyes.

Logan already knew the answer, but she asked it anyway. 'The brake lines on his truck were definitely cut?'

Cameron answered her. 'Our crime scene unit is very

good, Logan. The reports aren't finalised just yet, but the initial analysis suggests some kind of clippers, a sharp pair of pliers, maybe. There are traces of brake fluid in Lafitte's yard.'

Logan nodded slowly. 'Can we see Lafitte's yard?'

Behind her, the sheriff grunted and shifted his feet restlessly. Logan looked over her shoulder at him. 'Does the idea bother you, Sheriff?'

'You don't got no jurisdiction here, lady.'

'You're right. I don't. It's a request, not an order.' She looked back at Cameron. 'Do you have any objections?'

'No.'

'Good.' She stood up and smoothed the creases in her skirt. She looked again at the sheriff. 'D'you want to come with us?'

They followed Riggins's 4 × 4, riding with Cameron in his unmarked car. Logan sat up front and leaned sideways against the door. Cameron was grinning all over his face. 'You did it on purpose, didn't you,' he said suddenly.

Logan squinted at him. 'What?'

'You two gals. Two agents from Washington D.C. Not even Portland, but Washington D.C. Both of you women.' He shook his head. 'One of you black. Way out here in the boonies.'

Logan laughed then. She liked Cameron, and was suddenly glad this was a state police investigation. She had nothing against the county system, but sheriffs were elected and every now and again one like Riggins popped to the top of the pile. 'Tell me about the Orientals, Detective,' she said.

Cameron pulled off the highway and started to climb up a dirt road, dust rising to mist up the side windows. 'A lot of people saw them,' he said. 'Three men in grey suits, black ties, Ray-Ban shades. You know, the real deal.'

'And they were driving a black Chevy Suburban?' McKensie spoke from the back seat.

Cameron looked at her in the rearview mirror. 'That's right.'

'A federal government vehicle, the kind of thing Mel Gibson had so much trouble with in *Conspiracy Theory*.'

He pulled a face. 'That's about the size of it.'

'And the helicopter?'

'Black, of course,' he said. 'I don't know a whole lot about that. We only have Lafitte's word and he's dead.'

They were halfway up the mountain now and Cameron pulled over opposite an area which had been taped off by the police. He put on the handbrake and took his sunglasses and raid jacket from where they were stuffed under the windshield. The two FBI agents followed him and crossed the dirt road to the tape. The mountain fell away sharply here. Part of the landscape had been logged and was open, leaving the soil brown and scarred. Part of it remained thick with forestation. Logan stood with her hands in the pockets of her raincoat and studied the ground: a mishmash of tyre tracks. She could see where the vehicle had slewed as the driver tried to take the bend, then rocketed over the edge. A trail of broken-up ground and foliage led off down the mountain. Perhaps five hundred feet below them, she could see the back end of a truck wedged between two pine trees. Cameron pointed and pursed his lips. 'It's gonna take something to get it out. We're waiting for a truck with a big enough winch, right now.'

Logan nodded slowly. 'Where does this road lead to?' she asked him.

'The Lafitte place, that's all.'

She turned to him then. 'So who cut his brake lines, Detective?'

Cameron looked from her to McKensie and back again. 'You tell me, Logan.'

They drove to the top of the road and Cameron pulled up outside the property. Logan could see maybe seven vehicles stacked up along the driveway and people were milling about in front of the house. 'Lafitte was a popular figure round town,' Cameron told them. 'He ran the outdoor store, you know – fishing rods, guns, etc.'

Logan nodded. 'Are all these people local? That licence plate's Montana.' She pointed to a white Ford 250 truck. And then she saw BobCat Reece come striding down the drive towards them. Two younger men accompanied him, one on either side. They were wearing jeans, lace-up cowboy boots and baseball hats, the peaks curved into tunnels above their eyes. She recognised Reece from the picture the Bureau had taken of him, when he had been arrested and ultimately released over the shooting of a forest ranger near the Canadian border. There had been no witnesses and the ranger's weapon had been fired. Reece walked on a plea of self-defence.

'Those are Lafitte's sons,' Cameron said, pointing to the two younger men.

'Can we talk to them?'

He blew out his cheeks. 'If they'll talk to you. But I wouldn't step on the property if I were you.'

They got out and stood just on the dirt road. Reece stopped ten feet from them. 'Morning, Detective,' he said, then eyed Logan in particular, the hint of a sneer creasing the edge of his lip. 'These must be the G-men, or should I say women.'

'Good morning,' Logan said. 'I'm Agent Logan and this is Agent McKensie. We're with . . .'

'The FBI. We know.'

She looked at Reece and smiled. 'I'm sorry,' she said. 'You have me at a disadvantage. I don't know your name.'

Reece half closed his eyes then. He was a tall man, with dark hair and a heavy moustache reaching to his lower jaw. Lafitte's sons were in their twenties, both black-haired, heavily tanned, and with sharp eyes. One of them wore a shirt cut off at the sleeves and his muscles bulged as he hooked his thumbs in his horsehair belt.

'You ain't welcome here.' His voice was deep and

guttural. He sucked on whatever it was he was chewing and spat into the dirt. His brother leaned on the gatepost.

'Detective Cameron, sir, that don't include you. Not right now, anyways.'

The sheriff's been on the cellphone, Logan thought. She looked at Reece once more. 'Are you a family member, sir?'

'You know fine who I am, lady. I bet you got my picture pasted on your walls back east.'

Don't flatter yourself, she thought, but smiled. Cameron saved the situation. 'This is Mr Reece from Montana,' he said. 'These two gentlemen are Jim and Jacky Lafitte.'

Logan offered her hand. Reece kept his in his pocket. She looked at the two sons. 'I'm very sorry for your loss,' she said.

Neither of them replied.

'What's the FBI doing here?' Reece said then. 'Checking to make sure all went according to plan.'

Logan laughed lightly. 'You don't seriously think this was down to us, do you?'

'You got a good reason why I shouldn't?' Reece took a pace towards her. 'You wanna explain the presence of three Hong Kong soldiers driving a Chevy Suburban in Oregon?'

'Mr Reece.' McKensie spoke then. 'Do you really think if we wanted to kill Mr Lafitte, we would send in three Orientals driving a black Suburban?'

'I think you'd do what you damn well please, lady. Just like you people always do.' He stuck out his chin. 'Now, my reading of the law tells me this is a state investigation and I know I speak for everyone when I tell you you're not welcome in Hope Heights.'

'I expect you do, sir,' Logan told him. 'But the funny thing is we're just as concerned about this homicide as anyone else. It's why we're here.'

She took a pace forward and Jacky Lafitte, the elder of the two brothers, snapped his head up. 'Lady, you step on my daddy's property and I'm within my constitutional rights to shoot you.'

Logan looked at him, shook her head sadly and then turned to Cameron. 'Detective, I think we should leave these good people to their loss.' She turned for the car and somebody muttered the words 'nigger bitch', and she paused, almost turned, then bit her lip and walked back to the car.

The District of Columbia was sweating, eighty per cent humidity, and the traffic was backed up downtown due to the security surrounding the state visit of Israel's newly elected prime minister. Fachida Harada sat in his red security consultant's truck, with *C U SAFELY* painted on the side, in the no-waiting zone, watching the parks police officer on a Harley Davidson making his way towards him. He shifted the baseball hat, embossed in the same manner as the truck, higher up his head and picked up the sunglasses from where they lay on the passenger seat. The cop pulled up and revved the weighty V-twin alongside him. Harada rolled down the window and heat struck at the air-conditioned interior of the cab.

'Can't you read, buddy?'

Harada smiled at him. 'I'm sorry.' He pointed across the road to a hotel. 'We're working there. Security. My partner's on his way back.'

The cop looked at the side of the truck. 'You fitting alarms?'

'And CCTV. He'll only be two minutes.'

The cop twisted the throttle again, tight-fitting black gloves reaching to his bare forearms. He wore a shirt with no jacket and high-leg leather boots.

'It must be nice,' Harada said, 'riding round the city when it's this hot.'

'Are you kidding me?' The cop looked through mirror-lensed sunglasses at him. 'You can't get enough speed up to cool down.' Again he revved the engine, glanced over his shoulder at the traffic, then looked back at the driver. 'You got ten minutes, buddy. Then you get the ticket.'

Harada saluted him and smiled, but the smile dried on his face as he watched the bike roar off up the road. He stared across the street once again, then started his engine.

He drove down Pennsylvania Avenue, past the many flags flying outside the Hoover building. Here, he slowed and counted the number of black-uniformed FBI police who were guarding the place. Somebody in a dump truck hooted his horn behind, and he thrust his hand out of the window and waved apologetically before speeding up again. The traffic slowed to a crawl as he approached Capitol Hill.

He eased on to the ring road that skirted the seat of democracy and took Maryland Avenue as far as Stanton Park. Here, he pulled into a parking zone and let the engine idle. He sat in the truck and watched for a few minutes longer, hands lightly gripping the wheel, his flat features impassive. Then he shifted into first gear and pulled back into the traffic. He headed up 4th Street and when he drew parallel with the FBI's field office, he slowed, scoured the windows, but saw nothing. SCIF. That's what he had been told: a secret compartmented information facility. The windows were protected from unwanted eyes by dark, impenetrable glass.

He parked the truck in the self-storage unit he had rented in a large complex, not far from the US soldiers' and airmen's home off North Capitol Street, and stepped through the adjoining door into the next unit. Here there was a shower, and he undressed slowly, meticulously folding the red overalls he had made specially, then hanging them in the first metal locker set against the wall. The showerhead was wide and the water fell in an icy torrent, and Harada tensed every muscle in his body until they stood out against the skin. When he was finished, he stood on the mat and let the water dry naturally until he started shivering. It pleased him – the movement of flesh, the chilled freshness after the heat of the city. He had learned a little today, and then again, perhaps he had learned a lot. The police were as he had found them over the past six months. Ten minutes in a no-parking zone. That was close to the best. Thirteen minutes and thirty-two seconds was the actual record length of time that a cop had let him wait, but this one ran a close second. Not that he required anything like that amount of time. Preparation was everything and he had been preparing for a very long time.

He caught sight of his reflection, naked in the mirror alongside the locker, and it pleased him. Every muscle was visible: the horizontal layers against the flat of his stomach, the smooth arch of his pecs. There was not a single grey hair on his cropped black head and, after forty-four years, this pleased him. He opened the door to the second locker and took down his plain grey suit. He dressed carefully, his body still damp so that the white shirt stuck to him in places. When he was finished, he straightened his cuffs and picked up the briefcase he always set down beside the locker, and climbed into the sedan. He started the engine, left it running, then opened the roll-over door. He drove the car out and parked, then closed the door again and locked it. The self-storage complex had no guard, but twenty-four-hour access, which was why he had chosen it. Back in the car he looked at his watch, rolled the window up and switched on the air conditioning.

Across the road, an old man sat in his room in the old soldiers' home, dreaming of the past when he still had his legs. He tried to remember exactly when he had lost them, or for that matter, where. Sometimes he woke up, saw they weren't there and could not recall for the life of him when they had gone missing. But they were missing and the continuing shock of the discovery was debilitating. He thought (now that he tried hard) that it could have been Omaha beach, but he could not remember when that was. Some time in World War II, but he could not remember when that was exactly, either. He did not have much to do these days except read, and as he could not remember whether or not he had read something, he did not have to change his book very often. He wondered at his memory loss, thinking that if he could ever get out of here, he could tell the world about the conspiracy to keep him. Maybe the doctors took his legs to stop him walking out. He was a dangerous man with this knowledge.

He saw the red truck pull in again and the little man in overalls get out and open the lock-up. Then he saw the truck drive inside. Half an hour later, a door on the next unit opened and a car drove out. Then he saw another little man (who looked like a Jap from here) get out of the car and lock up. Funny thing: he watched every morning and every night and never saw the guy in the overalls leave. The guy in the suit came and went, but he never saw the guy next door. Again he shrugged his shoulders: it was all part of the same conspiracy, most likely. The door to his room opened and that young nurse came in, the pretty one whose name he could never remember.

'Charlie,' she called from behind him. 'It's time for your medication.'

'Will it make my legs grow back?'

'No. But it will make you feel better.'

'I ain't taking no medicine unless it makes my legs grow back. Which one of you stole them, anyways?'

Harada drove south on 95, the highway lined with trees all the way to Richmond. It was in truth a very boring drive, but one he would not have to make much longer. He drove carefully, watching for state troopers and never exceeding the speed limit. He had not exceeded the speed limit in the six months he had been here. Six months: he thought about that, thought about the suburb of Tokyo where his wife and children still lived, thought about the festival of the cherry blossom in April. Tadyoki, his son, would have taken part, as he had done every year since he had been able to walk, in the tradition of the family. He took part this year and would do so next year and all the years after that. Only nine years of life and every single one of them invested with the honour of generations. If Tadyoki knew only one thing of value in this world, it was the value of honour. Harada's wife, Akiko, would continue the tradition, and her father, still revered even by the young men, would see to it she did. Not that he needed to – he knew his daughter was a good and faithful wife, one who would remain so even in solitude. Harada could smell the trees now, that soft pungency, the delicacy of petals which, as soon as they bloomed, were lost for all time to the wind. For a long moment he dwelt on the image, and the blacktop rolled beneath the wheels at a steady fifty-five.

At Richmond, he turned off the highway and took 195 as far as the toll road, where he cruised south-west till he came to the junction for the Johnston Willis Hospital and Chesterfield Town Center. He parked the car and sat a long time behind tinted windows, watching the people on the street. There were not many of them. All the main stores were in malls and everyone drove everywhere else; the antithesis of Tokyo.

A police officer drove by, wearing sunglasses, a tanned forearm leaning against the doorpanel through the open window of his car. Harada let him pass, then locked and left the Ford and crossed to the antique shop at the far end of the street. A little wind-chime bell tinkled behind him as he stepped into the darkened interior. It was so dark that he had to allow his eyes a fraction of a moment to adjust, after the sun-baked glare of the street. Then, at the very back of the shop, he saw the kimono-clad Japanese seated as if he was asleep. Harada moved between the cluttered racks of oriental curios, not all of them Japanese. He recognised items from Manchukuo and Korea, as well as the Chinese-influenced areas of Siberia.

He had been lucky to discover this store and even luckier to observe the Shinto shrine arranged just beyond the counter. The shopkeeper was of the old code and the old code was honour and silence. He opened his eyes now, light blue and liquid, rheumy almost from a distance. His face was seamed with age and his thin moustache as white as the bones which buckled his hands at the knuckles. Harada paused and bowed.

The man returned the gesture. 'You are the gentleman who telephoned me last week.'

Harada nodded slowly, and the old man rose soundlessly, uncoiling himself from where he sat and led the way into the back room. He bent to a small wooden chest and, opening it, lifted out a gilt and velvet casket about two feet in length and six inches in depth. Harada could feel the breath drying the back of his throat. The old man set the casket on the small desk and unfastened the catches. Standing behind it, he opened the box so the lid lifted against his stomach, and subconsciously, Harada tightened the muscles round his mouth. The sword was a short samurai, not much bigger than a dagger, and the razor-sharp blade glinted in the half-light.

'The pedigree is exceptional,' the old man said. 'The sword was minted in 1797 and last worn in 1853 when the US fleet anchored in Tokyo Bay.' His eyes misted then. 'When the old ways were lost for ever.'

Harada shook his head slowly. 'Not for ever.' He looked at the intricacies of the blade, run with gold amid the silver. The hilt was covered in velvet and bamboo, with velvet again as the final layer.

He could feel the depth of emotion welling inside him, and for a moment he was in Jakarta, and then in the Bekaa Valley with the Arabs he despised so much for their trickery. He thought of Shigenobu and Korea, and how much money had been salted away after the incursions on behalf of the Libyan. For a moment, his past appalled him. Then he looked again at the sword and thought of the master whose name means 'snow at the foot of Mount Fuji'. He had been fifteen years old on 25 November 1970, when that last great deed of honour had been performed. He looked again at the old man and nodded. The old man smiled and snapped the casket shut.

Harrison walked the marbled length of the Vietnam War Memorial on Constitution Avenue. He had been here many times over the years and knew the first name was John H. Anderson, Jnr and the last was Jessie Calba. He passed a marine in uniform, who placed a US flag against the wall with a sheet of paper pinned to it. Harrison glanced at it; a photograph of a marine and the photocopied back of an envelope, stamped with the words: 'Verified missing in action. Chief casualty branch, US Marine Corps.'

The marine was dressed immaculately and, as he stood up, he squared off to the stone and saluted. Harrison went to the first bench across the stretch of grass from the monument, where the statue of the nurses, with the dying GI in their arms, stood in silence. He watched the marine at the wall, then glanced down at his own dishevelled appearance: ponytail hooked over one shoulder, singlet, scuffed jeans, and cowboy boots worn down at the heel. The marine stood very still for what seemed a long time. Then he dropped the salute, swivelled to the right and came up the path. As he passed Harrison, he glanced at him and stopped. His gaze rested on the rat tattooed on his upper arm. 'Excuse me, sir,' he said. 'Is that tattoo what I think it is?'

Harrison squinted through the sunlight at him. 'Well, that depends on what you think it is, son.'

The young man looked at it again, then into Harrison's eyes. 'Were you a Tunnel Rat in Vietnam, sir?'

Harrison pursed his lips and nodded to the memorial. 'Your daddy over there?'

The marine's eyes glassed. 'Yes, sir. He was killed in action in the Iron Triangle in 1969. He'd only been in Vietnam for three weeks and I was a month old. Today's the anniversary of his death.' He paused then. 'They told

71

my momma he was shot by a VC who came up out of a hole.'

'So was my best friend from Chicago.' Harrison gestured to the bench beside him. The marine sat down and Harrison plucked a cigarette from his pocket, snapping a match on his boot heel. 'Eli Footer. His name's right there on that stone.'

'Did *you* go underground?'

Harrison sucked smoke, thought back to muddy holes under steaming vegetation, and spiders, snakes and punji stake mantraps waiting to impale you. Darkness and fear. That's what he remembered most. Darkness and fear. He nodded and said quietly: 'I volunteered after my buddy Eli got killed.'

'Sir.' The marine was staring earnestly at him now and Harrison met his eyes. 'If you don't mind, I'd like to shake your hand.'

'You would?' Harrison looked at his gnarled fingers, cigarette burning between them.

'Some Rats went in after the VC that killed my daddy, sir,' the marine said. 'I don't know if they got him, but I'm proud to have met you.'

Harrison shook his hand. 'Thank you, son,' he said. 'I'm proud to meet you too.'

The marine stood up then, nodded to him, set himself square again and saluted. Harrison looked up into the marine's face and lifted his own hand to his temple. He then watched the marine walk away, smoked his cigarette and went to find a payphone.

Kovalski answered his direct line. 'ASAC.'

'Johnny Buck, Tom. How you doing?'

'Hey. Where are you, New Orleans?'

'Constitution Avenue. I'm on vacation.'

'And you're spending it in D.C.?'

'Kinda.' Harrison blew smoke into the breeze. 'It ain't so hot as New Orleans.' He paused. 'You fancy sipping beer with a fellow old soldier this evening?'

'Sure I do. Where?'

'Well, if I remember rightly, there's a good bar called the Seaport in Alexandria. Can you make it over there?'

'Sure thing. See you about eight o'clock.'

Harrison walked past the eastern gates of the White House towards Lafayette Park. Above him, unbeknown to him, Cyrus Birch, the CIA's national intelligence officer for the Near East and Africa, looked out of the corner office in the Old Executive building. Wendell Randall, the Director of Central Intelligence, sat at the Victorian desk and read the presidential finding Birch had drafted. Birch watched the scruffy man in the singlet and jeans, with a long grey ponytail dangling out the back of his hat, stroll past, then he glanced over his shoulder at Randall. Wendy (they called him that at Langley, when he wasn't listening) had been the President's campaign manager back at the last election and the DCI's job was his reward. Secretly, everyone knew that he had been after the State Department, but had had to settle for DCI instead. He had no intelligence experience whatsoever, and no military experience, save three years in the Marine Corps back before swords were invented. Little did he know when he took the job that he would end up as whipping boy for the intelligence oversight committees. And what Birch had just placed before him would put the cat among those pigeons like nothing he had seen before.

Birch was a veteran CIA case officer, one of the Ivy Leaguers, silver spoon and the best universities behind him. Some people were jealous. Birch dismissed it. He had seen many a prejudiced DCI come and go and *he* was still there.

When the President was sworn in, everyone out at Langley was hoping that Charles Wheeler, the deputy director for operations, would make DCI, but of course he didn't. Invariably, any incoming president owed too many favours to seriously promote from within.

Birch turned his back on the window and sat down once again in the chair across the desk from Randall. He had prepared his national intelligence estimate, in the wake of the bombings in Tanzania and Kenya, at the butt end of last year. Randall had had plenty of time to consider it before the finding was drafted. Birch was convinced in his own mind, but that meant nothing when a DCI had to persuade a president to make an executive order that had not been given for over twenty years. He *would* do it, however. Birch was sure of that. The President was a shrewd cookie for all his other weaknesses, and Birch was fairly confident he would be summoned to the situation room in the White House for the obligatory secret meeting. He hoped he would – the case would be better put if he got the chance.

Randall looked up at him, pressed half-moon glasses to the bridge of his nose and wagged his head from side to side. 'You know what you're asking, Cyrus?'

Birch looked at him. 'Funnily enough, I do, sir.'

Randall tutted like an admonitory schoolmaster. 'You know what I mean.'

'I know exactly what you mean.'

'This kind of thing hasn't been sanctioned since 1976. It'll never get past the oversight committees.'

'I think it will, if it has to, sir.'

Randall sat back again. 'What d'you mean if it *has* to?'

'Exactly what I say, sir.'

'You mean just steamroller on with it. Cyrus, the House Intelligence Committee has to see any finding that sanctions covert action.'

'Yes. But the worst they can do is draft a letter of protestation.' Birch paused for a moment. 'I know most of the members personally, sir. I don't think, given the past and what we believe about the future, they'll protest.' He sat down again. 'Everyone's attention has been grabbed by the Balkan situation. But this will not go away.' He tapped the paper, now laid flat on the desk between them. 'This man is the biggest single threat to US national security since the Cold War ended. He's way more dangerous than Milosovic or Saddam Hussein.' He stood up again. 'Can I suggest that I'm present when you put the finding to the President. In the meantime, I'll wine and dine a few congressmen at the Metropolitan. Send a few messages of my own.' He smiled then, his easy disarming smile. 'Sir, it's not as if this is anything like Nicaragua. No Contras, no massive funding, no harbour blockades.' He leaned one perfectly manicured hand on the desktop. 'It's just regular covert action, and not an Oliver North in sight.' He smiled reassuringly now. 'We get the OK from the President. The Talent set it up, and we go. I've had an operative *in situ* for almost a year in anticipation.'

'Simple as that, huh?' Randall looked unimpressed. 'You're that sure. Just waiting for the OK from the President.'

Birch smiled again. 'He will go with it, sir. Trust me. If you look at how we reacted last year, it's already been tacitly sanctioned.'

4

Kibibi Simpson wanted to get laid. She had that urge in her loins, brought on by a cocktail of alcohol, dance music and memories of her teenage years in Mississippi. Fifteen years ago: she had been eighteen, living with her parents and four brothers, close to the National Guard base at Meridian. She looked twenty-one and never got asked for ID, and she and her brothers used to go to the Howard Johnson disco on Friday nights and upset all the white folks. Her brothers were all big, black and in the Marine Corps, like their father before them. When Kibibi graduated from high school, she joined up too.

Nobody messed with her when the five of them went out together and her mom and dad could sleep soundly in their bed, knowing that their little Kibibi was just as safe as safe could be. She giggled to herself girlishly about it now as she sat on the lip of the stool, squeezed between two sweating night-clubbers with designs on the inside of her panties. They were white boys. She had a penchant for white flesh these days and they were both civilians. They already knew she was American, because it stuck out a mile every time she opened her mouth, but they did not know she was in the Service, even with the Grace Jones haircut.

She looked at the clock on the wall above the bar: 2 a.m. already; the lights would be coming on soon and the party-goers would spill like so much rubbish on to the London pavements. Camden Town on a Saturday night. It was either a cab or the night bus back to Paddington. The boy on her right rested his hand against her thigh, stroking lightly with one finger. Kibibi sucked the last of her cocktail through a straw and decided that he was not the one. She leaned towards him and, at the same time, grabbed hold of his

76

fingers and twisted them back. He yelped like a whipped dog.

Kibibi laughed, a long-nailed hand to her mouth. The nails were false and one of them had already fallen off. The boy looked at her for a moment and a pained expression broke open in his eyes, then he turned and walked away. The other one still looked keen, but Kibibi crushed his hopes with one shake of her head.

She stood on the pavement on her own, hopping from one foot to the other. It was colder than it ought to be for summer, and she wished she had gone to the toilet when she had the chance. Camden was busier now than on a Saturday afternoon, everyone looking for a cab. She figured her best bet would be to walk down towards Euston and hail one from there. She hugged her coat more tightly about her and lit a cigarette, the breeze whipping the smoke back over her shoulder. She got to Camden Palace, crossed the road and walked alongside the triangular stretch of park, where two lovers were making out on a bench. She felt a pang of jealousy, then remembered her options back at the night-club, shook her shoulders and walked on. Just north of Euston Station she flagged down a cab. As she climbed in, she got the strangest impression that somebody somewhere was watching her.

The driver dropped her in Southwick Street where she rented a flat above the wine bar. She had been sleeping with the old regional security officer for a year, before he transferred back to Virginia Avenue. His wife did not know, of course, and he had assisted with the rent as he had a real yen for covert black pussy. Kibibi had taken his money when it was offered, but she did not need it: she had a little extra coming in of her own and could cut off any lover at the kneecaps, whenever she had a mind.

She fumbled in her bag for the key and, as she did, she heard a boot scrape over stone. She tensed and listened, her training taking over, and then she looked back across the road to the shadows at the end of the street. Nothing moved in the silence. She looked closer and still saw nothing. She had had a lot to drink and figured maybe she was hearing things. Locating her key, she went up the three steps to the main door and let herself in. The wine bar was long since closed and she climbed the stairs to the landing. Two flats occupied the upper floors, hers and that of a nosy old lady who had her eye permanently stuck to the spyhole. Her feet made no sound on the heavy-pile carpet and all at once she felt tired. Still, she could sleep all day tomorrow if she wanted to, she was not on duty again until Monday week. She sought her doorkey, fitted it into the lock and went inside. The flat was in darkness, the curtains pulled on all the windows – she had done that before she went out. Tough-guy soldier or not, there was still something about walking into a house at night, with all the windows uncurtained, that had unnerved her since she was a child.

Dropping her bag on the hallstand, she tugged off high-heeled shoes, which just about ruined her feet. They made her feel feminine, though, which after weeks of uniform at a time was no bad thing. She had still not put the lights on, and she wandered through to the lounge and dumped her packet of cigarettes on the coffee table. Something moved in the darkness. Kibibi stood stock-still. A shadow took shape against the paleness of the window. Kibibi stepped backwards. She did not cry out; she had drunk too much for the alarm to register. She could hear the rasping sound of breathing. Then a hand clamped over her mouth and sudden, sharp pain bit between her ribs.

Jack Swann flew to New Orleans from Heathrow, with a stop in Detroit. He had hoped to spend at least one night with Cheyenne in Washington, but he had been busy right up to the moment he left, which meant he had to be in New Orleans that evening. He was annoyed: no Cheyenne, and not even Harrison to have a beer with. Still, at least his lectures were to be given in the FBI's briefing room and not upriver in Baton Rouge. That meant this whole week would be in New Orleans, with Thursday and Friday pretty much free. He had planned to fly to Washington for the weekend, but Cheyenne had been on the phone telling him that she might come to New Orleans instead. She had not seen her brother, James, for ages. He worked on the King's House charity project in the city.

New Orleans baked in a damp heat that visibly ate at your clothes. Swann could feel the sweat soaking his skin the minute he stepped outside the airport to wait for the FBI agent to come and pick him up. It was the white-haired former sheriff from St Charles Parish, John Earl Cochrane.

'Jack, good to see you.' Cochrane swept round the front of the car and they shook hands. 'Where y'all staying?'

'The quarter,' Swann told him. 'Provincial on Chartres Street.'

Cochrane drove him to the hotel and they sat in the bar and had a beer. Cochrane was the FBI co-ordinator for the terrorism joint task force, and he had arranged for the New Orleans lectures. 'Will you be going to Houston at all?' he asked.

Swann shook his head. 'Only here and possibly the LSU in Baton Rouge.'

Cochrane finished his beer and took his car back to the field office. They had still not moved, something that had been on the cards since the last time Swann had been in the city. Currently, they occupied three floors of somebody else's building, which was not a lot of good if the militia decided to lob a few mortars at them.

Upstairs in his room, Swann phoned his ex-wife in London to talk to his two daughters, then he took a shower. It was seven-thirty now and he was hungry. He did not fancy walking, so he made his way down to Nu Nus Café, which opened on to Decatur Street. A heavyset, blond-haired bartender commented on his accent. 'Are you Swann?' he asked.

Swann nodded.

'Dewey Biggs.' He offered a meaty palm. 'Johnny Buck

asked me to look after you. Said he didn't want to read about a limey getting his head blown off in the wrong part of the quarter.'

Swann laughed and took the beer Dewey offered him. 'Like I've never been here before,' he said, and drained half the bottle. He set it back on the bar and fished in his pocket for cigarettes. 'When's he due back, anyway?'

Dewey shook his head. 'I don't know. That guy comes and goes like a Louisiana rainstorm.' He scratched his head. 'Vacation, though, this time. I never knew him to take a vacation before.'

Swann nodded and yawned. 'D'you have an English lady staying here? She's Vietnamese to look at.'

'You mean Jean. Yeah, she's staying here. She's a doctor. Real nice lady.' Dewey wiped the counter with a cloth. 'She's out of town right now. St Charles Parish, I think.'

Swann finished his beer, ordered a sandwich to go and went up to bed.

The following morning, Cochrane picked him up and they drove up to Poydras Plaza. Swann was lecturing on the antiterrorism assistance programme which had been set up by the Bureau of Diplomatic Security, whose desire it was to promote the bilateral ties between the US and friendly foreign countries. This one, however, was sort of inverted, the participants being Louisiana police officers as opposed to visiting foreign security forces. Six months previously, Louisiana had had to deal with a tanker hijack on the Mississippi River, dangerously close to the Waterford 3 nuclear power facility. Swann had been on secondment with the FBI at that time, hunting an escaped fugitive from England, and with his local experience and expertise in terrorism they had asked him to lecture on this course. He was instructing on explosive incident counter-measures, bomb-scene management and counter-terrorist practice processing. Classroom stuff for six weeks. He did not mind: it meant he was closer to Logan.

He had twelve delegates for the two days' paper tuition: three of them were Feds; the rest were New Orleans cops, Louisiana state cops and two deputies from the sheriff's department in St Charles Parish, under whose jurisdiction the location of the nuclear plant fell. He noted the name of one of them, Joe Kinsella, the chief of deputies. Harrison had mentioned him and Swann thought about it as he wrote some additional notes during lunch. Harrison seemed to have something of a bee in his bonnet about this Jean Carey, but there was not much Swann could do except offer a little moral support. He had not met her yet, but could imagine why she had come here; the nothingness that she would be left with – how meaningless her job, her home and her friends would become. The lack of justice which would burn like an insult, an affront to the memory of her only son. Swann had come across the sentiments many times, the subconscious build-up of guilt, which haunted the relatives of murder victims for most of the rest of their lives.

Downstairs, he sat in the blazing sunshine of the parking lot with David Cimino, a cop from the NOPD, who told him he had been working surveillance with Harrison.

'Long-haired sonofabitch,' Cimino said, sucking on a Lucky Strike. 'He's gotta be the least likely looking Fed I ever come across.'

Swann smiled. 'That's why he's good, though, isn't it.'

'Oh yeah. And he's real good.'

'When's he due back?'

'I haven't got a clue.'

After class finished that afternoon, Swann took Joe Kinsella to one side. 'You wanna talk to me about the Carey kid,' Kinsella said, before Swann had a chance to say anything.

'You know all about it, then?'

Kinsella passed a hand over his moustache. 'I know all there is to know. But that isn't very much.' He made a face. 'Jack, the kid jumped on a freight train, which started out in Texas. I don't know what point he got on, but he never made it off again. He was shot in the head. Close quarters. We had powder burns on what remained of the right temple.' He paused for a moment and licked his lips. 'The only prints we could identify were his own.'

'On the gun, you mean?'

Kinsella shook his head. 'There was no gun.'

'So it wasn't suicide, then.'

'No. Somebody japped him up close. Somebody was on that train with him, probably more than one guy. The angle of trajectory makes the ME think that the shooter was sitting right alongside him when he did it, or Tom Carey was holding the gun himself.'

'Which means at least one other person was holding a gun on him.'

Kinsella nodded. 'There had to be two of them.'

Swann nodded. 'So, we're possibly talking some kind of Russian roulette. A game, maybe, that went wrong.'

'That's possible, I guess. But it's pretty unlikely given what the boy's mom tells me. He was a medical student with a real bright future. Not the type to go spinning the chamber on a freight train.' He shook his head. 'I'm treating it as a homicide. I don't know about the motive, but the Carey kid was part Vietnamese and looked it, so it coulda been racial.' He laid a hand on Swann's arm. 'Jack, there're a lotta crazy people riding those railroad tracks. This isn't the first stiff to show up. Whoever did it was long gone before that train rolled into Hahnville. The ME reckoned the boy had been dead at least ten hours before the security guard found him. You can get a long way on a train in ten hours. These guys jump one going east, then hop off and take one north, west or south. I got about a hundred and one different sets of fingerprints, a few scuffed boot marks and jack-shit else. I got no murder weapon. I got no motive. I got no record of anyone being on the train. There'll be no witnesses, Jack. There never are.'

Swann sat on the edge of the desk. 'Has Jean Carey been to see you?'

'Only about five hundred times.' Kinsella shook his head. 'I understand, but shit, what can I do? I can't just magic up the perp and hand him to her.' He sighed then. 'This is a cold case file, Jack, and every instinct I ever relied on tells me it's gonna stay that way.'

Jean Carey sat at a table in Nu Nus Café, aware that the bartender was glancing over now and again as if to make sure she was all right. She had been in town for well over a week now and had been back and forth to Hahnville to see Kinsella. He was apologetic but unhelpful, and she knew the chances of him solving Tom's murder were remote to nonexistent. Which placed her precisely nowhere and served only to accentuate the terrible feelings of isolation that visited her constantly. Everywhere she looked, she saw her son's face; not how she remembered him when he was alive – vibrant and smiling out of photographs at her – but how she had last seen him, five months ago now. And yet the image was as vivid in her mind as if she had seen it yesterday. They had been as careful and as considerate as they could be in the mortuary, but nobody could disguise the fact that half his head was missing. He haunted her dreams at night, standing at the foot of her bed like some macabre, ghostly image, with half his face gone. For the first three weeks back in England, she had woken up screaming.

She sipped her drink, aware of the barman's gaze, and felt like the refugee she had been in her youth, when every eye was a pitiful one, and her time and space and thoughts were barely her own. Kinsella had been kind enough and he listened, but she knew every ounce of control had been wrested from her and there was nothing she could do about anything. Every time she went out on to the street, just stood in Jackson Square, or on the banks of the river, she felt minuscule in comparison to everything, thoroughly insignificant in the world. And her son lay dead, with no justice, tossing and turning in a grave he was far too young to sleep in.

A tall man wearing a pair of chinos and a short-sleeved polo shirt came into the bar. He was good-looking, Jean thought, with short black hair and the beginnings of a suntan. He took a packet of cigarettes out of his pocket and she was suddenly reminded of Harrison. She liked Harrison, though he looked a bit of a mess. His eyes had that same hunted look she recognised in her own, as if he no longer felt sure where he stood in the world. The dark-haired man bought a beer, spoke to Dewey and came over to her table.

Swann had noticed her as soon as he came in. Very petite, dark hair, and large oval eyes that took in the comings and goings on Decatur Street, and yet did not take them in. He introduced himself and sat down. 'Harrison asked me to speak to you,' he said.

Jean smiled then and her eyes crinkled at the corners: they were deep and dark, with an air of intelligence, which Swann also recognised in Logan.

'Harrison asked you?'

'Yes. I hope you don't mind. He seemed concerned about you.' Swann stuck out his hand. 'I'm Jack Swann.'

'It was sweet of him to do that.'

Swann sipped from the neck of his beer bottle. 'He phoned me in London specifically. I'm a police officer, you see. Harrison knew I was coming over here and he asked me to look out for you.'

She sighed then. 'Everyone seems to want to look out for me. Do I look that fragile?'

'D'you want an honest answer?'

'Of course.'

'Yes. You do. You look lost, Jean.' He was not sure if he should say it, but it came out anyway.

She looked away from him then, through the window to the café across the road in front of Governor Nicholls Wharf, where the lone trumpeter was just getting started. 'I feel fragile. I think I shouldn't, but I do.'

'You've every reason to.' Swann said it quietly. He took a cigarette from the pack, and Jean looked at him for a moment. 'Can I have one of those?' she asked.

'Of course you can.'

'I don't smoke normally. Well, in my youth I did, but when I became a children's doctor, it seemed a little incongruous. Only lately, I've needed it again.'

Swann handed her a cigarette and lit it for her. He inspected the burning end of his own. 'My fiancée doesn't smoke,' he said. 'She never complains, but I really ought to quit.' He looked at the wedding ring on Jean's finger then. 'Is your husband not here with you?'

She stretched the finger and inspected the gold band. 'I'm not married any more. I really should take this off. I suppose I've just never got round to it.'

Swann watched her for a few moments. She did look lost. Her whole world had collapsed and she was desperately trying to deal with it. 'I spoke to Joe Kinsella today,' he told her. 'The chief of deputies in St Charles Parish.'

'What did he say?'

'The same as he said to you, I suppose.'

Her face fell then. 'There's not much they can do, is there?'

'No.' Swann made an open-handed gesture. 'It's a tough one, Jean. They're pretty sure your son was killed by a vagrant, and tracking him down, without a witness of some kind, is nigh on impossible.'

Jean tugged her top lip down with her teeth. 'I've been doing a little checking of my own. I hired a car and did some driving around. Tom's is far from the first death on a freight train.'

Swann watched her face, and she sat forward then, with a conspiratorial air. 'There's been two others in Louisiana, Jack. Three in Arkansas and, as far as I know, at least seven people in Texas.' She paused then. 'I've got the information upstairs, if you'd like to see it.'

Swann sat there for a moment, then nodded. 'Have you

had dinner?' he asked her. She shook her head. 'I tell you what then, you go and get the stuff, and I'll get menus from Dewey.'

Over dinner, he looked at what she had gathered. She had been to the library and the archives of the regional newspapers: the *Times Picayune* in New Orleans, various others in Baton Rouge and Shreveport, and as far north as Little Rock in Arkansas. Swann was impressed. 'You've done all this in a week?'

She laughed then. 'Jack, have you any idea how many hours I worked in a day as a junior doctor?'

She had driven all over the place and had put together quite a dossier. The Arkansas killings had been over a three-month period the year before last and each of the victims had been found alongside a railroad track. They had arms or legs missing, and two out of the three had their shirts pulled over their heads and their trousers round their ankles. Their possessions had not been found and it was assumed they had been stolen. He found similar situations in Texas. Seven murders over a three-year period, gunshot wounds in two of them, and again the same thing – shirts over their heads and trousers yanked down. Jean had compiled newspaper cuttings and quotes from cops and the odd photograph.

'And none of these have been solved?' Swann said.

'Not one.' Jean sat forward. 'Most of the victims are vagrants, Jack. Nobody cares overmuch.' She sucked breath. 'But Thomas was in the wrong place at the wrong time. And I do care.'

Swann laid the dossier to one side. 'Have you shown this to Kinsella?'

She nodded. 'He's not in a position to launch an interstate investigation, and he was candid enough to admit that given that ninety per cent of the victims were members of the homeless community, he was unlikely to get the budget anyway. He assured me that no stone would be left unturned in the pursuit of my son's killer, but that was as far as he could throw out the line. Those were his exact words.'

Swann nodded. 'Which leaves you precisely nowhere.'

'Unless I hire somebody.'

'You mean, like a private detective or something?'

'Yes.' She pointed to Dewey. 'He put me on to somebody. I'm going to speak to him later. He's a singer as well as a detective, apparently. He's playing at Tipitinas tonight.' She paused then and smiled. 'When Harrison asked you to look out for me, do you suppose he meant in the form of a chaperone?'

Swann tipped back his head and laughed.

The singer she referred to was very good. Gary Hirstius, New Orleans born and raised, standing about five foot eight, a Bruce Springsteen lookalike, who played his own songs at the fashionable French Quarter nightspot. The club was busy and smoke was thick in the air, but he played a good set, and Jean and Swann sat at a table and watched him. When he was finished he came over, introduced himself and sat down.

'You were very good,' Jean told him.

'Thank you.'

'Have you been playing long?'

'Yes, mam. I started on Bourbon Street when I was fifteen. I'm forty-three now.' He glanced at Swann. 'You a cop?'

'Does it show that much?'

Hirstius sat back, resting one arm over the back of the chair. 'Does to me. I've known cops all my life: good cops, bad cops, cops who'd help a guy out, others who'd kick him in the face when he's down. I've been dug outta trouble by some and kicked to silly-silly land by others. Right now, I got a homicide dick on my ass from Jefferson Parish, who figures I owe him a favour. He left a message on my phone and I figure he's looking for me to wear a wire or something for him.' He cocked an eyebrow. 'I don't even remember the guy.'

'Are you going to call him back?' Jean asked.

Hirstius laughed. 'No, mam. I'm not. There's no need to go looking for trouble, when it can find me all by itself.'

Swann offered him a cigarette and he shook his head. He rested both elbows on the table, and a waiter brought him a glass of Merlot and he sipped at it. 'What can I do for you, mam?'

'Find my son's killer.'

He blew out his cheeks and looked across the table at Swann. 'That's a job for a cop,' he said.

'The cops can't find him.'

He shook his head. 'I heard about your son and I'm really sorry. It sucks when somebody puts their faith in this country and it gets abused by some low-life sonofabitch. But the dicks out at St Charles did all there was to do, mam. Your son was killed by a vagrant. Now that's a whole different set of problems.' He gestured with a flat palm. 'Without a single witness to any part of the story, like when he got on the train even, where the hell do you begin?'

'There've been other similar murders.' Jean rested a hand on his arm and he nodded.

'You're right. There have. But the same thing applies. Besides, most of those guys were hobos and it's a sad fact of life, but very few people actually give a damn.' He sighed then. 'Mrs Carey. Somebody shoulda told you I do insurance work mostly. It's safer than most stuff, though not as safe as playing up there.' He jabbed a thumb at the stage. He sipped wine and stood up again, nodding to the drummer who was heading back to the stage. 'I tell you what,' he said. 'I'll make some noises and see what I can do. Then I'll call you. Hotel Provincial, right?'

Jean nodded and he made his way back to the stage.

Cyrus Birch paused under the Washington Memorial, wearing a pair of shorts and sneakers. He was lean, fit and tanned and knew he did not look anywhere near his forty-two years of age. Everything was set. The International Activities Division had been contacted as soon as the

President signed the finding and they were busy now with the 'stagehands', who had long ago started putting the background into place. Birch had known last fall that this was inevitable, and only too aware of how difficult it was to create a plausible background, he had started the ball rolling early. Just before the African bombs had gone off, they had come across an article written by an Australian journalist who lived in New York City. Birch knew that after the bombings, the reporter would be kicking down doors to get another interview.

Since then, the comings and goings between his office, the station chief in Egypt and Secret Branch 40 in Israel had been fast and furious. The NSA Umbra crypts had been thick on the ground, and people were watching and listening all over the globe. The background the IAD had set up was extremely good and, given the operative's capabilities, might just work. It was the partnership thing that really worried Birch: the Australian could easily become a victim.

He was not worried about the operative, but he did not like dealing with him personally. Normally, national intelligence officers did not get involved much beyond the initial estimate and the finding. Of course, he had to placate irate congressmen now and again and keep egos in Washington massaged, but it was rare to get this involved with the sharp end.

This situation was different, however. There were only four people who knew, thus far, exactly what the finding had sanctioned. With the way the President was going to handle the intelligence committees, only a further four would find out. The IAD had no idea what the job was about. They were just told to get the back-up operation set up at ground level. As far as the actual operative went, Birch had only ever had one individual in mind, and he knew the man was watching him right now. He did not know where he was, could not see him, but he knew he was under observation. There was no way he would want a face to face under the memorial, and Birch knew he had been lucky to get him anywhere near D.C. at all. Nevertheless, the memorial was a good place to start, and once he had 'rested' his legs for a couple of minutes, he knew that anywhere he went, the operative would locate him. He decided on the Native American history section of the Smithsonian.

'Very apt. Very applicable,' the voice said in his ear, as Birch looked at one of the Navajo displays. 'A pity they only record what they think is palatable. It took Dee Brown to write about people like Chivington.' The voice was soft, gentle almost, yet it never failed to chill him. It was like having Charles Manson around, only on your side, and it was at times like these that Birch found himself at a complete disadvantage. Put him out in the field and he would be eaten alive. Still, no matter, he only planned to go as far afield as the DDO's office.

He turned sideways and looked into the face of The Cub. Copper-coloured skin, jet-black hair untied and hanging beyond his shoulders from under the dust-coloured baseball hat. Round his throat he wore a medicine bead choker, and his face hollowed at the cheekbones. And then there were those incongruous blue eyes.

They sat across from one another in the refectory. The Cub was half Nez Percé Indian. Birch had never been too sure of the other half, although it was said his father was the product of a coupling in the thirties between a white man and his Chinese whore, in one of the Idaho mining towns.

The Cub had been earmarked for special forces work during his brief stay in the Marine Corps: brief, because after giving a friend a room in his house, the man ran off with his wife. The Cub had finally run the pair of them over in his truck. The court martial gave him five years for attempted manslaughter, notwithstanding the fact that The Cub had backed the truck over them *after* he ran them down. He served twenty-six months in Leavenworth, then went to Europe and spent seven years with the 2nd REP in the French Foreign Legion. Birch knew he had seen more action than most American soldiers ever would. These days he was freelance and had been used by the IAD on more than one occasion.

The Cub drank his coffee black and watched Birch, aware of just how uncomfortable he made the man. 'So what's the deal, Cyrus? You contacted me nearly a year ago and I've been practising my Kiwi accent and photographing cricket matches ever since. You ever watch cricket, Cyrus? It's like baseball, only with no home runs. But it's been a blast, really. I can tell you the batting averages of any Pakistani player you wanna mention.'

Birch sat back in his chair. The place was heaving: theirs just one conversation amongst a gaggle of others. School kids in oversized T-shirts, sneakers and bum-bags, baseball hats stuck on backwards, and overworked, exasperated teachers.

'The contract has been approved.'

The Cub thinned his eyes.

'It's taken us this long to get it agreed. I think the politicians hoped that certain military action would render it unnecessary.'

'But it didn't.'

'Absolutely.' Birch leaned across the table towards him. 'The Talent have located a reporter on a mission,' he said. 'His name's Jim Moore and he's an Australian based in New York. He's freelance and the only man who's conducted an interview with our target since the Afghan war.' He paused. 'For the last six months he's been trying to set up something, along with the Australian photographer he worked with before. They went on a little assignment to Afghanistan prior to August last year, and now Moore wants to follow that trip up. Our intel' indicates they got the green light only a week ago.'

The Cub said nothing.

'Moore can do it, because our target trusts him. He must be about the only westerner he does trust right now, and I think the fact that he's neither American nor British helps.

The problem he's got, though, is his photographer. He's just blown out on the trip. You see, he got an offer of an assignment to photograph bears in Alaska, which is gonna pay him about ten times what the Afghan trip would make him.' He smiled. 'And he's a greedy man. Moore's on his way to Pakistan right now and he still doesn't know about it. He'll find out when he gets there. The ISA are ready to help him out, though. You're the only Antipodean photographer who lives in Islamabad. Your pictures have been in all the good magazines and Moore *will* contact you. He's in a hurry and he's gonna cut corners.'

The Cub sat back now. 'And what about the opposition?'

'Oh, they'll check out the contract his friend was offered and find out that it's legitimate. The oil company, who've funded it, really need to put something back into the environment up there.'

The Cub nodded slowly.

'I want you to go home to your flat in Pakistan and wait for the phone call. He'll contact you first to make sure you're up for it, then he'll run you by the target's people. They'll have been watching you already. He likes to keep an eye on all westerners in that area, but we're confident you'll get a clean bill of health. Moore's a hardcase Aussie from the Northern Territories. You're from New Zealand. You ought to be able to swap a few war stories between you.'

'And who are we going to interview?'

Birch's features clouded. 'There's a man out there who poses a bigger threat to this country than anyone else we know. He's more dangerous than the Islamic Jihad, than the ANO, Milosovic or any of his cronies. He's supported terrorism all over the world. We believe he's operating in at least fifty countries and has training camps in another fifteen.'

The Cub pursed his lips. 'And last August he blew up two of our embassies in Africa, killing two hundred and sixty odd people. On February thirteen of this year, the

British press reported that he had abandoned his Afghan enclave, and that he's targeting the UK. But *we* think he's still in Afghanistan.' He paused then and sipped black coffee. 'You want me to kill Osama Bin Laden.'

5

Logan spoke to Swann on the phone and confirmed she was coming down to New Orleans at the weekend. She put down the phone and looked across the office at Harrison. 'When are *you* going back?'

Harrison shrugged. 'I'm driving down, anyways.'

They were both seated in Kovalski's office on 4th Street. He was at a meeting on Pennsylvania Avenue. McKensie sat at Kovalski's desk, working on his computer, trawling the militia websites, looking for responses to the murder of Billy Bob Lafitte. Since they got back, Logan and Kovalski had been working in conjunction with the Portland office on potential identities and subsequent motives for the three Orientals.

Logan sucked the end of a pencil and swivelled back and forth in her chair, watching the misty expression spreading on Harrison's face. 'You're gonna quit, aren't you, Johnny Buck,' she said quietly.

Harrison glanced at her, but did not reply. He got up and walked to the window.

Logan moved next to him. 'Why?'

He did not say anything immediately. He had been away barely a week and learned little of what he had hoped to find out about himself, although he was not exactly sure what that was. 'Maybe it's just time, Cheyenne. I'm fifty years old next birthday.'

'So? The Bureau doesn't put you out to grass for another seven years.'

'Yeah, I know.'

'So why now?'

He shrugged. 'Maybe I've done all I planned to.' He bit his lip. 'I got no life, Chey. Alls I do is sit in the back of surveillance vans or pretend to be somebody I'm not. Shit, I've been a guy called Harrison so long, I don't even know who John Dollar is any more.'

'Do you have any family?'

'I've got a sister in Marquette.'

'Michigan?'

'Right up there on Lake Superior.' He paused and shifted the plug of chew to his other cheek. 'I flew up there for two days before I came here. She'd moved house and never even let me know.' He looked back at her then. 'Some kinda family, huh.'

Logan laid a hand on his shoulder. 'Have you ever thought that maybe Harrison *is* John Dollar?'

He squinted at her. 'Yeah, I did one time. When I spent two years undercover in small-town Idaho. The two guys were one and the same right there, for a while.' He spat into the Coke can he was holding. 'Didn't last, though. There's another place I can't go back to.'

'You got a home anywhere other than New Orleans?'

He shook his head. 'Two rented rooms on Burgundy and Toulouse, Cheyenne. That and my Chevy, is all.'

'Money?'

'None of your damn business.' He laughed then. 'Just kidding you. No, I got some stashed away. Not a whole lot. But there's a log cabin up on Payette Lake I got my eye on.'

'Why don't you buy it?'

'I might do that. Sit there with my fishing pole. Hunt elk come the fall. That'd be some kinda life.'

'You'd miss the job, JB.'

'You think so?'

McKensie took a phone call and interrupted them. 'Cheyenne. I've got the resident agency from Billings Montana on line one.' Logan looked round at her. 'The Garfield County sheriff just recovered the body of a forest ranger from Fort Peck Lake. Gunshot to the back of the head.'

Logan picked up the phone, her eyes dark, deep and

intense. She spoke for a few minutes, listened, and then put down the phone and looked back at her colleagues. 'The forest ranger was a naturalised Korean,' she said.

Harrison moved away from the window and sat down at the table Logan had been using. He picked up her file on the Hope Heights murder and began to flick through it.

'BobCat Reece,' he muttered. 'I saw that sonofabitch a long time ago in Idaho. He killed a Montana ranger, too.'

The door opened and Kovalski strode back in. 'You still here, JB? You must be the only agent I know who spends his vacation in another field office.' He chuckled knowingly to himself. 'And you're talking about quitting the job.'

Harrison looked at him then. 'Guess I'm just a lost soul, Kovalski. Got nowhere else to go.' He stood up. 'This thing in Oregon looks real messy, though, don't it.'

Logan took the file from him. 'Why would three Orientals go to a small Pacific coast town, make themselves ultravisible and then murder the prominent militia leader?'

'Why indeed?' Kovalski said.

'Maybe they *were* government agents,' Harrison suggested. 'Maybe these psychos are actually right. Just because you're paranoid, doesn't mean they're not after you.'

'You got anything helpful to say?' Kovalski asked him.

'Hey, who knows, Tom? The websites are full of it. People surf them, don't they. "The Ride of the Valkyrie" playing in the background. The white race will overcome. The seed is planted and the mud people will be no longer.' He glanced at Logan. 'No offence, Chey.'

'None taken.'

'The government coming to get their guns,' Harrison went on. 'We'll see colour-wearing gang members in Strangeville, New Mexico, next.'

'It's serious, Harrison,' Logan said. 'Whoever killed Billy Bob Lafitte wanted it to look like it was us.'

'One hundred thousand Hong Kong troops.' Harrison's mouth puckered. 'Maybe it is us, Cheyenne.'

Kovalski gave him a withering look. 'When are you going back to New Orleans?'

'Now.' Harrison winked at him. 'I'll see ya, Tom. Cheyenne, no doubt I'll hook up with you and the duchess over the weekend.' He left then and closed the door behind him.

Logan shook her head. 'He told you he was gonna quit, then, Tom.'

Kovalski smiled. 'They dropped him from the SWAT team down there. It made him think about his age.' He made a face. 'So he's not on the SWAT team any more. Big fucking deal. He's still the best UCA I ever worked with.'

Harrison headed back to New Orleans. It would take him a couple of days, but he was in no hurry. So he drove steadily with the window rolled down, his elbow resting on the doorpanel, and listened to John Lee Hooker's gravelled voice on the tape. Jean Carey was on his mind and that was why he was going back to New Orleans. It was a weird reason, he told himself, although, on the other hand, maybe it wasn't. He had come away to get things straight in his head and in a way he had done that. The cabin by the lake in McCall was something he had been thinking about for some time, somewhere to go, relax and fish.

The marine at the war memorial had made him think. That had been a moment he knew he was not going to forget in a long time: the look of respect in the marine's eyes. Harrison wondered how often he did that, laid something on the wall to the memory of his father. It had concentrated his mind on the past. The things he had accomplished, the people he had been acquainted with. He was amazed at how many names on the Vietnam memorial he knew – kids lost to parents at a stupidly tender age. There were many names missing, though, thankfully, like his own and people like 'Batman' and the Rat Six he had worked with, the officer in charge of the unit. There was Billy 'The Wormhole' Wilson, and others like Ringo and

Ray Martinez. 'The Probe' they had called him. That guy had almost always worked alone, or at least liked to whenever he could. He loved it underground, knew no fear, and had been the guy to take over from Harrison, when he lost the plot and fired six shots in succession that last time underground. You never ever did that: three shots and swap guns with your back-up man. Let him reload. For a long time, the memory of that mess-up had haunted him, but not any more. He wondered what had happened to Martinez.

Driving south, he spent the night in Spartansburg, South Carolina, and drank large bottles of Bud for only two bucks apiece, shooting pool with the locals at the Sportsman's Bar. He got up at the crack of dawn and drove on, making Meridian, Mississippi, by three in the afternoon, and knew he could get to New Orleans before it got dark. At six-thirty he was stuck in traffic crossing the causeway on Lake Ponchartrain, and an hour later he was watching the rain fall vertically outside his bedroom window, at the junction of Burgundy and Toulouse.

In London, Detective Sergeant George Webb looked down at the body of the black woman, holding a handkerchief to his nose. She had been there for five days, which amazed him, considering she was a gunnery sergeant based at the US Embassy. That was until they told him she had been on a week's leave, which had commenced the previous Saturday. Webb looked at his boss, Inspector Frank Weir from the Paddington murder squad, who stood with his hands in the pockets of his immaculate, four-button suit. He chewed gum with his mouth open. The pathologist, wearing a white paper suit, with a mask over his mouth and nose, was on hands and knees, checking over the corpse. Kibibi had her eyes open and her lips drawn back, still showing traces of lipstick which had crusted into vertical lines on her mouth. She had a congealed angular cut on the right side of her forehead.

The pathologist rocked back on his heels and looked over

his shoulder at Weir. 'The head wound was made when she fell,' he said. 'A single stab wound killed her, under the ribs and right into her heart.'

'Somebody knew what they were doing,' Webb muttered.

Weir looked at him, still with the handkerchief over his nose, and smiled to himself. 'I thought you were in charge of picking up the pieces at SO13,' he said.

'I was. But that meat was still frying, boss. I never did like cold cuts.' Webb bent closer and looked at Kibibi's hands. She wore false nails and a couple of them had worked loose. 'Can you get any skin samples from those kind of nails?' he asked the pathologist.

'Sometimes we can, yes.'

Webb straightened up and looked round the flat once again. He had already followed the scene of crime officers as they dusted and photographed their way from room to room. It did not look as though anything had been stolen. Even her handbag, complete with thirty pounds in cash, was on the phone table in the hallway, and there was no sign of forced entry. He frowned and looked again at Weir. 'This is going to be very interesting, Frank,' he said.

'You're telling me. US Marine Corps. We could be camped in Grosvenor Square for months.'

Outside on the landing, Dan Farrow, the regional security officer, was waiting: US Diplomatic Security, Department of State. He had got the shock of his life when Webb phoned him. They had received a call early that morning, when the old lady who lived in the flat next door had complained about the smell. She had taken delivery of a clothing catalogue for Kibibi and had not been able to raise her on the three separate occasions she knocked. On the fourth, she lifted the letterbox and then the smell hit her. The past week had been the hottest of the summer so far and Londoners were walking round in pools of their own sweat. Farrow had been in the post exactly three weeks, his predecessor having transferred back to Washington. He stood in the hall now, restless, wanting a look at the crime scene, but unable to get one. He was in his thirties, something of a high-flyer, so the police liaison officer at the embassy had told Webb. This was a prime overseas posting for him. Many of the people who had gone on to dominate Washington had London RSO stamped on their CV. Farrow did not even know who Kibibi Simpson was until the police called and told him she had been murdered.

'Why did she have a flat?' Webb asked him, as he stepped back on to the landing. 'I thought the marines were billeted at Eastcote.'

'Most of them are. It's not mandatory, though.' Farrow lifted his shoulders. 'I don't know, Sergeant. I really only just got here myself.'

'You and me both, Mr Farrow.' Webb was short and stout, hair thinning, with disarmingly cheery eyes. He had spent ten years as the senior exhibits officer at the Antiterrorist Branch, when the IRA was at the height of its mainland bombing campaign. When the Good Friday agreement came, it was, in his opinion, a good time to quit, and he moved out of Scotland Yard and joined the South-West London murder squad. He was Weir's minder, watching his back and looking after the ship for him when his role of senior investigating officer became too demanding.

Weir came out of the flat, unwrapping another piece of chewing gum, and looked over Webb's shoulder at the RSO. 'Welcome to London, Mr Farrow,' he said.

Swann met Logan at New Orleans International Airport in a hire car provided for him by the FBI. He was amazed he had actually found his way to Kenner in the mass of New Orleans traffic. She was much earlier than either of them had expected, arriving at three-thirty, after Kovalski dismissed her early. Swann noticed her briefcase and laptop computer and guessed how much of the weekend was likely to be spent working. He did not care so long as they were together. She walked through from baggage claim and he took her in his arms and kissed her. Logan pressed herself against him, lips fixed so tightly into his that they hurt. 'Goddamn, I missed you,' she said. 'Where's the hotel?'

They drove to Chartres Street through the Friday afternoon rush hour and got stuck in the traffic coming off Interstate 10. Swann drummed his fingers on the wheel and Logan sat next to him in her two-piece suit, with the skirt riding up naked black thighs.

'I really missed you, Chey.'

'You and me both, sweetheart.' She squeezed his hand. 'I've been up to my neck up there, and I tell you, I could do without this thing in Oregon.'

He lifted one eyebrow. 'Militia.'

'They worry me. They worry Tom. They don't seem to worry anyone else, but they really worry us.' She shifted in her seat. 'Jack, why would three oriental males dress themselves in G-men suits, drive a G-man car and hang out in Hicksville by the Sea for two solid days . . .?'

'And then cut somebody's brake lines.' He finished for her.

'Not just anybody's. Billy Bob Lafitte's.'

'It might not have been them,' he said. 'It could be a coincidence. A nasty one, mind, but it's possible.'

'I know, although somehow I doubt it. As far as I can work out, they did not single Lafitte out for particular scrutiny. They weren't seen anywhere near his property. The closest any of them came to him was one guy in his gun store.' She took a spearmint Lifesaver from her purse and sucked it. 'But that's not how the militia are gonna view it. The main man in the movement was already in Hope Heights when I got there.'

'I didn't think there was a *main man*. Phantom cells, autonomous leadership units and all that.'

'That's how it was, hon. But for about a year now, Kovalski's been aware of BobCat Reece taking centre stage. He runs the West Montana Minutemen which, apart from the New Texas Rangers and maybe the Michigan Militia, constitute the largest group in the country. The three groups appear to be co-ordinating. They've set up what they call the FPA. "Free People of America". We think it's the beginning of the amalgamation we never wanted to see.'

Swann nodded. 'Leaderless Resistance causes one set of problems, but you give an organisation a central chain of command and you're looking at fighting a war.'

'Exactly. Reece has been buzzing around the websites ever since Lafitte got killed. Hope Heights has all the potential to become a siege town. Even the sheriff over there is pro militia.'

'Just how many law-enforcement officers are there, Chey? D'you know?'

'We have no idea. None whatsoever. Reece is ex-Vietnam and a Green Beret to boot. He's big-time Christian Identity and trying to get all the different groups to sing from the same hymn sheet. The Phineas Priesthood is all but in his backyard, then there's Hayden Lake and Wyoming. The Priesthood's a really nasty bunch. They took their cue from Numbers twenty-five, in the Bible. A man becomes an avenging priest after killing a Midianite woman who had sex with a Jew.' She paused. 'We arrested three of them from Washington State in 1996. They'd robbed a US bank in Spokane and were casing one in Portland, Oregon. Barbee, Berry and Verne Jay Merrell.' She shook her head. 'They don't believe in the federal system, Jack. Any US bank is just a stooge for the Federal Reserve, so it's OK to take the money. Funny how some people can do what the hell they like, when they believe they're in the right.'

They parked in the self-contained parking lot at the Provincial, and Swann carried Logan's bags up to the fifth floor and their room overlooking Decatur Street, the river and the ironwork bridge to the west shore. Logan immediately opened the window and all benefit of the air conditioning was lost. 'I know it's hot, honey, but I like to hear the street.'

Swann took her in his arms and kissed her, then he eased her out of her jacket. She was wearing a flimsy white camisole with no bra, and her breasts moved under his hand, the nipples pert and erect against the silken material. Her skin was very black, like velvet under his palm, and he hoisted the camisole over her head and kissed her breasts, tweaking the nipples between his teeth until she shivered.

They made love on the wide double bed, Swann pressing himself deeper and deeper inside her, until she squirmed and arched her back and the muscles stood out like cord against her neck. Her lips were full and painted red, and her eyes were the same olive hue as her skin. Swann roamed her face and neck with his tongue, kissed her along the shoulders, and let his lips trail her stomach and down her thighs. She gripped the sheet in one hand, twisting it into a knot, and then she worked him over on his back and rode him until she came with a muffled cry in her throat.

He sat naked at the window, smoking a cigarette, listening to the fall of the shower and watching the heat rising from the softening concrete pavement. Looking right, he could see the WESTIN building and the old Jax Brewery, where they no longer made any beer. Harrison had told him it tasted like shit anyway, much worse than Dixie, which was bad enough. The river was quiet today, the sun bouncing off flat, mud-coloured waves, which crested in a mush of greyed wake when a tanker ploughed under the bridge. Swann had been here a few times now and he was beginning to like the place. The French Quarter people were friendly, although they were always looking to make a buck. Harrison knew most of them and had told Swann about the Chicken Man dying, which had made the *Picayune*. The Duck Lady was still around, though, along with the Wizard with his long black hair, top hat and blue-lensed sunglasses.

Logan came out of the shower, naked, the water not quite dry on her skin, and Swann felt the saliva drying inside his mouth. 'You are the most beautiful creature I think I've ever seen,' he said. 'Will you marry me?'

'Jack,' she said. 'You asked me that and I already said yes. Now come over here and make love to me again.'

Harrison sat in Swartz and Penny's office in the gang squad section. Friday night, and everyone was about to head home. Cimino, his partner from NOPD, was going to the tiny ranch he had bought north of the lake, where he and his wife were trying to raise some horses. He had invited Harrison out there on many occasions, but Harrison had so far never made it.

'Come back with me now,' Cimino was saying. 'We got beer and steaks. Barbecue and fresh north shore air, Harrison. You'll shrivel up in the quarter.'

'I like the quarter, Davy. Besides there's someone I wanna see tonight.'

'A date.' Cimino poked him in the chest. 'You got a date?'

'Fuck you, asshole.' Harrison patted away his hand. He stood up as Agent Cox came in from the wire room. 'Little Nate's just been using his phone,' he said. 'His buyer's in town. They've got a face to face planned for this evening.'

Silence. Nobody wanted to go. Most of them had plans. But this was the buyer and if they were going to get Nate off the street, cleaning up his supply line of heroin would help them do it.

'Where?' Mike Hammond, the supervisor, asked.

Cox looked straight at Harrison. 'Jackson Square. Down by the cathedral.'

All eyes were on Harrison now and he shook his head wearily. 'What time?'

'Seven.'

Harrison looked at his watch. That gave him less than a half-hour. 'Fuck,' he said. 'Somebody give me a ride.'

Penny dropped him off on Royal, then left him and headed home to Slidell for the weekend with his wife and son. Harrison did not look back, but hunched his shoulders, flicked his ponytail out from his collar, and walked east to Canal. They were still working on the outside of the Holiday Inn, and he skirted the scaffolding and the dump trucks. Men in hard hats shouted orders to one another above him. Two black guys in shorts, singlets and Nike sneakers were hanging around on the corner by the street artists, as he turned into Jackson Square. Not many tourists were out; maybe they had finally realised that New Orleans was no place to be in the summertime.

He saw a hobo sitting on the concrete with his back to the railings and square of grass. Beside him he had a small, grubby backpack, and he sat with one leg under his butt, the other thrust out in front of him. Harrison could see his boots were almost as worn as his own. His hair was wrapped in a jet-black bandana which was tied in a knot at the back of his neck, and one of his eyelids hung lower than the other. He did not look up, intent on rolling a cigarette one-handed. Harrison walked on and stopped on Decatur, and bought himself a copy of the *Picayune* and a beer in a 'to go' cup. Then he crossed and climbed the steps of Washington Artillery Park, from where he could see across Jackson Square. He was not alone in the surveillance. Two cops from the Vieux Carre Precinct were in a van parked on Decatur and two other FBI agents were on foot, on the Royal side of Jackson Square. Harrison read the paper, smoked a cigarette, and sipped now and again from the beer. The wind was getting up across on the west shore and he knew it would rain later.

Little Nate arrived with a buddy driving his white Z28 Camaro. Harrison had an earpiece in and heard one of the NOPD guys signal his arrival. He had the eyeball now and muttered into his mouthpiece. 'Eyes on target. On foot now. Crossing the square.' Little Nate was an amateur. Swartz, who'd been busting gangs for ten years, had told them as much. He reckoned he had listened to over seventy thousand wire-tap phone calls in his fifteen years with the

Bureau and had only heard the words heroin and cocaine twice. Both times from Little Nate. Harrison shook his head now as he watched him. Nate squatted down next to the bandana-wearing hobo and started chatting to him. It surprised him: not the fact that Nate was talking openly in a very public place, but the fact that it was *that* guy he was talking to. Surely he could not be the contact.

'He's talking to a hobo,' Harrison muttered. 'Anyone else got eyeball?'

'Yeah.' One of the NOPD's officers again.

'That can't be who we're looking at, surely,' Harrison said.

'Beats me.'

Harrison watched, bored all at once, bored with the inevitability of it, and again thoughts of the mountains, the dry summer heat of the north, spread over him. He was restless and he knew it. This was not how he wanted to be spending his Friday evenings any more. He'd had about enough of low life such as Little Nate. Twenty-five years of watching shit like him was a very long time.

He continued to watch, saw Nate pass the hobo something, and then the hobo got up, leaving the backpack on the ground. Harrison saw that he had a larger one, which had been against the railings behind his back, and he shifted this between his shoulders. Nate picked up the other pack and walked back towards Decatur, where his Camaro had swung another loop.

'You wanna jump this guy's ass or what?' Harrison said.

One of the gang squad agents spoke in his ear. 'Not right now. We got pictures and we got the phone conversation on tape.'

'What about the other guy?'

'You wanna stick with him for a while?'

'I'll take him as far as the edge of the quarter. My wheels are back at the office.'

Harrison walked fifty yards behind the hobo, who cut his way across Chartres to Royal and then Bourbon Street.

Harrison thought he was going to head north, but he didn't – he walked the length of Bourbon Street, all the way down to the business district. A white United taxi was parked by the side of the road and the hobo got in.

Harrison got back on the radio. 'Somebody pick me up,' he said. 'That guy just got my attention.'

Swartz swung by in his Ford with the tinted windows and picked Harrison up. They followed the cab part way along St Charles Avenue, then it headed north again, before swinging west on Loyola. The cab crossed the river on 90 and headed through the swamps into St Charles Parish on Highway 310. Harrison sat and smoked. Next to him, Swartz was as puzzled as he was. 'A hobo taking a cab ride, all the way out here. It don't add up, Harrison.'

'It does, if the hobo's dealing.'

They followed the cab as it turned off and then headed north along the river towards Reserve. Just short of town, the cab pulled over and the hobo climbed out. He started across an open lot and disappeared into the trees beyond. Swartz pulled over and sat for a moment, drumming his fingers on the steering wheel. 'What the hell's through there?'

'Swamp and scrub and more fucking swamp.'

Swartz made a face. 'Let's forget it. We got the guy on film and we got him on the phone. He's a mule at best, anyway.' As he was speaking, the radio crackled and Harrison picked it up. Cox was still in the wire room. He had just taken a call from the Vieux Carre Precinct.

'You're kidding me?' Harrison said, then turned to Swartz. 'The NOPD just pulled Little Nate's Camaro and arrested the driver.'

'Oh, man.'

'They never got the backpack, but there were two weapons, a 9-millimetre and an AK, just lying on the back seat.'

'Little Nate?'

'Ran off, apparently.'

Swartz took the radio from him. 'Todd,' he said to Cox. 'Get on to Hammond. He's gonna have to talk to the district captain, let him in on the wire. We don't want the NOPD picking up Nate for illegal possession of firearms.'

Swartz dropped Harrison back in the French Quarter. 'You know, JB,' he said. 'You ought to move to a better neighbourhood.'

'I know it.' Harrison sighed. 'One of these days, I will.'

'So do it, buddy. Get a little life for yourself.' Swartz punched him playfully on the arm. 'If you're kicking your heels this weekend, we got beer and steak at my house. Some of the guys are coming over for the baseball.'

'Thanks, bro. But the limey cop's in town. If I get bored with him, I'll do that.'

He walked the length of Chartres and cut through the hotel parking lot to Nu Nus. It was nine-thirty now, dark and hot, but the wind was getting up and the streets would be awash with Louisiana rain before morning.

Dewey was bartending and he snapped the top off a beer. 'Some friends of yours were in, man,' he said.

Harrison looked around the empty bar. 'Where they at now?'

'They've gone on down to Levon Helm's club. They got a band playing.'

'That's on Decatur, right?'

'Yep. Other side of the street from the fire station.'

'Who's there?'

'Your buddy from England.' Dewey rolled his eyes. 'His *sweetheart* of a girlfriend and Jean Carey.'

'Jean's with them?'

'She sure is. Nice lady, Harrison. Way too good for you.'

'Don't count on that.' Harrison walked out on to Decatur.

The rain began before he made it to Levon Helm's club. He walked with his hands in his jeans' pockets, his red T-shirt getting very wet. The doorman looked him up and down, and Harrison slipped a five-dollar bill across his palm and the man stood to one side. Helm's club was spacious, the ceiling high and the bar running the length of one wall to the right. Tables were dotted here and there, and the people crowded the dance floor in front of the stage. Harrison had not noticed whose face adorned the billboard on the windows outside, but he recognised Gary Hirstius. He was midway through one of the tracks on his first album, a copy of which Harrison had back at his apartment. Harrison stood a moment just inside the door to dry off, and Hirstius caught his eye from the stage. Harrison peered through the smoke and the semi-darkness, and saw the three of them at a table on the raised section of flooring, just to the left of the dance floor. He took a cigarette from his T-shirt pocket and lit it. Menthol: Since Vietnam, he had smoked two brands alternately, and every shirt he ever wore had a pack of Marlboro in one pocket and Merit or Kools menthol in the other. He bought a beer at the bar and went over to the table, where he laid a hand on Swann's shoulder.

'Hey, bubba. What's up?'

Swann twisted his head back, looked into the weather-beaten old face, and at the wet, grey hair hanging in two plaits down his chest Indian-style. 'Harrison.' He jumped up and shook his hand. But then Harrison, suddenly very glad to see him, hugged him close.

'New Orleans-style,' he muttered, and caught Jean's eye over Swann's shoulder. 'Has he been looking out for you, Miss Lady Mam?'

'Him, Dewey and Cheyenne.' She smiled.

'Right on. Southern hospitality.' Harrison sat down in Swann's chair and Logan looked slant-eyed at him. 'Honey chile, you ain't in the South.'

'I know it. I'm in N'Awlins.'

They all laughed, and Swann grabbed another chair and sat down again. 'How've you been, Harrison?'

'Real good.'

'He's thinking of quitting the job,' Logan said. 'He's doing *that* good, Jack.'

Harrison sucked breath and felt Jean watching him. He

smiled at her. 'So, how're you, Miss Lady Mam? I wasn't sure you'd still be here.'

'I'm OK. How was your vacation?'

'Thought-provoking.' Harrison looked beyond her then to the stage, where Hirstius had finished playing and was cutting a path towards them, taking the plaudits and pats on the back as he did so. He paused in front of the table and Swann gave up his chair.

Hirstius shook hands with Harrison, then he looked round the table and saw Logan for the first time. 'Fed or state?' he said.

'It shows, then.'

'Only in the company you're keeping.'

'Fed,' she said.

'Oh, brother.' Hirstius rubbed the heel of a palm across his eyes. 'A table full of cops and me. I'll never get outta here alive.' He looked at Jean then. 'Mam, I did what I could.' He sat back and took a roll of A4 paper from the back pocket of his jeans. He passed it across to her. 'There's been over five hundred people killed on the railroad tracks since 1996,' he said. 'They've mostly been hobos, which is why nobody seems to give a damn, but there's also been some straights, like your boy.'

Harrison was staring at him and Jean laid a tiny hand over his. 'I asked Gary to try and find my son's killer, John. The police weren't able to.'

Hirstius was shaking his head. 'I ain't even gonna try, mam. I told you that already.'

He looked at Harrison then. 'I did a little digging, is all.' He tapped the pages of the mini-report he had prepared. 'It's all in there.' He glanced over his shoulder then, to see what was happening on stage, before going on. 'There's a gang out there known as the FTRA, that's Freight Train Riders of America. I've only found out a little bit, but there's something like two thousand of them.' He looked hard at Jean. 'Mam, you ain't gonna find your son's murderer. Those killings I just mentioned have pretty much been attributed to the FTRA. There's three separate gangs which all come together under the one banner. They're nazi, racist sons of bitches. You can tell them apart by the bandanas they wear round their heads. They ride the trains in groups and kill people who get in their way. Why they kill, nobody seems to know. Maybe they're running some kinda gig they don't want people knowing about. Maybe they're just sick.'

'You said bandanas.' Harrison sat forward. 'What colour bandanas?'

Hirstius shrugged. 'Like I said, there's three outfits. Some wear red, some blue, and I think the others are black.'

Harrison went very still; the ash was an inch long on his cigarette. Slowly, he tipped it into the ashtray. Hirstius got up. 'Anyways, I gotta get out of here,' he said. 'Before somebody figures out the company I'm keeping.'

Jean grabbed his arm. 'Thank you, Gary. How much do I owe you?'

'Mam, I'm really sorry for your loss.' He smiled. 'All I did was make a few calls.'

Swann went for more drinks and Harrison sat staring at Hirstius without really seeing him, as he set up for the next session. Logan laid a hand on his arm. 'What is it?' she said.

He glanced at her then. 'Tonight,' he said, 'before I came here, I did a little job for the gang squad. We're watching this headcase from the St Thomas Project. Gangbanger. Heroin-dealer. His source came into town tonight and I saw a face to face in Jackson Square.'

'So?'

'So the supplier was a hobo wearing a black bandana.'

Jean stared at him, and her round face with its high cheekbones and gentle mouth was still. Her hands were clasped in front of her on the table and she sat in silence for a moment, both Logan and Harrison watching her. Harrison laid his rough, calloused palm over the little mound of knuckles. 'You OK, Miss Lady Mam?'

She smiled, then pinched her lips again. 'Yes. Thank you. Just shocked, I suppose. Every time I find out a little more, it shocks me over again.'

Harrison picked up the papers Hirstius had left and leafed through them. Swann set the fresh round of drinks on the table and sat down next to Logan.

'Gary got his information from a cop in Texas,' Harrison said. 'If this was just a phone call, the guy owed him one helluva favour. It says here that the real information is with another cop in Spokane, Washington.'

Harrison passed the papers to Jean. 'You might learn something from this, Miss Lady Mam, but I think Gary's right. You're not gonna find who did it.'

Jean's face suddenly crushed and tears broke from her eyes. She got up, grabbed her cardigan and headed for the main door. Harrison watched her go and sighed.

Logan touched the back of his hand. 'You can't let her walk home, JB. This is New Orleans. Remember.'

Harrison went outside and the rain rattled off the pavement. Jean was on the other side of the road, trying to take shelter in the shadows cast by the balconies. He called to her, but she did not look back, and he broke into a run. She was likely to get herself killed. 'Jean.' This time she did stop and Harrison caught up with her. 'You can't walk these streets on your own, Miss Lady Mam,' he said gently. 'Somebody's gonna rob you or worse.' He nodded to the shadows. 'Especially along here. Nobody's on the street because of the rain. People that are, stick to the sidewalk. So do the bad guys. In New Orleans, if nobody's on the street, you walk right up the middle.' He took her arm then, cupped it against his bicep, and together they headed towards the hotel under the cover of the balconies.

Jean walked for a few moments in silence, and then said, 'Why are we not in the middle of the road?'

Harrison paused, then lifted the leg of his jeans, revealing his ankle holster. 'Because we don't need to be,' he said.

They walked on in silence and Jean listened to the

pounding of the rain on the road. It was so heavy and so thick she could barely see the other side. 'I've never seen rain so heavy,' she said.

'Does it a lot here.'

They walked again in silence and Harrison could feel the warmth of her body against him. He suggested a drink in Pat O'Brien's as they came to St Peter Street. They sat inside, and Jean had a brandy and Harrison a beer and a shot of peppermint schnapps. He knocked it back, slammed the shot glass on the table and whacked his chest with the heel of his palm. 'Now that hit the spot.' He leaned over the table and looked in her eyes.

'You OK now?'

'Yes. Thank you. You're very kind.'

Harrison pursed his lips. 'We're all sorry for your loss, Jean. Not one of us knows what it could possibly feel like.'

'It hurts like no hurt I could ever imagine, or would want to imagine again,' she said. 'That's what it feels like.'

Harrison nodded and shook a Marlboro from his shirt, saw the expression on her face and shook out another. He lit them both, popping a match on his thumbnail, and handed one to her.

She smoked nervously, looking at the glowing end every time she took it out of her mouth. 'I gave birth to him. It took me nine hours and ten minutes.' She drew smoke in through her nose, coughed, and stubbed the cigarette out. 'He was part of me, John. More than part of me.' She looked him in the face then. 'Nothing in my life is ever going to be the same. I left Vietnam when I was eighteen and I have never seen or spoken to my father since. I can remember the last time I saw him, the expression on his face, and I know the North Vietnamese killed him. I got over that. He was the father. I was the child. He was meant to die before I did.' She shook her head and her lip quivered, eyes misty again. Harrison sat quietly, his fingers steepled before him. 'I was meant to die before my son,' she went on. 'No parent should bury their own child.'

113

Harrison sipped at his beer and watched her face. She looked beyond him and she was lost in some memory of the past, which was nothing to do with him. She drank some brandy and then asked him for another cigarette, and he lit it for her.

'I'm sorry,' Jean said. 'I hardly know you and I'm pouring my heart out here.' She cupped his hand. 'You've been so very kind. And I know nothing about you.'

'There's nothing much to know,' he said.

'There must be.'

He sighed. 'I don't think this is the time or the place, Jean. Right now, I figure I'm here to listen to you.'

'Do you?'

He nodded. 'Yes, mam. I do.'

'What did you call me earlier?' she asked. '"Miss Lady Mam"?'

Harrison laughed.

'Where did you come up with that?'

'Oh, just some place, I guess. It's just a figure of speech. I call most people something other than their name. Swann is duchess, because he's a limey, I guess.' He shrugged his shoulders, then said: 'Gary *is* right you know.'

She looked at the tabletop. 'I know.' She was quiet for a moment or two, then added, 'But what do I do if I give up here?'

Harrison had no answer for that. 'Listen,' he said. 'There may be something I can do. That bandana thing's a helluva coincidence.' He touched her on the shoulder. 'Let me talk to some people on Monday.'

She nodded and smiled, and sucked on her cigarette. Harrison sank the rest of his beer.

'I'll walk you back to the hotel.'

'Would you mind?'

'You think I'd let you go by yourself?' He stood up. 'Besides, it's my pleasure.' He took her in via Nu Nus Café, as Dewey was thinking about closing up. Harrison stood at the connecting hotel door with Jean.

'Thank you,' she said. 'I really appreciate it.'

'What're you doing for the rest of the weekend?' he asked her.

She shifted her shoulders. 'Nothing.'

'You fancy going on a swamp tour?'

'With you? I'd love to.'

'You got it, then.' He tapped the watch on her wrist. 'I'll come get you about ten and take you down to the bayous.'

Tom Kovalski was still at his desk in the Washington field office. Everyone else had gone home long ago, and twice his wife had called and asked him what he was up to. He was working, he told her, and he would be home just as soon as he could. He had been due to leave at 7 p.m., when reception had taken delivery of a small package addressed to the assistant special agent in charge. It did not name Kovalski, but he was the ASAC. The parcel had been screened and found to contain an audiotape. They had checked it for booby traps, but found none. Kovalski had played it, rewound it and played it over again. He sat alone in his office, with only the desk lamp burning, and rewound the tape for the umpteenth time. He sat back in his chair, loosened his tie, and listened all over again. The voice was oriental, clipped concise tones:

'My name is Fachida Harada. Before me was my father Noruki and his father Akira. Our home was in Kobe and our business was herbal pharmacy. You are my enemy, the enemy of my father before me and my grandfather before him. I, Fachida Harada, will make war on you. I will honour you in battle until one of us is dead.'

6

Logan called Detective Cameron in Hope Heights, Oregon, and asked him how his investigation was going. 'Badly,' he told her. 'We've completed all the interviews and come up with pretty much nothing.' He paused for a moment. 'We'd really like to talk to three oriental gentlemen, though, who were seen in the area a couple of days before the killing.'

'Number one suspects, huh?'

'Them and their black Chevy Suburban.' Cameron laughed. 'If it wasn't so serious, it'd be funny. Certain people's worst nightmares are coming true, Logan. I don't know if you monitor the websites. I'm pretty sure you're not allowed to constitutionally, but maybe you've seen them in your spare time.'

'Maybe,' she said.

'Well, you might want to check out one I've come across. It's aimed at teenagers, called "Midnight Hour". The Hong Kong troops are here, sent in by the New World Order to take away our guns.'

'Thanks, Detective.' Logan hung up and sat with her hands in her lap. Hope Heights, Oregon, just a tiny west coast town, and yet she felt the cloud that had descended on that community was already spreading east.

Kovalski came in then. He had been attending a meeting with the Washington D.C. joint terrorism task force. His face was grave and he crooked a finger at Logan. 'Cheyenne, I've got something I want you to hear,' he told her.

Logan listened to the tape and stared across the desk at him. 'Fruitcake?' she said.

'They're *all* crazy, Chey. The question is – do we take him seriously?'

She turned her mouth down at the corners. 'Fachida Harada. I've never heard of him.'

'Neither have I.'

'It's probably not even his real name.'

'Then why give it to us?'

'Vanity.'

Kovalski looked unsure. 'The tape came in late Friday, which was a little ironic given that I had a meeting with the JTTF this morning.'

'Did you mention it?'

He shook his head. 'I thought about it, but I wanted your opinion first. We have no idea who or what he is, even if he's for real. You know how many crank calls we get, Chey.'

She smiled then. 'So why does this one bother you so much?'

He scratched his head. 'It shows, huh. I don't know. I just get a feeling.' He stood up. 'Call me an old fool, Cheyenne. Maybe it's just the timing that bothers me, what with this and the situation in Oregon.'

'It's 1999, Tom. The year of the millennium psycho.'

'Then roll on 2000.' He looked at her for a long moment. 'It might be totally unconnected, but somebody gave me a whisper the other day, somebody who has proved reliable in the past. The words "cherry blossom" were mentioned.'

'In what context?'

'In the context of us having a hometown problem.'

'The festival of the cherry blossom,' she said. 'That's Japanese.'

'Yes. And so is Fachida Harada.'

Back at her desk, Logan phoned Swann in New Orleans. She knew he had dealt in some detail with yakuza gangsters in the UK. New Orleans was an hour behind Washington and she got him just as he was about to leave for his class at the field office. She asked him if they had had anything to do with cherry blossom.

'Not as far as I know,' he told her. 'Cherry blossom was

117

the ancient symbol of the samurai. Arguably, and I mean arguably, the yakuza are the nearest thing to samurai, at least symbolically, these days – finger-cutting, dishonour, that kind of thing. Why?'

'I'm not sure yet. I'm just trying to piece something together for Kovalski.'

She put down the phone and went back to Kovalski's office. 'I just spoke to Jack Swann,' she told him. 'Down in New Orleans. He had an organised crime attachment back in England. Yakuza.'

Kovalski sat back in his chair. 'Yakuza? I never thought of the yakuza.'

'And, apparently, cherry blossom was a samurai symbol.'

Kovalski made a face. 'I'll talk to someone in organised crime, see if they can enlighten me.'

Harrison sat in the office of gang squad supervisor Mike Hammond, along with Swartz and Penny, the two case agents working on the Little Nate wire tap. 'We followed the guy out to the swamp in St Charles Parish,' Harrison was saying. 'Me and Andy.' He glanced sideways at Swartz. 'The only thing in that woodland, besides 'gators and mud, is the Kansas City Southern railroad.' He sat forward. 'Six months ago, that English kid, Tom Carey, was murdered on a freight train coming in from Texas. Body was found by a security guard out near Hahnville.'

Hammond nodded. 'I remember.'

'Well, his mom's in town. She's been doing some digging and found out that a whole buncha hobos have been killed all over the country.' Harrison paused and looked at the others. 'There's a cop in Spokane, Washington, that reckons a gang is behind it. A couple of the victims have been found gunshot like the Carey kid, with their pants pulled down to their ankles, shirts up over their heads, that kinda thing. There's been something like five hundred killings over the last three years, but nobody seems to have done anything about it.' He lifted his shoulders. 'The victims have been homeless, mostly, with nobody to care about them. But there have been one or two straights, such as Tom Carey.' He picked up the coffee cup that sat on the edge of Hammond's desk. 'The gang calls itself the FTRA – that's Freight Train Riders of America. They're allegedly split into three groups, who wear different-coloured bandanas to designate the crew they run with.' He looked at Swartz then. 'The guy we tailed, after he had the face to face with Little Nate, was wearing a black bandana. Right?'

Swartz nodded.

'That's the mark of the FTRA, right here, in the South.'

For a few moments nobody spoke.

'The cop in Spokane has done more work on the outfit than anyone,' Harrison went on. 'But there's been no investigation *per se*. As far as I know, he's just monitored the murders. My question is, why go around the country murdering a bunch of hobos?'

Penny cracked a smile. 'Why not, JB. Since when did the bad guys need a logical reason?'

Harrison nodded. 'You're right.' He looked again at Hammond. 'But maybe there's more to it than that. If a guy with a black bandana's been supplying dope to Little Nate, who else is he supplying? And is it just him, or is it his buddies too?' He paused again. 'How many cops do you know would stop and search a hobo smelling of piss?'

Hammond steepled his fingers. 'This Carey woman,' he said. 'Is she still in town?'

Harrison nodded. 'Right now, she is. But she's gonna fly up to Spokane.'

'She's really going for it, huh?'

'Mike, some sonofabitch murdered her only son. Nobody can tell her who it was or why. She's looking for any clue she can get.'

Hammond nodded. 'So, what're you proposing, JB? Our remit is gangs in New Orleans, not hobos on trains.'

'Yeah, but hobos travel interstate, Mike. What if Little Nate's gang is just one of a whole bunch that's being supplied. Vagrants shipping dope in the boxcars of freight trains. That *is* our business.'

'What d'you wanna do?'

'I wanna fly up and see this cop in Spokane. Find out what's going down. If I can get a handle on it, maybe we can pull down more than just the sonofabitch from St Thomas.'

Harrison stood in the parking lot, smoked a cigarette and considered his motives. He had been going to quit. That marine in D.C. had all but convinced him it was time. He had something of a past and perhaps he needed to sift through it a little bit, before settling his mind elsewhere. He could retire early, and with his service, still take a livable pension with him. He had a mind to get that old Chevy tuned up properly and cruise the blue highways for a while. Maybe track down some people he had not seen in a long time.

'I thought I'd find you out here.'

Harrison turned to find Swann standing behind him.

'Never creep up on an old soldier, duchess. You're liable to get yourself killed.' He plucked a fresh cigarette from his shirt pocket and stuck it in the corner of his mouth.

'You seem preoccupied,' Swann told him, 'this time around. Like you've got things on your mind.'

Harrison blew out his cheeks. 'Well, I'll tell you, duchess. I do.' He leaned back against the concrete parapet, with his arms folded across his chest and the heel of one boot resting against the toe of the other. 'I got dropped from the SWAT team, Jack.' He raised his eyebrows. 'No real problem in that. We got a guy down here who used to be in the Hostage Rescue Team up at Quantico. The team leader probably figured he could teach us a thing or two, so it made sense. I'm the oldest by about ten years. Hell, I'm fifty next birthday. It's time I quit the SWAT team.' He broke off. 'But it made me think all the same.' He looked Swann in the eye. 'You remember when I first met you, how I figured it was you that got me burned up in Idaho?'

Swann rolled his eyes. 'How could I ever forget?'

'Well, I told you then, that once that deal was done, I was getting outta here.'

Swann flipped away his cigarette. 'And now is the time?'

Harrison pursed his lips. 'I think it might be, bubba.' He looked beyond Swann then. 'But first I'm gonna fly up to Washington State with Jean Carey and help her find out a bit more about these freight train riders. If she can figure that maybe they were responsible for her boy getting killed, then maybe she can go home with something.'

'She's got no chance of a conviction.'

Harrison sighed. 'I know it. But that's not the point. The lady's got guts and she needs something. Maybe I can persuade her to quit and go back to her life in England.' He stepped away from the wall. 'Then I think I'm gonna quit. I could walk away right now, but I wanna do this for Jean first.'

'You like her, don't you?'

Harrison leaned and spat. 'Yeah, I guess I do.'

They walked downstairs together. 'When're you and Logan tying the knot?' Harrison asked him.

'As soon as she gets that London posting.' Swann smiled at the thought of it. 'My two daughters are going to be bridesmaids.'

'They don't mind their daddy getting hitched again, then?'

'They did at first. I think they liked having me to themselves, but they're up for the idea now.'

'Good.' Harrison laid a friendly hand on his arm. 'That Logan's a sweet lady, duchess, and a hell of an FBI agent. You treat her nice, y'hear?'

Hammond called Harrison into his office when he got back down to the gang squad. 'Johnny Buck,' he said. 'I think you got a point about this train business. Go up to Spokane and see what you can dig up. I've spoken to the boss and he wants the full story when you get back. Apparently, we're not the first field office to show interest.

Swartz checked with a couple of buddies in Chicago and they told him that a blue bandana-wearing hobo got busted supplying heroin to a Gangsta Disciple.' He made a face. 'You just might have something here, and if we can co-ordinate a response, we might get both ends at the same time.'

Harrison went back to the quarter and phoned Jean's room from the hotel lobby. They sat and talked over a cup of coffee in the open quadrangle behind reception. Harrison could smell the flowers and their conversation was punctuated by the sound of hosepipes keeping them fresh. He told Jean what had happened, and her eyes lit up when he explained that he was going up to Spokane and that they ought to travel together.

'I'm delighted, John,' she said. 'But why're you doing this?'

Harrison shrugged. 'It's my job.'

She nodded, but the expression in her eyes told him she thought there was more to it than that. All at once, Harrison was embarrassed and got up. 'The plane leaves at ten-thirty tomorrow morning,' he said. 'I'll swing by and get you at nine.'

Jean stayed in the quadrangle after he had gone, just sitting quietly and thinking. There *was* more to it than just his job. She thought about him then, the way he had treated her since that first night in the bar. He had been concerned about her ever since. Yes, it was his job, but there was a kindness about him that was hidden behind his appearance and his awkwardness. She wondered if kindness was all that it was.

Harrison packed a bag at his apartment. He was not going back to the office today, and he had arranged for Matt Penny to give them a ride to the airport in the morning. He had got the Spokane police officer's name and number from Jean: a Detective Spinelli. He called him.

'FBI?' Spinelli said. 'You guys finally interested in this, huh? I've been trying to get some kinda federal co-ordination for years. Does this mean that Mrs Carey won't be coming now?'

'No, she's coming along. I'm just accompanying her.'

'Good.'

Harrison frowned. 'Why is it good?'

'Because from the tone of her voice on the phone, I figured she was looking for the kinda answers I sure as hell can't give her. I can tell her a few facts about some of the murders, perhaps point out a few similarities which might identify this crew as the perps, but that's not gonna convict anybody, and it sure as hell won't bring her son back to life.'

'Don't worry, she's a tough lady, Detective. And she's intelligent. She can handle it.'

Harrison put down the phone, lit a cigarette and stared out of the window at the balcony across the street. The Sun and Moon hotel and boarding house. He could see Kathleen changing the beds. She waved to him, but his thoughts were all at once in Vietnam. Maybe it was Jean's connection, but his mind was in Cu-Chi and the past. Eli Footer being blown up and him finding a disembodied hand with Eli's watch strapped to it. He sat down on the bed and wondered at himself. Was this just because of Jean Carey, or was it age catching up with him? Never before in his life had he thought so much about the past.

They flew to Spokane via Denver and Salt Lake City. Jean sat in the seat alongside him and looked out of the window as they climbed above Lake Ponchartrain. Harrison watched the muscles in her neck; her head was twisted to get the best view of the glistening mantle of water. Her black hair was loose, but she had pushed it back so one ear was exposed, small, neat and nut brown, and Harrison found himself taking in every contour. She looked round once more as the plane levelled off and then she sat back, eyes closed, with both her hands on the armrests. Harrison rested his hands in his lap, looking at how small hers were and how beautifully she kept her nails.

Jean opened her eyes and smiled at him. 'Thank you for coming with me.' She touched his hand where it lay in his lap and Harrison squeezed her fingers briefly. 'It's my job, Miss Lady Mam.'

'I know. But thank you anyway.'

All at once he felt colour in his cheeks, as if she knew this was much more than just his job. 'What made you want to be a doctor?' he said quickly.

She thought about that and was not wholly sure of the answer. 'I think it was because I helped nurse a lot of people during the war. Would that make sense to you?'

'Perfectly.'

'When I got to England, I knew it was going to be for keeps, and I wanted to forget all about the war and the past and the terrible suffering everyone had been through. But I had been good at the science subjects at school, and I think I have an analytical mind, so medicine seemed the natural thing to do.'

'And your job's still open for you?' he asked her. 'Back in London?'

'Yes.' She smiled then, thinking of the wards and the faces of the children and the tremendous amount of laughter there was in the place. For the first time since coming here, she missed the work. But then she felt inexplicably guilty, as if in considering such thoughts she betrayed the memory of her son; and the need to understand, to do something about his murder was redoubled. She dismissed London from her mind.

'I'm not thinking about going back, John. I have too much to finish here first.'

Harrison looked sideways at her then and wanted to tell her not to get her hopes too high, and that all they could really expect was general information. But her eyes were fired with renewed strength and there was no way he wanted to dampen that spirit.

The flight attendant came by with her trolley and poured them both some coffee. Harrison sipped his black and thought about placing a surreptitious plug of chew under his lip. But the no-smoking policy extended to all tobacco products and he would have to wait. He took an elastic tie from his pocket and twisted his hair into a ponytail. 'Time I got this cut,' he muttered. 'I'm too old for it now.'

Jean smiled. 'How old are you?' she asked.

'Almost fifty.'

'Have you always been an FBI agent?'

'No, mam. I was INS before the Bureau. Border patrol agent on the New Mexico line.' He smiled. 'Trying to stop wetbacks crossing the river.'

'Wetbacks?'

He nodded. 'It's not a real nice term, but it's only because of the river.' He made a face. 'American-born Mexicans are called Chicanos. I lived with a whole bunch of them in a trailer park in Idaho.'

'Undercover?'

He nodded.

'Have you done a lot of that?'

'Too much.'

'Would you do it again?'

'No, mam. I wouldn't.'

They sat in silence for a while, Harrison half listening to the murmur of other people's conversation, half to the drone of the engines, and then Jean touched his hand again.

'Did you go to fight in my country?' she said.

He pushed out his lips and nodded. 'I did two years. Like the dumb sonofagun I am, I volunteered to go back.'

'Why?'

'Because I had unfinished business.' He squinted at her. 'A friend of mine, who should never have been out there in the first place, got blown up on my first tour. I had promised his mother I would look out for him, because he was about as streetwise as Mr Magoo.' He stopped then, and Eli's face was as clear in his mind as that day in 1968 when they had shared a last cigarette, while holed up in a firefight. Eli was a nervous individual and did not make a good soldier. But he had balls and refused to duck service for his country by going to college like he should have. 'I fought the VC underground, in the tunnels of Cu-Chi,' he said.

They looked at one another for a long moment and it was as if each could discern the level of pain in the other. Harrison finally smiled and patted her hand. 'It was thirty years ago,' he said. 'I was a punk kid with a hair stuck up my ass. It was real dumb, Jean, and I know better now. But right then, I just wanted to kill the sonofabitch who blew up my buddy. I think I got by on adrenaline alone.'

'Do you regret it?' she asked him.

'No, I don't regret it. I was true to my feelings at the time. I think as long as you do that in life, you don't regret much.'

They changed planes in Denver with a half-hour in between, and then an hour in Salt Lake City, before finally they flew into Spokane. It was raining and the wind was howling in from the Rockies. Harrison stepped out of the airport on to the pavement. 'And I want to move north?' he muttered.

Spinelli had told them to check into the Holiday Inn downtown, which was only a short cab ride from police headquarters, where he was stationed with the homicide squad. Harrison hailed a taxi and helped the driver load their bags into the trunk, then he settled against the back seat with Jean.

They took a room each on the second floor, and agreed to meet for dinner in the bar. Harrison showered, smoked a cigarette and thought once more about his motives in coming here. He was first down and had a beer going when Jean came in. She had changed into a sleeveless, light cotton dress. She wore no stockings and the skin of her legs was smooth, brown and rich. Her hair was piled on her head and looked very black against the artificial light. Harrison pulled out the stool next to him. When she sat down, the hemline of her dress rode just above her knee and it was all he could do to keep his eyes averted.

'You look beautiful,' he told her, and nodded to the barman.

She ordered a Long Island iced tea and Harrison sipped another beer, and they chatted with the bartender for a while, getting the lowdown on Spokane. It was an industrial city and all Harrison knew about it was that the FBI had arrested three members of the Phineas Priesthood there. But he had learned a long time ago that the best way to find out about a place was to ask the local bartenders.

In the morning, they got up early and went down to the station house only to find that Spinelli had been called out on a homicide. So Harrison and Jean took in what sights of the city there were, until one of the homicide dicks paged them.

Spinelli was a big man with a handshake that crushed bones. He was in his mid-thirties, with blond hair, sharp blue eyes and a bushy blond moustache. He wore a short-sleeved shirt, revealing heavily muscled arms, and had a .357 Magnum in his shoulder holster.

'I'm sorry for your loss, Mrs Carey,' he said. 'I'm afraid your son just got on the wrong train.' He stood up and reached for his jacket. 'Most of the investigation time I've put in on this has been my own.' He looked at Harrison and smiled. 'The FBI wasn't the only organisation to show no interest. The Spokane PD wasn't too hot on the idea of the legwork either.' He opened the little gate that separated the squad area from the corridor and turned down the collar on his jacket.

'I've done it all in my own time and keep the files at home.'

He drove them to a suburb on the southern city limits, a small development of single-storey houses in a four-block grid. Harrison rode up front and they talked about police work.

Spinelli's house was set to the back of his lot, which was

unfenced, and a newspaper still lay on the lawn where the paperboy had tossed it.

'My wife's at work and the kids will be at school,' he said, and led the way inside.

The front door opened into an open-plan living room and kitchen. Spinelli put some coffee on to boil, then he opened a door off the hall, and a desk and two metal filing cabinets seemed to bulge at them. 'Not a whole lotta space, but there you go.' He whipped his jacket off, spread it over the back of the chair and settled himself down at the desk. 'OK,' he said. 'Tell me what you know so far.'

Jean told him what Gary Hirstius had found out, and then Harrison put in his piece about the bandana-wearing heroin-dealer. Spinelli drew in his lips. 'Now that is interesting,' he said. 'I've come across that one other time, but it kinda bears out a theory I've had for a while now. Chicago. One of the Highrollers got popped up there. The Highrollers are the northern crew by the way.'

'Supplying dope to a gangbanger,' Harrison said. 'I'm wondering if we're looking at some kinda supply network.'

Spinelli pulled a number of files from the cabinets and gave them the picture he had built up over the past five years. He told them that the FTRA had upwards of two thousand members, split into the three groups that Hirstius had identified. The Blues, or Highrollers, rode the northern lines, from the North-West to Minnesota. 'As far as I can gather, their leader is a Canadian guy they call The Voyageur,' he said. 'I guess after the trappers that used to canoe Lake Superior in the old days. I've never got a picture of him and, like most of them, he's real secretive. But I know he's French Canadian and hails originally from Montreal.' He went on to explain that the Red Heads occupied the Midwestern railroads and were led by a man called Ghost Town. 'His real name is Nixon Bodie,' he said. 'From the Yosemite area of California. They named him after the town of Bodie, which is a sorta living museum now, up in the Sierras.' He looked at Jean then. 'The black bandanas roam the South, mam. Southern Colorado's as far north as they get, and they ride all the way to Florida, Georgia, and maybe even the Carolinas. All I know about them is that they call themselves the Southern Blacks, which is a play on words, because the whole outfit is racist through and through.' He paused for a moment. 'You said you were Vietnamese.'

She nodded.

'Forgive me. I haven't seen a picture of your son. Was he oriental to look at too?'

'Partially.'

Spinelli sucked a breath. 'They coulda killed him just because of that.'

The colour drained visibly from Jean's face and she bunched her lips together hard to stop them trembling.

'It may've been something else, but I can't pretend to you that it was.' Spinelli tried to smile.

Harrison touched Jean's arm and she took his hand in hers and squeezed really hard. He looked back at Spinelli. 'I've got a picture of the guy we tailed,' he said. 'You wanna take a look?'

'Sure.'

Harrison let go Jean's hand and she sat down while he fished out the surveillance photograph from his bag. Spinelli frowned, chewed at his lip, and then went back to his filing cabinet.

'I thought I recognised him,' he said, taking out a file. 'There you go. Harold Douglas. Goes by the nickname Limpet.' He passed Harrison a picture. 'I got that from a hobo who sorta went UC of his own accord.' His eyes narrowed then. 'Good old boy, he was. Musta been all of seventy, had been riding the skids since the forties. He got a whole bunch of information for me before he disappeared.'

'Disappeared?' Jean said.

'Yes, mam.' He took off south one day, two years ago, and I've never seen him since.' He made a face. 'I've got a bad feeling he became one of the statistics.'

'Why'd he do that for you?' Harrison asked. 'Go undercover.'

'I figure he was just sick of it all. Quite a lot of his friends had disappeared over the years, people he'd known for thirty years in some cases. He figured riding the rails was the last bastion of what used to be the spirit of America. The whole hobo thing started up after the Civil War. Lots of farmers went home to nothing after the fighting was over and some of them started laying track for the big railroad operators. They called them "hoe boys" because of their farming background, and that eventually shortened into hobos, and then they started taking to the rails instead of building them.'

He led the way back through to the kitchen and poured them each some coffee. 'I've spent quite a bit of time at freight yards up here in Spokane and Seattle, and down at Pendleton in Oregon. Some of the regular guys have started to trust me. The freedom of always being able to move on gets in their blood, like the early pioneers. All they need is a little shelter, a fire and some food. Only now they can't do it any more, because somebody formed a gang.'

Harrison nodded grimly. 'If they are freighting dope, then that's the other spirit of America kicking in, right there.' He looked at the file on Limpet. 'Got quite a rap sheet, this dude,' he said. 'Three-time loser.'

Spinelli nodded. 'He's been with the outfit about two years, I figure,' he said. 'Right after he got out of the can the last time.'

'The three groups,' Jean said. 'Are they completely separate?'

'I don't know for sure,' Spinelli said. 'It's shadowy, mam. The Southern Blacks are a really nasty bunch. They've got discipline squads who mete out punishment to members who step out of line. They might even be assassination squads, I couldn't tell you for certain. They're led by a really nasty guy called Southern Sidetrack. He's never been arrested and I've got no file on him.'

'And he runs the whole crew?' Harrison asked him.

Spinelli shook his head. 'I don't think so. I've heard other rumours, stuff about an ex-Hell's Angel who came back from 'Nam with more than one grudge. He went by the name of Whiskey Six and he's still wanted in Arkansas and Tennessee for the murder of two guards during two separate bank robberies in 1981.' He pulled a face. 'Trouble is, there's no picture of him anywhere and nobody knows his real name. Like I said just now, most of this is sketched together from bits and pieces I've picked up at the freight yards. The way the hobos tell it is, he quit the Angels in the mid-eighties, because he was pissed off about an FBI agent infiltrating the Alaska chapter.'

'Anthony Tait,' Harrison said. 'I know him. His evidence put a helluva lot of them away for a helluva long time. He did real well, worked his way up to sergeant in arms. Nobody had a clue he was an undercover agent.'

'Well, anyways,' Spinelli went on. 'Apparently, Whiskey Six quit the brotherhood and took to the tracks. Over time, he established a brand new gang of his own. That gang now runs the railroad from here to the Florida Keys and has over two thousand members. He lets the three wings run their own deal pretty much, and they say he sticks mostly to the northern routes, but he's liable to turn up any place, at any time.' He looked at Jean then. 'Forgive my language, mam. But he is one evil bastard.'

Jean sat very quietly at a table by the window in the bar, thinking how suddenly alone she felt. What the detective had described was ugly and brutal, and for a few moments she had been back in the past with her mother and her sister, fleeing the armies of the North. Her son was a victim of the same kind of brutality that had killed her father, only in a different place and in a different time. Names like Limpet, Southern Sidetrack, The Voyageur and Ghost Town, men who for some reason had to spill the blood of others – for money, for drugs, or just because the colour of their skin was different. What could make one person kind, gentle and loving, and another a raging beast who would kill you as easily as look at you?

Harrison stood at her table. She had not seen him come in, but now she looked up. His hair was washed, unbraided and hung over his shoulders, and the grey of his eyes seemed to share the sadness she saw these days in her own. He was not a tall man, slim still for his fifty years, with wiry muscles knotted against the skin of his arms. His neck had begun to show his age and his face was tanned like old leather. Yet there was something about him, some depth in him that she saw, sensed or felt, and it sparked something inside her. 'Hey, Miss Lady Mam,' he said gently. 'How you doing?'

'I'm doing OK.'

He sat down, steepling his fingers on the table, and looked evenly at her. 'I'm sorry,' he said. 'Every little piece of information must add to the shock for you. Strange country, strange people. Everything, everybody, feeling alien.'

She smiled, but a single silent tear glassed against her eye. 'I wish there was something more I could do,' Harrison said softly.

'Thank you.' She mouthed the words and looked at the floor between her feet.

Harrison left her for a moment then and brought some drinks from the bar. Jean had wiped away her tears, but her eyes were tinged red at the edges when he sat down again. He passed her a drink and she accepted one of his cigarettes.

'What're we going to do?' she asked him.

'Tomorrow, we're going to visit one of the freight yards with Spinelli, see if we can talk to some of these hobos ourselves. There's more than just random murder going on here, Jean. This is a gang – organised, disciplined and strong.'

'You think they're running drugs?'

'I know they're running drugs. What I don't know is, how big of a set-up we're looking at.'

'How will you find out?'

Harrison sucked breath, aware that he was not keen on the answer. 'There's a number of ways,' he said. 'But close-range surveillance is the best.'

Fachida Harada sat on the bare wooden floor of his house in Falls Church, meditating at the Shinto shrine he had built. He sat cross-legged, wearing a silk kimono, with the eighteenth-century sword laid to one side of him in the open casket. He prayed silently, as samurai had prayed before him, as he himself had prayed and chanted softly down the ages. He knew, all before him had known, that there was no equating the Buddhism of his religion with the way of the bushido. He had been a samurai and would remain so for all eternity, incarnation after incarnation, paying penance for the violent way of life. He thought of Tetsuya, and the last time they had been together as warriors, three years previously. He had been close by when the National Police Agency in Osaka had arrested him. That had been the worst moment of his life. Perhaps it was at that moment that the extent of his own betrayal and the depths to which he had fallen were laid bare before him.

The causes of the early eighties had seemed just at the time, and yet the Marxist philosophy followed by Shigenobu was in direct opposition to the bushido way of his father and grandfather. It was diametrically opposed to the nationalist way of the master. Yet the master was already dead when Shigenobu formed the group, and Harada was just a disillusioned teenager. But the way of Shigenobu quickly turned to the capitalism that bloated their enemies. The funds paid by the Libyan and others were enormous, and their members grew fat in the North Korean enclave. Harada had only remained with them until 1990 and then he had returned to Japan, endeavouring to set his feet back on the path appointed to him. But it was not easy and, as before, *they* trapped him, ensnared him with new possibilities, angry that he had returned to Japan. *They* had played on his disillusionment with Shigenobu, with the Marxist theme in general, and he had been pliable. But their anger was raw when he quit and went home. They had lost on a massive investment: time, money, resources. And all the while, Tetsuya had held fast to the old ways, somehow equating them acceptably with the work of Shigenobu. It had been that way ever since they set foot in the Bekaa Valley, all those years ago.

Both of them ultimately married, both of them had children to carry on the code, yet the love between them was that of the highest calling. Warrior to warrior, as it had been in the days of seclusion when Japan was closed to the world.

He opened his eyes, the meditation interrupted, disturbed by emotions that welled up from within. Once again he looked at the sword, its pedigree perfect for what might be required in the end. The moment was over. He got to his feet, bowed before the shrine and closed the lid on the casket. He blew out the candles and showered, then considered the words he would use. Before him on the bedroom floor lay a cardboard box, a length of ribbon and two ounces of C-4 plastic explosive.

The previous day he had visited one of his dead drops, just on the eastern side of the Appalachian Mountains. He had chosen it carefully, by the entrance to a culvert just off Highway 340. It was a hole in the ground that lay parallel to the twenty-five-mile road sign between Bentonville and Front Royal. From the rented house in Falls Church, it was a couple of hours' drive along Interstate 66. He alternated between the grey sedan, the black independent taxi cab, and the red security truck with *C U SAFELY* painted on the side. He had sectioned a chunk of earth, just to the left of the culvert, under the cover of darkness some six months before, and placed a large, dry cool-box into the hole. This time, four individual rolls of C-4 military-grade explosive had been delivered. One kilo per roll, plus a case of RD6 phosphorus grenades. He had slipped the rolls of C-4 inside two lengths of plastic plumbing pipe that he carried as a matter of course. Later, if and when they instituted their stop-and-search procedures, no cop or sheriff's deputy would see anything out of the ordinary. He stowed the grenades in a sectioned compartment where the spare wheel was housed, and climbed back into the truck. The mortars he had requested would come later, much much later, when panic was everyone's watchword.

Logan picked up Tom Kovalski's phone. 'ASAC's office,' she said.

'Agent Kovalski, please.' Something in the tone of the voice made her stiffen.

'He's not here right now. This is Agent Logan. Can I help you?'

'That depends, Agent Logan.'

There was an accent, but she could not quite place it. 'On what exactly?'

'On your role with the FBI.'

And then she recognised the voice as the one on the tape. 'I'm the terrorism response co-ordinator.'

'That's fortuitous.'

'Is it. Why?'

'Because I'm a terrorist.'

7

Logan paged Kovalski and he was on the line three minutes later. 'We've just had a call from Harada,' she told him.

'What did he say?'

'He said there's an improvised explosive device planted in the Arlington Cemetery and we have forty-five minutes to evacuate the area.'

'Forty-five minutes.'

'That's all. He gave us what he claims is a legitimate codeword. He told me it was for us only, but if we did not co-operate, then he would disclose who he is to the media, which he assured me would not be good news. He didn't say why.'

'Where in Arlington Cemetery?'

'It's in a garbage can by John F. Kennedy's grave.'

'Did he say why he'd planted it?'

'No.'

'What about the codeword?'

'Wind-blown.'

'That it?'

'Yes.'

Kovalski thought for a moment. 'What the hell does it mean?'

'I don't know. But Jack Swann told me the reason the cherry blossom is the symbol of the samurai is because as soon as it blooms, it's blown away on the wind.'

'OK. Evacuate the area. And see if you can get Swann to fly up here from New Orleans. I want to talk to him.'

Logan got everything rolling. The parks police began the evacuation, and the Office of Emergency Management for D.C. together with that of Arlington County were placed on standby. Kovalski called the chief of police for the District of Columbia and the chief at Arlington County and the parks, as well as the leading members of the joint terrorism task force. The EOD squads from the field office and headquarters rolled, together with the metropolitan police squad. The rendezvous point was set at the junction of Roosevelt Drive and Weeks Avenue, a hundred and fifty yards down the hill from Kennedy's grave.

Logan raced to the scene, down 4th Street and on to Constitution Avenue, then across the Memorial Drive Bridge. There was only one entrance to the cemetery off Memorial Drive and she could see the hordes of tourists being ferried out of the area on the blue sightseeing buses. McKensie was with her in the passenger seat. 'Do we know anything at all about this guy, Cheyenne?'

Logan shook her head, kicked down hard on the bridge, and the police package roared.

'He's Japanese and he might be something to do with the yakuza. That's it so far.'

'Are we talking a pipe bomb?'

'We haven't got a clue.'

Logan turned into the cemetery at the women's memorial and pulled up at the rendezvous point, where the police and other emergency services were gathering. She looked up the hill to where General Lee's mansion, with its white pillars and bright yellow fascia, dominated the skyline. The crisis site was blocked by trees and the concrete oval set directly before it. Both John Kennedy and Jackie lay up there, together with their son, Patrick. The eternal flame between them. Logan knew that there were two trash cans made of stone, one on either side of the grave. She looked round the open rendezvous point – the road, grass and small white gravestones, which had already been searched. She could feel her heart beating, her shield pinned at the breast of her jacket now, as she approached the uniformed parks police officers winding tape across the adjoining roads.

'Agent Logan,' she said to a sergeant. 'I'm on-scene commander. What's the situation?'

'Well, we got the cordons in at one-fifty yards, and the cemetery limits have been cleared. You want us back another fifty?'

Logan bit her lip. 'Have we got EOD here yet?'

'No, mam.' As he was speaking, the big blue FBI van came roaring in through the gates below them. The driver pulled up and an explosives officer climbed out of the passenger seat. He was Italian-looking: wiry, with a thin black moustache and equally thin hair. He shook hands with Logan. 'Callio,' he said. 'Bomb Squad. I want everybody back of that line.' He jerked his thumb to the outer cordon perimeter. 'Has this area been searched for booby traps?'

Logan glanced at the parks sergeant. 'Yes, sir,' he said.

'Good.' Callio scratched his head and looked up the hill. 'Where exactly is the crisis site?'

Logan pointed. 'There are two garbage cans on either side of the grave. We believe the IED's in one of them.'

Callio looked at his watch. 'OK. I want to know exactly what happened. The full sequence of events that led to you and me standing here.'

Logan told him exactly what had happened in the minutest of detail, the time of the call and the exact words spoken by Harada.

'Do we know who he is, who he represents?'

She shook her head. 'He's a new one on us, Callio. We don't know if this is a bluff or what.'

'Forty-five minutes.'

She nodded.

He looked at his watch. 'Which was precisely seventeen minutes ago.'

Again she nodded. Callio made a face and looked back beyond the cordon, to where the evidence response teams were gathering. 'OK,' he said. 'We wait the full forty-five and see if anything goes bang.'

Harada was watching things unfold on television, flicking the channels between Fox News, NBC and CNN. So far he had only told the FBI his identity, but he wanted to see how much had been unravelled by the media. The media was a weapon he would use but sparingly, and in his own time. The skies had been closed over the crisis site and the only helicopter shots were from a good distance away, but reporters and media vans crowded Memorial Drive. The FBI had instituted cordons at what looked like a couple of hundred yards and were clearly waiting. They were professional. He did not know why, but he had half expected them not to be. He thought they might go in physically, or send a robot with a coil and line to hook the device from the bin.

There was intense media speculation as to who had planted the bomb. So far, an 'unknown subject' was all the FBI had said. Everybody was being blamed: from the Islamic Jihad to the militia. One thing that was interesting, he thought. Historically, it was always some external force that was blamed first in this country, but since Oklahoma it was the militia. One reporter seemed to be being interviewed by another and Harada turned the volume up louder.

'I'm here with Carl Smylie,' the CNN man on the ground was saying, holding his microphone up to the face of a young man with long hair and round-rimmed glasses. 'Mr Smylie is a freelance journalist and an expert on the rise of militia groups in this country.' He turned to the long-haired man. 'Tell us what you know, Mr Smylie.'

'Larry, I've just got back from Hope Heights, Oregon, a small town on the Pacific coast, where the people are all but barricading their houses. The scene reminds me of the time a few years ago when the FBI and the National Guard descended on Reserve, New Mexico, and people fled from their homes. The authorities claimed they were helping local law-enforcement officers search for the body of a murder victim, but it was a year since that crime took place.' Smylie looked straight into the camera. 'Billy Bob Lafitte, a local gun store owner, was murdered in Hope

Heights a week ago, and it's the general belief that government agents were behind it.'

'Lafitte was a militia leader, wasn't he,' the CNN man said.

'A patriot. Yes, sir. He was. Three Orientals, driving what looked like a government vehicle, were seen in and around Hope Heights over a period of two days before Lafitte's brake lines were cut.'

'So, you're saying that this incident today is some kind of militia backlash.'

Smylie looked directly into the camera. 'Larry, I'm not saying anything. I've noticed the timing, is all.'

'There you have it,' Larry was talking again. 'Speculation right now, but a possible link with one of the unorganised militias. As we all know, the circumstances surrounding Billy Bob Lafitte's death were suspicious and, as yet, the investigating police officers have come up with no significant leads, other than the three alleged Orientals. That incident followed hard on the heels of the strange death of another militia leader, Daniel Pataki in Missouri. Pataki's post-mortem examination revealed his death was caused by yellow fever, which can only be contracted in the tropics. It was well known that Pataki had never stepped outside the United States.'

Harada looked on and waited.

Logan took a call from Kovalski on her cellphone. 'We're waiting right now, Tom. The EOD guy wants to see what happens when the forty-five minutes are up.' She checked her wristwatch. 'That's less than eight minutes from now. What's happening back there?'

Kovalski had remained at the central command post at the field office, from where he could talk by phone, radio or computer link to the tactical operations center, a massive Chevrolet Suburban, at the scene. He had an open line to the FBI Director, as well as the President's national security adviser – Robert Jensen. Everybody was breathing down his neck, but Kovalski was used to that. He had flown helicopters in Vietnam, and figured pressure in degrees of being fired upon, with no body armour, when you were trying to medevac wounded GIs from hot landing zones. He had been hit twice in the chest and upper arm. 'Did you get hold of Jack Swann, like I asked you, Chey?'

'Of course. Shit, Tom, you think I need an excuse to get his ass up to Washington?'

Kovalski laughed. 'How much does he know about what we know?'

'He knows I asked him about the yakuza, that's it.' She thought for a moment then. 'Tom, I've just seen a CNN monitor. That militia reporter Smylie's in town. He's already started the rumour mill turning with comments about Hope Heights. We've not released anything about Harada, have we?'

'No. And we're not going to.' Kovalski sighed then. 'It is an interesting coincidence, though, isn't it. Harada being a Jap and three Orientals showing up on the west coast.'

'Those three guys were *deliberately* meant to look like government agents.'

'Or they *were* government agents, depending on which conspiracy theory you adhere to.'

Logan switched the phone off and climbed into the TOC, where an analyst had the Cascade programme running and was logging every detail of what had happened. Logan glanced at McKensie, who checked her watch and twisted her mouth down at the corners. Logan looked across the open space to the inner cordon line, where the only vehicle was the blue truck housing the explosive officer's monitors, computer equipment, toolboxes and the Alvis Wheelbarrow. He was standing beside the vehicle, studying the crisis site through binoculars. Logan could hear the crackle of radios from the SWAT tactical ops center; and then the garbage can blew up.

The sound was not loud, a muffled whump, but she jumped where she sat and waited, and then climbed out of

141

the truck. The EOD agent was still watching through binoculars. Smoke rose and she could smell cordite, but it was not possible to see anything. Logan waited a full minute, then she and McKensie crossed under the inner cordon line and approached the bomb-squad vehicle. Callio was still standing with his driver and watching. He lowered the glasses as Logan came alongside.

'Phosphorus,' he said. 'That's my initial opinion, Logan. Lotta smoke, but not much else. Looks like an amateur to me.'

She nodded. 'You're saying, a lot of fuss about nothing.'

Callio lifted his eyebrows. 'Well, we don't know that now, do we?' He looked across the empty cemetery, then down on to Memorial Drive where the media were camped *en masse*. 'He sure drew some attention to himself, whoever he was.' He went round to the back of the van then and opened the doors. 'I'm gonna send in the robot,' he said. 'Check the area out through the drive cameras. No sense risking my neck till things are a little clearer.'

Logan reported back to Kovalski and watched as Callio sent in the Wheelbarrow, armed with disrupters for controlled explosions. He could sit in the back of his truck and monitor exactly what the drive cameras told him, and when he neared the crisis site he could search, using the attack camera on the extendable boom. 'I might be wrong, Tom,' she said. 'But my bones tell me the fireworks are over.'

'I think you're right, baby. He told us it was there and it was. Depending on what he's trying to achieve, it didn't need to be very big.'

'Callio said phosphorus. Just designed to burn.'

'Wait till he gives the all-clear, then hand over to the ERTs.' Kovalski paused for a moment. 'Tell you what, Chey. Leave McKensie in charge. It'll be good for her training. As soon as Callio gives the OK, let her take over. I want you back here.'

Swann landed at the National Airport at seven-thirty that

evening and Logan checked him into the Hyatt on Jefferson Davis Highway. The FBI explosives officer had given the all-clear, and the evidence response teams and the specialists from the Bomb Data Center began zoning the area for evidence. The section of ground around Kennedy's grave was completely sealed off and scaffolding poles and sterilised tarpaulins were erected to ensure there could be no evidence contamination. Sample swabs of the area were taken for explosive residue, RDX or PETN, and then forensic teams went to work. Logan and Swann drove in to the field office.

Kovalski was in the command post, together with the FBI Director and the heads of both the domestic and international terrorism sections, based at the Hoover building. The senior members of the task force were also present, and Kovalski introduced Swann.

'He's been with the UK's Antiterrorism Branch for seven years and, as he's in the country, I want some consultative help.' His face darkened then. 'OK. So far, we've got few details. The device was small and it was effectively only an incendiary – phosphorus – causing minimal damage. The bang was minor, but it was exactly where he said it would be and it went off exactly when he said it would.' He paused. 'We had a phone call telling us his name was Fachida Harada, but we don't know who he is or what he's playing at.'

Swann spoke for the first time. 'I might be able to help there. I made some phone calls from the plane on the way up from New Orleans. We've got a specialist Japanese crime unit back in London, with a former Hong Kong cop who infiltrated the Yamaguchi-gumi, the largest yakuza gang in the world, three years ago.'

'Are you saying Harada is yakuza?' the ATF agent seated at the end of the table asked him.

'After a fashion, he is. Although I'm not sure what that's got to do with this situation. The yakuza is a three-hundred-year-old organisation, which is supposedly descended from the ancient samurai warriors. It's claimed they're the last upholders of the ancient virtues of *giri* and *ninjo*: that's the obligation to repay favours and show compassion for the weak. These are things the samurai undertook in the past, and the yakuza claim to undertake them now. I think you have to take the latter with a huge pinch of salt, mind you.'

'Jack,' Logan interrupted him. 'Why would a yakuza want to bomb Washington?'

Swann made a face. 'I don't know.' He opened his briefcase and spread a sheet of paper on the table in front of him. 'You might want to get these copied,' he said. 'It's the scant bit of information we've got on him.' He passed the single sheet to Logan. 'Fachida Harada. He's about forty-five and he *has* got connections to the yakuza, but I'm not sure how strong they are. We think he might have been *sokaiya* – that's their business investment arm.'

Kovalski nodded. 'Gangsters buying stock and taking seats on company boards.'

'Exactly. We think Harada did that in Hong Kong for a while, till we handed it back to China.'

'What's he doing over here?'

Swann shook his head. 'I don't know.' He looked at Logan. 'He contacted you, didn't he?'

Logan gestured to Kovalski. 'He sent a tape in to Tom.'

'Addressed to you personally?' Swann asked him.

'Not by name, but addressed to the ASAC, which amounts to the same thing.'

Swann nodded then. 'And he told you his name, his father's name, his grandfather's, where the family came from and stuff like that?'

'Yes.'

'That is samurai. It's part of their challenge.' He broke off for a moment and sifted his notes. 'When a samurai warrior went into battle in the past, it was one to one, man against man, sword fighting. It ended in death for one warrior, generally involving beheading.'

Logan lifted an eyebrow.

'Before battle commenced, each warrior would announce his pedigree so that his opponent would know the value of who he was fighting. Killing an opposing warrior in samurai combat was a big thing in Japan. It was all about honour, skill and bravery.'

'So what exactly are you saying?' asked the district police chief.

'I'm saying he's announced himself in battle. I suppose to the FBI. He's personified that in you, Tom.' He gestured at Kovalski. 'I don't know why, but he's probably researched you and discovered you're the main man against terrorism over here.'

Kovalski stared at him across the table. 'You're telling me this asshole wants to fight me?'

'Metaphorically speaking, yes.'

Swann and Logan left the field office at ten and drove back to Crystal City and the hotel. Harada intrigued Swann. He had never come across anything vaguely similar in the past, and the thought of helping the FBI track him down was far more appealing than teaching a class of deputy sheriffs what to do at a bomb scene. They parked in the lot to the left of the main hotel building and went to the bar. A man seated on a stool at the far end spotted them and came over. He was in his early thirties, wearing chinos and loafers, with longish brown hair and gold-rimmed glasses. Logan saw him and groaned.

'Agent Logan. We meet again.' He looked at Swann and offered his hand. 'Carl Smylie, news and current affairs. You another Fed?'

Swann did not shake his hand.

'No, Carl, he's not.'

'Gotta be personal, then.' Smylie winked at Swann. 'Hey, Logan. I saw you in Hope Heights. Checking on the covert action were you?'

'Carl, I'm busy right now.'

'Sorry.' He grinned boyishly again. 'Was kinda strange,

though, huh. Three government types and then boom bang.'
He snapped his fingers under her nose. 'Billy Bob goes off
the mountain road. I wanted to talk to you in Oregon, but I
guess you were ignoring me. Sure talked to Cameron,
though. That state cop's got some opinions of his own.
Mind you, so does Sheriff Riggins.'

Logan sighed heavily. 'Carl, leave us alone, will you. It's
been a real long day.'

'You're not kidding. I was in Oregon this morning and
only came back by chance. CNN wanted to do a special
with me on the militia thing, but it's gonna have to wait till
tomorrow now.' He looked at Swann. 'Helluva thing today
out at the cemetery, wasn't it. Militia, you figure, Logan,
getting their own back?'

'Hey.' Swann stepped in front of him. 'The lady asked
you to leave us alone. Now why don't you do that.'

'Aha. A British accent.' Smylie cocked his head to one
side. 'Are you a UK cop or something?' He took a step back
and Swann guided Logan past him to a table with four low-
backed chairs. He signalled to the barman, but Smylie
sidled alongside him. 'How come you're in town? Is it
business or personal?'

'I tell you what,' Swann said. 'If you don't stop bugging
us, it'll become intensely personal.'

'My God. Attitude.' Smylie moved towards the open
lobby area. 'I like him, Logan. A Brit with style. That's a
first for ya.' He turned, flapped his hand over his shoulder at
them and walked across the lobby.

'Who the hell is he?' Swann took a beer from the barman
and passed it to Logan.

'He's a freelance reporter and he's right. He knows more
about what's going on with the militia movement than just
about anyone else. He makes good money out of peddling
conspiracy theory stories, but he does have his finger on the
pulse. He knows all the big guns. He's the only reporter in
America to interview BobCat Reece from Montana.'

'Reece,' Swann said. 'He's the guy with the compound.'

'Yeah. The one that trains SPIKE teams and claims they're only Minutemen looking to protect their families.'

'SPIKE?'

'Specialist integrated killing entities. It's his own acroynm, something he no doubt bastardised from his days with the Green Berets.' She sipped beer. 'The militia trust Smylie to tell their side of the story and he likes nothing better than mixing it up for the media. He earns a good living at it. All the major networks come to him when they want the lowdown on some new group or a slant on things. You watch the papers tomorrow. This bomb will be down to the militia.'

She was not wrong. Swann got up first and found a copy of the *Washington Post* outside their door. He flapped open the first page and narrowed his eyes. FBI BAFFLED BY GRAVE-YARD BOMBER. He read how the FBI was at a loss to know what the motive behind the attack on Arlington Cemetery had been and who indeed was behind it. Various groups were hinted at, and then he read Smylie's name, the connection with the mysterious deaths of Daniel Pataki and Billy Bob Lafitte. The murder of the park ranger was also cited, and there was an exclusive quote given to Smylie from a man described as 'millennial presidential candidate' Robert Reece of Montana. Logan was drinking coffee in bed, the sheet falling just below her chocolate-coloured breasts. Swann gazed at her: dreadlocked hair loose about her shoulders like strips of black rain. Her face was smooth as silk, eyes dark and wide.

'BobCat Reece is running for President,' he said. 'You were right. There's a comment in here from Smylie. Reece is linking this incident with what went on in Missouri and Oregon. He says: "If the government insist on subjugating the people with taxes, federal laws and now murder, they cannot reasonably complain if a few concerned citizens decide to hit back in order to protect the integrity of the Bill of Rights."'

'Bill of Rights – bullshit.' Logan threw off the sheet and got up.

'He says the presence of three oriental G-men in Hope Heights, Oregon, is proof of what they've been saying. The New World Order is being ushered in and the use of Hong Kong troops, first mooted by the militias as far back as 1992, is becoming a reality.'

'What an asshole.' Logan went into the bathroom, turned on the shower and came out again, still naked. 'If we *were* using them, we'd hardly send them into a place like Hope Heights, Oregon.'

'Reece has thought of that,' Swann went on. 'He claims that for years this was on a covert basis, along with gangs like the Crips and the Bloods taking away citizens' guns. He says the last covert display of action by the government was the federally organised Los Angeles riot in 1992, when the only people whose property was not harmed by marauding black people were the ones who openly displayed their weapons. He says the government has finally decided to enact the plans drawn up by the Bildebergers, the Trilateral Commission and the United Nations. From now on, he will be wearing his gun whenever he ventures from his property.'

'Good,' Logan said. 'Maybe a state trooper will arrest him.'

'Maybe that's what he wants.'

She pulled a face and took the paper from him. 'What I don't understand is why an incendiary device planted in Arlington Cemetery gives BobCat Reece so much newspaper time.'

They drove back to 4th Street, joined Kovalski in his car and went with him over the bridge to Arlington. Swann wanted to look at the crime scene, which was still sectioned off and being searched for evidence. They had zoned carefully and created a swept path in and out, leaving all other areas uncontaminated. 'Why send us a coded warning, Jack?' Kovalski asked. 'We've never had one before. The militia or the Priesthood – or any of the other groups – just plants the IED and bucks outta there. Why a phone call now?'

'The Provisional IRA are the only group to consistently phone in coded warnings,' Swann told him. 'Their plan was to disrupt as much as they could. Civilian deaths never did anyone's cause much good. The question is, what's Harada's cause?'

'And why choose Kennedy's grave?' Logan put in.

'Maybe it's the memorial factor,' Kovalski said. 'Kennedy still symbolises the United States.'

Swann nodded slowly. 'Maybe it's some kind of cementation of what he's already told you. Maybe he's proclaiming that he really is a warrior and therefore to be taken seriously.' He thought about it for a moment. 'That would fit. The device was phosphorus, yet there was very little to burn. The samurai honour thing. They didn't want to desecrate, and they would not want to harm civilians. The samurai didn't kill noncombatants in battle.'

'I guess that makes a sort of sense.' Kovalski pulled up at the outer cordon line and they got out.

One of the evidence response agents from the field office spotted Logan and beckoned them over. She introduced Swann. 'This is Matt Bremner, Jack. He heads up the 4th Street ERT.'

'I got something for you, Cheyenne. Boss,' he added to Kovalski. Fishing in a plastic evidence bin, he brought out a ziplock-sealed envelope and laid it flat on the table before them. 'What d'ya think of that?'

They all looked at it and Swann frowned. Like a piece of Plasticine, only the colour of putty and shaped into a flower. Kovalski was staring coldly. 'That's a lump of shaped C-4.'

'That's exactly what it is. I found it at the back of the memorial, in the bush, right there.'

Bremner pointed off to the left of where he had set up the automatic debris-sifter and table. Kovalski was still looking

149

at the polythene envelope. 'What's the betting that's the shape of cherry blossom,' he said.

They sat round the conference table in his office, the three of them and McKensie.

'Learning fast, huh?' Kovalski said to her.

'Very.'

'You did a good job when you took over as on-scene commander yesterday.'

McKensie glowed a little under the ears and Swann smiled at her. 'Why would he plant a grenade when he's got C-4?' he murmured. Bremner had told them that the Bomb Data Center had localised the seat of the explosion and recovered fragments of the device. It was enough to tell them that the bomber had used a phosphorus RD6 military-issue grenade. He had pulled the pin and set up a relatively primitive single-circuit timing and power unit. They had recovered a section of melted wiring and a burned piece of a lunch box. Swann had seen many similar things with the IRA. Over the years, they had perfected their home-made timing and power units up to a Mark 17. Harada must have left the device with a safety-arming switch in operation, to set off the forty-five-minute delay once the pin was removed. Crude it might be, but it had been extremely effective.

Kovalski was looking at Swann. 'Not only why, Jack. But where the hell did he get the C-4?'

'And why leave an unexploded shaped charge?' McKensie added.

'To tell us that he has it?' Logan suggested.

The red phone rang on Kovalski's desk and he sighed. 'Give me some space, people. That's the privacy channel.'

'Privacy channel?' Swann asked as they trooped out and Logan shut Kovalski's door.

'Yeah. He's the Washington ASAC, Jack. This office is responsible for counter-intelligence.'

Kovalski held the phone to his ear. 'Cyrus Birch,' he

said. 'Why're you calling me on the division chief's phone? I thought your interest was held in other parts of the world.'

'It is, Tom. But I'm a man of many interests, believe me. And Washington's where my heart is.'

Kovalski knew Birch of old. They were allegedly on the same side, but had sparred a few times, and even crossed swords once or twice when Kovalski thought the CIA went too far, as sometimes they were wont to do. They did not like the FBI because of their jurisdiction, plus the fact that the Bureau had got Aldrich Ames and made them look very silly for a while. 'I saw your little problem in Arlington. Anything we can help you with?'

'Right now, I don't think so. Unless *you* were behind it?'

'Ha ha, Tom. You gotta stop watching Mel Gibson movies.'

'So what d'you want, Cyrus? What made you call over this one? It's been a while since I heard from you.'

'Just keeping tabs on things, Tom. It's a personal thing with me. Important when a man has my ambitions.'

'The DCI's an external appointment these days, Cyrus, same as the Director is here. Unless you're on real good terms with the President, I wouldn't stick your house on it.'

'*Houses*, Tom. I'm Ivy League, remember? With us, it's *houses*. No, but you're right. The DCI is way out of my league.'

'Cyrus,' Kovalski said. 'I'm running a bomb-scene investigation this morning. Is there something I can help you with, or were you just fishing?'

'Who was it, Tom?'

Kovalski smiled. 'That was direct. Unexpected from you.' He sat forward. 'Right now, I can't tell you. It's the morning after the night before. We've still got the hangover.'

He put the phone down and sat in the silence of his office for a moment. Why would Cyrus Birch call him up over this: the CIA had no jurisdiction on the US mainland, and a small device, which hurt nobody, was nothing to do with them. Unless. He thought of Horowitz at the Israeli Embassy and the extent of his network of contacts. If Horowitz knew about a fly landing in his ointment, maybe he knew the identity of that fly. And if he did, maybe other people did too.

Harada woke early as he always did, washed his face and body, and dressed in his kimono, before meditating in the lotus position before the Shinto shrine. At seven, he changed into his grey business suit, collected his briefcase and drove the grey sedan down Highway 50, slowing, along with the rest of the rubber-neckers, to watch the gaggle of media vehicles still camped out by Arlington Cemetery. He listened to the radio news as the traffic backed up on the bridge across the Potomac, and it was almost eight-thirty when he pulled off North Capitol Street, across the road from the old soldiers' home, and into the small self-storage lot. He stopped outside the first unit, got out of the car, unlocked the chain on the roll-over door and hoisted it. Then he got back in the car and drove inside.

Across the road the old soldier, with no legs and little memory, watched him.

Harada changed into his overalls, then he took the case from the back seat of his car and transferred three more lengths of plumber's pipe to the store section at the back of the truck in the next-door unit. He had all kinds of items in there, from a CCTV unit to a video-monitoring system, and alarms with pipes, wires and batteries. He checked that the piping was stowed where it was warm and dry, and closed the doors on the truck.

Outside, it was hot and it took a little while before the air conditioning clicked in, and Harada found himself sweating. He did not mind: the summers in Tokyo were unbearable for a lot of people, but he had never had a problem with heat. He took it as another metaphorical flagellation, a purging of the failures of youth from his bones.

He drove down New Hampshire Avenue and made a

circuit of the Federal Triangle, monitoring the whereabouts of the cops and the secret service agents, as well as the diplomatic security men outside the State Department's buildings and along Virginia Avenue. He cruised up 4th Street and pulled over for a few minutes outside the redbrick Federal Museum, directly across from the FBI's field office. After six months, the black-uniformed Federal Protective Service cops were used to the *C U SAFELY* truck pausing while the driver made phone calls. Once, a uniformed secret service agent, close to the White House, had stopped him and asked for some ID. Harada had various drivers' licences, but this one was in the name of Joe Aoki, originally from San Francisco. He also had his full security consultant's résumé and his college degree certificates from Cleveland, Ohio. That was the one and only time he'd ever had to show his identification.

He swung the truck in an arc and drove across George Mason Bridge on 395, which took him south of Arlington Cemetery. He had seen the television news and read the reports in this morning's *Post*, and knew that nobody had been injured and there had been minimal damage. It was interesting, but unsurprising, that there was no mention of him or any tape of his phone call or coded warning. It was bound to go one of two ways; and he had thought they would prefer secrecy until they had more of an idea what they were dealing with. There were government experts to assist them, as well as people in their organised crime squads, who would be able to recognise the yakuza/samurai connections. Like everyone else, they would believe that the yakuza upheld the old traditions, which he had discovered was untrue. Yes, they had the codes, the black mist and the finger-cutting, but in reality it was as far removed from the old ways as anything in modern Japan.

He had read the reports thoroughly and remarked to himself on the commentary that came out of the militia movement. There he had sympathy, although they hated his kind, as seemed evident in the disturbance created by the presence of Orientals in small-town Oregon. Those men were *ninja*, the masters of stealth and secret killing techniques. He had read of Pataki dying in Missouri and was reminded of the strange accidents and illnesses of old.

But the people here had no idea of the master, or what he had created as long ago as 1970. He thought again of that day in November, when the news came through of the siege. The final act of honour from the final honourable man, whose name means 'snow at the foot of Mount Fuji'.

A car hooting its horn shook him from his reverie and seemed to prick at his purpose. Ahead of him, a metro transit police road unit was parked across the highway, cutting the lanes from two to one, and the drivers of each vehicle were being stopped and asked questions. Harada smiled to himself, practised the voice in his head and waited for his turn. The officer was young and in uniform. Harada rolled down the window.

'How you doing?' he said.

'Sir, we're sorry to interrupt your day, but there was a bombing incident in the cemetery yesterday evening and I have to ask you some questions.'

'No problem.' Harada leaned his elbow on the doorpanel.

The officer was looking at the side of his truck and writing the name down, then the licence number. 'Were you in the area yesterday?' he asked him. 'I've seen your truck around. Were you downtown yesterday?'

'Not yesterday, no. I wasn't working yesterday. Gave myself the day off.'

'Business is good, then.'

Harada smiled at him. 'In this day and age? You bet.'

'Where were you yesterday?'

'At home. I was a little sick, actually. Stomach flu, I think. I didn't work at all.'

'So you didn't pass this area and therefore didn't see anything or anybody acting in a manner out of the ordinary?'

'No, sir. I wish I could help you. Like you said, I'm

normally all over this area. I've got clients both sides of the river, but yesterday I was sick.'

'Not today, though, huh?'

'No, sir. Today I'm better and real busy.' He smiled again. 'I'm sorry I can't be more help. Unless you want an alarm fitted to your house.'

'No, thank you.' The cop glanced down at his notes. 'You have a good day, Mr . . .'

'Aoki.' Harada smiled, shifted the column change and eased back into the traffic.

He watched the cop hold up his hand for the next driver and pull him over. He laughed then, softly. The man could have searched his entire van, found all manner of things connected with bomb-making, and still not been any the wiser. He made a loop and drove north once more, and parked the truck in Georgetown, close to the university. Then he climbed into the back, selected one of four cellular phones and pressed in the numbers.

Logan and Swann sat in Kovalski's office reading the initial reports from the evidence response team. It was late afternoon now and they had been at it since lunchtime. Swann had been on the phone to London and cleared it with the commander to stay in Washington for a few days, and help. He had then contacted the State Department's course leaders in Louisiana and explained the situation to them. All of which meant he could spend more time with Cheyenne, and that pleased him immensely. All his life he had posed himself the question as to whether or not there was a woman out there with whom he could be totally at his ease, and he had all but decided there wasn't. He'd had a bad marriage (notwithstanding two delightful daughters) and one abortive relationship after that. Then Logan came along and bingo – all the right buttons were pressed.

Logan was on the phone to the technical support unit about Triggerfish, the FBI's system of tracing calls made on cellular phones. On Kovalski's desk the phone was ringing and Logan gestured for Swann to pick it up.

'ASAC Kovalski's phone,' he said.

'Who are you?' The voice on the other end was clipped and brusque.

'Jack Swann. Who are you?'

'Fachida Harada, the warrior.'

8

Swann signalled to Logan across the office and she picked up the connecting phone.

'This is Agent Logan.' The Triggerfish scanner was activated, searching the airwaves for the cellphone identification. 'What do you want, Harada?'

'I want you to know that I'm serious.'

'I think we figured that already.'

'I don't think you do. You see, a harmless grenade in a harmless location means nothing.'

'Why choose it, then?' Logan was desperately trying to keep him on the phone. She signalled to the Triggerfish operator, who shook his head. Swann sat listening on Kovalski's phone, with his palm covering the mouthpiece. 'Why a war memorial?' Logan went on. 'Why a cemetery, Harada?'

'Why not?'

'Was it your way of affirming your message? A former president – warrior in chief?'

He laughed quietly. 'You have no idea.'

'But you're a samurai. The challenge – the cherry blossom. You must be quite a sculptor. Where'd you get the C-4?'

Swann smiled. Logan had completely taken the wind out of his sails, posed questions that had to be thought about.

'What I have acquired and where I got it is irrelevant. What is important is that we are at war. The reason I have chosen you as my adversary, I will make clear at a later date. In the meantime, it is necessary for me to demonstrate my pedigree to you, in order that when I make my demands, you will be in a position to take them seriously.'

'Mr Harada, we do take you seriously.'

But he was gone. The phone clicked dead and Logan looked over at the Triggerfish operator. He shook his head. 'They didn't get a fix, Chey.'

'No location?'

'No. There's a helluva lot of cellphone activity in Washington.'

Logan looked at Swann. 'What did you make of that?' she said.

He moved his shoulders. 'I'd have thought he would make his demands known now.'

'So would I.' Logan turned to McKensie. 'Carmen, get hold of Tom, will you. He's over at the puzzle palace.' She sat down at her desk and Swann sat next to her.

'Samurai warrior,' he said. 'With access to C-4 explosives.'

Logan looked up at him. 'Yet he uses a phosphorus grenade.'

Swann got up again and went back to Kovalski's phone, which had an international dialling capacity without going through the central operator. 'He's told us he has C-4, Chey, which means, at some point, he intends to use it.' He phoned Christine Harris in the Special Branch cell at Scotland Yard. He had already asked her to look into Harada's background for him. She was not there, but he left a message on her voice mail for her to call him back.

Kovalski came back to the office and he brought with him a selection of experts from headquarters, bomb data, domestic terrorism and organised crime. He then chaired an open-forum meeting in the conference room, where there were sixteen blue chairs with the 'Integrity Bravery Fidelity' logo emblazoned on them. The evidence response teams had turned up little else from the crime scene apart from a few more pieces of the timing and power unit, some wire and the melted remains of a bulb for circuit-testing. Swann sat next to Logan, who had her jacket draped over the back of the chair. McKensie sat opposite, minuting the meeting.

Just as it was about to get under way, Swann was summoned from the room to take a call from London. When he came back, he carried three sheets of fax paper and his face was troubled. Kovalski was in mid-flow, talking about the model of the cherry blossom made out of C-4 explosive. He stopped as Swann took his seat and spread the sheets of paper in front of him.

'That was Special Branch back home,' Swann said. 'They've done some more digging on Fachida Harada.' He drew his lips together. 'MI5 had a file on him. Harada *was sokaiya* and had visited the UK on two occasions.' He paused. 'But we've found out a bit more since then.' He looked at Kovalski. 'He was in the Japanese Red Army from 1975 to 1990, although, from what we can gather, the organisation was pretty much dormant after 1987. The JRA was formed by Fusako Shigenobu in 1971, when he was a student at Meiji University. He had become very disillusioned with Japan and world politics in general, so he formed his own group. Their first action was a suicide attack on Lod Airport in Israel in 1972, using grenades and machine guns. Twenty-six people were killed. The PFLP employed them to do it on their behalf.' He glanced at Cheyenne then. 'That was how it was. They were contract terrorists. They claimed a militant Marxist ideology, but the bottom line was profit. They made a very lucrative deal with Qaddafi after the Tripoli airstrikes in 1986 and carried out a number of acts on his behalf under the cover name of the AIIB – anti-imperialist international brigades. Basically, anything that the AIIB claimed was funded by Libya and carried out by the JRA. Harada would have been very much involved by then.'

Logan looked at Kovalski. 'In 1986, the JRA attacked our embassy in Jakarta,' she said. 'They fired mortars from a hotel bedroom window, which landed in the courtyard but didn't go off. They did the same thing in 1987 in Madrid, and they also set off a car bomb outside the embassy in Rome. It was all on behalf of Libya.'

'In 1988,' Swann went on, 'we know they were planning to attack further US and European sites. Harada was in London, which is where we first came across him. Those attacks were intended to coincide with the anniversary of the military action against Libya, but they never happened. The JRA, like almost everybody else, was based in the Bekaa Valley during the eighties, but they also had an enclave in North Korea. That's where they disappeared to after they finished with Qaddafi. They haven't been active since.'

Kovalski was rolling a pen across the tabletop. 'In 1996, the Japanese National Police Agency arrested Tetsuya Shikomoto and handed him over to us.' He sat forward and looked at Swann. 'He was the only one we could get for the attack in Indonesia.'

'This is all fine,' McKensie put in, 'but what's any of it got to do with cherry blossom and the samurai?'

Swann glanced at his notes. 'Harada's family have a tradition of being samurai,' he said. 'In latter generations it died out a bit, but his grandfather was a kamikaze pilot, killed in the Second World War. They were the twentieth century's embodiment of the bushido philosophy, militarily speaking, anyway.'

The Cub sat on the balcony of his apartment building, with the phone on the floor alongside him. He was in the southern part of Islamabad, his home for the last year. He was used to waiting. He had done it before and, if he survived this operation, no doubt he would do it again. The city heaved, sweating under a mantle of cloud, which kept the heat close to the concrete, compressing the air into solid blocks of humidity. He looked at the phone. He had been waiting for the call since he returned from Washington. Behind him in the bedroom, there was enough camera equipment to make the most professional photographer green with envy. For the past year he had cultivated his skill and, through the covert contacts set up by The Talent and the Intelligence Support Activity's network of agents here in Pakistan, a good number of his pictures had found their way into magazines and the sports pages of newspapers. That had been vital for credibility. The Australian had been angry after his usual photographer had gone off to Alaska at such short notice, and a man like Bin Laden, whose influence stretched round the globe, would have scrutinised that in detail. Right now, they would still be checking everything that Terence Morgan, native of South Island, New Zealand, had ever done in his life. The Cub had confidence in his stagehands, however, and when the cue call came he would be ready.

He considered his target as if gauging a set of statistics. Bin Laden was forty-two years old, one of twenty sons of a Saudi Arabian construction magnate. As far as The Talent had been able to ascertain, the business empire was worth in excess of five billion dollars and the family maintained close links with the kingdom's royalty. Most of the work they undertook was road building for the government. When Osama Bin Laden was twenty-two, the Russians invaded Afghanistan and he left his homeland to join the fighting. But Bin Laden was no ordinary mujahedin warrior. He was one with a considerable amount of money at his disposal. He brought in his own trucks and bulldozers, and funded the recruitment, training and transportation of thousands of volunteers – Palestinians, Somalis, Tunisians and Pakistanis. That was undoubtedly a turning-point in his life. If the Russians had stayed away, he might have become something else, but with the invasion he embraced his religion and set the course for the rest of his life. He had effectively been funded by the US, only to blow up two of their embassies twenty years later. Still, it was not the first time that kind of thing had happened and it would not be the last. The Cub thought about the reports in the British press back in February, claiming that Bin Laden had left his Afghan stronghold and that his whereabouts were unknown.

But he had surfaced: some of his communications had

been picked up by the NSA's listening station in Egypt. The Cub had also received intelligence there in Islamabad that Bin Laden was actually still in Afghanistan, although in a new, secret location. The raids back in the fall of last year had dealt him some serious blows, but if the intelligence was to be believed, he had safe houses all over the world.

The phone rang and The Cub looked at it, his face expressionless. He let it ring three times and then reached for it. 'G'day.'

'Terry?'

'Yeah.'

'Jim Moore. I think the eagle has landed.'

The Cub was quiet for a moment. 'Do I get my gear together or is this another false alarm?'

'Who knows, mate. But I'm at the Marriott. Get a taxi down here and make sure you bring the appropriate clothing with you.'

The Cub hung up. The IAD's intelligence on Moore's last visit to Bin Laden, prior to the African embassy bombs going off, had him dressed like the rest of them – baggy trousers and knee-length shirt. The Cub had been wearing this garb now for almost a year, finding it considerably more comfortable than western clothing in this climate.

In his bedroom, he carefully packed his bag and stowed each item of camera equipment into the aluminium case that housed them. He selected two black 35mm film cases and slipped out the film. Then he replaced them with two different rolls of film, sealed the lids and fitted them into the spongy pocket in the case. He took two PP3 batteries, which he had spent a long time cutting, emptying and filling with high explosive before resealing. He had a slavemaster unit set up and ready, and his flashgun. That ought to be good for 800 metres. Out on the street, he hailed a cab.

Moore was drinking beer in the bar. He was a red-haired Australian, with a sun-burned neck where his hair was cut too short. The Cub's hair was Native American black and very long, and it was stretched back from his forehead with a single elastic tie. He walked through the lobby and set his bags down next to Moore's. The Australian looked up at him. 'That was quick, mate.'

'I got a cab right away.' The Cub's accent was well-practised Kiwi, differing from the Australian in words like 'fish' or 'Jim'.

'I'm sorry it took so long for them to get in touch,' Moore said, and snapped his fingers at the barman, indicating a bottle of beer for each of them. 'I've been up to my neck in panic over this thing. I really didn't think it would be a goer after the Americans bombed the fuck out of him. A yank tried to see him, a bloke I know in New York, but the main man would have none of it. I reckon anyone with an American accent is nothing more than a target to him now.'

The Cub sat down on the stool and sipped beer. 'So what's the plan?'

Moore chuckled then. 'The plan, mate, is we sit here and wait. It could be two hours. It could be two days.'

'Or it could be two weeks, or never.' The Cub made a face. 'Well, I reckon I'll share your room, if it comes to it. I pay enough rent in this city as it is.'

They waited for two days, The Cub hating every minute of the Australian's company. He did not cope with company well, and worked alone unless it was with his old captain from the Legion, who was freelance like himself these days. At five in the afternoon on the second day, a man walked into reception, and Moore, who was drinking tea in the lounge, looked up and saw him. The Cub, sitting reading the newspaper across from him, watched from the corner of one eye as Moore crossed the lobby, all smiles and handshake at the ready. The man was short and stocky, with a beard but no headgear. He smiled, shook hands and then Moore indicated The Cub. He laid down the newspaper and stood up. For a moment, the man looked doubtful, but then he smiled, and The Cub smiled back and crossed the floor to greet him.

'Terry Morgan. Meet Anwar. Anwar's our driver and guide. He's going to take us to meet our host.'

The Cub shook Anwar's hand firmly. 'Mr Morgan. A pleasure.' Anwar showed gold teeth this time as he cracked another smile. 'I have seen your pictures in the sports pages. Very good. The one of Shoaib Akhtar bowling out Tendulkar pleased me very much.'

'I'll bet it bloody did. Tendulkar's the best bat in the world right now. I wish we had him in our team.'

'Ah, New Zealand is not so bad for such a small country. I like Martin Crowe very much.'

'Crowe retired years ago, Anwar. We need new blood if we're ever going to get a five-Test series.' He looked at Moore and gestured with his thumb. 'This bloke lives in New York. He knows more about baseball than cricket.'

'I know Australia is the best Test-playing nation in the world,' Moore said. 'What more do I need?'

Anwar drove a battered Mercedes 230. This time it had been easier, according to Moore. He had been able to apply for the proper visas, having planned the trip for some time. The Cub, unbeknown to him, could have any visa he wanted, stamped in whatever passport. He sat in the back being jolted around on spongy suspension, as Moore rode up front with Anwar. Anwar was not, apparently, directly involved with Bin Laden, not one of 'his' men. But he was close and worked as a go-between with various western and subcontinental agencies.

Moore had intimated that if the route followed the same as last time, they would fly to Peshawar and drive from there. But Anwar drove them beyond the airport, and when Moore asked him directly, he just smiled and told him that the plans were likely to alter at any minute. He had a cellphone with him, which he patted from time to time. The Cub sat in the back with his arms folded and stared at the dust rising from the fields beside the road.

They drove all the way to Peshawar, being lurched and bounced over a half-ruined, half-metalled road, and were on the city limits before the cellphone rang. Anwar pulled over and answered it, listening with the engine off and one finger plugging his other ear. He muttered, nodded and finally switched the phone off, and looked a little troubled.

'What is it?' Moore's voice was edged with weariness and tension.

Anwar made a face. 'We are to continue to Peshawar and wait.'

'Where? A hotel?'

He shook his head. 'A safe house.' He started the engine and slipped the shift into drive and pulled back on to the highway. He looked in the rearview mirror and his eyes met those of The Cub.

The house turned out to be a hovel, a shack with one room; no sanitation or ventilation save the door. It was set in a choked area of the town, which was as shabby and run-down as the last time The Cub had been here, when the FBI were hunting Yousef Ramzi. Fires seemed to burn perpetually in Peshawar and for no apparent reason – tyres, piles of rubbish, vehicles, anything vaguely combustible. During the Afghan war, this had been the staging-post: the supply line for communications and weapons, with CIA and KGB agents bumping into each other on every street corner. You could still obtain a gun here more easily than a regular supply of rice. Abu Nidal had one of his many munitions centres here, from where he supplied any group prepared to pay his price. Unlike Ayman a-Zawahiri and his Islamic Jihad, the ANO had not thrown in with Bin Laden.

The Cub squatted on the dirt floor in the middle of the room and looked out of hooded eyes at Moore. 'You're nervous, aren't you?'

'Course I bloody am. This thing could go to ratshit at any moment.'

'Then chill out. There's nothing you can do about it, is there.'

Moore slumped to a sitting position on the floor. 'It's all right for you to talk, mate. It's not your story.'

'No, but it's my pictures.' The Cub sat cross-legged now and produced the short clay pipe he liked to smoke and filled it with rough-cut tobacco.

'You look like a bloody Indian,' Moore said. 'You got Maori in you?'

The Cub shook his head. 'Samoan and Filipino.'

Anwar came in then with some tea, meat and black bread. He brought sleeping mats from the car; and when The Cub looked out he saw a young kid of about fourteen, sitting the watch with a 9mm on his lap. He chewed at the dry bread and sipped hot tea, and smelled the dust and smoke in the atmosphere. The kid looked round at him and two pairs of cold eyes met through the twilight. Neither of them smiled.

They waited in the heat and dust of Peshawar for two more days, The Cub spending his time sleeping or moving between the hovels and junkyards, looking at places he recognised. Moore was becoming agitated again and The Cub could not stand the man's nerves for more than an hour at a time. Anwar came and went, disappearing for long periods, but whenever he left the Mercedes, the same kid with the black eyes and the 9mm stood guard over it. On the evening of the third day, Anwar returned looking troubled, but ushered them and their belongings into the car. He started the engine and the heat intensified, sweat dribbling in slow drops down his forehead. He rested one arm on the back of Moore's seat and spoke to both of them. 'You are to fly from here to a small airfield north-west of the Khyber Pass. From there, you will be met at the Afghan border by members of the Taliban. They will want to ensure your papers are in order, so be ready.'

The plane was a twin-engined eight-seater, and they were the only passengers. The pilot and co-pilot sat up front, and they were ushered on board by two bearded men, wearing traditional Muslim clothing and dusty white turbans wrapped round their heads. Nobody spoke. The two men checked their bags meticulously. They searched the aluminium camera case completely, taking out each piece of equipment and replacing it. They tried to remove the sponge that was sectioned so each piece fitted snugly, and The Cub explained to them that it did not come out. They appeared to understand a little English, but when they spoke to one another it was in a dialect he had no comprehension of. He took his seat and strapped himself in.

'Wonder what the in-flight movie is today,' he muttered and raised a smile from Moore.

The plane took off, immediately banking sharply, and then climbed north above the mountains. The land beneath them was rugged and barren, all but inaccessible by road. Moore was staring out of the window.

'I take it this isn't the way you came the last time,' The Cub said quietly.

Moore shook his head. 'No, we went to Bannu and then overland from there. I haven't got a clue where we're headed this time.'

'But he trusts you.'

Moore snapped a glance at him. 'D'you think we'd have got this far if he didn't?'

The Cub settled back and closed his eyes. The two men, who were travelling with them, sat in seats which faced them and watched. Moore tried to talk to them, practising his rudimentary grasp of their dialect, but either they did not understand or they ignored him. In the end, he fell silent.

They landed in darkness and, as soon as the engines died, The Cub heard the protracted rattle of automatic gunfire. The door opened and a set of steps were wheeled up, and he went to pick up his bags. But they were already held by one of their escorts. The Cub looked at the man holding his. 'You be careful of my camera, now.'

The man stared at him and said nothing. The Cub touched an index finger to his temple and considered how he would kill him if he had to, then descended the steps.

They were in a narrow mountain pass, which was more of a flat stretch of road than an airstrip, and the wind whipped the dust into a storm of little devils. The Cub waited at the bottom of the steps for Moore and quickly took in his surroundings. Two vehicles stood beside a shadowy, hangar-like shed fifty yards to his right. He could see a windsock billowing on top of a wooden pole, where the lighter mass of the sky pierced the gap in the mountains. The gunfire was coming from the vehicles and he made out three figures shooting automatic weapons into the air. The vehicles were US army trucks that must have been left over from the war. The engine started on one and the headlights hit him full beam in the face. He stood where he was, blinking hard, and waited.

Next to him, Moore was restless. 'Taliban,' he said. 'Get your papers ready.'

The truck pulled up in front of them and two men got out of the passenger side. Both had AK47s on chest slings and they rattled a few words of Afghan at The Cub and gestured with open palms. He handed them his papers, which he carried in the linen pocket stitched inside the knee-length shirt. They shone a torch at the documents and then into his face, and the younger of the two – dark-eyed and with a black beard – stared him right in the eyes. The Cub smiled at him, and the man shouted something, waved the passport and then tucked it away inside his pocket. Moore lost his passport too, and he explained that the men were Taliban, but they were Bin Laden's and they would return the papers when they took the journalists back to Pakistan.

'So this is Afghanistan, then,' The Cub said.

Moore nodded. 'You know, you're dealing with this much better than I thought you would.'

The Cub laughed as they were ushered round the back of the truck at gunpoint.

'Listen, mate. You learn a bit of philosophy when you watch New Zealand play cricket.'

They sat in the back of the truck – which was covered in military green canvas and had bench seats along either side – wedged between Taliban fighters with Kalashnikovs and ammunition belts doubled across their shoulders like

Pancho Villa. The Cub tried to talk to the young lad next to him, who was no more than eleven if he was a day, but the kid just glowered at him and plucked at the ammo belt that all but crushed his chest. Their bags were nowhere in sight, but the other truck followed, and The Cub could only hope they were in that one. He had a tiny global positioning system built into one of his cameras and right now it was signalling the NSA's listening post in Egypt. The chances of hitting Bin Laden on this trip were slim if he wanted to get out alive, but he had his equipment should an opportunity present itself. The GPS would enable the boys in Egypt to get a handle on his movements. They wanted to pinpoint Bin Laden's new location, which might, or might not be, where they were headed now. If The Cub could house him, then he would plan the hit from there.

The trucks wound a path between the mountains and then climbed once again. The Cub had a mini-compass in the bowl of his pipe and he knew they had flown north-east initially, before looping away west. Now they were driving due west, deeper into Afghanistan. They drove for four hours into the night before they heard gunfire and the sky was lit up by tracer bullets.

'Welcoming party,' Moore said. 'Either that or a warn-ing. Sometimes, the communication between his various factions isn't as professional as it's cracked up to be. They show both their displeasure and pleasure by shooting off their guns.' He made a face then. 'When I met him last time, they fired off their weapons like applause. He's got bodyguards, but if a round hit him they would never identify the shooter.'

The gunfire grew steadily louder until it seemed as though it was right outside the truck, and then the vehicle stopped and flashlights were shone in their faces from the tailgate. The Cub shaded his eyes and counted a dozen different heads bobbing behind the lights. The tailgate was unfastened and they were manhandled to the ground, where the lights were shone in their eyes and, for the second time, their identities were checked against their papers. Still, the documents were not returned to them, and they were moved from the first truck to another, with fresh guards and fresh arguments.

The Cub watched with interest: each group of men they encountered was different and seemingly disorganised. Gunfire was a consistent feature; the rattle of assault rifles being let off with abandon. He studied the group, who now escorted them along the pitted roads leading ever deeper into the mountains, and put most of them under twenty. They were volatile, undisciplined, and probably unreliable. These were the ultimate boys with the ultimate toys, which they relished playing with. He was absolutely positive now, given the opportunity, he could execute this mission with relative ease. Moore had fallen into a weary silence and his head lolled on his chest as they were bounced and battered from one hole in the road to the next. The Cub sat with his arms folded and rested his eyes while remaining fully awake and listening to the drifting conversation, sometimes quiet, sometimes animated, from the men around him.

'You are from New Zealand?' He opened his eyes and looked into the face of the man seated directly opposite him. He was young and his beard was straggly, his features dark and smooth and as yet unmarked by age or life in the mountains. He was leaning forward, AK flattened across his knees, with a single belt of ammunition hanging from one shoulder. The Cub nodded.

'What part?' The man's English was perfect.

'South Island.'

'Whereabouts?'

The Cub sat up straighter now.

'Invercargill.'

'The very south, then.'

The Cub nodded. 'Have you been there?'

The man shook his head. 'I was educated in England. Harrow.'

The Cub squinted at him. He knew that Harrow was a public school. 'What're you doing here?'

The young man smiled then and glanced at his colleagues who looked on blankly.

'Fighting for Islam.'

'You believe it all, do you?'

'Most certainly. We read only the earliest versions of the Koran. Our religion must be pure, uncorrupted – the religion of the prophet. We leave nothing to chance.'

'I'll bet.'

The man sat more upright again. 'How long have you been a journalist?'

'I'm a photographer.'

'How long?'

'Years.'

'I've never seen your pictures.'

'You like cricket?'

The man laughed then.

'It's true. I take pictures of cricketers. It's why I base myself in Islamabad. There's always some side playing down here. Most of the other guys trail after Australia or the West Indies, but the market for Indian, Pakistani and Sri Lankan stuff is brilliant. Then, of course, you've got Bangladesh, and I can get to South Africa and Zimbabwe if I want.'

The boy thinned his eyes then. 'So why are you here?'

'Because somebody asked me to come.' The Cub shrugged his shoulders. 'I live in Islamabad. I'm a Kiwi and he wanted somebody he could trust.' He jabbed a thumb at Moore. 'Apparently, your boss isn't keen on Americans.'

'None of us are keen on Americans. Or the British either. They are just puppets of the Americans.'

'But you went to school in England.'

The boy made a face. 'My father paid for me.'

The Cub nodded again and sighed. 'You know, I'm beginning to wish I'd stuck to cricket matches. How much further is it?'

The boy laughed then. 'I like you,' he said. 'But I get the feeling you care about very little.'

The Cub looked evenly back at him. 'I care about cricket,' he said. 'Cricket and good pictures. Which reminds me. I'm going to need my cameras.'

The boy sat back. 'You will get them. Don't worry.'

The Cub waited for maybe five more minutes of lurching and bouncing, before he sat forward and beckoned. The boy leaned towards him. 'I thought your boss had gone walkabout.'

'He did. After the Americans attacked us, he removed himself for a while.'

'So where are we going, then?'

'You'll see.'

Dawn had broken before the trucks slowed and took what turned out to be a final bend in the mountain road. Moore was awake, very stiff and sore, and The Cub gazed past him to the roadside, which was chipped and broken by stones. It fell away sharply and the whole world seemed to be one rugged line of mountains. He could tell by the ease of his breathing that they were not very high, and he figured they were somewhere east of Kabul, yet still west of the Khyber Pass. The road narrowed where the cliffs dropped away on one side, and then all at once the mountain reared on both sides and they were in a narrow, natural tunnel. The Cub moved to the back of the truck and looked up, where the curve of the walls formed a natural roof. He could not see the sky. The sound of a Kalashnikov being racked made him look round and he stared into the face of the young boy. The boy motioned with the weapon for him to resume his seat, which he did.

Moore leaned against him. 'I've got a feeling we're close now,' he said. 'I always knew he had a refuge high in the mountains.'

The Cub was watching the faces of their escorts and the sudden restlessness told him that Moore was right. Ten minutes later, the tunnel of rock widened and the trucks rolled to a stop. They were either very sure of themselves, or this location was not that important, because there had been no blindfolds since dawn broke. The Cub gauged the time and the probable truck speed, and therefore the distance. It was hard to calculate in this type of terrain, but so long as that tracker was working, the NSA would have it down to the last centimetre. Their guards trooped out first and then manhandled them down, and The Cub took in their surroundings. The tunnel of rock had opened into a sort of amphitheatre, with cliff walls rising in a natural circle about them. He noticed wooden walkways strung across the walls and rope ladders that climbed to makeshift goon towers, where men stood with AK47s bearing down on them. Men were everywhere, as were jeeps and trucks, and in one corner of the rock floor, a herd of camels chewed hay. Moore stood with his hands on his hips, shading his eyes from the sun, and also took in the surroundings.

The floor was perhaps a hundred yards wide at the widest point and, on each side, natural caves in the walls had been filled in with breeze blocks. Bulldozers sat idle, together with dump trucks, some still loaded with great lumps of rock. The Cub realised that this was no temporary hideout and the adrenaline eased into his veins. There was only one way in that he could see: the narrow stretch of road forming a natural choke point. The rock walls rose up like a funnel and he noticed that all the vehicles and buildings, even the walkways, were set under the lee of the actual walls. Very clever, he thought. An AWACS flying high overhead would pick up the natural formation but nothing else, except maybe a camel wandering loose.

The public schoolboy in the turban walked past him and The Cub caught his arm.

'Hey,' he said. 'Where's my camera?'

The boy looked at him then and said nothing. Something in his eyes was disturbing and The Cub's instincts were suddenly heightened. He gazed round the walls and noticed various heated discussions going on between their escorts and the men of the encampment. Glances were cast their way from all directions and, looking up, he could see that every step they took was being traced by the goon squads.

The Cub looked over at Moore. 'They don't seem that pleased to see us,' he said. 'What's going on?'

'I don't know. Don't worry about it. We're westerners, Terry. They're going to be on edge.'

They stood for five minutes longer, before the public schoolboy came back and gestured to a cave with a wooden door built into the concrete blocks that fronted it.

'You can rest in there.'

'Where's Bin Laden?' Moore said.

The boy just looked at him and motioned with his rifle. Inside the cave, it was quiet and naturally cool. Electricity had been rigged up via a whole raft of diesel-driven generators and the cave was well lit. Two sleeping mats lay on the floor, together with a water jug and a portable toilet. The Cub drank a long draught from the jug and then lay down on the mat. 'Wake me when the action starts,' he said, and, rolling on his side, went to sleep. When he woke up it was dark, and their bags and his camera case were standing in the middle of the floor. Moore was looking through the hole that formed the permanently open window. The Cub ignored him, and, laying his camera case flat, he unfastened the catches and checked the contents. The cameras and lenses had been taken out of their casings and replaced somewhat haphazardly – he could tell that much – along with the collapsible tripod and the plastic boxes of film. He checked them all carefully and then set them back in their allotted pockets of foam. When he looked up, Moore was watching him.

'All set?' Moore asked him. The Cub nodded, and Moore returned to the window once again. The Cub moved to the door, opened it a fraction and saw the elbow of the guard poking out from where he stood alongside. Through the crack he could see little hives of activity all along the walls. Gasoline was being pumped from a truck into the jerrycans attached to the back of a jeep. Everywhere he looked, men were hurrying back and forth waving weapons, shouting; and then the choked atmosphere of the amphitheatre would suddenly be split by a burst of gunfire as some hothead loosed off his weapon. Ill disciplined, The Cub thought, and closed the door.

Something was brewing, that much was clear, although Moore didn't seem to be aware of it. Perhaps he thought this was normal. Perhaps it was. He was standing by the window again, looking at his watch.

'I don't think he's here,' The Cub told him.

Moore looked up. 'What did you say?'

'I said, I don't think he's here.'

'Of course he's here. They wouldn't have brought us all this way if he wasn't. Relax. This is how it was the last time.'

The Cub sat down on his mat and filled his claystone pipe, lit it and drew the acrid smoke deep into his lungs. He sat cross-legged like his mother and meditated quietly, allowing his heart rate to slow so he could still his being and consider what was going on around him. Bin Laden was not here. He knew it with as much certainty as he knew he was sitting on cold stone. He had never been here. It had never been his intention to be here. He considered the jeep and he wondered.

At 10 p.m., a great hubbub of noise started up outside, shouts and yelling followed by the rattle of automatic rifle fire. The Cub shook his head sadly. If they popped enough tracer fire up into the air, the AWACS could get a fix on that alone.

Moore was on his feet, fiddling with his recording gear and his notepad. 'I hope he answers the questions properly this time,' he said. 'I don't want to have to wait until I get back home to translate them.'

'You don't need to worry.' The Cub was watching the door. 'He isn't here.'

'Will you stop saying that.' Moore stared at him then, face bunched up. 'You're beginning to piss me off.'

The Cub smiled, smoked his pipe and tugged his ponytail out so that his hair fell across his shoulders, very thick, very black and very long.

The door opened suddenly, harshly, with a rattle of the handle, and then it swung in on them soundlessly and four men with Kalashnikovs came into the room. The Cub stood up and reached for his camera gear. Moore smiled at him. 'See,' he said. 'It's showtime.' He grinned at the four men and they stood aside as he eased past them. The Cub followed him outside.

The night air had cooled considerably, the amphitheatre not holding anything like the level of heat as the scrubbed high desert. The Cub followed Moore past one of the canvas-covered trucks. In his hand was a black circular tube that housed 35mm film. Only this one was different, and he let it slip with an imperceptible flick of his palm and it rolled out of sight under the truck. He walked on, shouldering his bag and calculating exactly how much time he had. They passed the jeep with the three full jerrycans strapped to it and he noticed the public schoolboy sitting in the driver's seat. He looked tired, but as they passed, his dark eyes met those of The Cub and a scowl itched away at his lips. The Cub slipped the empty clay pipe into his shirt pocket and followed Moore across the yard.

Given the amount of gunfire that had gone off earlier, Bin Laden's men were now surprisingly careful. They were crossing open ground to the other side of the amphitheatre, and open sky, stitched with stars, stretched above them. They carried no torches and there was no shooting, and the whole place seemed to have descended into a strange, unworldly silence. The escort of guards stopped on the far side of the arena where the camels grazed, and The Cub looked quickly back the way they had come. The rock floor was empty again and lights burned only dimly on the far side where their room was housed. Somebody said something guttural and unintelligible to him and he felt the barrel of an assault rifle jab him in the ribs. Moore was silent and they both had to duck their heads as they were shown into another cave. The floor was completely covered with matting this time and there were a variety of Persian-looking cushions to sit on.

Moore laid down his gear. 'He'll be along in a minute,' he said.

'Right.' The Cub quickly, expertly, scanned the room for weapons. Nothing caught his eye. Tripod: he opened his case and laid it on the floor alongside him. Three black rubber bungs formed the feet of the hollow alloy tubes. While Moore was busy testing his tape recorder, The Cub slipped off one of the bungs and peeled the stiletto blade from where it was taped to the inside of the leg, then slid the blade up his sleeve. At that moment gunfire sounded again, deafening in the confines of the room as it echoed off the walls outside.

'They're bringing him,' Moore said. 'I told you. They shoot their guns instead of clapping. They're bringing him in now.'

The Cub nodded, sat back on his haunches and waited.

The door flew open and two men with rifles came in. One of them had a sort of kukri knife in his rope belt and the other a 9mm pistol. Then another, very tall figure ducked his head and entered the room. He was wearing the same knee-length shirt as the rest of them, with a muslin shawl about his shoulders. Moore got to his feet, a smile of anticipation on his face. The Cub got to his feet, the point of the stiletto pressing against the heel of his right palm. The tall man straightened and the lamps on the walls lit his face. The expression on Moore's face was replaced by one of puzzlement. The Cub felt his heart move in his chest. At six foot three, the man was as tall as Bin Laden, and at forty-two, he was also the same age. But Bin Laden was Arabian to look at, with a long, wide-nostrilled nose and heavy black beard. This man's skin was black, and his beard was short and cut square to his face. He was heavier set than Bin Laden and his eyes were black and dead in his face. He stood there, towering over his guards, looking down on the two westerners. The Cub had seen him before – only once and a long time ago. He was Mujah al-Bakhtar, the Butcher of Bekaa.

The Cub said nothing. He held his camera. Moore opened his mouth to speak, but al-Bakhtar raised a hand for silence. His face was impassive, expressionless. He was a Somali national, but like his mentor he had left his homeland some years ago, and he, too, had embarked on a battle with the Russians. Unlike Bin Laden, he had no wealth and had always been a front-line fighter. Halfway through the war with the Russians, he left Afghanistan for the training camps of the Bekaa Valley, where he ritually slaughtered meat for the various Muslim factions. They gave him the *nom de guerre*. The word from the ISA had been that he was back with Bin Laden, but no one had been able to verify it until now. The Cub eased his weight gently to the balls of his feet. Now he knew for certain that Bin Laden was not here, although he would be close by. The two men were rarely seen in the same place, but al-Bakhtar was, to all intents and purposes, Bin Laden's most trusted body-guard.

'Please.' His voice was soft yet deep, welling up from his chest. 'Sit.' He gestured to the cushions and then moved to the far side of the room, so he could sit with his back against rock. He lowered his massive frame and drew his heels together. Still, his face betrayed no expression. Two guards flanked him and two more stood behind the two journalists. The Cub guessed at least two more would be stationed on the door, and then there was the small matter of the five hundred or so gathered in and around the base.

Al-Bakhtar was silent now, not looking at either of them, his chin low to his chest so his eyes were hidden, as if he was deep in concentration. When he did speak, his voice had lowered another octave and he did not look up. 'Unfortunately, gentlemen,' he began in perfect, accented English, 'the interview with Mr Bin Laden cannot go ahead as planned.'

The Cub said nothing. Moore shifted restlessly and let go a stiff little sigh. Al-Bakhtar looked up at him, slowly, like a snake's laconic movement before it strikes. 'I am sorry.'

'Why?' Moore said. 'What's the problem? I thought we had ironed everything out.'

Al-Bakhtar was looking at The Cub then and his eyes took on a glazed expression. 'You don't look like a man from New Zealand,' he said.

The Cub looked evenly back at him. 'Filipino and Samoan,' he said. 'You don't look like an Afghan.'

Al-Bakhtar laughed then, a slow hollow sound that burbled in his throat, but had no effect on his face or eyes. He stopped the sound as suddenly as it started and looked back at Moore. 'And you're from Australia.'

'Yes.'

Al-Bakhtar nodded. 'Gentlemen, it is unfortunate,' he said. 'But we have to be extremely careful about these things. You see, the devils from America would like nothing better than to see Mr Bin Laden dead, and it's come to our attention that an assassin has been loosed against us.' He stopped talking and looked from one of them to the other. The Cub held his eye and considered how good Bin Laden's intelligence actually was. The finding would have been signed by the President after it was drawn up by Birch. The only other people who would know it existed at that point would be the DCI and possibly the national security adviser. Post-signature, they may even have bypassed the Senate and House intelligence committees, but if they didn't, then Wendell Randall had the provision in law to inform only four people on each committee – the chairman and vice-chairman and the leaders of the two parties. A maximum then of twelve. Nobody in IAD knew what his mission was, only that they had to furnish him with his home and cover in Islamabad. Twelve people from the White House to here, and yet the Butcher of Bekaa was calmly telling them that *it had come to their attention.*

Moore was stunned, visibly. The Cub considered his own demeanour and decided it did not matter any more. The Butcher was here because neither of them were leaving, so reaction now was irrelevant. 'I don't understand,' Moore was saying. 'What on earth are you talking about?'

The Cub knew from hearsay that al-Bakhtar got tired of people easily and he wondered how much of Moore's whining the man would put up with. He eased the stiletto further down his palm and judged the distance between himself and the man behind him.

'Are you trying to tell me that you believe one of us is a CIA assassin?' Moore's voice was incredulous.

Slowly, a little wearily, al-Bakhtar nodded. Moore blinked several times, and The Cub counted down the seconds it would take him to think back and figure how his buddy had gone off to Alaska, and, albeit by a circuitous route, he wound up with a Kiwi already based in Islamabad. On the count of five, Moore's head tilted his way, and The Cub rolled backwards, stabbed one of the guards in the heart and ripped the AK out of his hand.

Al-Bakhtar leaped to his feet, grabbing both Moore and another guard as shields. The third guard took a heel kick in the testicles and lost his gun as The Cub stepped out of the door. He shot the remaining guards, then ran round the outer perimeter as fast as he could. The gunfire brought no one running right away, clearly because they heard a lot of it in this base. By the time the shouts rang out from the room and the lights came on in the goon towers high on the walls, The Cub was by the truck where he had dumped the film case. He pointed an AK47 into the face of the public schoolboy, who still sat in the jeep. 'I hope you can drive,' he said.

9

Harrison flew back to New Orleans with Jean, having spent two nights in Spokane. He was troubled. Together with Detective Spinelli, they had been out to the freight yards and spoken with a number of ageing hobos whom Spinelli had befriended. Harrison liked Spinelli. He was a straight, honest cop who had been looking into this thing pretty much of his own volition. The murder victims were vagrants, so nobody gave a damn – the Spokane police department and the FBI in particular. Normally, with a bunch of potentially related interstate murders, the VICAP co-ordinator in some field office or other would run a mini task force linked to the behavioural profilers at Quantico. But not in this case.

They had learned quite a bit from the hobos who were prepared to talk. The word was that the FTRA killed you if you were black, Asian or Hispanic, just because they wanted to. But it was not only ethnic minorities that were turning up dead, with their pants round their knees and their shirts up over their heads. A hell of a lot of people must have been killed simply because they were in the wrong place at the wrong time. Harrison had talked to the old-timers himself. They told him that every year there was a hobo convention at Britt, a nothing town at the end of one of the Midwestern lines in Iowa. For years, that place had been the gathering point for hobos from all over the country. They would come together to play music, to sell the odd trinket or leatherwork, and generally have a good time. But the FTRA had come muscling in, dealing dope and other stuff to the 'Flintstones', or younger hobos – the twentysomething generation, drawn to the railheads by stories of old-timers, like latter-day Jack Kerouacs.

Harrison had questioned an old man about the dope, and told him in great detail about the lazy-eyed Limpet and the psychopathic gangbanger they were looking to nail in New Orleans.

The old man, rheumy-eyed and with grey hair tied in a ponytail like Harrison's, had pursed up his toothless mouth and nodded. 'I figure they run shitloads of drugs,' he said. 'I figure that's why so many of us get killed. If they're doing their thing and you get in the boxcar, they don't take no chances. They just dump your ass right there.' He flapped out a hand. 'Who the hell's gonna give a goddamn. Just more homeless vermin taken care of. Lotta people'd be happy at that.'

Harrison phoned the office and Penny came out to pick them up from the airport. They dropped Jean back at the hotel and Harrison stood on the sidewalk while Penny waited in the car. 'You gonna be around tonight, Miss Lady Mam?' he asked her.

She nodded. 'What're you planning to do?'

He blew out his cheeks. 'I don't know yet. There's things I gotta figure, things I gotta talk to the gang squad about. We've latched on to something here that's a lot bigger than just a New Orleans deal, honey. I got to talk to people about it.'

She touched his face then, her palm suddenly warm against his cheek. 'Thank you so much for coming with me,' she said.

Harrison stood watching her as she went into reception, feeling the sensation of her hand on his skin – the first hint of affection he had received from a woman in a long time. His eyes misted a fraction and he knew then he really was getting old. In the car, Penny squinted at him. 'You OK, Johnny Buck?'

Harrison looked through the windshield. 'Sure I am,' he said.

He sat at the table in the tiny conference room at the gang squad's office, waiting for Mike Hammond to finish his meeting. Swartz told him that he was interviewing another guy from the state police, who had applied to join the task force. Harrison stared at the white screen wall, at the tape machine and headset, and the pad of notes scribbled by the last agent who had been listening to Little Nate on the phone. When he came back from Washington, he had been determined to quit this job and go find himself a life before he got too old, or croaked from all the cigarettes he had smoked. But now, after having been up north with Jean, having seen her face when the three of them hit those old freight yards, and having witnessed the pain in her eyes as she cast a long glance over the open-topped boxcars and imagined, as she must have done, her young boy lying in one with his brains blown out, he had faltered. Something about this had got to Spinelli so much, he had a whole filing system set up on FTRA members going back five years. He had members from each of the three crews, had identified the leadership chain and the wrecking squads they employed to keep discipline. With a bit of concerted effort, they might bust this thing wide open. Up until now, however, nobody cared enough, which bothered him for its own sake. Hoboing had always been a rough life, but not one where you feared for it every time you jumped on a train. Not only that, it was probably the last outpost of the kind of freedom America represented, and should be preserved for that in itself. His mind was wandering and where it was going bothered him, because he was old and it was dangerous, and he questioned his motives for even considering it.

Hammond opened his office door and showed out the detective from the state police. When he came back, he laid a hand on Harrison's shoulder. 'OK, JB. I'm all yours.'

Later, Harrison and Penny had a beer together at Pat O'Brien's. 'What happened to Swann?' Harrison asked.

'They seconded him to Washington after that bomb in Arlington Cemetery.'

Harrison raised his eyebrows. 'For a limey, that boy gets about.'

Penny looked out of the corner of his eye at him. 'So what's eating you – apart from the English lady?'

Harrison stared at him. 'What are you talking about?'

'Come on, Harrison. It's written all over your face. You got it real bad for that gal.'

'You think so?'

'You know you do.'

Harrison was silent for a moment. 'You figure that'd cloud my judgement?'

'I don't know.' Penny pondered that for a moment and then shook his head. 'No, I don't think so.'

'I spoke to Hammond about the Spokane thing, and he's talking to the field office up there and the VICAP people in Virginia. I figure these guys could be running dope all over the country, Matt. That's a big deal and it's probably why so many hobos have turned up with bullet holes in their heads.'

Penny looked at him. 'You think that's what's going on?'

Harrison nodded. 'We don't know for sure. Hell, until the other day, we never knew how Little Nate was getting supplied.' He lit a cigarette and flapped out the match.

'So where does your judgement come in?' Penny asked him.

Harrison blew a stream of smoke at the ceiling. 'I was gonna leave the job, Matt. After Mackon dropped me from the SWAT team. Hell, I'm fifty years old and I don't have a whole lot in my life besides this.'

'Sounds like a mid-life crisis to me.' Penny sipped beer. 'If this is all you got, why give it up?'

'I don't know. I guess I must be restless for something else, is all.'

'So what's the deal, then? You said you were gonna quit. You changed your mind now?'

Harrison sighed. 'Matt, I figure we're gonna look into

184

this dope scam big time. We scratched at something till it bled and now it won't stop.'

'So?'

'So, you know what I'm saying. How're we gonna figure out what they're doing? How're we gonna collect enough evidence to do something about it?'

Penny looked stiffly at him. 'Take a train ride, I guess.'

They sat round the table on the twenty-second floor. Charlie Mayer, the special agent in charge, was there, along with Hammond and Swartz from the gang squad, Harrison from the special ops group, and two members of the Violent Criminal Apprehension Program from Quantico. On conference phone lines were the ASAC from Seattle, the chief of police from Spokane together with Spinelli and two other detectives who had done work on the railroad murders, the man in Texas that Gary Hirstius had spoken to, and another cop from Arkansas.

Harrison sat quietly while they debated, thinking about Jean, already pretty positive what the upshot of the meeting would be. It was the only reason he was here, and looking round the table it was more and more obvious. They looked like Feds – either wearing suits or polo shirts and jeans, sneakers or the soft-soled black boots the SWAT team wore. They were clean-cut Middle Americans all of them, and he looked like a rapidly ageing surf bum. He had told Jean about the meeting and she had wanted to attend, but he smiled gently and told her that she couldn't. He was due to meet her later that evening and report back, however.

He sat there and watched: Mayer chairing the thing, talking on the phone to Spokane, Texas and Arkansas. Harrison chewed a plug of tobacco and spat every now and then into an empty Coke can. He wore a T-shirt, faded Levis and a dusty pair of boots. The gun itched in its holster against his shin and he was sure the air conditioning was not working properly. For an FBI meeting, the decision was made pretty quickly. Matt Penny would act as the contact agent, with Swartz running the case from New Orleans. There would be constant liaison with the other people involved and a task force would officially be formed. The whole thing would be co-ordinated by the specialists up at Quantico. All it needed now was the undercover agent.

Silence round the table, nobody looking at anyone else. Harrison sat there aware of the tingling sensation against his palms. He had experienced it before, in similar circumstances, on three occasions in the past. Only this time, he had promised himself never to go there again. He was too old and it was too dangerous. His reactions were slower now and he was not sure he could keep up the pretence for a prolonged period.

'So we need somebody to go undercover,' Hammond said at last. He gazed directly across the table at Harrison. 'What about it, JB?'

Harrison looked at him and spat into the Coke can.

Jean was waiting for him, talking to Dewey in the bar, when he arrived at Nu Nus Café. It was dark outside and had been raining all afternoon. Harrison got a ride back to his apartment when the meeting finally broke up, showered and changed, and took a cab down to the waterfront. The rain hissed against the pavement and nobody was on the street. The café across from Governor Nicholls Wharf was empty and nobody was in Coop's Place or the Palm Court: a really dead summer's night in New Orleans. Jean looked up as Harrison came inside, shook his clothes and sat down on a bar stool. Nobody was eating and Lydia, the waitress, was reading an Anne Rice novel at one of the tables. Dewey whipped the top off a bottle of beer and changed the music over. Harrison took Jean to a table by the door and looked into her expectant face.

'What happened?' she asked him.

He sipped beer and plucked a cigarette from his shirt pocket. 'We're going for it,' he said. 'I'm going undercover. I shouldn't tell you, but I figure America owes you that much. You can't tell anyone, but I'm gonna try and infiltrate the FTRA in the South.' Her eyes sparked, but he shook his head. 'We won't find your son's killer, Miss Lady Mam. Or if we do, we'll be very lucky. I'm doing it so that we can try and bust their drug cartel.'

Jean's hair fell across her forehead to kink at her right eye, a dark oval eye, soft and gentle, and suddenly full of something for him. He felt his heart beat in his chest and all at once his hands were clammy.

'Thank you,' she said, and, for the second time in her life, she lifted her palm and laid it across his cheek. He looked into her eyes, and he saw the softness of her face and neck. The cleft of skin where her clavicles met was warm and brown, and he had to fight off the urge to lean forward and kiss it.

'I want to help you,' she said.

He shook his head. 'There's nothing more you can do. When I'm under, the only contact I'll have is with one other agent.'

'But I need to help, John. D'you understand? I really need to.' Her face had clouded again, the darkness troubled now in her eyes. 'My son is dead and he was all I had. I have to do something.'

'Jean, you've done enough already. If I hadn't met you and you hadn't hassled everybody, none of this would've happened.'

She shook her head. 'It's not enough. Not enough for me: I need to do something tangible.'

Harrison sat back and thought about it then. There *was* something she could do and in a way it was better than the alternative, but it was dangerous for her and dangerous for him, and again he questioned his motives.

'No way, JB. Not a cat in hell's chance.' Hammond sat on the other side of the desk and shook his head. 'Shit, I can't believe you even told her you were going undercover.'

'Mike, she's got a right to know. If she hadn't shown up down here, we wouldn't be having this conversation.'

'Maybe, John. But come on. You know how it is when we set something up like this. Nobody gets told.'

'You're not listening to me, Mike.' Harrison rested both fists on Hammond's desk. 'She's the last person on the planet to shoot her mouth off. And she's the only reason we have it set up.' He sat back. 'Besides, if she's up for it, and it makes sense – what's the . . .'

'I don't care what she's up for. She's a civilian. She cannot be part of any FBI investigation, let alone one as delicate as this is.'

'But she's perfect fucking cover.' Harrison whacked his hand on the desk. 'What am I gonna do, hobo along to meetings with Penny?' He shook his head. 'This is gangland at the very bottom of the pile, Mike.'

'Hey.' Hammond jabbed a finger at him. 'Don't talk to me about gangland. I know fucking gangland.' He gestured at the successes the task force had had, spread on the wall behind him.

'Yeah, with confidential informants, controlled purchases and wire taps. We're talking UC, Mike. Deep cover. I'm gonna put my neck on the line here. You figure that? It's my neck. I'll be the asshole riding the fucking boxcars with a bunch of shitkickers from Nowheresville. If one of those mothers sees me with somebody who looks like Penny, I'm dog meat.'

Hammond stared at him now.

'This ain't like anything I've done before, Mike. Every other time I've been under, I was still in the regular world. This ain't the regular world. Hobos do not frequent the company of clean-cut anybody.' He paused then, licking the spittle from his lip. 'But if they see me with a woman, hell, everyone gets a piece of ass now and again.'

'A Chinese piece of ass, Johnny?'

'It doesn't matter. Even the Klan fuck black women.'

Hammond sat in silence for a long time then, gently

kneading a balled fist with the fingers of the other hand, 'I'm not gonna sanction this, John. No matter how you put it to me.' He broke off. 'But, she's a civilian and I assume her visa's in order.' He shrugged his shoulders. 'I guess she can go any place she wants to.'

The Cub sat next to the terrorist who had been to Harrow public school in England, the barrel of the AK47 pressing him under the ribs. The boy was driving the jeep full tilt along the tunnel of rock where no light could get in. Still, there was no sound from behind them. The Cub looked at his watch and counted down the seconds; and then the explosion sucked at the air and he felt the shattering sound in his ears as the pressure wave compressed rock behind them. The boy jerked his head sideways at him. The blast was too far back to knock the jeep off course, but the army truck had been close to the entrance of the tunnel and The Cub hoped some damage had been done. That might slow up the inevitable pursuit. The most important thing, however, was that they would not know where the blast came from, which would give them vital seconds. The Cub's camera case had been left behind, along with the tiny global positioning system and signalling device. He had a 'one-time pad' in the pocket of his shirt and the code in his head, but no means of sending it. So it would be just him, the boy and the desert.

They exited the far end of the tunnel and were on the dirt road that twisted like a bad roller coaster all the way through the mountains. The Cub was thinking back over the journey up here and calculating the distances he had mentally plotted between the sporadic bursts of gunfire, which would tell him when they were likely to encounter trouble. They would be contacted immediately. Al-Bakhtar was no fool. He wondered how long they would torture Moore before they killed him. Moore was unfortunate: he was an innocent with an overactive sense of curiosity. The Cub would have liked to have got him out of there, but there

189

was no time and no chance, and the bottom line would always be self-preservation. He could smell the chilled air of the high desert at night and for a moment was back in Chad, or training in the Namib, listening to lions roaring far off in the night. The desert was his terrain. He was no Afghan mountain man, but five years with the 2nd REP's covert reconnaissance team was the next best thing. He knew he could survive longer than almost anyone else.

'How much gasoline have we got?' The Cub's accent was gone now and the boy sneered at him.

'American.' He curled his lip.

'Don't judge. Drive. How much gas?'

'Enough. All the vehicles are kept stocked.' The boy spat into the wind. 'In case we have to flee all of a sudden.'

'You knew Bin Laden wasn't there, didn't you.'

The boy smiled then. 'Of course. We had just come from the mountain. He hasn't been there in months.'

'Where is he?'

'Oh yes. I'm really going to tell you that.'

The Cub laughed then. 'Son,' he said. 'You may think you're some kinda mujahedin tough guy looking for early martyrdom, but believe me, if you know – you'll tell me.'

The boy did not look at him. He kept his face forward and concentrated on driving. 'Where are we going?'

'Just drive until I tell you not to.'

The Cub settled back and considered his options, which as usual were few. But he had a vehicle, a driver who presumably knew the country, and a weapon. He looked at the boy again. 'How much water have we got?'

The boy spoke without looking round. 'A gallon.'

Enough. The Cub thinned his eyes against the horizon. There was a good moon tonight, which had not been visible from the amphitheatre. The desert scrub of the uplands that bordered the twisted road was shadowed and grey, darker here and there, where boulders jutted or the hillside fell into nothingness.

'What are you – CIA?' The boy spoke over the whine of

the engine as he took another corner quickly. The Cub ignored him. He was doing calculations in his head – not far now until the first set of watchers in the hills. 'You ought to give yourself up,' the boy said. 'We won't make it off this mountain.'

The Cub was studying the road ahead and trying to remember the layout of the landscape when the last burst of gunfire and angry voices had hit them. It had been night, though, and he had not been able to see. Suddenly, a thought occurred to him and he sat more upright. 'Have you got a radio?' The boy did not reply. The Cub shook his head and leaned over the back to where tarpaulin covered the trunk area. Keeping the rifle pointed at the boy's head, he tore back the tarpaulin and smiled. Not only was there a short-wave field radio, but a box of US-made grenades which must have been left over from the war.

Ten miles further, they were halfway down the mountain and the night was brighter still. The wisps of cloud that had threatened to cover the moon a little while earlier were gone now and The Cub's night vision was focused. He worked well at night and once his eyes were accustomed, they picked out features that other people did not see. Many times he had been deep behind enemy lines with the *commandos de renseignements et de l'action*, where every move they made had been under the cover of darkness, often without NVGs. He had learned to operate almost as effectively as he could in the light. There were many advantages with night, the most important being – you were harder to see. He figured they were close to the area where the guards had been now and he put the gun to the boy's head. 'Pull over.'

'What?'

'Stop the jeep.'

The boy pulled over and killed the engine. The noise died away and without the movement of the vehicle, so did the wind. The Cub sat in absolute silence and listened.

'OK,' he said, pointing to the short wave. 'I assume you can work that thing?'

The boy thought for a moment, then nodded. The Cub eased sideways out of the jeep and motioned for him to do the same. 'Get it working.'

The boy picked up the headset. 'Who am I calling?'

'Everybody. I want to know exactly what's going on. I want you to speak to the folk down the hill there, and tell them that the jeep went off the cliff and you're hurt. This radio was made to bounce, so they're gonna believe you. And, boy.'

The boy stared at him.

'Think real hard about martyrdom.'

He stood with the action worked on the rifle and pointed it. 'Now,' he said. 'I want you to speak with the mountain Taliban dialect.'

'How do you know I can?'

'Because I figure it's your common language. I heard various dialects up at the camp, and I want you to use Taliban.'

The boy looked sourly at him.

'Go on.' The Cub said it to him now in the Taliban dialect. 'I'll be listening.'

Ten minutes later, they were rolling again. The Cub could only speak the few words he had picked up when they took Yousef Ramzi, but that was a long time ago and he had not had much call to use it since. But he believed he had said enough to convince the boy, and the ensuing conversation had been stilted and breathless. The boy was not bad: they must have given him acting lessons at that school in England.

Another ten minutes passed and The Cub saw the wash of headlights climbing the mountain road. He knew another truck would be coming down from the camp, but he ought to have enough time. He told the boy to slow and then stop, and then he waved the AK in his face. 'Out.'

'What?'

'Get out.'

The boy climbed out of the driver's seat and stood beside the jeep. All at once he looked small, scared and incredibly young. The Cub moved into the driver's seat.

'What will they do when they find you?' he asked.

'I've failed.' The boy's face was still. 'They do not tolerate failure.'

'They'll shoot you, huh?'

The boy shrugged. 'I don't know.'

The Cub looked forward again, one hand on the wheel and the other holding the Kalashnikov. He levelled it between the boy's eyes, and they balled and stalked, and his mouth fell open. 'I can shoot you right now. Make it easy on you,' he said. 'Or you can climb back in here and help me.'

The boy stood still, not speaking . . .

'You've got three seconds. One, two . . .'

The boy got in and The Cub shifted across to the passenger seat again.

He could hear the engine of the truck labouring up the hill, moving slowly, much slower than they were. The road was narrow, making it very difficult to pass. The Cub was thinking hard, looking left and right as the road dipped and twisted, opening the hill on one side of them and closing it on the other.

'There.' He pointed into the darkness ahead, at a slight slope backing into the hillside away from the cliff edge. It was on the height of a bend in the road and would have to do. 'Pull over and back up there,' The Cub told him. The boy did as he was instructed, less sullen now, much more mentally malleable. The Cub watched as he backed and backed until they were at an angle, facing down on to the road. 'Cut the engine.'

The boy did as he was told, and again stillness settled on them. The Cub lifted his head, like an animal hunting, to listen. Vaguely, far in the distance, he heard the sound of an

193

approaching engine. 'How many men are posted down there?'

'Ten.'

'How many will they send?'

'Most of them.'

'That's what I figured. Maybe just a couple left for us to contend with.'

The boy looked at him, face pale all at once in the darkness. 'What're you going to do?'

The Cub just smiled at him. 'Give me your belt.'

The boy looked a little quizzical for a moment, then took the rope belt that held up his trousers and handed it to him. The Cub tied him to the steering wheel, then took the turban from his head and tore off a strip, which he stuffed into his mouth. Then he took the rest of it, wound it freshly about his own head and slung the AK over one shoulder. He hummed softly to himself as he reached behind and picked up two grenades, then he climbed out of the jeep and moved down to the side of the road. He chose the cliff side, which was not sheer, but steep and loose with sand, broken shale and stones. His feet slithered and slipped as he sought a position behind a jutting chunk of rock, and, as he did so, headlights appeared down the road ahead.

He waited, pins pulled on the grenades with the fly-off levers pressed in, one in each hand, the rifle hanging at his chest. He kept low as the headlights washed over his rock and then disappeared again round the first bend, before reappearing and vanishing. The saliva dried in his mouth and all his senses were alive. His mind was fixed on what he had to do and he waited. The truck rolled nearer. Headlights again, and he ducked lower behind the boulder. Then the lights were gone, but the engine strained louder and louder. Slowly the truck came into view, first the lights, then the shadow, and it rumbled right by him, the canvas top swaying, yawning open at the back. He had kept his eyes away from the lights, and when he popped his head up now, he could see the shapes hunched with their guns in the back of the truck. He licked his lips and expertly lobbed the grenades, which sliced soundlessly through the air, one after the other. He did not hear them land. Seconds passed, then he heard a shout and then the explosions, a millisecond between each. Orange flames shot up and he saw the truck lift clear of the ground, land and swerve dangerously close to the edge of the cliff. It arced and teetered on two wheels, and then collapsed on its side, a mass of sharded burning metal.

The Cub leapt up, emptied two short volleys from the AK at the wreck, then jumped back in the jeep. With the stiletto, he slit the rope round the boy's wrists and told him to drive. 'Remember,' he said, as the boy fired up the engine. 'You've got nothing to hold your pants up if you run.'

They drove down the mountain and, without stopping, negotiated the second set of watchers with machine-gun fire and more grenades. Then they were on the valley floor, racing towards the border.

'Will the plane still be at the airfield?' The Cub demanded.

The boy stared at him.

'This isn't the time to start lying to me, boy. Will it still be there?'

The boy bit his lip, disgust mixed with the fear in his face. 'Yes,' he said.

'And the pilots?'

'They'll be there too.'

They flew into Peshawar. The Cub had sent a message on the ancient, but highly effective and unbreakable one-time pad to the back-up he had from the ISA. The kid was sitting in the only other passenger seat, in tears. The Cub had given the boy the interrogation of his young life – while sitting with a gun trained on the pilot's back – and his particular war was over. He had spoken quietly and menacingly, and managed to extract the information he was looking for. It was not definitive, but it was a start.

'They'll kill me,' the boy said, as the plane banked above the airfield. 'They will now definitely kill me.' He stared through at the cockpit, where the co-pilot still nursed an open gash on the side of his head. 'They are witness to what I told you. They will kill me now.'

The Cub nodded slowly. 'Probably.'

The boy stared at him coldly then. 'You should have shot me back there.'

'You had the choice, remember. You chose to live.' He looked out of the window as the small airfield came into view and he wondered how successful the man on the ground had been. Money usually did the trick with officials in a remote outpost like this, but the town was a hotbed of anti-American rhetoric and he wondered if money alone would be enough. He still had his identity as Terry Morgan the photographer, but knew that would not wash. The airfield got closer and closer: another country, passports and questions; and the fact he held a gun in his hand, and the boy and the two pilots. He stood up and stuck his head into the cockpit.

'Fly over the airfield.'

'What?' The co-pilot twisted round to look at him, blood congealing above his eye where The Cub had whacked him with the rifle butt.

'You heard me. Overshoot the runway and keep on south-west.'

'But we're low on fuel.'

The Cub grinned then, showing his teeth. 'Good. The kinda landing I got planned, we need to be.'

'We can't do it. There's nowhere else to land.'

The Cub worked the action on the rifle. 'Trust me. There will be.'

He squatted behind them now, as they overshot the runway and flew over the sprawling slums of the town towards the mountains. They were heading for Bannu, where he figured he would have a better chance of survival, but he doubted they'd have enough fuel to get there.

Halfway across the mountain range, the co-pilot looked round at him again. 'We've got the Pakistani authorities on the radio,' he said.

'Tell them to fuck off.'

'They're sending up a fighter to make us land.'

'I tell you what, then,' The Cub said, getting up. 'Let's not wait for it. The first decent stretch of ground we come to, I want you to put this baby down.'

The co-pilot swallowed, then nodded and translated to the pilot, and The Cub strapped himself in.

They landed on a stretch of open scrub desert at the southern crown of the hills, north of Kohat. The wings tilted badly from side to side as they swept in low, and the boy gripped the armrests of his seat. They came down with a terrific bang and the undercarriage was ripped off, the plane almost bucking into a somersault. Then they were airborne again for a few moments, and through the open cockpit door, The Cub saw the nose dip. The pilot yelled and they slithered along the ground, and the boy screamed as all the windows popped. The Cub sat where he was, gun on his knees, gripping the arm of the seat with one hand and the gun butt with the other. The slide went on for ages, and then the whole plane shuddered and span ninety degrees as the right wing was torn off. He saw the fear on the boy's face and again he wondered how he had ended up with an outfit like Bin Laden's. He was still staring at him, teeth gritted, jaws clamped together, when the plane lurched to a stop and the single engine died.

The sudden silence was chilling, like the lull before the storm, when the electricity gathers in the atmosphere before unleashing itself on the earth. The Cub scrambled his senses together and unbuckled the belt that fastened him into the seat. The AK47 was still attached to him by the sling, but the wooden barrel casing had shattered and the gun was useless. He had the 9mm he had taken from the pilot, however, and he took it from his belt, glanced at the boy and then into the open cockpit. Neither the pilot nor co-pilot was moving. Quickly, he checked himself for injuries, then got up and went to the air-locked door. The boy sat where he was, breathing hard; little flakes of blood bubbling up into his mouth. His ribs must have shattered and punctured a lung. He was bleeding internally. The Cub twisted the two-handled door and pushed it open. Hot, acrid air filled his lungs and he could smell the leaking aviation fuel. He did not look back, just adjusted the pistol where he had stuffed it back in the rope belt and leapt to the ground, buckled at the knees and rolled parachute-style, before rising and sprinting away from the stricken plane. The ground was rough, choked with stones, and he feared for his ankles. It was some kind of a crop field and in the distance he could see two peasant workers staring in incredulity at the plane. He kept moving, ducking low and working his way across the field to the thin line of broken tarmac, which was the road to Kohat. Halfway across the field, the plane blew up behind him.

He lay in the dried mud, with his hands over his head, as bits and pieces of debris showered him, shards of glass and metal and little bits of wood and burning foam. Hoisting himself to one elbow, he looked back and saw the flames – red, gold and black shooting up at the sky – then he got up and made it the rest of the way to the road.

He stood there, ignoring the fire now, and briefly he considered the local back-up in Peshawar. He was glad that no one had been compromised. Long after he was gone, they would have to live there and, when it suited their purpose, bribed officials have a habit of remembering who had given them money. He looked up and down the road. He was on his own now, but he was dressed like a local and his skin was dark enough to get away with most situations. Also, his grasp of the language had been greatly enhanced by a year in Islamabad. The year was over now and he was glad. He liked the food, but hated the humidity, and the whores had never been to his liking: so much for the *Kama Sutra*.

He sat down by the road and rested, amazed that he had made it through the crash landing without a broken bone. He needed water and rued the fact that the containers had been left in the jeep. There had been water on the plane, but no time to think about it and no way of carrying it either. But there was a road and there were people further up that field, and where there were people, there was water. He straightened, slipped the 9mm from his waistband and checked the action and the clip. Smooth enough, one round already in the chamber, no safety catch, just a hair trigger. He replaced it in his pants and wiped the sweat from his brow.

The road ran from east to west, and he stood shading his eyes from the sun and looked for traffic. Nothing moving, just the heat, shimmering like water in the distance. He walked east, the sun on his back, where it burned through the cotton of his clothing, and he longed for the mountains of Idaho. It was not often he thought of home, but he had been out of sight for a full year and this deal had gone to ratshit. It needed to be refigured and re-evaluated, and might have been aborted altogether if he had not taken the boy hostage.

He paused and looked back across the field to where the stricken plane had attracted quite a crowd of peasants. He could see them migrating towards it from hidden places of work in the fields. What he needed was a truck to Kohat, where he could disappear, establish fresh contact and get the hell out of this country. But there was no truck and he walked on for an hour without seeing anything. The plains here were still quite high and he thought it ought to be cooler, but no cloud broke up the sky and the blue was so perfect it became a haze. The gun chafed his skin through the thin cotton clothing, and he shifted it to the back and then the other side, and finally walked with it openly in his hand.

He heard an engine behind him suddenly, just a faint hum in the distance, and he turned round but initially did not see any vehicle. Then the heat deepened and he saw the unwieldy front of an ageing Ford truck gradually moving closer. It looked military green and, for a moment, The Cub wondered, but as he narrowed his eyes and squinted into the sunlight, the green became a dull grey coated with dust. He held his hand out, as he had seen local people do on these underused highways, when he had been doing early reconnaissance work last year. An old man was driving, both hands at the top of the wheel, and at first The Cub thought he was not going to stop, but then he suddenly ground the gears and slowed the truck without using the brakes. He did not look sideways, but brought the truck to a stop alongside him. The Cub opened the door. The man looked at him then, grinned a toothless smile and gestured for him to get in. The Cub asked him how far it was to Kohat, and the man muttered, gesticulated and nodded all in the same moment. He chucked over a water bottle and pulled away again. The Cub drank it dry, then settled against the door and went to sleep.

10

Swann lay in bed with Logan in his arms and brushed his lips against her hair. 'We've got Harada at a disadvantage,' he said. 'If some form of negotiation starts, that could be useful.'

Logan lifted her head, rested her chin on his chest and looked him in the eyes. 'We do?'

'Yes. He thinks he's got the upper hand, which, of course, he has right now. But we know he's ex-JRA and we think this may have something to do with the man you've got in custody.'

'And that's having him at a disadvantage?'

'Well, it's better than knowing nothing at all.'

'Why should he want to warn us, Jack?' she said. 'And why the codeword?'

'I don't know, unless he intends to make himself public. If he does that, he needs to use codewords that tell you it's not a hoax.' He sat up and placed his arms behind his head. 'The threat of being able to do something is far more effective as a weapon than actually doing it. Fear becomes your greatest tool. The IRA proved it with twenty-five years' attacking the UK mainland. Harada doesn't want to kill civilians, Chey. We know that from the fact he phoned a warning in the first place and set his device in an area where no one would get hurt. Also, he believes he's a warrior – a samurai. The samurai did not kill noncombatants in war, and he's declared this to be a war of sorts.' He sat up straighter. 'He'll contact you again when he's ready and issue another warning. When he does, you'll be armed with much more knowledge, much more information than he thinks you've got. That's an advantage.'

Harrison had his black Chevy truck parked on Burgundy Street, with a police notice pasted on the windshield. On his bed he had laid his battered old army pack, which dated him to Vietnam. He had dug out his scuffed fatigue jacket with the name patch missing from above the breast pocket and poked his fingers through one or two of the holes. Then he had selected his oldest, most battered cowboy hat, with the sides curled up and a red-tailed hawk's feather stuck in the sweatband. There was a bullet hole in each end, which he had stitched together with staples. Jean picked up the hat, watching him as he sat down on the bed and removed the pack of Marlboro from one pocket of his shirt and the Merit menthols from the other. He pointed to the small cabinet by the bed. 'Jean, in that drawer, right there, is a leather tobacco pouch. Hand it to me, would you?'

She passed him the pouch, and he took the packet of hand-rolling tobacco he had bought, plus a tin of chew and some papers, and stowed them all in the pouch.

Jean was still fingering the hat. 'This is a bullet hole, isn't it?'

'Yes, mam.'

'Were you wearing it at the time?'

'Yes, mam.' Harrison shook his head then. 'Jeanie, you really don't wanna go there.'

Jean laughed. 'Ah,' she said. 'I see.'

Harrison looked up at her then and saw for the first time since he had met her, something like hope in her face. 'You look happier than you have in a while,' he said.

'I am. At long last, I feel as though I'm achieving something. I don't feel impotent any more.'

'That's good.'

'Thank you,' she said gently. 'I know you're risking your life.'

Harrison stood up and stretched. 'Wouldn't be the first time. In fact, it's the third since I joined the Bureau.'

'You're doing it for me, though, aren't you?'

Her words cut into him as he looked out of the window at

his truck. He did not reply. And then he felt her hand on the small of his back. He turned and looked into her face. 'It's my job, Jean. It's an FBI investigation.'

'Even so. Thank you.'

He had all his gear laid out now: a spare shirt, his combat jacket and hat, and a tightly rolled sleeping bag. He also had his ancient Coleman stove and a small set of folding billycans he used whenever he went hunting. Next to these, he had a snub-nosed .38 with the serial number filed off, a 9mm Beretta and a bowie knife. Two guns, he thought: one in the bag, one in his boot. He had had to discard the ankle holster in favour of a home-spun leather affair he had rigged up during his days undercover in Idaho. It enabled the gun to sit just in the top of his boot, so that only a portion of the handle rested against his calf. A regular holster was a giveaway every time. He lit a Marlboro from the crumpled pack, sucked smoke and exhaled without removing the cigarette from his mouth. 'There's one thing in my favour,' he said.

'What's that?' Jean rested her back against the window ledge, her head framed in the sunlight, hair in silhouette.

'Nobody knows who the hell these assholes are.' Harrison tapped the ash from his cigarette. 'No law-enforcement agency has taken any official notice, apart from the odd arrest here and there, and I reckon they've been running this scam for years. They won't be looking for anyone to go in undercover.' He glanced at his weary features in the mirror. 'I look the part, too, don't I?'

Jean laughed then. 'You most certainly do.'

Harrison sucked on the cigarette. 'I talked to the office about you and, of course, they won't go for it,' he said.

Her face fell.

'Officially,' he added quickly. 'There's no way they can, Miss Lady Mam. D.C. would hang Mayer by his balls if he approved it.'

'I'm going, anyway.'

Harrison nodded. 'I know. You got enough money for the gas and stuff?'

'Money isn't a problem, John. I want to help. I need to.'

Harrison smiled. 'I might be gone a while. These things can take a whole lotta time, and I mean years, in some cases.'

'Well, I don't have years, but I do have months. I took a year-long sabbatical, and rented out my flat to fund this.'

'OK.' He stood up. 'We'll swing by the office and then I hit the road.' He reached under the mattress and took out another 9mm pistol. 'This is a Glock,' he said. 'It's automatic. Once you rack in the first round, you just keep pulling the trigger. There's no safety catch, just a hair trigger.' He handed it to her. 'You figure you can use it?'

Jean stared at him. 'Yes. But why?'

'Because you're a lady driving an old pick-up to God knows where. Keep it in the glove compartment. Now, you've got Matt Penny's pager number?'

She nodded.

'OK. Any trouble, you get hold of Matt.'

He opened the closet and took down an old five-string banjo from the shelf at the top. He had not played it in years and there were only four strings on the fingerboard.

Jean stared at him. 'Do you play that?'

Harrison nodded. 'I'm taking it for company.'

They walked outside where the heat was softening the pavement and Harrison climbed into the passenger seat of his truck. He nodded to the other side. 'You drive, Jean. You're gonna have to get used to it.' From the glove compartment, he took his cellphone and the charger that plugged into the cigarette lighter in the dashboard. 'Keep this charged and wait for my calls. When I've got something to report, I'll get in touch and we can meet up.'

'Will you be wearing a wire?'

He shook his head. 'Not from the get-go, I won't. If I get accepted, then maybe. Any time you wanna bail out and head on home, you just drive the truck to Poydras Plaza and tell Matt Penny. Y'hear?'

Jean started the engine and looked at the stick shift on the column. 'It's a three-speed,' Harrison told her. 'Third used to jump out all the time, so you had to hold the stick, but I got that fixed. She's been tuned and she's ready to go. Get yourself some Wranglers, honey, and a hat maybe, and you'll pass for one of the gals from Galveston Bay.'

She drove him out of the city on Interstate 10 and then they crossed into St Charles Parish and headed north-west. They left Hahnville and bad memories behind, and Harrison sat with the window rolled down and chewed tobacco. Jean drove the truck a bit jerkily and he cringed for his clutch now and again, but by the time they had done a hundred miles, she was getting the hang of it. The highway opened up and then Harrison directed her to leave the main road and head north. The railroad was ahead of them at Donaldsville, and a few miles the other side of town, he asked her to pull over and stop. They sat there in silence for a long moment, then Harrison opened the door.

'I'm heading west to begin with: Texas, and New Mexico, maybe. Be careful in the small towns. Keep out of the bars and stay in the best motels.'

She smiled at him and nodded. 'It's you I worry about. I escaped from Vietnam before I was twenty, remember. I'll be OK. Honest.'

Harrison looked at her then, a softness in his eyes. 'Course you did. Regular tough guy. Don't worry about me, though. I got outta Vietnam as well.' For a few moments, they just sat there, Harrison with his hand on the door catch, the door half open and the heat of the morning on his thigh. Then Jean shuffled across the bench seat and kissed him on the lips. 'Be very careful,' she said.

Harrison could feel the lump congeal in his throat and at that moment he vowed to himself that he would. 'Don't expect too much,' he said, and climbed out of the truck. He stood on the side of the road and hauled the pack between his shoulder blades. Jean handed him the plastic bottle of water he had filled before they left New Orleans. 'Get outta here, Jeanie. Before another truck comes by.'

She looked at him one last time, then gunned the engine, clunked in the gear and took off up the highway, with a shot of dust from the tyres. Harrison stood and watched until his Chevy was no more than a black dot shimmering against the horizon, and then all was quiet and he was alone again in the world.

He squatted and rolled a cigarette, aware of the gun sweating against his leg on the inside of his boot. He licked the gummed edge of the paper, popped a match on his belt buckle and cupped both hands to the breeze that was not there. He flapped out the match, letting smoke drift, and looked up and down the highway. 'Well, Johnny Buck,' he muttered to himself. 'Fifty years old and going under again. Good job you don't have a wife.' He looked into the distance and thought of Jean, saw her face, felt her lips on his. He stood up and pushed away those thoughts, consciously working them from his mind, and cold professionalism began to seep like iced water into his veins. Flipping away the butt of the cigarette, he stood up, shouldered his pack again and headed towards the railroad.

He jumped a grainer running north out of Donaldsville on the Union Pacific line. The sun had gone and thunderheads gathered in anger above him. He jogged alongside the open boxcar and threw the water bottle in ahead of him, then he slid the banjo over and jumped up, swinging his legs away from the iron clank of the wheels. He got to his haunches and then the train jerked, couplings bruising one another, and he rolled on to his side. He groaned and felt his gun work loose a fraction, and made a mental note to check the strapping. The interior of the boxcar was dark, but Harrison was alone and he sat by the door and dangled one leg over the side.

The train rolled north through the swamplands, heading for Pineville, and the sky darkened still further before the first big gobs of rain slapped the dirt. Harrison rolled a cigarette, sipped from the water bottle and sniffed the air as the rain mixed up with the earth. For a moment he was at peace, at one with the motion of the train, the massed expanse of the cloud and the landscape unravelling around him. Under different circumstances, he could get used to this life and he wondered what he might have done if the border patrol and then the Bureau had not beckoned. The train took him north towards Shreveport, where he would switch lines and head west into Texas.

The rain fell harder; a wind had whipped in from the gulf and was blowing due north, sending sprays of warm rainwater in through the open door. Harrison sat there long enough for it to dampen his face and then he moved into the shadows and dozed.

When he woke, he was not alone. He heard the voices first, talking low as if not to disturb him, and he opened his eyes without moving the hat from where it was set across his face. He was lying full stretch with his head on his pack, and his banjo against the wall. He moved his left leg a fraction until he felt the weight of the .38 and then he took the hat from his eyes. Two hobos sat opposite him, cross-legged. One was much older than the other, with a shock of white hair and a red and white bandana tied about his neck. He was playing cards by himself, but talking to his buddy, a younger, long-haired man in military green, who sucked on a bottle. Harrison looked at the younger one, and he looked back and gestured with the bottle.

'Howdy,' he said.

Harrison nodded, but said nothing. The older man half closed one eye and peered at him through the shadows. It was growing darker now, the rain still hissing past the open side of the car, and Harrison was stiff and sore from the boards. The couplings clanked and metal grated against itself, and the boxcar rolled slightly as they swung into a bend.

The old man grinned at him then, showing a set of long grey teeth. 'Ain't seen you afore,' he said.

'Ain't seen you.' Harrison sat more upright, then he flipped his feet underneath him and stood up. He stretched and yawned, then bent to his bottle and sipped the warm water.

'You ride this section often?'

'Nope.'

These two were not Southern Blacks. They wore no colours, which in itself meant nothing, but Harrison just had the feeling. The old man leaned forward and offered a hand. 'My name's Uncle Ted,' he said. 'This here's Billy.'

Harrison ignored the hand, but nodded. He rolled a cigarette, wetted the paper and lit it. 'You wanna share that bottle, Billy?'

Billy looked a little doubtful and glanced at the old man, then he shrugged and passed it over. 'Swap you for a smoke,' he said. 'Ain't had a cigarette in days.'

Harrison took the bottle and tossed him the pouch. 'Make it jail time, Billy. That's all I got.'

Billy nodded and rolled himself a skinny cigarette, and then Harrison split one of the paper matches he carried in half and popped the head with his thumb. He put the other half back in the pouch and swigged cheap vodka from the bottle. It made him gag, but fired up his throat the way only hard liquor can, and he whacked his chest with the heel of his fist. 'Goddamn,' he muttered. 'You make this stuff yourself?'

'Bought in a liquor store,' Billy mumbled. 'Just like reg'lar people.'

Harrison took another stiff pull and handed the bottle back.

They sat awhile in silence, and Harrison moved to the lip of the door and gazed out into the night. The rain eased, then ceased altogether, and then started up again as soon as the darkness was complete.

'Where did you jump the train?' Uncle Ted asked him.

'Donaldsville. Hitched me a ride from New Orleans.'

'New Orleans's too hot in the summertime. Too much fucking humidity.'

'What's humidity?' Billy asked.

'The stuff that makes you sweat.'

Billy nodded. Harrison glanced at him and let smoke escape from his nostrils. 'Where y'all from, Billy?'

'Arkansas. I's born in Junction City. S'right on the state line thar. Ain't been back in a while.'

'What about you?' the old man asked him.

Harrison shrugged. 'Upper Michigan.'

'Right up there, by Canada?'

'Right up there by Canada.' Harrison crushed out the stub of his cigarette.

'Cold in the wintertime.'

Billy was looking at the banjo. 'You play that thing, mister?'

'Some.'

'You figure to play it some now?'

Harrison drew breath in through his nose and then shrugged. 'I could, I guess.'

'Be nice to have some music. Can't play a note myself.'

Harrison reached behind him and took up the instrument. He tweaked the tuning keys and made a face. 'Darn thing's only got four strings.' He showed the banjo face to the other two. 'Shoulda had five, but one got busted in Jackson Square.'

'You play music down there?'

'Enough to bum a smoke now and again.' Harrison took the fingerpick and plucked a little ditty that Dewey had played him once in Nu Nus Café: a James Booker song.

'I like that, mister. You're real good.' Billy's simple face opened in a smile and he settled back as the rain drummed on the roof above their heads. Under them, the wheels rolled and Harrison picked up the rhythm and beat time with the banjo.

They rode through the night, and Harrison dozed and

woke near dawn to find Billy and the old man gone. Opposite him, in their place, sat two heavyset men in their thirties. Both were tattooed, both had black bandanas wrapped round their heads and both of them were staring at him. He sat up slowly and reached for his water bottle. It was still dark outside, but the rain had stopped and the clouds were being swept away by the wind coming up from the south.

'Hey, bro. What's happening?'

Harrison looked at the speaker. He was bearded and there were flecks of grey among the black. He wore a leather waistcoat over a T-shirt and spiders' web tattoos spread over his arms. His partner was ginger-headed and bigger, belly bulging at the waistband of black jeans. He wore German parachutist boots with the jeans tucked in at the top. Harrison sipped water and eyed them both, easy smiles slack across their mouths. He remembered Spinelli's words in Spokane: *We'll drink with you. We'll be your best friend; and then, when you turn your back, we'll kill you.*

'Where did the other two fellas get to?' he said, as he fished in his pack for his stove. He had cold biscuits, some ham, two apples and a packet of chocolate-chip cookies that Jean had brought over.

'Never saw no other two.'

The ginger-headed one spoke then. 'Where you from, fella?'

'What's it to ya?' Harrison eyed him carefully.

'Hey, no problem, man. Just bein' neighbourly.'

Harrison set the stove on its legs and pumped up the pressure. Then he lit it and poured water from his bottle into a tin mug. It boiled and he lifted it off using his jacket sleeve, and set it down by his feet to cool. He shook granules of coffee in, then took his bowie knife from his pack, looked the ginger-headed man in the eye and stirred the coffee. He opened the packet of cookies and took out two, which he dipped into the coffee and then sucked dry. The two men watched him and he watched them, the knife stuck in the floor between them. Harrison ate another cookie, deliberately not offering them any, and wondered where their guns were hidden. His pack lay open at his feet and he could see the butt of the Beretta, loosened from the shirt it was wrapped in.

'Guess you don't know the rules of the railroad. Do ya, mister?' The black-haired one was eyeing the open packet of biscuits.

Harrison followed his gaze and then looked him in the eye. 'I guess not.'

The ginger-headed one laughed. 'Friend, you got an attitude problem. We're set here trying to be friendly and you're set there like somebody shoved horse hair up your ass.'

Harrison didn't answer him, just chewed his cookies, sipped thin black coffee and swallowed. When he was done with the cookies, he screwed the packet down again and stuffed it back in his bag. Then he rubbed his palms on the thighs of his jeans and stretched out his legs, crossing them at the ankle. Laying his tobacco pouch in his lap, he set about making a cigarette. The two men said nothing, did nothing: they just watched him roll one thin cigarette, then split another match and place the unused half back in the pouch.

'Where'd you come from, bro?' the ginger-headed man asked him.

'Quit asking me that.' Harrison looked him in the eye as he spoke. 'If I wanted to tell ya, I'd have answered you the first time.'

The black-haired man gestured to the skinny cigarette and the split dead match lying just inside the doorway. 'Where was you at – Angola?'

Harrison pursed his lips.

'Angola, then. You just got out, didn't ya?'

'What's it to ya?'

'It ain't nothin' to me, bro. But I can understand you

211

being jumpy now, is all.' He looked at the knife. 'You bought that the minute they cut you loose, didn't you?'

Harrison smoked the cigarette, stared at the night and said nothing.

The two Southern Blacks dozed, and Harrison sat with his hat just above his eyes and pretended to. So far, he had played it about right – the moody, mistrustful ex-con, just out of the farm. The stagehands had set him up with a background in Angola State Penitentiary, and the man sitting opposite had cottoned on very quickly. Matches were at a premium in jail, and every ex-con Harrison had ever met was splitting match stems for years after. The two Southern Blacks would have automatic respect for a man fresh out of Angola, which, as prisons go, is about as tough as they get. Harrison had been there on two separate occasions to interview a guy who was serving life for heroin possession. It was not a pretty place and not one he would like to visit in any other capacity.

With the morning came the sun and he stood by the doorway with his jacket off, just a loose-fitting, yellow singlet exposing sinewy arms and his Tunnel Rat tattoo. Somebody scuffed a boot behind him, and he whirled, crouched and balled his fists.

The bigger of the two, the ginger-headed one, was on his feet and he stood much taller than Harrison. His thighs bulged at the material of his jeans and his belly was exposed at the belt. He lifted a palm as if to calm a child and shook his shaggy head. 'You are one jumpy motherfucker.'

Harrison straightened and looked him in the eye. 'It's why I'm still alive.' He crouched by his pack once more and unscrewed the lid on the water bottle.

The ginger-headed man slouched against the doorjamb. He rolled a cigarette, licked the paper and stuck it in the corner of his mouth.

'Where we at?' his partner asked, and Harrison glanced at him. He was looking at the other man, shading his eyes from the sun. Harrison noticed he was resting one arm on a square package, which was inside a canvas holdall.

'Lufkin.' The ginger-headed man looked back. 'We're coming into Lufkin.'

'Good. I need to get me something to eat.' The black-haired man got up, stretched and looked down at Harrison, who was busy fastening the straps on his pack. The train would stop at the freight yard and he had no option but to get off. The man stared at him, and Harrison ignored him, and then he nudged his partner.

Harrison saw him motion, out of the corner of his eye. 'Am I wearing something of yours?' he said without looking up.

'Brother, you got a bad mouth.'

Harrison stood up and looked him in the eye. 'I ain't your brother.' He shouldered the pack and stepped towards the door. This was the moment: the train was slowing down and if they were going to whack him, it was going to be now. But they did not. They looked at him strangely, their gaze shifting to his arm, and if they were carrying guns, they did not think of going for them. Harrison stood at the edge of the boxcar until the train slowed a little more and then he dropped down, bending his knees to absorb the impact. The train rattled on and he looked up and left, the wind catching his hair, and saw the pair of them still staring from the open doorway.

It took three minutes for the rest of the train to pass and then Harrison could step across the tracks. He could see Lufkin City limits to his left, and, shouldering his pack, he took the banjo by the neck and started walking. He considered his actions and figured he had made the right choice. It pleased him. Instinct. A tight situation and his instincts had been spot on. Like being an animal again. He always felt like an animal when he went undercover. He worked on his guts and so far they had not failed him.

Those last few minutes puzzled him, though: there was something about the way they had looked at him, which he could not quite comprehend. He walked on towards the city, hungry, and the pack all at once weighty between his shoulders. A vacant lot, concreted flat, stretched between himself and the highway, and he paused as an Angelina County sheriff's cruiser idled by, the deputy behind the wheel giving him the once-over from behind Ray-Ban aviators. Harrison ignored him and walked with his head down, hair hanging loose to his shoulders from under his hat. The sun beat on his back and he could feel the straps of the pack chafing as he made his way towards the neon lights of the town.

He ate a breakfast of pancakes and molasses, followed by eggs, hash browns and strips of crispy bacon. He sat on a swivel stool and had to place a fistful of cash on the counter before the waitress got rid of the bad taste in her mouth. She poured him a glass of iced water, which he downed in one, and then some coffee. A couple of good old boys sat at a table, drinking coffee and smoking, but apart from that, Harrison was the only diner. Halfway through his meal the door opened, and he felt rather than saw the two Southern Blacks walk in. They stowed their gear in a booth and slid into the vinyl seats, and he heard one of them mutter something about him, but he ignored it and kept on eating. He had thought it likely that they would get off here, with the train pulling into the yard to be unloaded. There would be guards everywhere, and workers, and he assumed they must have ditched the ride somewhere after he did. He wondered where they were going, and determined, if it was possible, to be on the same train when they left.

He finished his breakfast, accepted some more coffee and rolled a thin cigarette. The waitress watched him and she watched the two guys in black bandanas, and then the diner started filling up. A couple of truckers rolled in and Harrison was flanked on either side, his banjo up against his knees. He considered his next move, toying with a packet of sugar, then glanced over his shoulder at the two men in the booth. The ginger-headed man caught his eye and Harrison looked away again, and placed a toothpick in the corner of his mouth. Getting up, he hefted his pack. The water bottle was empty and he passed it over the counter and asked the waitress to fill it for him. The old man on the stool next to his looked distastefully at him. Harrison met his eye and the old man looked hurriedly away.

The action was not missed by the two Southern Blacks and the ginger-headed one leaned towards his buddy. 'Thinks he's a mean sonofabitch, don't he?' he muttered.

Harrison collected the water bottle from the waitress and picked up his change. She glowered at him, shook her head and tutted. The last thing he was going to do was leave her a tip. He drew alongside the men in the booth, then he bent and looked the ginger one right in the eye.

'Yeah, he does,' he said, and for a second the man's face burned. 'Seeing as how you're so talkative,' Harrison went on, 'where'd a fella go to get a train outta here?'

The ginger-headed man stared at him then and Harrison knew what was running through his mind. Normally, people backed off him. Nobody would backchat him. He wore the colours. He was all of 240 pounds and here was this skinny, ageing ex-con badmouthing him every step of the way.

The dark-haired man spoke. 'Take a right outside the door and keep walking,' he said. 'Keep right on through town and you'll hit the skids in the north-east.'

Harrison nodded once. 'Obliged,' he muttered, and then the red-headed guy grabbed him by the forearm. Harrison looked at the man's hand and then into his eyes; and his own gaze dulled, and his face set cold as it had in the tunnels of Cu-Chi all those years ago.

The man stared back at him and squeezed his arm slowly. 'See you around,' he said.

Harrison walked through town and bought some more biscuits and some fruit. He stocked up on rolling tobacco and purchased a tin of Copenhagen, and saw the same deputy eyeing him from the cruiser, which stood at the lights. Harrison ignored him and walked on. The last thing he needed was to be stopped, what with two guns and Rambo's knife in his bag. He kept walking right through the town and, as the buildings thinned into nothing and mesquite and sagebrush took over, he saw the deputy for the third time. 'Don't worry, asshole,' Harrison muttered to himself. 'I'm outta here.'

He sat on a hill overlooking the Texas South-Eastern line and watched the grainer, empty now, take on a fresh cargo. The railroad hands worked hard – cranes, trucks and men all over the yard, a hive of activity. Below him, the tracks swept in an arc of sunlit iron, before heading south across the flatlands as far as the eye could see. Harrison had never liked Texas and had spent as little time here over the years as he could. The land was flat and featureless, and the weather either blisteringly hot or cold enough to freeze your feet off. The sun was at its height now and Harrison sweated where he sat. He wanted a good vantage point, though, because he needed to see when the train pulled out and he wanted to keep a lookout for his two bandana-wearing friends. There was no sign of them right now, however, and he moved down and sat on a gravel bar in the partial shade of a cottonwood tree.

A rattlesnake moved out from behind a rock, slithering soundlessly at the edge of the trickle of water, and paused to soak up the sun. Harrison watched it. The snake was a diamondback and very thick about the middle, its head flat, low and unmoving. It was no more than five feet away from him, but he did not move and neither man nor beast bothered one another. They both remained exactly where they were, taking in the stillness broken only by the scraping of crickets in the grass. For some reason, Harrison was back in Vietnam, watching one particular hole where one of those thin, black and deadly poisonous serpents was weaving through the grass. No one would go near the hole or try to shift the snake. It was the kind that the VC liked to place in the punji stake mantraps, so you'd be bitten to death once you'd been impaled. The snake was nervous, unsure of which way to go with so many people around. No one would touch it and old Ray Martinez was positively sweating. The Probe: that stone-cold killer who would prefer to crawl alone underground than buddy up. Nothing frightened him, not anything, except that was, the snakes. It occurred to Harrison that maybe he only went underground as some form of macabre metaphorical flagellation. Martinez was a God-fearing Catholic, who had done some pretty nasty things in his life. Harrison often wondered if being a Tunnel Rat wasn't some uneducated way of trying to avoid purgatory. One night in the hootch, while Martinez was high on grass, Harrison had put it to him. Martinez had rolled on his side and looked dull-eyed at him. 'Yeah, right, Johnny. Go to hell to avoid purgatory.'

The rattler moved off again, as softly and soundlessly as it arrived, heading away from Harrison and under the lip of a flat, platter-like boulder which stood up from the gravel bar. A red-tailed hawk screeched high in the sky and Harrison shaded his eyes with a palm, but could not see it. He drank some water, thought about the past and then got to his feet. Back at his vantage point, he could see the train was still being loaded, but coming along the tracks were two figures dressed in black.

The Cub flew into Dulles Airport and transferred to the main terminal on the weird buses that lifted on hydraulics. He cleared customs, stepped out on to hot tarmac and tied back his hair. A yellow cab idled beside the stop for the Washington Flyer and The Cub climbed in the back.

'Where'd you wanna go, buddy?' The black driver leaned over the seat and looked at him. The Cub wore sunglasses and a white T-shirt that stretched across the tightly woven muscles of his chest. 'The Best Western in Leesburg,' he said, and settled against the seat. The driver shoved the old Buick into gear and took off with a jerk. He dropped The Cub in front of the hotel and helped him with his small, lightweight travel bag. The Cub paid and tipped him, and walked out of the heat into the air-conditioned lobby. The receptionist looked up and smiled at him.

'Mr Johnson,' he said, 'from Montana.'

'Oh yes, Mr Johnson. I have your reservation right here.' She passed him the registration card to fill out and The Cub scribbled down the details. 'Are there any messages for me?' he asked.

She went through to the office and came out with a slip of paper. 'Mr Goodby called and said he would meet you as arranged tonight.'

'Thank you.' The Cub took the paper, picked up his key and bag and went up to his room. He showered and changed, flicked through various mind-numbing channels on television and then went out. Birch had said an Irish bar in the parade of shops on the right-hand side of the road, across from the Ford dealer. The Cub walked past the all-night store and got the eye from a bunch of punk kids. Cars passed him as he traversed the three hundred yards of highway and he got the usual strange looks. Nobody walked anywhere in America. He had been stuck in Pakistan for so long, he had forgotten.

He was there first, and ordered a tall glass of beer and drank it slowly. The bartender was chatty and told him to stick around for the band later – some girl and a guitarist. At seven-thirty, the bar was pretty full and The Cub sat at a table by himself, well away from the door. Every now and then a few single guys on their own would approach the table to sit down, but he would lift his head just slightly, look through his sunglasses and they would walk away again. At a quarter to eight, Birch came in, dressed in beige chinos and a bottle-grey polo shirt. He wore no socks, just a pair of very soft loafers that exposed his suntanned ankles. He sat down opposite The Cub and signalled the bar for a vodka and a fresh beer. Birch sat forward then, hands clasped and smiled.

'Well,' he said. 'I didn't expect to see you here.'

The Cub sat easily, one arm on the table, flicking the dirt from under his nails.

'So, he wasn't there?'

The Cub shook his head.

'It made the papers. He's used it as a propaganda weapon. We're denying we know anything about it, of course, but the journalist was shot and his body dumped. They left him with a sign round his neck saying "Made in America".' Birch stopped talking as the waitress returned with their drinks.

'You live out this way?' The Cub asked him, when she had gone.

'You think I'd tell you that?' Birch sat forward again. 'The Australians have made a few noises in private, asking us if we knew what was going on. The President is pissed off about it all.'

'Is he? There's a thing.' The Cub sat forward then. 'You tell the sonofabitch that I'm pissed off, so he should worry.' He looked left and right. 'They knew. They knew right from the get-go. He was never there. They knew something was going down. We never saw the main man. We got Mujah al-Bakhtar instead.'

Birch's face lost its smile. 'The Butcher of Bekaa?'

'In person.' The Cub made a face. 'Tell me something, Cyrus, there's no more than twelve people apart from me who knew about this, right?'

'In totality, yes.' Birch nodded. 'But you know the game. The Talent set the thing rolling, that involves people on the ground in Pakistan. We send in one man to sit and scratch his ass for a year. Pakistan neighbours Afghanistan. Someone could work it out.'

The Cub sipped beer. 'The kid I mentioned.'

'What about him?'

'We had a conversation.'

Birch felt the familiar shiver run down his spine. He could not recall a single face-to-face meeting with this man when he did not experience the sensation. 'What was that about?' he said quietly.

The Cub looked at the bar. 'He said the game's changed, Cyrus. Gone are the days of big compounds and massive infrastructure.'

'So what were you in, if not a big compound?'

'They were winding it down, shifting everything out. Every vehicle in the place was being gassed up ready to roll.'

'Why?'

'Because Bin Laden really has disappeared. His own crew don't know where he's at.' He rested on his elbows. 'The last time Moore interviewed him, before he blew us up in Africa, he figured something out. With all those men and all those guns around, the chances of somebody taking him out were growing by the day.'

'So he took off?'

'Exactly. He's still the master of the game, but he's playing by different rules now.'

'Somebody must know where he is.'

'I figure one man does, and where *he* shows up, so will Bin Laden.'

Birch looked at him over the top of his glass. 'The Butcher of Bekaa,' he said.

11

Swann and Logan were working their way through a print-out of Japanese Red Army attacks over the years, when Carmen McKensie came into Kovalski's office. 'Chey, I think you better look at this,' she said. Logan took the paper from her and scanned it.

'What is it?' Swann asked her.

Logan looked back at McKensie. 'Has Kovalski seen it?'

McKensie shook her head.

'Get a hold of him.'

'What is it?' Swann asked her again.

'It's from the National Crime Information Center,' she said. 'A deputy sheriff in Lander County, Nevada, has just reported an abduction.'

'A child?'

Logan laughed. 'Hardly. A six foot three, two-hundred-pound male, Jack. Tommy Anderson, a miner who helped form the Nevada Unorganised Militia. He was drinking in Austin, comes out of the bar to get in his truck, and a witness from the motel across the street sees three oriental men take him and his truck at gunpoint.'

Swann stared at her. 'You're joking.'

She shook her head. 'I wish I was, because it gets worse. The sheriff's department is called and they start to search. There's only two ways out of Austin, so they commandeer a chopper from the BLM and find the truck, abandoned in the mountains. Right beside it are the marks from the skids of another helicopter.' She drew in a stiff breath. 'This is gonna send the militia loco, Jack. Either we've got some very bad agents out there, or somebody is fucking with us big time.'

'It better be the latter.' Kovalski spoke from where he stood in the doorway.

Logan and Swann flew to Reno. Tim Reilly, an FBI man with the resident agency office in Carson City, met them. Carson City, rather than Elko, had been designated to deal with the Tommy Anderson abduction and Reilly did not look overly enamoured with the situation. Logan rode up front with him and Swann leaned between their seats. Reilly was talking: 'I guess the "blue flamers" at the puzzle palace are getting pretty concerned.' He glanced at Logan's thoughtful face. 'Pataki and Hope Heights, and now this thing here in Nevada.'

They left the interstate for Highway 50, which entered the desert at Fallon, and rode all the way to the Utah line. Austin was about a hundred and fifty miles due east. Logan gauged the trip to take normally about three hours, but Reilly had the light flashing on the dashboard and was leaving what little traffic there was back in his wake.

She had persuaded Kovalski to let *her* go and leave McKensie in D.C. co-ordinating the Harada bombing investigation. Somehow, she had also managed to persuade him that Swann's impartial presence was invaluable. Kovalski had been less convinced about that, but cut her the slack nonetheless.

'Have you got any leads as to what happened after the truck was dumped?' Logan asked Reilly. He shook his head.

'We're working on it with the Highway Patrol homicide dicks,' he said.

'Already?' Logan looked squarely at him. 'Since when was this a homicide investigation?'

'It's not yet.' Reilly pulled a face. 'But it's the third militia-linked attack in the last three weeks, Logan. Both the other two ended up as DOAs, so why should this be any different.'

'Abduction,' Logan said over her shoulder to Swann.

'Kidnapping is FBI jurisdiction, because more often than not, it involves the perps going interstate.' She looked again at Reilly. 'You got TOCs on-scene in Austin?'

He nodded.

'What's the atmosphere like?'

'I'll let you guess.'

They drove through New Summit Pass in the Desatoya mountain range and headed down into the sagebrush and scrub once again. Logan explained to Swann that eighty per cent of Nevada was range land of sorts: most of it owned by the Bureau of Land Management and leased to ranchers for grazing cattle and sheep. The state also housed the largest population of wild horses left in the country, but a number of them had been slaughtered by the ranchers during the really bad drought years at the beginning of the decade. Swann looked out of the window as they reached the flat land again and the basin floor stretched into nothingness as far as the eye could see. 'Even now, you can see how water's at a premium,' Reilly added.

They could smell the atmosphere in Austin as they drove up the hill and pulled over at the vacant lot on the westerly edge of town, not far from the Battle Mountain road. The FBI had set up a mobile incident room, using one of the tactical operations centers with the computer link to Washington, as well as a silver-coloured trailer towed by another massive truck. The trailer housed three FBI agents and two Nevada Highway Patrol officers from their criminal investigation division. The area was cordoned off with police tape and two state troopers stood at the makeshift gateway. The town, though, was all but deserted and Swann could sense the air of malice as soon as they drove in.

The state troopers, both white men with grunt haircuts, eyed Logan curiously as they got out of the car. She already had her shield open and propped it in the breast pocket of the short black jacket she was wearing. The trooper nodded and stepped back. Swann followed Logan into the TOC, and one of the support staff, seated at the fold-out computer screen, looked up. He was in his early twenties, suntanned, with slicked-back hair.

'Good afternoon,' he said.

'Hi. My name's Logan: terrorism response co-ordinator from D.C. How're we getting on?'

The young man sat back and rested his palms in his lap. Swann thought he looked a little effeminate. 'Not good. The mood here is as bad as I've ever seen it. Austin always was a rough little town. The population now is only about two hundred. The miners all live out on-site in trailers and they only come in to get drunk.'

'And the local mood is ugly.'

'To say the least, mam.' He gestured over his shoulder. 'The media circus is at the top end of town. BobCat Reece is holding a meeting right now.'

'Reece is here already?'

The man nodded.

'What kind of meeting?' Swann asked him.

'An anti-federal one.'

'Have we got anyone up there?' Logan put in.

He shook his head. 'The local people don't want us anywhere near the town, let alone their meeting. One agent tried to go up to talk and was told he was violating their First Amendment rights.'

Logan rested her elbows on the edge of the table. 'Have you got any history on Tommy Anderson?'

'Some.' The man reached forward and handed her a paper folder. Swann moved alongside and looked over her shoulder as she read it. The picture pinned at the top left-hand corner showed a rugged-looking, bearded man with a cowboy hat. He had one conviction for assault from his youth, but apart from that his sheet was clean.

Logan pursed her lips. 'Looks like a regular stand-up guy.'

'He led the militia on manoeuvres out by Mount Callaghan.' The voice came from behind them. A young woman in uniform, with a Lander County sheriff's department badge on her sleeve, was standing there. She was no more than five foot five and the gun on her hip looked incongruous, as if she had to stand at a slight slant to hold it up. 'He took them out into the boonies to shoot their guns and lay mini-explosive charges. I know because I watched them.'

Logan held out her hand. 'Cheyenne Logan,' she said. 'This is Jack Swann, a cop from London who is giving us a hand.'

She shook hands with both of them. 'Dorothy Becker. I can tell you all you want to know about Anderson.'

Logan looked over her shoulder at Swann. 'Sense in a small town,' she said. 'Female.'

The three of them walked the short distance up the road to a diner. The two women sat down at a window table and Swann ordered coffee for all of them from a bald-headed, short-order cook, who scowled consistently at him. 'Goddamn G-men ever'where you turn your head,' he muttered. 'Should be looking at Washington D.C., not here. Only for goddamn show, anyways.' Swann paid him, took the coffee and sat down.

'The people think the government is behind the kidnapping?' he said.

Becker nodded. 'Three Orientals showed up in a black Chevy Suburban, two days before Anderson was taken. They had a good look round, as if they were casing the place.'

'Did you speak to them?' Logan asked.

'No, mam. The sheriff did. They told him they were businessmen who were considering buying out the mine.' She poured a packet of sugar into her cup and stirred vigorously. 'They stayed the two days, then headed for Carson City. A day later, Tommy Anderson's truck is found out on the Battle Mountain road and there were signs of a fight. The Chevy is found the same afternoon, just east of the Yomba Indian Reservation. That's south of here; and what look like helicopter skids are located about fifty yards the other side of the road. Two Indians from the reservation will swear under oath that they witnessed a black, unmarked helicopter coming in low over their land the day before.'

She broke off as the bell tinkled above the door and two men in baseball hats walked in. They eyed the table coldly, particularly Logan. 'Good afternoon, gentlemen,' she said.

They looked beyond her to Becker. 'Deputy,' one of them said, 'you're hired by the county. You shouldn't be hanging out with scum.'

'Hey, Earl.' Becker jabbed a finger at him. 'Who I hang out with is my business. And you ought to think about some manners before you get much older.'

He snorted phlegm into his mouth and eyed Swann then. Swann stared evenly back at him, arms resting on the back of his chair.

'You're fraternising with the enemy, Dorothy,' Earl went on. 'Not good in a time of war.'

'There ain't no war, Earl. Don't be such an asshole.'

Earl snorted again and looked at Logan with a sudden curl of his lip. 'Maybe there ain't yet,' he said. 'But there's gonna be.' He looked at Becker again. 'You better think about that, sweetlips. Figure out whose side you're on. Sure ain't gonna be no prisoners taken.' He opened the door again and looked across the counter at the cook.

'Sorry, Udal,' he said. 'You got a bad smell in here.'

'Don't you think I know it?'

They moved outside once more and stood on the sidewalk. Becker eased her gun higher against her hip. 'The meeting's up the street, if you wanna see what's going on.'

Logan felt for the snub-nosed .38 housed under her armpit. 'Yeah, why not,' she said.

The three of them wandered up the hill, with the church on the right-hand side and the road winding like a snake into the foothills of the Toiyabes. The town was old, comprising just one street, with wooden sidewalks and skinny pillars holding up the porches of the buildings that

226

overhung the street. Some were rickety in places, their paint stripped by the sun. They passed a bar on the left-hand side and Swann took in all the media trucks parked in a long line. He noted ABC, CNN, Fox, CBS, NBC. 'They're all here, then,' he muttered.

'Oh yeah.' Becker lifted her eyebrows. 'Regular circus. This is real big news after Hope Heights and Daniel Pataki's death.' She glanced at Logan. 'Who's running the investigation in Oregon?'

'The state police.'

'They come up with anything yet?'

Logan shook her head.

'It's the New World Order. One hundred thousand Hong Kong troops to take away our guns.' Becker made a face. 'I read somewhere that Billy Bob Lafitte's rifle was taken from his truck the night before his brake lines were cut.'

'That's right.'

They paused on the corner of Hope Street, which ran up to the church. A great scrum of people were gathered outside the building. Reporters, cameras, monitors and cables were everywhere.

'What d'you figure is really going on, Logan?' Becker asked her. 'What's the federal angle?'

'We don't have one yet.' Logan made a face. 'But it looks like everything they talk about in their conspiracy theories is coming true, doesn't it?'

'It sure does.'

Swann looked up the street, then back at Becker. 'You don't believe it, though, do you?'

Becker glanced at him and shifted her pistol where it sat in the holster. 'Nope,' she said. 'But that doesn't make it any less dangerous.'

They could not get close to the door, but Swann could hear somebody's voice booming out of a microphone, and the reason the streets were so deserted was because the building bulged with the town's inhabitants. The TV cameras were rolling and he stood next to one group from

227

ABC and watched their video monitor. A tall, rangy-looking man with dark hair was standing in the pulpit, eyes wild and with fist clenched like the old pastor in *Moby Dick*.

'I tell you, good people,' he said. 'We cannot take this lying down.' He banged his fist on the lectern. 'For years, people have branded the likes of Tommy Anderson a fool. What is it they like to call us? What is it *you* like to call us?' He levelled a stiff forefinger at the cameras trained on his face. 'Conspiracy theorists. Scaremongers. Fools.' He broke off and wiped a strand of spittle from his lip. 'Well, Tommy Anderson was such a fool that he's gone missing, abducted by three men of, shall we say, Asian extraction. Three men in a black Suburban, just like the three seen by hundreds of people in Hope Heights, Oregon, where Billy Bob Lafitte was murdered. And what of Dan Pataki in Missouri? Dan Pataki who'd never been east of Kentucky in his whole life, yet still manages to die of *yellow fever*.'

He gripped the lectern now with both hands, knuckles raw against his skin. 'It's happening right under our noses. It's been happening for years – the erosion of everything that this country ever stood for. Our Bill of Rights. Our Constitution, written to oppose the very tyranny we're now witnessing, tossed in the garbage along with all of our rights. No wonder the President was on the tube this year under the pretence of concern about shootings in our schools. I put it to you that those shootings were perpetrated by government agents, the same government agents who are behind the killings in Oregon and Missouri *and* the abduction of Tommy Anderson. What a perfect excuse for the liberals to take our guns. They're not content with the Brady Bill and other such Second Amendment infringements, they're prepared to sacrifice our children to go one better.'

He leaned forward then, clearly aware that his audience was nationwide, and stared into the sea of cameras pointing up at his face. 'Don't you see what is happening? We're not just a bunch of tobacco-chewing Okies sitting up in the boonies. This is going on all over the country. They're after your guns so they can come and get you, just like they came for Tommy Anderson.' He stood tall again and shook his head. 'The FBI will tell you it's a kidnap, an abduction. But we know we won't see Tommy again. His wife told me as much only this morning. His sons, just like those of William Lafitte, will be orphaned. Let me ask you this: are we, the free citizens of America, gonna stand by and let this government make slaves of us with their FBI, their ATF and their foreign troops?' He banged his fist into his chest. 'I for one am not.'

Swann looked at Logan and then out of the corner of his eye he saw Carl Smylie, heading straight for them. Logan looked up as Smylie pushed his thin face into hers.

'Well, Special Agent. What you got to say to that?'

Logan drew breath, flaring her nostrils a little. 'Not a whole lot, Carl.'

'You don't think he's got a point?'

Logan looked at him then. 'Talk to the Office of Public and Congressional Affairs. I'm not the Bureau's spokesperson.'

'No,' he said, folding his arms. 'You're a terrorism response co-ordinator, with her eye on the leg-att's job in London.'

'You're well informed.'

He tapped the side of his nose. 'Gotta be, don't you. If you wanna stay ahead of the game.'

'So what's the story here, then?' Swann asked him. 'What's going to happen?'

Smylie shrugged. 'You tell me, Inspector. But think about it. Old BobCat there has just made a broadcast nationwide. Nobody in his position ever had a national audience like that before. You figure he made the best of it?'

Logan took Swann's arm and guided him away, but Smylie came after them, trailing like a dog. 'Logan, I thought you'd be tied up in D.C., what with the Arlington bomber still on the loose.' He stopped and stood there. 'I see you in D.C. and I see you in Hope Heights, and now I see you out here. You wouldn't give me a quote about Dan Pataki, but you're interested enough to be nosing around here. Now, is that being weird, or is it just me?'

Logan looked round at him. 'I don't know, Carl. Go figure.'

They walked back down the hill. Behind them, the meeting was breaking up and members of the media were interviewing various townspeople. BobCat Reece came bustling out of the church and was collared by a whole gaggle of reporters, with their cassette recorders and microphones stuffed under his nose. He gave them another interview and Logan watched him from the sidewalk. 'Leaderless Resistance,' she said. 'Each cell doing its own thing.' She looked at Swann. 'That's fine in peacetime, Jack. But in war, you need a leader.'

Back in the tactical operations center, she spoke to Kovalski in Washington. 'Did you see that, Tom?'

'Yes, I saw it. Everybody saw it. The Director's been on the phone down here. He's had the national security adviser asking him what our response is to this. What's happening on the ground?'

'Not a lot,' Logan told him. 'It's much the same as in Oregon. Jack and I will have a look round and then head back. Have we heard anything more from Harada?'

'Nothing.' Kovalski sighed then. 'I put in a request to speak to Tetsuya Shikomoto in jail, but he refused to see me.'

'He hasn't said a word since we arrested him. Why should he start now?' She looked at Swann as she spoke. 'We don't know for sure that Harada's bomb is anything to do with him, anyway.'

'We don't know anything about Harada's bomb,' Kovalski said. 'You ever feel like you're getting the run-around, Chey?'

'All the time I've been working for you.' Logan laughed and hung up the phone.

Reilly was busy talking to the Highway Patrol detectives and Logan asked him for the use of his car. Then she and Swann headed west once more, out of town, until they came to the dirt road south towards Ione and eventually Tonopah. Dust lifted from the tyres as she drove through the afternoon heat. The road was bumpy and rippled with tyre tracks left by 4 × 4 trucks.

Swann sat next to her and sighed. 'You can smell the powder drying, can't you, Chey,' he said. 'I mean back there, that small town full of hate and mistrust. It's tangible.'

'The people are scared, Jack. And it doesn't take much from the likes of BobCat Reece to really shake them up. People are scared of what they can't understand and they can't understand this. Two people dead and one gone missing. The one thing they have in common is their distrust of federal government. Not to mention their racist views and probable Christian Identity religion.' She gripped the wheel with both hands, as the car bumped and lurched over the ruts in the unmade road. 'What do you think is happening?' She glanced sideways at him as she said it.

Swann sat back in the seat and thought about it. 'I don't know,' he said. 'It's baffling. You have a society built on the gun, Cheyenne. Everyone has a gun, or at least has easy access to one. I can't think of another civilised nation on the planet that's built on ownership of guns.'

'I know.' Logan shook her head. 'It's the way it's always been. Which is why we can't just ban them. It's not just because of the Second Amendment, although that presents a nightmare in itself. It's the very essence of what this country is.'

'It's not possible that some government department you're not aware of *is* doing this. Is it, Cheyenne?' Swann looked at her as he said it and for a moment she did not reply.

'Well, Jack. Once upon a time I'd have laughed at you. But now.' She twisted her mouth down. 'Now, I think just about anything is possible.'

The area where the truck had been was still cordoned off, although there was no deputy or state trooper there to keep people away. The land was flat and it stretched grey-green with sagebrush and scrub desert as far as the eye could see. 'It's awful hot today, Jack,' Logan said, as she laid her coat on the seat and got out. 'Watch where you put your feet, it's prime rattlesnake country.'

Swann stared at his shoes, partially covered by sand. Rattlesnake country – that was all he needed.

There was nothing to see, just wheel marks and the long flat indentations, which looked like they had been made by a helicopter. Swann wiped his brow with his handkerchief, and suddenly he thought of London, his flat and his children, and how far from this they all were.

Logan's cellphone rang where it was clipped to the belt on her skirt and she looked down at it. 'I never knew it could work this far off the tracks,' she said. She looked at the number, did not recognise it, and answered the phone. 'Logan.'

'Agent Logan, this is Carl Smylie. I just thought you'd like to know that Tommy Anderson's been found.'

'Are you kidding me?'

'No, mam. I'm not kidding you. Of course, he's not saying much. Hard to, when your palette's been blown clear through the top of your head.'

Logan signalled to Swann. 'How do you know this, Carl?'

'Because a rancher friend of his has just called CNN and told them.'

Logan stood, one hand fisted on her hip, and looked at the brilliant blue of the sky. 'He didn't think to call the police first.'

'Why would he do that, Agent Logan? He thinks the police are his enemy.'

232

Swann squatted beside the corpse, still being photographed by the evidence technician from the Highway Patrol. They were just off Highway 50, on a slip road where the rancher had found Tommy Anderson lying face down in an irrigation ditch, with his head blown apart. 'Shotgun,' the medical examiner was saying. 'Twelve-gauge I would say, but don't quote me on it yet.' Logan was standing with him, listening. 'It's as if he put it in his own mouth and pulled the trigger.' The ME pressed his glasses against his nose and wiped sweat-moistened gloves on a piece of muslin cloth. 'But somehow I don't think he did that. Again, we'll find out at the autopsy.' He stepped back and nodded to the two paramedics who were standing by. 'OK,' he said, stripping off the surgical gloves. 'You can wrap him up now.'

Swann and Logan exchanged a glance. Behind them, backing up the road was the mass of television vans with their masts waving in the breeze that was drifting in from the north. Helicopters were flying overhead and Swann knew that live pictures were being beamed into every home in America. This was not his country. This was nothing to do with him, but he had a sense of trepidation that dug deep into the pit of his stomach. The doctor was right. Anderson had not shot himself. He had been murdered just like Lafitte and Daniel Pataki.

FBI agents from all over Nevada had gathered now and they were working the crime scene in conjunction with the Highway Patrol. Swann caught Dorothy Becker's eye and admired her taciturn indifference to the locals who wanted to hang her. He walked away from the crime scene towards the photographers and news crews, and saw Smylie talking on a mobile phone. Their eyes met and Smylie waved at him.

'You OK?' Logan touched his arm.

'Yes, I'm fine. I'm just thinking, that's all.'

'Have you ever come across anything like this before?'

Swann shook his head. 'It's a different mindset, Chey. Different mentality. What I dealt with, the Irish thing, the

differences are historical. It goes back five hundred years.'
He scanned the faces in the crowds, not just the media, but
the townspeople who had driven out from Austin in their
trucks, cars and vans. He bunched his eyes to the sun and
looked back at Logan. 'For a population of two hundred,
there's a hell of a lot of them,' he said.

The freight train, now reloaded, pulled south out of the
Lufkin loop to join the Union Pacific tracks. Harrison stood
up, stretched and reached for his pack. He had watched the
two Southern Blacks moving along the railbed to beyond
the signal point before setting their stuff down. Now they
were on their feet.

Harrison had circumnavigated their position to the west,
moving along the riverbed and crossing the gravel bar into
the hills, before setting himself down some two hundred
yards further up the track. The sun was going down behind
him now, rendering him all but invisible to anyone looking
west, and he shaded his eyes and counted the cars till the
two men jumped. Then he shifted the pack over his
shoulder. By the time the train reached him, it would be
moving much faster and he would have to trot along at a fair
crack to get aboard. He would be vulnerable in that
moment, both to the train wheels and to the two men in the
boxcar. But they would not be expecting him and he was
well armed. He moved off the hill and picked his way
between cactus stalks until he could smell diesel and hear
the groaning metal as the train clanked its way south.

The first few carriages thundered by; Harrison started
counting and at the same time he broke into a run. When he
got to the tenth car, he tossed his pack ahead of him and
hauled himself up, slipped and almost fell, whirling his legs
back behind him to keep them away from the wheels. Then
a hand gripped his arm and he was hauled into the boxcar.
He rolled and knelt, and looked into the faces of the two
Southern Blacks. Again, Spinelli's words rang in his head:
We'll be your best friend, but when you turn your back,

we'll kill you. He muttered his thanks and scrabbled up his pack, banjo and water bottle, then squatted for a moment at the far side of the door. He glanced at his two travelling companions and the ginger-headed one leered at him. 'Didn't expect to see us again, huh? We knew you was coming. You asked me yourself, back in Lufkin.'

Dumb fuck, Harrison thought, but said nothing. Both of them leaned against their packs and then Harrison noticed that the smaller canvas one was missing. He smiled inwardly. So the dealers of Lufkin had fresh supplies on the street.

The ginger-headed man rolled a cigarette and offered it to Harrison. He stared at it for a long moment, then slowly, reluctantly, took it. He snapped a match on his boot, cupped his hands and lit the cigarette.

The black-haired man grinned, showing long yellow teeth like those of an ageing horse. Harrison thought of Jean Carey's son. He wondered where Jean was, how far she had driven. She would be somewhere in Texas, but he had no idea where. He missed her, could see the moon shape of her face in his mind, skin clear and unmarked by age; just the trace of silver lightening the black of her hair.

'You play that thing?' The red-headed guy motioned to the banjo, and Harrison picked it up, stroked the strings and then plucked at them with the thumbpick.

'You got a string missing, bro,' the black-haired guy said. 'That's a five-string banjo with only four strings.'

'Four-string.' The other man laughed then, and nudged his partner. 'Four-string.' He looked at Harrison. 'Hey, you gotta road name, brother?'

'I ain't your brother.'

The ginger-headed man nudged his partner again and jerked a thumb at Harrison's chest. 'Four-String.'

The other guy laughed. He leaned forward then and stuck out his hand. 'Van Horn Hooch. Or just Hooch. I first got on a train at Van Horn, Texas.' Harrison looked at the hand, then reached over and shook it. He wondered if this was how it had been with Tom Carey. Were these two there? Did one of them give the young kid a name, other than Charlie or gook, before they killed him? He could feel the sweat inside his boot where the butt of the pistol chafed the skin. Hooch was still talking. 'This here's Carlsbad the Bad.'

'And is he?' Harrison looked across the semi-darkness at them.

'Oh, yeah. I'm one mean motherfucker.' Carlsbad widened his eyes.

'Carlsbad, New Mexico,' Harrison said.

'You been there?'

'Seen it on a map, is all.' Harrison squatted cross-legged now and inspected the burning end of his cigarette. 'I had a map in Angola. Alls I did when I wasn't working the fields was stare at that map.'

Hooch looked at him, his head slanted to one side. 'How long was you in?'

Harrison had to be careful here. The stagehands had set him up with the identity of a dead man who bore an uncanny resemblance to him. It was a pure coincidence that they found him. One night, one of the gang squad was at the Vieux Carre District station house when the guy's rap sheet was pumped through the NCIC. He had been out of prison for only three weeks, when he robbed a drugstore in Jefferson Parish and was shot dead by a state trooper. The Vieux Carre dicks had been trying to speak to him about a similar robbery in the French Quarter.

'A while,' he said.

'Whatcha do?'

Harrison looked him in the eyes then and said nothing. Hooch held up his hands. 'Just being friendly.'

'I ain't the friendly type.'

'You figure we didn't notice?' Carlsbad showed him dirty teeth. 'Reg'lar Mr Nice Guy, ain't you.'

'Where's this train going?' Harrison asked them.

'South.'

'Where's it finish up?'

Hooch looked slantedly at him again. 'Why? Where you headed?'

Harrison bunched his eyes at the corners and looked beyond him.

'Nowheresville, huh?' Hooch nodded. 'You and us both, brother.'

Harrison lit another cigarette without offering his tobacco, then he worked his pistol looser in his boot with his other heel and took a chance. He pointed with the lighted cigarette. 'What's with the matching headgear? You two a coupla faggots?'

Hooch stared at him. Carlsbad stared at the gap in the door.

'Hit the nerve, huh.' Harrison was aware of how dry his mouth was and hoped it didn't show. He had the bowie knife slung under one arm in its sheath and he would pull it before either of them could drag their bulk across the floor. Slowly, Carlsbad looked up at him. It was darker now and Harrison could no longer see his eyes.

'If I was you, I wouldn't fall asleep tonight.'

Hooch stood up suddenly and Harrison was on his feet with the knife out, blade glinting in a shaft of moonlight breaking through the open doorway.

'Mister,' Hooch said. 'You got a real attitude problem.'

Harrison looked up into his face. 'I'm fifty fucking years old. I survived three years in Vietnam and twenty years in holes you can't even imagine. I figure I can survive a coupla hobos on a goddamn freight train.'

Then he heard a metallic clicking sound that was all too familiar. 'You know what they say, asshole.' Carlsbad's voice came from the shadows. 'Don't bring a knife to a gun fight.'

Harrison still held the knife on Hooch and they looked one another in the eye, and Harrison could feel the sweat gathering under his hat. The adrenaline was pumping and he went for broke. 'When I was in the hole,' he said softly, 'I saw a cop video about knives that one of the bulls smuggled in.' He licked his lips. 'Your buddy there's packing, but I can still cut you real deep before he slots me.'

Hooch slowly raised a palm. 'Nobody's gonna shoot nobody and nobody's gonna cut nobody,' he said. 'We's three guys sharing a ride, is all. Ain't that right, Carl?'

No reply.

'I said, ain't that right, Carl. Put the gun up and chill the fuck out.' He looked in Harrison's eye. 'And you – get the hair outta your ass.'

Harrison stood his ground, aware of the pulse at his temple, at his wrist. He put the knife up and waited. If they were going to kill him, now was the time. If not, all his front would be worth it. He said nothing, just continued to stare at Hooch, while sliding the bowie back into its sheath. Nobody spoke. Nobody moved. The wheels rattled and groaned underneath them, shaking the boxcar; and moonlight poured silver through the side of the train. Harrison heard the click of the hammer coming down. He sucked breath and took off his hat, letting his hair fall across his forehead. He squatted and swigged from his water bottle.

'Here.' Carlsbad sat forward and nudged his arm. 'Have yourself a shot.'

Harrison took the bottle, sniffed cheap bourbon and drank. The whiskey burned his throat, but sent warm feelers into his chest and upper arms. He handed the bottle back and sat down on his pack.

For a good few miles, nobody spoke. Harrison sat where he was and smoked, legs drawn up to his chest, avoiding eye contact and staring into the night. He could feel their gaze picking over the shadows of his face and he could almost hear the wheels turning inside their heads. 'We're Southern Blacks,' Hooch said suddenly. 'Normally, we don't share our boxcar.'

Harrison cocked one eyebrow at him. 'You look like white boys to me.'

Hooch grinned in the darkness. 'It's a play on words,

Four-String. What you might call an irony.' He glanced at Carlsbad, then he rolled up his sleeve to reveal a small tattoo which Harrison had to pop a match to see. It was the letter A, crudely drawn in a capital, with FTR set round it in an arc. Hooch said: 'Freight Train Riders of America.'

'Club, is it?'

'Oh, yeah.' Carlsbad drank from the Kessler bottle. 'Real exclusive. You gotta be white and mean and homeless to get in.'

'Sounds like jail to me.'

Carlsbad shook his head. 'They let anyone into jail, asshole. Niggers, spicks, gooks.'

The train rolled on again and the conversation stilled. Harrison sat in the darkness, listening to the whistle and the thunder of the wheels, and watching the two men through the shadows. He left the conversation-making to them, but a major hurdle had been vaulted and he knew now they were not going to try and kill him. He imagined most of their victims, kids or old men, unarmed with nothing backing them up. They respected force, strength, violence. Anything less was weakness, and weakness to men like this was there to be crushed. Strength, on the other hand, gave him an edge. It unnerved them, knocked them off their course and made them think. Here was a man unafraid enough to back up his mouth with a blade, even in the face of a gun. It had been a while since Harrison had placed himself in such an openly dangerous situation and the blood was still fizzing round in his veins. He was happy to sit and watch and let the beating still in his heart. Around dawn he dozed, and when he opened his eyes, the two men were gone. Quickly, he checked his pack and found that everything was intact. His other gun was still there, his roll of cash was still there and the knife still hung in its sheath.

Cyrus Birch sat in his office in Langley, Virginia, and looked at his watch. The Cub was back in northern Idaho, doing whatever he did when he was not killing people, and

The Talent were on standby. Everything had gone quiet, though, and every feeler imaginable was probing away at the silence. Birch had contacts with the French, the British and the Germans. He had a courier in the Russian Embassy in Islamabad, as well as Secret Branch 40 on his side. And it was the Israelis who he figured would come through. Their intel', coupled with the NSA listening stations and GCHQ in England, had located Bin Laden's whereabouts in the first place, and it was only later, after The Cub had been despatched, that the shit hit the fan. They knew Bin Laden was missing within an hour of The Cub's departure from Islamabad, but it was too late to get him back. Birch had been the most surprised man on the planet when his phone call came through. That had chilled him even more. He did not believe that anyone could get out of a situation like that, especially when the rumour factory had spilled the name of Mujah al-Bakhtar long before The Cub did.

It was why Birch used The Cub whenever he could, and the way he looked was always a bonus in the Middle East. God bless his grandfather for running Chinese whores. Right from the off, notwithstanding his own feelings about the national intelligence estimate and the seriousness of the threat, he had doubted they would achieve their goal. The barrage of missiles back in October had not managed to get him, so how could one man. He would never admit it to Wendell Randall, but he was surprised the President had gone for the assassination finding at all.

Right at that moment, however, Birch had other things on his mind. He was trying to read the analysis gleaned by one of his intelligence officers in Cairo and put forward his own recommendations *vis-à-vis* covert action against Gama al-Islamaya, but he could not concentrate. Tom Kovalski at the FBI had played the counter-espionage cards really close to his chest when Birch had phoned him after the Arlington bomb. Initially, the CIA had thought it was the Priesthood or some other militia faction. But then a little bird had squawked something in his ear that worried him greatly.

Right now, he was waiting for confirmation from a fresh source inside the Israeli Embassy. This source needed paying and Birch was pretty sure he was also the FBI's source, but would happily play one agency off against the other. Birch was aware that Kovalski had personally built up a raft of embassy contacts, and not just in Washington.

He looked at the phone and then at his watch, and then, as if in further confirmation, the clock on the far wall. He checked his pager was switched on, scooped his jacket from the back of his chair and went out to the main office. 'Jenny,' he said to his assistant. 'If anyone's looking for me, I'll be in the Metropolitan Club massaging congressmen. Metaphorically speaking, of course.'

He drove into Washington, let the valet park his car and breezed into the Metropolitan Club, where various craggy-faced alumni members liked to gather and imagine they still had influence within the intelligence community. He noticed Admiral Pavell, who had been a long-time friend of his father, and nodded to him. Pavell was talking to Erickson who had worked briefly with Bill Casey when he had been DCI, before Woodward wrote his book detailing the Iran-Contra scandal. But the man he was looking for was not there, which was not unusual. Birch was not usually flappable, but he did need to know what was going on. If the information he had received was right and it became public, then he might have some questions to answer.

He drank a cocktail and perused the grill menu, while watching the comings and goings for a few minutes. The pager vibrated against his hip and he unclipped it and read the message. Outside on the street, he sought a payphone. 'I got your message,' he said, when the line was answered. 'What've you got to tell me?'

The man on the other end of the line was still for a moment, then he said: 'His name is Fachida Harada.'

Birch felt the sweat form in a line beneath his hair. 'You're sure?'

'I'm absolutely positive.'

12

Fachida Harada sat in the small office attached to the self-storage unit he had rented. Next door, the red *C U SAFELY* security consultant's truck stood idle. Seventy-two hours had passed since he had planted the device in Arlington Cemetery. He looked above his head at the street plan pasted to the wall and considered the array of different-coloured stickers he had marked. The first incident had been by way of introduction: a device set off in the middle of their dead; a warrior laying down his warning at the memorial to US dominance. There had been no casualties, but the selection of different newspapers he had collected on his way in all still headlined with the story. The FBI were saying nothing about who the telephone warning had come from, other than an 'unknown subject'. Harada sat back and weighed their reaction in his mind. They had been on the scene pretty quickly, highly visible in their Chevrolet Suburban trucks with the blacked-out windows and array of computer equipment inside. They had been backed up by the parks police, the metro police and the metropolitan police. He had seen *Washington JTTF* stamped on the back of some of their raid jackets, which meant the various agencies were working together.

Harada stood up and tugged at the knot of his tie, then slipped off his shirt and placed it on a hanger alongside his suit in the closet. Today was hot, warmer than yesterday, and he would wear nothing but a pair of shorts under the cotton one-piece coverall. He fired up the truck and then backed out into the lot, before swinging the nose round and heading down past the Catholic University. He sat in traffic for a few minutes, listening to the newscasters on the radio, with his arm dangling out of the window. The truck was fitted with a scanner for the police radio channels. He drove south on North Capitol as far as Bloomingdale, before turning east to Edgewood and the second self-storage lot, where he kept the black independent cab. Here he changed quickly, this time into a pair of blue slacks and an open-neck shirt, and pocketed the false cab driver's licence, this one under the South Korean name of Hu Li.

Dressed and ready, he opened the back door of the security truck and carefully took out the three separate devices he had prepared. He laid them on the workbench and inspected the packaging, the first in a McDonald's 'to go' bag, the second and third in plastic garbage sacks. He had shaped three separate charges, exactly half a kilo of C-4 in each, and wired them into the short-fuse military timers. These had been rigged with separate safety-arming switches, assembled from the components he carried in the truck, which would give him enough time to place and arm all three.

Back in the cab, he headed downtown, easing through the weight of the traffic. As with his truck, the cab was fitted with a radio scanner and he had three cloned cellular phones in a box under the seat. The Federal Triangle was choked as usual. Harada watched the city cops moving the traffic on as he hit Pennsylvania Avenue and passed the FBI headquarters. He knew exactly where he was going, having done the necessary research over the past six months. He drove south-east on Pennsylvania until he hit Constitution Avenue and the US Capitol building dominated the skyline. 'Land of the free, home of the brave' – the very epicentre of the democratic world. Harada thinned his eyes at the memory of Jakarta all those years ago, and considered all that had taken place in between. Again, the level of his own betrayal stung him, urging on his resolve to complete this task and make his own peace. He swallowed briefly at the thought, then recalled the courage of the master, and stepped on the gas pedal once more. He swung the cab past Capitol Hill and slowed at the junction with Delaware Avenue, where a traffic cop was issuing a speeding ticket. Harada pulled over and deposited the McDonald's bag in the garbage can on the side of the road. The police officer did not look up.

Back in the cab once more, Harada waited for the traffic to slow and then pulled out and headed south of the Capitol building to Maryland and 7th. Here, he placed the first of the plastic garbage sacks in another trash can, before driving to George Washington University Hospital, across the street from Foggy Bottom metro station. The last sack he placed in a trash can to the left of the bus shelter, where an old man sat looking at his shoes. Across the street, the hot-dog and novelty vendors were busy serving commuters who came up the escalators from the station. Harada looked at his watch. Twelve minutes had passed since he placed the first device at Delaware. Sitting back in the cab, he picked up the telephone and dialled.

The operator took the call at the Hoover building. 'FBI.'

'My name is Fachida Harada. Listen to me very carefully.'

Logan was talking to Kovalski, and Swann was preparing to head back to New Orleans, finish his lectures and then return to London. Kovalski's phone rang and Logan picked it up. The muscles tightened round her mouth.

'How did he sound?' she said.

'Calm,' the operator told her. 'Very calm.'

'What exactly did he say?'

'That he had planted three bombs.'

'Where?'

'Delaware and Constitution, Maryland and 7th, and right across the street from Foggy Bottom metro.' The operator's voice was agitated. 'He said we had exactly forty-five minutes before they would detonate.'

Logan put the phone down and related the conversation to Kovalski. 'It was definitely Harada?' he said.

'He gave her his name.'

'What about demands?'

Logan shook her head. 'Another forty-five minutes, Tom.'

Kovalski picked up the phone.

Swann could hear the sirens screaming, as the task force rolled for the second time in three days and got the evacuation started. Forty-five minutes was not a long time. He stood at the window on 4th Street, looking across at the Federal Museum and thinking. He knew that Harada would be watching the chaos. He would be monitoring the response of the authorities, timing vehicles, gauging the directions they came from. Logan came off the phone to a colleague on Pennsylvania Avenue.

'What's the distance between the devices, Chey?' Swann asked her.

She indicated the locations on the wall map. 'We're smack bang in the centre,' she said. 'Maryland and 7th is just across Stanton Park.'

Swann stared at the map for a few moments, considering. 'What're the cordon settings?'

'The bomb squad want to go for two hundred metres. We don't know how big the devices are.'

Swann nodded. 'He'll be in the area, Chey. He's a specialist. Right now, I think he'll be checking your response times and seeing if he's picked the correct RVPs.'

Logan stared at him for a moment. 'So he can booby-trap them. Don't worry, they're being searched.'

They got her car and drove down 4th, under the Labor building and on to Pennsylvania Avenue. Traffic was backing up everywhere as people were forced away from their workplaces. Harada had effectively placed one of his devices at either end of Capitol Hill and both ends of the building were being evacuated. 'He picked a helluva day for it,' Logan said. 'They're considering the President's extensions to the Brady Bill.'

'What's that?'

'Gun control.' Logan glanced at him. 'The House is full of congressmen.'

They made it to the rendezvous point at Delaware and Constitution, and Logan met up with her counterpart from the metropolitan police. The evacuation was proceeding, but there was an air of panic about it and Swann was reminded of London in the old days. He scanned beyond the barriers of police tape, from where they had formed up to the east of Capitol Hill on Maryland and 1st Street. He looked at his watch. Seven minutes had elapsed since Harada's call. The police had reacted quickly, but the evacuation was still in its early stages. They had been up and down the streets within the immediate vicinity, using loudhailers and phones to get everybody out of the buildings.

At Foggy Bottom, the hospital evacuation was taking longer, and Logan was monitoring the progress with McKensie, who was on-scene commander. Swann watched Logan as she organised things: thoroughly professional, crisp, calm and concise. She stood with her back to him now, one hand on her hip, speaking into her cellphone. Beyond her, police cars cruised up and down the street, shepherding people across the perimeter line and out of danger. The rendezvous point had been chosen quickly, the most obvious location given the proximity of the devices. Three of them. Swann thought about that. Three of them all at the same time, spread across the centre of the city. A strike at the heart of government. Harada was a professional. He knew exactly what he was doing. But the JRA had not been active since the spate of bombings they carried out on behalf of Qaddafi. So why now? he wondered.

Logan came over to him. 'We're spread a bit thin, Jack,' she said. 'Tom Kovalski wants to know if you'll go to the Foggy Bottom rendezvous point and help out. Carmen's down there, but it's bedlam because of the hospital. We've got EOD coming in from all over the place, our own bomb squad, the Washington PD, and the Navy at Indian Head.' She pointed to where her car stood with the door open and an agent in the driver's seat. 'That guy'll drive you.'

The agent got him across town in a matter of minutes and

they screeched up to the rendezvous point with a howl from the siren, light flashing on the dashboard. The team had formed up on a patch of grass and flowerbeds, just off a roundabout with a statue of George Washington in the middle of it. The RVP overlooked a parking lot – still being cleared of vehicles – which formed the roof of the metro station. The explosives officer was already there, watching the crisis site through binoculars. The police had got their initial cordons in, but there were twenty-nine minutes to go and the evacuation was slow because it involved bedridden people. The media were everywhere now – cars, vans and helicopters from all over the city. McKensie was co-ordinating from a tactical operations center, speaking to Kovalski at the command post. Swann climbed into the truck beside her.

'What can I do to help?'

'Look at the scene, Jack. Tell me what I'm not seeing.' Sweat was forming on McKensie's brow. 'The parking lot worries me.'

Swann looked where she looked. A uniformed cop was directing drivers away from the area. Lots of the cars would have to stay, though, and Swann imagined all the places a professional like Harada could find to lay booby traps.

'There's not enough time to search every vehicle, Carmen.' He shook his head. 'But something tells me he won't have laid any traps.'

Harada eased his cab past the rendezvous point and saw Swann watching the parking lot. This had been where he had figured they would set up, and, right now, they would be worrying about all the cars in the lot above the station. He had timed how long it had taken the bomb-squad van to react and from which direction it had come. He already knew where the police department housed their specialist vehicles, but he was not sure if the FBI used the field office or the underground car park at the Hoover building. Now, he had that answer and could calculate their ETA at any of his proposed locations. A cop waved him on and he was forced away from the tapes. He gauged the distance in metres from the potential seat of the explosion. Two hundred. They had done their homework and were being very careful. Two hundred was far more than was required, but they did not know that. Professional. He had imagined they would be. They showed as much at Arlington and they were more on their guard now. Spinning the wheel under the palm of his hand, he turned the cab and headed for Pennsylvania Avenue. He doubted he would make it back to the lock-up before the bombs went off.

Swann called Logan's cellphone. 'Cheyenne, it's me,' he said. 'Everything's set here, the cordons are in at two hundred yards and the RVP is clear. What's happening with the third one?'

'It's clear.'

Swann looked at his wristwatch. 'I make it eight minutes. What's your plan if nothing goes bang?'

'I gotta talk to the EOD guy about that yet, but I figure he'll let things sit for a while longer.'

She had to go then, as another call came in from the Bomb Data Center at headquarters. Swann looked at his watch. Six minutes. He lit a cigarette and moved back beyond the outer cordon with McKensie, so only the explosives officer and his driver were left inside the perimeter. Swann scanned the faces of the police officers and firefighters, the paramedics, and men and women running around with FEMA written on their backs. The Federal Emergency Management Agency, McKensie had told him. They always attended situations like this. She smiled as she said it. 'The FBI is the lead agency, but the politics can be almost as bad as the bomb. Not only do we have FEMA, we've got all the different jurisdictions to think about, not to mention the ATF. The task force should've superseded all the politics, but it doesn't seem to work that way.'

Swann looked at his watch. 'In a way, it's just as well,

Carmen. I'll tell you, you'll need every ounce of manpower you can get to find this guy. He's planned this for a long time. There's nothing random about it. He's got a specific agenda and he'll make sure he stays ahead of the game.'

She looked at him with her mouth half open.

'Sorry,' he said. 'I hate to be a harbinger of doom, but he's done his homework. Look at what he's achieved today – taken a line across the city and stretched resources. Forty-five minutes is not a long time, Carmen. But it's long enough to get the media hassling you, believe me.'

Swann counted the minutes down, aware of the tingling sensation in his gut, the anticipation edged with fear that he had experienced so many times before. He could smell the tension in the air – the air of uncertainty. Police cars were still milling around this side of the cordons, and he hoped to God they had got everybody out of the hospital.

And then the bombs went off.

Swann was standing at Carmen McKensie's shoulder and felt the sudden surge of heat in his face, as the blast wave swept between the buildings and glass shattered in a maelstrom of fragments. Swann steadied himself against the impact, one hand over his ear. High explosive, not very much of it, maybe half a kilo, stashed in a lunch box or a paper bag or rubbish sack. One of the first things he had noticed when he got to Washington were the garbage cans on every street corner. He looked round at McKensie.

'Are you all right?' he asked her.

She grinned. 'I'm fine. Guess you're used to this, huh?'

Swann nodded. 'What you just heard was about a pound of high explosive.'

'How can you tell?'

'Pressure wave. Low-grade explosive pushes at buildings, high-grade makes them fragment.' He shrugged. 'It's all about heat, blast and fragmentation, a solid becoming gas instantaneously.' He borrowed her cellphone and called Logan.

BobCat Reece was in his compound on the banks of the Missouri River, north-east of Great Falls, Montana. He was watching CNN broadcasting from three different bomb scenes in Washington D.C. With him were Jerry Freer and Olaf Mayberry, his lieutenants. Like Reece, both were ex-Green Berets and, right now, both wore military fatigues. Mayberry leaned one elbow on his knee and studied the screen, a military-style dog tag and a crucifix dangling from silver chains round his neck. 'Who the fuck did that?' he muttered.

Reece glanced at him, pressing the heel of his thumb against his jaw. They had only just got back from Nevada, where the ideas behind the new network had been discussed. Up until now, everything had been random – unorganised cells with no special affiliation to anyone. But with the recent deaths in Missouri, Oregon and now Nevada, the time had come to move up a gear.

Swivelling round in his chair, Reece scrutinised his encrypted Internet access – the kind of encryption the FBI wanted the government to ban. He tapped the keys and saw that messages were coming in from all over the country. It was loosely agreed that the West Montana Minutemen would take the lead in the new-look star system of resistance: a chain of operatives and different groups linked to the hub in Montana. Reece read a few of the messages, then sent out an encrypted all-points bulletin to every e-mail address he had on his system. He wanted to know who had planted the bombs in Washington.

Harada drove the security truck slowly back from Edgewood. The streets were still clogged with traffic, people leaving all parts of the city, not just the downtown federal area. The beginnings of panic. This was something the citizens of Washington were not used to. He could hear sirens wailing from every direction and he imagined the mêlée down by the White House: congressmen being removed from Capitol Hill, workers from the State Department and the university, and every other type of government facility. Chaos in their minds, in the minds of the authorities, but nothing compared to what he was planning. Carefully, he listened to the radio for word on casualties. As yet none had been reported, which was how he had planned it. But it was still early and they may not have got everybody out. Noncombatants in a war zone. It would be regrettable, unfortunate, but that's what happened in war.

He considered all that he had witnessed. As with Arlington, it had been the police who arrived on-scene first and they who managed the evacuation. Clearly, they had some form of standard operating procedure and they had taken no chances by evacuating as far as two hundred yards.

He slowed the truck for a roadblock. They had got them in quickly and, as he approached the cathedral on Massachusetts Avenue, he could see three cruisers stopping the traffic. He sat and drummed his fingers on the wheel, inching forward until it was his turn. The policeman was young, fresh-faced, with cropped black hair and sunglasses. Harada could see his gun was housed in a holster you could not yank the gun from. It was one of those twist-and-release affairs. He rolled down the window and smiled. The policeman looked him squarely in the eye and Harada knew then that the FBI had released minimal details. They had probably told the cops they were looking for an Oriental, maybe they had gone as far as to say Japanese. He was Joe Aoki, however, a refugee from the war in Vietnam. The policeman looked at him, then at the side of the truck, and then he stepped closer to the window. Harada had both hands on the steering wheel. It put the officer more at his ease and Harada smiled at him. 'Hi,' he said.

'Can I see your driver's licence, please?'

'Sure.' Harada reached for the glove compartment and took out the licence. He had his other papers there, but handed over only the licence.

The policeman took it and looked it over, then glanced at the truck once more. 'Is this your vehicle, Mr Aoki?'

Harada nodded. 'Yes, sir.'

'How long have you been in the United States?'

'Twenty-two years.' Harada handed over his naturalised US passport and work permit.

The officer nodded, then took the licence over to his female colleague in the cruiser.

Harada sat easily, the papers were in order: the preparatory work for this had been done a long time ago. The cop came back again and looked at the truck.

'What d'you carry in here?'

'Everything.' Harada jumped down and opened up the back for him, where it was decked out with racks and shelves carrying all manner of pipes and wires, batteries, switches and locks. 'You name it, I can make it happen,' Harada said. He pointed to the side of the truck. '"C U Safely". I like to think I do.'

The other cop brought the documentation back and Harada climbed into the driver's seat. He swung north now, past the zoo, and parked back in the self-storage lot. Closing the roll door, he turned on the interior lights and went into the little office section where he kept a desk and a television set. Switching on the TV, he sat back, arms folded, and watched. The cab was safely back in Edgewood.

The pictures were of the bomb scenes in the Federal Triangle and the reporters were all speculating on what might have happened. The word was the militia, which Harada thought was vaguely ironic, given how the US normally blamed Islamic fundamentalists first. That had all changed with Oklahoma, though, and he had sympathies with the militia and their calls for a return to the old ways. Like him, they had witnessed the erosion of all that had been sacred; and over time it had forced their hand. He thought then of the master, his one hundred chosen men, the Tatenokai, formed as a protest against the new Japan, after the 1969 treaties with America. Another irony: here he was

252

in America, carrying out work that perhaps the master himself might have approved of. He closed his eyes for a moment and then he was back in Jakarta with Shikomoto.

The hotel room overlooking the walls of the US Embassy: 1986, and he was a young man. The two of them lying naked together, in that sweat-filled room, waiting for the moment. The work that had gone into setting up the mortars they would fire remotely, and all of this for Qaddafi, and even more than that – for the money demanded by Shigenobu. He was no more an idealist than the Americans they were bombing. Harada felt that perhaps that had been his weakest moment, the moment when the misplaced idealism of his youth had finally caught him up. That had been nothing to do with the master's way, it was just amassing wealth.

He stood up and walked the office floor like an animal suddenly aware of its cage. He looked back at the TV screen, but he paced and paced and the thoughts burned uncontrollably in his head. Shigenobu and his Japanese Red Army, the work for the PLO, and for Qaddafi and Carlos. Shikomoto lying naked in that hotel room, with the heat building in his skin and the two of them together through the night. Then later, in the safety of the enclave, away from the clutches of the Americans, or so it had seemed. He stood very still, fists bunched. Everything had crumbled inside him: everything he had ever been, his father and his grandfather before him. All those lives, those generations, those incarnations of warriors – betrayed.

He looked again at the screen and an FBI agent was being interviewed. Harada turned the volume up higher and listened with renewed interest. The man was some kind of spokesman from the Office of Congressional and Public Affairs. He spoke about the bomb and was asked questions about the speed of the evacuation.

'We did receive a telephone warning,' he said, 'exactly forty-five minutes before the three devices were detonated.'

'What kind of a warning?' one of the reporters asked him.

'Just somebody telling us that three devices had been placed and roughly where they were.'

The official gave them no more information than that and Harada pursed his lips. So they were not releasing anything about him at this time. That was interesting. They had clearly primed the police as to who they might be looking for, but that information had not yet been made public. They were playing it close to their chest; a difficult decision, weighing the balance between help from the public and the amount of false alarms they would have to investigate. Later, if they did not accede to his demands, he would ensure they got those calls and their resources would be stretched to the limit. Sitting down once more, he contemplated his next move, then he went to the back of the truck and took a selection of stolen mobile phones from the spare wheel panel. He moved back to the desk and switched the first one on.

Swann and Logan had returned to the field office where Kovalski was liaising with the bomb data agents, now busily combing the blast scenes for the first strands of forensic evidence. Swann poured them all some coffee and Logan answered the phone when it rang.

'This is Fachida Harada.'

It was his voice: Logan would recognise those clipped tones anywhere now. 'Why're you doing this?' she said.

'Because you are my enemy. Because this is a war and these are my rules of engagement.'

'Why're you at war with us?'

'Because you are my enemy. Because you have always been my enemy.'

'I understand.' Logan was thinking hard. 'You're a warrior. A samurai. We are warriors also. Is that right?'

'The defenders of your country. Your Constitution.'

'OK, Mr Harada. My name is Cheyenne Logan and I'm from Atlanta in Georgia. My father was a worker in a . . .'

He hung up. Logan yelled through to McKensie. 'Carmen, did you get it?'

'We sure did, Cheyenne. It's bouncing off the Brookland beacon.'

Kovalski looked admiringly at Logan. 'Good going, Chey. He had to listen to you.'

'That's what I figured, Tom. Declare myself in battle, just like he did.'

'There's only one problem,' Swann said.

'What's that?'

'Now you've got to fight him.'

Harada was smarting. She had almost caught him out. Perhaps he had hung up in time, perhaps he had not. Soon he would see. Carefully, he placed the phones in the grey sedan in the adjoining lock-up garage, and then changed into his grey suit without showering first. Hanging up his coveralls, he opened the doors to the second unit and drove out. He was pulling on to North Capitol Street when a dark blue Ford Crown Victoria came up the other side of the road. There were two men behind the tinted glass. They had been quick indeed. Their equipment for monitoring cell-phones was better than he had imagined. Still, it did not matter. All they would have is the serial number and the fact that the phone had used the Brookland beacon to bounce off. They would not locate the phone itself because it was a clone, and he had access to as many as he wanted. He drove south and then east and, after a further ten minutes, he phoned Logan back.

She, Swann and Kovalski were sitting in the office waiting for information from the road units to come in. McKensie fielded calls from the media people. The President had been on television to make a brief statement, and every news and radio station in the city was humming with speculation. Three bombs in Washington D.C., coming only a few days after the grenade attack in Arlington Cemetery. Nobody had publicly claimed the attacks and the rumour factory was churning product fast and furiously. Kovalski's phone rang again and he nodded for Logan to pick it up.

'Agent Logan.'

'You're very clever, Agent Logan. You will make a fine adversary. I look forward to doing battle with you.'

'Why do you want to fight at all? What's all this about?' Logan was looking at Swann, who stood in the doorway watching the technical team in the outer office.

'Because you have something I want.'

'What is it? Maybe we can give it to you and stop all this.'

'I hope so. If you do, then honour will be satisfied, and I will not have to kill you.'

'That'd be nice. What is it you want?'

'The release of Tetsuya Shikomoto.'

Swann sat in the meeting room down the corridor from Kovalski's office. Kovalski chaired the meeting, and in addition to Swann, Logan and McKensie, there were representatives from the other task force agencies, as well as the Bomb Data Center, the evidence response teams and Fugitive Publicity. The Director was linked to them by conference line from his office at the Hoover building. With him were the heads of the domestic and international terrrorism units, and they were linked to the White House and the national security adviser. Kovalski relayed what they had just discovered.

'At least we know what he wants,' he was saying. 'Tetsuya Shikomoto was an active member of the JRA. He was charged and subsequently convicted of attacking our embassy in Jakarta, Indonesia. Mortars were fired remotely from a hotel bedroom next door to the embassy compound. Nobody was caught right then. In fact, it took us ten years to get Shikomoto. We always knew there was a second suspect, but have never been able to identify him.' He glanced at Swann. 'You wanna go over what you know, Jack?' he said.

Swann stood up then, glanced at Logan and gave them his opinion of Harada.

'Special Branch, back in the UK, identified him as being a one-time member of the Japanese Red Army, which was pretty much disbanded within two years of the mortar attack that Tom's just outlined. They hid out in an enclave in North Korea, probably living off the millions of dollars they generated from various Palestinian factions and Colonel Qaddafi in Libya. Our information is that Harada then returned to his native Japan, along with a chunk of money, and bought his way into one of the yakuza circles.

'Anyway, the point I'm making is, he's a serious terrorist, well versed in the practice. This afternoon's bombings, I would argue, have been planned for a long time. He identified the Federal Triangle and stretched resources within it. Just enough explosive to cause a problem, but still minimise casualties.'

One of the agents from the Bomb Data Center interrupted him. 'Your initial thoughts were correct,' he said. 'We estimate the explosive was about a pound to a pound and a half of plastic.' He paused for a moment and glanced at Kovalski. 'C-4, sir. We found traces of it. It's easily identified by the lab. About thirty to forty per cent nitrate, the rest is PETN, with two per cent colourant and about three per cent oil and plasticity.'

'C-4,' Kovalski went on, 'is military-grade, US army explosive. It cannot be bought on the street.' He paused. 'Not only that, you don't need to buy it on the street. You can make just as big a bang by using sugar and nitrate fertiliser mixed with a little diesel fuel.' He scratched his head. 'Which, of course, is what our friends in the patriot movement do. Two questions. Where did Harada get C-4? And why bother with it in the first place?'

'The bombings have been claimed by three different nazi

groups so far, boss,' McKensie put in. 'The Priesthood being one of them. They claimed it was in retaliation for the murder of Billy Bob Lafitte and Daniel Pataki.'

'This is nothing to do with the militia,' Kovalski said.

'But the public don't know that.' The voice was from the telephone squawk box: Robert Jensen, the national security adviser.

Kovalski lifted one eyebrow. 'The irony kinda strikes at you, though, doesn't it? The militia are all jumping up and down about Orientals, the so-called government-funded Hong Kong troops in their black Suburbans, and now we're looking for one too.'

'The situations are totally unconnected, though, aren't they?' the adviser said over the phone line.

'We think so, yes. Coincidental but unnconnected.' Kovalski squinted round the room. 'Harada's demanded the release of Tetsuya Shikomoto. What're we going to do about it?'

'Well, we're not going to release him, that's for sure.' The FBI Director spoke for the first time.

'The question is,' Swann put in. 'Why does he want him out? And why three years after he was arrested?'

For a few moments nobody spoke, then Logan clasped her hands together, leaning on the table. 'There are things we can work on here. Harada is a samurai. He came out and challenged us openly, declared himself – name, background and everything. He's made no attempt to hide his identity.' She glanced at Swann. 'There's a psychology behind all this that we need to look at very carefully.' She turned to Kovalski then. 'Given what we know, Tom, I think we ought to get one of the behavioural people in from Quantico. Run an evaluation.' She looked again at Swann. 'Jack, can you get any more background information from the UK?'

'I can certainly try.' Swann sat forward then. 'There's something else we should consider, something your behavioural people will be interested in.' He tapped the desk before him. 'The samurai declared his pedigree before he went into battle with his adversary, so that they knew who they had conquered, if that's what happened. To kill a samurai was a great deed and the whole affair was about honour.'

'Honour,' Kovalski said. 'We can maybe work some kinda angle on it. Use it against him somehow. How much honour does it take to bomb a fucking hospital?' He paused. 'What we need to do is stall him for a while.'

Swann looked at him, face clouded. 'I wouldn't hold your breath,' he said. 'Carlos used the JRA to bomb the hell out of France in 1982, when the authorities refused to release Magdalena Kopp from prison. Harada may well have been there. If he was, he'll have learned something.'

13

The streets of London were muggy. Low cloud pressed bad air against the roof of the city and tempers frayed below. George Webb, from the South-West London murder squad, sat in the air-conditioned comfort of the office that he and Frank Weir had been allotted, down the corridor from the FBI legal attaché in the US Embassy. Webb leaned his elbows on the polished wood of the desk and looked at the file the US Marine Corps had provided for him. Dan Farrow, the recently appointed regional security officer, kept hovering about the doorway like a cat on hot bricks. Webb, in a perverse sort of way, enjoyed his apparent discomfort – just a few weeks in the job and already one of his marines had been murdered.

Weir looked over at Webb. 'So who was Kibibi Simpson, Webby?' He walked across the office and bent over Webb's shoulder. 'Thirty-one years old. Impeccable career since joining the US Marine Corps in 1989. Three postings. Germany, Italy and now here.'

'And this one.'

Weir leaned again for a closer look.

'Wichita Falls.' Webb looked at the entry on the file record. 'It looks like a National Guard base. She was only there for three months. Probably just a training exercise or something.' Webb sat back and laid the file down. 'How many men can we draft in, sir?'

'In here, just you and me.'

'What about interviews? We can't do them all.'

'No, we'll run the normal incident-room principles, Webby. It's just that here, it's you and me.'

They went back to the flat in Paddington, which was still sectioned off with blue and white tape and had a uniformed guard on the door. He moved aside as Webb and Weir came up the stairs. Webb closed the door behind them and they both stood in the hall, looking down at the place where the body had lain, bloodstains dried brown now on the carpet. The forensic team had just about finished, but Webb and Weir were still careful where they placed their feet. The normal path a walker would take on the carpet had been scanned by the electronic static lifting apparatus to try and discern a footprint. They were still waiting for the results from the lab.

Weir looked back at the door. 'No sign of forced entry,' he said. 'So either she answered the door or the killer had a key.' He tapped the spyhole at eye level. 'Would she open the door to anyone she didn't know?'

'Would she use the spyhole?' Webb shifted his shoulders. 'She was a marine, Frank. She probably thought she was tough.' He paused. 'Nothing stolen, or even disturbed.'

Weir looked again at where the body had fallen. 'Not even made to look like burglary.'

'Not made to look like anything at all.' Webb went through to the living room and stood with his hands on hips. 'That means the killer was either very cool or very scared.'

Weir nodded and made a face. 'I hate to say it, Webby. But I'd reckon the former. Nothing was disturbed. If he did ring the bell and march her in backwards, he did it slowly, deliberately, making sure nothing was knocked over.'

'And he didn't leave in a rush.'

Webb sat down on the settee. The furniture was good quality. There were brushed cotton covers on the chairs, and ornaments and little crystal knick-knacks littered the mantelpiece. He got up and looked at a picture of Kibibi and two black guys also in uniform. 'Who do you think they are?' he asked.

'Brothers, probably.' Weir looked at their faces. 'I spoke to her mother in Mississippi. She's got brothers in the service.'

'Where are they?'

'On a posting in Italy.' Weir slipped a hand into his pocket. 'The parents are being flown in this evening, though, so they can accompany the body home when the time comes.'

'But we're not going to release it yet.'

Weir shook his head. 'They could be in for a long stay.'

They interviewed her parents the following morning. They were staying at the Marriott Hotel, round the corner from the embassy in Grosvenor Square, and the RSO sent two marines in a car to escort them. Weir and Webb waited in their office, while the Simpsons were greeted by the US ambassador and the FBI delegation. Finally, they were brought down to the office.

'You don't mind if I sit in, fellas, do you?' Farrow asked them.

Weir shook his head and offered his hand to Kibibi Simpson's father, a very tall, very slim black man, with tightly cut hair. His wife was smaller and her skin was slightly lighter. She wore a dark suit and black patent shoes. 'We're very sorry to have to meet you in such difficult circumstances,' Weir said.

Mrs Simpson nodded in a dignified way and her husband leaned forward, elbows on his knees, and stared at Weir. 'Who killed her, Inspector? Who killed our little girl?'

'That's what we're trying to find out,' Weir said. 'Right now, we have a major incident team working round the clock, trying to establish her movements and whereabouts on the night she died.'

'Stabbed,' Mrs Simpson said quietly. 'With a knife.'

'We think so. We haven't been able to recover the murder weapon as yet.' Webb sat forward and looked at

262

each of them in turn. 'Do either of you have any idea who might have had a grudge against your daughter?'

Mr Simpson frowned. 'Here in England? It coulda been anybody breaking in.'

Webb made a face. 'It could've been, but we don't think so.' He explained that nothing in the flat had been disturbed, nothing had been stolen and that there had been no sign of forced entry.

Mrs Simpson sat with both hands holding her handbag across her knees and looked round at her husband. 'We didn't even know she had an apartment,' she said. 'We always used to write to her at the base.'

'She never told you?'

'No, sir.'

Weir looked up at the RSO. 'Is it normal for a gunnery sergeant to have a flat?'

'Depends what you call normal. Some people prefer to live off base. It's not a problem for us, if that's what you mean.'

The five of them went to Southwick Street, so that the parents could look at her belongings and perhaps give them some clue. Webb and Weir drove separately. 'Are you thinking what I'm thinking, George?' Weir asked him.

'Yeah. Southwick Street is a bloody expensive place to have a flat.'

Weir looked sideways at him. 'It is, isn't it? I wonder what a gunnery sergeant takes home a month.'

Later, after the parents had looked over the flat, Weir and Webb drove along Ealing Road, which was like a mini-India, with Muslim, Hindu and Sikh living in varying states of tension. Webb liked the area. The atmosphere was always buzzing, with shops selling all kinds of different things at any time of day and night, and some of the best curry houses south of Bradford. He had spent quite a lot of time in Bradford, undercover as a cab driver during his time with the Antiterrorist Branch, and he could never decide whether northern or southern curries were best. He parked the car on the side of the road, stuck the green Met police book against the windscreen and led Weir into the Taj Mahal.

'Not a very original name,' he said, 'but the food's bloody good.'

Weir sat down, ordered a Bacardi with ice but no coke, and kneaded his eyes with his thumbs. 'That was a long day, Webby.'

'And not a very fruitful one, to boot.' Webb ordered a beer and looked out across the road to the new halal butcher's shop that had recently opened up. Two men were serving the ritually slaughtered lamb, in time for the weekend's ceremonies. He yawned and stretched, and noticed a tall bearded man, in traditional baggy pants and long shirt, come out and go into the shop next door. Webb looked across the table at Weir, who was swirling his drink round the bottom of the glass. 'How much shit's come down from on high, then, Guv?' he said. 'I'm sure the Home Office love this one.'

Weir shrugged. 'I don't give a fuck about the Home Office, George. After twenty-seven years in this job, the politics wash over me. Besides, we've got an area superintendent to take all the flak. I'm just a lowly inspector who gets to play SIO now and again.'

'Seriously, though,' Webb went on. 'I hate to be negative, but I get the feeling we're going to struggle on this one.'

'I always ignore those feelings, George. Feelings don't come into it. Stick to the facts.'

'Which are, we've got a seemingly motiveless murder and a thousand people to interview.'

Weir leaned across the table. 'How hungry are you?'

'What?'

Weir stood up. 'Let's get a drink in the Foxhole. That's where the marines hang out. Maybe we'll pick up some gossip.'

Webb stared at him as he got up, a pained expression in his eyes. 'What about my curry?'

Weir patted the weight of his belly. 'I think you can do without it.'

They got back in the car and, as they did so, a very tall, very black man watched them from the halal butcher's window. His features were smooth and sharp, and his eyes dull and cold. He watched them drive away, then went behind the counter where two young men were cutting meat. The black man brushed aside the bead curtain and went down the steps to the basement. The other man, the man with the long beard and hooked nose, was seated at a table with an array of computer screens in front of him. Intermittently, he would tap at the keys of one, then switch his attention to another. He looked up as the black man filled the doorway. 'You look a little bored, my friend,' he said. 'How can you be bored when there is so much going on in the world?'

Cyrus Birch watched the news on CNN in the Director's office, in the Old Executive building close to the White House. Randall was not in the room, having gone down the hall a few minutes previously, and Birch was watching all the speculation and considering the implications. Nobody at the FBI was saying that they knew who it was, only that they had received a warning, which was why the only damage was to buildings. As yet, they had not said what the make-up of the devices was, but Birch's sources told him that C-4 had been hinted at. Where the hell had he got C-4, and with his background, did he actually need it? He looked at the phone and considered giving Kovalski a call to see if there was any update. But that would only get his back up.

The DCI came back, face flushed, the tension of hours in front of the oversight committees showing round his eyes. 'You know, Cyrus,' he said. 'When I was the presidential campaign manager, I wanted Defense or State.'

Birch laughed lightly. 'They all want State, sir. What they get is the DCI's post.'

'You mean the congressmen's whipping boy.'

'Exactly.' Birch sat forward. 'Helluva reward for getting the old man back in the White House, isn't it?' Getting up, he went to the window and looked out across the square. The DCI's office was in the corner of the building and you got a good view in more than one direction. The area was just about getting back to normal, although there were still dozens of uniformed secret service agents running around the place. He sighed and looked at Randall. 'Sir,' he said. 'I have to tell you. We've got a bit of a problem.'

'What problem?' Randall was back at his desk, half-moon spectacles suspended on the bridge of his nose. Birch sat down in the chair directly opposite him.

'Those three bombs yesterday, and the grenade at the Kennedy memorial.'

'What about them? That's an FBI problem, Cyrus. We've got enough of our own.'

Birch nodded. 'Yes, sir. I know. The thing is, I think I know who planted them.'

Jean Carey drove Harrison's Chevy pick-up truck with the three-speed manual gearshift on the steering column, and felt like a latter-day Calamity Jane. For the first time since she got the news in February, she felt active and alive. She drove the truck at a steady fifty-five, keeping her eyes open for state troopers. The mobile phone Harrison had given her was plugged into the dashboard cigarette lighter and lay permanently charged on the bench seat beside her. This morning, Harrison had phoned her from somewhere called Como, which he said was in Cherokee County, and asked her to meet him in Henderson, south of Kilgore, the following evening. Jean had been in Baton Rouge, Louisiana, and had been driving ever since. She was excited – excited about seeing him again, about finding out what had happened. She had been four days on the road alone, aimlessly driving, or sitting around in cramped motel rooms with poor-quality television and beds that were way too soft for her. She had been eating junk food, except for the bits and pieces of fruit she had been able to buy, and had not gone into any bars on her own. She had Agent Penny's phone number to hand and Harrison's gun in the glove compartment. She wore jeans, T-shirts and open-toed sandals, and her hair was piled on her head, hidden beneath a baseball hat.

She looked at her watch, then checked the road map and worked out there were still fifty or so miles before she got to Henderson and booked into the motel. Once she was checked in, she was to drive out of town on Highway 135 to the junction with 323. There she would find Harrison waiting for her. In the truck box behind her she had clean clothes for him, and he could dump all his hobo gear in the box out there on the highway. They would drive back to the motel together and stay the night. Jean felt a strange tingle of excitement when she thought about that. There would be two beds in the room, but she had not spent the night in the same room as a man for over five years. There had only been one relationship since Tom's father had gone back to South Africa. Her work had completely taken her over, that and bringing up Tom. But now Tom was gone and here she was driving an FBI agent's truck across the Texas plains.

Harrison had left the train at Sulphur Springs. It had been a difficult decision: he was still not totally sure of Hooch or Carlsbad the Bad. The conversation after the incident with the gun had been amiable, as if something had passed between them, and Harrison knew that the point at which they might have killed him for fun was gone. About an hour out from Sulphur Springs, they asked if he wanted to ride along with them. He took a chance and declined, telling them he was not going to ride the rails for the rest of his life, but would try to get some kind of work and lodging in Texas. They laughed and said they'd see him again, and he laughed with them and asked where they were heading, just in case. They told him Oklahoma territory.

He could see Sulphur Springs coming up against the flat of the horizon and he jumped off the train just south of the town. He hitched a ride on a farm truck to a place called Como and called Jean from a payphone. Then he jumped a train going south through Tyler, leapt off it near Jacksonville and hitched a ride to Black Jack. He knew he was being overcautious, but that was a habit he had developed the very first time he went undercover.

He squatted by the side of the highway on his backpack, hat pushed up so the sun warmed his face, smoking yet another hand-rolled cigarette. He had asked Jean to stop at a gas station and buy him a carton each of Marlboro and Merit menthols for when they hooked up. He was sick of spitting threads from his teeth and longed for that tang of menthol hitting the back of his throat. He sat, smoked and drank water, and thought about what he had discovered in the few days he had been out. He had discovered the Southern Blacks and he had discovered he liked life on the road. His mind wandered then and he thought about going back and fishing in Lake Superior, but he figured his Upper Michigan days had disappeared with his youth. Instead, there was the possibility of the cabin in McCall. He might settle there or he might buy a camper top for his pick-up and just drive. He looked at the height of the sun and figured out the time, deciding he had at least a couple of hours before Jean got there. So he lay back, tipped the battered cowboy hat down over his eyes and went to sleep.

He was woken by a shadow across the sun and instinctively reached for his boot. Then he smelled her scent and, shading his eyes, he saw the strands of black hair flying loose about her face. 'Hello, Miss Lady Mam,' he said.

He stood for what seemed like hours under the needle-points of water, only too aware of what he must have smelled like when Jean first got to him. She had stood guard on the road, while he changed into better-looking clothes and stowed all his gear in the truck box. Then she had driven him into Henderson and the motel. The railroad tracks ran through Kilgore and he wanted to avoid them. The shower water plastered his hair against his shoulder blades, and it chilled when he turned off the water. He wrapped a towel round his middle and stepped into the bedroom. The motel was small and built on one level, and Jean was sitting on the stoop with a bottle of beer in her hand, taking in the afternoon sunshine. Harrison stood a moment and watched her: petite, with back bent as she hugged her knees, the jeans clinging to her flesh. The skin of her arms was smooth and her hair was loose now to her shoulders. He fished in his shirt pocket for a Marlboro and she looked round at the snap of the lighter.

'Better?' she asked.

'Oh, yeah. Loads better.' Harrison sucked smoke and wandered to the door. A couple of other trucks were parked in the motel lot and every so often they would hear one rattle down the blacktop, but apart from that, there was nothing but Texas stillness. He had a report to write for his case agents before he went back to the tracks, but that could wait for now. He had no idea how long he was going to spend here with Jean. He might get her to drive him north and dump him somewhere near the Oklahoma State line. But that, too, could wait for a while. Right now, he wanted some food, a few beers and some sleep.

They ate dinner at a small, family-run diner on the edge of town. Harrison had chicken *enchiladas* and bottles of cold beer, and Jean had peppers stuffed with chilli. He told her what had happened so far, making light of the incident with the gun.

'Get Matt Penny to check the names with Spinelli up in Spokane,' he said. 'Van Horn Hooch and Carlsbad the Bad.'

Jean squinted at him across the table. 'Weird names.'

'Aren't they?' Harrison smiled then. 'They christened me Four-String.'

'Why?'

'That old banjo I took with me has only got the four strings.' He pushed away his plate, sat back in the booth and lit a cigarette. He watched her sipping at the glass of red wine and sighed. 'I think I'm getting too old for this,' he said.

'Really?'

'Really. My bones don't take kindly to jarring on the floors of boxcars.' He sat forward then. 'Apart from that, though, I like it. Being on the road, I mean. Just travelling.'

Jean looked at his cigarette, and he fished in his pocket and handed one to her.

'Freedom,' she said. 'I've quite enjoyed it myself, well, the driving part anyway, not so much the hanging around in motels.'

'You like that old pick-up, huh?' Harrison watched her tuck a strand of hair behind her ear and tap the end of the cigarette against the ashtray. She looked at him again.

'Why didn't you stay on the train with them?'

Harrison made a face. 'It's a hard one to call, Miss Lady Mam. I've played it real tough so far, which is gonna do one of two things, either get me in a fight or get me respect. Either way, I've made it look as if I don't give a damn, that I go my own way. They think I've just been sprung from Angola, which is fine, and they know I've got a knife. I figure I can find them again if I need to and the word'll spread across the tracks. Spinelli figured there were something like six hundred of these guys in the South. I'll bump into some more, or possibly the same ones again. I'm gonna head up to Oklahoma, and I want you to get the report back to the field office for me.' He sucked on the cigarette. 'Is anybody keeping in contact with you?'

'Not officially, no. But Matt phones all the time.'

'He's a good boy. Talk to him. In fact, send the stuff via him at his house. Let him get it to the office.' He took a napkin from the pile and wrote down Penny's address. As

270

he passed it to her, their fingers brushed and she looked him in the eyes for a moment.

They had a beer in a small tavern where a couple of cowboys were shooting nine-ball pool. They sat side by side in a booth, where Harrison could see everybody in the room. His hair was washed and brushed, and hung against his shoulders. He had grown a partial beard and had left it unshaven. He hadn't met a hobo yet who took a razorblade to his face. He could feel Jean sitting close to him and could smell the scent of her hair. Every now and again he would glance sideways and catch her face in profile – the fine line of her cheekbones, like porcelain in this light.

All at once, she looked at him. 'Matt told me you were about to leave the FBI. Before this blew up, I mean.'

Harrison blew smoke at the ceiling. 'I was, Miss Lady Mam, but after we visited Spinelli, I figured somebody had to find out what was going on.'

She touched the back of his hand, just brushing his skin with hers. 'This has given me back some purpose, John. I was wandering around like a blind woman. Nothing seemed to be going anywhere, until I bumped into you.'

Back in the hotel, he lay in the other bed with the sheet up to his chest. The moonlight filtered through the curtains and he watched Jean's face as she lay sleeping, her hair very black against the pillow. In the morning, he rose early, showered and dressed in his old clothes before she was even awake. He had written his report and left it in a plastic file for her. Shouldering his pack, he wrote her a brief note, then left the motel with the dawn and hitched a ride to Kilgore, where he hopped a train heading north.

Just south of the Oklahoma line, two hobos wearing black bandanas got on. One was thicker set with tattoos crowding the flesh of his arms. He rolled a cigarette one-handed, and when he opened his mouth to lick the gummed edge of the paper, Harrison noticed that the overlong canine tooth on the right side of his mouth dominated his features. The other man was skinny, with lank hair and one lazy eyelid. Harrison had seen him before, dealing drugs in New Orleans. Spinelli had told him his name was Limpet.

The man with the tooth stared coldly at him and Harrison stared back. Two other hobos were in the boxcar, both of them old and neither of them wearing the black bandanas of the FTRA. They moved closer together when the two Southern Blacks jumped aboard and Harrison knew they would be gone just as soon as the train slowed down.

It slowed to almost a stop just north of the Oklahoma line, taking a curve round the base of a hillside with a silver-topped lake glinting in the brilliance of the sun. The two old-timers gathered their belongings together and scraped their way across the dusty boards to the open door. As the train rattled and clanked to a stop, they jumped off. The two Southern Blacks, neither of whom had said anything since joining the train, looked at one another and smiled with no laughter. Harrison squatted on his haunches and placed a pinch of Copenhagen under his bottom lip. He sucked the tobacco threads and spat a stream of dark juice on to the wooden floor. The two men stared at him and he stared right back, elbows resting on his knees, fingers splayed just above his boot top, inside of which the butt of the snub-nosed .38 was concealed.

'How come you didn't get off with your buddies, dude?' Limpet spoke softly.

Harrison looked him in the eye and spat another stream of juice.

'They ain't my buddies.'

'This is our boxcar.'

'You figure.'

Limpet had his thumb hooked in the top of his belt. 'They belong to us, all of them. You can't just hop any train you please.'

Harrison ignored him and slipped off his battered combat jacket. The day was stifling and the enclosed wooden space accentuated the heat. All he wore underneath was a singlet; and his hair hung loose against his back and the rat tattoo crawled on his arm. The older one, with the long tooth, looked at it and frowned. He exchanged a glance with Limpet, and Harrison recalled Hooch and Carlsbad doing much the same thing. He sat back, perched his hat higher on his head and looked straight at the one with the long tooth. What he saw was recognition in the man's eye. Harrison unscrewed the lid on his rapidly warming bottle of water and sipped from it, then he leaned back against the wall and closed his eyes.

When he woke up it was cooler, the sun had gone and a freshening breeze was picking out the holes in the boxcar. Harrison yawned and scratched his head, and looked across the car to where the two Southern Blacks had been joined by two more. All four were resting against the far side of the boxcar and all four were watching him. The two newcomers were younger and cold-eyed, and one of them sat on a small wooden crate that had not been there before. Harrison sat up, sipped water and rolled himself a cigarette. All the time they watched him and he could feel the steady rise of the pulse at his temple. His jacket lay behind him now and the sinewy muscle of his arms stood out as he worked at the cigarette.

'Where you from, man?' The man with the long canine tooth spoke.

Harrison licked the paper down and stuck the cigarette in the corner of his mouth. 'Nowhere.'

He lit the cigarette, scraping a match against his boot heel, then he stood up and stared out of the open doorway. The sky was darkening visibly in the east and he frowned. There was a stillness in the air despite the breeze and the movement of the train, and a feeling of anticipation settled in his stomach. A movement next to him and the man with the long tooth stood there. This was his opportunity to push Harrison out if he wanted to. Harrison leaned nonchalantly, smoking, but he was already sprung on the balls of his feet, ready to take the man down with a spin-kick to his knees.

'Storm blowing in.' The man pointed east. 'Could be a tornado.'

Harrison said nothing.

'You ever see a twister hit ground?'

'Nope.'

The man screwed up his lip. 'Ain't a pretty sight. Not a good time to be on a freight train.'

Harrison looked at him. 'I figure if the railroad thinks there's one coming, they'll pull the train off the tracks.'

'Yeah. That's what they usually do.'

'You been on one when they done that?'

The man nodded. 'One time near Oklahoma City.' He looked again at Harrison's arm. 'Where'd you get that thing?'

'Tattoo shop.'

The man looked at him and then he smiled, showing that one tooth. 'Where?'

'What's it to you?'

'Just interested. Just being neighbourly.'

Harrison leaned against the wall of the boxcar. 'You guys – neighbourly? Kiss my ass, brother.'

For a long time they looked at each other.

'That's what you heard, huh?'

'That's what I heard.' Harrison flipped away his cigarette and immediately reached for his pouch.

The man looked once more at his arm. 'You got that in Vietnam, didn't you?'

'You know what it is?'

'I heard about it one time.' The man showed his tooth again. 'Not worth a rat's ass.'

Harrison laughed then and sat down. He took a drink of water, then lifted a paper-wrapped bottle from his pack, some cheap bourbon he had bought last night in Henderson, to keep him warm at night. He took a swig, rescrewed the lid and set it back in his pack. He had worked the Beretta loose from its oil cloth, and he sat now, legs stretched and crossed at the ankle, resting his hand on his pack.

'Boys,' the man with the tooth said. 'Our friend here doesn't think we're too neighbourly.'

Harrison felt his heart begin to pump and he let his fingers dance up and down the butt of the Beretta.

'What d'you figure to that, Limpet?'

Harrison watched Limpet's eyes. They were shifty, nervous. He figured he could take him out just by looking at him. Limpet laughed, a liquid cackling sound like an old mad woman. The two younger ones just sat and stared at Harrison. The one with the tooth nodded to the open doorway.

'We're coming to the yard at Broken Arrow, Mr Rat Tattoo,' he said. 'That's a twister blowing in, right there. The railroad'll haul the train off the tracks, so we'll be pitching camp in the freight yard.'

'So what?'

'So we'll have a fire and if you wanna share it, you can.'

They built a fire in a space surrounded by bits of blackened sleepers and stones. Clearly, there had been many before, in the lee of the concrete wall. There were no security guards that Harrison could see and before long they were huddled in their jackets round the flames, as the wind blew in from the south. Harrison had seen a few tornadoes in his time and he thought the Southern Black was wrong. There was a big storm coming and some pretty high winds, but he did not think it would build to a twister.

Some of the men had food and they shared it out and set it on the fire to cook. Harrison sat slightly apart from the others and kept his own counsel. He was suspicious and it showed, which was OK with his cover, because of his recent release from Angola and the fact that he was aware of who these people were. After an hour or so, three more men in black bandanas strode into the yard and now the odds were stacked heavily against him. Seven to one. Even with three weapons, those were serious odds. The man with the long tooth was clearly some kind of leader: the three newcomers acknowledged him with respect and eyed

Harrison warily. He was just as wary and sat with his blanket draped round his shoulders. He brewed a little coffee, sipped it and gnawed at some beef jerky. He thought about Jean Carey and how she had looked in bed last night; how he had lain in that other bed restless to go over there and slip between the sheets alongside her.

'Hey, bro.' He looked up and the guy with the long tooth threw a bottle at him.

Harrison caught it deftly in one hand and looked at the label. It was mescal, yellow with the agave worm in the bottom.

'Go ahead. Sup.'

Harrison looked at him, nodded and lifted the bottle to his lips. The mescal was warm, sweet and sickly against his teeth. He preferred the sharpness of whiskey, and he followed the shot with another of Kessler and then hefted the quart bottle at the man with the long tooth. He caught it one-handed, pulled off the top and drank. Silence descended round the fire; eight men, seven in black bandanas, all with their backs to the wind.

'What's your name, partner?' Limpet spoke to him. He had long dark hair, but no beard, and his face was so pockmarked it looked as though he had never got beyond puberty.

'Four-String.'

'Four-String?'

Harrison nodded and brought his banjo round from behind him, tweaked the strings and grinned suddenly. He looked across the fire at the man with the long tooth. 'I ran into a couple of your guys just the other day,' he said. 'Hooch and a red-haired sonofabitch called Carlsbad the fucking Bad.'

They all laughed. 'Sonofabitch is right,' Limpet said. 'You was lucky he never blowed your head off. He's one mean motherfucker.'

Harrison strummed his banjo. 'Hooch called me Four-String on account of this banjo only having four instead of five.' He looked sideways at Limpet then and began to pick at the strings, fingers deft and lightning fast all at once. 'I can still play the fucker, though, huh?' He stopped as abruptly as he began, laid aside the banjo and rolled another cigarette.

The man with the long tooth was staring through the flickering flames at him. 'Was you in Vietnam?' he asked.

Harrison sucked smoke, looked at the men around him, all of them just a little too young to have been there. 'Why?'

'Was you?'

Harrison sat cross-legged. 'You know somebody who was there, then?'

The man looked at him darkly, irritation in the dead of his eyes. 'Maybe.' He gestured with the bottle to Harrison's arm. 'I knew somebody one time had a tattoo similar to that one you got right there.'

'Is that a fact?'

'Yep. Where'd you get yours?'

'Saigon. Where'd he get his?'

'I don't know. I never asked him.'

Limpet frowned. 'You talking about . . .'

The other man looked sharply at him and Limpet tailed off, recoiling under the gaze.

Harrison pretended to ignore them and stared into the fire. He took another sip from his bottle. For a moment, the man with the long tooth watched him and then he glanced at Limpet, who looked away again. 'They call me Southern Sidetrack,' the man said. 'I run this outfit.'

Harrison sipped again from his whiskey bottle, aware of the gooseflesh on his arms. All he could hear was the crackle of the flames and the wind lifting dust from the concrete walls. The shadows crawled over the broken-down freight cars scattered about the yard, and somewhere off in the desert a coyote howled for its mate. Harrison watched Sidetrack watching him.

Sidetrack's voice was low in his chest. 'You just got outta the can, right?'

Harrison didn't say anything.

'Being on your own out here ain't good for you. Man needs friends on the skids. If we ain't your friends, then nobody is. You understand what I'm saying to you?'

Harrison looked coldly at him then, hating him all at once. 'I spent ten years on the farm. I survived without getting butt-fucked.' He paused. 'You understand what I'm saying to you?'

Limpet roundhoused him, swinging his fist backhanded at Harrison's head. But Harrison was ready for him, ducked and grabbed the hand and had it twisted up behind his back. He pressed him into the dirt, knee to his back, bowie knife to his throat. His eyes were mad and rolling and he leaned close to Limpet's face. 'Don't ever come at me, asshole. You understand me? Not unless you're gonna kill me.'

Sidetrack was on his feet. 'Let him up.' Two of the others had drawn handguns and were pointing them at Harrison. Harrison stared at them and then he released Limpet, throwing him to one side. He got to his feet.

Sidetrack was staring at him. 'Nobody fucks with us, man.'

'That's what I heard. "Be your best friend, buddy, but when your back's turned, we'll kill you."' Harrison spat into the fire. 'I trust nobody in this world, bubba. And nobody fucks with *me*. I crawled underground in Cu-Chi and learned how to kill gooks one on one, with no fucker to help me. You think I'm scared of a buncha chickenshit assholes who hassle old men on freight trains?' It spilled out of him like venom, and all at once he was not acting. He was back there in those sweating jungles, with nothing but his wits and six bullets to protect him. Snakes, spiders and punji stake mantraps, and up ahead, a VC ready to blow your brains out.

Sidetrack stared at him and then he raised a hand and indicated for the others to put their weapons away. 'What you heard about us is right. And I don't care how mean you are, you can't ride the skids without my say-so.' He paused

then. 'So you can put your blade away and sit down. Either
that or get outta here. And the next time any guy in a black
bandana sees you, you're dog meat.'

14

Swann spoke to Special Branch in the UK from the hotel bedroom telephone, while Cheyenne showered. He asked them for every scrap of information they had on both Fachida Harada and the Japanese Red Army. He then contacted the National Police Agency officer who was resident at the Japanese Embassy and asked him to get the same from his people back in Tokyo. Swann had spoken to him many times before and they had worked together on some of the yakuza activities in London. The policeman said he would work as quickly as he could and pass all the information to the FBI team resident at the US Embassy in Tokyo. That way, they could wire it to Washington over the encrypted lines. When Swann came off the phone, Logan was standing naked in front of the mirror, her jet-black hair glistening with globules of water. Swann looked at her and felt the tightening in his throat.

They made love frantically, passionately; Swann pressing her against the bed – their fingers entwined – holding her under him until they both came, she with a cry in the back of her throat. Then he rested against her, smelling the scent of her skin. He kissed her on the face and neck, working his tongue over the cords of muscle that fell from jaw to clavicle. Eventually, he sat up and reached for a cigarette. 'Why does he want Shikomoto out three years after he was picked up, Chey?' he asked.

She sat up and crossed her legs under her like a Native American. The sweat still clung to her body, her nipples points of dark flesh.

Swann sucked on the cigarette and prodded a pillow into shape under his head. 'Why wait three years?'

'Maybe that's how long it took him to set this up, Jack. You said yourself, it was very well planned.'

Swann twisted his mouth down. 'But what's the relationship? The JRA's been dead and buried for years. Harada was back in Japan, a bloody gangster for God's sake. That's a far cry from the idealistic world of the terrorist.'

'Is it?' Logan cocked her head to one side. 'From what you said, the JRA were little more than mercenaries, anyway.'

'I did, didn't I?' Swann got up, crushed out the cigarette and paused at the bathroom door. 'How did you get Shikomoto?'

Logan followed him into the bathroom and twisted on the shower taps. 'We had him fingered after the attack in 1986. The CIA identified him for us initially, and we tracked him from then on. He disappeared for a while, no doubt to the same enclave that Harada was in, and then we lost touch till the CIA got word he was in Osaka, Japan.'

'What was he doing?'

She shrugged. 'Not a whole lot from what I can gather. But we had an international warrant out on him and we tipped off the Japanese that we thought he was there. They did some digging and – bingo – we extradited him back here.'

'Why don't we talk to him?' Swann suggested.

Logan sighed. 'I ran that by Kovalski again this afternoon, honey. Shikomoto isn't interested in saying anything to anyone.'

They ate dinner downstairs in the restaurant and Logan told Swann about Harrison's visit to Washington. 'I think he'll quit the job after this thing he's working on now,' she said. 'I've never seen him so thoughtful as the time he came up here. You know, he'd spend hours just sitting out by the reflecting pool, looking at all the names on the Vietnam War Memorial.'

'The man's got no family, Chey. Maybe you get to an age

when that really matters. I don't suppose he has anyone in the world to really care about him.'

'I told you before, Jack. Johnny Buck's a dinosaur, one of the old school. A serious "kiss my ass" agent. All those guys were married to the job.'

Swann nodded. 'Maybe he thinks it's time to get divorced.'

Logan sipped wine. 'I was really surprised he went UC one more time. Mind you, I can't think of anyone who'd make a better hobo.'

Swann laughed then. 'I'm sure he'd take that as a compliment, Cheyenne.'

He looked beyond her then and saw a man smiling at them from the restaurant door.

Logan recognised him instantly: Carl Smylie, the free-lance reporter. 'Hello, Carl. How's BobCat Reece?'

'He's fine, Logan. If a mite pissed off.' Smylie chuckled and sat down, flicking his lank hair back and pressing his glasses on to his nose. 'Helluva situation going down in Austin right now. The people are really pissed about what you're doing to the Second Amendment.'

Logan laid down her fork. 'Carl, we're not doing anything to the Second Amendment and you know it.'

'Well,' he said, sitting back. 'That's not how they see it.' He picked up the wine bottle and examined the label. 'That looks good.'

Swann took it from him. 'Buy your own.'

'Ah, English chivalry.' Smylie rested his elbows on the table. 'I bet you could teach the Feds a thing about bomb scenes. Did you see how bad they fucked up at Oklahoma?'

Swann did not reply. Smylie turned to Logan again. 'Mr Reece is one unhappy man, Logan. So is every other patriot leader in the country.'

'Patriot's your word, Carl. Not mine.'

'What would you call them, then. Subversives?'

'I'd call them cerebrally challenged. They keep seeing

black helicopters and Russian tanks, and the US government training Crips and Bloods.'

'Ah, but there *are* black helicopters, aren't there? And there are unmarked trucks and oriental gentlemen in suits abducting US citizens.' Smylie tucked himself further under their table. 'You know, you ought not to dismiss this so lightly. Ordinary citizens have seen those guys. The bartender in Hope Heights, the gas station attendant in Austin, to name but two. Have you seen the website activity, Logan? It's not just recognised patriots that are pissed off, it's ordinary, regular people. If you guys don't watch yourselves, you'll be dealing with something ten times the size of Waco.'

Logan pushed her plate to one side. 'Are you all done, Carl?'

'Unless you wanna give me an exclusive on why the government's targeting the militia.'

'Nobody's targeting anybody.'

'OK. If that's how you wanna view it.' He leaned forward again. 'Tell me about this bomber. You got a warning today, right?'

'Talk to the press officers, Carl.'

'They don't tell me anything, Logan. Come on, this is Carl Smylie, the people's investigative reporter. I'm the guy that always gets his stuff from the horse's mouth.'

'Is that how it is?' Logan pushed back her chair. 'Well, this stable's empty.'

She and Swann went down to the bar and ordered a couple of whiskies. Smylie followed them and took the stool next to Swann.

'Piss off, Carl.'

Smylie wagged a finger at him. 'Mr Swann,' he said. 'This is the USA. In this country, we have what's called the First Amendment. The First Amendment says I can sit pretty much where I like.' He looked at Logan. 'Why don't you tell me what's going on? I hear a whole bunch of patriots have claimed the bombings.' He sat back then, with his arms folded. 'But to me, that doesn't make sense. Nobody in the patriot movement, as far as I remember, ever bothered to warn you guys about a bomb before.' He looked at Swann. 'That was the sole domain of the Irish freedom-fighters, wasn't it?'

Swann did not say anything.

'Ah, that British reserve I've heard so much about. Refreshingly on the fence.' He looked back at Logan. 'I'm right, though, aren't I, Logan? They don't warn you about their bombs, they just set them off. Whoever planted those three today managed to destroy a lot of government property without killing anyone.' He thought for a moment. 'Of course, it could be a new tack on behalf of some of the Second Amendment groups. They pissed people off when McVeigh killed all those babies in Oklahoma. Maybe they've learned something.'

Detective Andrew Cameron of the Oregon state police parked his car outside the church hall in Hope Heights and sat for a moment. Not only the parking lot, but the whole street running up and down the hill was chock-full of cars, trucks and vans. He could see at least three of the sheriff's vehicles, including the 4 × 4 truck that Riggins himself used. He did not like Riggins, and certainly didn't trust either him or Maplethorpe, his deputy. He got out of his car and took his windbreaker from the back seat and slung it over one shoulder. His pistol was clipped to his belt and he rested the heel of a palm against it. Perhaps he should not have come here alone. Perhaps he shouldn't have come at all. Since Billy Bob Lafitte died, the people in this town were as paranoid as any he had seen, and more and more out-of-state vehicles seemed to be arriving. Even now, as he walked slowly up the hill, he could see plates from Idaho and Montana, Washington and Nevada. The thing with Tommy Anderson had not helped. For years, the right-wing basket cases had been ranting on about G-men and the United Nations sending black helicopters and Hong Kong troops to round up the people and take their weapons. He thought they were all crazy, most regular people did; but now, well, who could argue with the facts? Three Orientals had been seen in Hope Heights and Lafitte had his brake lines cut. Three more were seen in Nevada, and Anderson turns up dead after being abducted. Cameron paused by Sheriff Riggins's vehicle and pondered. New World Order: a phrase used by George Bush after the Gulf War.

At the door of the meeting hall, he had to stop. There was no room and no way to get past the hordes of people that had filled every seat, every available standing place, right up to the doors and the edge of the sidewalk outside. He could see the raised stage, however, occupied by Millicent Lafitte and her two sons. Next to them were a couple of men he did not recognise, and at another table sat Riggins and Maplethorpe.

Millicent was tapping a thin finger against the formica tabletop. 'My husband is dead,' she was saying. 'It's still hard to take in. I wake up in the morning and roll over, but he's not there.'

Cameron watched her force down tears and he felt for her. This was his investigation, a murder in a town where there had never been a murder, and he was no closer to solving it than he had been when he first got the call.

'Nobody can argue with the facts,' Millicent went on. 'How long was Bob saying this? How many years did he stand up for his rights? He only had his driver's licence under duress, and you all laughed at him. You didn't listen when he argued that a driver's licence changed his constitutional right to travel. You all laughed when he said they were coming to take our guns, that a concentration camp was being prepared in Jerome, Idaho. Well, I've been to Jerome, Idaho, and I've seen it for myself. An old Second World War intern' camp for the Japanese. It's being refurbished. Now, what would anyone wanna go refurbish an intern' camp for, if not for more interns.' She broke off as a murmur of acknowledgement rippled through the audience.

Cameron leaned against the doorjamb and listened as she talked about her husband's belief that somebody was going to take his guns. One of her sons leaned towards her and nodded in Cameron's direction. The table was still for a moment, then a murmur started up again and Cameron realised that the Lafitte boy was pointing at him.

'Detective Cameron.' He jumped when Millicent spoke his name. 'I can see you at the back there. What is it – have you come to spy on us? Is the government gonna take the First Amendment from us as well now?'

Every eye was on him then and Cameron was suddenly nervous. 'Not that I'm aware of, mam.' He tried to lighten the atmosphere but failed. The mood was ugly. He looked to Sheriff Riggins for support, but he just sat with his arms across his chest and looked on with the others.

'You wanna explain to the good people of Oregon why the state police haven't solved my husband's murder yet?' Millicent was on her feet now. 'You wanna come up here and do that, Detective?'

Cameron stood where he was and the crowd moved as one. His mouth dried and his hand crept towards his trouser pocket just below his gun. 'Well, mam,' he began, but his voice cracked and now he knew he should have stayed away.

'Go on, Detective.' Millicent's eyes bored into him from the stage, and Cameron moved away from the doorjamb as the young men nearest to him began to shift uneasily.

'We're working on every lead, Mrs Lafitte. You've seen me yourself. Right here in town.'

'I've seen you sitting there in your government-owned trailer in the parking lot, Mr Cameron. Funny how you should do that, instead of taking some space in the sheriff's office.'

'Mam, there is no space in the . . .'

'Maybe it's because he's an elected county official and

nothing to do with your masters.' Her voice was splintered now, broken like straining wood, and both she and her sons were on their feet. Cameron watched the crowd and took a pace backwards and, as he did, he bumped into somebody standing behind him.

'There is only one lead, Detective,' Millicent was saying. 'The three Hong Kong troopers who showed up in their government-sponsored vehicle. No wonder you can't find them. You work for the same people.' She looked round at the crowd then – men, women, children, all of them with their gaze fixed on the detective. The two men standing closest to him took a pace forward and Cameron lifted a hand.

'Now take it easy,' he said. 'I work for the state. I'm one of you people. You all know me.' He could hear the panic in his voice and, as he turned, he realised that the crowd was now behind him as well as in front. They advanced on him as one and then he pulled his gun.

Somebody screamed – a child, a woman, he did not know which. He felt something chop down on his arm and the gun was on the ground. Then they were on him, one mass of people. He was on his knees in seconds; blow after blow on his head and body, from fists and boots. He felt his collarbone snap, then his right wrist, and then he was doubled up in agony as a boot flashed into his groin. He tried to cry out, tried to call for help and to scrabble for his fallen gun. But the blows kept coming, and then he couldn't feel them any more and he opened his eyes one last time and thought of his wife. He thought he saw her holding their baby in the crowd, but it was not her, it was somebody else and she was holding the baby in one hand and beating at his head with the other.

'Jesus Christ.' Logan tore off the paper print-out from the Strategic Intelligence Operations Center.

'What is it?' Swann looked up from where he was

287

studying the information he had received from London. 'Harada?'

'No.' Logan's eyes were onyx orbs in her face. 'Detective Cameron was beaten to death at a public meeting last night.'

'What?' Swann stared at her.

'The state cop investigating the death of Billy Bob Lafitte. Apparently, he showed up at a meeting in Hope Heights and they beat him to a pulp. Killed him. The sheriff's put in a report saying that Cameron pulled his gun on the crowd.'

They sat in silence for a moment and then Logan looked at Swann. 'We met him, Jack. Carmen and me, when we flew out there.'

'They must have a suspect.'

She shook her head. 'Riggins says he saw nothing conclusive, just a mass of heaving people. Nobody else is talking and Riggins says Cameron was gonna shoot people.'

'That's bullshit, Chey,' McKensie said from the doorway. 'Cameron was a decent guy.'

'Of course it is.' Logan was on her feet. 'Where's Kovalski?'

'He's being grilled by the Director and the national security adviser over at the puzzle palace. The President's pissed about his town being bombed.'

'Well, there's a thing,' Logan said. 'I'm going up there. Are you coming, Jack?'

Swann followed her down to the car park and they drove up to the street. At the corner, she had to wait for traffic and somebody rapped on the window. Swann looked round and rolled down the window. Carl Smylie's smug-looking face was gawping at them.

'Told you, Logan. The people are pissed off. You wanna know how many folks were at that meeting? Twice the town's population. There's one tonight in Elko, Nevada, and another in Kilgore, Texas. They'll be happening all over the country. The ordinary God-fearing American is suddenly pissed off.'

'And you're happy about it?' Logan shook her head at him. 'Go crawl back under your stone.' She revved the engine and pulled out on to the street.

They parked underneath the Hoover building and then had to go round the front to get Swann cleared to go in. Kovalski was in conference with the FBI Director and Logan insisted they go right in. She apologised to the Director, who looked up and smiled at her. 'Nothing like a zealous brick agent, Logan. I used to be one myself.'

Logan told them what had happened and passed the SIOC print-out to Kovalski. His eyes darkened and he looked across the desk at both the Director and the President's national security adviser. 'Sir,' he said. 'I think you should get the President on television. He's got to talk to the people about this.'

'Don't you think that's a bit of an overreaction, Mr Kovalski?'

Kovalski stared at him. 'No, I fucking don't. Goddammit, I've warned you people about these groups since before Ruby Ridge. This is mob rule. It's mob murder of a police officer.'

The national security adviser took the paper from him. 'It says here he drew his gun. That's come straight from the sheriff.'

'Sir,' Logan put in. 'The sheriff is one of Jack McClamb's Operation Vampire Killer converts.'

The national security adviser looked puzzled. 'Come again?'

'It's an organisation set up to educate law-enforcement officers about the New World Order. Some people have claimed that the vampires to be killed are cops who follow the law.'

'Logan's right,' Kovalski went on. 'We've left these groups alone for too long. If they were the Black Panthers, we wouldn't.' He stood up. 'You need to get the President to talk to his people, sir. And you need to do it now.'

Back at the field office, Logan spoke to the special agent in charge at Portland and got an update on what was happening. The state police and the FBI were swarming all over Hope Heights, but nobody would admit to being at the meeting, and the sheriff could not identify any of those who were closest to Detective Cameron when he drew his gun. His attitude was that whoever they were, they were just defending themselves, anyhow.

Logan then took Swann over to headquarters again, where they sat down with the domestic terrorism analytical unit, who were now monitoring the more notorious militia websites. The main difficulty faced by the FBI was the ever-increasingly sophisticated methods of e-mail encryption that were being used. Today, though, the militia groups themselves were not the problem. The problem was the ordinary members of the public making hits on websites normally reserved for psychos.

'It's worrying,' the analyst monitoring the Missouri Breakmen was saying. 'Since Pataki bought it, the website activity has gone up fifty-fold. We've calculated the same with the Oregon situation and we reckon it'll be the same in Nevada.' He looked round at Swann. 'All these groups have websites.' Then to Logan, 'The busiest by far right now, though, is the West Montana Minutemen.'

When they got back to the field office again, Kovalski was talking to Special Agent Mallory from the Violent Criminal Apprehension Program at Quantico. She was a behavioural scientist, with a master's in psychology, and she was talking about Harada. Swann scooped up the papers he had received from London and sat down at the table.

'Terrorists are hard to quantify,' Mallory was saying. 'There's no distinct psychological pattern. They're indoctrinated by a group or a cause or some sense of religious fundamentalism, which does not necessarily produce predictable patterns of behaviour.'

'Harada issued a challenge to the FBI in the manner of an ancient samurai warrior,' Swann interrupted. 'Fundamentally, the samurai were dealers in honour. Honour came above everything else – friends, family, warlords, even the emperor.' He offered his hand when Mallory looked a little puzzled. 'Jack Swann,' he said. 'Detective Inspector, UK Antiterrorist Branch.'

'Jack's been lecturing in Louisiana on the State Department's antiterrorism assistance programme,' Kovalski explained.

'Samurai.' Mallory chewed on the word. 'And his demand is the release of Shikomoto?'

Logan nodded. 'We don't know why, or what their connection was, other than the JRA.'

'There was a second player in Jakarta in 1986,' Kovalski said, 'but we never found out who it was.'

'You think the other player might be Harada?' Mallory said.

'We think it's pretty likely.'

'Harada was in North Korea,' Swann told her, 'then he went back to Japan, joined the yakuza and became part of the *sokaiya*, the white-collar brigade.'

'That would make sense. The yakuza allegedly hold fast to some of the samurai values.' Mallory sat forward. 'What we need to know about is Harada himself.'

'We're already doing some digging,' Logan said. 'When he issued the challenge, he did it in the formal samurai way, naming his father and his grandfather, where they came from and what the family business was.'

'I spoke to the Japanese police liaison in London this morning,' Swann said. 'He told me something that I thought was interesting.'

'What's that?' Kovalski asked him.

'The word samurai means to serve.'

15

Webb and Frank Weir were back in Kibibi Simpson's flat in Paddington. They had traced the landlord and he had confirmed to them that she had paid the rent each month in cash: £850. Webb sat on the couch with one leg crossed over his knee and looked at the stacked CD system, the Sony television set and the polished mahogany coffee table. Weir was in the kitchen and Webb could hear him poking around.

'What're you looking for?' he said, as he went through.

Weir stood up and his knees cracked. 'Showing my age again.' He held a bottle of Veuve Cliquot in his hand. 'This was in the fridge,' he said, 'and have you clocked the wine rack?'

Webb followed his gaze and noticed that the rack, which formed part of the main kitchen cabinets, was very well stacked. Weir slid out a bottle with a label Webb did not recognise. 'This isn't your average Hungarian Bull's Blood,' he said. 'We're talking expensive taste here.'

Webb leaned on the kitchen cabinet. 'Eight hundred and fifty quid every month in cash. Who pays their rent in cash in this day and age? It's not as if she didn't have a bank account.'

Back at the embassy, Dan Farrow was waiting for them. The FBI had sent a delegation of observers over from Washington, together with one investigating officer from the State Department. They tagged along with Weir and Webb, and attended the daily briefings back at the Paddington offices of the murder squad.

'The ambassador has actioned your request for everybody who knew Simpson to come forward,' he said. 'He's issued a negative response notice, so we'll have an answer one way or the other from everyone.'

'Good.' Weir unwrapped a piece of chewing gum. 'I'd like to get the interviewing underway as soon as possible.' He glanced at Webb. 'There's a couple of things troubling us, Dan,' he went on. 'Number one, she rented that flat six months ago and it's always been paid for in cash.'

Farrow stared at him. 'That's kind of odd.'

'It is in this day and age.' Weir sat down on the edge of the desk. 'The other thing is the flat itself. We found champagne in the fridge, good-quality red wine in the rack and a lot of designer labels in the wardrobe. How much exactly does a gunnery sergeant earn?'

'I'll find out. You can have access to all her financial records.'

Weir nodded. 'In the meantime, we're going to try and figure out what her last movements were. The pathologist gave her time of death as circa three in the morning, on Sunday the tenth.' He took a selection of photographs from his case, copies of those taken at the crime scene, and spread them on the desk. 'So far, the scenes of crime boys haven't thrown up anything we can get DNA from, but we're still hopeful.' He sat back again. 'She was wearing a nice dress and the neighbour has confirmed that she went out the previous evening around seven o'clock. We don't know how she travelled. She may have called a taxi or taken the tube. It's a bit of walk to Paddington tube station and she was wearing high heels, so we think she took a cab at least that far.' He paused and looked at Webb. 'With a bottle of bubbly in the fridge and the wine and everything, we don't think she was short of money. I'd bet my pension she didn't walk anywhere.'

Farrow nodded. 'Can you check with the cabs in London? There must be a helluva lot of them.'

Weir smiled. 'We've issued a public request for any cabbie to come forward who either picked up or delivered to that address that night. If no one's got anything to hide, we should get something. In the meantime, we've requested the security video tapes from Paddington tube to see if she got on there. If she did, we can start to check her journey.'

'That's a helluva long job.'

'It certainly is, Dan. But we've got enough bodies back at division to cope with it. It's man-hour intensive, which means nothing happens in too much of a hurry, though, I'm afraid.'

Farrow eased the door closed and leaned on it, hands behind his back. 'What about the cash?' he asked. 'Even without salary records, right now, I can tell you that's an expensive apartment. Most of the sergeants live in quarters.'

Webb jangled the change in his pocket. 'There's lots of possibilities,' he said. 'Kibibi was a good-looking girl.'

'Smart, too, from what I can gather.' Farrow pulled a face. 'Me only being *in situ* a couple of weeks doesn't really help you guys that much, huh?'

'No.' Weir looked evenly at him. 'We might want to talk to your predecessor, though.'

'I can arrange that. He's based back in D.C. right now.' He pushed his cheek out with his tongue. 'What about the money?'

'Sugar daddy somewhere, maybe?' Webb said. 'Rich parents?'

Farrow laughed. 'You've seen them, George. They're downhome Mississippi folk, just real proud they got their kids in the service. If anything, the kids send them money, not the other way round.'

'There's other things she could've been doing,' Webb went on. 'It's a nice apartment, and well located. She could have been tomming.'

'What?'

'A hooker,' Weir cut in. 'Prostitution. It would account for the cash.'

Farrow looked wide-eyed at him. 'A serving US marine sergeant – a hooker?'

'It's possible, Dan. Everything here is possible.'

'In which case, her killer could've been just about anyone in London.'

'That's right,' Webb said. 'Man or woman.'

Farrow blew out his cheeks. 'Well, gentlemen,' he said. 'I'll get the responses from all staff to you just as soon as they come in. UK and US personnel.' He paused in the doorway. 'By the way, the ambassador wants to be kept up to date at all times on this thing. Is that OK?'

'Of course.' Weir smiled at him.

They drove back to Southwick Street and the wine bar below Kibibi's rented flat. Two Australian girls were serving. They told them that Kibibi did frequent the place quite a bit.

'She drank a lot of wine,' one of them said. 'Always red, unless it was champagne.'

'Expensive red?' Webb asked her.

The girl nodded. 'I'd say so.' She looked at her colleague. 'That'd be right, Gail, eh?'

'Yeah. I reckon.'

'Who did she come in with?' Weir asked her.

'What d'you mean?'

'I mean, regularly. Did she come in with anyone on a regular basis?'

The girls said that they had only been working there a month and had not noticed anyone in particular, but they called the Italian manager, who was very helpful. He leaned on the bar, sleeves pushed up, hairy arms making up for the lack of it on his head. 'Yeah,' he said. 'You could not help but notice. Very pretty girl. Even in this bar, where we get lots of pretty girls.'

'Was there anyone who accompanied her or met her here regularly?' Webb asked him.

'One guy, sometimes. They come in late, maybe two, three times a week.'

'What did he look like?'

The Italian lifted his shoulders. 'He's not been here in a long time. Maybe four or five weeks.' He made an open-handed gesture. 'But he was white and he was a lot older than her, I think. Maybe forty-five, maybe fifty. I don't know.'

'Can you describe him?'

'Sure. He was always well dressed. Nice suits. Armani mostly.' He gave a wry smile. 'He had grey hair, lots of gel, always flat and right back on his head. You know, like Michael Douglas in *Wall Street*. Good-looking guy. He always liked to look at himself in the mirror.' He tapped the glass behind the bar. 'Vain, I think. You know.'

'Would you recognise him again?'

'Oh sure. He was American, I think.' He gestured with his fingers to his mouth. 'You know the accent.'

Webb glanced at Weir. 'If we sent an artist down here, could you describe him more fully?'

'Sure.'

Weir got up off the stool. 'What about anyone else?'

'She was with one other guy a couple of times. Black. Tall, I think. With the haircut right up here.' He rubbed his hand up the back of his head.

'American?' Webb asked.

'I don't know. I didn't hear him speak.'

They walked outside and Weir unlocked the car with the remote. 'A grunt,' he said.

'The one with the haircut.'

'Yeah.' Webb leaned on the roof. 'A grunt and Gordon Gekko.'

'Grey hair, slicked right back, about forty-five.' Farrow sat at his desk and looked at Webb standing opposite him. Weir had gone back to divisional headquarters to see how the video-watching session was going.

'Well dressed,' Webb added.

'Shit.' Farrow sat forward. 'That sounds like Mitch Arnold, my predecessor.'

Webb cocked one eyebrow. 'The previous RSO?'

Farrow nodded.

'D'you know him?'

'He's a lot older than I am, but yes, I know him.'

Webb sat down. 'What's he like?'

'Well, he's in his mid-forties, very fit, always tanned. Likes to play tennis and golf. Hangs out with the right kinda people.' Farrow broke off. 'George. The guy's been back in Washington for weeks. He couldn't have done it.'

'I know that, Dan. But I'm thinking of something else.'

'Like the apartment?'

'Yeah. Somehow, she must've paid for it. You said yourself, it's out of a gunnery sergeant's league.'

Farrow squinted at him. 'You figure maybe Arnold was playing sugar daddy. He's got a wife and four kids in college.'

'That must be expensive.'

Farrow nodded. 'In the United States. No kidding.' He laughed then. 'Kibibi was a good-looking gal, George.'

'It wouldn't be the first time.' Webb stood up. 'I want to talk to him.'

'I figured you would. Listen, he's real well thought of in the department. Can you make it discreet?'

'Initially, I can. But I can't guarantee to keep it that way.'

'I'll try and get hold of him for you.'

Webb got up and turned for the door, then a thought occurred to him. 'Has he been in touch since the murder?'

Farrow nodded. 'I got one call and then an e-mail. The call was right after it happened and I passed the e-mail on to her folks.'

'How did he sound on the phone?'

'I don't know. As shocked as everybody else, I guess. Why?'

'No reason. I just wondered, that's all.'

Back at the incident room, Webb relayed the information to Weir.

'So, you're thinking that maybe Arnold was paying for the flat so he had somewhere they could sleep together,' he said.

'We'll have to ask him. But in and out of the wine bar with her, fancying himself – it's got more mileage than her being on the game.'

Weir nodded. 'We've had a result with the tube station,' he said. 'No cabbie's come forward yet, but she definitely caught a train from Paddington at eight o'clock on the night she died.'

'But we don't know where to yet?'

Weir shook his head. 'She had a one-day Travelcard in her wallet, which doesn't tell us anything.'

Webb groaned. 'So now we have to look at the tapes from every possible tube station in London.'

'Well.' Weir sat forward. 'Not every one. Think about it, George. The girl was all dolled up. It's got to be somewhere up west.'

'Not necessarily. Some of the trendiest clubs are in the East End now, or Tulse Hill, or even Brixton.' Webb went on. 'She was black, wasn't she?'

'Yeah. But with a penchant for well-dressed, middle-aged white men. I think we can discount Brixton, George.'

The Cub flew into London under the mutual visa waiver system. A tourist looking to see the sights – the Tower of London, Buckingham Palace, etc. He was booked into the Marriott, close to the US Embassy, which he thought was a nice touch on Cyrus Birch's part. The last time they had met, when Birch flew out to Boise, he had been agitated. He had tried not to show it: Mr Cool, as ever. But years of covert action had taught The Cub to detect the simplest of changes in behaviour. It was an art he had perfected and one that had saved his life on more than one occasion.

He had driven down from Kamiah where he was visiting his mother, still a shaman for the Nez Percé tribe; and he had put himself through the purification ceremony after what had gone on in Afghanistan. He had never told her what work he did and she had never asked. She had stood by him all the time he was at Leavenworth, and then been amazed at his perfect French when he returned from five years with the Legion. That was when Birch had first approached him. Unbeknown to him, he had been earmarked for special ops way back, when he graduated with the Marine Corps. His superiors had marked him out as instinctively special and the IAD boys from the Agency had looked him over. But then he got mad with his wife, tried to kill her and her boyfriend, and did the seven-year stint in Leavenworth for attempted manslaughter.

His father had been born to a white man and one of his imported Chinese whores, and had grown up as a ridiculed half-caste during the heavy mining days in southern Idaho, back in the thirties. When he got old enough to quit school, he had travelled north and wound up on the Nez Percé reservation amongst Chief Joseph's descendants. He fitted in. Dark-haired and dark-skinned, he looked more like an Indian than a white boy. He married a shaman and they had one son, but he had died in a hunting accident when his son was only four. For the first twelve years of his life, the boy had slept in animal skins and one day he came home with a mountain lion cub, not thinking that its mother would come looking for it. She did, and from that day to this, he had been known simply as The Cub. It was a story he liked to tell to the whores he slept with, especially the bit about his grandma.

He knew he made Birch nervous – the man was a pen-pusher, an Ivy League turtle-hopper, no doubt with his sights set on the DDO's desk or even the DCI's. To him, men like The Cub were something of an enigma: in some ways no better than criminals, yet working for the United States government. Birch had met him at the Kopper Kitchen by the airport. The only other patrons were a couple of maintenance men bullshitting at the bar, one wearing a Navy Seals T-shirt, which meant he had probably been a cook on the *Nimitz* during his time in the service. Birch had been in a side booth and The Cub sat down next to him.

'What news?' he said.

Birch picked at the paper beer mat. 'We've had word. It appears your information was correct. The rules of the game have changed.'

'Cyrus.' The Cub sat forward. 'When I get information from somebody, they don't get a chance to lie to me.'

Birch looked at him, and The Cub's eyes were dead and cold.

'He's gone underground.'

The Cub sat back and nodded. 'Where?'

'Well, we don't know exactly, but al-Bakhtar showed up in London.'

In the mêlée on the pavement at Heathrow Airport, the Cub stood waiting for a cab. The day was cool and cloudy, and the air stank of traffic fumes. He closed his eyes and thought back to the mountains of Idaho twenty-four hours earlier. Then he let his mind focus on Mujah al-Bakhtar: that tall black Somali who wanted to rip his head off in Afghanistan. That would be a good meeting. But wherever the IAD had got their information, it was not as good as they would have liked. The word was that al-Bakhtar had taken a flight from Orly Airport in Paris to London, under one of his West Indian pseudonyms. But that was the only word. What happened to the West Indian when he landed, where he went and who he met was a mystery. But the word was out and both the Agency here in London as well as the NSA back home were scouring the British intelligence landscape for signs. Nobody knew what Bin Laden was doing – whether he was planning some other major action or merely hiding out. But wherever al-Bakhtar went, Bin Laden would be close by.

He jumped in a cab and rode to the Marriott. His long hair had been cut short and he was travelling as an American businessman on vacation. Charles Canning had a reservation for two weeks at the Marriott. After that, it was up to The Talent to shift him, get fresh ID if needs be, until his quarry could be run to ground. The Cub was as relaxed as he had ever been on a covert mission alone. This was the

West after all, a friendly town like London where they all but spoke the same language. It could have been Beirut or Pakistan again, where he had hunted Yousef down for the FBI. In comparison, London was easy. He would spend his days looking the place over and reconnoitring until such time as word came. Not only that, but he had other plans as well. The one thing he needed and lacked in Islamabad was somebody he knew he could trust to watch his back. In his line of business, people like that were few and far between, and not once had The Talent or the Intelligence Support Activity ever come up with a local operative who was up to it. He was not sure how much he would need to watch his back, but he was on British soil and, whatever Birch told him, he knew that the British secret services were good. If word had leaked to Afghanistan, it sure as hell had leaked across here. He was as adept as anyone at counter-surveillance measures, but it would be reassuring to have some back-up of his own. He had basically told Birch that he now had a second man on the payroll. After that, it had been a covert phone call to a small restaurant in the mountains of northern Spain.

He walked up the steps of the Marriott and nodded to the doorman in his top hat and tailcoat. Inside, he stood at reception and waited while two fat Venezuelans checked out, then booked himself in as Mr Charles Canning.

'Would you like a porter to help with your bags, Mr Canning?'

'No, thank you.' The Cub took the elevator and pressed his swipe card into the lock. The room was in darkness, the curtains pulled, and, as he let the door swish closed, he knew there was somebody there. He stood very still for a full thirty seconds, taking in every tiny sound, every chink of light. Gradually, his eyes grew accustomed to the half-darkness and he made out a shape on the bed.

'*Oui. C'est moi.*'

The voice came out of the darkness and The Cub let his travel bag drop to the floor.

'Je sais. Ça va bien?'

'Bien sûr. Je suis toujours bien.' The lamp came on by the bed and The Cub stared at a lean man in his late thirties, with blond hair and blue eyes.

'How did you know what room they'd give me?'

The man swung his legs over the side of the bed and stood up. They were the same height, the same build, only the guest was lighter-skinned. 'I just utilised certain skills similar to the ones that got me to be referred to as "*mon capitaine*" when we were in the Legion.'

They sat on the bed. This was probably the only man The Cub had ever called, or would ever call, friend in his entire life. Jean-Emmanuel Haan: medically discharged from the 2nd REP commando team, after taking a bullet in the head in Bosnia. He had been part of a rapid reaction force trying to secure Mount Igman. He had medevaced a woman whose baby had just been murdered by the Serbs, and had taken the bullet intended for her. Now they lived together with the Basques high in the mountains of Spain.

Haan sat with his hands resting in his lap. 'I've swept the room and it's clean,' he said. 'No bugs. No cameras. No ultrasound.'

'They know I'm here, then.' The Cub pursed his lips. 'I thought they would. It's why I called you in.'

'Oh, they know you're here all right. England's been a veritable hive of silent activity.' Haan smiled. 'They just don't know why and it's really making them nervous.'

The Cub got up and walked to the window looking out on to Duke Street. Two cars were parked, one where it should not be. He looked for footpads and saw two possibles. Nothing to worry about yet. He turned back into the room. 'Do they know you're here?'

Haan shook his head. 'Of course not. Now, tell me what's going on.'

The Cub went back to the window. The cars were gone and two different footpads were on the street. 'This is gonna be interesting,' he muttered, and turned to Haan once more.

'Mujah al-Bakhtar is in London. We don't know where, we just know he flew in from Paris under a West Indian *nom de guerre.*'

Haan's eyes thinned. 'The Butcher of Bekaa,' he murmured. Then he looked sharply at The Cub. 'If he's here, then ...'

The Cub nodded. 'That's what we think.'

'You're not.'

The Cub smiled. 'Oh yes, I am.'

Fachida Harada rewatched the videotape he had made of the CNN coverage of the three Federal Triangle bombs. He sat in his living room in the sparsely furnished house he had rented in the quiet suburb of Falls Church, and re-examined every frame of the authorities' reaction to the threat. He knew that the FBI led the fourteen formal joint terrorism task forces, and that the New York one had been effective in apprehending the bombers behind the attack on the World Trade Center. On that occasion, however, the perpetrators, except perhaps for Yousef, had been inept to say the least. One of them had even gone back for a refund on the van used in the attack.

Harada studied the screen, identifying the different vehicles in use. He recognised the black Suburbans as the FBI's tactical operations centers. They had computer links to their headquarters and fixed command posts, which, in this case, would be the field office on 4th Street. The Washington police were simple to identify and their task force members had inscriptions on their raid jackets that were similar to those of the FBI. He calculated their response times and how quickly they had begun to instigate the evacuation. This had been done on the ground, initially in the cab and later in the security truck. Harada had set up the videotape to run from the moment he phoned in the coded warning, and was now able to rewatch the whole thing again. It was extremely useful – the US media doing much of his surveillance work for him.

He watched the screen and then replayed the interview given by Carl Smylie. He furrowed his brow, rewound the tape and played it through again. Then he thought for a moment, got up and put another tape in the machine. He wound this one forward until he got to the section at Arlington Cemetery and stopped. Another interview with Carl Smylie. This was the freelance reporter he had seen on national television in Oregon, Missouri and Nevada. This was indeed a unique country – a gross free-for-all, where moderation and manners no longer existed. No wonder the master had been so aggrieved by the 1969 American treaties. He recalled his words now, and then a thought struck him. The Tatenokai: one hundred chosen men to protect what must be protected. Freezing the frame on the television, he moved to his computer and his encrypted e-mail. He sat for a long time and considered the weapons hide where he collected the government C-4 that had absolutely been insisted on. He paused and thought about somebody else's words, words that had been whispered softly to him, while still back in Japan: 'Listen to us you people of America, if you hold worth in your lives, in the lives of your children and your children's children, then change your way in the world . . .'

He sat for a long moment considering the irony and then he summoned the website he wanted, encrypted the source and sent the message on. He switched the computer off and unfolded the copy of the map he had on the wall of the self-storage unit. He had it marked exactly as the other one: red, blue and yellow dots, with road junctions and possible rendezvous points circled in black. He looked again at the blank computer screen and the fresh videotape set to the CNN news channel, then he went out to his grey sedan. Pressure: little by little, gently increasing pressure.

The INS agent attached to the task force was briefing Logan at the Washington field office. They had been scouring the immigration records going back the last six months, but so far had come up with nothing. That morning, the agent had been back at his headquarters instigating a fresh computer scan, with every various possible connection added into the equation. 'It's a helluva task,' he said. 'And even if we locate a possible, I don't see what good it'll do.'

'We have to cover the bases,' Logan told him, irritated. 'You know we have to cover the bases. We never know what they're going to lead to.' She went over to where Swann was finishing a phone call to London.

'I've got some stuff on Harada and Shikomoto,' he told her.

Kovalski looked up at him from behind his desk. 'Shoot, Jack. We need all the leads we can get.'

Swann spread the scribbled notes before him. 'OK,' he said. 'We know they were in the JRA together. In fact, they joined at the same time. They both attended Meiji University, which is effectively where Fusako Shigenobu founded the organisation in the first place, although that was 1971 and both Harada and Shikomoto would have been only about sixteen then. It seems these two guys were pretty inseparable, both during their time in the Bekaa Valley getting trained and while they were operational. According to MI5, they worked as a two-man unit on more than one occasion – in France with Carlos, and later when Shigenobu was contracting them out to Colonel Qaddafi.' He looked at Kovalski. 'You already have Shikomoto banged up for the mortar attack in Jakarta, and it's more than likely that the other player was Harada.' He made a face. 'What I don't get is how you could never ID him. If the CIA knew it was Shikomoto and knew there were two of them, then the other one almost had to be Harada.' He glanced at Logan. 'They couldn't find him?'

'They couldn't give us an ID, Jack.' She made an open-handed gesture. 'Shit. Sometimes it happens that way.'

Swann looked back at his notes. 'They both must have gone to North Korea, because we lost sight of them after MI5 learned there were plans to attack targets in the UK, in the aftermath of the Libyan air raids. Harada did not show up in Japan again, according to the NPA over there, until 1992, when they began to monitor his activities with the *sokaiya*. There were only ever twenty or so hardcore members of the JRA, so I guess the money they made, which was literally millions of dollars, must have been divided between them. No doubt Shigenobu took the lion's share, but Harada must have had a bucketful or he could never have made *sokaiya*. The yakuza are extremely careful who makes their way into the white-collar ranks.' He paused and scanned the notes again. 'Maybe they trusted Harada because of his samurai connections, I don't know. But his family seem to have kept the tradition alive for generations. The NPA have done a family tree going back as far as 1790. They're going to beam it over to us here.' He paused again. 'Harada's married. He's got two kids living in Tokyo. I guess the yakuza are taking care of them for him.'

Logan cut in on him. 'Are the yakuza involved in this, Jack?'

'I don't know. The NPA have been pretty discreet in their enquiries.' He lifted his hands, palm up. 'As far as we can see, Shikomoto was nothing to do with any form of organised crime in Japan. He was in North Korea with Harada, but left two years earlier. He didn't return to Japan till 1995.' He looked at Kovalski again. 'I guess that's when you first caught up with him.'

Kovalski nodded. 'We think he moved around quite a lot after he bombed our embassy and he certainly hid out in North Korea. But the National Security Agency checked him out in Manchuria and Mongolia as well as back in Lebanon, before he assumed a new identity and went home to Japan.'

'There's nothing there to suggest why Harada is so pissed off about his friend, other than the fact that they worked together for the JRA.' He got up and paced to the window. 'The other thing I can't really get my head round at the moment is this samurai connection. The JRA didn't adhere to any samurai traditions. They were radically left wing to begin with and then just plain greedy. The samurai were right wing, if anything, and they were all about honour.'

'What about religion?' Logan asked him.

'You mean like a sort of Japanese equivalent of an Islamic fundamentalist?'

'Why not?'

Swann shook his head. 'Chey, the samurai followed the Shinto sect. They were Buddhists.'

Kovalski ran a hand through his hair. 'How the fuck can anybody as aggressive and warlike as the samurai be a Buddhist? They're pacifists for Christ's sake.'

Swann smiled. 'Puzzling, isn't it? One thing I do know is that the only way the samurai could reconcile their religion with their way of life was, ironically, the Buddhist belief in reincarnation. They believed that being samurai was a punishment. Every time they died, they would be reincarnated again as samurai, as an atonement for their previous lives. Every life lived, every generation, destined never to attain Nirvana, doomed to live eternally as reincarnated samurai.'

Logan got up and shifted the gun under her arm. She shook her head and bent to the water cooler for a drink. 'You think Harada believes all this, Jack?'

'Yes, I do. If he genuinely sees himself as samurai.'

Kovalski stared at the wall. 'Makes him a fucked-up sonofabitch, doesn't it?'

Smylie was busy at his computer screen, typing an editorial for the *Washington Post*, when a fresh e-mail envelope interrupted his flow. He cursed and looked at his wristwatch, considered the editor's deadline and figured he had enough time to make some fresh coffee. Things had been pretty hectic of late, and all the years of work he had done on the rise of the far right was beginning to pay off. He thought of the hours he had spent listening to Butler or Trochmann, or Bo Gritz back in 1992. He thought of Billy

Bob Lafitte and Jack McClamb, and Louis Beam when he first called for the single-cell Leaderless Resistance in Colorado, after Randy Weaver was arrested. Hours of rhetoric from demented men, or so he had thought. At that time, it was anti-government and a good source of story fodder for an aspiring freelance journalist. Nobody had listened to him then, but after Oklahoma, he had got his first piece taken by the *Washington Post* and it was syndicated to the London *Times*. From then on, whenever anything happened which had militia or patriot connotations, he was the guy they called. Since those three gooks showed up in Hope Heights, Oregon, he had more videotape of himself than he did of Jack Nicholson, and he loved old Jack.

He had no idea who these Orientals were, though, or why Lafitte, Pataki and now Tommy Anderson had been murdered. It made no sense to the regular rational man, but it fulfilled the prophetic judgements of the militia-minded. Black helicopters and one hundred thousand Hong Kong troops in America. The phone rang: the features editor at the *Post* trying to hurry him along. Back at his computer, he looked again at the e-mail envelope, then opened it. He stared at the screen, sitting very still, and sweat gathered on his palms.

Swann and Logan sat at the bar of the Hyatt by the National Airport, drinking shots of Jagermeister with cold beer chasers. It had been a long and arduous day, the sort of day Swann remembered during the height of IRA activity, when one set of twenty-four hours just rolled into the next and your headache was kept at bay by a cocktail of painkillers, coffee and willpower. Logan, seated next to him on the stool, yawned and lifted a hand to her mouth. Swann noticed that even in this day and age, a number of people cast curious glances their way when he kissed her or they held hands, or she rested her head on his shoulder. A white man with a black woman in America. It was still less than accepted.

He swallowed cold crisp beer and ate handfuls of pretzels. Logan smiled and placed her hand over his. 'You sure you don't want dinner, Jack?'

'It's too late,' he said. 'I can't be bothered to go through the hassle of sitting at a table.' He glanced at the menu lying on the bar. 'I might just order a bowl of chilli "to go",' he said.

'They do good salt crackers.'

'Do they?' Swann looked at her, but she was staring at the TV set above the bar. The picture was flickering, but there was no sound. Swann followed her gaze and recognised the long hair and round glasses of the sneering Carl Smylie.

'Turn that up, please,' Logan snapped at the barman. He picked up the remote control and increased the volume, and both Swann and Logan sat in silence and listened.

Smylie was in the ABC newsroom talking to the news anchor. On the desk before him, he had a single sheet of paper and was reading from it. 'It came right through to me on my e-mail,' he was saying. 'I'm under no doubt that this is from the Washington bomber.'

Looking down at the sheet of paper, he read the message through again. It talked of the Shield Society being the shield of the emperor. The society was a standby army whose day would come. There would be no demonstrations or Molotov cocktail-throwing, no placards, just patience until the last desperate moment, and then the SS, the Shield Society, would strike.

When Smylie finished reading, he sat up a little straighter and swept his hair back from where it fell across his forehead.

'And you have no idea of the identity of the sender?' the news anchor asked him.

Smylie shook his head. 'Even if I did, I'm a journalist with protocols to think about. I couldn't reveal my source.'

'But you're sure this is the bomber?'

'Positive. The e-mail address was encrypted, technically

withheld.' He gestured towards the camera. 'It would appear to me from reading this that the Shield Society must be some form of collective code for the movement I've been studying over the past seven years. Why else would someone send it to me?'

'And the initials SS?' the news anchor said. 'They're pretty emotive, not to say apt, given the alleged Nazi sympathies some of the more radical groups hold.'

Smylie nodded. 'I can understand the connotations that spring to mind, but I believe the wording is the most significant thing. "A standby army. No way of knowing when our day will come. The least armed, most spiritual army in the world."' He looked at the camera again. 'For years, certain groups of people in this country have been predicting the rise of the New World Order under the auspices of the United Nations. These predictions were accompanied with what many have described as anti-federalist paranoia: black helicopters, Crips and Bloods, one hundred thousand Hong Kong troops covertly trying to disarm the people. Well, just a few weeks ago all that so-called paranoia changed. Daniel Pataki was found dead in Missouri. The FBI had a UFAP warrant out on him, and lo and behold he shows up dying of yellow fever. Then there was Billy Bob Lafitte, a vociferous opponent of federal agencies. He had his brake lines cut. Then Tommy Anderson in Nevada. Three oriental men in a black, unmarked helicopter.' Again, he looked at the camera. 'You know, I've studied this for over seven years, and like most people in this country I'm against the bombing of federal buildings or abortion clinics. I figured all this was just overactive imagination, peddling that great American export – the conspiracy theory. But now we've had three citizens murdered. There are no suspects except a bunch of mysterious Orientals wearing government suits and driving what look like government vehicles.'

Swann stared at Logan. 'Can he say all this on national TV?'

She laid a hand on his arm. 'Honey, this is America. He can say what the hell he likes.'

Swann looked back at the screen. Smylie was saying that, in his opinion, the bombings in the Federal Triangle were the work of one of the right-wing groups, in retaliation for what they perceived to be government-inspired murders. 'If this government's not real careful,' he said, pointing a finger at the camera, 'it's gonna have a civil war on its hands.'

16

In Kovalski's office, the clock ticked beyond midnight. Logan was waiting for the phone to ring. Carmen McKensie had paged her as soon as Smylie appeared on TV, and she and Swann had gone back to work. Half the task force was still there. Kovalski's eyes were dark hollows of flesh and he sat with his tie undone, sleeves pushed up, sipping at a cup of water. 'Well, at least Smylie got his facts wrong,' he said. 'If that message did come from Harada.'

Swann sat forward and hunted for a cigarette in his pockets, then remembered he was not allowed to smoke in the building. 'It's unlikely that it did, Tom, surely. The language, the rhetoric, sounds like militia to me.'

Kovalski made a hopeless gesture. 'I don't know, Jack. Normally, I'd agree with you, but this whole situation is so damned weird. Anything goes, as far as I'm concerned.'

Logan yawned. 'If it was him, he'll call. It's time he called, anyway.' She stared at the phone, but it remained silent.

'It's got to be the militia,' Swann went on. 'SS. Standby army. Spirituality. They think they're Christians, don't they?'

Kovalski nodded. 'Christian Identity. British Israelism. The twelve tribes of Israel being the children of Satan, not God. White Anglo-Saxons are the true chosen ones and America the promised land.'

'Yackety, yackety, yah. And I'm one of the mud people.' Logan got up and unfastened her shoulder holster, laying it across the back of the chair. She winked at Kovalski. 'Jack still can't figure me packing, Tom. I don't think he's up for the idea of me defending him in a firefight.'

Swann ignored her. 'What about the emperor?' he said. 'That doesn't sound like the militia.'

Kovalski lifted a palm. 'Who knows, Jack? The Klan has a grand dragon. Why can't they have an emperor?'

'Japan *has* an emperor.'

Kovalski nodded. 'Anyways, there's nothing doing on that front till the morning. All the dweebs are sleeping right now.'

The phone rang. For a moment they all stared at it, then Kovalski picked it up. 'ASAC.'

At first he heard nothing, and then: 'Smylie's interpretation is interesting, but that doesn't help you. You have till noon tomorrow to release Shikomoto.'

'Harada,' Kovalski said.

'Noon.' Harada put down the phone.

Swann had three hours' sleep and then Logan woke him with a kiss. He half opened his eyes, blinked and smelled her hair against his face. It was just about light outside the hotel bedroom window. 'Rise and shine, sweet thing,' she murmured.

'Ah, Cheyenne. I'm not even being paid for this.' Swann rolled on his side and she moved herself next to him, slowly letting her hand drift across his belly. Swann woke up.

'Bastard,' he said, flicking shower water at her as she came into the bathroom, still naked.

'You loved it.'

'I know. It's the fact that you know it that pisses me off.'

She thumbed her nose at him and went through to get dressed.

Kovalski did not look as though he had been to sleep and his office was crowded with the senior members of the task force. The liaison officers from the metropolitan police were there, together with the ATF and Mallory from the VICAP. Kovalski looked up again as Swann and Logan came in. 'Noon, today,' he said. 'What d'you reckon?'

Swann shrugged. 'Everything he's said so far has been right. He's done what he said he would do.'

'It's six now,' Kovalski said. 'That gives us six hours.'

'Where exactly is Shikomoto, anyway?' a Washington cop asked.

'He's at Eastpoint in Georgia.'

'Why not talk to him? See if you can find out what the hell is going on here?'

Kovalski looked at him then and nodded. 'I've thought of that, believe it or not. But right now, we got a clear field in front of us. Harada, for reasons of his own, has chosen not to reveal his identity or his war cry to the press, which is to our advantage. It's in our interests to discuss him publicly as an "unknown suspect" only. If we talk to Shikomoto, then the word will spread. It just takes one prison guard to mutter it outside.' He shook his head. 'Besides, Shikomoto doesn't want to talk to us, and finding out why Harada wants him released so badly is not necessarily gonna help us catch him.'

'It might create an angle for negotiation,' Mallory suggested.

'It might, but we're not gonna release Shikomoto, so I want to keep him out of it for the time being.' Kovalski looked at Swann again. 'Jack, your research threw up nothing that links Shikomoto with Harada other than their days in the JRA. Am I right?'

Swann nodded. 'They were in the JRA together. They're both married and both have families in Japan.'

'Which excludes Japanese organised crime connections, or at least makes them very unlikely.' Kovalski sat back in his chair. 'OK. We've got till noon.' He looked at the police chief. 'Let's get as many cops on the street as we can. Visible show of force.'

'Legion patrols,' Swann muttered.

'What?'

'It's what we call them in London. It's a good idea.'

Kovalski looked at the police chief once more. 'Can you organise it with the parks, the metro and the counties?'

'I'll get right on it.' The police chief got up from his chair and left.

Swann looked at Kovalski. 'Why d'you think Harada's chosen to keep his identity secret?'

'I don't know.'

'Weird that he should send that message to Smylie.'

'Perhaps he's keen to exploit the militia links, Jack. The inference has been there from the get-go. Maybe that's not coincidence.'

'You could go public and dismiss the militia thing.'

'I'd like to. The militia link is far more dangerous in its implication than Harada's own agenda.'

'Unless they really are linked,' Logan put in. She stood up. 'He sent that message to Smylie to perpetuate that rumour. Tom, I figure we ought to find out what it really means.' She picked up a copy of the *Washington Post* that lay on the circular table.

Swann looked up at her. 'How?'

'George Washington University. The Japanese history department.'

They were met by a small, quietly spoken Japanese woman in her fifties. She introduced herself as Akiko Habe, the chair of the faculty. Logan had cut out the section of newspaper where the message from Harada to Carl Smylie had been reproduced and showed it to her.

The woman offered them seats in her office, then sat behind her desk and took her glasses from the case at her elbow. 'I heard this on the television last night,' she said. 'I thought it interesting then, and now it's in print, I can see just what it is.'

'Does it refer to some kind of militia group?' Logan asked her.

The woman smiled, steepled her fingers under her chin,

and looked from Logan to Swann and back again. 'After a fashion, yes.'

'Dr Habe,' Logan went on. 'You need to understand that this conversation must remain confidential. We're trying to catch this bomber, and we want as many cards in our hand as possible. If too much is made public too quickly, our job will be that much harder.'

The woman nodded. 'I understand,' she said. 'Don't worry. This conversation will remain entirely confidential.'

'Can you tell us anything about the message?' Swann said.

'Young man, I can tell you everything about it.' She picked up the paper and reread the message aloud. Then she paused and sat back in her chair. 'The Shield Society,' she said. 'In Japanese, it is the Tatenokai, a group of one hundred men. It was a private army, or was purported to be such, at least. Formed in 1970 in Japan, by Yukio Mishima.'

Swann stared at her. 'Mishima.'

'D'you know him?'

'I've heard of him.'

'He followed the way of the samurai, Mr Swann,' she said. 'Or, at least, he tried to. He certainly died that way. On 25 November 1970, he committed *sepukko*. Are you familiar with the ceremony?'

Swann nodded. 'Hara-kiri. Stab yourself in the stomach, then draw the knife from one side to the other and cut upwards.'

'Indeed.' Dr Habe sat forward again. 'A friend close by to decapitate you when the suffering becomes unbearable. If it were not for the beheading, death could take hours, days even. The warrior chose the abdomen because it was the centre of being, the soul – the basis for all the emotions.'

'What was the Tatenokai for?' Logan asked her.

'Mishima believed that Japan was falling into spiritual ruin, particularly after the treaties of 1969 were signed with

316

the United States. He saw Japanese society as being infected and all that was pure being eroded.'

'Was he from a samurai background?'

She shook her head. 'In reality, no. He did not have the lineage. But he chose to adopt it. In sentiment, given his suicide, it's hard not to accept that he embraced the tradition wholeheartedly. The Shield Society was there to protect the emperor when the rest of the country was falling into western degradation. That's how Mishima viewed it, at least. Other people thought he was mad.' She looked at Logan again. 'In answer to your original question, it does indeed draw some parallels with the patriot movement here. The reporter on television believed this message came from the militia.' She smiled again. 'After a fashion, it did.'

Logan nodded. 'We know who it came from, Dr Habe. And you're right, it certainly was not the militia in the given sense of the word.'

Swann was chewing his lip. 'Dr Habe,' he said. 'Mishima was married, wasn't he?'

She nodded.

'But didn't I remember reading somewhere that he was homosexual?'

Again she nodded. 'You did. Many of his novels had elements of that theme, most explicit in *Confessions of a Mask*.'

'But he *was* married.'

'Yes.' She clasped her tiny hands together. 'You must understand that Mishima really did embrace the way of the bushido. In ancient Japan, many of the samurai warriors had male lovers. Love between warriors was the highest form of that expression.' She shook her head. 'Terms such as heterosexual or homosexual were not even thought of. There were no words for them. There was no single essence of sexuality. The warriors had wives and children; the whole family was samurai. But the greatest expression of love was between warriors, both platonic and physical love. The samurai were the fiercest swordsmen who ever lived,

317

but equally they were some of the most delicate and refined people. They would spend as much time painting or writing poetry, arranging flowers perhaps, as they would practising their swordsmanship.'

Swann was staring at Logan. 'Homosexual love.' He looked back at Dr Habe. 'Doctor,' he said. 'Would one warrior go to war over the love of another?'

'Certainly,' she said. 'If his honour had been besmirched in some way.' She smiled then. 'Honour was everything to a samurai. If he fell from his own grace, he would fall on his own sword.'

'Harada's gay.' Logan rested her fists on Kovalski's desk. 'He's in love with Tetsuya Shikomoto.'

Kovalski stared at her. 'You're sure?'

They told him what they had discovered from Dr Habe. 'She's an expert on ancient Japanese history,' Logan finished.

Kovalski drew his brows together in a frown. 'So, you're telling me Harada's bombing us because we arrested his boyfriend.'

'Possibly.' Swann looked at him. 'Carlos did it to the French, Tom. The Paris–Toulouse Express. Cafés, discos. He killed a lot of people just because his girlfriend was banged up.'

Kovalski sat back. 'So he's gay.' He chipped at his teeth with his knuckles. 'We can use that.'

'If he gives us the chance to talk to him.' Logan made a face. 'Which, so far, he hasn't.'

'He holds all the aces,' Swann said. 'He's been a terrorist for twenty years. He knows just what to do and just when to do it.' He looked again at Kovalski. 'We know he was in Japan up until six months ago. He must have entered the US on a false passport after then. If he's been here six months, he will have all the groundwork well and truly covered.'

Kovalski looked back at him. 'Jack, you're a real barrel of laughs in the morning, you know that.' He looked at the clock on the wall. It was nine-thirty. 'We got two and a half hours.'

There was nothing they could do but sit and wait, with every FBI agent in the capital on standby. Kovalski had warned everyone up the line; the FBI Director had had another meeting with the national security adviser, and the President was being kept informed. Everybody was agreed that they would not release Shikomoto.

At eleven-thirty, Kovalski's direct line rang and he picked it up. 'Kovalski.'

'There is snow at the foot of Mount Fuji.'

'Harada, listen. We . . .'

'Puddington Place and 3rd Street. You have thirty minutes.'

The phone went dead and Swann could see the sweat on Kovalski's brow. He was on his feet looking at the map, and then he jabbed his index finger into the junction of Puddington Place and 3rd. 'Capitol Hill again.'

'Tom.' Swann laid a hand on his shoulder. 'The device will be in a rubbish bin. He's going to continue to use them until you get them all off the street.'

Kovalski stared at him. 'Yes. And then he'll use the garbage dumps that spring up in their place.' He looked at Logan. 'Let's roll.'

Logan went through to the outer office and sent the warning out over the city. All the elements of the task force would come together again, but this time there was only half an hour to evacuate. Swann stood where he was, as Kovalski strapped on his gun.

'You coming?'

Swann shook his head. 'I'll stay here if you don't mind. Man your phone for you.'

'OK.' Kovalski ducked out of the door.

Swann sat down behind Kovalski's desk and picked up a copy of the Constitution, which Kovalski always kept there. A small white booklet entitled *We the People*. He flicked it open and read the Second Amendment: 'A well regulated militia being necessary for the security of a free State, the right of the people to keep and bear arms shall not be infringed.' He thought about Smylie and his comments on the television. He thought about the death of the detective in Hope Heights, Oregon, and the murders of Tommy Anderson and Billy Bob Lafitte. Three oriental men. He thought about what Dr Habe had told them this morning: Yukio Mishima and the Tatenokai. Then he considered the similarities between Mishima's sentiments and those espoused by the modern US militias. Was this all just a wonderful coincidence for Harada? Or was there something else going on here, something far more sinister?

He sat, thought and watched the clock as it ticked towards twelve o'clock. He heard the sirens screaming outside, vehicles racing from every part of the city. Then a thought struck him and a shiver rippled across his scalp. He called Logan on her cellphone. 'Chey, it's me. Listen, where's the RVP?'

'I'm standing in it.'

'It's an obvious place, right?'

'Yeah, it's two blocks down the street.'

'Search it.'

'It's been searched already.'

'Get them to search it again. Listen, Chey. He'll have monitored what happened the last time. Search that RVP again. He may not want to kill civilians, but anybody connected to law enforcement is the enemy. Get them to search it again.'

'OK. I'll do it.' She hung up, and Swann could feel the sweat on his brow. He got up and went into the outer office where the Triggerfish operators were sitting, just waiting for Harada to call. They had been working round the clock since the equipment had been set up; double shifts, then changeover. Swann looked at his watch. Three minutes to twelve.

'It's gonna go bang again, isn't it?' one of the technicians said to him.

Swann nodded.

'Gonna piss people off real quick.'

'Yes.'

'Not used to it, you see, us Americans. This doesn't happen too often here.'

'I know.' Swann turned back into Kovalski's office. Two minutes to twelve. The phone rang and Swann jumped. He glanced over his shoulder at the technicians and then reached for it.

'Harada,' he said.

'Who is this?'

'Jack Swann, the Englishman.' Swann watched the clock ticking down. 'Listen, we know about Shikomoto. We know about Mishima. It doesn't have to be this way.'

'Oh, but it does, Mr Swann.'

'"Snow at the foot of Mount Fuji", that's what Yukio Mishima means, isn't it?' Swann watched the clock. 'Mishima wasn't his real name, was it?'

'The master.'

'Is that what you think?'

'You cannot keep me talking. Thirty-third and Prospect. You have another thirty minutes.'

'Harada, wait.'

Harada hung up. Swann held the phone, and then the bomb went off and the glass rattled in the windowpanes. Frantically, he dialled Logan's cellphone. She answered and he breathed more easily. 'Are you OK?'

'Yeah. The RVP's safe, Jack. It's OK. It's gone off, though.'

'I know. I heard it. It's bigger than the last ones. Listen.' Swann told her what Harada had said.

'Oh, Jesus.'

Logan put the phone down and Swann looked up to see one of the Triggerfish technicians looking at him. 'We got a fix on the phone,' he said. McKensie was standing behind him. 'It's a payphone right outside.'

Swann went out on to the street with McKensie and she

321

led the way past the Judiciary Center to where two payphones stood outside the Lutheran church. Some of the traffic had been redirected this way and everywhere was chaos, police cars and sirens. Swann touched McKensie's arm as they got closer. 'Gently, Carmen. We're the enemy, remember?' They stopped fifty yards away and Swann scrutinised the phones.

McKensie crossed the street to the little park, chasing up an evidence response team on her cellphone. They were struggling, though. All resources had been directed at the first threat and now there was another one – Prospect and 33rd Street – right in the middle of Georgetown.

Swann could see something on the phone booth, but he could not make out what it was. 'Have you got any binoculars, Carmen?'

'Upstairs.'

'Send somebody down with them, will you?'

One of the support staff came out on to the street with the binoculars, and Swann lifted them to his eyes, focused, then surveyed the booth again. On top of the coin box, he could see a small plastic sandwich box. Slowly, he shook his head. 'He's booby-trapped the phone booth,' he murmured. 'He deliberately stayed on the line long enough so we'd know.'

Harada phoned in three more coded warnings and exploded five bombs in various parts of the city. The fifth was just across the Maryland State line. By the end of the day, two civilians had been killed and thirteen were in hospital, two of them critically injured. The city had been brought to a standstill and every news station across the world was broadcasting the chaos. The Cub lay on the bed in his hotel room and watched the BBC news show an FBI spokesman giving a press conference in the quadrangle at the Hoover building.

'My name's Kovalski,' the spokesman said. 'As you know, today has been the worst in Washington's history as far as active terrorism is concerned. We've had to deal with five separate improvised explosive devices, in five separate locations.' He paused and looked into the camera. 'Last night, CNN broadcast an interview with Carl Smylie, a reporter who received a message allegedly from the bomber. Mr Smylie's interpretation of that message was that the bomber was part of a militia group taking revenge on us for the murders of three militia leaders.' He took a breath. 'Firstly, the bomber here in Washington is not, I repeat *not*, connected to any group, organised or otherwise. As you are aware, we have received warnings about the devices. Initially, forty-five minutes for the Arlington one. This enabled us to evacuate the area without loss of life. Today, however, that warning time was reduced to just thirty minutes. Subsequently, two civilians have been murdered and a number are in hospital.' He paused long enough to let his words sink in.

'Secondly, neither the FBI nor any other federal agency has any connection with the killing of alleged militia leaders. On the contrary, we're offering the local police departments every possible assistance in order to apprehend those who are responsible. Our opinion is that the three Orientals who have been sighted have been used deliberately to feed the conspiracy theories that, if we are not very careful, will undermine this society.' He broke off and looked at the camera again. 'We know the identity of the bomber here in Washington. Thus far, we've not released the information publicly because we did not want to initiate a spate of hoax sightings and callers. In the light of today's events, however, and those of last night, *vis-à-vis* the telecast, we have decided to issue the following statement.

'The bomber's name is Fachida Harada and he was formerly a member of the Marxist group, the Japanese Red Army. He is a Japanese national and has nothing to do with any US militia group. He is working alone and is demanding the release of a former colleague, arrested in

Japan three years ago for his part in the mortar attack on our embassy in Jakarta, Indonesia, in 1986.'

'Mr Kovalski.' Carl Smylie was seated in the front row of the benches in the FBI quadrangle. 'How do you explain the contents of that message? The references to standby armies, to the Shield Society and the connotations that the initials SS suggest?'

Kovalski looked coldly at him. 'Mr Smylie. I think it might've been helpful if you'd brought the information you received directly to the FBI, instead of going on national television to spread rumours.' He leaned on the lectern. 'I'm not going to answer any questions at this time. Further statements will be issued through the Office of Public and Congressional Affairs.' He paused. 'The important thing here is to catch Fachida Harada. We will be publishing photographs of him and welcome any support the public can give us.'

The Cub got up and switched off the TV. He yawned, stretched and looked out of the window. The two spotters were still there, parked in their cab at the bottom of the road. He shook his head at them and smiled, then he flicked open his cloned mobile phone and dialled.

Kovalski was back in the field office, having been grilled like a trout by his superiors. The pressure was bearing down like a ton of bricks now: the city in a panic, and business and government departments alike, all wanting a result and wanting it yesterday. Swann and Logan were in his office, taking calls like everyone else about sightings of Harada, particularly around the phone booth in 4th Street. They had issued a picture to the television stations, which Swann had acquired from the National Police Agency in Japan. It was three years old and showed a slightly built Japanese man, with short-cropped hair and square, indistinctive features.

'Could be anybody.' Logan looked at Kovalski's ravaged face. 'You did a good job, boss,' she said. 'Mind you, we've had thirty-three separate calls since you went on TV, claiming that you're a liar and Harada is one of the Hong Kong troops whose "programming" has destabilised. They reckon the microchip the CIA inserted in his brain must be malfunctioning. He's gonna be something of a hero amongst the militia because of it.'

McKensie came through then and her face was very grey. 'Tom,' she said. 'We just had the Denver field office on the line. The central post office in Colorado Springs has been blown up. No warning. Nobody claiming it.' She paused. 'The ERTs are on-scene now.'

Logan looked at Swann and bit her lip. 'Copycat,' she said. 'There'll be more.'

'There is.' McKensie sifted paper in her hands. 'A state trooper in Michigan was gunned down an hour ago. He stopped a speeding pick-up truck and they shot him dead as he approached the vehicle.'

Kovalski got up and paced the office floor. He thought for a minute, then sat down again and picked up the confidential telephone. Logan looked at him.

'D'you want us to leave, Tom?'

'Hell, no. Stay right where you are.' Kovalski sat back and swivelled in the chair.

'Cyrus Birch, please,' he said. Swann watched him, and Kovalski's eyes were dark and thoughtful in his head. 'Cyrus,' he said, suddenly sitting forward. 'Why don't you guys know anything about Fachida fucking Harada?'

Birch put down the phone and sat in silence for a moment. He thought about Kovalski's words and he pondered. Then he pressed the buzzer on the phone and got his secretary. 'Get me the Tokyo station chief,' he said. 'I don't care what the time is over there.' He sat back again and thought about calling the deputy director of operations just in case, but decided against it.

The station chief came on the line from Tokyo. 'Hello, Maybelline,' Birch said. 'This is Ivy House. I want to see your entire file on Tokyo Joe.' He put the phone down once more and then buzzed through to his secretary again. 'Get me The Talent, will you?'

Harrison rode the boxcar with Southern Sidetrack and Limpet. The Texas plains rolled out on both sides of the train and the breeze did nothing for the heat that scalded the walls. Harrison had survived that first night in the Oklahoma freight yard and nobody had tried anything since. He had woken in the morning to find himself alone, but, with Limpet's pack lying by the embers of the fire, he knew he was being tested. That had been a difficult moment. The temptation to search the pack for drugs was strong, but they had left it deliberately, and Harrison knew from one of the hobos he had met up in Spokane that this was the FTRA's first initiation test. The situation both puzzled and intrigued him. He had known these people a matter of days, had done nothing but get in their faces, and yet they were already testing him for recruitment. Either that, or they figured he might be some kind of undercover agent and were trying to catch him out. He had left the pack alone and Limpet had come back with Sidetrack and the others. They jumped a train heading west on the Southern Pacific line. That had been three days ago now and two more Southern Blacks had got aboard, but they had jumped off north of Wichita Falls, carrying a spare backpack. Now they were heading south for Abilene and had been joined by Hooch and Carlsbad the Bad, who appeared to have three rucksacks between them.

Limpet, Hooch and Carlsbad sat playing five-card draw in a little circle on the floor of the boxcar. Sidetrack sat on his own, sipping from a bottle of mescal. Harrison was standing by the door in his singlet and he could feel Sidetrack's gaze on his arm. It was the tattoo that intrigued them and the tattoo that, for some reason, had kept him alive. He had no idea why. Maybe they just respected Vietnam Vets or maybe there was something else. He ran through the intel' he had stored up in his head. So far, he had identified Limpet, who he already knew from the surveillance in New Orleans, as well as Hooch and Carlsbad, and, most importantly, Southern Sidetrack himself. He considered the rest of the information Spinelli had furnished them with: the Blues or Highrollers up north, led by the Canadian Voyageur; and the Red Heads out west, led by Nixon Bodie, known as Ghost Town.

Harrison looked at Sidetrack again and found him still staring at his arm. 'You keep staring and I'm gonna get nervous. I do strange things when I'm nervous.'

Sidetrack looked at him and shook his head. 'You're one fucked-up sonofabitch. You gotta mouth on you like the Hudson River Tunnel. You know, we could kill you as easy as swatting a fly.'

'I know you all think you could.' Harrison squatted in front of him. 'But I think you'd die trying.'

Sidetrack stared bug-eyed at him and his face flushed red at the jawline. 'Fuck,' he said. 'I figure we'll do it, just to show you we can.'

'Your call, big guy.'

Suddenly Sidetrack laughed. The others looked up, and he shouted to them over the rattle of wheels and the sudden, long whistle blast from the locomotive, a quarter of a mile ahead of them. 'Can you believe this guy?' he yelled. 'He's calling the four of us out.'

Harrison looked him in the eye. 'I'm calling nobody out, Sidetrack. Alls I'm saying is, you better get the drop on me real good, 'cause if you don't, I'll kill you.'

Sidetrack looked at his arm again. 'How many gooks you kill underground?'

'Enough.'

'On your own?'

'Sometimes.' Harrison took out tobacco and papers. He looked down at his arm. 'You got a real thing about this, don't ya?' He looked at the other three. 'You all do.'

Sidetrack shook his head. 'Distinctive tattoo, is all.' He was quiet for a moment, then he said, 'You got brains, Four-String. And for a man your age, you got balls.'

'That's a compliment, is it?' Harrison licked down the paper on his cigarette.

'I like you.' Sidetrack looked at the others. 'Carlsbad over there told me how you was when you ran into the two of them. Takes balls to do that to an FTRA member.' He looked him right in the eye. 'We kill people just because we don't like them.'

Harrison sucked smoke soundlessly. 'I'm fifty years old, Sidetrack. There ain't a whole lot I haven't seen in this world. And nothing that really scares me.' He pointed to the men playing cards. 'When I met up with those two, the odds were two to one. I figure I can adapt to those odds.' He looked back in his eyes. 'Right now, those odds are way out there.' He smiled coldly. 'You'd kill me, all right. But some of you'd die trying.'

Sidetrack sipped mescal. 'We ain't gonna kill you, Four-String. You're free to ride the skids in this part of the country.'

'That's your say-so, is it?'

'You better believe it.' Sidetrack tipped the neck of the bottle again and wiped his mouth with the back of his hand. 'I get to say who lives and who dies in the South. Up north or out west, it's a different story. You travel out there without one of these' – he touched the bandana that pressed his hair to his scalp – 'you're gonna end up in the slicer.'

'You mean there's more of you?' Harrison said.

'Oh yeah. There's more.'

'I'll try to remember, if ever I head out west.' Harrison leaned and spat into the wind.

They rode without conversation for an hour. The game was still going on and Carlsbad called Hooch out as a cheat. They were almost fighting when Sidetrack whacked the floor with the heel of his bottle and told them to quit it. He looked across at Harrison, who sat against the far wall now, with his hat half over his eyes. Harrison could see him squinting again at the tattoo.

They hit the first of the Abilene yards, with dusk falling

like rain clouds across the breadth of the sky. The train slowed and slowed, and they assembled at the door and one by one dropped into the dirt at the trackside. They stood there, Harrison a little apart from the others, watching as the train rumbled on, and then Sidetrack led the way into the yard. There were no guards anywhere that Harrison could see, just the shadowy shapes of the boxcars, some still in use, others clearly broken and beyond commercial value. A small fire burned in a trash can in one corner and three old men sat huddled round it. The Southern Blacks materialised out of the darkness and the old men gathered up their belongings and shuffled into the shadows. Sidetrack bent to the fire and warmed his hands. The temperature was dropping rapidly now, and Harrison threw a blanket round his shoulders and cut some beef jerky from his pack. Carlsbad and Hooch were laughing about the rapid exit of the old hobos and bemoaning the fun they had been denied. Sidetrack was on his second bottle of mescal and Harrison was watching him closely. During the daytime, Sidetrack was rational, even thoughtful. His eyes darted like tiny burning coals and he weighed up each situation. At night, though, he liked to sit round the fire and drink till he passed out, and his words became slurred and evil.

Harrison sat cross-legged, the blanket over his shoulders, and cut himself some more jerky. Limpet squatted next to him and looked at it enviously. 'That the kind with pepper in it?'

Harrison nodded.

'You gonna share?'

Harrison looked at him, sighed and cut a chunk, which he stuffed greedily into his mouth. Hooch produced some *tortillas* and some steak meat, which he dropped into the blackened cooking pot he carried. He had some carrots, which he chopped up, and then Harrison took some potatoes he had bought and cut them into slices with his bowie knife. He added them to the pot and Hooch nodded to him.

They ate out of the one pot with spoons. The stew did not

taste of much, but it was hot and kept the cold from their bones. Afterwards, Hooch broke open a bottle of Kessler. Carlsbad rolled a joint and passed it round, and Harrison sucked the pot deep into his lungs. He lay on one side and watched Sidetrack watching him. 'You gonna play that thing some?' Sidetrack asked him.

Harrison looked at his banjo. 'Only if somebody gets me that missing string.'

Hooch laughed. 'Then we gotta change your name, bro.'

'So buy me the string and keep the fucking name.' Harrison sat up and played them a bad version of 'Me and Bobby McGee'. He watched Sidetrack watching him, as he sang softly and picked away at the strings. 'That's it,' he said. 'There ain't no more till I get me that fifth string.'

There was silence round the fire, just the wind plucking at their clothing through the gaps between the boxcars. Sidetrack looked across the flames into Harrison's eyes. 'You did well the other morning.'

'Excuse me?'

'We left you with Limpet's pack, and when we came back it was still there and so was you, and from the look of things you hadn't touched it.'

Harrison smiled thinly. 'Touch a man's stuff in the hole and you're pushing up dirt.'

Sidetrack nodded. 'You betcha.' He paused, made a face and looked at the others. They were all silent and Sidetrack looked back at Harrison again. 'You wanna run with us for a while?' he asked.

Harrison did not reply. He looked into the fire. 'Figured I might head north,' he said eventually. 'Who do I need to look out for, if I do?'

Limpet flicked a cigarette stub into the fire. 'Highrollers, man. Blue bandanas. Got some mean motherfuckers up there.' He glanced self-consciously at Sidetrack then, as if he had said the wrong thing, but Sidetrack was still looking at Harrison.

'Why go north? It's cold up north.'

'Not at this time of year, it ain't.'

'You got something up north?'

Harrison looked into the fire. 'I guess once upon a time I did.'

'Stick around. Run with us for a while. Nobody's gonna give you no shit.'

Harrison squinted at him. 'You mean you guys or other people?'

'Either.'

'And do what, exactly?'

Sidetrack smiled. 'Who knows? Stick around, Four-String, and you might get a little something for yourself.'

Harrison did not say anything for a moment, then: 'Where you all headed, anyways?'

'All over. We got stuff we gotta do.'

'So this ain't just wandering for the sake of it, then. You got purpose to your travels.'

Sidetrack smiled. 'Four-String, do biker gangs just ride motorcycles?'

'I don't know, man. I never was one for motorcycles.'

'Man.' Sidetrack was beginning to slur. 'We're more powerful than any biker gang you could name. We got connections, brother. And we got a country fulla railroad tracks to ride on.' He broke off and drank. 'And you know what the best thing about it is – no cop, no Fed, nobody knows we're out here.' He tipped his head back and laughed.

In the morning, they moved south again, walking from the freight yard and hooking up with the train as it pulled away from the driver swap. Sidetrack was quiet, evidently suffering from his two bottles of mescal, and Harrison kept his distance and his mouth shut. They jumped an open-topped car, which worsened Sidetrack's mood still further and he cursed the thought of spending the day under the heat of the sun. Harrison sat down in one corner and rested his hat on his knee. This was the fifth day since he had had any contact with Jean and that meant his case agents had no

331

clue where he was. It was not a problem, although they normally liked contact every second or third day when someone was undercover. In the past, he had gone as long as two weeks without surfacing and nobody worried overmuch. He was as experienced at living the lie as just about anybody, but he missed Jean, and images of the one night he had slept in the motel room with her burned with the sun in his head.

Sidetrack watched him even more carefully today, or so it seemed to Harrison. He thought about calling him on it, keeping up with the lippy bravado, but his instincts told him today was the day when Sidetrack might have him killed. So he kept his lip buttoned, held Sidetrack's gaze if he stared, but did nothing else to provoke him.

Sidetrack slept till noon and, when he woke, Harrison shoved a water bottle under his nose. He said nothing, but took the bottle, swallowed noisily and complained about it being overwarm.

'I'll pack an ice box the next time,' Harrison said.

Sidetrack laughed suddenly and stood up. He sucked air into his lungs, shaded his eyes from the sun and looked out at the mesquite plains. 'Where are we?' he said to Hooch.

'I figure we're heading towards Brownwood.'

'Where we picked up that gook that time? Was that south of here?'

'What gook?'

Sidetrack frowned at him. 'Naw,' he said, 'that wasn't you. It was me and Limpet. Hey, Limpet, we pick up that gook about here?'

'The young one?'

Sidetrack nodded.

'Aways south of here, Sidetrack. That was Kinney County.'

Sidetrack leaned and spat into the wind. Harrison stared at his back and pretended not to listen. Limpet got up and unzipped, then stood by the door and urinated, being careful not to let it blow back on his pants. Sidetrack stood at the

332

other end of the doorway and scanned the horizon with one hand shading his eyes. He said something to Hooch, which the wind took and Harrison did not pick up on, but then the train began to slow and Harrison got to his feet.

The four of them were crowding the doorway now, so he could not see out, and then to his surprise, Sidetrack ducked back in the car and took a cellphone from his pack. Harrison stalked one eyebrow, and Sidetrack winked at him and punched in a number, then half turned away and lifted the phone to his ear. 'Hey,' he said, finger in his other ear to block out the clatter of wheels. 'We're just south of the lake, coming into Coleman.' He paused and listened. 'OK.'

He switched off the phone and stowed it back in his pack. Harrison leaned against the wall of the boxcar and Sidetrack leered at him. 'Not just riding motorcycles,' he said and turned to the door again.

The train slowed as they approached the town of Coleman and, as it did so, Harrison saw a pick-up truck kicking up dust on the dirt road. The truck was moving fast, converging on the train at an angle of thirty degrees, bouncing its way through the scrub. The four Southern Blacks watched as it got closer, and then Harrison noticed that Hooch and Carlsbad had the spare pack between them. Carlsbad picked it up by both straps and seemed to strain a little under the weight. Harrison thinned his eyes, and, as their boxcar rounded the bend in the tracks, Carlsbad hefted the pack into the sagebrush. They watched it land as if to make sure it did not break open, and then the train gathered pace again and Carlsbad ducked inside. Harrison took his place and looked back. He could no longer see the pack, but the dust trail rose from the pick-up.

That night, they camped well away from any freight yard and were joined by two other Southern Blacks, at the edge of a group of caves once used by the Comanche. Sidetrack was in good spirits and was especially pleased when the newcomers showed up with beer, steaks and two bottles of mescal. Hooch had built up a big fire, using dried brushwood, mesquite stalks and tumbleweeds broken down for kindling. Harrison laid out his bedroll on the desert floor and lay with his hands behind his head, looking up at the night sky. He picked out the names of stars he knew and listened to the conversation. Neither of the two newcomers had spoken to him and he had said nothing to them. Hooch was busy cooking steaks in their own fat on a skillet and Limpet squatted by the fire. Southern Sidetrack sat on a rock, with the cap off a bottle of mescal, and was chewing delightedly on the worm. Carlsbad hefted a can of beer at Harrison, who caught it one-handed and snapped off the ring pull. He took a long draught and raised the can to Carlsbad, who raised his in return. One of the newcomers, a short, thickset man, with cropped hair and lots of earrings, stared through the flames at him. He wore his bandana cowboy-style round his neck and smoked tailor-made cigarettes one after the other. He looked at Harrison, but spoke to Sidetrack.

'Who's this asshole?'

Sidetrack sipped mescal. 'Just some dude we picked up along the way. Reckons he's outta Angola.'

The man squinted at Harrison. 'The farm, huh? You know Curly Brown?'

Harrison felt his hair prickle with sweat. 'Nope.'

'What block you in?'

'A.'

'How long?'

'Too long.'

The man stared at him. 'What you do?'

'That's my business.'

'What's your name?'

'That's my business, too.' Harrison had his palm resting lightly on the top of his boot.

The young Black glanced at Sidetrack. 'This mother know who he's fucking with?' He stood up then.

He was not very tall, maybe an inch or so shorter than

Harrison, but a lot wider and younger. He started round the fire, fists balled. 'Motherfucker, I asked you a question. You know who you're fucking with?'

Harrison stared at him and still said nothing.

'You don't fuck with the man.'

'You a cop, bubba?'

The others laughed then, a great guffaw between them. The hoods in New Orleans, the hoods everywhere, referred to cops as 'the man'.

The young guy hesitated, looking Harrison up and down.

Harrison stared, unblinking, right back in his eye. His fingertips were half an inch from the butt of the concealed .38. 'You're in my space, man. Back off,' he said quietly.

The man narrowed his eyes, then looked to the others for support. Nobody said anything. Harrison could tell by the way he had his right hand cupped that there was some kind of knife up his sleeve – maybe a switchblade, maybe a short stiletto. He decided that if the knife appeared, he'd draw the .38. The man stared at him.

'Which bit of *back off* don't you understand, bubba?' Harrison's fingers caressed the butt of the gun.

'Hey, Jackson,' Limpet spoke softly and the young Black looked at him. 'Man's got a rat tattoo on his arm just like Whiskey Six.'

The young man's eyes balled then and he stared through the darkness at Harrison.

'You know Whiskey Six?'

Harrison continued to stare at him, but said nothing. The man stood a moment longer, then shrugged and sat down. He looked at Sidetrack. 'If this guy's with you, then I guess I don't got nothing to say about it.'

'You're right, man. You don't.' Sidetrack had all but finished the first bottle of mescal and he picked a steak from the fire. He ate it, pulling it to pieces with his fingers, then wiped the grease on his jeans. He came round the fire and sat down next to Harrison.

'I'll say it again, bro,' he said. 'Either you're just plain crazy or you got balls of steel.'

Harrison blew cigarette smoke at the fire. 'Who's Whiskey Six?' he said.

17

The list of US Embassy personnel came through to Webb within a day of the ambassador's negative response directive. A pretty girl from the support staff brought it to him, a great pile of A4 paper with the names and details of every person employed at the embassy, both US and UK nationals, from the ambassador to the cleaners. All the US marines were listed, together with those working at the naval building across the square. The girl laid it on Webb's desk with a smile.

'Did you know her?' he asked.

She shook her head. 'No, sir. I don't have a whole lot to do with the marines. My job's in the post room.'

Webb nodded. 'What's your name?'

'Amanda.'

'Amanda what?'

'Robertson.'

'Thanks, Amanda Robertson.'

She smiled. 'Will you need to see me?'

'Probably not.' Webb smiled again. She left and he watched her cross the corridor. 'But then again,' he muttered.

James Carragher, the FBI liaison agent, was from Washington D.C., in his late twenties with a grunt haircut and a taste for Italian suits. There had been two of them initially, but his colleague had returned to the States. He was late in this morning and Webb was on his own. Weir was busy checking the tube station videos with the rest of the team. Carragher came in a little after nine and Webb had already sifted most of the responses into Yes and No piles.

'Morning,' Carragher said. 'Sorry I'm a little late, I've been on the phone to my boss.'

Webb glanced at his watch. 'It's four in the morning over there.'

'Yeah, but the shit's hitting the fan.' Carragher sat in the chair on the other side of the desk. 'We've got a member of the Japanese Red Army bombing D.C. Five devices, just yesterday.'

Webb scratched his head. 'A friend of mine is over there.'

'Jack Swann. I know. He told me to look out for you.'

'How is he?'

'Up to his neck. Kovalski, that's my boss, has got him on secondment. He was supposed to be lecturing in Louisiana, but I figure Kovalski wanted his experience.' He paused for a moment. 'Are he and Cheyenne Logan an item?'

'You mean you haven't noticed? I always found it difficult to part them at the tonsils.'

'There you go.' Carragher sat forward. 'We got all kindsa shit going down with the militia as well.'

'Tell me about it.' Webb stared at him then. 'What's the story with these Orientals killing the leaders?'

'Beats me.'

'The CIA playing silly-buggers?'

Carragher shook his head. 'I don't think so.'

'Rogue FBI agents. ATF, maybe?'

'I don't think it's that either.' Carragher shrugged. 'We had a state cop killed in Oregon and a bomb in Michigan. Another state cop was killed just the other day.'

'Paranoia.'

Carragher nodded. 'That's what these guys thrive on. The stuff they believe is incredible.'

Webb smiled. 'I know. I used to trawl some of their websites when I was at SO13.'

Carragher looked puzzled.

'Antiterrorist Branch. We've had our fair share of right-wing extremists over here, too.'

Carragher nodded. 'The thing is, we've never had a groundswell of public support for the militia, even though most people agreed with the defence attorneys after Ruby Ridge.'

'And now it's different?'

'It could be. More regular people than we figured gave tacit support to some of these anti-federal groups and they've had their share of political support from some of the more radical congressmen. But now, they're not the only ones who think there might be a government conspiracy.' He sighed. 'On top of that, we've got this Jap bombing the shit out of us.'

Webb looked back at the pile of papers in front of him. 'Not to mention people killing your marines over here.'

Between them, they worked through all the responses and separated them properly. Then Webb began setting up the interviews, bringing in the people who did claim to know Kibibi Simpson in alphabetical order, starting with her fellow marines. It was going to be a long-winded and laborious task. The levels of relationship would no doubt vary enormously and he had to speak to every single person. When that was done, he had to look at those who said 'no' and cross-refer the information. At ten-thirty, he was interrupted by Frank Weir, who told him they had located footage of Simpson leaving Camden Town tube station at 8.45 p.m. the Saturday she was murdered. Webb left the pile of paperwork and, together with Carragher, he met Weir at Camden.

They had a whole team of officers trawling the nightspots with photographs of Kibibi. Officers were also interviewing shop staff and checking for street-facing CCTV. Webb and Carragher joined them, and at Eagles nightclub just off the high road, an Irish barman recognised her picture. 'Yes,' he said. 'I've seen her.'

'In here?'

'Aye.'

'That Saturday night?'

The barman blew out his cheeks. 'I don't rightly know

for sure, but it's possible. She came here on a few occasions.'

'On her own?'

He made a face. 'Not always, but sometimes, aye.'

'The last time you saw her, was she alone?'

'I think so. Aye, right enough, she was. She was sitting here at the bar. Late on it was, about two, just before we closed.'

Webb looked up at the security cameras on the walls. 'Are those taped?'

'I don't know. You'd have to ask the boss.'

They did ask the boss, another Irishman, in his forties, with thinning black hair which he combed forward. The security cameras were taped and he thought he would still have the video from the day of the murder. Webb at last began to feel as though they were getting somewhere. He phoned Weir who was asking similar questions at Camden Palace.

'Get the tape, George, and I'll meet you back at Paddington.'

They sat in the incident room and watched the video: four different cameras, which alternated automatically. Webb concentrated on the one at the bar. 'Wind it on, Frank,' he suggested. 'The barman reckoned she was talking to him late on.' They wound the tape forward and then Webb paused it. 'There she is,' he said. 'Good as gold.'

Carragher and Weir looked at the pictures closely now, as Webb flicked the film on frame by frame. Kibibi Simpson was sipping a cocktail at the bar. On one side of her was a man clearly trying to talk. They watched him slip his hand down towards her leg and then jerk back suddenly.

'I want to talk to that man, right there,' Weir said. 'Get his picture on the news, George.'

Swann listened to the briefing Kovalski was giving on the squad-room floor. He used the lectern with the microphone and the 'Fidelity, Bravery, Integrity' symbol on the drape that hung from it.

'We know Harada used the phone booth right outside the field office here,' Kovalski was saying, 'and we've got pictures of him from three years back, which should have been distributed to you all by now. That picture's gonna hit the lunchtime news specials, by way of Fugitive Publicity, and, as you know, we've already gone public with his ID.' He glanced at Swann then. 'I didn't want to do that right off, because we all know that ninety per cent of the calls we get are gonna be man-hour intensive, with nothing at the end of them. But we also know that given the reports coming out on the TV and this sudden upsurge in militia activity, we have no real choice. The joint task force is going to be augmented from the Washington PD as well as the domestic terrorism ops unit. We've got county police coming in from Arlington and Alexandria, and secondments in from Fairfax as well as the Virginia state police. All activity will be co-ordinated from the SIOC, with this field office as the command post. Cheyenne Logan will be deputising when I'm placating politicians. We've got Jack Swann here from the UK as a consultant on urban terrorism and he also has specialist knowledge of the suspect.

'Ladies and gentlemen, we're dealing with a man who believes he's a samurai warrior. He's declared war on us and his intention is to get Tetsuya Shikomoto released from the federal pen, which, surprise surprise, ain't gonna happen. We have to find this guy and do it quickly. Already we've got the district breathing down our necks and you all know what that means. I've had the Capitol Hill police on the wire and the secret service demanding to know whether they need to ship the President out to Camp David.' He rubbed tired eyes with his palm. 'Let's go to work. You know the angles. Who is this guy? Where does he live? Where does he go to work?'

Back in the office, he summoned Logan and Swann. 'Chey,' he said. 'Given we've now gone public, I want you to fly down to Georgia and pay Shikomoto a visit. Maybe there's something he can tell us, something that might be useful.'

'But no deals, Tom.'

'Right now? No, no deals.'

Swann looked at Kovalski. 'You wanna go with her, Jack?'

'Unless there's anything I can help with here.'

Kovalski shook his head. 'Agents are hitting the bricks, buddy. There's not a whole lot you can do.'

They flew to Atlanta and were picked up by a thickset field agent from the Georgia office, who would drive them to Eastpoint and the federal penitentiary, thirty miles out of the city. 'Bill Pryce,' he said, shaking hands. 'Two pipe bombs exploded this morning outside the federal building in Macon.'

Cheyenne had her laptop computer open already. 'Militia?'

'They even claimed it.' He looked at Swann. 'That's unusual.'

Swann nodded. 'In retaliation for the abductions and murders.'

'Yes.'

They got in the car. 'Have you been able to gauge public reaction down here, Bill?' Logan asked him.

'We've done some stuff with the state police. Public reaction to law enforcement is more suspicious than it's ever been. The newspapers are full of conspiracy theories and interviews with militia leaders, and people purporting to be militia leaders.'

'What about regular people?'

Pryce gunned the engine and headed on to the freeway. 'The regular people are pretty confused, Logan. The militia rhetoric has lost its venom. You know, the racist bullshit. It's anti-government, but in a victimised, plaintive kinda way.'

'Looking for the sympathy vote, you mean.'

'Yeah. The Constitution is being quoted left, right and centre, the fourth of July, etc. They're comparing this to the days of enslavement by the English.' He glanced at Swann then. 'No offence, buddy.'

Nobody spoke after that and then Swann said: 'It's important they don't get the public support they've been missing. That's what gives movements credibility. It's what forces governments to give away what they shouldn't.'

'What's the word at the puzzle palace, Logan?' Pryce asked her. 'Who d'you figure is doing this shit?'

'We haven't got a clue. The sightings of the Orientals have been verified by a number of different people, that and the black helicopters.'

'Weird that, isn't it? Like playing into the militia's hands. You know we had one group here claiming they ran into the Crips and the Bloods at a diner on Interstate 85.' He glanced at Swann, then back at Logan once more. 'This isn't my opinion, but rumours have gotten around – does anybody figure it *is* some federal agents gone off at the deep end?'

Logan looked sideways at him. 'Nobody's saying anything officially, Bill. But who the hell knows?'

Tetsuya Shikomoto had a young face and a neatly cut moustache. He was brought into the police interview room wearing a one-piece orange suit, with chains round his wrists and ankles. It looked to Swann as if somebody had given him a black eye recently.

Logan picked up on it immediately. 'Did you get yourself in a fight, Tetsuya?'

He looked at her, but did not reply.

'Don't tell me. You walked into a door.' She took out her FBI shield and slid it across the table. 'My name's Logan,' she said. 'I'm with the FBI. This is Jack Swann, from London.'

Shikomoto looked squarely at Swann, but still said nothing.

'Tell us about Fachida Harada,' Logan said. 'He's planting bombs in Washington D.C. right now.'

Shikomoto looked beyond her.

'You do speak English, don't you?' Logan glanced at Pryce. 'We don't need an interpreter or anything?'

'Not as far as I know.'

'I speak perfect English.' Shikomoto's tones were clipped. 'When I choose to.'

'Will you speak it to me? Will you tell me why Harada is doing this?'

'Harada is a warrior.'

'We figured that bit out. Samurai, right?'

Swann sat forward then. 'Right now, he's *ninja*, isn't he, Tetsuya.'

'It would appear so, yes.'

Logan sat back. 'You're an educated man, Tetsuya. You gained a master's degree in psychology from Meiji University. Is that where the two of you met?'

'Why is this relevant?'

She smiled then. 'Come on. You're not gonna sit there and tell me you wouldn't prefer a philosophical discussion with me, than the plebeian chatter back there.' She pointed to the door.

'Philosophical?' He looked at her with his brow slightly furrowed.

'Yes, the whys and wherefores of the samurai. The role of the warrior in ancient and modern Japan.'

'There is no role for them in modern Japan.'

'That's not what Yukio Mishima thought,' Swann put in. 'He committed *sepukko* with the Tatenokai around him.'

'Has Harada got links to the militia over here, Tetsuya?' Logan interjected. 'Or does he really just want to get you out of jail?'

Shikomoto looked down the length of his nose at her. 'Discussion has its own unique virtues, Agent Logan. But to me, in here, they are insignificant. Debate, the formulation of agreements are of far more interest.'

'I'm not looking to make any deals with you.'

He laughed all at once. 'Then I shall return to my cell, because though I might value some intellectual stimulation, I doubt I'll get it from you.'

'He was your lover, wasn't he?' Logan leaned across the table and looked him right in the eye. 'Homosexuality,' she added. 'It's probably useful in here.'

Shikomoto had the hint of scarlet smouldering in his cheeks. 'It's more useful than being black,' he said.

'*Touché*, Tetsuya. See, you've lost none of that sparkling wit we've read so much about.' Logan sat back again. 'Harada was your lover, wasn't he? Yet you're both married. I can't get my head round that one.'

Shikomoto placed his hands flat on the table. The chains rattled as they slid back and forth through the links. 'Agent Logan. I've been sentenced to ninety years in jail. You really need to tell me something to my advantage before we can get into a conversation.'

'Maybe you've got nothing to tell us.'

He laughed again. 'How absurd. You come all the way from Washington to sit there and tell me that. How nonsensical.'

'Have you got something you could tell us?'

'What do you think?'

'Is Harada doing this just because you were lovers?' Swann asked again.

'Do you have any idea what you mean when you say that?' Shikomoto looked sourly at him. 'You make a statement based on western ideals, of which, I might add, there are few. You make a statement based on western religious philosophy and western prejudices, and yet you have not the remotest idea what you are talking about.'

'So it's different in Japan, then,' Logan said. 'Sex. Being gay. Sleeping with men when you're married.'

Shikomoto's face darkened. 'Do you really think I'm going to rise to this cheap bait? Do you not think I might have trained myself to ignore the jibe of ignorance?'

'I think you might have. But you've got a lot of time to think in here, and if you were any kind of a samurai, you wouldn't have allowed yourself to get caught in the first place.'

The silence was so complete that Swann could hear paper rustling on a desk in the room next door. Shikomoto stared at Swann, his fists clenched on the desk in front of him. Pryce, who was standing behind him, tensed.

'Harada's way is not the way of the warrior,' Logan went on. 'Yours may've been, but Harada has just killed two noncombatants and injured thirteen others. You're not going to sit there and tell me that's the way of the bushido. Are you, Tetsuya?'

Shikomoto took a long stiff breath and looked beyond them to the window, where the sky was grey and cloud-blown. He sat for a while, lips compressed, nostrils flared slightly.

Swann watched his face and saw the depth of passion beneath the calm exterior. 'Why would Harada send a message about the Tatenokai to a reporter?' he said.

Shikomoto looked at him then. 'What do you know about the Tatenokai?'

Swann lifted his shoulders. 'I know it was formed by Mishima before he killed himself in 1970. I know they wore uniforms and peaked caps and there were a hundred of them.' He sat back. 'There's something special about Mishima for Harada, isn't there? What is that? Is it just the homosexuality? When Harada phoned in his last warning, the codewords he used were "snow on the foot of Mount Fuji". That's what Mishima means, isn't it? He's got a fixation with him. Is it militia-linked, hence the Tatenokai?'

Shikomoto just looked at him.

'What about the samurai? Harada's family go back to samurai warriors, don't they? His grandfather was a kamikaze and the lineage can be traced back to before the US Navy sailed into Tokyo harbour last century.' Swann sat

346

back again. 'Mishima was flawed, wasn't he, Tetsuya. He was not samurai, yet he claimed samurai descent.'

Shikomoto shook his head. 'Mishima was more samurai than anyone else this century.' He stood up. 'I will say nothing further.' He shuffled to the door, then turned and looked Logan in the eye. 'You,' he said. 'Black woman. The nature of sexuality is irrelevant. You should understand that the love between warriors is love in its purest form.'

Logan looked back at him. 'Go figure,' she said. 'And there's me thinking you two were just a couple of faggots.'

They flew back up to D.C. and Logan talked to the SIOC via her laptop. 'Not much is happening, Jack, although we've had hundreds of phone calls from people claiming to have spotted Harada.'

'You surprise me. How many people does he live next door to?'

'About fifty so far.'

'And you're checking them all?'

She sighed. 'No stone unturned, you know how it is.'

'I think you dealt with the inscrutable one really well.'

She laughed. 'I was trying to goad him, yes. I don't think it worked, though.'

'Give him time. He knows something, Chey.'

She glanced at him. 'You think so?'

'Don't you?'

'Yes, I do.' She looked back at the computer screen. 'I don't see how we can get at it, though. Kovalski isn't gonna make any deals.'

'He might have to, darling. Harada's not finished by a long chalk.'

Harada had watched Kovalski's press conference dispassionately and allowed himself a laugh at the three-year-old photograph which they must have acquired from the NPA in Japan. His days with the *sokaiya* were over now, as was everything else. He had been at home, and this morning he was back in his security truck, touring D.C. and considering the intense police activity. He had been stopped at least three times, along with every other Japanese, Chinese, Korean or Vietnamese person in the city. Pretty soon, the authorities would have to contend with another outcry over that. He thought about Smylie and his interpretation of the Tatenokai message, words spoken by the master himself, not long before the *sepukko*. He had heard one media comment from the militia, saying that if he was an Oriental, then he was a government agent gone wrong. 'Their own plan was backfiring on them,' was how the unnamed individual had put it. What was surprising, though, was the editorial leader in one of the newspapers that morning, considering the possible validity of such an observation. American conspiracy theory was running away with itself.

Three separate troopers had stopped him and compared his face with the picture of himself and let him go. His papers were intact and his truck was well known, and he had fitted systems in cars and buildings all over the city. The money had been unimportant, but visibility was necessary and he knew that the average traffic cop, whose job it was to look out for the suspect, would consider that one gook looked much like another.

He sat in traffic now – yet another roadblock, more lights and sirens. He drummed his fingers on the wheel and thought about Shikomoto. There had been no way to get word to him, to tell him that he was here in the United States and that his mission would not be complete until he had his freedom, or honour had been restored. The yakuza families had informed him that Shikomoto was at Eastpoint Prison in Georgia, but they had refused to carry messages. Shikomoto was not yakuza and Harada himself was *persona non grata*, and he knew that if the old codes did not hold firm, they would inform on him themselves. But they would not do that, because whatever the situation here, he had married into the Yanagawa-gumi, the largest, most success-ful syndicate in South-East Asia. His wife's father was of the old order and he saw as much in Harada, but he also saw the US dollars that Harada brought from his days in the North Korean enclave. With hindsight, another error, mistakenly believing that the criminal network in some way adhered to the old codes, which, of course, they did not: another misguided action for which he had to atone.

Now, however, Shikomoto would know he was here and he would recall, as Harada had done, the days in Indonesia before the mortar attack, when they had lain together like warriors of old. And on the day of the attack itself, they had painted one another's faces and tied back their hair in the traditional manner. The FBI spokesman had been careful not to put forward the reason for his actions, thus far. Of course, it was possible he did not fully understand them, but Shikomoto would know that the day of atonement had finally come. He drove through the roadblock and his ID was checked. He glanced briefly at Union Station as he headed for North Capitol Street. If they thought they had problems yesterday, by the time the next round was complete, the whole city would be thrown into a panic.

'You've got to get all the rubbish bins off the street.' Swann leant on Kovalski's desk. 'If you don't, he'll use them again and again.'

Kovalski nodded grimly. 'I know that. The district is removing them from sensitive buildings in the Triangle already.' He looked over at Logan who was talking to McKensie. 'What happened with Shikomoto?'

'Tom,' McKensie interrupted him. 'Before you talk to Chey, I thought you'd want to know.'

'Want to know what?'

'Two militia members from West Virginia have been abducted from their truck.'

'Oh, Jesus.'

'It's worse. *Six* Orientals were allegedly seen in the area, and the victims were both women. One of them was pregnant.'

Kovalski rapped his knuckles against the desktop. 'What the fuck is going on out there?'

'The state police are on high alert because the word's been spread over the websites. Right now, the town of Cassity, West Virginia, is a no-go area for cops.'

Kovalski bit his lip. 'OK, Carmen. Thank you.' He looked at Logan again.

'Shikomoto?' he said.

'Nothing doing. I wound him up a bit, told him we knew he and Harada were gay, but got pretty much nowhere.'

'Does he know anything useful?'

'I don't know. He won't talk unless we deal.'

'No chance. No way is the Director gonna let me deal. We deal with him, we have to deal with every piece of shit that crawls from under a rock.' He sat down heavily. 'Somebody get me some coffee.'

The Cub rode on a London bus round Piccadilly Circus, with Haan sitting seven rows behind him. Between them was one of the footpads, the third change since The Cub had openly walked out the front door of the Marriott. There was still no word on the target and, at this stage in proceedings, The Cub had no desire to 'clean' his movements. This was merely an exercise in assessing the level of resource. Haan was along for the ride, to verify the numbers that The Cub himself figured made up the team. It would be an MI5 surveillance team, specialists; people who did nothing other than this for a living. They were good, and right now he was not sure whether he had got the numbers correct or not. Later, when they did finally lose them, he and Haan could compare notes. Haan was better at this than he was. MI6 had used him on numerous occasions and he knew their surveillance methods better than many of their own spotters.

The Cub was moving freely around the city, taking advantage of the tourist cover story The Talent's stagehands had set up. He had visited the Tower, the waxworks at

Madame Tussaud's and Regent's Park zoo. Today, he had visited the London Dungeon and he was either giving the watchers the run-around or a good day out, depending on how they looked at it. He had had one contact with the ISA since he had been here and word would have been sent back to Cyrus Birch in D.C.

The British clearly knew he was here, but they did not know why. So he and Haan had devised a plan: after two weeks' vacation time, The Cub would fly to Paris and from there, purportedly, on to D.C. The British would be finished with him as soon as he left their airspace and, given the nature of the ongoing relationship between MI6 and the DGSE, he doubted the French would be alerted. After that, he would forget the Intelligence Support Activity: the only way the Brits could have known he was here was via a leak from them. The Cub would contact Birch himself when he made a routine visit to the station chief in Paris. Then it would be fresh papers, fresh ID and a return flight to England.

The bus slowed, and he yawned, got up, stepped past the watcher and went down the stairs. The man stayed where he was, but as The Cub waited for the driver to pull over, another passenger got up from a seat at the back – a woman, middle-aged with a half-empty shopping bag. The Cub jumped down, crossed the road and went into McDonald's, where he bought a hamburger and sat down to eat it by the window. The street outside was heaving with tourists and, even with his experience, it was impossible to spot who the watchers were. Couples walking hand in hand, women with babies, businessmen, tramps and beggars, just about any-one.

He took the tube back to the hotel and glimpsed a van parked at the end of the road with the hood lifted. A man looked as though he was trying to assemble some leads, and The Cub grinned to himself and walked over. 'You wanna hand there, buddy?'

The man smiled at him. 'Thanks, but you're all right. The AA is coming.'

'You got a drink problem as well?' The Cub looked in his eye then and his gaze belied the fractured smile on his lips.

The man looked puzzled, then laughed. 'Oh, I see,' he said. 'Of course. You're American.'

The Cub looked at him for a moment longer. 'Of course.' He turned then and walked up the street.

Haan was in his room, seated on the bed overlooking the street. He had swept it again for bugs. He indicated the broken-down van. 'He's been there as long as I have,' he said.

At that moment, a yellow AA van pulled up and the driver got out. The Cub pursed his lips. 'See how long it takes to get it going.'

They watched for a few minutes longer, then lost interest. The Cub sat down on the bed and took a cold bottle of beer from the minibar. Haan tore the wrapper off a stick of chewing gum and stuffed it into his mouth. 'I've heard a whisper,' he said. 'It's only that, right now. But I'll check it myself and then meet you in front of Notre Dame the day after tomorrow.' He smiled. 'Let them follow you, Cub. Let them have their fun. Then they can pack you off on a plane and forget about you.' He paused. 'You've told no one in ISA what your plans are?'

The Cub shook his head. 'Birch is doing a deal with Secret Branch 40. Somebody's leaking stuff in our team. We'll see if we can use theirs when I get back.'

'The chances are they'll find him quicker than your boys, anyway,' Haan said.

'Well, they sure did the last time.'

'Only he wasn't there.'

'I don't think that was their fault.' The Cub moved to the window. The white van was gone.

He flew into Paris the following morning and took a taxi into town. He changed the cab three times and then walked through a department store, left by the rear exit, re-entered

352

and left again by a different one, before taking the metro into the centre of the city. There he took another cab, which dropped him by the Seine, and he walked to Notre Dame, as positive as he had ever been that the route he had taken was clean. He was being extra-vigilant, probably for nothing. Haan was likely to be right. The Brits would want him off their turf and would leave it at that. They knew who he was and whom he worked for, but he had done nothing suspicious.

Haan was there, on his hands and knees, doing a street painting with chalk. The Cub did not recognise him at first, having never seen him in such a pose. He knew he could draw, however. During the more boring covert watches while they had been behind enemy lines with the 2nd REP, Haan had caricatured everyone in the unit. The Cub watched him for a while, then bought a beer at a café and sat down by the river. The sun was full and the sky empty of clouds, and sweat gathered at the nape of his neck. Haan worked away for another half an hour, then came and sat next to him. The Cub ordered more beer. Haan lit a Gauloise.

'Those things smell like cigars made of camel shit.'

The beer came and Haan requested some cheese and *saucisson*. He looked at the glowing end of the cigarette. 'You think so?'

'Don't you?'

'I never thought about it.' Haan crushed the cigarette in the ashtray and lifted the glass of beer. The sun reflected off the muddied waters of the Seine and they both sat in silence as a boat crammed with tourists floated beyond Notre Dame. 'When are you meeting Birch?' Haan asked him.

The Cub looked again at the water and took a pair of sunglasses from his pocket.

'Tonight.'

'Do you want me along?'

The Cub shook his head. 'No. It'll only make him nervous. I'll meet you back in England.' He looked sideways at him then. 'So tell me, your little whisper – what did you discover?'

Haan smiled widely. 'There's a very tall, very black Somali living in West London.'

18

Harrison parted company with the Southern Blacks outside the town of Coleman, Texas. The newcomers went west, and Hooch and Carlsbad headed east. Sidetrack stood with Harrison by the remnants of the previous night's fire, on the hill with the caves hollowed out of the rock. 'We're going north,' he said. 'Me and Limpet.'

'Right.'

'You can come with us if you want.'

'Right.'

'You wanna?'

'I don't know.'

Sidetrack looked at him. 'Well, north is where we're headed. We're meeting up in Arkansas one week from now, just beyond the Saratoga freight yard, by Millwood Lake. The KCS line. Swing by, if you wanna.' He smiled, showing the protruding canine tooth and signalled to Limpet.

Harrison crouched down by the fire and picked up his tin mug of coffee. 'I might be going to Michigan, Sidetrack. Don't figure on me showing up.'

Sidetrack waved a hand and set off towards the railroad tracks with Limpet in tow. Harrison sat and sipped coffee and watched the sun come up over the mountains. A scorpion moved from its burrow not three feet from him and Harrison watched the sectioned arc of its sting. He thought of the night Jean Carey's son died, and when Sidetrack and Limpet were gone, he walked into Coleman and phoned her.

'Thank God,' she said. 'I was really beginning to worry about you.'

'Jeanie,' he said. 'Never worry about me. I'm old, obstinate and really hard to kill.'

'Where are you?'

'Coleman, Texas. It's south-east of Abilene on Highway 84. Where you at?'

'I'm in a town called Tyler.'

'OK. I'm gonna go down to a place called Brownwood, because I just split from the goon squad. Can you find it on the map? I figure it'll take you most of the day to drive, but you oughtta make it by this evening. I'll call you again when I get fixed with a motel. Head for Corsicana, Waco and Gatesville. Gatesville's on Highway 84.' He hung up, sipped some water and thumbed a ride to Brownwood.

Jean arrived at six that evening, and Harrison was bathed and rested, having slept most of the day away. He recognised his own truck's engine coming from some distance away and got up to open the door. Jean had her hair tied up and was wearing a camisole with no bra. She hauled on the wheel of that old Chevy like a veteran. He watched her as she shifted the three-speed stick into neutral and killed the engine. The door still squeaked when she opened it.

'Hey, Miss Lady Mam.' Harrison leaned against the porch of the motel room. She wore flat, open-toed sandals and she slipped her arms about his waist and hugged him. Harrison stood there a little awkwardly at first, and then he just delighted in her touch and felt himself relaxing. 'I'm showered and scrubbed, Miss Lady Mam,' he said. 'But these are the same duds I been wearing since the last time you saw me.'

'I don't care.' She laid her face against his chest. 'I've missed you, Johnny, and I was worried about you.'

He went to the truck box for his case and found she had cleaned and pressed all of his spare clothes. Jean was in the bathroom and he could hear the shower falling. He stood just outside the door with his back to her.

'Have you spoken to Penny?' he asked.

'This morning, after you called.'

'I want to meet with him and Andy Swartz. Where'd you put the cellphone?'

'It's still in the truck.'

Harrison stepped outside into the cooling Texas evening and sat in the cab of his truck. It was familiar and yet unfamiliar, and he wondered at that for a moment until he realised it was the smell. He smiled widely to himself. The cab smelt of Jean. He dialled New Orleans and got hold of Penny. 'Matthew,' he said. 'Johnny Buck. I'm in Brownwood, Texas, and it's time I met with my case agents.'

Jean was out of the shower when he went back inside, sitting on the bed and massaging her wet hair with one towel, another wrapped round her. Harrison felt the dryness in his throat and stepped back outside. He pinched a Marlboro from his shirt pocket and stared west toward the sunset, a strange sense of loneliness coming over him.

'How've you been getting along?' he asked Jean quietly. 'You must be real sick of that truck by now.'

She moved into the doorway alongside him. He could smell a burnt quality in her hair; maybe it was her shampoo, maybe the heat of the water, but it mixed with the natural scent of her skin. He looked round at her: onyx-coloured eyes and a clarity to her skin he had only seen in oriental people. All at once he was in Vietnam, evacuating the South Vietnamese from their villages. There was one woman in particular, with seven young children huddled round her like chicks. She had not wanted to go, but the NVA were shelling the place and half the buildings were on fire, smoke and yellow flames licking about their heels. He grabbed her round the waist and hefted her over his shoulder, yelling at the children to follow. They did, and he bundled them all into the open door of a helicopter. That was his first tour of duty, before he had volunteered to go underground. They had been pinned down in a firefight that lasted two weeks. The choppers couldn't get them out, but dropped C rations and menthol-flavoured cigarettes.

Jean suddenly reached up and cupped the side of his face. Harrison felt his flesh pucker and he smiled.

'Where were you?' she said softly.

'I was in your homeland, Miss Lady Mam.'

She let go his face, sat on the bed again and helped herself to one of his cigarettes. He popped a match and lit it for her.

'Did you like the fighting?'

'No, mam. I didn't.'

'But you went back because of your friend.'

Harrison squatted on the edge of the bed next to her. 'I was young and pissed off,' he said. 'So I went back and fought underground.'

She touched his arm where the tattoo was under the shirt. 'Hence this.'

Harrison looked past her to the open door, where little dust devils were rising in the parking lot. 'Kinda dumb thing to do,' he said. 'But I was a kid and the Tunnel Rats were a sort of family, I guess. Close-knit. Elite. A really tight group of men. I got the tattoo done when I finished with them. I was drunk at the time and for a long time I regretted it.'

'But not any more?'

Harrison sighed. 'Jeanie, I'm near on fifty years old and I got no family, no regular home or anything. When I went on my little vacation, I spent a lot of time thinking about the past. The Rats were a big part of my life. I've never again been quite so up against it, never had to rely on my wits, my own instincts, quite like I did back then.' He looked into her face. 'Shit, I'm sorry. There I go rambling like some sad old soldier and it's your country I'm talking about.'

Jean shook her head. 'No it's not,' she said. 'I've never been back. The Communists killed my father. I fled with my mother. England's my home. It has been for twenty years.'

Neither of them spoke for a few moments after that. Outside, the wind was getting stronger and it whistled through the wooded eaves of the buildings, and reminded

Harrison of the sound it made in the boxcars. A single truck rolled by on the highway. Jean still sat on the bed with the towel wrapped round her and Harrison looked at her then, the gentle arc of her neck, the shape of her collarbone and shoulder. His gaze roamed the towel to her knees and the smooth skin of her calves. She reached forward, cupped his face in her hands and pressed her lips into his. Harrison trembled with the weight of sudden emotion. It was a long, long time since he had felt anything vaguely like this. He kissed her on the mouth, the bridge of her nose, under the eyes and dragged his face through the scent of her hair. The towel gradually slipped and her breasts pushed against him, tight mounds of flesh thrusting at the material of his shirt. Jean pressed him back on to the bed and, standing naked above him, she unbuttoned his shirt.

'It's been a long time, Miss Lady Mam. I'm not as young as I was.'

'It's been a long time for me too, John, and I'm nearly as old as you.' She stripped off his shirt and singlet and traced the crude lines of the tattoo.

'I got it from a picture we used to hang on the door of the hootch,' he explained.

She touched his lips with a finger and worked at his belt. Then she took his penis in her hand while he lay back, eyes closed, and when he was ready, she climbed on top of him.

The door to the parking lot was still open, but nobody walked past and the dust devils hurried themselves out to the street. Harrison rolled her on to her back and, raising himself on his hands, made love to her, his hair hanging loose in her face. Afterwards, they lay on the bed in their own sweat and talked quietly together for an hour. Eventually, Harrison got up, closed the door and looked at her, still naked there in the bed. Her breasts were small and perfectly round, and the nipples lifted under his gaze. Her belly was flat, with dark hair curling at the top of her thighs.

'You're beautiful, Jeanie.'

'Thank you.'

They shared the shower and Harrison soaped her breasts and shoulders for a long time, then gently rinsed her off. He dried her with the towel and brushed her wet hair, aware of a new lightness in his movements. They got in the truck and drove north towards Dallas and the diner on the Stephenville city limits. Penny and Swartz had jumped a National Guard helicopter from New Orleans to Shreveport, and another from there to Dallas. They had picked up a rental car from the Texas field office and driven down Highway 377. Harrison and Jean got there a little before them and were sharing a carafe of wine in a booth when they walked in.

'Well, you two look cosy,' Penny said, and he and Swartz slid into the seat across from them.

Harrison told them what he had accomplished so far. 'Check all the names with Spinelli's file in Spokane,' he said. 'See what else he can come up with.' He told them that Sidetrack had invited him up to Millwood Lake in Arkansas.

'So you're in, then?' Penny asked him.

'Not yet. I've played it pretty carefully, you know, like I don't give a shit. I think I might've rode my luck once or twice, but that's just the colour of the territory.' He told them about the first little test they had put him through and then he mentioned the drop they had made north of Coleman.

'Pick-up truck?' Swartz said.

Harrison nodded. 'The Blacks travel in twos and often when they jump the trains, there's a spare pack between them. We're talking large quantities of drugs, Andy. Three or four keys per pack.'

Penny rested his elbows on the table. 'Have they talked much about it?'

'Innuendo, is all.'

'What about a wire?'

'Not yet.'

'But later?'

'Matt,' Harrison lit a cigarette. 'There's not a whole lotta point being out there unless I can get some evidence.'

'Isn't wearing a wire dangerous?' Jean asked then.

Penny and Swartz looked at her. 'Jean, the whole thing's dangerous,' Penny said.

Harrison squeezed her hand. 'Don't worry, Miss Lady Mam. I've worn a wire before.'

He looked back at Penny. 'I'm gonna make the trip to Arkansas. See what happens there. Once I'm in, I'll wear the wire.' He sat back for a moment and thought about the attitude he had built so far. The Blacks he had met knew not to get too physically close to him, which lessened the danger of some stray finger running an exploratory line up and down his back. The mobsters had done that in Florida, fortunately in the early days and not when he was wearing a wire. Harrison had taken a leaf out of Joe Pistone's book and threatened to kill the wiseguy who did it. He doubted the Freight Train Riders of America were that sophisticated, anyway. Southern Sidetrack himself had said that nobody knew who they were. That had pretty much been true. Nobody would ever have really known, if Spinelli had not been so vigilant. He sipped some more wine and put out the cigarette. 'We knew from Spinelli that the overall leader, the one who strings the three bands together, is a guy they call Whiskey Six. I've had that confirmed.' He sat back and rolled his sleeve high on his arm. 'Apparently, he's got some tattoo like this. That might make him a Tunnel Rat.' He looked at Swartz, then back at Penny again. 'There weren't that many of us. It's possible I might even have known him. Matt, I want you to check with the military records office and find out what you can. Who is dead, who is still alive, etc.'

'That won't be easy, JB. Have you kept in touch with the army since you quit Vietnam?'

'Actually,' Harrison said, 'I have. Or at least, I tried to. From time to time over the years, I tried to find out what happened to the other guys in my battalion. Rats were a strange breed. You had to be pretty damn crazy to volunteer to go down there in the first place. Check it out. You might be surprised.'

When the two case agents had gone, Harrison stayed a while longer with Jean. They sat in the window, watching the rain blow in from the south. Jean hunched against him, resting her head on his shoulder. 'Are you happy to go on with this?' he asked her.

She nodded, pressing her hand against his arm.

'I can't tell you how long I'm gonna be undercover. How long can you keep trucking round the country waiting on a phone call?'

'John.' She turned to face him then. 'My only son is dead. I've leased my flat and taken a sabbatical from my job. I can't think of a better way of spending my time and money than tracking down his killer.'

'And what if I don't get any evidence to link any of the Southern Blacks with the murder. The FBI might put some people away for drug-dealing, but you'll be no further forward.'

She looked at the floor then. 'That's a chance I'll have to take, isn't it? I know there are no guarantees.'

They went back to the motel and made love again; and afterwards they lay together long into the night, listening to the rain sweeping across the parking lot outside.

Fachida Harada drove his cab into the Federal Triangle unhindered by any of the police officers that seemed to be everywhere now. It was what he had expected, a massive show of force, as if in some way their obviousness alone would deter him. Fools. His mission was sacred and nothing would get in his way. They had begun to remove some of the trash cans. He had used them twice now and they had finally reacted, but there were still both trash cans and waste paper bins on the metro.

He regretted the two civilian deaths, but no war in history had ever been prosecuted without some collateral damage.

He pulled over outside the Metro Center station and waited. There were two cops, in a road unit, moving down the street ahead of him. He saw their tail-lights come on at the stop sign, then go off again as they eased forward. Three sidewalk stallholders were selling various goods to tourists: Washington D.C. shirts, sunglasses and hamburgers. All that was America. Harada got out of the cab and walked into the heaving mass of the Metro Center station. It was on two levels where the lines crossed, and he stood for a few minutes reading the street map and considering which receptacle he would use. A uniformed cop was stationed by the platform-entry booth, where hordes of people were passing beyond the barrier. Harada went back to the cab.

He drove out of the Triangle, beyond Capitol Hill, where he was stopped by a cop and his ID and cab licence were checked. The cop looked carefully at him, then handed back the documents and waved him through. He headed due east past Lincoln Park and made a circuit of the Robert F. Kennedy Memorial Stadium. Then he crossed the Anacostia on the Whitney Young Bridge and took the freeway towards Barry Farms. He recrossed the river on the Douglas Bridge and cruised past the naval yard, watching, thinking, assessing. He crossed the Washington Channel and the Potomac, then made a right turn towards the National Airport. He parked in the short-stay lot and locked his cab, before entering the metro station and crossing to B terminal.

It had recently been finished and was very ornate with yellow metal pillars and glass everywhere. He went down the escalator and saw the aircraft being prepared beyond the glass wall, then headed for the men's room just ahead of the escalator on the left-hand side. He had been here before, three months ago now. Fortunately, the third cubicle was unoccupied and Harada closed the door. He crouched over the bowl and scrutinised the inspection hatch, behind which the cistern was hidden. From his trouser pocket, he took a small screwdriver and deftly undid the screws, peeked inside using a pencil-light torch and rescrewed the hatch. He urinated into the bowl and then flushed the toilet, and spent a long time washing his hands, watching the all but hidden security cameras. They covered the main area and urinals only. The American public would, no doubt, take umbrage at 'big brother' watching them shit.

Outside, he checked on the police patrols and then went back to his cab. From the glove compartment, he took his little coded diary and checked the dates and times, and made some additional notes. He would give them a few days and then he would take a train ride.

Swann and Logan were trawling Chinatown, a four-block section of D.C. between Pennsylvania and Massachusetts Avenue. 'Jack,' Logan was saying. 'Chinese people can tell the Japanese apart.'

'I know. But we have to cover all the bases. Is there a major Japanese community in town?'

Logan made a face. 'There's more Vietnamese and South Korean, I think. Residentially, they're north-west of Georgetown.' She glanced at him again. 'They can tell each other apart as well.'

'So, are you telling me there's no Japanese people working in this part of town?'

'I'm telling you that the Chinese and Japanese don't exactly get along, unless they're Triad or yakuza, who sometimes work together. God, this guy's giving us the runaround.'

They stopped the car and moved from store to store, restaurant to restaurant, showing Harada's picture and asking if anyone had seen him. Nobody had. In the end, they walked back to the car, hot and defeated. Swann listened to the sounds of the city: engines, horns blaring, sirens. It served to accentuate how vast the place was, how many people there were in it, and how difficult their job really was.

Back at the field office, agents, police officers and additional support staff drafted on to the task force were sifting the massive public response to the information put out by the Fugitive Publicity unit. They had taken literally hundreds of phone calls from all over the country – people claiming that he was living next door, or they had seen him on the metro or walking the street. The best lead was from a witness who had seen the picture and claimed to have used the phone booth on 4th Street just before Harada made his call. Carmen McKensie had the man in Kovalski's office. Kovalski was at headquarters in yet another meeting with the Director and members of the National Security Council.

The witness was in his fifties, an office worker from the United States Labor building that fronted Pennsylvania Avenue, a couple of blocks from the field office. He was small and bald, wearing a bad suit, and clearly enjoying the sudden attention heaped on him.

'I was making a personal phone call,' he said, as Swann and Logan returned. 'We're not allowed to make them from the office. House rule.'

McKensie nodded. 'What did you see?'

'I was on my lunch break. I went a little early as it happens, ten before twelve. Usually I take my lunch between twelve and the half-hour, but that day I was a little early on account of other people changing theirs. I like to be flexible when I can.'

Logan sat down and he smiled a little self-consciously at her. 'Go on,' she said, 'don't mind me.'

'Well, I wanted to call about how my cable TV's not working. So I go to the stand of phone booths, only one isn't working. It's always the same in this city. Try to find a phone booth that's working. Goddamn phone companies need more competition. I get to use one finally and then I can't make the connection.'

'What did you see, Mr Riddington?' McKensie asked him.

'Oh, sorry. I saw your Japanese guy come to the phone right after me. I stood a while, thinking how I'd maybe try again. I saw him dial, speak for a few seconds, then I left.'

'Did he look like he did in the picture?'

'I guess.'

'Would you recognise him again?'

'Oh sure.' He sat forward then. 'There's one other thing I wanna say.'

'What's that?'

'I got halfway back to the office and thought about trying again. When I turned round, I saw him getting into a black independent cab.'

Logan looked at him now. 'A passenger?'

'No. He was the driver.'

Kovalski came back at two and Logan filled him in on what Riddington had said. 'Is he a reliable witness?' Kovalski asked her.

'I'd say so, Tom, yeah. The guy sure talks a helluva lot, but it made sense and his timings were spot on.'

Kovalski chewed his lip. 'Well, it's a lead. An independent cab. Have we put the word out?'

Logan nodded and Kovalski looked at Swann. 'I put forward the idea of some kinda deal for Shikomoto, but as yet they don't wanna go for it.' He scratched his head. 'They might, if we don't catch Harada real quick. But the best it'll be, will be some kinda privilege situation. There's no way that guy's gonna walk.'

Logan furrowed her brow. 'Harada must know that. Surely.'

'He might,' Swann said. 'But you could argue that Carlos must've known the French wouldn't release Magdalena Kopp. He still bombed them senseless.'

Harada watched the six o'clock news in the comfort of his air-conditioned living room. The Venetian blinds were lowered, and he sat with a glass of mint tea by his side and listened to what the newscaster was saying. The FBI had a new witness, somebody who had seen the suspect making a telephone call from a booth on 4th Street, at 12 p.m. on the day of the last attack. The suspect had climbed into an independent cab and driven away. They were now appealing for anyone else who had seen the cab, or had been driving in the vicinity at that time, to come forward. Harada sipped tea and digested this new information. They had stepped closer to him, not enough to make a difference, but a pace closer. He could feel it as something physical and it unnerved him just a fraction. He sat a moment longer, then went up to his bedroom and slid the trunk he had bought from under the bed. Carefully, he lifted out the ceremonial costume that had been in his family for almost a century. He took out the natural face paints and the parchment chart his grandmother had given him, which traced his heritage back through the ages. He held that closely for a moment, again considering the nature of his failure – the misguided footsteps of youth, the vain attempts at remedy through *sokaiya* and fool's gold. Perhaps he would do better in the next life. Lastly, he lifted the ceremonial wooden case and took out the half-length sword.

Standing, he made one or two kendo moves, and then he was in full swing, mind clear, stepping on the balls of each foot, whirling the sword above his shoulder, under his arm, across his neck, before him and behind. He paused, sweating lightly, and felt the surge of adrenaline in his veins. He would not be human if he was not touched by etchings of fear. But fear was a thing that the warrior banished. If a samurai was to fight bravely, he must not consider such inconsequential concerns as his own survival. Time moved on and there were things he had to do today. Throughout his stay here, he had been careful to carry or store only the minutest amount of bomb-making paraphernalia. He could get away with tilt switches, infrared sensors, etc. in his truck because of the nature of the security business, but not much more than that.

Still sweating, he replaced the sword in the casket and stowed the casket under the bed. As he got up, he caught sight of himself in the mirror. Perhaps it was the cab discovery that unnerved him, but he thought then how much his face did resemble the photograph the FBI had put out. He could not continue to rely on his nerve alone. He moved to the mirror and stood there for a moment, turning his face this way and that, raising his fingers to the height of his cheekbones. His face was sharp and angular, and his lips were full and very red in colour. All at once he smiled. Ancient warriors used to rouge their cheeks and lips with paint. It showed their disregard for danger and allowed the mind serenity and concentration in battle. One old master, renowned for his valour and prowess with the sword, was so beautiful with his face paint on that his adversaries, before they died, swore a woman had killed them on the battlefield.

He drove into West Virginia, heading for the second dead drop. He was careful, even though the wig fitted well and fell in a fringe across his eyes, in the style of so many oriental women. But he felt vaguely self-conscious. This was the first time a woman had left his house and got into the car. He had been shopping for clothes as soon as the idea struck him, gauging his size as he went. He was slightly built, so a little padding created curves in the right places, and because he had painted and sculpted many things in his life, the make-up was all but perfect. He looked like a demure Japanese lady in her late thirties, dressed sensibly and driving a sensible grey sedan. When he rode the metro now, it would be so much easier.

He left the city, making sure he did not break the speed limit. Throughout the six months he had been here, he had ensured the police had no reason to stop him. His brake lights worked, he never drank alcohol and never broke the speed limit. He checked the mirrors now as he left the freeway and headed into the mountains, aware of the time ticking away on the clock set in the dashboard.

He had made the call the day before yesterday, outlining his exact requirements, and the voice on the end of the phone intrigued him. He had no idea who it was that left the materials for him, but so far the system had worked well. It had not been his place to ask who or why: the materials were there and they served his purpose. He was especially cautious when he visited the dead drops, however. These trips were one of the two points of maximum danger. In making the collections, as with laying the improvised devices, he exposed himself to the possibility of being stopped, the car being searched and him being caught. The cab was obsolete now and he would have to think that one out carefully. An error of judgement, a single mistake on his part – it was a good thing. It would ensure he was even more vigilant in future. He was not even half done and to lose now would be the biggest loss of honour he could begin to contemplate. It was a long drive to the dead drop, which further increased the risk on the way back, but the goods were well packaged, having been transferred from the military cases into bottomless hot-dog tins. He would stow them on the back seat, with the top of the box left open, so that if he did get stopped, any cop could lift the lid and see that he had stocked up for a barbecue.

Vernon Jewel, leader of the Mountaineer Militia, woke up in his pick-up truck. His Thermos of coffee had gone cold on him and he wished he had brought some more. Fifteen hours now and still no sign. Again, he considered firing up the rig and heading back into the hills. He was at the rest area and had already stowed the box of hot-dog tins under the drainage cover. The contact could not leave it more than twenty-four hours, and if it was *him*, he'd be there a whole lot sooner than that. Who knew when a county works vehicle would pull in to do an inspection.

He was parked in the trees, off the main rest area, which was on a wide lay-by with the mountain climbing behind it. Jewel did not usually make the deliveries himself. Some of the young bucks took care of that, those with a taste for adrenaline and a hair stuck firmly up their ass. But he always insisted they took the dirt road, which climbed into the hills from the highway ten miles up the road. It wound back on itself and forked in various directions, one of which came out at the back of the rest area. The only potential hazard was a ranger's truck: no cops ever rode that trail. Out of season, a ranger might pull you over if he suspected you'd been poaching, but even in these days of paying lip service to the Constitution, he still had to have probable cause.

Jewel had come himself this time because of the story the FBI were putting out about this guy Fachida Harada, the so-called member of the Japanese Red Army. After those gooks showed up in Cassity and kidnapped Vera-Mae Brown and Angela Appleyard, Jewel had to see this for himself. Cassity was all but barricaded and the potential for a stand-off grew with every passing hour. His outfit had been servicing this dead drop for a while now, the word coming in from BobCat Reece in Montana about six months previously. He had met Reece at the gun show in Iowa and Reece had told him his theory. Reece reckoned the munitions were being paid for by a German outfit who wanted to assist the US cause. Where they were going after they were dropped off, he had not said, and Jewel had not been sure that even Reece knew. But when the bombs started going off in D.C., Jewel had begun to wonder, and now this claptrap handed out by the FBI made him wonder even more.

He had contacted Reece, who seemed as baffled as he was and it was Reece's idea that he stake out the place to see for himself. Old BobCat had become something of a big man these days, and his membership in Montana was the biggest in the country. Jewel used to joke with him about it, how easy it was to run a militia, given how many miles they were from D.C. Reece seemed to be co-ordinating a lot of things lately, though, and with his military background, he was the man to do it. He was the most suspicious, anti-federal man Jewel had ever met. But even he was surprised when the government sent those gooks to Oregon.

Tactics had altered from that moment on and every member in the country was now at a one-minute call to arms. It was for just these circumstances that the Founding Fathers ratified the Second Amendment back in 1791. So many of the liberals called them outdated, but Jewel figured those men had been blessed with the gift of foresight. He sat up straighter all at once, as a car drove by the rest area. He squinted into the gathering darkness and could not make it out. Some kind of sedan, he figured. It went on up the highway, though, and he settled back again, yawned and bemoaned the lack of coffee. Then he heard the same engine rolling back down the hill and he stiffened. Sure enough, the headlights swung into the rest area and the car stopped by the toilet building. Silence and gathering darkness. Jewel fumbled on the seat next to him and took out the pair of night-vision glasses he sometimes used when poaching deer. He strapped them over his head and slipped out of the truck, making sure the interior light was switched off, so it would not come on when he opened the door. He stood in the shadow of the trees, the toilet block between him and the sedan now, and he moved quickly, silently, across the grass to the wooden sign that designated the foot trails leading into the hills.

He heard a car door open, then close, and he crouched behind the sign and waited. The footsteps on the path were light and quick and a figure drifted into his line of vision, before disappearing inside the toilet block. Less than a minute later, it came out again and Jewel twisted the focus wheel on the glasses. His jaw dropped open. It was a woman bending over that drainage cover. She had black hair and slanted eyes. He watched her lift out the C-4 and carry it back to the sedan. He heard the engine fire up and then she pulled out on to the highway.

For a long time he sat in that truck and felt the shadows growing around him. The FBI had claimed that Harada was working alone, no group structure to back him. Yet here was a woman picking up the C-4. Now it fell into place. The gooks in Oregon and Nevada, and right here in West Virginia. A gook woman here at the dead drop. The government was using its own munitions to bomb the people and was blaming some fictional Japanese man. All these months his group had been depositing weapons here and it was the US government that picked them up. That implicated the militia. The whole thing was a massive infiltration exercise. He stared into the shadows and saw movement that wasn't there. He thought he heard the whump whump of a chopper in the distance, or was his imagination playing tricks on him? The breath tightened in his throat and he knew he had to get home and get hold of Reece in Montana. This thing was way deeper and way dirtier than any of them could have expected.

Swann read the newspaper, an interview with Robert BobCat Reece of the West Montana Minutemen, given to Carl Smylie. According to Reece, the militia had proof that the Washington bomber was indeed a US government agent. Reece said that the people of America were no longer fooled. The government had shot itself in the foot when it sent the Hong Kong troops after Lafitte and Tommy Anderson. They had underestimated the level of outrage that followed, not from militia members, but the ordinary US citizen. That had been bad enough, but then the abductions of the two women in West Virginia, one of them being pregnant: a sure sign by federal officials that the seed of revolution must be snuffed out. Reece commented on the fact that no sooner had there been an outcry about this tactic of using the much-threatened oriental army, than the Feds had used an Oriental as the scapegoat for the Washington bombs. They had badly miscalculated: the Bilderbergers and the leaders of the Federal Reserve and the United Nations. Never before in the history of America had anyone phoned in warnings before a bomb went off. So why now? Because the government wanted to minimise collateral damage. Initially, the belief had been that this so-called scapegoat 'Harada' had been an agent gone AWOL, but now the militia had obtained indisputable proof that there was no such person as Fachida Harada. The whole sham was a deliberate attempt by federal agents to subvert the will of the people, abrogate the Second Amendment and infiltrate constitutionally viable groups, starting with the Mountaineer Militia in West Virginia.

'How the hell does he come to that conclusion?' Swann asked Logan, who was reading the same piece.

'I haven't got a clue. It's just BobCat shooting off at the lip, trying to generate some more publicity for himself.'

Swann glanced at her. 'Are you sure? What does he mean by an attack on the Mountaineer Militia?'

'The town of Cassity,' she said. 'Where the two women were kidnapped. That's Mountaineer territory.'

Swann went through to the corridor and got himself some coffee. He wondered what had happened in West Virginia to make Reece come up with something like this. Was he merely talking about the abduction of the women or was there something else, and how did any of it tie in with Harada?

Harrison left Jean for the third time and hitched a ride back to Coleman. He walked then, pack on his back, gun in his boot, hauling a bottle of water and his banjo, out beyond the freight yards, where the plains rolled in scrub, sagebrush and clumps of dry cactus. He was heavier-hearted than he had been for a while, Jean in his mind, like a candle that would not blow itself out. It felt like his steps were dragging. He had no desire to jump another freight train and even less inclination to go north and meet up with the Southern Blacks. What he wanted to do was stay with Jean, get in his truck and drive off somewhere with her, the sunset maybe or some other such dumb idea. He had never been married and none of his girlfriends had stuck by him for very long, or indeed him by them. He often wondered if the possibility of some kind of love might have passed him by.

He watched the drivers changing on the grainer, which was heading north, and waited while the diesel cranked up. Then the train rolled away from the swap point and he was trotting alongside an open-doored boxcar. He jumped up and rolled across the dirt floor to the back of the car. Sitting up quickly, he saw that the boxcar was empty and he was glad, because right now the last thing he wanted was company. He sat with his knees drawn up and rolled a cigarette, fingers working automatically, his mind transported by the rhythm of the wheels that beat time in his ear. He thought about the two rooms he rented on Burgundy and Toulouse in the quarter, and he thought about New Orleans and the field office, and Gerry Mackon dropping him from the SWAT team. Then he wondered if going UC again, like this, was not also a way of reminding himself, reminding them, that he could still cut it when it really counted. He thought about D.C. and the Vietnam memorial and that woman thirty years ago with her brood of seven crying children. He thought of the marine laying the flag down for his long dead father. 'God, JB,' he said, aloud. 'You're a maudlin sonofabitch. If this is what hanging out with a woman does for you, don't do it.' But his mind was off by itself and he thought about childhood and Marquette, and lake fishing in winter with his grandfather. He thought about the sister to whom he had not spoken in ten years and decided that when this was over and Jean was gone, that was something he would rectify. Jean gone: that's what this mood was all about; he figured that as soon as this deal was over she would be heading back to the UK.

'Goddammit. Cowboy up,' he said to himself and got to his feet. He moved to the door and leaned there, the wind in his face whipping the cigarette smoke away from him as soon as he exhaled. He ought to quit smoking, but he'd smoked and chewed for so long now, he didn't think his body would recover anyway.

He left the train at Abilene and headed for the tracks, which ran east towards Fort Worth and Dallas. He had to walk for three miles before he was able to jump another train. Three Southern Blacks occupied the car and Harrison did not recognise any of them. He was already in a bad mood, and their sullen expression, copious earrings and black bandanas got under his skin even more.

He had to keep forcibly cool, the animosity building, as the train lurched over the bridge, with the three men staring at him. Harrison put them all in their thirties, older than some he had seen and younger than others. He sat with his back to the wall on the left of the open door. Two of the Blacks were against the longest wall, the third directly opposite him. Nobody spoke.

The one facing him continued to stare and Harrison held his gaze. In the end, the man leaned and spat. 'Quit staring, asshole.'

Harrison continued to look him in the eye. 'You're the only view I got, unless I wanna crick in my neck.'

The man squinted at him, looked at his friends, then stood up. 'You disrespecting me, man?' he said.

Harrison tensed fractionally. The bottom of his jeans' leg was half hooked over his boot top and he had a huge desire to draw the snub-nosed gun and put a bullet right between the Southern Black's eyes.

'Get off this fucking train,' the man said.

Harrison stood up, glanced at his two companions and wondered what his chances were in a gunfight in such a confined space: not good. He looked at his tormentor.

'Listen, asshole,' he said. 'My buddy, Southern Side-track, calls me Four-String on account of my busted banjo. Now I ain't going nowhere, so if you can fight like you talk – make your best move.'

The man was looking squint-eyed at him now. His companions were gawping, trying to register the fact that Sidetrack's name had come from his mouth. Harrison was ready, every sinew working, every muscle knotted, his whole body coiled like a spring.

'Come on, asshole. Let's see what you got.' The anger was genuine, the mood that had gnawed at him earlier was breaking now and he beckoned the man with his fingers.

The man stared at him, suddenly in two minds. 'You're Four-String?' he said slowly. 'The Tunnel Rat?'

'That's right, bubba.' Harrison screwed up his eyes.

The man stared at him a moment longer and then he raised a conciliatory hand.

Harrison wanted to hit him. He wanted to pound on his head and not stop. Jean was in his mind and her son's meaningless death. He let air hiss from between clenched teeth. Then he leaned against the door to roll a cigarette. He looked at the Black, who had now backed right off, and he could spit blood. Just another so-called hard man. He had lost count of the so-called tough guys he had rounded up on SWAT rolls. Give them something real, like an MP5 and a man who knows how to use it to think about, and they shit in their own pants. Again, he thought of Jean's son, the pictures she had shown him – just a wide-eyed kid with a bright future in front of him. He thought of the pictures Joe Kinsella had shown him, with half his head gone and his pants round his ankles. To guys like this jerk, Tom Carey was weak and they only preyed on the weak.

Harrison looked at the man again, sitting down now against the wall. 'You ever come at me again, I'll tear out your heart and eat it.'

19

Harrison rode with the three Southern Blacks across north-eastern Texas. His mood had brightened a little and the man who had threatened him had spent the rest of the trip since then trying to befriend him. Just beyond New Boston, the train slowed and Harrison saw two other bandana-wearing hobos waiting by the trackside. He recognised Hooch and Carlsbad the Bad. The other three helped them into the boxcar. Carlsbad had an open bottle in one hand and he sat with his back against the doorjamb and sipped from it. Hooch squatted down next to Harrison.

'So, you figured you'd come after all, Four-String,' he said. 'You'll have a blast. The whole squad are getting together for this one. Six, himself, might even blow in. He does that sometimes, man. Just shows up when he feels like it. Rolls in on a train from the north and then rolls out again.' He felt in his waistcoat pocket. 'Here,' he said. 'I got something for you.' He took out a small paper package and handed it to Harrison.

It was light, and he screwed up his face, opened the package and then a smile stretched his craggy features. It was the missing string for his banjo.

'Way to go, bubba.' He took the banjo from its case and fitted the string across the frets. Then he sat there with the instrument across his knees and plucked with his thumbnail, while tightening the twist key to tune it. 'Sounds about right,' he said after a while and strummed the full five strings.

Hooch slapped him across the shoulders. 'Four-String-Five,' he said, and his arm lingered a little and Harrison thought, if ever there was a time to check for a wire, this was it. But Hooch didn't and Harrison decided there and then that the next time he saw Jean, he would hook himself up.

They crossed the Arkansas line in mid-afternoon; the sun was gone and the sky had clouded over. The train ran to Ashdown and then Saratoga. Hooch told him that Blacks would be coming in from right across the South, literally hundreds of them. They would take over their usual camp grounds by the lake and stay for a day or so. Harrison gazed across country as the first spots of rain began to drift through the open door.

They left the train at the Saratoga yard and Harrison could see the spread of Millwood Lake to the north. It was only a short distance and he walked a little apart from the others, all of them wearing a black bandana, either round their heads or necks. Blacks he had not seen before gave him the eye, but Hooch walked one side and the big, lumbering, ginger-headed Carlsbad on the other.

'Hey, Hooch,' one man said, 'got yourself a prospect?'

Hooch glanced at Harrison and grinned. 'Something like that, man.'

Southern Sidetrack was already by the lake, with Limpet building a fire. The Blacks filed up in a straggly line. Harrison counted over twenty-five of them.

'Regular hobo convention,' Hooch muttered to him. 'Like Britt, Iowa, but no straights allowed.' He cackled to himself and dumped his pack and sleeping bag on the ground.

Harrison took himself off slightly and laid out his gear on a small hill. He sat down and rested on his elbows, caught Sidetrack's eye and Sidetrack nodded to him.

Limpet came sauntering over. 'You made it then, brother,' he said.

'Just for a while, Limpet. Arkansas's on the way north.'

Limpet laughed at him then. 'You ain't going north, man. There ain't nothing up there for ya. If there was, you'd be gone already.'

'You figure?'

'Yeah, dude. I figure.'

Harrison leaned and spat tobacco juice.

Limpet took a bottle from his pocket and offered it to him. 'Look, bro. I been in the can. I know what it's like when you get out. There ain't nobody and there ain't nowhere. You been away so damn long, anybody who might give a shit is long gone. The world's gone crazy on you and the only thing you can do is keep rolling.' He shrugged. 'It's why I hit the skids.'

That evening, they cooked steaks and drank cheap whiskey. Sidetrack, as usual, supped from his bottle of mescal and chewed on the worm, with bits of it poking through his teeth. More and more Blacks were arriving, and Harrison counted in excess of two hundred now.

'Quite a party, Sidetrack,' he said, when Sidetrack sat down next to him.

'We do this once in a while. I figure it's important. Get everybody together.'

'Where you headed after?'

Sidetrack looked at him. 'I thought you was going north?'

Harrison made a face and spat.

'You could tag along with us if you wanted.' Sidetrack nodded to where Hooch was bullshitting with Carlsbad and two other guys. 'Hooch, over there, put you up for membership.'

Harrison sat up straighter. 'Me, join your gang?'

'Family, Four-String. A place to be. A place to go. The whole of the southern United States for your backyard, riding any damn train you please and taking bullshit from nobody.' He reached in his pocket and took out a new black bandana. 'I spoke to Whiskey about you. Told him how you were gonna kill anyone who laid a hand on you. Told him about that rat tattooed on your arm.'

'Yeah? What did he say?'

'He asked me how old you was. I figured fifty or so.'

'That's about right,' Harrison muttered. 'Last time I counted.'

'Whiskey wants to hook up with you, man. He's never come across another Rat on the rails before.' Sidetrack looked at him. 'He wanted to know when you was in the outfit and for how long.'

Harrison nodded. 'It was 1969, Sidetrack, and I did six months underground. Rocket City, Lai Khe base in the Iron Triangle.' He took tobacco out of his pocket. 'Supposing I wanted that.' He nodded to the bandana. 'What would I have to do to get it?'

Sidetrack laughed then. 'You'll see.' He stood up and his knees cracked. He nodded to the banjo. 'Hooch tells me he got the string you needed. You better play us a tune, bro.'

At midnight, with the fires burning against a velvet sky, Sidetrack got to his feet and called everyone to be quiet. He waited until the conversation and laughter had subsided, and then he looked across the fire at Hooch. 'You got something you wanna say, brother?'

Hooch rubbed his palms on grimy jeans and got up. He was part drunk and he slurred a little as he spoke, but he looked at Harrison and told the gathering he was putting him up for initiation. 'You wanna join this crew, Four-String?' he finished.

Harrison looked him in the eye. 'I'm sat here, ain't I?'

Hooch looked at Sidetrack. 'I needed somebody to back me.'

Sidetrack looked at Limpet, then at Carlsbad and the others. Silence. Harrison was aware of the pulse at his temple. Then Sidetrack nodded. 'I'll back you. Get up, Four-String.'

Harrison spat, then got up and stood there with his hands loose at his sides.

Sidetrack looked round the gathering and selected four of the biggest, ugliest Blacks seated round the camp fire. He signalled to them and then looked back at Harrison. 'No weapons, bro. Anything you're carrying, you gotta lay down.' His eyes had dulled to the chill blackness Harrison had witnessed when he first met him. 'Lay them down, Four-String. You've come too far now. You don't, we're gonna kill ya.'

Harrison stood a moment longer, then he let the stopped-up breath ease out of his chest and he reached to his belt for the bowie knife. He was about to be as exposed as he ever could be, and he knew then that either way he might not survive the next few minutes. He hesitated, spat and then reached for his boot and took out the snub-nosed .38. From the waistband of his jeans, he took the black 9mm, weighed it in his hand and then dropped it on the ground.

Carlsbad stared at the array of weaponry, with his eyes popping. 'This guy believes in packing,' he muttered.

Sidetrack stared at the weapons and then at Harrison, who was stripping off his jacket. All he wore underneath was a singlet and the rat grinned wickedly on his upper arm. 'Guess old habits die hard, huh?' Sidetrack said to him.

Harrison nodded. 'Handgun's the only friend you got underground.' He looked at the pile himself. 'Needless to say, I'm gonna kill any fucker who touches them.'

The four men advanced on him then and Harrison moved sideways to give himself room. He could see the flames and the faces dulled by drink, and he was aware of the adrenaline tumbling in his veins. The biggest guy first; he had always been taught to take out the biggest one first. He knew he was going to take a beating and he just prayed his old bones were still up to it. He stepped back and the four men circled him now. He concentrated on the big one: bearded, fat-bellied, somewhere in his forties. The man lunged for him and Harrison sidestepped and stamped hard on the side of his knee. The man yelped and went down. Harrison pivoted on his left leg and ducked under another a massive roundhouse punch from the second man coming in. The momentum of the punch carried him forward and Harrison caught him under the ribcage with a right. At the same time, the third man swung a kick and hit him above the knee. Harrison staggered but did not go down. Fists up, he gave the man a combination under the jaw which jerked his head back, and then he hit him as hard as he could with a spin-kick and sent him reeling towards the fire. Two more Blacks had got up and were heading to join the fray. Harrison took in their bulk and movement, and aimed another kick at the first man. Then somebody lunged and he ducked too late and the blow caught him on the side of the eye. He regained himself again, only to take a kick under the ribs which knocked the wind right out of him. He swung with a left, caught one guy, but then he was down and they were raining kicks at him. He rolled and twisted, caught one man's foot in both hands and twisted it as savagely as he could. Harrison got to his knees, but was knocked back again, and then fists were smashing him in the face and he rolled again, dirt in his mouth. He could feel the heat of the flames. And then the attack just stopped and he lay there for a moment, breathing hard. He thought he was about to pass out, but then somebody jerked back his head and poured water into his mouth. He coughed, spluttered and sat up. One eye was closing rapidly: he could tell by his dulling vision. He saw Sidetrack's face and felt a hand on either side of his own, slapping the sense back into him. He aimed a punch at the slapper and staggered to his feet, spitting gobs of blood at the fire. Out of the corner of his eye, he could see half a dozen men taking a piss at the same time, and he could not figure out why.

He staggered back to his pack, sat down and checked his guns. He spat more blood and checked his teeth to make sure none of them were loose. Then he unscrewed the cap on his water bottle and poured it over his head.

'You OK, dude?' Limpet's voice.

Harrison nodded. 'Roll me a cigarette, will you.'

'The game ain't over yet.'

'Tell somebody who gives a fuck. Roll me a goddamn cigarette.'

Harrison looked up as Limpet set about making him a

cigarette and he saw Southern Sidetrack walking towards him, with what looked like a soaking rag in his hand. Harrison stared at it and realised what it was, and then he thought about the men pissing and groaned aloud to himself.

Sidetrack made him stand up and then he tied the urine-soaked bandana round Harrison's neck. 'You're one of us now,' he said, their faces pressed close. 'Part of the brotherhood.'

In the morning, Harrison washed the bandana in the lake, and, stripping off all his clothes, took a bath himself. When he was dressed again, he tied the still wet, but no longer foul-smelling, bandana round his neck and rolled himself a cigarette.

Sidetrack was talking to Limpet and Hooch. He beckoned Harrison over. 'How you feeling?' he asked.

'How do I look?'

'Put it this way, you ain't pretty.'

Harrison snorted. 'I was never pretty, Sidetrack.' He squatted down. 'Nothing's busted.'

'You fight real good.'

'I know.'

'Why'd you carry all those guns?'

'Habit. I got out of it in Angola. Soon as I got out, I got back in it.' He looked Sidetrack in the eye. 'It's why I made fifty.'

Sidetrack grinned and slapped him on the back. 'You're hanging with us now,' he said. 'I want you close to me, man who can fight like that.'

Harrison noticed then that Sidetrack's pack was already strung up ready to go. He looked round the rest of the campsite and saw hobos still laid out in their sleeping bags and blankets. 'Are you splitting already?' he said.

Sidetrack shook his head. 'No, *we* are. You're coming with us, Four-String. We got work to do.'

They headed back to the freight yard, where a coal train was hissing and cracking metal on the westbound line.

Harrison noticed that Carlsbad and Hooch each carried spare packs and he frowned. 'You bring the kitchen sink with you?' he asked.

Sidetrack smiled. 'Something a bit more valuable than that.'

Harrison made a face and stuffed a plug of chew into his mouth.

They rode west again with the early morning. The coal train was long and slow and strung out for two miles. The boxcar they had jumped was halfway down the train, which Harrison had noticed was always where Sidetrack tried to pitch it. Easier to get on and off undetected, not that the guards in the yards or those who rode on the trains seemed overly bothered about the presence of hobos. One thing that had been very apparent, though, was the declining number of regular hobos Harrison had seen on these tracks, particularly through Texas.

He squatted on the floor, fingered the bandana tied at his throat and looked at his travelling companions: the twin bulk of Carlsbad and Hooch; the skinny, insipid-looking Limpet who dealt heroin to Little Nate in New Orleans; and Sidetrack with his dead eyes and overlong canine tooth. Harrison looked again at Limpet, recalling the first time he had seen him in Jackson Square, before the face to face with Nate. Nate was a heroin-dealer and gangbanger and Limpet his source of supply, yet on the occasions he had been riding with these men he had yet to see a single class A drug. He caught Sidetrack's eye and they exchanged a glance, and another thought struck him. It was going to be that much more difficult, now he was initiated, to get away and see Jean.

'Where we headed?' he asked Sidetrack.

'Wichita Falls.'

'What's at Wichita Falls?'

'You'll see.'

They rode the Burlington Northern line and late that evening rolled into Wichita Falls. They leapt off the train just before the freight yards and, when the last of the cars had passed, Sidetrack took out his cellular phone. Limpet came alongside Harrison.

'Gotta make a drop,' he said. 'Then we'll split.'

Harrison said nothing and waited till Sidetrack came off the phone. Then the five of them crossed the tracks and picked their way through the bunch-grass to a small hill with a gravel bar running off it. The twilight was falling in the east, the blue of the sky giving way to strands of grey and purple. Harrison looked at Sidetrack, who was staring down the dirt road that led away from the hill.

Limpet was watching the sky and listening. He glanced back at Harrison. 'Gotta keep an eye out for those fucking black helicopters. Government's watching the whole damn country.'

Harrison could feel the threads of a chill working into his veins. He sat in the dirt and rolled a cigarette, and every now and again he would look up and see Limpet still scouring the skyline. Sidetrack was watching the dirt road, and Carlsbad and Hooch had the two big packs between them.

'Anybody wanna tell me what the fuck's going on?' Harrison asked.

Sidetrack looked down at him. 'Four-String,' he said. 'Today you joined the revolution.'

Harrison spat. 'So what's in the packs then, gunpowder?'

'C-4 explosives.'

Quietly, he licked the gummed edge of the cigarette paper and pasted it down. He stuck it in the corner of his mouth and popped a match on his boot. In the distance, he could hear the sound of an approaching vehicle.

Sidetrack had climbed to the top of the hillock now and was looking up the road. The gloom had deepened to a half-darkness and he snapped his fingers at Hooch. 'Gimme that flashlight.'

Hooch fumbled in his bag and tossed a long-trunked flashlight to him.

Sidetrack caught it, flicked it on and made an arc in the sky. 'Keep watching, Limpet. Those gooks are fucking everywhere.'

Harrison looked up the road and saw the driver of the approaching truck flash his lights once. Three minutes later, the dust rose as a massive Ford 350 slowed to a halt. Harrison got to his feet. Two men got out of the cab and came over. The first one, bearded and wearing a cowboy hat, nodded to Sidetrack and looked at the packs.

'That it?'

'That's it.'

'Good.' The man shifted a plug of tobacco to his other cheek and crouched down. 'You don't mind me taking a look, now do you?'

'Go right ahead.'

Sidetrack shone the flashlight for him, as he fumbled with the rucksack drawstrings and opened the neck of each pack in turn. Harrison could not see properly from where he was, but the man stood up again, a smile playing across his lips.

'Excellent,' he said. 'DeWitt, haul over those coolers.'

Harrison strode over to the pick-up where the younger of the two men was already in the back. 'Here, I'll give you a hand.' He reached up and took down two giant Coleman coolers, which he set on the ground.

The cowboy bent to the packs again and began to lift out the rolls of grey C-4. He talked as he transferred them to the coolers. 'When's the next load coming in?'

Sidetrack leant against the door of the truck. 'Whenever you want it.'

'We want stuff as soon as you boys can deliver. And we need more M16 rounds. Those G-men sonsabitches are all over the fucking place.' He looked up. 'They took two gals the last time. And one of them was pregnant.'

'They didn't show up yet, huh?'

The cowboy shook his head. 'When they do, they won't be talking about it.'

Harrison watched him work until the packs were empty

and the coolers were full, and then he helped him hoist them back up to his partner. The cowboy was a big man, much taller than Harrison, at well over six feet. 'I ain't seen you before,' he said. Then he turned to Sidetrack. 'I ain't seen this guy before.'

'He's cool, Randy.'

The cowboy looked down his nose at Harrison and Harrison looked evenly back at him, but said nothing. Sidetrack stepped between them. 'It's OK, Randy. This guy is just outta Angola. He was in Vietnam, a Tunnel Rat like Whiskey Six. He's one of us.'

He looked at Harrison. 'Four-String, meet Randy Meades.'

Harrison looked at Meades and nodded. 'Howdy, Randy,' he said.

Meades looked a little doubtful. He turned to Sidetrack: 'Tunnel Rat, you say?'

'Yeah. Killed gooks hand to hand. Something, ain't it?'

Meades looked back at Harrison again. 'Don't mean to be suspicious of you, partner, but these are dangerous times we're living in. Government spooks are everywhere. They've killed Billy Bob, Dan Pataki *and* Tommy Anderson.'

Harrison shifted his shoulders. 'I don't read no newspapers.'

'Well, you're in the fight now, so you better start.' Meades seemed to relax. 'At least you chose the right side.' He looked at Sidetrack again. 'The people are coming round, Sidetrack,' he said. 'For years, they thought we all was just a buncha rednecks, but now they ain't so sure. We got more and more of the regular people coming out on our side and they're keeping their powder dry. Goddamn, I always knew it would come to this, but I never figured on it being this quick.' He looked up and down the road, then back at Sidetrack once again. 'We gotta get moving. There's still some good cops in this country, but the state troopers ain't among them.'

They climbed back in the truck, swung it round and headed off the way they came, raising a cloud of dust in their wake.

In London, the murder squad had put the picture of the man they had taken from the nightclub CCTV tape into the papers. They wanted to speak to the man so that they could eliminate him from their enquiries.

Webb was back at the embassy with Carragher from the FBI, and he was gradually working his way through the interviewees. 'James,' he said, 'Kibibi Simpson had a fridge full of good food, a bottle of champagne and a wine rack fit for a decent cellar. The flat cost eight hundred and fifty pounds a month and she only earned a Marine Corps sergeant's pay. Her bank balance was healthy and the clothes in her wardrobe all had designer labels on them. How d'you work that out?'

Carragher sat back and steepled his fingers under his chin. 'Sugar daddy.'

'We thought about that,' Webb said. 'But it only works so far. She was sleeping with the RSO before Dan Farrow got here. We spoke to him and he admitted that he helped her get the flat in the first place, but only with the deposit. After that, she paid for everything herself, including her clothes and stuff. The State Department investigated the RSO's finances, but there's no sign of any incoming money that shouldn't be there and nothing regularly going out.' He ran his fingers over his moustache.

'Maybe she was a hooker,' Carragher suggested. 'You said the rent was paid in cash.'

'We thought about that, too. If she was, then the flat would be a good place to take her punters, but she's got one of those really nosy old neighbours and she told us that only a couple of men showed up at the place. We know one of them was the RSO, from the barmaids in the wine bar. According to the neighbour, he was the only white guy. She said that at least two different black guys visited now and again, but not what you would call regularly.' Webb got up and wandered over to the door and stood with his back to it for a moment.

Carragher smiled at him. 'George, if they wanted to eavesdrop, they wouldn't have someone bent at the keyhole.'

Webb ignored him and put his hands in his pockets, crossing his legs at the ankle. 'I don't get it,' he said. 'Lots of cash and no apparent reason for it.'

'What about her folks?' Carragher asked.

Webb shook his head. 'They're just a normal working family from Mississippi. There's no money there.' He sat down once more at the desk and picked up the next interviewee's résumé from the stack in front of him. Alton Patterson. Marine. His main occupation was guarding the naval building opposite the embassy. Picking up the phone, he dialled the extension for the police liaison officer and told her he was ready to talk to Patterson. Two minutes later, there was a knock at the door and Carragher got up to open it.

Patterson was black, very tall and lanky, wearing the standard grunt haircut. Webb looked up into his face even when he was sitting down. 'You're a big lad, aren't you?' he said.

Patterson's smile was slightly lopsided. 'I got a basketball scholarship to college,' he said. 'Coulda made the NBA, but I had a problem with my knee.'

'That's a shame,' Webb said. 'Is the knee OK now?'

'Oh sure. They don't let you in the Marine Corps if you got a busted knee.'

Webb nodded. 'How long have you been over here, Mr Patterson?'

'Just a year, sir.'

'D'you like it?'

'Yessir. London's just fine.'

'Where were you before?'

'This is my first overseas posting. I was attached to a

National Guard base at Wichita Falls, Texas, before coming here.'

'You live at Eastcote?'

'Yessir.'

Webb sat back, spreading his fingers across his stomach. 'You know why we're talking to everyone?'

'Yessir. On account of Sergeant Simpson dying.'

'Being murdered, actually.'

Patterson looked briefly at his feet. 'That's what I meant, sir.'

'Of course.' Webb glanced at Carragher, who was sitting at the other desk watching. 'I'm going to caution you, Mr Patterson,' Webb said. 'And tape the interview. There'll be two tapes, one of which you can have at the end. OK?'

Patterson looked doubtful. 'I guess.'

Webb smiled at him. 'It's normal procedure. Just the way we do things over here.' He nodded to Carragher. 'Special Agent Carragher there is from the FBI. He's listening to make sure I do it properly.'

Patterson glanced at Carragher. 'OK,' he said. 'It's no problem. I got nothing to hide.'

'Good.' Webb cautioned him, then checked his watch and switched on the tape. 'So,' he began. 'Sergeant Kibibi Simpson. Did you know her?'

'I knew who she was, sir. I didn't exactly know her. We worked in different departments.'

'I see. So you knew her just to talk to?' Webb was looking at the answer sheet Patterson had sent in and he had put down much the same as he was saying now. Webb looked at him again. Patterson sat with rounded shoulders as if, like a lot of big men, he was self-conscious of his height. 'Speaking terms, but not a lot else.'

'Yessir. I mean, I knew who she was and all. I spoke to her. She was a gunnery sergeant.'

Webb was flicking through Simpson's file as he spoke. He came to the page detailing her service record and he paused. 'Did you ever see her socially?'

'No, sir.'

'You never visited her flat in Paddington?'

Patterson shook his head.

'Did you remember her from Wichita Falls?'

Patterson looked at him then. 'Excuse me?'

Webb smiled. 'She was posted to Wichita Falls, too.'

'I saw her there, yes, sir. But not for long. I think it was only about six weeks that we were there at the same time.'

'I see.' Webb was quiet for a moment. 'But you didn't hang out with her.'

'She was a gunnery sergeant, sir. They don't hang out with us.'

Webb nodded. 'Who d'you room with, Mr Patterson?'

'Excuse me?'

'Your room mate. Who is it?'

'Dylan Stoval, sir.'

'Stoval.' Webb flicked through the pages of responses and found Stoval's name. He sat for a moment, then looked up at Patterson once more. 'Well, Mr Patterson. Thank you for your assistance.'

Patterson looked at him a moment longer, then scraped back his chair. 'That's it, sir?'

'That's it.'

Patterson's face broke open in a smile and he turned for the door. 'Thank you, sir. Have a nice day.'

Webb smiled back at him. 'You too, Mr Patterson.'

When he was gone, Carragher got up and closed the door. He looked over at Webb and frowned. 'What're you thinking, George?'

Webb did not reply right away. He sat and pondered for a moment, looking again at Patterson's sheet. 'It's just something that a barman said.' He looked up at Carragher. 'Kibibi was seen in the wine bar in Southwick Street with a very tall black guy.'

They drove back to the incident room and found Frank Weir on the phone in his office. Webb left Carragher talking to a couple of the detectives and knocked on Weir's door.

Weir beckoned him in and Webb sat down opposite and yawned.

'Are we keeping you up, George?' Weir said, when he came off the phone.

'You have been, sir. You have been.'

Weir rubbed a palm across his bristling scalp. 'So, tell me some good news. It's not as if I get much.'

Webb hunched forward in the seat. 'I've just interviewed a marine called Alton Patterson,' he said. 'He told me he was on speaking terms with Kibibi, but no more than that.'

Weir was looking at him closely now. 'Go on.'

'Well, this could just be pure coincidence, but both he and Simpson served some duty time at Wichita Falls National Guard base in Texas.'

'So?'

'Like I said, probably just coincidence. Another thing bothers me more. Patterson is really very tall.'

'Is he indeed?' Weir sat more upright. 'Didn't the barman at the wine bar talk about a tall black bloke?'

'He did, sir, yes. But Patterson told me he'd never been to the flat. Somehow, I doubt he would've gone to that bar without meeting her first at the flat. He also told me he never socialised with her.'

They sat for a long moment in silence, then Webb lifted his palms. 'But there must be lots of tall black men in London. There's nothing to say that either of the two visitors were marines.'

'No.'

They looked at one another and Webb said: 'Did the subject in the nightclub come forward yet?'

'No.'

'But we've got Kibibi leaving Camden Town tube on video.'

Weir nodded.

'I hate to say this, sir, because the boredom will probably kill me, but I want to watch those tapes.'

'George, be my guest.'

392

Webb and Carragher sat in front of the television and watched the tape made by the camera above the exit barriers in Camden Town underground station. It was boring, but the time Simpson had been seen had been confirmed and Webb worked the tape half an hour either side of that.

'Are we looking for Patterson?' Carragher asked.

'Yes. He'll stand out a mile, with his height.' They watched the full hour, but there was no sign of him. Webb sat back and blew out his cheeks. 'Well, that takes care of that little theory,' he said.

Carragher was still watching the images. 'Stop the tape,' he said. 'I mean freeze the frame.'

Webb snapped the remote at the screen.

'No.' Carragher shook his head. 'Wind it back a bit.' Webb did and Carragher pointed again. 'There. Stop.'

Webb froze the frame and looked at the screen. Carragher was off his seat and looking very closely. 'That guy's American,' he said. 'I can spot them a mile away.' He pointed to a black man collecting his ticket from the pop-up slot. 'Look at his clothes, George.'

Webb looked more closely now and he could see that Carragher was right. 'He's got a grunt haircut, too,' he said. He checked the time: eight minutes after Kibibi went through. 'I'll get hold of somebody technical,' he said. 'Get a still of this and take it back to the embassy.'

The still was ready at four-thirty that afternoon and Webb drove back to the embassy. Carragher was in the office on the telephone and two agents from the legal attaché's office were with him. Their expressions were very serious. Webb sat down and looked at them. 'Did somebody die?' he asked.

Carragher put down the phone. 'As a matter of fact, they did.' He looked at his colleagues, then back at Webb. 'I was just on the phone to Washington,' he said. 'One of our agents has been shot dead in Jackson, Mississippi. The killer used military-grade rounds.' He stood up and exhaled heavily. 'That's not all. Two more members of the Missouri

Breakmen were gunned down in their beds last night. In two separate incidents; fully automatic fire and MP5 rifling on the shells.' He glanced at his colleagues and then at Webb again. 'The only people in the US with access to fully automatic MP5s are FBI SWAT teams.'

Swann lay in bed, holding Logan close to him. The room was on the eleventh floor of the Hyatt and faced across Jefferson Davis Highway. He held Logan very tightly. Earlier she had been crying, something he had never seen her do before. The murdered agent in Jackson had been a friend of hers from when she first joined the FBI. He had graduated from Quantico with her and they had been friends ever since. He was married with four children. She had fought her emotions all the time they were in the office, though the mood on 4th Street was as black as Swann had seen it. Nobody knew what was going on, and now an FBI agent had been gunned down.

When they got back to the hotel room, Logan had turned to him and said: 'It's war, Jack. That's how they think of it. Nobody shoots an FBI agent very easily. They know if they do, we'll hunt them to the ends of the earth.'

'You'll get the guy who did it, Chey.'

'That's not the point.' And then she had broken down.

Now he held her in his arms, aware of the rhythm of her breathing. She was asleep and he was awake, thinking about Fachida Harada and the Tatenokai. Why bring that to the attention of the media? The obvious link with the militia, the connotations of the SS initials in the English translation. The FBI had put forward their interpretation by way of counterbalance, and the demand made by Harada for the release of Shikomoto had also now been made public. Kovalski was making decisions on the hoof, in order to try and deal with the growing swell of public opinion. Then there had been the interview with Reece in Montana and his claim that he had indisputable proof that Harada was a government tool being used to blame the militia. Reece's final point was that the militia groups did not start the killings, the government did. None of it made sense.

There was a correlation between Harada's samurai posture and his homosexual relationship with Shikomoto, according to what Dr Habe had told them. But was that the only reason he was doing all this? The planning was reminiscent of an organised campaign, something that had been devised over a long period of time. Harada had a wife and family in Japan. Shikomoto had a wife and family. Could it just be the love between them that had sparked all this? If it was, why would Harada send the message about the Tatenokai to Carl Smylie? Swann could see how the militia would interpret Harada's actions, given what was happening to their members. But how could they have their indisputable proof?

He slipped his arm out from under Logan's shoulders and walked to the window. He wanted a cigarette, but the smell would only wake her. He was wide awake, though, and he got dressed and went downstairs. The bar was closed, but he sat in the lobby, smoked a cigarette and thought. Harada would attack again, that much he knew, but where? And where was he hiding? Again, he thought about the Tatenokai. Mishima obviously played a vital role in Harada's psyche. Samurai. Mishima. Tatenokai. He tossed it around in his head. Perhaps the *sokaiya were* involved, but, as far as he knew, Japanese organised crime had never been involved in terrorism. If Harada's sole reason for doing all this was to procure the release of Shikomoto, then why bring the Tatenokai into it? That just did not add up. If anything, it detracted from his purpose. He thought back to the beginning. Make your challenge, fight and protect your honour. That made sense. But then another thought struck him. The word samurai meant to serve. Was that just another coincidence? If not – who was Harada serving?

To Harrison's surprise, the five of them split up after delivering the C-4. Sidetrack instructed them all to go their separate ways and meet in four days' time, back at the Saratoga freight yard. Harrison grabbed his opportunity, jumped a train heading south-east and called Jean from a payphone in Corsicana. He then called the field office and instructed Penny and Swartz to run a check on Randy Meades and meet him at a diner he knew in De Ridder, Louisiana. When he was finished, he jumped another train and shared the car with a slim, silent hobo, with a multicoloured bandana tied round his neck. He seemed to be asleep and Harrison didn't bother him. He jumped off the train and met Jean at Lufkin. She stared at his face and the fear showed in her eyes. Harrison frowned, then remembered the battering he had taken and realised he had not looked in a mirror since. He adjusted the door mirror on the pick-up. His eye was bruised where he had taken the blow on the right-hand side and his lower lip was puffy and blackened.

'My God, John,' Jean said. 'What happened?'

'I got initiated, Miss Lady Mam. You're looking at the newest member of the Southern Black faction of the Freight Train Riders of America.'

He took a shower in the motel room, and she bathed his cuts and bruises with iodine. Then she took him to bed. Later, they sat naked in the heat and drank bottles of cold beer from the cooler he kept in his truck. 'After we meet with Penny and Swartz, I want you to go back to New Orleans,' Harrison said.

Jean looked a little doubtful, but he took her hand in his and squeezed. 'I've got to meet up with the crew in Arkansas again, and I aim to get as much on tape as I can.'

'You're going to wear a wire?'

'Yes, I am. Jean, these guys might be freighting drugs round the country, but it's not their main business. They're shipping military-grade weapons to the unorganised militia. We've got all hell busting loose and the weapons are being transported by the FTRA.' He shook his head. 'No wonder hobos are being killed. You get in a boxcar with a bunch of

396

guys arming a revolution and they ain't gonna take any chances.'

Her face clouded and Harrison laid down his beer bottle. 'I'm sorry, honey. I didn't mean to . . . I forgot myself for a moment.'

'It's OK. In a way, it's something.' She looked at him then, eyes glassed with unfallen tears. 'At least I know he wasn't just murdered for no reason at all.'

'No.' Harrison brushed her hair back with his fingers. 'He was in the wrong place at the wrong time. He looked oriental and he musta jumped a boxcar of Southern Blacks freighting military weapons.'

Jean got up then, walked to the door, still naked, and Harrison watched her: slim, lithe and petite. She opened the door a fraction and let the warm night air penetrate through the screen. 'You know,' she said. 'I think I might go back to New Orleans. Perhaps it's time I started to think about going home.'

Harrison did not say anything at first, then he shrugged lightly and nodded. 'Maybe you oughtta get your life going again, Jean. Go back to work or whatever. Your job in that hospital in London – that's a worthwhile job right there. I bet those kids really miss your face of a morning.'

She looked over her shoulder at him. 'Do you think so?'

'I sure do.'

'Oh, John.' She came to him then, and he took her in his arms and held her with her head against his chest. A lump was coagulating in his throat and he tried to swallow it, but could not. 'I don't know,' she said. 'I've come so far but . . .'

He held her at arm's length then. 'Jean, you've probably done as much as you can now. We've probably learned as much as we're gonna learn. You know the Southern Blacks killed your son and you probably know why. I tell ya, that's more than a helluva lot of families ever find out.'

She took her robe from the bed, slipped it round her shoulders and sat down again.

'No,' she said. 'I can't go home just yet. I can't go without knowing you're safe.'

'I'll be just fine.'

'I mean, I need to know you're not with them any more. You know – that the job's finished.'

Harrison smiled then. 'Miss Lady Mam,' he said gently, cupping her chin in his fingers. 'D'you know how long I was undercover one time?'

'No.'

'Three and a half years. I can't see you sitting in New Orleans for three and a half years.'

She laughed. 'No. Neither can I. There's a part of me that wants to go home, John, but there's another part which feels this isn't finished.'

They met Penny and Swartz in De Ridder the following afternoon. The diner was quiet and they occupied a booth at the farthest end of the room. Harrison set his back to the wall so that he could survey every corner. There were a couple of truckers eating in one booth and a kid and his girl in another, and one old guy who came in behind them and ate apple pie at the counter. The waitress brought coffee, and then Penny and Swartz showed up and sat down opposite them.

They made some fairly audible small talk and then Penny leant over. 'Randy Meades is one of the main players in the New Texas Rangers. That's the biggest militia outfit in the state. The cops have busted him three times for driving with no licence plates or valid documentation. Every time he goes to court, he claims the government has abrogated his constitutional right to travel and replaced it with a privilege.'

'Usual fodder, then,' Harrison said. Then he told them what he had learned and afterwards the two agents sat in silence. Harrison looked squarely at them. 'The Southern Blacks referred to it as revolution. They're arming the militia for war.'

They left the diner an hour later, and the man at the

counter was on his third piece of pie. He chewed, sipped coffee and watched them cross the parking lot. Five minutes later, he left the diner, stood on the step and looked at the night sky. It was warm and moist and he took off his denim shirt, leaving only his singlet. He lit a cigarette and then took a multicoloured bandana from his pocket: red, blue and black. He tied it round his neck, then flicked his shirt over one shoulder and headed for the railroad tracks. He had a rat tattooed on his arm.

20

The Cub flew into Manchester Airport on a Canadian passport provided by Secret Branch 40. He had met with Cyrus Birch in Paris, and Birch had confirmed that the Intelligence Support Activity's role in London had been terminated and was being taken over by the Israelis. Haan had been right. Mujah al-Bakhtar had been spotted in West London, which set alarm bells ringing throughout the UK's security services. There had only been one sighting, but by a reliable PLO source, who was based in London and was also an Israeli asset. Mossad, in consultation with Birch, had informed the British.

The intelligence community thinking was simple: the Americans wanted Bin Laden dead. Wherever al-Bakhtar went, Bin Laden was usually there too. By informing the British, they were increasing their chances of locating him. Birch was happy to have Haan on the payroll now, to covertly monitor MI5 activities and to see if they could lead The Cub to Bin Laden's location. The PLO source had had one sighting only. Al-Bakhtar had walked into a shop in Wembley and bought a newspaper. The source witnessed him getting into a BMW car and driving west on the A40.

So now, The Cub returned to the UK as a Canadian businessman, ostensibly heading for Sheffield to buy table knives. The UK authorities had previously seen him on to the plane at Heathrow and Haan had informed him that they had no idea he was returning. At Manchester Airport, he boarded the shuttle for Piccadilly Station and headed south to London.

He took a room at a small hotel overlooking the recreation ground on Kilburn Park Road. The accommodation had been arranged through the Israelis. The Cub studied his watch; the schedule had been tight, coming down from Manchester and getting across town. He had a number to ring three times if he was delayed. But since he was not late, he left his bag on the bed, stepped back into the sunshine and headed for the recreation ground. A footpath divided the large grassed expanse, with tennis courts and a cricket pitch occupying half of it. The pavilion overlooked the cricket ground on the far side of the path and The Cub made his way towards it. Wednesday evening and getting dark now, beyond nine o'clock. He was hungry and needed a shower, but this had to be done first. Only a handful of people were in the park – mainly kids playing cricket, a game that The Cub considered himself expert at after Pakistan. Apart from them, there was only the odd walker such as himself. He carried a small black attaché case, which was empty.

The Cub walked to the pavilion and then crossed behind it to where the large metal dustbins on wheels were standing. The rubbish was collected on Thursday mornings, so this had to be done now. He quartered the area with great care, leaving and re-entering the park to make sure it was clear of surveillance, before he approached the bins. He hefted the case up into the first one. The second bin was right beside it, but partially hidden by the ever-lengthening shadows. The Cub stepped up on the wheels, reached over and grabbed the other case. Another covert look round told him that nothing was amiss. The attaché case was an exact replica of the one he had been carrying, only this one was much heavier.

He did not return immediately to the room, but jumped on a bus that took him west. During the two weeks he had stayed in London as a tourist, he had familiarised himself with the bus and underground train routes to ensure his options (if attempting to shake surveillance) were varied. The bus took him as far as Wembley, then he took another back towards Willesden and walked up to the Neasden roundabout. The Indian tandoori house was still open, and

The Cub sat down in the window and ordered a curry, wondering how they would compare to those he had eaten in Islamabad. This was close to where the PLO man had made the sighting of the Butcher of Bekaa. The Cub sat in the window seat on his own and waited for his meal to come. At his feet, he could feel the comforting weight of the attaché case. Al-Bakhtar could have come from anywhere and disappeared back to anywhere. This part of London was full of ethnic communities, Asian and Afro-Caribbean predominantly. Thousands and thousands of them. Al-Bakhtar had not been dressed in any traditional garb, merely a dark suit, and he was bareheaded – just another black man amid a sea of black men. He ate the curry and decided it was not too bad, then he paid in cash, picked up the case again and travelled back to the hotel.

He laid the case on his bed, then turned the key in the doorlock. When he arrived, he had been over every inch of the room for bugs or microsurveillance cameras. Birch believed that the Israelis were clean, but if the ISA ground support had been infiltrated by the British, then it was entirely possible the Israelis had too. The Cub was in no doubt that the Brits would pay more attention to Israeli personnel than they would to Americans. But Haan had corroborated Birch's opinion. He said that Mossad recruited from within the ranks of the Jewish community for their ground support personnel. The UK was a friendly country, which always made it that bit easier, and there was a substantial Jewish community in Stoke Newington. It was they who had prepared the way for the assassin. Satisfied that no one was watching him, he flicked the locks on the case and lifted the lid. Expertly, he cast his eye across the rifle, broken down and secured in pockets of cut polystyrene foam. Next to the gun was a full clip of 10mm ammunition and a mobile telephone with battery charger. The Cub took out the phone, switched it on and laid it beside the bed. Then he closed the curtains and set about putting the sniper's rifle together.

It was a hybrid, no particular make, and certainly not traceable. It reminded him of the ones that the FBI used – hand-made by ex-marine armourers at Quantico. It took him less than five minutes to assemble it and adjust the sights. The breech was set in glass. Most importantly, the barrel had a screw-on silencer. He took it to pieces again and cleaned each section with the oilcloth housed in the lid of the case. He checked the sights again and took the corner of his shirt to a tiny smudge on the glass. The mobile phone rang and he looked at it for a moment before picking it up.

'Hello.'

'Everything OK?'

The Cub smiled. 'You're here already, then.'

'I'm on the payroll now.'

'When this is over, I'm coming to your place for a few weeks.'

'Fine. I'll let Natalia know.'

'She's still putting up with you?'

'Her, my grandmother and Yannick.'

'I thought he went back to Puyloubier.'

'No. They didn't want him back. He drinks too much wine. Anyway, he looks after my grandmother, or she him, one of the two.'

The Cub checked the street below through the curtains. All was quiet. 'What news?'

'Nothing. Our hosts are very anxious. He's got a lot of people in this country, a support network that makes some of ours look amateur.'

'So I sit tight.'

'I'm afraid so. Watch some of the cricket. There's a World Cup in progress.'

The Cub grunted. 'With my knowledge I could contribute to *Wisden*.'

George Webb drove along Kilburn Park Road and turned south on Maida Vale. Ten minutes later, he was parked at the US Embassy in Grosvenor Square and Carragher looked at him from the passenger seat. 'I'll get the door opened,' he said.

The building was quiet, just the marines on guard and a light in the legal attaché's office. 'Your buddy Swann's girlfriend is moving over here, isn't she?' Carragher asked.

Webb looked sideways at him. 'His fiancée, you mean.'

'Really? That serious, huh?'

'Oh yeah. Old Jack's going for it hook, line and sinker.'

Carragher smiled as he unlocked the office door. 'I gotta tell you, George. She is a bit of a babe.'

Webb sat down at his desk and sifted through the papers. The technical support unit had created the still photograph from Camden Town tube station, and had blown it up so the picture was pretty clear. Webb laid it on the desk and began leafing through the pile of military personnel.

Carragher took half the pile over to his desk. 'There's no law against being in the same tube station on the same night, is there, George?' he said.

Webb looked at him. 'Course not.' He smiled then. 'Keen to protect your own, huh?'

Carragher shrugged. 'I just figure Kibibi's killer could be anyone in London.'

'You just keep talking.' Webb was staring at a sheet of paper in front of him. It came from the file of a black marine, with portrait and profile photographs attached. He looked at them closely, then laid the blown-up image from the video alongside. 'I think that's bingo,' he said quietly.

Carragher looked up from his own pile. 'What've you got?'

'Dylan Stoval,' Webb said. 'Alton Patterson's room mate.'

Stoval sat across from him at eight-thirty the following morning. Carragher was there, plus two of the officers from diplomatic security. Webb looked over fisted hands at Stoval, who looked back laconically. He sat easily in the chair, his beret secured under the epaulette on his shoulder

404

and his tie tucked inside his shirt. Webb could almost see his own reflection in the shine on his boots.

'You room with Alton Patterson, don't you, Mr Stoval?' Webb said.

'Yessir.'

'Have you known him long?'

'A couple of years, I guess.'

Webb looked at the file in front of him. 'You've shared one or two postings, haven't you?'

'Yessir. Here and the National Guard base at Wichita Falls.'

Webb nodded. 'How well did you know Gunnery Sergeant Simpson?'

'Not real well at all, sir.'

'Did you ever visit her apartment?'

'No, sir.'

'And you didn't socialise with her at all?'

'No, sir.' Stoval's eyes were clear, his expression sure of itself. He sat with his hands resting in his lap in an easy manner.

Webb glanced at Carragher. 'Who do you hang out with over here?' he said.

'Alton mostly. We're buddies. I shoot pool with a coupla guys up at the Foxhole. There's a crowd of us, I guess.'

'But none of your acquaintances had much to do with Sergeant Simpson.'

'No, sir.'

'Did you know her in Texas?'

Stoval shrugged. 'She was there when I was, for about a month, is all.'

'Six weeks.'

'Was it? There you go.' Stoval smiled. 'We'd met as soldier and sergeant, sir. That's about all there was to it.'

'She was a good-looking woman, though, wasn't she?' Webb said.

'I guess so.'

'You didn't fancy her?'

'Excuse me?' Stoval looked puzzled.

'You know – fancy her?' Webb made an open-handed gesture.

Stoval looked at the diplomatic security officers and then his face cracked open in a grin. 'She was an OK gal to look at, but she was a gunnery sergeant, sir. She wouldn't have nothing to do with guys like me. Besides,' he said, 'when she was in Texas, she was dating a white guy. I figure she musta liked them better.' He looked evenly at Webb. 'Lotsa white guys like a piece of black ass.'

Webb stood up then and walked round the desk. 'So you never saw her socially?'

'No, sir.'

'And never visited her.'

'No, sir.'

Webb nodded. 'This is just routine, Mr Stoval, but we're asking everybody the same thing. Where were you on the night she was murdered?'

'I was in my room some of the time and shooting pool the rest.'

'Where?'

'The Foxhole, then two local bars.'

'Which bars?'

'The Red Lion and the Cat and Fiddle, sir.'

'And people saw you there?'

'I was playing with Alton. But yeah, I guess some people woulda seen us.'

'Nobody that you can name, though.'

'No one except Alton, sir.'

Webb nodded and sat down again. 'You didn't go anywhere else?'

Stoval shook his head and Webb gestured towards the tape machine. 'For the tape, Mr Stoval.'

'No, sir, I didn't go no place else.'

'Thank you, Mr Stoval. That'll do for now.' Webb leaned over and switched off the tape. Stoval got up, saluted and left the room.

Webb sat back and placed both hands behind his head. 'We've found our first liar,' he said.

He, Carragher and an agent from diplomatic security went back to the incident room at Paddington. They sat down with Weir and Webb relayed what they had discovered.

'You didn't ask him directly?' Weir said.

Webb shook his head. 'He's cocksure of himself, Guv. I wanted to hold that in reserve.'

'So what do you want to do now?'

'I want to get the barman in here to look over some pictures, see if he picks out Patterson. If he does, I want to lean on him a little.'

'Why Patterson?'

'Because he's weaker than Stoval. Stoval lied through his teeth to me just now. He claimed to be with Patterson all night, but he's on that tape in Camden Town. Patterson's his alibi.'

'What about the nightclub tapes?' Weir asked.

'We've been through them, but nobody has spotted him there.' Webb sat forward. 'I know what you're thinking, Guv. The trip to Camden could be innocent. But if it is, why lie about it to me?'

Weir sat back and lifted one foot to the edge of the desk. 'OK,' he said. 'Go for Patterson. I'll get the barman in here, see if he can give us anything.'

Harada rode the metro in Washington D.C., dressed as a woman. His make-up was perfect, painstakingly applied that morning. He had taken a razor to his head and shaved off all of his hair, then fitted the net over his scalp and the black-fringed hairpiece over that. He wore a skirt and jacket combination, flat black shoes, and had shaved the hairs on his legs so that nothing showed under the black nylon stockings. The whole thing set a charge in his veins and his thoughts of Shikomoto were concentrated into memories of the past. For three years they had been lovers, men with a passion born of generations before them. Harada had never dressed in women's clothing before, but both he and Shikomoto had applied make-up, in the manner of their forebears, before they launched their attacks. Those thoughts brought back other memories – more recent ones – thoughts and deeds he would much rather forget.

He concentrated on the map above the opposite window. At his feet, he carried three large plastic store bags from the shops in Pentagon City. They contained clothes he had bought to cover the separate packages he had built in the early hours of this morning. Last night, he had driven his *C U SAFELY* truck to the Kennedy stadium and then to the B terminal at National Airport. Complete with tool belt hanging like a *pistolero* round his waist, he had wandered into the men's room and closed the door of the cubicle. Fifty-five seconds to whip out each of the four screws on the inspection hatch, then set the timers and replace the hatch once more. After that, he headed back to the scene of his second attack, the hospital opposite Foggy Bottom metro station, and laid another device. Then he had walked through Station Park until he found the appropriate trash can. And now he was on the final leg of this particular trip, with a journey on the metro.

He rode the Blue line, got out of the train at the Metro Center and dumped a Burger King drink carton into a rubbish bin on the platform. Then he got back on the train and rode to Rosslyn, where he discarded a sealed hamburger carton, once again in the trash can. Switching lines, he made a drop at Union Station, then took a cab to Constitution Avenue and the Smithsonian Museum of Natural History. He climbed the stairs in the cool of the building and paused briefly in front of the massive stuffed elephant that dominated the lobby. In the ladies' room, he went to the disabled cubicle and placed his final device behind the inspection hatch. He was working hard now and alone. This was more difficult than he had first envisaged.

He was conscious of the summer heat and the last thing he needed was sweat starting to smear his make-up.

When the final stage was set, he hailed a cab and rode up town as far as the old soldiers' and airmen's home. He got out, paid the driver and walked to the self-storage units.

Across the road, the legless old man was vigilant as ever. Sentry duty in the goon tower. He sat in his wheelchair with his twin stumps sticking out and wondered where the hell he had lost his legs. His pyjama jacket was open, revealing matted white hair on the hanging folds of his chest. He gurgled on his own saliva and spat at the floor as if it was tobacco juice, then thinned his eyes at the woman opening the door to the lock-up.

'Nurse,' he yelled. 'Goddammit. Nurse!' Reaching out, he pressed the bell and kept his finger there until the intern appeared in the doorway.

'What is it, Charlie?'

'Goddamn Japs. It's Pearl Harbor all over again.' He looked round at the nurse, eyes rolling. 'I was in Hiroshima, or was it Nagasaki.' He thought for a moment, his finger still pressing the bell button.

'Charlie, take your finger off the button,' the nurse said gently and walked round the bed.

'Goddamn, would you look at that.' The old man threw a hand in the direction of the storage lot across the street. 'One minute it's a man, now it's a goddamn woman.' He gripped the nurse's arm and looked into her face. 'I tell you. They're damn near everywhere.'

The nurse smiled at him. 'You wanna take your nap, now, Charlie? I think you're getting tired.'

'No.' Charlie squeezed more tightly on her arm. 'Call the marines, goddammit. Call the President. The Japs are everywhere.'

'Your nap, Charlie.' The nurse wheeled him away from the window. 'Come on, you'll feel better after.'

'Where're my damn legs?' Charlie muttered as the nurse

lifted him on to the bed. 'Who in God's name ran off with my damn legs?'

Swann could smell the tension in the field office when he went in that morning. Logan was up and gone without waking him. Neither of them had got to bed before 3 a.m., and he took the metro in from Crystal City, switched lines and got out at Judiciary Square. She was on the phone when he got upstairs, and Kovalski and McKensie were in a meeting with the people from Fugitive Publicity. Swann sat down opposite Logan.

'Carl,' she was saying. 'If you're so sure BobCat Reece has the proof he talks about, show it to me. Until then, why don't you think about how you might just be making the situation worse.' She sat back, smiled at Swann and rolled her eyes to the ceiling.

'The FBI is not running round the country killing people. I know somebody is, Carl. But it's not us. We're doing all we can to stop it. Tell that to your friend Reece.' She put the phone down and shook her head. 'Every time I change my internal number, that reporter gets a hold of it.' She blew out her cheeks. 'How are you, honey?'

'Fine. Why did you leave without waking me up?'

She shrugged. 'This is our fight. Besides, you're looking tired. I figured you needed some beauty sleep.' She tried to smile again, but it didn't really work.

Swann sat forward. 'Are you going to Mississippi for the funeral?'

'If I possibly can. It depends what Harada's got planned.'

'I was thinking about him last night,' Swann said. 'Why bring the Tatenokai into it, Chey? Why go to all that bother of sending Carl Smylie an encrypted e-mail about Mishima's Shield Society? I mean, given the remit Harada's laid out for us, why do all that?'

'I don't know, Jack.' Logan got up. 'But when I pop the sonofabitch, I'll ask him for you. OK?'

Swann followed her to the coffee-maker. 'What about

some kind of deal with Shikomoto – privileges or something?'

'Nothing doing.' Logan poured coffee.

Back in the squad room, the phone she had left was ringing. Swann walked over and picked it up. 'Agent Logan's phone,' he said.

'This is Fachida Harada. Listen very carefully.'

Swann snapped his finger at the agent seated in the next booth and made a whirling gesture above his head. The Triggerfish team set about trying to locate the source.

'Fachida, listen,' Swann started. Everyone in the office looked up. Logan dumped the coffee in the sink and all but ran to Kovalski's office.

'You listen,' Harada said in Swann's ear. 'The FBI has done nothing by way of accession to my demands. So this is what will happen.' Now, half a dozen agents were listening in, including Logan and Kovalski. 'There's a bomb at Union Station, another at the Metro Center, another at Rosslyn. There's one at the Smithsonian and one at National Airport. I've placed a really nice one at the Kennedy stadium, one at Station Park, and, because your vigilance is so pitiful, another at Foggy Bottom.' He paused for a moment. 'There is a total of two hours before they all go off. The first will go in thirty minutes and then at intervals after that. This time, we play a guessing game. Which is thirty minutes and which is two hours?' He hung up.

Logan came out of Kovalski's office and yelled at the Triggerfish man. 'Did you get a fix?'

The agent looked at her and sighed.

'Fuck it.' Logan turned to the gathered members of the task force. 'Eight separate devices and thirty fucking minutes. I don't believe the sonofabitch.'

The city ground to a standstill: eight separate devices, placed strategically to cause the maximum confusion. The people around Foggy Bottom were evacuated for the second time in as many weeks and feelings were running high. City cops, parks cops and even the secret service cops were drafted in to assist the task force with what was becoming a massive logistical problem. Kovalski and Logan remained in the command post this time and Swann hovered impotently in the background. The Office of Emergency Management was on the phone to Kovalski, so were the Department of Water and Power, the State Department, FEMA and the Department of Defense. The FBI Director drove the short distance from Pennsylvania Avenue to be on hand at the command post. Everyone outside wanted to know what they were doing about Fachida Harada. Was the militia right? Was this some renegade government agent gone wrong, or was it even more sinister than that? How could one man be causing so much mayhem?

Kovalski somehow kept his cool, but exactly thirty minutes from the time the warning came in, the device at Union Station blew up. Already the metro was at a standstill and the thousands of commuters who had travelled in on the trains had no way of getting home. Ten minutes after Union Station, the Foggy Bottom bomb went off. It was much bigger than the previous one and windows for a hundred metres were blown out. This time, there was not enough bomb-squad support in the city and the naval EOD team had to come in from Indian Head to deal with both the airport and the Kennedy stadium. Kovalski had ordered a full evacuation of the National Airport and its metro station – the whole area back to four hundred metres. Incoming flights were rerouted, the air-traffic control tower had to be abandoned and contingency plans were being implemented. Bolling Airbase assisted and Andrews out in Virginia. Some of the flights were sent into Dulles, which was rapidly clogging up.

'This is the worst we've seen in the city,' Logan told Swann. 'Somehow, we're gonna have to negotiate with this guy.'

Swann moved alongside Kovalski. 'Tom,' he said quietly. 'Something occurs to me. The delay on these devices is complicated. So far, there's been not a single error and, as far as we know, Harada is working alone.'

'So?'

'So he's using military hardware. Not only has he got access to C-4, he's using sophisticated timers. This isn't just a central heating programme with a safety-arming switch.'

Kovalski's direct line, rerouted to the command post, started ringing. Logan picked it up. 'Agent Logan.' She knew even before he said anything and she snapped her fingers at the Triggerfish team. 'You're making your point, Fachida. Stop this and we can start talking.'

'Talk is cheap, Agent Logan. You know what my demands are.'

'Call it off, Fachida, and I promise we'll talk.'

'Interstate 395. There's a car bomb between junctions 7 and 8a. You'll know the vehicle, because the hood is up and the hazard lights are on. You have another thirty minutes.' He hung up.

Logan held the phone for a few seconds, then set it down, and turned to Kovalski. 'You're not gonna believe this,' she said.

Kovalski was on the radio to the EOD units and every available state trooper in the area. Interstate 395, one of the busiest routes into the city, had to be sealed off. Sweat was visible on his brow now: resources were being stretched to breaking point.

Fifteen minutes later, Harada called again. This time he spoke to Kovalski. 'I hope you're having a nice day. I want Shikomoto released within the next twenty-four hours. In the meantime, Interstate 66 between junctions 73 and 74. You need to close it down.' He hung up. Kovalski was glaring at the Triggerfish man.

'Mr Kovalski,' he said. 'Quit looking at me like that. This guy is on the move and every call's on a different electronic serial number. There's fuck all I can do about it.'

Kovalski sat down heavily and looked at the Director. 'Sir,' he said. 'He's given us a further twenty-four hours,

413

including the time it takes to sort this mess out. What're we going to do?'

They could hear the explosions from the command post, and Swann stood at the tinted windows and watched the pandemonium round the metropolitan police headquarters in the next block. When this happened in London, people got upset, but they were relatively used to it. It had never happened in Washington D.C. and the people were panicking. The TV sets were on in the outer office and he went to watch the coverage from various vans and choppers. CNN showed the massive snarl-up of traffic on 66 and 395. They showed the Federal Triangle in disarray, people herded into the parks round the White House and the Washington Monument.

Various members of the public were being interviewed by reporters. One man, well dressed in a business suit and crisp white shirt, was gesticulating wildly. 'We wanna know what the hell is going on here!' he was saying. 'Twice now, twice there's been a bomb at Foggy Bottom. What the hell is up with that? What does the FBI think it's doing?'

The reporter moved to the next person and the next, and the sentiments were exactly the same, just varying degrees of venom in the verbal vilification. 'The goddamn militia's got it right,' one woman was saying. 'The government's brought this on itself. There's gonna be war in this country and it'll be the government's fault.'

Swann shook his head. Then another man, bearded and sweating, was talking. 'This is either some loco agent gone AWOL, or it's a deliberate ploy to deflect public opinion away from the murders these Orientals have been committing. I think the patriots are right. I tell you, I thought they were just a buncha fruitcakes, but not now. Oh, no. The government can take my gun if they want to, but the barrel's gonna be smoking and they'll find the clip empty.'

In the command post, Kovalski's phone was ringing again. 'Have you been watching TV?' There was ice in Harada's voice. 'If you do not release Shikomoto within

414

twenty-four hours, I will make public a fact that will have the people of this country storming every federal building in the fifty-one states.' He hung up before Kovalski could say anything.

Kovalski did not even look at the Triggerfish man. He stood for a long moment, thinking. Swann could almost see him count from one to ten. Then he looked up, caught Swann's eye and called to Logan. 'Cheyenne. Get a chopper up and get to an airport,' he said. 'I want you at Eastville, Georgia, talking to Shikomoto.'

Swann went with her. The roof of the 4th Street field office was flat and the SWAT team had a helipad painted on it. The Department of Defense flew in a Blackhawk and airlifted them to Andrews Airforce Base, where the Hostage Rescue Team's plane was waiting. Swann buckled himself in and looked round at Logan. They were the only passengers. The plane was cleared for take-off and they were away, flying south across Virginia for the Carolinas and Georgia.

They landed at Atlanta and Agent Pryce from the field office collected them again. 'We've set it up,' he said. 'Shikomoto's agreed to see you. From what the guards down there tell us, he's really enjoying this.'

They were shown straight to the interview suite, where Shikomoto was already seated in his leg and wrist irons, a packet of cigarettes and an ashtray on the table before him. He looked up when they came in, but his face was as impassive as ever and he did not smile. Logan sat down opposite him.

'Hello, Agent Logan,' he said. 'I expected to see you again, but Fachida has hurried things along a little, hasn't he?'

'What do you want?' she asked him.

'My freedom.'

'Freedom's gone already. Second option?'

Shikomoto laughed then. 'There are no second options, Logan. You knew that before you came here.'

Logan shook her head. 'Get real, Tetsuya. You know we're not gonna free you.'

'What choice do you have? Your capital city is in panic. Your people are revolting.'

'Nobody's revolting.'

'They're beginning to. They will, Logan. They have the fear of God himself in them right now, and they will react. With some countries that's not a real problem, they might riot, smash things, demonstrate, but there are two hundred and fifty million privately owned weapons in this country. When your people revolt, they do it with guns in their hands.' He took a cigarette from the pack, his manacled hands making the movement awkward. He blew the match out from the side of his mouth and looked at her once more. 'Release me.'

Logan sat back and drummed long-nailed fingers on the table. 'Who is Harada working for?'

'Nobody.'

Swann sat forward then. 'What he's doing is not the work of just one man.' He held Shikomoto's eye. 'Samurai means to serve, Tetsuya. Who is Harada serving?'

Shikomoto shook his head. 'People believed that the samurai served the emperor in the old days. In a way they did. They might have collected taxes for him, or they might have done so for their warlords. But, ultimately, a samurai warrior served no one and nothing, save his honour.'

'Honour.' Logan curled her lip. 'What has blowing up innocent people got to do with honour?'

Shikomoto shook his head at her. 'As far as I am aware, only two innocents have died.'

'Until today. There's been three more today.'

'Unfortunate. Fachida will mourn them. He will atone for them in the next life, but, right now, his honour is more important than anything.'

Logan stood up then and paced behind him. She bent over his shoulder so her mouth was close to his ear. 'Tetsuya,' she said softly. 'If we understood what this honour thing was about, maybe we could figure out something to do for you.'

'The only thing you can do is release me. Fachida will not stop until either you do or he is dead.' He looked over his shoulder at her. 'That's how seriously he takes the restoration of his honour.'

'Restoration.' Swann said. 'Has Harada's honour been tainted?'

Shikomoto looked at him then and his eyes were narrow slits in his head. 'I will tell you what I know, and if you do not agree to Fachida's demands, I will make it public in this prison. Word will spread and every fear that is plaguing your citizens will be realised. When that happens, you will have a civil war on your hands.' He leaned his elbows on the table. 'After we attacked your embassy in 1986, the faction was all but disbanded. Shigenobu led us to the enclave in North Korea.'

'We figured that much,' Logan said. 'So what?'

'North Korea, the great Communist stronghold that has proved so irksome to the Americans over so many years. How many of your soldiers died fighting the Chinese?'

Swann was staring at him now.

'The FBI was hunting me after I had been identified by the CIA. But they did not know about Fachida.' Shikomoto's voice was quieter now. 'Both of us escaped to North Korea with Shigenobu. He had amassed a fortune from the PLO and Qaddafi. I had no time for this act of pure capitalism. It made him as weak as those he was fighting. I was a warrior. Like Mishima, I was samurai. I took a new name and returned to Japan. I obtained work, married and had a family in Osaka. Fachida remained behind. Shigenobu did not want anyone leaving the enclave, ensuring he had warriors for the future. But I slipped across the border to China, travelled through Manchuria and crossed the Sea of Japan in a fishing boat. Fachida remained in the enclave for three months, but then he, too, grew tired of the existence and vowed to follow me.'

'Did he get to Japan?'

Shikomoto shook his head. 'He was captured by CIA agents in Shanghai. They had discovered he was the second man and they monitored his movements.'

Logan was staring at him now. 'What happened?' she said.

'They offered him a choice.' Shikomoto looked sour now, as if his mouth was suddenly rancid. 'They showed him pictures of his sister in Kobe and told him of the unforeseen accident she would be having, while he was being handed to the FBI. You see, they had wanted an asset in North Korea for years and years. Fachida was free to move about the country. He was in a position to gather intelligence.' He broke off for a moment, then said: 'I think that time was his weakest. The old ways were gone and, with them, all form of ideals. The Communist ideal had been a good one, but Shigenobu did not adhere to it. We had become fat cats of capitalism, yet under the red flag. Fachida returned to the enclave for the sake of his sister and for four years he worked for the CIA. Then he took his share of the money and escaped to Japan.'

Logan stared at him. 'You're telling us that Fachida Harada was a CIA asset?' she said.

'That's exactly what I'm telling you.' Shikomoto laughed then. 'He is every bit the government agent gone wrong that the militia are proclaiming. Think about it, Logan. If either he or I make this public, the worst fears of the militia will be realised. Those fears will translate to the general public and you will have war in your country.'

Swann nodded slowly. 'So his honour went when he succumbed to the CIA,' he said.

Shikomoto looked witheringly at him. 'Of course it did. Fachida spent time in the enclave, then escaped them and did everything a warrior might to try and re-establish his line. He married into the Yanagawa-gumi. He became *sokaiya* with money he took from Shigenobu. He thought the yakuza would protect his sister from the Americans. For a while this was successful, but then the CIA found him again. They came for him a second time and showed no regard for his yakuza employers. Fachida was foolish. The Yanagawa-gumi would not fight the Americans.' He paused long enough to fish another cigarette from the packet. 'The FBI had been hunting me for ten long years and they really wanted me badly. Fachida succumbed for a second time. You see, unfortunately, he is not a strong man. He could never have fought in open combat; always with him it was *ninja*.' He paused for a moment. 'I had been living in Osaka since 1989. I had married. I had a family. I had been true to the ways of the master.' Again, he looked beyond them. 'Fachida gave me up to the FBI. And after that, the CIA left him alone.'

'His honour gone for all time.'

Shikomoto looked at him again. 'Not quite,' he said.

Logan had been looking through him, hearing his words and not hearing them. In her mind's eye, she could see the crowds of angry, salivating people by the Washington Monument, and in the parks and outside the White House. She could hear Smylie's words about the militia and Tatenokai. Harada *was* a government agent gone wrong. Shikomoto was right: if that ever came out, their worst fears could be realised.

They flew back to Washington in silence, sitting side by side on the twenty-four-seater plane. 'I hope the Hostage Rescue Team weren't called out,' Swann said, trying to lighten the atmosphere. Right now, he missed London. He missed his own job and, above all, he missed Charlotte and Joanne, his children. Logan was linked into the SIOC via her laptop computer and was getting an update on the situation in D.C. So far, she had not imparted their discovery to anyone. If it leaked, the repercussions did not bear thinking about. As far as she was concerned, it was for Tom Kovalski's ears only. She tapped the keys of her laptop and then looked round at Swann.

'They're beginning to get things under control. The Indian Head EOD team were hoping to perform a con-ex on the Interstate 66 car bomb, but it blew before they could send in a robot.'

'Is there much damage?'

She shook her head. 'A lot more than before. But they're still not massive bombs, nothing like Oklahoma City. They're there to cause minimum casualties and maximum disruption.' She snorted. 'Judging by how jammed up the Bureau switchboard is, they're proving pretty effective.'

Swann leaned his head against the edge of the window. 'He's using the terrorist's greatest weapon, Cheyenne. Fear. He's showing everyone exactly what he can do and just how easily.'

'Both the National Airport bomb and the one at Kennedy stadium were in the men's rooms,' Logan interrupted him. 'The same with the Smithsonian. The initial reports from the explosives' officers say that they were behind the cistern inspection hatches.' She looked at Swann. 'Jack, they could've been there for weeks, months even.'

'They probably were. It's what I said to Kovalski earlier. Harada's got access to some very sophisticated timing and power units.'

It was late when they got back to the field office, but most of the task force were still there, taking phone calls, some of them with sightings of Harada, but most of them from people screaming vitriol at the FBI's ineptitude. BobCat Reece was on prime-time TV again, and, across the country, militia leaders' views were being aired. People were calling for a suspension of Congress and the arrest of the President. The FBI, ATF and just about every other federal agency were being publicly castigated, and not just by the extremists.

The following morning, Kovalski took Logan and Swann down the road to Pennsylvania Avenue and the Hoover building. They went up to the Director's office and were confronted by the mayor, the chief of police, the head of the Washington office of the Federal Emergency Management Agency and the national security adviser. Kovalski looked at the gathering, shook his head and took the Director to one side.

Two minutes later, only the three of them remained, plus the Director and the President's national security adviser. Kovalski told them what Logan and Swann had learned and everyone was silent. 'Sir,' he said, at length. 'I'm not one for doing deals with terrorists, but if this story gets out, I believe the whole situation could spiral out of control. The country has seen happen everything the radicals ever said would happen – Hong Kong troops, the taking of weapons, black helicopters, abductions, citizens being murdered. Now they see an Oriental bombing the capital. Half of them already believe that we're behind it. If Harada or Shikomoto goes public, then we've got a state of emergency on our hands.'

Robert Jensen, the national security adviser, sat in his chair with his arms folded. 'We don't do deals, Mr Kovalski. We will not be held to ransom. The whole world is looking on. We've got a foreign policy mess to clear up in the Balkans, and we can't afford to be seen to be weak when dealing with threats in our own capital city.'

Kovalski nodded. 'Ordinarily, I'd agree with you, sir. But I think it's equally politically damaging to fight a civil war. If we ignore the realities of this, then we're really fucking stupid.' He looked at each of their faces. 'Yesterday at two o'clock, Harada gave us twenty-four hours. We've had eighteen of them already.'

Jensen frowned across the desk at him. 'Then you have six left to find him.'

21

'Six hours,' Logan was saying as they rode up in the elevator. 'What does he think we are – miracle workers?'

Kovalski looked round at her. 'No, but he thinks we need to be.'

McKensie was waiting for them as they came in. 'Sir,' she said. 'Mr Mayer's been on the line from New Orleans. He wants you to contact him immediately. He was going to page you through the SIOC, but I told him you were with the national security adviser.'

Kovalski breezed into his office and dropped his leather briefcase on the desk. Logan and Swann followed him. 'You want some privacy, Tom?' Logan asked him.

Kovalski laughed out loud. 'Fuck privacy, Cheyenne. Hell, take a seat.' He flicked through the Rolladex on his desk and located the New Orleans number.

'Charlie Mayer, please,' he said. 'Tom Kovalski.' He sat back, one foot up, swivelling from side to side. 'Charlie, it's Tom,' he said, when Mayer came on the line. 'What can I do for you?'

Then he sat up straighter. 'Right. OK. Can you get me the details right away? Thanks, Charlie.' He hung up the phone again.

Logan was watching him, and the colour had drained from his face. He worked his tie loose at the collar. 'What's up, Tom?'

'Shut the door, Cheyenne.'

Logan did as she was asked and both she and Swann moved over to Kovalski's desk.

'Have you heard of the Freight Train Riders of America?' he asked.

'The freight train murders,' Swann said. 'Jean Carey, an Englishwoman. Her son was killed in Louisiana.'

'Right.' Kovalski pursed his lips. 'New Orleans put Harrison on to the trains undercover, because they thought the gang was using the freight network to haul class A narcotics to their dealers.'

'And were they?' Swann said.

'No. They're shipping military-grade weapons to the militia.'

For a few moments, the three of them just sat there.

'Harrison witnessed the transfer of C-4 explosives from members of the FTRA to a man called Randy Meades,' Kovalski went on. 'Meades is an active member of the New Texas Rangers.'

'Militia,' Swann said.

Kovalski nodded. 'This is about the worst news I coulda heard today.'

'You think they're preparing for a showdown?'

'Well, it's not a Sunday school picnic.' He made a face. 'But if they've got any sense, they won't create any kinda stand-off situation. No, they'll be preparing for a new hit-and-run campaign, much like they've been doing already, but on a larger scale. The big difference is the military ordnance, that and public opinion.'

'Who is behind the murders of their leaders, Tom?' Swann asked.

'I don't know. If I did, we could do something about public opinion.'

'Maybe it *is* rogue agents,' Logan said. 'Maybe there really is a New World Order, a global conspiracy. Who knows?'

Kovalski curled his lip. 'Whoever it is, they're destabilising this society like it's never been done before.'

'I can't help thinking that this all blew up at the same time,' Swann said. 'Harada, the Orientals killing militia leaders. Is there a link between Harada and the militia? They've both got access to military-grade ordnance.'

'You've heard the rhetoric, Jack,' Kovalski said. 'Read the newspapers. BobCat Reece claims they've got proof that Harada's a government agent. He's not working with them.' He stood up. 'New Orleans is gonna co-ordinate a nationwide task force with this FTRA thing. We have to stop the militia getting those weapons.'

'Another thought occurs to me,' Logan said.

He nodded. 'I know. Where are the weapons coming from in the first place?'

Harrison left Jean again and this was the hardest parting yet. He could feel himself falling for her badly, something he had not wanted to do. They made love into the night, and in the morning she woke him with the softness of her hand across his thighs, and they made love again. He buried himself deep inside her, her ankles crossed tight behind his back. He lay for a moment, breathing hard and sweating, the Texas heat rising outside, though it was still early morning.

Jean lifted herself on one elbow. 'Are you OK, John?' It was as if she could sense something, feel the sudden pain he was going through.

He sat up and got out of bed. 'I'm fine, Miss Lady Mam.' He turned then. 'I guess I'm just getting old, is all.'

'You and me both.'

'You're not old, Jeanie. You're young.'

'I'm almost forty-five.' She looked up at him then; the sheet thrown back so that only part of one leg was covered.

Harrison shook his head and smiled. 'I gotta tell you, you are one beautiful lady.'

She was. Her skin was smooth and youthful; just a few lines across her lower belly which she had gained in childbirth.

Harrison sat down again and let his fingers fall on to her thighs, where the wisps of black pubic hair lifted. He could feel himself getting aroused once more, but knew he had to get going. He touched her lips with his, then stepped into the shower.

'Are you going back to New Orleans?' he asked, when he was dressed in his old clothes with the wire fixed under his shirt.

She made a face. 'I'm not sure. Part of me wants to, but another part doesn't.' She touched his cheek. 'I don't like to think of you all alone out here. If I'm driving around, then I'm sort of still with you.'

Harrison kissed her fingers. 'Then drive around some more. Shit, I'll miss the hell outta you if you go back to New Orleans.' He shouldered his pack. 'Jean, do what you need to do. I'll understand. If you do head back, though, just leave the truck at the field office. And give the cellphone to Penny.'

'OK.'

They looked at one another for a long time and then Harrison stepped outside. He closed the door quietly and stood for a moment, plucked a cigarette from his shirt pocket and then walked to the roadside. A hundred yards out of town, a truck rolled by and he stuck out his thumb.

He met Hooch and Carlsbad first. They were running across country south of Dallas. Harrison had been on two trains, crisscrossing the counties, with his black bandana tied about his throat. He picked up the train heading east for Louisiana and was trotting alongside an open-topped boxcar when Carlsbad shouted at him from another, further back down the train. Harrison waited for the car to catch up, then grabbed Carlsbad's outstretched arm.

'Hey, bro. What's happening?' Carlsbad said as he hauled him up. 'Where you been hiding?'

Harrison squinted at him. 'Nowheres, buddy. Sidetrack told me we was splitting up after the drop.' He was acutely aware of the wire taped across his flesh and eased himself over to the far side of the car. 'Where *you* been at?'

'On vacation.' Carlsbad grinned at Hooch. 'You oughtta come with us next time.' He smiled lopsidedly. 'We always take a little holiday after a big one.'

'You lost me, bro. You're gabbling.'

'A drop-off, man. Like the one to the Texas Rangers.'

'Oh, right.' Harrison rolled his cigarette. 'What the fuck are they gonna do with so much C-4, anyways?'

Carlsbad shrugged. 'Blow something up.'

Harrison sucked smoke. 'Tell me about the vacation, Hooch. Carlsbad's not making any sense.'

'He's talking about the whorehouses.' Hooch sat more upright. 'We like to get laid some, after we've been working hard. We've got a good trail of whorehouses right across southern Texas. All kindsa gals in there.'

'Next time, I might just tag along with you.'

'So where did *you* get to?' Hooch asked him.

Harrison shrugged. 'Nowhere really. I kinda didn't know what to do. I was all for heading north, when you guys decided to beat the fuck outta me at Saratoga. Then you take me halfway across Texas with a load of fucking explosives.'

Hooch laughed. 'Four-String, you're FTRA now. You'll get used to it. Sometimes we is all running together and sometimes we split up. We're regular hobos, man. The tracks are in our blood. We just come together so we can make a little money.'

'Yeah,' Carlsbad said. 'And bust a coupla heads.'

Harrison squinted at him. 'When I first ran into you guys, I noticed how the regular hobos didn't stick around too long.'

Hooch nodded. 'Except you, you asshole.' He pinched forefinger and thumb together. 'You know, man. You was this close from getting wasted.'

'You figure, huh?'

Hooch shook his head wearily. 'Four-String, you might figure you're a tough guy, but I killed more guys on the skids than you ate hot dinners.'

Harrison squinted at him. 'Is that a fact?'

Carlsbad interrupted them, lying on his side on the boards. 'Anyways, man. How come you was packing so much hardware?'

Harrison flicked ash from the end of his cigarette. 'Are you kidding me, Carlsbad? I was fresh outta Angola. You figure I'm gonna go anywhere without packing?'

'Yeah, but two guns, man.'

'And the knife. Don't forget the knife.'

Carlsbad looked sourly at him. 'How can I forget the fucking knife?'

They switched trains east of Dallas, and Hooch told Harrison they were due to meet up with Sidetrack in Paris, twenty or so miles south of the Oklahoma line.

'How come you know when to hook up with him?' Harrison asked.

Hooch looked at him then as if he was stupid. 'You from the dark ages or something?' He produced a cellphone from inside his pack. 'I call him up on the phone.'

Harrison shook his head. 'I thought this riding the skids was getting away from regular life,' he said. 'Next, you'll have fucking e-mail.'

Sidetrack, as always, was with Limpet, plus four other Southern Blacks, some of whom Harrison recognised from his initiation ceremony. The three of them left the train in Paris, and found Sidetrack and his cohorts already settled beside a campfire at the far end of the freight yard. Harrison walked next to Hooch, who towered above him, wheezing a little as he moved.

'How much do we pay the guards?' Harrison asked.

Hooch looked round at him. 'What d'you mean?'

'I mean, I've been in a dozen fucking freight yards and I've never seen one of them.'

Hooch grinned at him and dumped his bags by the fire.

Sidetrack seemed preoccupied and Harrison's survival instincts prickled. He sat across the fire from him and leaned with an elbow resting on his pack. Carlsbad had a bunch of steaks laid on top of one another in waxed paper and he set them on sticks to cook. Sidetrack was sipping mescal and Harrison watched him. He was wearing his thoughtful expression, exemplified by the canine tooth pressing down on his lower lip. Neither of them had spoken as yet. They looked at one another across the fire and Harrison licked the edge of his cigarette paper.

'What you been doing, Four-String?' Sidetrack asked him suddenly.

'Just bopping along.'

'Where did you go?'

'No place in particular. I hooked up with a gal I know, for a day or so.' He could feel Hooch's eyes on him. 'Woulda been rude not to, seeing as how I was in the area.'

'Where would that be?'

'De Ridder, Louisiana.'

'Who's the gal?'

Harrison wanted to keep everything as close to the truth as possible. Ninety-five per cent of the undercover agent's story is true: that way, lies don't catch up with you. Sidetrack had no idea where he had been, but this was his first major test since initiation.

'Just a gal, Sidetrack. If you wanna know, I first met her when I was in 'Nam. She came here with the rest of the refugees.'

'A gook?' Hooch said. 'You been fucking a gook?'

Harrison smiled along with them, but he was thinking of Jean and just how precious she was to him. 'That's right, Hooch. And you know what? When they lie with you all night and tell you how much they wanna be with you, it's a whole lot better than paying for it.'

Everybody laughed then, including Sidetrack, who corked the bottle of mescal and tossed it to Harrison. He took a swig, got up to stretch his legs and sat down on the other side of the fire. He handed the bottle back to Sidetrack. 'So where you been at?'

Sidetrack looked at the flames. 'Here and there. Setting up some deals. You know how it goes.'

'Tough at the top, huh?'

Sidetrack leered at him. 'Somebody's got to do it.'

428

Harrison sucked on his cigarette, then took one of Carlsbad's steaks from the fire and chewed on it.

Later, Sidetrack had drunk most of his bottle and they had all begun to relax. Harrison wanted to know what their movements were, whether they were making any more shipments, whether the crew with Sidetrack was carrying any cargo of weapons. He wanted to know where the C-4 had come from and what Randy Meades planned to do with it, but he knew better than to ask any questions. He plucked at the strings of the banjo, with the breeze pulling at his hair and sending smoke from the fire drifting this way and that. Sidetrack watched him and nodded appreciatively.

'You ain't bad on that thing, now you've got five strings.' He looked in his eye then. 'I guess I don't mind having you around, even if you do sleep with gooks.'

'Sidetrack.' Harrison laid the banjo aside. 'A gal is a gal is a gal.'

'Not if she's a gook.' Sidetrack slurred slightly and then he looked at Limpet. 'Remember Kinney County?'

Harrison had the tape running.

'She weren't no gal.'

'I know it, asshole. *She* was a he.' He looked back at Harrison. His eyes were black and dead and, with his tooth glinting in the firelight, he looked like a misshapen vampire. 'You wanna hear a war story, Four-String?'

'If you wanna tell one.'

Sidetrack sat up and supped mescal. 'How many suckers we killed, boys? Hooch. You done plenty.'

'Carlsbad done the most.'

'What about the gook?' Harrison said.

Sidetrack looked back at him. 'You wanna hear about the gook?'

Harrison leaned on his elbows. 'I haven't looked one in the eyes that wasn't a gal since Cu-Chi.'

Sidetrack rolled on his belly. 'You'd a liked this one, bro. Me and Limpet was coming outta Kinney County and found this gook kid in a boxcar on his own. He was bright-eyed and bushy-tailed, and looked as if his momma just quit with the diapers. We thought he was one of those motherfuckers who took all the shrimp fishing in Galveston Bay, but he weren't.' He looked back at Limpet. 'He was some kinda tourist, wasn't he?'

'Yeah. Some kinda tourist.'

Sidetrack looked back at Harrison again, supped mescal and wiped his bristled chin with the back of his hand. 'You talk about a six-gun, Four-String. We got this kid and gave him a handgun with three shells in it. Old Limpet kept him covered and I spun that chamber, and the sucker blew his brains all over the boxcar. Man, that was as funny a thing as I've seen. Kid going to Mardi Gras, ends up painting the tracks with his head.'

Harrison looked at him then, trying to smile, while inside his heart leapt against his ribs. Sidetrack had killed Jean Carey's only son, and he had just recorded him admitting it. He thought of Jean, her pain, her loss, and the five months of wandering. He wondered then whether to give up the tape to the Bureau or find the right moment to cut Sidetrack's throat himself. 'You gave it *The Deer Hunter* routine, did ya?' he said slowly.

'What?'

'Russian roulette. It's a game the VC liked to play on prisoners. You musta seen the movie.'

'Nope.' Sidetrack slurred. 'I figured it out all by myself.' He was on his second bottle and pretty drunk now. Harrison watched his eyelids flutter and then his head flop on to his pack. Within minutes, he was snoring. The rest of them had eaten and drunk and were quiet.

Harrison lay down himself and looked up at the stars. He was wrapped in his blanket, with his heavier coat over the top of that. The fire had burned low and the Texas night was cold. He lay for a long time, thinking of Jean. At least now she would know. He wouldn't kill him. He'd arrest Sidetrack and indict him for murder, along with Limpet. With any luck, he'd get the death penalty anyway. Jean needed to *see* justice done. The moon drifted behind a cloud and a new darkness settled over the freight yard. Behind him, the aged wooden cars creaked in the wind, metal contracting with the steady drop in temperature. When he was sure every one of his companions was asleep, he changed the tape on his back.

Every FBI agent, every member of the joint terrorism task force, every police officer in Washington D.C. was looking for Fachida Harada. He drove his truck round the city and observed the results of his handiwork. They had five hours to release Shikomoto and he was watching their attempts to catch him. When he had got an idea of their exact tactics, he returned the truck to the lock-up and changed back into the woman's clothing he now wore when driving the sedan to 'work'. Her name was Chiang Soo Li and she had been resident in the US for seven years since coming here from Seoul. The police had not stopped her yet, but given time they would. They were targeting every Oriental in the city. He sat for a long time in front of the mirror, shaving for the second time that day and then making sure that the make-up was perfect. He enjoyed the routine – it was part of the battle, part of his life with Shikomoto, and part of the long process of restoring his honour. When he was finished, he straightened the stockings under his cotton skirt and opened the roll-over door. He had to get out of the car to close it once again.

Across the road in the old soldiers' home, Charlie, with no legs, watched him.

Logan and McKensie, with Swann's help, were co-ordinating the task force response to the hundreds of calls they were getting. Not all of the calls were helpful by any means; some were abusive, accusing the FBI of lying and blowing up their own city. There were more and more of those type, and there had also been a number of telling editorials even in the more sensible newspapers. Swann had heard one TV commentator talk about the FBI's track record in such events, citing the illegal activities over the American Indian Movement, Ruby Ridge and Waco as just three obvious abuses of power.

Other calls came from the Japanese, Chinese and Korean communities, accusing the authorities of harassment. Two people were claiming civil rights' violations against the Washington PD, and all of it was flowing across Kovalski's desk.

The support staff and analysts were pumping everything into the Cascade computer system for cross-referencing. Swann sifted papers in the operations room alongside Logan, and his thoughts drifted to New Orleans and Harrison going undercover again. The Freight Train Riders of America: killing hobos who got too close to their weapons-supply operation. That discovery had unnerved the whole office and Kovalski had been buried in meetings pretty much ever since. The big question was, where were the weapons coming from?

Right at that moment, Kovalski was in the Old Executive building with the FBI Director and Wendall Randall, the Director of Central Intelligence. With them was the national security adviser and Cyrus Birch, the national intelligence officer for the Near East and Africa. Kovalski was doing the talking. Ever since Louis Beam had made his Leaderless Resistance call back in October of 1992, he had been voicing his fears about the growing threat posed by militia-type groups. Yes, they had a constitutional right to gather together and to bear arms, but they were progressively conducting military-style manoeuvres, generally under the auspices of BobCat Reece's SPIKE teams. Local law-enforcement officers in Montana had commented on the growing security levels at Reece's compound and his 1998 purchase of a three-thousand-acre tract of land from the Bureau of Land Management, which he subsequently used for additional paramilitary training.

'Reece is just an old-fashioned, New World Order

paranoid,' Kovalski was saying. 'But with his expertise and his influence, that makes him very dangerous. I think the days of single-cell resistance are numbered. There's a new terrorism at work.'

'What about these Orientals?' Jensen cut in on him. 'The President wants to know what you've done about them.'

Kovalski sat back. 'They haven't been located, sir,' he said. 'Our best estimate is that they're yakuza. It's hard to prove, because trying to get a source in the black mist is like finding rocking-horse shit. But they've clearly got access to a lot of money, what with their trucks and those black helicopters. They are specifically designed to look like the Hong Kong troops that the militias have been so paranoid about.'

Randall frowned at him then. 'You don't think, Mr Kovalski, that they could actually be rogue agents, carrying on their own little war?'

Kovalski bit down on his lip. 'They could be, sir. We have a number of Asian agents in the Bureau, as do the ATF. But if you're asking my opinion, I don't think so. They're much more likely to be yakuza, which suggests a link to Fachida Harada.' He swivelled in his seat then. 'But talking of rogue government agents – BobCat Reece is using that freelance reporter, Smylie, to promulgate his theory that either Harada is a government agent gone wrong, in other words one of the Hong Kong troops, or someone paid by us to implicate the militia. Harada has given us till two o'clock this afternoon to release his lover, or he'll go public on some piece of information that'll play right into the hands of the militia.' He looked coldly at Cyrus Birch. 'Tetsuya Shikomoto told us that Harada was a CIA asset.' He paused, then added hopefully: 'You're gonna tell me that isn't true, aren't you?'

Birch shifted in his seat and his tan seemed to fade in his face. The DCI was looking at him. The national security adviser was looking at him. They were all looking at him, seated, as they were, round the Victorian conference table.

433

Birch looked at nobody. He sat forward and clasped his hands together. 'We did use Fachida Harada,' he said. 'Some years ago. We'd been looking for a humint source in North Korea for as long as I can recall. The JRA were our best bet.'

'So Harada *was* the other bomber in Jakarta,' Kovalski said.

'Tom, nobody got hurt in Jakarta. Shikomoto was the bomber. Harada just fetched and carried. We made a deal. You got Shikomoto and we got our source in North Korea. It was a good trade.'

Kovalski clenched his fist on the table. 'Was it? It's why Harada's here now. Why he's bombing the shit out of us.'

Birch did not say anything.

The national security adviser was on his feet. 'Gentlemen,' he said. 'This is all very well, but getting us nowhere. The fact is, we've got a problem. Harada is right. If word of this gets out, God only knows what the repercussions are going to be.' He looked at Kovalski. 'We can't let him go public.'

'Then release Shikomoto.'

Jensen shook his head. 'We can't do that.'

Kovalski sighed. 'Then he'll go public.'

'And if we do release Shikomoto?' Jensen said. 'What then? We'll be a target for every terrorist organisation going. What an advertisement. Hold the FBI to ransom and look what a result you get.' He shook his head. 'There's no way the attorney general will go for it. You've just got to find Harada before the deadline is up.'

Kovalski snorted. 'With respect, sir, we've now got just four hours to do that. It's ridiculous.'

'Mr Kovalski, you're probably right.' Jensen flared his nostrils. 'But that's all the time you've got.'

In London, Webb and Weir interviewed Alton Patterson for the second time, with Carragher sitting behind Patterson to unnerve him. Since they had identified Dylan Stoval at

Camden Town tube station, Webb had taken photographs of them both back to the wine bar below Kibibi Simpson's apartment, and had shown them to their witness.

The Italian barman looked at them very carefully. 'It's hard to say,' he'd said. 'I think he could be the tall one.' He had handed the picture of Patterson back to Webb.

'You only think. You're not sure?'

'No. I might be, if I saw him in the flesh. It was his size that stuck out, Sergeant. It's difficult to tell from a picture.'

Neither Webb nor Weir spoke immediately and Patterson sat there with his beret lying in his lap. 'Thanks for coming to see us again, Alton,' Webb said at last. 'This is Detective Inspector Weir. He'd like to talk to you as well.'

'Fine.' Patterson smiled. 'I've got nothing to hide.' As if to emphasise his point, he swivelled in the seat and looked at Carragher. Carragher looked back at him. He did not smile.

'Mr Patterson, tell me about that Saturday night,' Weir said. 'Tell me exactly what you did.'

Patterson turned again and shrugged his massive shoulders. 'I already told your colleague, sir. I was with Dylan all that night. We were shooting pool at the Foxhole, then a couple of pubs.'

'Dylan Stoval. Your room mate.'

Patterson nodded. 'All evening, sir. We do it most Saturday nights.'

'On your own?'

'Not always. We've got a little league going with some of the other guys. You know, a bit of rivalry – embassy guards against the naval building guards.'

Weir nodded and smiled. 'So what time did you start playing?'

Patterson thinned one eye at the ceiling. 'I don't know exactly, sir. We were both off duty. You don't keep count of the time so much when you're off duty.'

'Roughly, then,' Webb said. 'What time was it roughly?'

'In the Foxhole. I guess about six, six-thirty maybe.'

'When you started playing pool?'

'Yes, sir.'

'And you stayed there till when?'

'I guess around seven-thirty, eight o'clock maybe.'

Webb glanced over Patterson's shoulder at Carragher, then back at him again. 'Where did you go?'

'Just to the pub. The Red Lion.'

'Straight there.'

'Yes, sir. Straight there.'

Webb nodded. 'And what time did you get there?'

'About seven forty-five, eight o'clock maybe. It's only a short walk.'

'Just you and Dylan?'

Patterson looked back at him, leaving his answer for a fraction of a second. 'Yes, sir,' he said slowly. 'Me and Dylan.'

'You don't sound too sure, Mr Patterson.' Weir's voice was sharper than Webb's and Patterson looked at him then.

'It's not that, sir,' he said. 'It's just the time. Like I said just now, you don't take so much account of the time when you ain't working.'

'But it was no later than eight o'clock.'

'No, sir. No later.'

'Is it just you and Dylan sharing the room, Mr Patterson?'

'There's four bunks, sir.'

Weir looked at the sheet of paper on the desk. 'Of course there is. Who else is with you?'

'Dyer and Williams, sir.'

Weir was quiet for a moment, then he smiled and stood up. 'Thank you, Mr Patterson. That'll be all for now. But we might need to speak to you again.'

Patterson nodded, working his beret between his huge, pink-palmed hands. He glanced once more at Carragher and left. Webb closed the door, turned and stuffed his hands in his trouser pockets.

Weir was sitting on the edge of the desk with his arms

folded. 'He's lying,' he said. 'Stoval was in Camden at eight-thirty, so if Patterson did go to the pub when he said he did, it was not with Dylan Stoval.'

'What do you wanna do, Frank?' Carragher asked him.

'I want covert surveillance in their billet.'

At the field office on 4th Street, they sat and waited for Harada to call. Kovalski had come back from the Old Executive building and was at his desk, drinking coffee out of a massive polystyrene cup. Outside, the office was buzzing with task force agents, still following up the sightings. All morning, Swann and Logan had been helping them, along with every other available person. Logan had a whole stack of report sheets on the table and they had been through their share, contacting the callers by phone and then visiting various business and private addresses. They had been concentrating on business addresses: a number of callers from the Chinatown area claimed that various people working within the Chinese business district were Fachida Harada. They interviewed or tried to interview three Chinese waiters and two hotel porters, before Logan shook her head and they went back to the field office. 'This is ridiculous,' she said. 'We're just wasting our time.'

'It's how he planned it, Chey,' Swann said. 'He forced Kovalski's hand, made him go public, when it was probably better not to. Harada will have known this would happen – the world and his wife calling in. He knows how much manpower the subsequent investigation takes.' He shook his head. 'For one man, he's stretching the response every which way he can.'

Kovalski was in conference with the chief of the metropolitan police department, but he waved Logan and Swann in. 'Close the door, Cheyenne,' he said, and he indicated for Swann to sit down.

Swann looked at his watch: six minutes before the 2 p.m. deadline. 'What are you going to say to him?' he said.

Kovalski pursed his lips. 'I'm going to tell him we need more time. See if I can stall him a little.'

'And if you can't?'

Kovalski scowled at him. 'Let's just see if we can.'

'Tom,' Swann said. 'Everybody says they never negotiate with terrorists, but everybody always does.'

'Not on this occasion. There's no way they're going to release Shikomoto. And they're right. We'd just be setting ourselves up.' He sat back. 'If Harada won't stall, then so be it. We'll get him in the end and in the meantime we try to contain any militia activity.' He looked across the desk. 'In your experience, what d'you think he'd do next?'

Swann pondered for a moment. 'I think he'll really try and bring the city to a complete standstill,' he said. 'If I were him, I'd target the main roads in and out of Washington. Like he did with 395 and 66, only more effectively. He did those two in the way he did just to let you know that he could.' He paused then. 'The other thing I'd do is go for public buildings. He's already done the Smithsonian and National Airport. I'd go for more. The devices in the toilet areas had been there for a while. He may well have sited more.' Swann lifted his shoulders. 'The other thing he could go for is power stations, that kind of thing. The IRA tried to do it to us, black out London for a couple of weeks.'

'You really think one man can do all this on his own?' Logan butted in.

'Yes, I do. If he's been here long enough.'

Kovalski looked at his watch. 'Two minutes,' he said.

'D'you want me to talk to him, Tom?' Logan asked.

'No. I'll do it.' Kovalski looked at her. 'You just pray I keep him going long enough for Triggerfish to click in.'

Exactly two minutes later, the phone rang. For a second or so they all looked at it, then Kovalski pressed the speaker button. 'ASAC Kovalski,' he said.

'It's two o'clock. The twenty-four hours are up and I see

nothing on the television, no announcement concerning the release of Tetsuya Shikomoto.'

'Fachida, listen,' Kovalski said. 'We're working on it. I've just come from a meeting with the National Security Council. But these things can't be done in a hurry.'

'Of course they can.' There was almost a note of weariness in Harada's tone. 'They can, if there's enough will.'

'Fachida, there is a will. It's just that we need more time.'

'There is no more time.'

'Please. Don't do this. Your beef is with us, the establishment. If you make a public announcement now, you're going to create chaos.'

'I know.' Harada laughed lightly. 'Your militia – your Tatenokai – think I'm a government agent. How ironic.'

Kovalski sat back then. 'You betrayed Shikomoto, didn't you? Gave him up to the CIA.'

Harada faltered and Kovalski was watching the seconds ticking away. 'Listen, I understand why. And, believe me, I'm trying to get agreement to release him. But I need more time.'

'There is no more time.' Harada put down the phone. At the same moment, an agent from the Triggerfish team burst through the door. 'Got him,' he said. 'He's within four hundred yards of the Annalee Heights beacon.'

Logan was on her feet at the wall and running her finger over the street map. 'There,' she said. 'Between highways 50, 649, 613 and probably 244.'

Kovalski was already on the radio.

Harada, dressed as Chiang Soo Li, was in the grey sedan heading for home when he heard the first siren. They had picked up the electronic serial number from the phone. He thought they might this time and the phone had been discarded. He did have a cellphone in the car, but a different one, one that he had not used before. It was good to have had so much money at his disposal. He drove with both

439

hands on the wheel, false nails polished crimson, and headed for the Leesburg Pike. Police cars were converging from everywhere and roadblocks were going in. He had talked to Kovalski for too long. There was the chance of capture now and that was something he could not afford. He had two guns with him, each one set in a false shelf, which slid out from under the seats. If they really took the car apart, they might find them. He glanced at the street map and ducked off the main road. Then he heard the whirr of rotor blades and realised they had a chopper up. He turned north again and came back on to 613, just north of Belvedere. Ahead of him, a single white Ford from the Fairfax County police department blocked the road. Harada was the third car back. He debated what to do. His ID should be good enough, but in his heart he already knew the FBI would not let Tetsuya go. He was only putting off the inevitable and perhaps it was time for more direct action. Reaching down, he slid the gun from under his seat.

The trooper had stopped his car as soon as he got the call from the terrorism task force: all roads in the immediate vicinity of the Annalee Heights beacon to be blocked, suspect Fachida Harada believed to be in the area. They rode these units alone, but he had already called headquarters for back-up. He had nosed his car across the street and drivers in both directions had to ease their way round him. He needed somebody for the southbound carriageway, but in the meantime he would do the north.

The first two cars carried white Caucasian males. He looked at the third car, a grey sedan with an oriental female behind the wheel. He held up his hand and she stopped, rolled down the window and smiled at him. 'Good afternoon, mam,' he said.

She smiled and reached for her driver's licence. He had his radio to his lips and was about to walk round the front of the car.

'Officer.'

'Yes, mam.' He came back to the window and the smile

died on his face. Harada pointed the black automatic and fired. The trooper lifted both hands to his face, reeled a few paces and fell with a scream caught in his throat. Harada put the shift in drive and drove right over him.

22

Swann went back to see Dr Habe at the faculty of Japanese history at George Washington University. Logan had remained behind at the field office, co-ordinating the fresh hunt for Harada. Dr Habe was teaching a class, but when Swann explained the situation to her assistant, she met him in her office.

'What can I do for you, Mr Swann?' she asked him.

Swann sat down opposite her. 'It's about Fachida Harada,' he said. 'A Fairfax County police officer has just been shot dead and the FBI know Harada was in the vicinity.' He broke off for a second. 'The witnesses said the killer was an Oriental, but a woman.'

Dr Habe nodded. 'What is it you want to know exactly?'

'Doctor, I've got no jurisdiction here. But I do observe and I do have time to think. I've done some more reading on the samurai, and sometimes they painted their faces in battle, didn't they?'

She nodded. 'Like women. To show their disdain for danger.'

'That's what I thought.' Swann sat back again. 'The whole thing with the samurai was about honour. We discussed it, remember?'

She nodded.

'I want to ask you a question. If a samurai warrior's honour was truly compromised, what would he do about it?'

'He would kill himself. The *sepukko*, Mr Swann, ritual suicide.'

'Like Yukio Mishima.'

'Exactly.'

'That's what I thought,' he said. 'Thank you.'

He took the metro back to 4th Street and went up to the

442

field office, where he could almost taste the excitement in the air. Logan was in the squad room, studying the large-scale map of the city on the wall. She had ringed the section where the cellphone's electronic serial number had been picked up and marked off highways 50, 649, 613 and 244. Kovalski was standing at her elbow and he looked round as Swann came up.

'We're positive he was dressed as a woman,' Kovalski said. 'Driving a grey Chrysler sedan.'

Swann nodded.

'The picture we've got must be a very good likeness.'

'That and the samurai in battle.'

Kovalski arched one eyebrow at him. 'Excuse me?'

Swann leaned against the desk. 'Tom, I think you should go public about Harada's CIA involvement.'

'What?'

'He's going to. Right now, he's probably e-mailing Carl Smylie.'

Logan was staring at him. 'What are you saying, Jack?'

'I'm saying, get in before he does. Explain the situation to the public before he does. Create the advantage.' Swann folded his arms. 'This whole thing is allegedly about Harada's honour, or fall from it, or whatever the expression is.' He looked Kovalski in the eye. 'Call him on it, Tom. Make him look silly. Go public about him and Shikomoto, make a big deal about them being gay. It's not politically correct, but, right now, who will give a shit. Tell the newspapers about his work for the CIA, how he betrayed his past, betrayed his alleged Communist ties, the North Koreans, his colleagues in the JRA. Talk about his criminal links with the yakuza. But most of all, major on how he stitched up Shikomoto.'

'And the militia reaction?'

'It'll be what it'll be. But if you tell the public before Harada does, the full story can come out and not just the bits he wants them to hear.' Swann looked at them both. 'The point is Harada's honour. If you call him on it, he'll know there's no way Shikomoto will be released and therefore no way he can win.'

Kovalski frowned. 'So what happens then?'

Swann licked his lips. 'With any luck, he'll kill himself.'

Harada stood under the shower and let hot water ease the tension from the muscles in his shoulders. He had taken cream to his face and removed the bulk of the make-up, but now tiny rivers of lipstick-red water rolled down his chest. He stood with his head bowed, the force of the water on the back of his neck, and chewed over the events of the morning. They had held him on the phone for too long. He probably had been safe with that police officer, dressed as he was like a woman, and yet he had shot him dead. The battle was intensifying in his head; he could feel it, building with the frustration. How he longed to stand toe to toe with his enemy, his sword an extension of his arm. The FBI were stalling. They were bound to stall: a classic western tactic, no honesty in their warfare.

He dried himself, wrapped the towel round his waist and went through to the bedroom where his computer was housed. He sat on the edge of the bed, towelled his hair until it stuck straight up, then he took the ceremonial short sword from the casket and practised a series of moves, watching the fluidity of motion in the full-length mirror. Replacing the sword, he lit incense sticks and knelt for a while, meditating before his Shinto shrine. Then he took the laptop computer downstairs and switched it on. While it was booting up, he turned on the television news and, with the volume mute, considered how he would word the message to Smylie and fuel the militias' worst fears.

He glanced at the TV and recognised the black FBI agent, the woman. She was standing in the quadrangle at the Hoover building and hordes of press corps were seated on the fixed benches in front of the 'Fidelity, Bravery, Integrity' statue. Harada turned the volume up, as Logan spread what looked like some kind of prepared statement on the lectern before her.

'Ladies and gentlemen,' she was saying. 'I'm Special Agent Logan, the terrorism response co-ordinator for the District of Columbia. As you all know, this city has been facing a threat over the past few weeks that has murdered, disrupted lives and brought many of our services to a standstill. For the first time, the metro has been bombed, major highways have been sabotaged and federal buildings targeted. The perpetrator has made no secret of his identity. He is Fachida Harada of the Japanese Red Army.

'In 1986, Harada and his accomplice, Tetsuya Shikomoto, attacked the US Embassy in Jakarta, Indonesia, with mortar bombs. It took us ten years, but with the help of the CIA we finally apprehended Shikomoto in Kobe, Japan, in 1996. He was extradited and is now serving life in a federal penitentiary. Shikomoto is the reason Harada is in D.C. right now, and Shikomoto is the reason we are being bombed. We believe Harada has been here for at least six months, which is more than enough time to prepare his assault properly. There is no doubt that this bombing campaign is far more professional than anything we've seen from the FALN in the past, or the various right-wing groups based here, or indeed the World Trade Center. However, we need to explode a couple of myths about Harada.

'The reason he wants Shikomoto released is because the two men are lovers. They have been since 1986, yet they both have wives and families in Japan. There is a rumour circulating through the militia groups that somehow we are responsible for what Harada is doing, rather like we were apparently responsible for the Oklahoma City bomb in 1995. Certain people are promulgating the theory that we are controlling Harada or that he is a government agent gone wrong.' She paused then and looked right into the camera, looked right into Harada's eyes as he watched the screen.

'After the 1986 Indonesia bombs, Harada and Shikomoto

were tracked to North Korea, where the Japanese Red Army had an enclave. Around that time, Harada, whose role in the Jakarta bombings had been secondary, became an agent for the CIA. He agreed to assist them to avoid being arrested for the Jakarta bomb. His job was to gather intelligence in Communist North Korea.'

A murmur rippled through the gaggle of reporters. One of them called out: 'So BobCat Reece was right then. Harada is a government agent.'

'No.' Logan said slowly. 'Mr Reece could not be more wrong. Harada is his own man. He stopped working for the United States after he gave up Shikomoto to us.' She paused then and looked at the camera. 'You see, Fachida Harada wanted to save his own skin after the attacks in Jakarta. He reneged on his agreement with the CIA and gave up Shikomoto in return for his own freedom. Harada claims to be a warrior. He claims to be a man of honour, but any honour he might have had was lost the day he compromised his lover.' She paused again. 'He's demanding we release Shikomoto now, but the only reason he's in custody in the first place is because Harada put him there.'

Harada stared at the screen and globules of perspiration built on his forehead. He clenched his fists and the sweat rolled into his eyes. He could feel every muscle trembling and the emptiness gnawed at his gut; the emptiness he had suffered since the day they took Tetsuya.

On the TV, Logan was still talking. 'It's important we track Harada down before he does any more damage. We've prepared a handout sheet for the members of the press, which details the man and his organised-crime connections in Japan. The militia groups have alleged a connection between the Orientals killing militia members and Fachida Harada. Their claim is that Harada is somehow proof that there is an overall federal conspiracy against them. The reality is that the FBI, together with the sheriffs' criminal investigation divisions and state police, are hunting the killers of Billy Bob Lafitte, Tommy Anderson and the two ladies abducted from Cassity, Virginia. We do not know who the killers are yet, but if there is a connection with Harada, it'll be through organised crime syndicates like the yakuza.' She folded the papers. 'Harada was part of the yakuza in Japan. He is, at best, a criminal. And he has a grudge. It's manifested as a grudge against the FBI, but in reality it is against himself. We're dealing with a very mixed-up creature, a man who does not really know his own mind, a man who claims to have the strength of the ancient samurai warrior, but who appears to have lost any sense of the honour that set the samurai apart. Thank you, ladies and gentlemen, for your attention. With the help of the media and the general public, we can catch this man and put a stop to the bombings and, along with them, the rumours.'

Swann clasped her hand as she stepped off the rostrum and headed away from the gathering. 'Excellent,' he said. 'Spot on, Chey.'

Logan looked at him and grimaced. 'I hope so. I mean, it could really backfire. Send him off at half cock or something.'

Swann nodded. 'Let's hope it does. Up until now, he's been the consummate professional. If he gets mad he'll make mistakes, and when he does, we'll get him.'

Harada sat very still as the news programme cut back to the studio. The anchorman was talking to a colleague, but Harada could not hear what they were saying. He stared beyond the TV to the wall and through the wall into the darkest places of his mind. Logan's face dominated his thoughts, her words reverberating in his head. He knew now that they would never release Shikomoto. They had stolen his sword and used it against him. The silence lifted from inside him and he could feel the moisture on his palms and the sudden weakness in his limbs. It was over. He had lost.

His jaw quivered physically and he had to bite his teeth together to stop the tick in his cheek. He closed his eyes and he thought of April in Japan, and the festival of the cherry blossom and the faces of his children. He knew then that he would never see them again. He thought of his wife and her family, and knew that the FBI broadcast would bounce off satellites round the globe and every country in the world would carry the news item. In Japan, he would be disgraced; in Korea, China and the Bekaa Valley, too. Throughout Europe, where his contacts were still considerable, everybody would know that Fachida Harada had failed. He physically trembled at the thought. And then he thought back to the original approaches in Japan, approaches from the most unlikely source; how he must have been studied from afar and finally, after Shikomoto was taken, contacted. And as he thought about it, pieces of the puzzle clicked into place: the Tatenokai, the unorganised American militia, the so-called Hong Kong Troops, the media attention and the movement of weapons. A chill broke through him as he began to appreciate how far that arm could stretch, and the power that arm wielded. Then he marvelled. The Americans had no idea how much was stacked against them and how carefully, how cunningly, the weapons had been arrayed. This was truly the work of the *ninja*.

He got up and went into the kitchen, where he poured himself a glass of water and looked out on to the street. A police cruiser was moving steadily through the neighbourhood; two officers watching driveways for vehicles. The sedan was safely tucked out of sight in a garage. He drank the water slowly, poured a second glass, and very calmly he made his decision. There had been another phase planned: devices set in ten separate locations, all installed months ago, when the man with the *C U SAFELY* truck came to inspect security. But that could be left to another generation. Setting down the glass, he went back to his laptop and called up his electronic mail system. He set the single encryption code that had been insisted upon and then he began to type.

Harrison stood at the open door of the boxcar and let the wind blow through his hair. He had his snub-nosed .38 in his boot and the Beretta stuffed in his waistband, and he watched the countryside roll by as the train slowed for Sulphur Springs. The sun was high, though it was not yet noon, and he could see the dust rising from the speeding pick-up truck. He glanced at Sidetrack, who leaned against the other doorjamb with his arms folded and his canine tooth exposed. 'Ain't this a little risky?' Harrison called to him.

'What?' Sidetrack cupped a hand to his ear. 'I can't hear ya.'

Harrison moved across the door space to him. 'I said, ain't this risky?' He jabbed a thumb at the three big packs that the group were carrying between them. 'It's the middle of the fucking day.'

'So what?' Sidetrack jerked his shoulders. 'Nobody knows we're here. Nobody knows what we do. Besides, we ain't even stopping.' He squinted in the sunlight. 'How come you're so jumpy?'

Harrison shrugged. 'Hell, I don't know. I guess I'm just not used to working in the daytime.'

Sidetrack tipped his head back and laughed. 'Relax, man. We've been making this drop for years.'

Harrison nodded. 'How come we ain't getting off like we did the last time?'

'Because this train's headed for Wichita Falls and that's where we need to be.'

Harrison squatted down and looked across the darkened car at the packs: three of them – big old army-style backpacks – with a crate of something in each. He took tobacco from his top pocket and rolled a cigarette.

Sidetrack crouched down next to him. 'Need you to give me a hand,' he said. 'The truck's running alongside.'

Harrison tucked the cigarette behind his ear and got to his feet. Carlsbad was sitting on one of the packs, playing cards with the others, and Sidetrack kicked him lightly in the backside. 'Shift it, brother. We got work to do.'

Carlsbad got up and Sidetrack took hold of one of the straps. 'You'll need to support your side from the bottom, Four-String,' he said. 'This mother is heavy.'

Harrison helped him get it over to the door, then he squatted again, stuck his head into the wind and saw the pick-up racing up the dirt road towards them. The locomotive had slowed considerably and Harrison could have jumped down and landed on his feet with no bother. 'We're just dumping it over the side, right?' He looked at Sidetrack, who nodded.

'Just the one?'

'Yep.'

'OK.' Harrison took his strap. 'You ain't kidding she's heavy. What the hell's in it?'

Sidetrack showed his tooth. '120-millimetre mortars.'

Harrison lifted one eyebrow. 'And we're just chucking it over the side?'

'It's packed and sealed, man. What you might call bomb-proof.'

Harrison shook his head at the joke. 'Where's all this stuff come from, anyways?'

'All over the fucking place.' Sidetrack was looking over Harrison's shoulder, concentrating on the truck. He got to his feet and took hold of his side of the pack. Harrison followed suit and between them they dumped it on to the heaped sand at the side of the rails. It landed with a dull whump and then the train rolled on.

The pick-up pulled up and Harrison recognised the tall, lean figure of Randy Meades. Although there were fifty yards between them, Meades saw him and Harrison touched one finger to his temple. Meades looked a moment longer, then bent down for the fallen pack. Harrison turned to find Sidetrack already at the mescal bottle. It used to be just at night, around the fire, keeping out the cold, but over the past few days it had become a regular fixture in the daytime as well. Harrison used it to his advantage. Sidetrack liked to talk when he was sipping liquor.

'Those boys looking to start a new republic?' he asked.

Sidetrack laughed in his throat. 'Old Meades figures he's still at the Alamo.'

Harrison nodded. 'Only it ain't the Mexicans he's fighting, huh?'

'No, sir. Not the Mexicans.'

They rolled on, mile after mile of iron railroad. Sidetrack got a little buzz from the mescal and dozed with his head on his pack, eyes closed, an ugly leer spread across his face. Harrison sat down between Hooch and Limpet, who were still in the card game. Carlsbad was clearly out of funds.

'So what's at Wichita Falls?' Harrison said to Limpet.

Limpet played his winning hand and grinned wickedly at Hooch. He glanced sideways at Harrison. 'Rambo,' he said.

They left the train before they hit the city and Harrison hefted one of the two remaining packs, with Carlsbad on the other strap. It was something of a mismatch, and Harrison moaned about carrying all the weight.

'Y'all get used to it,' Carlsbad muttered. 'Build up some of those muscles you've been wasting.'

They walked beside the singing iron tracks for a while, then Sidetrack took his cellphone from his jacket, checked the signal, grimaced, and walked on. Half a mile nearer the city he stopped abruptly, inspected the face of the phone once more and dialled. The wind had got up and the sun was down, the sky a mass of moonwash and speckled stars.

'Sure is pretty,' Hooch muttered. Harrison followed his gaze and nodded.

'OK. We're all set.' Sidetrack snapped his phone closed and tucked it away again, then led off due north away from the tracks. Harrison looked behind him to where Hooch and Limpet were hefting the other pack and saw that Limpet was struggling.

'How far we gotta carry these damn things?' Limpet said.

'Just up that hill there.' Sidetrack pointed to where the

scrub lifted in a series of small hills, scarred here and there with shadowy outcrops of rock. 'Man's coming up the trail on the other side.'

Limpet muttered something under his breath, then all was quiet save the screech of an owl and Carlsbad's laboured breathing.

Sidetrack strode ahead of them now, climbing the hill and watching for snakes at his feet. 'Keep your eyes open,' he said. 'Goddamn rattlers like the night out here.'

Limpet giggled. 'No wonder Six don't come by too often.'

Harrison heard him and his senses were suddenly heightened. Limpet was behind him and cursing now. Harrison looked at the ground, thought about snakes, and all at once he wondered.

Carlsbad suddenly dumped his side of the pack. 'Fucking thing's pulling my arm outta the socket.'

Harrison laid down his side more gently and took a sip from his water bottle. Not only were they hefting the backpack, he had his own bag, bottle and banjo to think about.

Sidetrack was at the crown of the hill, scanning the horizon. Limpet sat down on his pack and rubbed his upper arm. 'I wasn't born to hump boxes across no desert,' he groaned.

'Stop whimping on, Limpet, and get me that other bottle.' Sidetrack was still watching the horizon.

Limpet grabbed the fresh mescal from his own pack, and Harrison took it from him, walked up the hill and handed it to Sidetrack. He looked where Sidetrack looked and saw nothing. A coyote called from out among the scrub and sagebrush. The wind caught Harrison's hair and blew it over his shoulders, the ends whipping at his face. He took a fresh tie from his jeans' pocket and bunched his hair into a ponytail. Next to him, Sidetrack sipped mescal and stared into the darkness.

The moon lightened the night and the landscape was

silhouetted in shadow rather than pitch-black. Harrison could make out small stands of scrubby trees and darker patches where the bunch-grass was thickest. Sidetrack passed him the bottle and he took a sip of the oily, sweet liquor and gagged. 'I don't know how you can drink so much of this shit,' he said.

Sidetrack did not respond. He was still watching the landscape, and then Harrison saw two tiny lights at the edge of the horizon. Sidetrack looked at his watch, smacked his lips together and took another long swallow from the mescal bottle. 'The man's on time,' he said.

Harrison watched and saw a second set of lights behind the first. He looked back down the hill then, to where the two backpacks were waiting, and screwed up his eyes. 'Gonna take two trucks to haul those packs, uh?'

Sidetrack shook his head. 'The other one's our ride, Four-String.' He smiled in the darkness, showing that one long tooth, and laid a hand on Harrison's shoulder. 'Don't I think of everything?'

He went back down the hill, but Harrison remained where he was for a few moments and watched the approaching headlights. They were still a long way off and he figured at least half an hour before the trucks got to their position.

Sidetrack was sipping mescal and Limpet was rolling him a smoke. 'Put a little grass in it, man,' Sidetrack muttered. 'I'm in that kinda mood.'

Harrison sat and watched Limpet expertly make the joint, twisting up one end and sticking a cardboard roach in the other. He passed it to Sidetrack and struck a match on a rock. Sidetrack sucked on the joint, gripping it between his third and little fingers and drawing in a great lungful of smoke. He held it, dipped his chin to his chest and let the smoke creep out through his nostrils. He passed the joint to Harrison, who took a long toke himself. It was grass, and he had not come across such good stuff in a while.

'Where did you get this shit?' he said. 'This is good.'

Sidetrack chuckled. 'This comes from Mexico, Four-String. A little sideline we got going.'

Harrison took another long pull and held the smoke in his lungs before handing the joint back. The wind had died away now and he could hear the vague hum of an engine far in the distance. Limpet heard it too and pricked up his ears like a dog.

'That'll be Rambo,' he said.

'Who's Rambo?' Harrison asked him.

Limpet just smiled.

Sidetrack moved back to the top of the hill and the others joined him. Harrison could see that the trail cut through the scrub – just a dust road, pitted and broken by mud holes and rocks of varying sizes. It twisted right up through the cluster of small hills, and passed at the northern edge of the one they were standing on. Sidetrack watched as the headlights got closer and closer and the engine grew louder and louder, and then he nodded to Limpet. 'Get the stuff shifted down to the road there.' He pointed to the track and the four of them went back for the packs.

Sidetrack stayed on top of the hill while they manhandled the stuff down the northern side. The engines were much louder now, the unmistakable rumble of a V8 from one of them. Harrison rolled a cigarette and lit it, cupping his hands to the new breeze that had lifted. Limpet stood next to him, with his lazy eye half closed. The trucks got louder and Harrison heard gears being ground in, and then the headlights shone in his face and the first truck lurched to a halt right alongside them.

The driver's window was rolled down and Harrison looked at a flat-faced man with a grunt haircut, and a plug of chewing tobacco bulging at his cheek. The sleeves of his light jacket were pushed up and Harrison could see he was wearing a military shirt. He spat a stream of juice that just missed Harrison's foot. He spoke to Limpet and jerked his thumb at Harrison. 'Who's this sonofabitch?'

'Name's Four-String. He's one of us.'

The man revved the engine of the V8 and looked through skinny-lidded eyes at Harrison. 'Load the gear in the other truck, then haul your butts into this one. And make it snappy, Sidetrack. I don't got all night. The fucking state troopers in Texas are a pain in the fucking ass. Every mother's son is looking to be a hero.'

Sidetrack told them to load up the gear and two men climbed out of the second truck to help them. Harrison noticed their clothes: jeans and jackets; but their hair was cropped and both were wearing military shirts. The vehicles were private, licensed in Texas, and Harrison made a mental note of the numbers.

When the gear was loaded, Sidetrack and Limpet got into the cab of the V8. The driver jerked his head at the back, and Harrison, Hooch and Carlsbad hoisted themselves over the tailgate.

The drive was about as uncomfortable as it could get – bumpy and winding – and Harrison had to grip the rail to hold on. Carlsbad swore at every divot in the road and Hooch just sat there scowling. 'How come Limpet gets to ride up front? That's what I wanna know.'

Harrison said nothing, but took in their bearings and ran over the licence numbers in his head. They drove along the pitted trail for perhaps twenty miles before the V8 slowed briefly and Harrison could make out the thin dark strip of the blacktop, running diagonally across the flat land ahead of them. A few minutes later, they left the dirt road and headed west along the highway.

Hooch had just got settled, half lying against his pack, with his head out of the wind, when the driver took a right turn and they were racing along another dirt road. 'God-dammit. Makes a boxcar look comfortable. What the hell's he think he's doing?'

'He's avoiding the state troopers,' Harrison said. 'Who highballs through the night with a buncha low lifes like us in the back of their truck?'

They ran north for a while and then east again, for

perhaps another thirty miles. Theirs was the lead truck; the lights from the second one, some way back down the road. 'I guess that guy is Rambo, huh?' Harrison yelled in Carlsbad's ear.

The big man nodded. 'Some kinda soldier, I think.'

'Militia?'

Carlsbad shrugged. 'I don't pay no mind to nothing but the money, Four-String. But I figure he's still in the service.'

'What we hauling?'

'Mortars. Same as we dropped in Sulphur Springs.'

Harrison fell silent once more and they rolled on, lurching and bumping across the Texas plains in the middle of the night. He could no longer see any lights from the highway. Ten miles further on, the truck slowed and the driver mashed the gears, then took a right turn off the main dirt road. Harrison was slammed against the back of the cab, his ribs crashing into the metal. Angrily, he banged his right fist hard on the cab top and saw Rambo look over his shoulder through the glass. Harrison gave him the bird and Carlsbad shook his head. 'Not very smart, Four-String. That guy can be an asshole.'

Ten minutes later, the truck slowed again and they pulled up outside a set of wire-meshed gates that looked as though they were fixed between two massive boulders. The driver honked the horn and, a moment or so later, Harrison saw a fresh pair of headlights coming up from the other side. Carlsbad tapped him on the shoulder. 'We gotta get down, man, haul the gear to that other truck.'

'Then what?'

'Then we're outta here. The railroad's half a mile thataway.'

Harrison nodded. 'Where we at, anyways?'

'North of Wichita Falls.'

'So what's this place?'

Carlsbad shrugged. 'Beats me, brother. Some kinda weapons dump, I guess.'

Hooch was jumping down from the truck. 'It ain't used any more,' he said. 'I think the marines did use it one time. There's caves back beyond those gates, like some kinda natural storage. I don't know. I think this place is still Texas Guard, though.'

Harrison was helping with the first pack and he shifted it over the tailgate of the second pick-up with Hooch. They dropped it to the ground, then Harrison straightened and rubbed his back. He felt breath on his neck and looked round. The flat-faced driver with the thick arms was looking down his nose at him. 'If you made a dent in my truck, you shitkicker, I'm gonna use your head to knock it out again.'

Harrison said nothing, but held his gaze evenly. Sidetrack came between them. 'Hey cool off.' He looked at the driver. 'Chill out, Rambo. Four-String'd eat you for breakfast.'

The driver's eyes balled then and he took a pace forward. Harrison tensed and clenched his fists. Sidetrack placed a hand against each of their chests. 'We don't want two old soldiers fighting. We want to shift this shit and haul ass to the skids.'

The driver flared his nostrils and stood back. 'Soldier?' he said. 'What service?'

Harrison held his eye. 'Marine Corps.'

'Vietnam?'

Harrison nodded.

'OK. I'll forgive you.'

'You better,' Limpet muttered from behind them. 'Guy crawled the dirt like Six.'

Sidetrack spat on the ground. 'If you two ladies are done, let's get this stuff shifted and get the fuck outta here.' He looked sideways at Harrison. 'Goddammit, Four-String. Wherever you go, there's trouble.'

They loaded the two backpacks of mortar shells, then Harrison shouldered his own pack and picked up his water bottle. Rambo, the driver, was still watching him and he had a quirky expression on his face that sparked new tension. He came over again.

'Do I know you from some place?' he said.

Harrison looked beyond him. 'Not unless you been to Angola in the last ten years.'

'You been in the pen'?'

'Well, there was fences and goons and shit, so I figured that's what it was.' Harrison leaned, spat and stood up. 'Guess I just got one of those faces, huh.' He walked away to where Limpet and Hooch were standing, but he could feel the driver's eyes on his back.

Limpet saw the look and nudged Harrison. 'That dude's looking at you like you're bad kin, brother. You been screwing his wife?'

Harrison smiled. 'You figure he's got one?'

They camped in a stand of cottonwood trees fifty yards up the hill from the railhead. Sidetrack and the others had ridden this way many times in the past, and they told Harrison there was no train till the morning. He helped Hooch collect brushwood for a fire, and they sat huddled in sleeping bags and blankets against the chill Texas night. Sidetrack supped mescal and chewed on some strips of peppered jerky, and Harrison picked at the strings of his banjo. Limpet had a bottle of cheap bourbon and he broke it open, and handed it round the fire. Harrison took a couple of shots and let the liquor warm his chest, before taking a couple more. He rescrewed the lid and handed the bottle back to Limpet.

Sidetrack laid down the mescal and looked across the fire at Harrison. 'I wonder about you,' he said. 'Where did you get that attitude?'

'Just born lucky, I guess.'

Sidetrack shook his head. 'That Rambo's a mean motherfucker, Four-String. If I hadn't told him you was in the service, he'd've kicked your ass.'

'Maybe.'

Sidetrack snorted. 'You sonofabitch.' He took another

long pull at the mescal bottle and chewed on the worm before swallowing.

'Who is he, anyways?' Harrison asked him.

'He's a sergeant in the Texas State Guard is who he is.'

'Oh right. So he's gonna make general in Randy Meades's republic.'

Sidetrack cackled then. 'You're really something, Four-String.'

'I try.' Harrison rolled a cigarette and looked over at Limpet. 'How's this place for snakes, Limpet? I don't wanna wake up and find a diamondback cuddling up to me.'

Limpet shook his head. 'Way too cold, brother. You'll be just fine.'

Harrison bit his lip, thought for a moment, then said: 'So Six don't like the snakes either, huh?'

Sidetrack was looking hard at him. 'Who told you that?'

'Nobody. Old Limpet made a crack, is all.'

Sidetrack's features softened again. 'You'll meet him one of these days, Four-String. You can ask him about snakes yourself.'

'He knows about me, then?'

'Oh, he knows about you.'

'When's he blowing in?'

'Can't say.'

Harrison nodded. 'But he's scared of snakes.'

'Never knowed anybody sweat so much over one before in my life.'

Harrison nodded again and the past grew up in his mind: soaking vegetation and holes in the ground, and the fevered features of Ray Martinez, as one of the deadly black serpents slithered over his arm.

Paulie Caulfield, a.k.a. Rambo, was back at home: a trailer just outside the National Guard base at Wichita Falls. He lived alone, had never been married and would still have been a regular soldier if it were not for his ankle ligaments. They were too weak, after a bad break, to hold him up every day. He had had to settle for the guard. But that was ten years ago and things had altered radically since then. He had watched the events at Ruby Ridge, had been at Estes Park, and had petitioned the FBI at Waco: to no avail. Good, honest people had died at Waco, children among them, and ever since then, his own course had been set. He switched on his computer, connected with the Net, then took a can of Lone Star from the refrigerator. He snapped off the ring pull and beer bubbled in yellow froth over the top of the can, which he sucked through rubbery lips. Tonight had been a good night in many ways and the weapons they were holding were stacking up well. The old site was just temporary storage until others, like Sidetrack, freighted them on elsewhere. Pretty soon, the people would have as many and varied armaments as the military did.

Sitting down in front of the screen, he scrolled through the menus, typed in his password and began to trawl the old website pages he sometimes kept for reference. He knew he had one somewhere, but could not remember where he had filed it. So he just sat there and searched until he turned up what he was looking for. The picture was bad, a grainy old black and white, and he stared at the screen for a long time. He could not be sure, but his instincts prickled and he printed a hard copy. Now, he stood under the light and looked at it again and, as he did, a cold sweat came over him. Back at his desk, he typed an e-mail message, closed it under encryption and sent it to Montana.

BobCat Reece heard the little plink from his computer screen, which told him he had mail, and he got up out of his chair. He was not normally up this late and his wife had long since retired, but that black bitch from the FBI had been on the TV and he had to figure out what tactic she was employing. He moved over to the bureau where his computer was permanently switched on and he clicked into the mail. He looked at the scribble, selected a decoder and the words sprang to life on the page.

He read it once, then again, and finally he sat back. Caulfield was talking about Idaho a couple of years ago, when the FBI had an undercover agent watching a militia compound. When it all came to light, a bad picture of the Fed had been circulated over the Internet. Reece read the message again, then looked at his watch and stood up. He went outside to his truck and took the cellphone he had bought in Mexico from his black leather attaché case. He sat in the cab, watching the darkness through the windshield, and dialled. He waited while the phone rang and rang. He would have switched it off had he been calling anyone else, but this length of time was no time at all and, two minutes later, a lazy voice sounded in his ear.

'Yeah?'

'This here's the Lynx.'

'Hey, what's up?'

'I think you got a problem.'

'Do I?'

'I just had word from Texas. There's a fella running with the Southern Blacks who might be a federal agent.'

'Ah, that problem.' The voice was thin in his ear. 'I know about that problem. I been watching that myself.'

23

Webb worked with the regional security officer Dan Farrow and the technical support unit. The only other person who knew what they were doing, apart from the US ambassador himself, was James Carragher, the FBI agent from Washington. Webb had been very careful and arranged for the TSU operatives to pose as electricity board technicians, sending in a whole team of them, purportedly to check the wiring in the billet. Every single section was looked at over a period of a week and, during that time, the covert surveillance equipment was installed in Patterson and Stoval's room. The job was done in less than an hour. At the same time, five other workmen were fiddling about in other rooms. Webb hoped it would be enough to assuage any suspicions on the part of their suspects.

The surveillance cameras were radio-linked to a van parked round the corner from the billet, which would be monitored and videotaped round the clock for three days initially, with the US ambassador wanting it reviewed after that. Webb could smell the wariness in the embassy. The last thing anybody wanted was Kibibi Simpson's murderer to be a US citizen. Webb sat in the back of the van with Carragher, watching the screen and listening in on the headphones. There were long periods when there was nobody in the room at all, largely during the working hours, and they let the video run. But at shift changeovers and early and late evening, the van was occupied. At quarter past five, Dyer and Williams, the two marines who shared the room with Stoval and Patterson, were getting ready to go on duty. Forty-five minutes later, Patterson ambled in, changed into some sweats and headed for the gym. Webb sat and watched as Stoval came back, cracked a couple of jokes with the two men going on duty, then went to the gym himself.

'Shoulda wired up the basketball hoop,' Carragher said.

Webb took off the headphones. 'Jim,' he said. 'The sun was over the yardarm six hours ago, it's time to slake my thirst.'

They sat in a pub in one of the residential backstreets, close to the Eastcote barracks, and drank pints of Guinness. Carragher told him about life in the FBI, how he had been to England just once before, when he was part of the investigation looking into the African embassy bombings.

'Osama Bin Laden,' Webb said. 'He's been quiet for a while.'

'I think the CIA have lost him. They tell us he's still in Afghanistan, but I doubt it.'

'I don't think anyone's got a clue where he is.'

'We had a SWAT team land here,' Carragher said. 'Coupla buddies of mine from New Orleans. Washington was rotating the African guard as the investigation got underway. Their plane caught fire over the Atlantic and they had to land here. British Airways took them on to Tanzania.'

They went back to the van and sat there in the heat, watching the empty screen.

'They're probably shooting pool somewhere,' Carragher said. Just then the door opened and Webb sat up straighter. He put the headphones on and twiddled with the volume control. The tape would start automatically as soon as someone spoke. The angle of the camera was not good, but it had been housed high up and took in most of the room. The only area they could not see was the wall directly below the camera, where Dyer's bed and footlocker were housed. Patterson and Stoval had their beds against the other wall, with footlocker space between them. They were laughing about two women in the pub and Webb again twisted the volume control. Stoval sat on the bed and pulled his sweat top over his head.

'So the man ain't asked to talk to you again,' he said. Patterson shook his head. 'Not since the last time.'

'That's cool.'

'They don't know nothing. How could they?' Patterson stood up and stripped off his jeans, folding them neatly on his chair.

Stoval bent to his locker and took out a packet of cigarettes. He lit one and flapped out the match. 'Exactly,' he said. 'How could they?'

In the van, Webb looked at Carragher, who was frowning heavily. 'Who's he trying to convince, us or himself?'

'I don't know,' Webb said. 'But tomorrow, we lean on Patterson.'

Weir joined them, together with Dan Farrow, in the office Webb used. Patterson was summoned from duty over at the naval building. He crossed the square to the embassy and came down the corridor. Webb was fetching some coffee and saw him, but did not nod or smile. Patterson's expression was easy, though there was a flicker of consternation way back in his eyes. Webb motioned for him to go into the office and sat him down in the chair in the middle of the floor. No desk to lean on, nowhere to put his hands except his lap. Webb sat behind his desk, and Weir rested against it, with his arms folded, his face unsmiling as he worked chewing gum round in his mouth. Patterson looked awkward, incongruous in the chair, with his long legs and heavily built upper torso. He waited for somebody to say something to him, but nobody did.

'You all wanted to see me,' he said at last.

Still nobody spoke, though four pairs of eyes were trained on his. He looked from one blank face to another, like the kid on his own looking for a friend in the playground.

'You lied to us, Mr Patterson.' Weir's voice was soft yet cold.

Patterson stared at him. 'Excuse me?'

'You heard. Why did you lie to us?'

'When? When did I lie?'

'The last time we spoke. You lied about what happened on the night Sergeant Simpson was murdered.'

Patterson shook his head. 'No, I didn't.'

'OK.' Weir leaned forward to look more closely at him then. 'Tell us again, Alton. Tell us exactly what you did on that Saturday night.'

'I was shooting pool with Dylan, is all.'

'Where?'

'In the Foxhole and then at a coupla bars.'

'No.' Weir shook his head. 'You didn't do that at all. Dylan wasn't there all the time, was he?'

Patterson blanched then. His expression sallowed and Webb moved in. 'Hit a nerve, Alton? Your face is a dead giveaway.'

Patterson was struggling. He opened his mouth to speak, then shut it again like a fish. Finally, he looked at Farrow. 'Mr Farrow, sir. I don't know what these gentlemen are talking about. I'm not lying, sir.'

Farrow did not say anything. He sat with Carragher and just looked at him.

'Mr Patterson.' Weir was talking to him now. 'This is a UK murder investigation. Neither Mr Farrow nor Mr Carragher can help you.' He worked the gum to the other side of his mouth. 'Now, I'll ask you again. Tell us what really happened.'

Patterson looked at him, drew breath through his nose and lifted his shoulders. 'Sir, it's like I already told you. I played pool with Dylan Stoval all that Saturday night.'

Weir suddenly smiled at him. 'All right,' he said. 'If that's how you want to play it. You can go now.'

When Patterson was gone, Farrow squinted at Weir. 'So it's back to the van, then.'

Weir winked at Webb. 'Softly, softly, catchee monkey,' he said.

Webb had the headphones in place. Stoval and Patterson

did not work together, which meant their optimum time for discussion was back in the billet. This time, both Weir and Carragher were crammed into the small hot space with Webb, and Weir had the second set of headphones.

At six-fifteen, Patterson came back and tugged at the knot of his tie. Stoval was already there, ironing a shirt for the morning. He looked up sharply. 'What happened?'

Patterson sat down heavily on his bed. 'The two cops told me I was lying.'

Stoval stared at him. 'Lying?'

'S'right.'

'What about?'

'About shooting pool with you that Saturday night.' Patterson got up again. 'They just said I was lying. They said to tell them what really happened.'

'And what did you say?'

Patterson shrugged. 'I told them I wasn't lying.'

'They don't know anything.' Stoval pressed the iron to his shirt collar. 'How could they know anything? We were both in the Foxhole, hundreds of people woulda seen us, and that pub was real crowded when I got there.'

'It wasn't earlier,' Patterson said. 'I'm a tall guy, Dylan. Maybe somebody said I was there on my own at first.'

Stoval shook his head. 'Who're they gonna find as a witness? People don't take that much notice. You are just another marine, Alton. There's hundreds of us over here. Nobody gives a damn.'

'Then how come they said I was lying?'

Stoval was quiet then. 'I don't know.'

'Maybe they know you followed her.'

Stoval shot a stiff glance at him. 'How could they? Anyways, I didn't follow her. I knew where she was going, is all.'

'Well, they know something.' Patterson flopped down on the bed again. 'They wouldn't be asking all these questions if they didn't know something.'

'Maybe.' Stoval sat down now. 'What could they have

got, though, man? I mean she musta known hundreds of guys. She was screwing the RSO.'

'Farrow?'

'Naw. The other guy.'

Patterson thought for a moment. 'That fat guy – Webb. He picked up on the fact that I knew Kibibi at Wichita Falls. Did he do that with you?'

'Yeah.'

'Well maybe they do know something, then.'

'Get a fucking life, man. How the hell could the British cops know anything about Wichita Falls?'

'I don't know. I'm just guessing.'

'Well quit it.' Stoval shook his head. 'I was real careful. I left nothing for them to find.'

In the van, Webb looked at Weir. Weir lifted a finger.

Patterson had got up and walked to the window, tension in the set of his shoulders. He spoke without looking round. 'I told you we shoulda called her bluff.'

'Well, it's too late now. Bitch got what was coming to her. Poking her damn nose in. She didn't know the half of it.' Stoval rubbed a hand across his brow. 'If we'd let her open that can of worms, man, then all hell woulda broken loose.'

'It's already doing that.' Patterson turned to look at him. 'Don't you read no newspapers?'

Stoval shrugged. 'I don't give a fuck about that. I got no allegiance any more.'

Patterson scooped a towel up from his bed. 'I gotta take a shower,' he said, and walked out of the room.

The Cub left the hotel in Kilburn High Road and crossed the recreation ground, walking with his hands in the pockets of his cotton sports jacket. He was wearing blue jeans and shoes without socks. His hair was neatly trimmed and combed back from his head, and he wore dark glasses against the brightness of the sun. He could see Haan reading a copy of the *Daily Telegraph* by the cricket pavilion. He scanned the rest of the park as he walked, looking for footpads – watchers who should not be there. He did not expect to see anyone: the Israelis were renowned for being thorough and his own side did not know he was here. All he could see were a few women with their children, a gardener driving a lawn mower and Haan seated on his own.

The Cub sat down on the bench next to him and rested his arms on the back. 'Good morning,' he said. 'What news?'

Haan spoke without lifting his gaze from the newspaper. 'The British are agitated. They're running round like headless chickens.'

'They know, then.'

'They think they know, but they're not certain.' Haan flapped out the paper. 'The Irish problem hasn't gone away for good yet, and now they might have *him* somewhere in their midst.'

'What's he doing here?'

Haan lifted his shoulders. 'That's what worries them. Nobody seems to know.'

'Have they located al-Bakhtar?'

'No. But every feeler they've ever cultivated in the coloured community is out. MI5 are tripping over themselves to be nice to people they've not dealt with in years.'

'Just the one sighting.'

'So far.'

The Cub pursed his lips then. 'Perhaps it wasn't him.'

Haan laughed lightly. 'You don't know the man who made the sighting. He knew our friend in Lebanon. There's no way he was mistaken.'

'Where is he now, the sighter?'

'In hiding. He's convinced "the butcher" is in the UK for the sole purpose of finding and killing him. Apparently, that was the gist of their last conversation in Lebanon.'

The Cub took off his sunglasses and wiped them. 'Have the Israelis come up with anything else?'

Haan smiled then. 'Not yet, but they're resourceful people.'

'Fifty years at war. Does it surprise you?'

'They're watching your back. Have you noticed?'

The Cub smiled then. 'No.'

'You have a third eye, my friend. If the game changes, they will let you know.' He folded the paper away then. 'Which is very useful, because it means I've been free to look in other areas.'

The Cub sat back, and Haan took a packet of Gauloises from his pocket and lit one. 'The British have a theory,' he said. 'Where would you hide a butcher?'

'In a field of butchers.'

Haan pulled a face. 'Not quite the answer I was looking for, but the sentiment is right.' He looked directly at The Cub now. 'In a butcher's shop,' he said. 'The word is that the Butcher of Bekaa is doing what he does best.'

'Preparing meat, you mean.'

'Not just any meat. Halal meat.' Haan gazed across the recreation ground. 'The question is, where?'

Webb, Weir and James Carragher watched the video of the conversation between Patterson and Stoval. Weir sat back, legs crossed at the knee, and rubbed his jaw with a palm. They watched it through twice and then Weir switched off the tape.

'So something must have happened at the National Guard base in Wichita Falls,' he said.

Carragher glanced at him. 'Like what?'

Weir shrugged. 'I was hoping you could tell *me*. Simpson was only there for six weeks when Patterson and Stoval were posted at the base. What could have happened in six weeks?'

Webb was silent, sitting with his arms folded across his stomach and thinking. 'Stoval killed her,' he said. 'Not Patterson. Patterson wasn't there.'

'You're basing that on the conversation?' Weir took a piece of chewing gum from his pocket.

Webb nodded. 'He left nothing for us to find. No forensics, no clue that he was ever there. I think we should lean on Patterson again.'

'So do I.' Weir looked at his watch. 'We could do it now, or pull him off watch again tomorrow.'

Webb made a face. 'Let's just pull him in properly, sir. Arrest him. That way, we'll spook Stoval just enough.'

Weir thought for a moment and then nodded. 'We're going to want to search that room,' he said to Carragher. 'We'll get the necessary warrants, but you need to inform your people.'

'No problem.'

'We'll do it simultaneously,' Weir said then. 'Pull Patterson in and search the room.'

Patterson was back on duty at seven-thirty the following morning, looking as imposing as ever at his post at the doors of the naval building. Webb was supervising the search warrants with Dan Farrow, and Weir drove back to the embassy with another officer from the incident room. Carragher met him on the steps, and they drove round the block to the naval building and bumped up on to the pavement. They all got out, leaving the car with the passenger door open, and climbed the steps to where Patterson was standing guard. He saw the car, and he saw Weir and Carragher. Weir watched the fear light up his eyes. Another sentry stepped into his path. Weir held up his warrant card and kept his eyes on Patterson's face. Carragher took the other sentry to one side, FBI shield flapped open.

'Alton Patterson,' Weir said. 'I'm arresting you on suspicion of the murder of Gunnery Sergeant Simpson.'

Patterson gawped at him, mouth open, spittle spread on his lip.

Weir read him his rights. 'You can come quietly, Mr Patterson,' he said. 'Or we can handcuff you.'

'I haven't done anything,' Patterson stammered.

'Which is it to be?'

Patterson looked at his colleague, who was staring wide-eyed at him, and then at Carragher.

Weir held up a set of plastic handcuffs.

Patterson shook his head and walked down the steps.

Webb, Farrow and two officers from the incident room searched the four-man billet. The three other occupants were summoned, and they stood by under Farrow's supervision while the search was carried out. Dyer and Williams looked bemused. Neither of them had even been interviewed over the murder. Stoval tried to look impassive, but Webb sensed the tension in him. He whistled while he worked. It did not take long, as the room was pretty sparse – just the beds, the cupboards and the footlockers.

'How come Alton ain't here?' Williams asked suddenly. 'You got us three. Where's Alton at?'

Webb looked up from Patterson's footlocker, which Farrow had just opened with a set of pass keys. 'Alton's in custody.'

Williams stared wide-eyed at him, then glanced at Stoval, who was standing against the wall, watching Webb. Webb smiled without any mirth in his eyes. 'Would you open your locker, please? My colleague would like to inspect it.' He jerked a thumb at one of the incident room team who was standing by. Stoval fished in his pocket for keys.

Webb rummaged through Patterson's locker: T-shirts, underwear, a couple of pairs of trainers. Under the clothing, he found a copy of *Penthouse* magazine and a badly printed journal of some kind. He picked it up and flicked through the pages.

Farrow stepped up to him. 'What you got?' he said.

Webb showed him the magazine. *The Resister*: spring issue, 1995. 'Bit out of date, isn't it?'

Farrow was squinting at it. 'I don't even know what it is.'

Webb flicked through the pages, and he came across one

with the corner folded down and marked with a felt-tip pen. An open letter to the readers was printed on the page. It had also been marked in two places by an asterisk. He frowned and flicked back to the inside cover again. 'Official publication of the Special Forces Underground.' He looked at Farrow, who was frowning heavily now. Webb could feel Stoval's eyes on him.

'Recognise this, Dylan?' he asked.

Stoval shook his head. The officer had been through his locker and closed it again.

'Why would Alton have something this much out of date in his footlocker?'

'Beats me. I don't even know what it is.'

Williams came over then and looked at the journal. 'That's a military magazine aimed at people who support the militia,' he said.

Farrow scratched his head. 'I've never heard of it.'

'Do a lot of military people support the militia?' Webb asked.

Williams twisted his lip. 'I guess. Enough to print a magazine, anyways.'

Weir was leaning across the table and staring into Alton Patterson's face. The tape machine was running and James Carragher was seated next to him. Patterson was looking at the floor between his feet.

'Where were you on Saturday the tenth, Alton?' Weir was saying. 'I don't think you were in that pub with Stoval.'

'Yes I was, sir. I was.'

'Not all night.'

'Yes, sir. All night.'

Weir hissed air through his teeth. 'You know, you really ought to stop lying to me. I really hate people who lie to me.'

'I'm not lying.'

Weir shook his head. 'Yes, you are, Alton. I know you

are. You see, I have proof that you were not with Stoval all that night.'

Patterson stared at him, bit his lip and shook his head. He looked at Carragher then, his compatriot, hoping to see some sort of support in his eyes. But Carragher was impassive, arms folded across his chest.

'Tell me the truth, Alton.' Weir got up and took off his jacket. 'Sergeant Simpson was stabbed in the heart, one long thrust up through the ribs, as if somebody had bayoneted her. A big man like you, a trained man, he could've done that.'

'I didn't kill anybody.'

'Didn't you?' Weir made a face. 'Then how come you lied to us? And don't tell me you didn't, because I can prove that you did.'

Patterson did not say anything. He clasped his hands together and looked at the space between his feet.

Weir sat down and leaned across the table again. 'Alton,' he said more gently. 'At this moment in time, you are my number one suspect for the murder of Kibibi Simpson. I've got a witness who can pick you out in an ID parade as having visited her flat on several occasions.'

Patterson looked sharply at him then. 'I never went there but once.' He closed his eyes and sat back.

Weir smiled and sighed. 'Thank you. Now, maybe, you'll tell me the truth.'

There was a knock on the door then and Weir looked up. Webb stuck his head round it and Weir glanced back at Patterson. 'Time for a break,' he said. 'Give you something to think about.' He stood up and nodded to the uniformed sergeant who stood behind Webb in the doorway. 'Don't get used to the cell, Alton. You'll have to share in Brixton.'

Weir followed Webb down the corridor, with Carragher right behind him. Patterson was escorted back to the cells by the uniformed sergeant. Webb led the way to the incident room and sat down at a desk. Farrow was already there, sipping coffee.

'We found this in his footlocker,' Webb said. 'There's an open letter I think you should read.' He handed Weir the journal and Carragher thinned his eyes.

'*The Resister*,' he said. 'Patterson had this in his locker?'

Webb nodded. 'You know what it is?'

'I've seen a copy. It disturbs a lot of people back at the puzzle palace in Washington.'

'I'm not surprised.' Weir was scanning the letter marked with the asterisks. '"The co-ordinating staff of the Special Forces Underground believes that our current federal state and local government represent the antithesis of everything we hold true. The only secure way to communicate our beliefs within the military is by clandestine publishing. Thus, *The Resister*. One uncontrollable consequence of publishing *The Resister* was its spread outside the Special Forces into the patriot movement."'

He read on to himself, scanning the lines, then read aloud again: '"You cannot reasonably expect to form a militia, voice your opposition to the federal government and its domestic policies, and expect to remain untargeted by its internal security apparatus."'

Weir stopped reading and handed the magazine to Carragher. He looked over his shoulder at Webb. 'George, wheel Patterson back to the interview room, will you?'

They both sat across from him now, with Farrow and Carragher seated against the wall. Patterson had declined any form of legal counsel, be it US military or UK civilian. Weir had the copy of *The Resister* laid out on the table before him.

'What's this, Alton? Why was it in your locker?'

'In my locker?' Patterson stared at it, then reached over and picked it up. He looked at the open letter and pushed out his lips.

'Mr Patterson, that's a very serious publication to be in possession of when you're in the Marine Corps,' Farrow told him. 'I think you've got some explaining to do. The stuff they espouse isn't far short of sedition.'

Patterson looked at him then and swallowed. 'Sir, this isn't mine.'

'Then whose is it?' Weir demanded.

Patterson did not reply. He licked his lips, laid the journal down and looked at the wall.

'Whose is it?' Weir was watching his face, the pronounced, angular muscle at his jawline.

'It's Dylan's,' Patterson said at last.

'Dylan Stoval?'

'Yes, sir.'

'Why was it in *your* locker, then?' Webb looked at him. 'Are you saying that Dylan Stoval planted it there?'

'I don't know that, sir. But it's not mine. It's his. I ain't never read it. I never cared to.' Patterson sighed then. 'I was only ever in it for the money. Dylan says the same now, but he was in way deeper than I ever was.'

'Deeper in what?' Weir said.

Patterson looked at Farrow then. 'Into the whole thing – Special Forces Underground, their links with the militia. The group at Wichita Falls.'

'What group?'

'The Rambo group. The Texas State Guard boys that were shifting all the guns.'

Weir looked at Carragher then. 'Mr Patterson, we'll come to all this in a minute, but first I have a murder to solve.'

Patterson looked back at him. He glanced at the journal and nodded as if to himself. 'You were right, sir. I did lie. I wasn't with Dylan that whole evening.'

'Go on.'

'Dylan wasn't with me is how I oughtta put it.' Patterson leaned his elbows on the table. 'He told me to say that he was, because he needed an alibi for the whole night, not just the early part.' He paused then. 'The early part he was in the Foxhole, then he took off after Kibibi. I don't know why. I think he was gonna follow her, maybe frighten her a little bit.'

'And then later he killed her?' Weir said.

Patterson thought for a moment. 'Williams and Dyer were working all that night, so there was only me and Dylan in the billet. He wanted me to stay behind and be the alibi, say that he had gone to bed and been there all night. Say that I got up to go to the toilet and saw him there at three o'clock, or whenever it was that he done her.'

'He went to Kibibi's apartment?' Webb said.

Patterson nodded. 'He had a key cut. She never knew it. Dylan's cunning like that. I was there one time.' He looked at Weir. 'Just the one time and we were all talking, and Dylan took a print of the Chubb key in a piece of clay.'

'Why did he kill her?'

Patterson looked at the floor again, then at Carragher and Farrow. 'Wait a minute,' he said. 'I done nothing here, except tell a few lies to save his black ass. What am I looking at?'

Weir sat back. 'There're two ways of playing it,' he said. 'I can get a warrant from our Home Secretary and put you up before a British court to be tried.'

'For what?'

'If you're telling the truth, accessory to murder.'

Patterson sucked breath.

'The other way of dealing with it is to hand you over to your own authorities and let them deal with you.' Weir glanced at Farrow, who nodded.

Patterson was thinking hard. 'It's all to do with this.' He tapped the copy of *The Resister*. 'There's stuff I can tell you about this. But you gotta cut me some kinda deal.'

Weir looked at Farrow. 'I'm sure you'd like to try them, Mr Farrow. I know we'd like you to.' He glanced at Patterson again. 'Save the British taxpayer the bother.'

Farrow stood up and fisted his hands on his hips. 'What've you got to say to us, mister? Tell me that first and maybe then we can talk.'

Patterson sighed. 'Dylan killed her,' he said. 'Because Kibibi was blackmailing the both of us. She's been doing it ever since Wichita Falls. We had enough money, so we paid her off for a while. But when we were all posted here, Kibibi got that snappy apartment and wanted a whole lot more money for clothes, rent and shit. Dylan got pissed off.'

'Why was she blackmailing you?' Webb cut in.

Patterson looked at Farrow then. 'Because we were part of the scam that steals weapons from the government,' he said. 'Anything from M16 rounds to C-4. It's stolen from all over the United States, but goes to Wichita Falls. Kibibi found out when we were all posted there at the same time.' He looked at Farrow again. 'The stolen munitions are stored there, sir, in an old dump away from the main Texas Guard base. I can give you names, places, the whole shooting match. But I ain't doing it for nothing.'

24

Harrison rode south with Sidetrack and the others, crossing the Brazos before it ran into Possum Kingdom Lake. They rode in an open-topped car, the sun beating down without mercy, and Harrison sweated beneath his battered cowboy hat. He had much on his mind and much, he hoped, on tape. He had a nagging fear that Whiskey Six might be Ray Martinez, the Rat who pulled him out of his last hole in Vietnam. It made a terrible sense: the interest in his tattoo; how Martinez hated snakes. He had been a year older than Harrison when they were in Cu-Chi and was one of the meanest men Harrison had ever come across. He thought about what Spinelli had told him, how Whiskey Six was wanted for killing two security guards in Arkansas and Tennessee, when he was still running with the Hell's Angels. He thought back to Vietnam: Martinez almost always worked alone. They had called him 'the Probe' because he just dived into a tunnel and kept going until he came across a VC and killed him, or came back up again so they could blow the hole. Martinez had been scared of no one and nothing, except those little black snakes. Everything else made sense too – the weapons, the Texas State Guard, that soldier they had just run into and the whole neo-Nazi attitude. Nobody hated gooks more than Ray Martinez. He even hated the South Vietnamese they had gone to help. Harrison thought of Jean then and her son, and realised that it was Martinez's mentality that infected people like Southern Sidetrack.

But he had no way of getting the information out. He had been hoping that Sidetrack would disband them again like he had done the last time, to give him enough time to contact Jean and feed her this new information. He would not tell Jean that Sidetrack was her son's killer just yet, not until he was out and they could make their bust. It occurred to him then that he already had a lot on tape and maybe he could surface with what he had got. But these new thoughts about Martinez had really struck a chord. Here he was, thirty years after he last saw him, riding freight trains with the FTRA. He sat there, rolled a cigarette and reflected silently on the vagaries of life.

Limpet squatted next to him. 'You wanna shot?' he asked and waved a bottle under Harrison's nose.

Harrison shook his head. 'Too hot, man. Think I'll stick to water.'

'Damn open-topped cars.' Limpet shaded his eyes from the sun. 'Never jump an open-topped boxcar in the Texas summertime.'

'You wanna tell Sidetrack,' Harrison said.

Limpet looked across to where Sidetrack was sipping mescal. 'You know, I don't think I'll bother.'

Harrison chuckled. Sidetrack's demeanour had been less than pleasant today. 'How long's he been running this outfit?'

'About five years. He ain't a guy to fall out with. We got discipline squads, you know.'

Harrison nodded. 'You ever come up against them?'

Limpet shook his head. 'Always stuck close to the man over there. Never needed no goon squad on my ass.'

'How often d'you see Whiskey Six?' Harrison asked him.

Limpet squinted into the sunlight. 'I only saw him once in five years. He rolled into a freight yard on the Colorado/New Mexico line one summer. It was me, Sidetrack and Hooch there. Ghost Town was visiting from California. He's the dude that runs the Red Heads out west.'

'How many of them are there?'

'About five hundred, I guess.'

'And they do the same stuff as us?'

'Ship the guns and that, yeah.' Limpet laughed then and

tipped the whiskey bottle to his lips. 'It's a good living, Four-String. That's for sure.'

'Yeah? I ain't seen any of it. When do we get paid?'

Limpet laughed again. '*You* don't, brother. *You* is on probation.'

'How did I know you were gonna say that?' Harrison leaned and spat. 'Where did all this hardware come from in the first place?'

Limpet shrugged. 'I don't ask no questions, man. That way, I don't get told no lies and I can't say anything to anybody I shouldn't.'

'Right on.' Harrison leaned against the side of the boxcar as they crossed a wooden bridge, with the ravine falling into dirt, rock and hollowed-out holes one hundred feet below them. Sidetrack was dozing, his head bobbing. Limpet sat with his eyes closed and his legs pushed out, feet splayed before him. Both Carlsbad and Hooch were sleeping. Harrison stared into the flat Texas plains, watching dust devils rise here and there. Clouds were gathering over Mexico.

The train slowed near the town of Morgan Mill and Sidetrack got up to take a piss.

Harrison stood upwind of him and leaned on the doorjamb. 'So, what's happening, Sidetrack? Where we going now?'

Sidetrack did not reply right away. He finished peeing, zipped up and spat into the wind. 'Gimme a cigarette.'

Harrison rolled him one and passed it over.

'Gimme a light.'

Harrison bit his lip, snapped a match on the back of his thigh and lit the cigarette. The wind took the match and he let it fall to the dust below.

'We're just cruising,' Sidetrack said. 'Just rolling for a while.' He looked into Harrison's eyes then. 'Why, brother? You got something planned?'

Harrison shook his head. 'I was never one for just wandering, is all.'

'Who said anything about wandering?' Sidetrack spat threads of tobacco. 'Nobody said anything about wandering. Wanderers, we ain't.'

Harrison nodded. 'How long am I gonna be on probation?' he asked.

Sidetrack smiled wickedly, showing that long tooth. 'As long as I say you are.'

'And in the meantime I don't get paid.'

'You got that right.'

Harrison looked him in the eye then. 'Well, don't take too long, big guy. I might just get bored.'

He sat down cross-legged and took out his tobacco and papers. He looked up at Sidetrack again. 'When this runs out, I'll smoke yours.'

Sidetrack laughed and sat down next to him. 'If you need anything, alls you got to do is ask. It's like I told you already, we're family here.'

They camped that night near Waco and Harrison thought about the stand-off with the Branch Davidians in 1993. The freight yard was big and low-walled, and they built a fire in the lee of two broken-down locomotives that sand and corrosion were taking over. Harrison ate dinner provided by Hooch and he sipped some of Limpet's whiskey, and longed for the comfort of Jean Carey's arms. The stars came out full that night; the Mexican cloud stayed south of them and the temperature dropped rapidly.

Around midnight, Sidetrack made a call on his cellphone and spoke in a low voice. He glanced over at Harrison briefly. Harrison held his eye, then looked into the fire. Sidetrack came off the phone and put it away in his pack. Harrison made cigarettes, smoked and thought, then tucked himself in his bedroll and went to sleep.

When he woke in the morning, Sidetrack was already up and talking again on the phone. Harrison built up the fire, boiled some coffee in the small tin pot and handed a cup to Sidetrack. The others were still asleep.

Sidetrack cupped the coffee between both hands and

blew on it. The steam rose through his fingers and he sipped, looking over the rim of the cup at Harrison. 'We got business to do today,' he said.

'Where?'

'East.' Sidetrack took a roll of weathered railroad maps from his pack and spread them out in the dirt. 'We gotta make the Saratoga yard by nightfall.'

'Going back to Arkansas. What's happening in Arkansas?'

'Got an important meeting to attend.' Sidetrack leered at him and Harrison cocked one eyebrow. 'Don't worry, Four-String. You been initiated already.'

They rode all day, swapping three trains, heading northeast for the Arkansas State line. Sidetrack's maps were good and he knew the southern railroads like the back of his hand. He knew which train would be along when, where the driver swap points were and what freight would be unloaded in what yard. Harrison stood in a rattling boxcar as they climbed north of Tyler once again. 'We ain't carrying no cargo, then,' he said.

Sidetrack shook his head. 'We're picking up later.' He looked sideways at Harrison then. 'Got to see some people here first.'

Hooch was standing behind them both. 'You gonna run us in some whores like you did that last time?' he said.

Sidetrack shook his head. 'No whores, man. Not on this trip.'

The train was not stopping at Saratoga, but rolling on to Hot Springs. Sidetrack led the way and they jumped off before they got to the yard. They watched the train thunder across the plains as they walked the final few hundred yards. Darkness had fallen and again the temperature was dropping. Above them, there was a perfectly cloudless sky, vast and purple. Harrison carried his banjo and walked between Hooch and Carlsbad.

As they approached the yard, he could smell burning, and passing between two disused trucks, he saw the flickering

482

flames of a fire. Eight men were seated round it, two slightly apart from the others. Harrison squinted in the firelight and could see both blue bandanas and red. The Highrollers and the Red Heads were in town; a gathering of the clans.

Sidetrack walked round the fire and the two men seated together got up. One wore a red bandana and the other a blue. Sidetrack greeted both of them. 'You got the call, too,' he said.

The two men looked at Harrison across the fire. 'Oh yeah,' the one with the red bandana said. 'We got the call.'

'Looks like zero hour.' Sidetrack beckoned Harrison over and laid a hand on his shoulder. Harrison was desperately aware of the wire. He looked into the drink-bruised faces of the two men.

'Four-String,' Sidetrack said. 'This here is Ghost Town.' He nodded to the Red Head. 'And this guy's from up north. We call him The Voyageur.'

Harrison nodded, but said nothing. Sidetrack looked round at him and his eyes were cold and black. 'Now go sit with the others. We got things to talk about.'

Swann watched his fiancée down the Budweiser in one long swallow. She placed her glass on the hotel bar and nodded to the bartender for another. Her cellphone rang where she had laid it on the counter. 'No peace for the wicked,' Swann muttered and handed it to her.

'Logan,' she said, holding it to her ear.

'There will be no more warnings. People will die and the responsibility will be yours.'

She bit her lip. 'Give it up, Fachida. You lost. We called your bluff. Your honour's in tatters. You're not fit to fight any more.'

Swann was staring at her.

She could hear Harada hiss the breath through his teeth. 'I will make Oklahoma City look like a kindergarten party, Agent Logan. And the responsibility will be yours.' The phone went dead then. Logan switched it off and lifted the fresh glass of beer to her lips.

'What did he say?' Swann asked her.

'He obviously caught my little news broadcast. I think I've pissed him off.'

They went back to 4th Street and passed the information to Kovalski. 'No more warnings,' he said. 'That's helpful.' He looked at Swann. 'Random strikes. You figure he's got stuff already set up?'

Swann nodded. 'I think it's likely. The way he's operated so far.'

Kovalski pursed his lips and exhaled slowly. 'Maybe we'll luck out on a lead.'

Logan lifted her eyebrows. 'Maybe I'll make president.'

The murder squad arrested Dylan Stoval as he came out of the shower at Eastcote. Patterson was already locked in a cell awaiting further interviews. Weir, as senior investigating officer, had agreed with Farrow that once the two men were formally charged, they would release them into his custody until the Home Secretary made his decision about who would prosecute them. Stoval was shampooing his scalp and singing a rap song when Weir, Webb, Carragher and Farrow turned up. They stood behind him in the shower block, and Webb folded his arms and waited for him to stop singing. Stoval twisted off the taps and turned. He stopped and stared, mouth falling open. Then the fear sparked in his eyes. Webb cautioned him and he got dressed.

They drove him back to Paddington police station and sat him down in an interview room. Webb fixed him with a cold-eyed stare. 'You made mistakes, Dylan,' he said. 'You were sloppy.'

Stoval shook his head. 'Sir, I have no idea what you're talking about.'

'You weren't with Alton Patterson all that Saturday night.'

'Yes, sir. I was.'

'You're a liar, Dylan.' Weir shook his head at him.

'No, sir.'

Weir got up then. 'We've got video footage of you coming through the barrier at Camden Town tube station.'

Stoval stared at him.

'We know exactly what's been happening. Alton's told us everything. We've got a witness who will pick both of you out as having been in the wine bar below Kibibi Simpson's flat.'

Stoval was staring beyond him to Farrow, whose features had darkened considerably.

'Sir,' Stoval said to him, but Farrow shook his head.

'Quit lying, Stoval. You're getting yourself in deeper and deeper. We already know all there is to know. We know about the stabbing. We know that you followed Sergeant Simpson. We know why you killed her.' He nodded again. 'We know all about the National Guard base at Wichita Falls and the rogue outfit down there. We know you've been stealing weapons and shipping them to Wichita Falls. We know that you read *The Resister*.' He stopped then. 'If I have my way, you'll be court-martialled for all of this back in the States. That's murder one and treason, soldier. I could have you executed.'

Stoval's eyes were wide.

'What Mr Farrow's saying, Dylan,' Webb said more gently, 'is that you might just have a choice.'

'I want full information,' Farrow went on. 'I want your statement detailing everything you know. We've got it from Patterson and now I want it from you. If you do that, then maybe, just maybe, I won't have your ass fried in the chair.'

The phone call from London came into the Strategic Intelligence Operations Center and was transferred to Tom Kovalski's office. Logan picked it up and then handed the phone to Swann. 'It's for you,' she said. 'London.'

Swann took the phone from her. 'Hello?'

'Jack. It's George Webb.'

Swann sat down in Kovalski's chair. 'Hey, Webby. Long time no speak. How are you?'

'Better now.'

'Why?'

'Because we solved the embassy murder.'

'That was quick.'

'Some of them are, Jack. We were dealing with amateurs and got lucky. The motive was blackmail.'

He went on to tell Swann exactly what had happened and the fact that Kibibi Simpson had been murdered because she had stumbled across a weapons-pilfering racket that was centred on Wichita Falls. 'Stuff goes missing all over the country, Jack,' Webb told him. 'We've got full statements from two marines, who have named names for the regional security officer. The chances are that we'll let the US military try them in the States and they've been keen to make a deal. The Fed they sent over is compiling his report, but I wanted to let you know that the weapons have found their way to the militia groups. I'm not sure how, but there's a lot of money involved, enough to get a marine sergeant murdered. We don't know what's at the back of it, but there seems to be some funding coming from neo-Nazi groups in Germany. You might want to pass that on.'

'Thanks, Webby. We already know part of the militia angle. Listen, if you find anything else out, let me know, will you?'

'Of course. The Nazi groups are new ones, you know, not Combat 18 or any of the others. We've got two names. The Shield Society's one of them. The other is ...'

'Shield Society?' Swann gripped the phone that bit harder.

'You've heard of it?'

'Yes, I have.'

'The other's the AMA. It apparently stands for American Militia Abroad.'

'Thanks, George. Keep me posted.' Swann hung up and looked at Logan. 'Where's Kovalski?' he asked.

'I'm here.' Kovalski walked into the office, followed by Carmen McKensie and two other investigating agents.

'He's called twice,' McKensie was saying to Kovalski. 'Not here, but headquarters. He always asks to speak to the Director.'

'Who does?' Logan asked.

'Some old nut from the airmen's and soldiers' home. We've checked him out with the staff there and he's got a couple of marbles missing. He lost his legs in Korea and still can't remember anything about it. Apparently, he relives the shock most days.' She tapped her skull with a fingernail. 'That's not good for the grey matter.'

'Tom,' Swann said. 'I've just had a call from George Webb. He's on the murder squad in West London, been working the embassy stabbing with Agent Carragher.' He related what Webb had told him and Kovalski's frown grew deeper.

'The Shield Society,' Logan drew up her face. 'Where are they based?'

'Germany, somewhere,' Swann said.

Logan wagged her head. 'That's got to be more than just a coincidence.'

'You mean Harada and the militia working together? That would be a weird alliance.'

Kovalski rested the knuckles of one fist on his desk. 'I'm gonna run these groups by the CIA,' he said. 'Get the people over at Langley to check them out.' He looked at Logan. 'In the meantime, get this information about the military ordnance and *The Resister* down to New Orleans. Somehow, they're gonna have to let Harrison know what's going on.'

Harrison was sitting cross-legged by the campfire, with the southerly wind at his back. He was rolling a cigarette, water on one side of him, and a whiskey bottle wrapped in brown paper on the other. Across the fire, Sidetrack sat next to The Voyageur and Ghost Town. The Voyageur's voice was husky from too many cigarettes and Harrison had to bend out of the wind to hear him. 'You got a special job,' he hissed. 'Whiskey blew in to South Dakota day before yesterday. Somebody's got to make a pick-up and take it to West Virginia.'

Silence. 'The Southern Blacks?' Sidetrack said.

'Your turf, man.'

'How come you got involved?' Limpet asked him. 'How come Whiskey didn't call us hisself?'

The Voyageur looked at the fire. 'The man is laying low, brother. Word is we might have somebody watching us.'

For a moment, nobody spoke. Harrison sat where he was, heart high in his chest, but he sucked on the cigarette and blew smoke from the side of his mouth. The Voyageur looked at Sidetrack. 'The days are getting more dangerous, brother. We figured person to person. The fucking FBI can tap almost any phone they please.' He looked at Harrison then. 'You say you was in Angola?'

Harrison nodded.

'For how long?'

'Seven and three.'

The Voyageur squinted at Ghost Town. 'That man, right there, was in Angola. He don't recall seeing you.'

Harrison looked across at Ghost Town, who had fixed him with a stare now.

'You know something, bubba,' Harrison said. 'I don't recall seeing him either.'

'Who were your buddies?' Ghost Town asked him.

'I hung out with Mad Mike Moore's crowd in A block.'

'I was in D block.'

'Then you ain't gonna know me, are ya?' Harrison had his hand at his boot top. 'You may not even know Moore, but I figure you know Klein.'

For a long moment, Ghost Town thinned his eyes. 'You knew Klein?'

'Everybody knew Klein, bubba. Even Mad Mike was scared of Klein.'

Sidetrack set his bottle down in the dirt. 'Who the fuck was Klein?'

'White Knights leader.'

The Voyageur leaned back on his palms. 'Forget this shit, man. We gotta talk about the pick-up, man. And then we gotta blow.'

Sidetrack nodded. 'The 2–18's heading north.'

Ghost Town was still staring at Harrison. He got up and walked round behind him. All he had to do was to run a finger down his spine and he would feel the wire. Harrison was tense, ready to pull his guns and try and shoot his way out. He could feel sweat in his hair and a clamminess on his skin, but he sat where he was and looked into the fire. Ghost Town squatted, resting his elbows on his thighs. 'So you were in Angola and you crawled tunnels in 'Nam.' His voice was a whisper. 'Tunnel Rats are rare, brother.' He patted Harrison on the shoulder. 'Real rare.'

The three leaders moved away from the fire and consulted together. Ten minutes after that, The Voyageur and Ghost Town melted into the darkness.

Hooch was watching Harrison. 'Didn't seem to like you a whole bunch,' he said.

Harrison made a face and spat tobacco juice.

They heard the whistle of the 2–18 heading north and then Sidetrack walked back into the pool of light cast by the fire. He squatted on his haunches and reached for his mescal bottle. He stared into the flames and his eyes were dull, black and cold. He did not say anything to anyone, just quietly sipped on the mescal as if deep in thought. Limpet rolled a cigarette and passed it to him. Sidetrack took it without speaking and lit it from a stick in the fire. Harrison was watching him out of half-closed eyes, lying on his side now, facing the fire, with the wind fresh at his back.

'So this is a big deal, then?' Hooch asked.

Sidetrack glanced at him. 'We got to go back to Wichita Falls.'

'Then West Virginia?'

'That's what the man said.'

Harrison took a long pull on his cigarette and let the smoke drift in the wind. 'What's in West Virginia?'

Sidetrack looked directly at him. 'The Mountaineer Militia.'

Jean Carey was driving the truck close to the Texas/Louisiana border at Kildare Junction, when Harrison's cellphone rang. She picked it up immediately and pulled off the road. It was days since he had contacted her and she had been wandering aimlessly, toying with the idea of heading back to New Orleans. 'Hello?' she said.

'Jean.' It was not Harrison, but Matt Penny's voice.

'Hello, Matthew.'

'Has John been in contact with you?'

'Not since the last time.'

'Where are you?'

'A place called Kildare Junction.'

Penny paused as if thinking. 'Drive to Dallas,' he said. 'I'll meet you at the airport.'

'Why, is John in trouble?'

'I don't know, Jean. But there's been a development.'

He hung up and Jean laid the phone down on the bench seat beside her. She sat by the roadside for a moment, then hauled the wheel round and headed south for the interstate.

As dawn broke, the Southern Blacks were up and heading back to the railroad. Sidetrack had been quiet all night, preoccupied it seemed, and the others gave him a wide berth. Even Limpet, who had got his name because Sidetrack was never without him, kept his distance. Harrison could feel the tension. Something had happened with the other two leaders – something which had made Sidetrack really pause for thought. Perhaps it was just this deal. Hooch had told him it must be serious if they had to head all the way back to the weapons dump to collect the goods themselves. Normally, whatever was being freighted would be routed to them. Whatever it was for, Whiskey Six wanted Sidetrack taking personal charge of the delivery.

They hopped a grainer heading for New Mexico and shared a car which stank of rotten alfalfa. Harrison sat close to the door and wondered how he could get word to the field office. He couldn't. There was no way he could leave the group long enough to make a phone call without raising suspicion. He pursed his lips, sipped water and felt the comforting chill of gunmetal against his shin.

Sidetrack got up from where he was sitting and came over. He stood next to Harrison and looked down at him. 'I need you riding shotgun, Four-String,' he said.

Harrison got to his feet. 'Shotgun?'

'Yeah.'

Harrison thinned his eyes. 'What about Limpet?'

Sidetrack shook his head. 'No good. He don't got the experience I need for this one.'

Harrison furrowed his brow. 'You're gonna have to explain a little better, brother.'

Sidetrack leaned against the doorjamb and looked him in the eye. 'We've got a long journey ahead of us,' he said. 'All the way to West Virginia. If I was humping shit that far, usually I'd pass it on to other sections of the outfit. Break it into smaller chunks. But this seems to be a rush job.' He broke off again and looked at him. 'It's big, too. We each got a box of C-4 to shift.'

'That's got to be one hundred pounds, man.' Harrison frowned. 'You could blow up a city with that.'

'Why d'you think we're shipping it to West Virginia.'

Harrison looked keenly at him then, his sixth sense tingling. 'Why you telling me all this, man? I thought I was on probation.'

'You are, brother.' Sidetrack let the words hang for a moment. 'But I need you riding shotgun. I want you on my shoulder at all times. We've got to cross a whole buncha states and end up in turf I don't know real well.' He paused. 'Things ain't what they used to be. The government, the cops and everybody are on high alert. We've got to be on our guard.'

Harrison drew a stiff breath through his nose. 'Why me?'

'Because you got balls of steel, man.' Sidetrack patted him on the shoulder and showed that wicked tooth. 'You must have, to do what you do.'

Jean got to Dallas that evening, parked up and then crossed to the terminal building, where she met Penny and Swartz. They were with two other men in business suits and Penny introduced them as FBI agents from the Dallas field office. Swartz rode with the agents and Penny climbed behind the wheel of Harrison's pick-up. He was wearing a faded baseball hat and a T-shirt. Jean climbed into the passenger seat next to him.

'John's not been in touch,' he said.

She shook her head. 'Not a word.'

Penny chewed his lip.

'What is it?'

'I'm not sure I can tell you.'

'Matthew, if it involves John, I don't think you can avoid it.'

Penny looked sideways at her then. 'Did something happen between you two?'

'That's none of your business.'

'Jean.'

She glanced through the windshield. 'If you must know, yes it did.'

Penny drummed his fingers on the steering wheel and started the engine. 'We're driving to Wichita Falls.'

'What's at Wichita Falls?'

He looked at her again as he eased the truck out of the parking space. 'A terminal for stolen military hardware.'

They drove north-west on the interstate as far as Fort Worth and then headed for Wichita Falls on 287. Penny explained to her what had happened in London and what had been discovered.

'A murder in the US Embassy led to this?' She shook her head.

'They uncovered a whole barrelful of bad apples,' Penny told her. 'We're mounting a massive surveillance operation. That's why Andy's gone to the field office in Dallas. We've got a joint terrorism task force running here in Texas.'

'How does all this affect John?'

'I don't know that it does as yet. But we've received information from London, which we have to act on now. If it comes out, then we'll publicise the London connection. It won't make any difference to John.' He looked at the cellphone, which lay on the bench seat between them. 'Anyways, maybe you'll get a call from him.' He winked at her then. 'I figure he won't wanna go too long without getting in touch.'

Jean sat back, the window rolled down and her arm resting on the ledge. Night had fallen, but the air was warm and balmy, and the breeze ruffled her hair. 'I was on my way back to New Orleans,' she said. 'Well, almost. I'd just about made my mind up.'

Penny looked across at her. 'Were you gonna go back to London?'

'No. Not yet, at least.' She sighed then. 'I will have to think about it, though. At some point soon.'

Penny was quiet. 'You don't sound too enthusiastic about the prospect.'

'Oh I am, in one way, at least. I miss my job, the hospital, working with the children.'

Penny nodded. 'But you've got unfinished business here.'

'Yes.'

'John must've told you, Jean. The chances of us catching anyone for your son's murder are slim to nonexistent.'

'I know. But I can live in hope.'

'You can, and at least you know why now.'

'Yes. That helps. It wasn't just random or racist. John said he would've just been in the wrong place at the wrong time.'

493

'It's why all the hobos have been killed,' Penny said. 'The FTRA don't want anyone busting in on their operation. It must make them a fortune.'

'Who is stealing the weapons?'

'Soldiers, marines, national guardsmen.'

'Why?'

'For money, I guess.' Penny shifted down a gear to overtake a truck. 'A lot of them are sympathetic to some of the militia or patriot causes, though. Timothy McVeigh, the guy that blew up the federal building in Oklahoma City, was a model soldier.' He sighed. 'But we know from London that money is involved. Apparently, there's a couple of European Nazi groups who are helping fund it. God only knows where they get their money from.'

'But why do it in the first place? What do they hope to achieve?'

'I don't know.' Penny wagged his head from side to side. 'They think the United States has deviated from its Constitution, the spirit of what was written down.'

Jean frowned. 'But that was two hundred years ago. Things change, alter, evolve.'

Penny laughed then. 'Try telling that to a Missouri Breakman who thinks a driver's licence is the abrogation of his right to travel.'

They drove on through the night and Jean dozed with her head against the window. Penny kept on Highway 287 as far as Bowie, then he pulled over and took a nap. Jean woke with the dawn, saw him dozing and crossed the road to the gas station. She washed her face in the ladies' room, and bought two cups of coffee and some muffins.

Penny was rubbing his eyes when she got back to the truck. He smiled at her and tapped the dashboard. 'We're gonna need to gas up, anyway.' He took the lid off his coffee and sipped it, the steam rising against his face. 'You know, Jean. Nobody gets to do this.'

'Do what?'

'Ride along with the FBI.'

Jean smiled then. 'I thought you were riding along with me.'

Penny laughed. 'I oughtta find a motel and let you out. Pick you up later.'

'Why? What're you going to do?'

'Just drive by a couple of locations and report back to Dallas. After that, we'll put up an airplane.'

'Then it's a good job I'm here with you,' she said. 'It's better cover – a man and a woman together.'

Penny smiled at her. 'And you'd fight like an alley cat if I tried to leave you behind. Right?'

'Ask Johnny Buck.'

Harrison rode shotgun. Sidetrack was focused. Last night he had drunk nothing but water, and this morning, as they rolled towards Wichita Falls, he stood by the open door and stared into the distance. Limpet and the others had noticed the change too; Limpet directing the odd look Harrison's way now and again. But nobody commented on it. Harrison stood and watched Sidetrack watching the world go by, and chewed over his situation. He was still wearing the wire. There was no way of taking it off now without being seen and he had no way of contacting Jean and his case agents. He was underground, alone, and visions of the past rolled back to him: Ray Martinez and his mortal fear of snakes.

He wore the Beretta concealed in his waistband, having shifted it out of his pack. The snub-nosed .38 was still stuffed in his boot and his bowie knife was accessible.

They headed due west towards Wichita Falls and the weapons dump. Harrison was working it all through his brain; one hundred pounds of C-4 was a massive amount of explosive. West Virginia: a finger of fear crawled the back of his neck. Half a day's drive from Washington D.C. and Fachida Harada, the bomber. Somehow, he had to get word out or this could go very bad, very quickly. But Sidetrack was jumpy and suddenly suspicious of everything. He had made such a big deal about wanting him close and then that crack about balls of steel. Was this his first really big test? What was it that The Voyageur and Ghost Town had heard? The Voyageur was right: Tunnel Rats were rare and Whiskey Six would know that. Before Harrison went undercover out here, the militia were the farthest thing from his mind. This was an undercover drugs deal. Coldly, chillingly now, he remembered the picture of him the militia had put out on their websites.

Penny and Jean drove north from Bowie to Ring Gold, then west towards Henrietta. Jean had the window down again and the day was getting hotter. Penny sniffed the air and made a face. 'There's one helluva storm coming,' he said.

Jean looked round at him. 'You can tell?'

'Oh, yeah. I spent half my life in Texas, Jean. You get to know when the weather's gonna change.'

'A tornado?'

'No. No. Just a mother of a rainstorm.' He smiled at her. 'They think they get rain in New Orleans, but you oughtta see it blowing across the plains.'

Jean leaned out of the window and heard the whistle of a freight train in the distance. She looked north where she could see it, grey and serpent-like, car after car stretching back into the distance. Penny looked across her to where the tracks ran to the north of them. He knew that the road crossed a few miles up ahead. 'We'll probably have to wait till that one passes,' he said.

Jean looked back at the train again and grimaced. 'That'll take a little while.'

Penny's cellphone rang. He fished it out of his pocket and rolled his window up against the noise of the wind. He spoke for a few minutes, then switched the phone off and put it away again. 'That was Swartz,' he said. 'The task force surveillance unit's been scrambled. We've got a lot of bodies on their way up here.'

'This is a very big deal, then,' Jean said.

'Jean, it could be the biggest deal in this country's

history.' He shook his head. 'I don't wanna sound melodramatic, but weapons have been going missing from military stores for years. Nobody seems to have done a whole lot about it until now. If they're being used to arm the militias, then it's very serious indeed.'

They drove on and Penny was right – they did not make it to the railroad crossing before the locomotive got there. He pulled up, knocked the gearshift into neutral and switched off the engine.

'We're gonna be here for a while,' he said. 'Get out and stretch your legs if you wanna.'

Harrison leaned in the doorway next to Sidetrack, watching the Texas landscape: scrub, dirt and sagebrush. North of them was the dustbowl of Oklahoma, and south, the vast stretch of country between Dallas and Abilene. Wichita Falls was coming up fast and, at that moment, all he could think about was how long it would take them to ship the C-4 to West Virginia. Sidetrack had been silent for most of the journey, not looking at anyone. He seemed lost somewhere in thoughts of his own. Harrison had never witnessed him in this kind of mood before and kept his own counsel unless Sidetrack actually spoke to him. The other three seemed relaxed enough. They lay around the boxcar on their packs, playing cards and joking. Harrison glanced at them now and again, but when they asked him to join the game, he refused.

Sidetrack was standing on the northern side of the car. The door was pulled right back, but the heat was still intense. Harrison wiped sweat from his brow and the back of his neck, and then crossed to the other side. He hauled open the south-facing door to let the wind blow through, and rested his back against the doorjamb. His hair was tied back and the dry heat of the wind prickled his face. The train was crossing a highway and he saw a black Chevy truck parked at the railroad crossing. He smiled as he thought of his own black Chevy and Jean behind the wheel.

Then he looked again and saw her face framed in the passenger window. Matt Penny was driving.

Jean watched the train rumble slowly by at no more than fifteen miles an hour. She was thinking of Harrison and wishing he would phone her. Then she saw him standing in the doorway of a boxcar passing right in front of her. 'Matthew, look, there's John.'

Penny leaned across her and saw Harrison's face as the train rolled by. He was half hanging out of the door now, clearly having seen them. Penny opened the driver's door and stood up in the well. There was nothing he could do; nor was there any way for Harrison to signal to him. He was obviously not alone.

The train passed and the crossing was clear. Penny got back behind the wheel and Jean looked into his face. 'What're we gonna do?'

'Follow that train.'

'Can we do that?'

'Watch me.' Penny put the truck in first, and they bumped across the tracks and swung north. He sped up and gained on the train, and then he eased off, just keeping the relevant boxcar in sight. He scooped up his cellphone and dialled Swartz's number in Dallas.

On the train Harrison stood still, not quite believing what he had just witnessed. His truck sitting at the railroad crossing: Jean and Matt Penny. What was Penny doing there? Something must've happened. He gazed the length of the train, but it bulged into a curve and he could no longer see them.

Penny kept with the train, which was not difficult. He stayed well back, though, and looked across at Jean. 'In a funny kind of way, it makes sense.'

'What does?'

'Seeing JB on a train up here.'

'Because of Wichita Falls.'

Penny nodded. 'The weapons are stolen from all over the country. Not only are the FTRA freighting them to the militia, they're shipping them to this central point.'

'It must be a big operation.'

Penny nodded. 'Didn't that cop in Spokane say there were in excess of two thousand FTRA members?'

'Something like that.'

'That's a lot of bodies, Jean. And there's us thinking they were drug-dealers.' His face was lined and serious.

'D'you think they pose a real threat?' Jean asked him.

'The militia? They didn't used to. But then their leaders started dying in suspicious circumstances.' Penny shook his head. 'Hong Kong troops running amok, just like they predicted.'

'You don't believe that, do you?'

'What – Pat Robertson and his New World Order?' Penny laughed. 'That was a phrase coined by George Bush after the Gulf War. The Iron Curtain had just come down and that was the New World Order. No more Cold War.' He looked at her. 'No, Jean, I don't believe the United Nations has deployed one hundred thousand Asian troops on US soil.'

25

BobCat Reece spoke to the assembly gathered in Cassity, West Virginia. Over two-thirds of the population had gathered at the high school to listen to him. Vernon Jewel stood with two of his lieutenants to one side of the stage and watched the faces of his fellow citizens with a certain amount of pride. Only a few months ago, none of these people would have given Reece the time of day. That was before Billy Bob Lafitte got killed, before the deaths of Daniel Pataki and Tommy Anderson. It was before two women had been abducted in a black helicopter. Jewel watched the door as yet more people filed into the building, then he looked at his watch. Reece was halfway through his speech and still people were showing up. At last, they were finally remembering who the Constitution had been written for. He watched Reece speaking: hawkish to look at, but totally in command of his audience. Jewel, along with a number of his team, both men and women, had attended a survival school in Reece's compound up in Montana. Reece was ex-Green Beret and it showed. His SPIKE teams were as good as any soldiering outfit Jewel had ever seen.

Reece finished speaking, took questions and then climbed down from the stage to shake hands with the throng that pushed towards him. 'Bless you,' he said to them. 'God bless you all.'

When the crowd had thinned, he stepped into the fresh evening air with Jewel and looked across the concourse to where two state troopers stood by their road unit.

'Panic-stricken,' he said. 'Look at them, openly watching us. We've got them on the run, Vern.' He laid a hand on Jewel's shoulder. 'Listen, our time is coming. Our moment of history is almost upon us. Vern, I've been using this whistle-stop speaking tour to gauge public opinion and our rating's as high as it's ever been.'

Jewel lifted one eyebrow. 'You sound like a politician, Bob. Our rating's high because we've got the truth.'

'I know that. But what I'm saying is, *they* didn't know it till now. They being the people who've ignored us for years.' He glanced across to where the state troopers were now back in their car and pulling out of the lot. 'Vern, the hour is at hand, the clock is about to strike and I have a job for you to do.'

Sidetrack signalled to the others to finish their card game. Harrison stood with him by the door to the boxcar and looked towards the line of hills in the distance.

'We going right to the dump, Sidetrack?' he asked. 'Wouldn't that be a little bit stupid?'

Sidetrack grinned then, for the first time in days, and he slapped Harrison on the shoulder. 'That's what I like about you, Four-String. You think.' He pointed to the hills. 'The man's gonna meet us up there with his truck. We take delivery and then hide out in the arroyo waiting for the 3–17.'

'Which takes us back east.'

Sidetrack jabbed a dirty forefinger at the dog-eared railroad map he clutched. 'Via Fort Worth. We got a lotta trains to jump before we hit West Virginia.' He took his phone from his jacket and tapped in a number, then he stood with his finger in one ear while it rang.

Limpet came alongside Harrison. 'What's happening, bro?'

'The man is making a phone call, Limpet. Setting up the drop.'

Limpet sucked wetly on the cigarette he had rolled. 'One hundred pounds is a lotta fucking gunpowder, man.'

'What d'you figure we're gonna do with it?'

Limpet shrugged. 'Ship it to West Virginia, like the man said.'

'And then?'

'Who gives a fuck. Alls we do is use the network. This is our turf. It's where we start and finish.'

'And get paid.'

Limpet looked at him and smiled. 'Unless we's on probation.'

'Kiss my ass, brother. For this, I'm getting paid.'

Limpet picked tobacco threads from his teeth. 'Looks like you might at that,' he said. 'Old Sidetrack's got you riding shotgun.'

'You noticed, huh?'

'Oh yeah.' Limpet was staring at him now, one eye half-closed as always. It gave him a macabre look and you could never tell his genuine expression. 'I guess he figures you're meaner than I am.'

Harrison shook his head. 'I figure this is my big test, Limpet.' He leaned and spat. 'I aim to come through it and then I aim to get paid.'

They jumped off the train fifty yards from the hills and a few miles east of Wichita Falls. Harrison fell awkwardly and winced, then rolled over and sat up, rubbing his ankle. He looked at the train and figured how long it would take to trundle past and expose them to the highway on the other side of the tracks. Sidetrack was looking down at him. 'What you done?'

'Twisted my damn ankle. Just give me a minute.'

Hooch bent down. 'You want me to carry you, Four-String?'

'Nope.' Harrison eased off his boot and rubbed at his ankle. 'Just give me a minute, is all. I'll walk. I'll be just fine.'

Sidetrack was watching the train, then the line of hills. 'Come on, man. I want to be out of sight of the road.'

'We are out of sight of the road, Sidetrack. The fucking train's still going by.'

Sidetrack nodded to Hooch. 'Get him up.'

Harrison waved him away and tugged his boot back on. The train was almost past and he gingerly got to his feet.

'You wanna lean on me?' Hooch said.

Harrison shook his head and pressed his weight down on to the foot. It didn't hurt. Nothing hurt, but he was buying precious time. 'I'm OK. Let's go.'

He started to hobble forward and the others strode towards the break of arroyos that led to the hills. Harrison was last and he could hear the ding-ding-ding of the track bell. He glanced over his shoulder: the train would be gone by the time they made the arroyo.

Sidetrack disappeared into the gully first, followed by Hooch and Carlsbad. Limpet glanced back and Harrison stopped, then leaned on his knees and looked behind. He could see the black Chevy way back on the highway. He stood tall then and looked at Limpet, who disappeared into the arroyo. Harrison turned and frantically waved his arms.

Jean saw him. 'There,' she said, leaning out of the window. 'Look, Matt. They've got off the train.'

Penny slowed the truck. He took the binoculars that Harrison kept in his glove compartment and directed them at the waving figure. 'It's JB, all right,' he said. 'He's pointing north.' At that moment, Harrison disappeared from view and Penny scanned the immediate horizon. 'He must mean the hills. I can't see anything else. God, I wish we had a tracker on him.'

He grabbed the road map and looked at what was around them. He found where they were on the highway and picked up a series of dirt roads that sportsmen used in the hunting season. He looked across at Jean and she guessed his thoughts.

'Don't even think about it, Matthew,' she said. 'I know what I'm doing. I escaped from Vietnam when I was barely twenty. I spent months at sea in a boat that should have sunk. So don't worry about me.'

Penny smiled widely. 'I'm not worrying about you. I'm

worrying about my pension when I have to explain how you got killed on surveillance with me.'

She shook her head. 'I don't plan to get killed. Besides, if we're spotted, we'll just be another necking couple in a quiet corner of the country.'

'I'm gonna take that as a promise,' Penny said, and pulled back on to the highway.

Harrison climbed out of the arroyo and dropped his pack in the lee of the hill. Sidetrack was at the top, with a pair of binoculars and his cellphone. Hooch was swigging water from a bottle and he wiped his mouth with the back of his hand. Harrison motioned for him to pass it over and he took a long drink. The plastic container had warmed the water, but it still slaked his thirst.

Limpet was looking back at the railbed and gauging the distance in his mind. 'One hundred fucking pounds,' he said.

'Lotta blast potential right there,' Harrison said. 'It'd do what they did in Oklahoma, for sure.'

'That was a Ryder truck packed full of the damn stuff,' Hooch said.

'Fertiliser. You need more of it than high-grade C-4.'

'How come you know so much about it?'

Harrison leaned an elbow on his pack. 'I blew a lotta holes in Vietnam, Hooch. If we found a VC and couldn't get him in a firefight, we'd come up and blow the hole.'

Hooch was tearing strips off a piece of jerky. Harrison looked up at Sidetrack framed against the skyline. It was late afternoon now and the sun was low in the west. 'He ain't coming till it gets dark,' Harrison said to him.

'Course not.'

'You're kinda jumpy, Sidetrack. What makes this one so different? So we're hauling one hundred pounds of explosive. We can handle it.'

'I told you. We're hauling it right across the country. The word from the main man is caution. The Feds are everywhere because of this guerrilla war that's been going on, or didn't you notice.'

Harrison looked evenly at him. 'I never read the papers.'

Sidetrack sat down and took a bottle of mescal from his pack. He unscrewed the lid and took a short swallow before stowing it away again. Then he stood up once more and scanned the horizon with binoculars.

Penny and Jean lay in the bunch-grass just to the south of the arroyos and saw Sidetrack on the hill. Penny was watching him through shielded binoculars to ensure there was no glare off the lens. He was wearing Harrison's desert gilly suit and Jean was wearing his summer one, which was way too big for her. But so long as they both lay still, no one would know they were there. Penny had driven the truck into a stand of cottonwoods and given their position to Swartz over the short-wave radio.

Swartz was on the ground in Wichita Falls and a number of the other agents were watching the Texas Guard base. The exact location of the munitions dump was not known by the two marines arrested in London, but the FBI had a name and a few discreet enquiries had given them a picture. Sergeant Paulie Caulfield, a.k.a. Rambo because of his attitude and alleged exploits in the field, was the lynchpin of the Wichita Falls operation. They had been watching his house ever since the call came in from Washington. Agents from the Texas special ops group had tailed him and their initial report detailed extensive 'cleaning' and counter-surveillance techniques. That had been passed to Swartz and the task force was exercising extreme caution. Either Caulfield always worked that way or something had recently spooked him.

Penny and Jean lay very still, watching Sidetrack on the hillside as the light faded around him. Jean stifled a little cry when Harrison suddenly poked his head out of the arroyo to join him. They lay between the rocks and the sagebrush as the sky visibly darkened, the clouds that Penny had forecast building in from the south. Sidetrack disappeared again and Penny lifted himself on one elbow. 'I think we're gonna get wet,' he said.

He left her then and made his way back to the truck, where he called in their new position to Swartz. Swartz told him that they had a tracker on Caulfield's truck and his movements were being monitored by a fixed wing. 'We could do with a tracker in Johnny Buck's pocketbook,' Penny had replied, before making his way back to the lay-up point.

Harrison had not spotted Penny and Jean, but he had the feeling they were out there somewhere. Whether they were alone, he did not know, but he doubted it. His instincts told him otherwise. Whatever had happened to send Penny in search of Jean, it would be enough to send more than Matt Penny. He looked through the twilight at the crew and smiled inwardly to himself. Nobody knew who they were, Sidetrack had said. They came and went and killed just as they pleased, because nobody knew they were out there. He thought of Spinelli and the months of painstaking work he had done on his own, to build up the picture of what was happening on the railroads of America. He had cared that bodies were turning up here, there and everywhere, with bits missing to make it look like locomotive accidents. If Spinelli had not spent his own time and his own money on people like Southern Sidetrack, Harrison would not be sitting here now. He thought of Jean – her face framed in the window of his truck – and the pictures of her boy with his head shattered, lying on that slab in St Charles Parish.

'You wanna shot, Four-String?' Limpet waved the neck of a bottle under his nose, but Harrison pushed it away. He heard a noise and lifted his head. Sidetrack, too, was listening. It was the drone of an engine in the distance.

Harrison followed Sidetrack as he scrambled up the hill and they both saw the glimmer of headlights in the distance. Sidetrack looked back at the others. 'Get ready, you fellas,' he said. 'I wanna make that train.'

Penny and Jean heard the truck approaching, and Penny stood up in his gilly suit and looked back the way they had come. He turned to Jean then. 'Listen,' he said. 'This is the really dangerous part. I want you to go back to the truck.'

Jean opened her mouth to argue, but Penny lifted a finger. 'No arguments. I need you to do it, Jean. If anything happens out here, we have to get word to Swartz. Go back to the truck and then find yourself a hiding place a little way away from it. We don't want any third eye finding you sat in a pick-up in the middle of nowhere.' He smiled through the darkness at her. 'If I'm not back in two hours, you call the cavalry. OK?'

Jean bunched her lips, then nodded and moved away into the darkness. Penny watched for a moment longer, then began to pick his path towards the hill. He had spent eighteen months with Force Reconnaissance, the Marine Corps special forces, and he could move as silently at night as anyone he knew. Within a few minutes, he could hear low voices from the other side of the hill and he lay as still as the grave, the gilly suit camouflaging him completely. He knew Harrison had always kept his covert gear in his truck box, part of his work for the Louisiana special ops group. It suited Penny's purpose now and he inched between the rocks further up the hill until the voices became intelligible. The truck was getting nearer, but not so near as to drown out the sounds of conversation. He strained to pick up words, listening for Harrison's voice. He heard others, but not him.

'We gonna make that train?' somebody said.

'We'll make it.'

'When's the next one, if we don't?'

'We'll make the fucking train. Alls you got to do, when the truck gets here, is load up your packs.'

'One hundred pounds, man. That's twenty apiece.'

'It's nothing.'

'OK, big guy. You can carry mine.'

Penny frowned in the darkness. The conversation stilled

and he wondered what had happened. Then, steeling himself, he ventured to the top of the hill and spotted five shadows in the darkness making their way along the arroyo. Up ahead, the lights from the truck were getting brighter. He began to inch forward.

Harrison stood with Limpet, watching the approaching truck. Sidetrack had a flashlight, which he waved in an arc, and the truck slowed then, swung to their left and pulled up where the dirt road met the arroyo. They moved forward quickly now, Sidetrack urging them into action. Two men occupied the cab of the pick-up. They waited, engine running, until the five hobos took shape in the darkness and then they jumped to the ground. Harrison looked for Rambo, but did not see him. Further down the arroyo, Matt Penny was watching.

'Let's get it done,' Sidetrack said. 'Haul ass. Come on.'

The two men climbed into the back of the truck and opened a wooden crate. Harrison swung up next to them and they began to lift out small, square cartons wrapped in oiled paper. They handed them gingerly one by one to Harrison, who passed them down. Hooch, Carlsbad, Limpet and Sidetrack made space in their backpacks for the packages. Harrison stacked the final few on the flatbed of the pick-up and then placed them in his own pack.

'Where's Rambo at?' he said to one of the militia men.

'He's got other things to do.' The man lowered the lid on the wooden crate and snapped the catches to. He swung himself over the side and landed in the dirt. Harrison handed him his pack, then swung down after him. The man helped him get his arms through the straps, then he and his accomplice were back in the cab and spinning the wheels in the dust. Harrison had made sure he got a close look at both of them, so he could identify them later. Lying not ten feet from where he now stood, Penny had done the same.

'OK, let's move.' Sidetrack hefted his pack and led the way back along the edge of the arroyo towards the hills and the railbed beyond it. 'Four-String,' he said. 'Stick close to me. The state troopers patrol round here of a night-time.'

When they were gone, Penny rolled on his back and looked up at the stars. He had counted fifty packages in all. He recognised the oiled paper used by manufacturers of explosive and figured the packages were about two pounds apiece. Getting to his feet, he stripped off the gilly suit and followed the hobos back down the trail. He passed the stand of cottonwoods where Harrison's truck was parked, but he could not see it, which meant they couldn't either. He followed them through the scrub and the clumps of crested wheat-grass as far as the railbed. He kept fifty yards behind them and could make out their movement by the line of shadows against the sky. The land beyond the arroyos was flat and broken by cactus and sagebrush, lending an eerie edge to the night. When they hit the tracks, they paused, then moved to the east where the tracks curved round the dry lake. There, they sat and waited. Penny checked their position in his head and then cut his path back to the truck.

Jean had got back in the cab. She did not see Penny coming back until he arrived and opened the passenger door. She jumped, hand to her throat momentarily, and he smiled at her. 'Sorry,' he said. 'But I had to be quiet.'

'What's happening?'

'They've made some kind of collection and now they're back at the tracks waiting for a train. He took the railroad map that Harrison had given to Jean and checked the co-ordinates of their position. Then he picked up the phone and called Swartz. He related what had happened; and Swartz told him that Paulie Caulfield had led them on a wild-goose chase into town, then to a bar and finally back to his house. 'I'm gonna keep him under surveillance,' Swartz said. 'Sooner or later, he'll go to the munitions dump.'

'Yeah, well in the meantime, somebody else did.' Penny gave Swartz the hobos' position and what track they were camped beside. 'I'm gonna set up a lay-up point,' he said. 'Make sure I know what train they're getting on, the number and everything. In the meantime, check with Burlington Northern and see what they can tell us about times and destinations.' He paused. 'They transferred a whole buncha packages, Andy. My guts tell me explosives. Two delivery boys, and Johnny Buck right up there on the truck with them.'

'Why do you figure Caulfield didn't supervise the drop?' Swartz asked him. 'From what we got from D.C., he likes to do the quartermaster routine himself.'

'I don't know, Andy. But we're gonna need fixed wing on that train all the way to wherever.' He paused then. 'I'm gonna follow it myself. If they switch trains, the overhead might not pick them up.'

'OK. You want back-up?'

'Sure. The more eyes on target, the better.'

He put the phone down and started the engine. 'There's a better place to park up, Jean. I'm gonna leave you with the truck again and go back to my lay-up point. I need to know exactly when they get on the train.'

Harrison smoked another cigarette, but it tasted foul and he considered quitting once and for all as he flipped it away in the darkness. Sidetrack was sitting against a rock with one arm draped over his backpack, as the dawn sent out orange feelers in the east. Limpet sipped water. Hooch and Carlsbad just sat and watched the distant lights of the train rolling in from the west. Harrison looked at Sidetrack, but Sidetrack was looking at a patch of grey dirt and neither of them said anything. The wind was cold and Harrison pulled his jacket more tightly about him, turning the collar up under his ears.

The train drew closer and Carlsbad hauled his massive bulk to his feet. 'Could do with some breakfast,' he muttered.

Harrison stood up next to him. 'You and me both, bro.' They watched the headlight breaking open the country in front of the train and now they could hear the thunder of iron wheels on the track.

'Hope that mother slows some before it gets to us,' Carlsbad muttered.

Fachida Harada took the metro into the Federal Triangle, dressed once again as a woman. His hair was now longer than it had been when he was the girl who had shot the Fairfax County trooper. He carried a small purse on a strap, which hung from his shoulder, but no other bag. He got out opposite the Old Post Office building, just off Pennsylvania Avenue. Traffic was busy, so he had to wait to cross the street. He then walked up to the corner and stared at the weird-shaped windows of the Hoover building. The flags were fluttering in the light breeze and he counted the black-uniformed FBI police who were posted at various stations round the building. His face betrayed no emotion. He looked at the watch on his slim wrist and made his way to the Hard Rock Café. Harada had been here once before, but that had been three months ago, and he realised, as he walked in, he had given himself a problem. He paused by the door, glancing across at the counter, then made his way to the toilets. He wanted the men's room, but now he was a woman, and the ramifications had not fully dawned on him until he had got on the metro that morning. Looking left and right, he took a breath and walked into the men's room. Nobody. He smiled and entered the first cubicle. The door closed behind him and he took a screwdriver from his purse and opened the cistern inspection hatch. Two minutes later, the bomb was primed. He replaced the hatch and walked outside.

Nobody took a blind bit of notice of him: how utterly complacent, when on two occasions already he had brought their city to a standstill. There were more police on the street, and some cars were still being stopped, but America was a business and business rolled on.

Jack Swann was seated in the lobby of the Four Seasons hotel on 9th Street, where he and Logan had bought some lunch. She was in the toilet and he was waiting for her. He sat reading a copy of the *Washington Post* and looked up briefly when an attractive oriental woman walked in off the street. He looked at the paper again, then folded it away and got up to stretch his legs.

He glanced at his watch and clicked his tongue against his teeth. 'Come on, Cheyenne.' He wandered, hands behind his back, through the lobby, and as he passed the toilets, the door to the men's room opened and the oriental woman walked out. Their eyes met for a fraction of a second, then head down, she scurried out to the street.

Swann smiled to himself and shook his head. This country, he thought. Then all at once, he froze.

He raced for the door and stopped, looking left and right. People milled about the spacious sidewalks, but there was no sign of the woman. Cabs eased up and down on either side of the road. Swann turned and looked back towards Pennsylvania Avenue, and the explosion tore at his ear drums. He felt the shock wave and windows shattered in buildings barely fifty yards from where he was knocked against the wall. The doorman staggered, losing his hat, and the rush of wind tore at the awning over the entrance. Down the street, cars piled into one another and smoke billowed. People were screaming, that terrible high-pitched screeching that only shock can bring. Swann stared for a second and then dashed into the lobby. He almost ran into Logan.

'Thank God,' he said.

'Jack, a bomb just went off.'

'Chey, we've got to clear this hotel.'

'Why?'

'Harada just primed one here in the men's room.'

'Jack?'

'No time, Cheyenne. Come on.'

They went up to reception and Logan stuffed her shield under the receptionist's nose and demanded to see the manager. He was already on their side of the counter, having appeared as soon as the blast was heard.

'I'm Special Agent Logan,' she said. 'You need to evacuate this hotel and you need to do it now.'

'But . . .'

'Listen,' Swann cut in. 'There is a bomb in the men's room. You just heard that one down the road. Well, you've got one too.'

The man stared at him for a moment, then picked up the house phone on the desk. A lot of people had already come down to the lobby and were milling about the entrance, trying to see what was going on.

Swann went into the dining room and calmly told everyone to get up and leave as quickly as possible. 'Do not pick up any belongings,' he said. 'Do not go to your rooms. Get outside and keep going north until you are at least two hundred yards away.'

Logan was still in the lobby, on the phone to the field office. A minute earlier, the Tannoy system had been in operation, requesting that everyone vacate the premises with immediate effect. Swann looked at his watch: four minutes since Harada had left the building. He figured that gave them between six and eleven minutes until detonation. Harada was wandering round the city, priming devices he must have planted months before. If he were on foot, he would need fifteen minutes to clear the area. But he might not be on foot.

Swann grabbed Logan. 'Get out of here now, Chey.'

People were piling down the stairs and streaming out of the lounge and dining room. The manager, at Swann's request, had expressly forbidden use of the elevators and the stairs were jamming up. Swann stood at the bottom, ushering people across the lobby until the flow dwindled and then finally stopped. Again, he looked at his watch. The ten-minute mark had passed. He looked at the manager. 'Is everybody out?'

'I don't know.'

'Well, you can't go up and check.' Swann bundled him towards the door.

On the street pandemonium ruled; people were running this way and that. Cars were backed up and some of them had been abandoned. Police officers down on Pennsylvania Avenue were trying to take control of the first bomb scene. Logan grabbed Swann's hand and they headed away from the hotel, pushing people before them. Swann looked at his watch. 'I reckon we've got four minutes.'

'How do you know?'

'Because like a dumbfuck I watched him come out of the men's toilet dressed as a woman. It didn't register until he was on the street. I chased after him, but he was gone. Then the first bomb went off.'

Logan looked him in the eye. 'No warnings,' she said.

Four minutes later, they were at the field office and the explosion sucked oxygen from around them. The noise was more muffled than the previous one, but windows shattered and concrete was flayed from the buildings on 5th Street. Swann looked back, one hand to his ears, as he felt the sudden heat on his skin. 'I hope we got them all out.'

Logan was clutching his arm. 'Christ, Jack. If you hadn't been in the lobby . . .'

Swann felt the shiver gather at the nape of his neck and race down his spine to disappear in his buttocks. He opened his mouth to let the air escape from his chest. 'Let's get upstairs,' he said.

Every phone in the building seemed to be ringing when they appeared on the squad floor. Kovalski was there with Carmen McKensie. He looked up at Logan. 'The Four Seasons,' he said. 'Did you get everyone out?'

'We think so.' Logan leaned on the desk. She told him exactly what had happened and Kovalski looked at Swann. 'You didn't see where the woman went?'

Swann shook his head. 'She was gone when I got outside. I should have worked it out immediately, a woman in the men's room.'

Kovalski made a face. 'Forget about that. You did a good job.' He sucked a breath. 'Damn this sonofabitch.'

'Tom.' McKensie got up from where she was sitting, with a phone cupped in her hand. 'It's the Director for you.'

Swann went to the window and looked out. Round here, there was not much activity – Judiciary Square was pretty empty, most people leaving the federal area by the major routes and bridges. He looked at the TV screen on the wall and watched the news broadcasting the carnage. Paramedics were at the first scene, the Hard Rock Café, but there was panic in the air. Two bombs and no warnings. Just then, he heard a third explosion. He thought about the ring of steel the task force had been implementing and how easily Harada had breached it. The stop-and-search procedure had been completely circumvented. Logan came alongside him.

'Chey,' he said. 'This took a whole lot of planning. I really don't think Harada could have done it all by himself.'

Harada got out of the taxi by the old airmen's and soldiers' home and crossed the street to the self-storage lot. He walked the length of the units, nodding to a couple of workmen, and entered the one adjacent to where the security truck was housed. Inside, he stripped off his wig and tore at the buttons of his jacket. He had a long drive ahead of him. Quickly, he showered and changed into his grey suit, then rolled up the door and backed out the blue Ford he had bought to replace the grey sedan that every cop in Fairfax County was looking for. He parked, then got out of the car to close the door.

Across the street, Charlie, the old soldier, squeezed the nurse's hand. 'See that,' he said. 'Happens every time.'

'I only saw a man come out, Charlie,' she told him gently. 'A man in a blue car.'

'Yeah, but he's a Jap, goddammit. I told you. You just think I'm stupid on account of having lost my legs. But I ain't stupid. No, sir. Not when it comes to the Japs.'

'Charlie.'

'It was a woman that went in and a guy that come out. I know what I seen. It's my legs that's gone, not my damn eyes.'

The TV set was on behind them and the newscaster was describing how Detective Inspector Swann of Scotland Yard had witnessed the Japanese woman coming out of the men's room in the Four Seasons hotel. Charlie wheeled himself round, and he and the nurse both stared at the screen.

'The FBI have already alerted the public to the fact that Fachida Harada was dressing as a woman,' the newscaster went on. 'If Inspector Swann had not been there and recognised the signs, hundreds more people would have been killed. The woman is described as small, oriental and wearing a long black wig. It is believed she made her escape in a taxi.'

'See!' Charlie said it with such venom that spittle flew from his lips. He jabbed a finger at the window. 'I seen her get out of a cab right there. *She* goes inside and *he* comes out. It's Pearl Harbor all over again.' He grabbed the nurse's sleeve. 'Dammit, woman. Call the FBI.'

Logan was manning the telephones. Swann was manning the telephones. He took a call from a cab driver who said he had picked up a Japanese woman outside the Four Seasons at the time given on the TV. 'Where did you take her?' Swann said.

'I dropped her up on North Capitol, by the soldiers' and airmen's home.'

'OK. Thank you. Can you come into the field office and make a statement?'

'Sure I can. Just as soon as the traffic dies down.'

Swann put down the phone and looked at Logan. 'I've got a location,' he said.

The phone rang again and McKensie picked it up and listened. 'Oh, yeah,' she said. 'He's phoned us a couple of times.'

'Well, I think he might be right this time,' the nurse said in her ear.

The three of them rushed upstairs to where Kovalski was back in his office, the door wide open, and agents and other members of the task force bustling in and out.

Kovalski was on the phone and Logan leaned over the desk. He flapped a hand at her and hung up the phone. 'Goddammit, Logan.' He looked at Swann. 'How the hell do you put up with her?'

'We might have a lead,' Logan said.

They drove out of the federal area, siren wailing, blue lights flashing, carving a path between the vehicles jamming the roads and sidewalks. Kovalski had summoned a helicopter and the SWAT team was already rolling. He commanded the largest force of SWAT-trained agents outside the Hostage Rescue Team and half of them were deployed by Blackhawk chopper. Logan and Swann were almost at the self-storage complex. To save time, the nurse had agreed to bring Charlie to the gates of the home, so he could show them exactly what he had seen.

They parked on the kerb, as she wheeled the old, frail-looking man through the gates. Swann and Logan got out of the car and Charlie looked out of liquid eyes at them.

'Goddammit, a woman,' he muttered. 'And she's black, too.'

The nurse looked apologetically at Logan, who ignored the comments and knelt down by the old man's chair. 'You must be Charlie.' She offered him her hand. 'I'm Agent Logan. This is Jack Swann from London.'

'London.' Charlie frowned stiffly at Swann. 'What's a damn limey doing here?'

Swann smiled at him. 'Learning the ropes, Charlie.'

'Aha.' Charlie nodded. 'I gotcha.'

'What did you see, Charlie?' Logan asked him gently.

He brought his other hand out from under the blanket that covered his withered legs and laid a notebook on his lap. 'It's all in here. Dates, times, the whole damn report.'

'May I?' Logan reached for it.

'I want it back, lady. Got to get it to the general.'

'Of course.' Logan took the book and stood up. Swann moved to her shoulder and together they flicked through the pages. Charlie had drawn a map of the storage complex and marked out two units in red. He noted that a man arrived in one, but he never saw anyone arrive for the next unit along. Yet that unit was opened up and the red *C U SAFELY* truck came in and out. Nobody ever left the first unit, but at the end of most days, a little Japanese man in a suit drove a grey sedan away. Recently, Charlie had seen a woman going in and out instead of the man.

Swann stared at Logan. 'Where's that SWAT team?' he asked. 'I think you're going to need them.'

'There ain't nobody there,' Charlie said from behind them. 'It's why I made her call you.' He nodded to the nurse. 'I saw the woman go in from the yellow cab and the man drives out in a blue Ford.'

'You didn't get the index number,' Swann said.

'What's that?'

'The licence tag, Charlie,' Logan said.

He shook his head. 'Can't read that far. You don't need no SWAT team. There ain't nobody there.'

They crossed the street and entered the storage lot. As they did, the Blackhawk swooped down from above them and the SWAT team fast-roped to the ground. Logan stopped and ushered Swann back.

The team leader came up and Logan gave him the rundown on what they had discovered. Immediately, he deployed his men: two sniper observer teams and the main attack force. He sent in two men to clear the other units of innocents. Swann and Logan were suddenly impotent, waiting at the entrance to the small industrial park.

Swann was chewing his lip. 'He's taking chances now, Chey. I think this might be his last throw.'

'I hope so.' Logan looked at him then, a macabre smile

518

on her face. 'Maybe the bastard will top himself and do us all a favour.'

Swann was looking at the row of lock-up units. 'If we can get a news blackout on this, he might come back.'

'Oh, yeah. Right.' Logan pointed at the sky where two separate helicopters were circling in the distance. 'They monitor the radio channels.'

'I thought the SWAT channel was encrypted.'

'It is. But they watch the field office. As soon as the Blackhawk is up, you can bet your life they follow.'

Harada drove out to Falls Church and then dumped the blue Ford. He had the keys to an old Buick station wagon which he had parked three streets from his own, and he walked briskly to it. They were looking for a woman and he was a man again, only his cropped black hair was gone. He wore thick, black-framed glasses and a baseball hat which hooded his eyes still further. Time was less important now: he had managed to get out of the city without being stopped and the Ford had been dumped. He got behind the wheel, adjusted the rearview mirror and gazed at his reflection. For a moment, the past stung him and his hands trembled, then he felt under the passenger seat. His fingers closed on the ornate scabbard and the breathing eased in his chest. Again he looked in the mirror, then checked his road maps before twisting the key in the ignition.

26

Mujah al-Bakhtar sat in traffic at the junction of Ealing Road and Bridgewater Road in West London. He had been out of the city and had driven the black BMW, with the tinted windows, east along the A40 until he came to Hangar Lane. From there, it was but a short distance till Ealing Road branched right and he was back in the heart of the subcontinent. He was too tall for the car and the top of his head brushed the velour ceiling. He drummed thick black fingers on the steering wheel and waited for the lights to change. What he had heard did not surprise him and, equally, it did not overly disturb him.

The halal butcher's shop was halfway down on the right-hand side and al-Bakhtar bumped the BMW on to the kerb, being careful to avoid the array of silk saris being sold on pavement racks by the shop next door. He climbed out of the car and smoothed his palms down his thighs, straightening the creases in his trousers.

Across the road, Jean-Emmanuel Haan was having an Indian snack of *samosa* and thick black coffee. Sitting across the table from him was Sinil Kapoor, one of the best Mossad agents he had ever worked with. Haan watched the Somali climb out of the car and nodded at Sinil. She smiled, showing a set of perfect white teeth. 'When have I ever been wrong?'

Haan stared at her now. 'And he works there?'

'Oh yes. You know, it was never really that difficult once we knew what we were looking for.'

Haan nodded. 'It was just a hunch.'

'Yes. But one that we never thought of.' Sinil looked out of the window again. One of the boys, who helped behind the butcher's counter, was getting into the BMW.

'Valet parking,' Haan said and chewed at a corner of *samosa*. He looked up and down the street then and saw a white car parked on their side of the road. Two men were in it, one Asian and one white; one was reading the paper. 'Mr Plod's here,' he said.

Al-Bakhtar had seen the white car as he drove in and it confirmed everything his sources in Windsor had told him. He went into the shop and descended to the basement, where the tall, bearded man with the hooked nose was working at his computer. Al-Bakhtar leaned in the doorway, listening to the bustling sounds of custom coming from upstairs. 'My friend,' he said quietly. 'I believe it is time to move our business. Somebody does not like what we are selling.'

Haan watched one of the shop assistants drive the BMW up the street and saw the men in the white car glance his way, then look back towards the butcher's shop once more.

'They really have no idea,' Sinil said wearily. 'They've only seen al-Bakhtar.' She leaned across the table again. 'They've never seen our friend leave, but he worships at the mosque on Chevening Road. Fridays at seven o'clock. Sometimes he likes to walk across Queen's Park.' She got up then and fished in her purse for cash.

Haan shook his head. 'Lunch is on me, my friend.'

He met The Cub in the cinema on Shaftesbury Avenue, the third row from the back on the right-hand side. It was a matinée performance and business was slow. The Cub sat hunched in his chair, with his foot on the back of the seat in front of him, sucking Coca-Cola through a straw.

Haan sat in the seat behind him. 'The word was good,' he said quietly. 'We have a location. Unfortunately, so do the British.'

The Cub stopped drinking. 'You saw them?'

'They stick out like a sore thumb. I imagine it's regular policemen.'

'That changes things. How do they know he's here?'

Haan laughed lightly then. 'They don't. They've only seen al-Bakhtar.'

'So how do *we* know he's here?'

'The Israeli source has seen him. If he is in that butcher's shop, somehow he still manages to worship at the mosque on Chevening Road.'

The Cub put down his carton of Cola.

He took the tube back across London, and read his *A–Z* like any other tourist. He found Chevening Road and Queen's Park, and his hotel was not far from both. He changed to the Bakerloo line and rode as far as Queen's Park. Here he got out and then walked up Salusbury Road, with the park a street away on his left. He walked the full length of Salusbury Road and moved in and out of shops. One of them had a back entrance, which was for service staff, but The Cub ducked through and retraced his steps to ensure the route was clean and he was not being tailed.

The mosque was small, directly across from the junction of Chevening Road and Carlisle Road, and he walked past it on both sides of the street. Three steps leading up from the pavement to ornate oak doors, one of which stood open. There was no obvious location for an assault point and he checked and rechecked, then stood and considered it all. He walked along Chevening Road and crossed the park, pausing briefly at the bandstand, and then he walked the circuit again. He knew beyond all doubt that he was not under surveillance; and pausing again at Carlisle Road, he made his decision. He phoned Haan on his mobile. 'I need a small van,' he said. 'Make it so the windows are tinted and the back ones roll down.'

'Anything else?'

'Yes, a resident's parking permit for Carlisle Road, NW6.'

Swann watched the SWAT team attack the first unit. They breached the small door to the side of the roll-over, using a remote breaching device on an Alvis Wheelbarrow robot. No booby-trapped explosion and Swann breathed his first sigh of relief. But then he and Logan had to wait while the SWAT team did their work, searching the premises until they could give the all-clear. Time ticked away and he thought about Harada and the blue Ford. As yet, there was no word over the radio that any vehicle had been located. And there probably wouldn't be. There were hundreds of blue Fords in the city. He stood at the edge of the lot with the evidence response team standing by, and waited. Eventually, the SWAT team leader came out and gave them the all-clear. Logan motioned to the ERT and they all moved forward.

The first unit was empty except for a small office, two lockers and a shower room. Swann stood in the doorway and studied the street map pasted to the wall. 'This is Harada's lock-up, Chey,' he said. 'There are his locations.' He stepped closer and looked at the coloured pins stuck into the map: National Airport, Kennedy stadium, the Smithsonian and the Four Seasons hotel.

Logan tapped the map with her fingernail. 'Look.' She pointed to two more downtown hotels where no device had gone off. 'If he's planted these, we can get the bomb squad to render them safe.'

They moved through the adjoining door to the second unit, where the red security consultant's truck, with *C U SAFELY* painted on the side, stood in the cool of the garage. Swann placed his hands on his hips and looked at Logan. 'Thinks he's a comedian, doesn't he?'

Logan stretched sterile rubber gloves over her fingers and opened the back of the truck. It was decked out in racking and shelves, and all manner of electrical equipment was stowed in little compartments. Swann could see wire and batteries, tilt switches, bulbs and circuit boards. He pushed the breath through his teeth.

'This is brilliant cover, Chey. He can sit in the back and wire up any kind of improvised explosive device he likes.'

Logan was already talking to one of the field-office agents accompanying them. 'Get on to the support staff,' she said. 'I want a check on every establishment in the city that's had dealings with this firm in the last six months.'

The agent nodded and ducked back through to the other unit.

Back at the field office, there was still no word on the all-points bulletin. The Federal Triangle was in chaos and emergency teams were fighting their way through the rubble and debris of three major buildings, looking for survivors. So far, the body count was eighteen.

Logan sat at Kovalski's conference table, toying with a ballpoint pen. 'So much for noncombatants,' she said.

Swann was very quiet. 'It looks like my plan backfired.'

Kovalski was standing behind him. 'Jack, it was better that we went public with the CIA angle than he did. We were never going to release Shikomoto and he was always going to do this.'

'Tom?' Mackensie was at his door.

'What is it, Carmen?'

'The Director and the national security adviser are here.'

Harrison dozed, his head against the wooden slats of the boxcar, the rhythm of the wheels working away in his head. Vaguely, he could hear the drone of Hooch and Carlsbad playing their perpetual game of cards, interspersed by Limpet snoring.

Sidetrack had been quiet ever since they jumped the 3–17 and had remained so across the various switches they made through Texas. They had been riding this train for twelve hours now and the only stop had been to swap drivers. They were through Arkansas and into Mississippi, and, as far as Harrison could gather from his railroad maps, their route would take them north through Tennessee into the mountains of Kentucky and West Virginia. The train jerked, and he wobbled, banged his head and sat up. Sidetrack was sitting at the far side of the car on his own, and their eyes met as Harrison got to his feet. It was midday outside, and Harrison stood in the doorway and took a leak, being careful not to let it blow back on his jeans. The .38 felt uncomfortable in his boot and, sitting down, he took the boot off to rearrange the strapping he used for a holster. Sidetrack watched him.

'You're pretty good around guns, ain't you, Four-String?'

Harrison snorted. 'You wanna tell me someone who isn't in this country?'

'But you really know what you're doing.' Sidetrack's elongated fang was showing against his lip. 'Sorta professional.'

Harrison snorted, but his senses were up. He looked through the shadows at Sidetrack's dull eyes. 'Sidetrack, I was never real professional at anything. If you're telling me that I am around a weapon, then I guess it's because I was a soldier.' Harrison looked at him and their eyes locked, and again he felt the fingers of unease against his scalp.

He opened the .38 and checked the rounds. Then he snapped it shut again and spun the chamber. Very deliberately, he took the Beretta from his waistband, knocked the magazine out and again checked the rounds. He worked the action, popped the cartridge out of the breech and fed it into the top of the clip. Then he replaced the clip in the butt and worked it back into the chamber.

'You getting ready for a war?' Sidetrack said.

Harrison looked him in the eye. 'Sidetrack, you're jumpy as fuck. I figure we must be looking at trouble somewhere along this line.' He got up and pushed the .38 back into his boot, then he folded his jeans' leg down and fished in his jacket for tobacco.

Sidetrack took a bottle of mescal from the top of his pack and swallowed a mouthful. He offered it to Harrison, who shook his head. 'Make me a cigarette,' Sidetrack said.

Harrison squatted on his haunches and rolled him one. He gummed down the edge and passed it to him, then popped a match on his boot heel. He held it for Sidetrack, who gripped his wrist hard to steady it. Sidetrack blew out the match, still holding Harrison's arm, and then he let him go. He swivelled to a sitting position, both legs tucked under him, and smoked without taking the cigarette from his mouth.

They rode on through the heat of the day and Sidetrack remained as sullen as he had been since they left Texas. Harrison sat slumped in a corner, nursing his water bottle and wondering what he was doing there. Hooch and Carlsbad finished their game and slept. When they stopped for a driver swap on the Tennessee State line, two ageing hobos tried to get aboard, but were discouraged. Harrison watched their expressions fade as soon as they caught sight of Limpet's black bandana.

Penny and Jean took turns driving the pick-up, stopping only for gasoline, sandwiches and coffee. Each drove four-hour stints while the other slept, and every now and again Penny would check in on the cellphone. The pursuit was being handled from the Dallas office, where Swartz had remained behind. The New Orleans SWAT team had mustered and they were currently using a National Guard helicopter to follow the train. Every FBI office along the route, be it a field or resident agency, had been informed and the regional SWAT resource was on standby. Penny drove with the train in sight and when he lost it, due to the road configuration, the fixed wing gave him the location. His was not the only pursuit vehicle: they had drafted in the state police in Mississippi and Tennessee, as well as the Tennessee Bureau of Investigation. The difficulty for everyone was when the outfit switched trains, which had happened five times since they hopped the 3–17. Twice Penny almost missed it, but maybe luck was with them or Harrison was just being extra-vigilant, because he picked them up on foot before it was too late.

Jean woke up and asked Penny where they were and he

showed her on the map. They pulled off to fill up the truck and replenish their coffee cups, and then it was Jean's turn to drive. She got behind the wheel and fired up the engine. Penny leaned in the far corner and sipped coffee. 'Are you OK to drive?' he asked her. She smiled, nodded and worked the steering wheel through her hands.

Harada drove north out of Washington D.C., heading for Interstate 270. He rode it as it became 70 and bent to the west, then crossed the turnpike into Pennsylvania. As usual, he drove within the speed limit. He was grey-haired now, wearing a baseball hat, and with his Joe Aoki ID in his pocket. If he got stopped, he was on vacation, heading for Canada and a date with the maple leaves of Toronto. But he did not get stopped. Once he was out of D.C., the pressure eased and with it the traffic, but he listened to the radio news for constant updates on the carnage he had created in Washington. The body count had risen above thirty, which made him the worst offender ever in the District of Columbia. The President gave a nationwide broadcast from his hidey-hole out at Camp David and said that the US authorities would stop at nothing until Harada was apprehended. He reiterated that calm was required and that undoubtedly Harada and the Orientals responsible for killing the militia, the so-called Hong Kong troops, were in some way connected. What had gone on in downtown Washington was grisly proof that federal agencies were not involved. When questioned hard by reporters, he justified the aims of the CIA in recruiting Harada in North Korea, after the atrocities against US nationals by the Japanese Red Army. Harada listened and shook his head. He regretted the collateral damage, but it was not his fault: his hand had been forced and they must carry the blame. Again, he felt under the seat for the comfort of his sword, and wiped the sweat from his brow.

He drove west on the highway through Bedford County, again conscious of his speed and mindful of the Highway

Patrol, which passed him both ways. He entered Somerset County and his palms began to moisten on the wheel. He rubbed them each in turn against his thighs, then he left the road at the town of Somerset and headed south-west for New Centerville. Here, he checked his map. There was a truck lay-by about ten miles further on, towards Bakersville on Highway 31. Harada looked at his watch. He had made good time and he was early. But he did not want to hang around; his nerves were more frayed than they had ever been, and he was suddenly unsure of his own resolve. He sat in the car for a few minutes, deepening each breath and concentrating until the calm descended once again. Then he started the engine and pulled out on to the road.

Clayton Morgan of the Pennsylvania Unorganised Militia drove east on 31. He had a sheet of tarpaulin fixed over the back of the old Ford pick-up and his brother followed in his Toyota. The road was quiet, though, and Morgan figured they would have more than enough time to dump the Ford and leave. The sky overhead was grey with summer rain clouds and the twilight fell earlier because of it. Morgan had his window rolled part of the way down and he could smell the moisture in the atmosphere. He pressed a plug of chew deeper into his cheek and spoke to his brother over the radio.

'I didn't really wanna volunteer us for this one, Mitch,' he said. 'Not with all that's going on.'

His brother's voice crackled back over the airwaves. 'I don't trust those fucking train-hoppers. But I guess somebody's gotta do this. Our part in the game, maybe, huh?'

'Yeah, I guess.' Morgan looked back along the blacktop, but no lights were following them. 'We'll be OK. What's it gonna take, a coupla minutes to dump the truck and skedaddle.'

Harada was cruising Highway 31. He had passed the lay-by shown on the crude hand-drawn map, spotted the parked

Ford, and was now heading for Bakersville. He looked at his watch and then concentrated on the road. He had not pulled directly into the lay-by because he wanted time to assess the area for unwelcome surveillance. He drove at a steady fifty-five and saw the lights of the approaching truck up ahead. He slowed a fraction as they passed: two men in the cab, neither of whom glanced in his direction. His palms began to tingle. He drove on, speeding back up to the limit, and went almost as far as Bakersville. He pulled off the road before the city limits, though, not wishing to be seen in the town. He made a U-turn with the wheels wheezing under the sudden redistribution of weight and headed back the way he had come. Now he sped up and, for the first time since he had set foot on US soil, he broke the speed limit. There were no other vehicles in the lay-by, and he pulled off the road and stopped the car. The keys to the Ford were in the tailpipe and Harada whipped them out. Then, standing in the lee of the vehicle, he hoisted the tarpaulin. The baseplate was screwed into the floor of the truck, with the legs of the bipod lying flat. The box of ammunition lay alongside it and quickly he counted. Twelve 120mm mortars for the Lockheed lightweight system. He could fire them all in the first minute, and a minute was all he needed.

27

Harrison and the Southern Blacks crossed into West Virginia, with Harrison hanging out of the doorway, holding the slat above his head to steady himself. They had made their last switch and were riding the CSX transportation line south of Huntington, which crossed the state southeast and hit Virginia at Covington. They had been riding boxcars for over thirty-six hours and everybody was raw at the edges. Harrison said nothing unless he was asked a direct question. Nobody was drinking. There was nothing left to drink and their cigarettes were skinnier than they would see in any prison. Limpet sat with Sidetrack on the far side of the car and Carlsbad mooched around like a bear stuck in a cage. Harrison glanced over his shoulder at him now and again, then looked up at the sky. Drifting far in the distance was a helicopter.

He ducked back into the semi-darkness and sat by his pack. He took his banjo and strummed a few chords, but the music was incompatible with the atmosphere and he laid it aside once again.

Hooch squatted beside him and spat into the dirt on the floor – a gob of oily saliva that suddenly drew their attention. 'Shit,' Hooch said, looking over at Sidetrack. 'How much longer?'

'A while.'

'That all you're gonna tell us – a while?'

Sidetrack stared coldly at him. Hooch looked down again and shook his shaggy head. His breath was rancid and irritatingly close to Harrison. He sat and said nothing, then felt in his pocket for what threads of tobacco he had left. Carefully, he rolled a cigarette and lit it. Sidetrack was on his feet now and at the door. He leaned a long way out, which was dangerous as the track was running through a cutting hewn from solid rock. The confines of the rock forced the rattle of wheels and thudding of the locomotive back at them, so conversation was impossible. Sidetrack was looking back the way they had come and then forward again, but the cutting obscured any view. He rested his hand where Harrison had and looked up at the sky.

'What you looking for?' Limpet yelled at him. 'Black helicopters?'

Harrison felt a prickle of unease, but smiled along with the rest of them.

Penny was on the phone to the agents watching the train tracks south of Huntington. The D.C. field office covered West Virginia and Swartz had already informed Tom Kovalski about what was going on. Agents had hit the 'bricks' from the resident agency offices all over the state and the progress of the train was being monitored.

In Washington, Kovalski briefed the joint terrorism task force. 'We know the FTRA are freighting weapons to the militia. Because of what went on at the embassy in London, we now know where the weapons are coming from. An hour ago, four FTRA members and our UCA crossed from Kentucky into West Virginia.'

'Harada is getting his C-4 from somewhere,' Logan said. 'This could be the supply line.'

Kovalski looked at her and nodded. 'If we're lucky, we can take all our birds with just the one stone.'

'We've got that train under surveillance,' Kovalski went on. 'But we don't know what their destination point is.'

'Does Harrison know you're watching?' Swann asked him.

'There's been an agent following in a vehicle ever since Texas. Yes, we're pretty sure he knows.'

'There was no way to get a tracker fixed up?'

Kovalski shook his head. 'No,' he said. 'We've had to do

this the hard way. The New Orleans SWAT team are following in a chopper. I'm gonna augment them with some of ours, if they need it.'

'What's the plan?' Logan said.

'There isn't one yet. It's a suck it and see situation.'

Vernon Jewel had thought long and hard about what Reece had told him and considered whether to send somebody else. Reece seemed pretty sure of himself, though, and told Jewel that the weapons-distribution programme had been running completely undetected for three years now, so there was nothing for any of them to worry about.

'Who's been paying for it, BobCat?' Jewel had asked him.

Reece had smiled and scratched his jaw, still basking in the turnout from the good people of Cassity. 'That's the joke of it, Vern,' he said. 'Especially after what you saw that night at the dead drop.' He had laid a hand on his shoulder then. 'There's two groups in Europe supporting us. Best you don't know more than that, just in case.'

Jewel sat in the stolen truck now, sipping coffee and waiting for Ricky Tomlinson to come back from the john. Goddamn that kid and his bladder. The truck had been provided for them – stolen three states away – and was now bearing West Virginia licence plates. A state trooper drove by in his cruiser, a pair of Ray-Ban sunglasses pressed against his eyes. Jewel could see the pump-action Remington, standing upright between the driver and passenger seats. Tomlinson jumped in beside him and passed a strip of jerky over.

'I got the peppered kind that you like, Vern.'

'Thanks.' Jewel took it from him and put the truck into gear. 'You all set for this?'

Tomlinson looked a little quizzically at him. 'It's what we've been planning for years, ain't it?'

Jewel nodded once and pulled out on to the highway.

Sidetrack rode by the door all the way across West Virginia. Five miles west of Covington, he looked round at the others. 'Get set,' he stated. 'We're outta here.'

Hooch was on his feet first. 'About fucking time.'

Harrison got up and shouldered his now very heavy pack. His water bottle was empty and he had tied it to a loop in the strapping. He carried his banjo in one hand and the other one was free to help him get off the train. The wind was fresh now; it was late afternoon and the sky grey with cloud.

'Typical, three days in a boxcar and when we get off it rains,' Hooch muttered.

Sidetrack shook his head. 'Hooch, why don't you shut the fuck up and think about the payday we're looking at. You and Carlsbad can buy all the whores you want.'

Hooch looked at Carlsbad and his features visibly brightened. 'Never thought about it that way.'

'Never thought, you mean.'

Limpet ducked out of the way of a mock blow and winked at Harrison. 'You set, Four-String?' he said. 'You been pretty quiet this trip.'

'I've been as bored and pissed off as Hooch,' Harrison said. 'But I figured I'd keep it to myself.'

Limpet sniggered, and Sidetrack looked round and his eyes were dead in his face. 'You all be careful when we jump down,' he said. 'We got a precious cargo.'

'C-4 ain't volatile, Sidetrack,' Harrison said.

Sidetrack looked through him. 'Like I said, we got a precious cargo.'

They jumped off the train as it slowed for the final driver swap that would run them into Virginia at Covington. Harrison leaned far out of the door and the train wheezed and groaned, the wheels hissing on the skids until it shuddered to a halt, and they all braced themselves. When all was still, they jumped down one by one.

Sidetrack stood straight, shifted the weight of his pack and looked up at the sky. 'It *is* gonna rain,' he said.

'How far we got to walk?' Harrison asked him.

'Just beyond that stand of trees.' Sidetrack pointed back along the track. 'There's a dirt road running up, right there.'

Matt Penny pulled the Chevy over to the side of the road and pointed through the windshield. 'There, Jean. Look.'

She followed the line of his finger. They had left the highway and four-wheeled up a dirt road that shouldered the tracks. The train had moved off again and she could see five men walking back down the line. Penny picked up the cellphone and dialled the Washington field office.

Logan spoke to him and he gave her the hobos' position. 'They're heading for the dirt road,' Penny said. 'I'm gonna follow on foot. Make sure that SWAT team is rolling.'

'The New Orleans SWAT team's in the air,' Logan said. 'Ours is on standby.'

'OK. Just don't leave my ass hanging out in the wind.' Penny hung up, looked round at Jean and checked his guns. 'You really have gotta stay here this time,' he said.

Sidetrack led the way, as the five of them walked back down the track to the stand of trees and the dirt road leading up into the hills. Hooch wheezed under the weight of his pack. Harrison walked with his head down, but his eyes were scanning the limited horizon ahead. He could see nothing, no movement whatsoever, and he had no idea whether he was alone out here or not. Sidetrack's mood bothered him. There had been a perceptible difference in the man since the visit of The Voyageur and Ghost Town. He had drunk less mescal, as if he had a problem which he needed to focus on properly. That problem could, of course, just be the delivery of one hundred pounds of C-4 to West Virginia. But it could also be much more than that.

Harrison watched him now, walking slightly in front and to his left-hand side. He looked up at the sky, but it was empty of all except rain cloud. The trees deepened and they left the line of the tracks and headed up the dirt road. From up ahead, he heard an engine and saw Sidetrack stiffen. The others moved up and Sidetrack climbed the short rise until they looked down on a mini-turnoff on the other slope of the hill. Sidetrack was watching the road for the approaching truck, straining his eyes, but the engine noise gradually died away. They walked down the hill, passing the turnoff, and Harrison looked back the way they had come.

Penny moved like a wraith through the thinly trunked trees, wearing the gilly suit from Harrison's truck box. He had an MP5 over one shoulder and his Sig-Sauer strapped to his hip. He could see the hobos fifty yards ahead of his position. The light was fading and they made five dark shapes against the pale dust of the road. He had his radio working and Gerry Mackon, his New Orleans team leader, updated him on the SWAT team's ground location.

Vernon Jewel and Ricky Tomlinson were labouring up the far side of the dirt road in the stolen pick-up truck. There was nothing in the back, save the twin truck boxes that were bolted to the floor just behind the cab. Reece had told them that the beauty of what they would be carrying was that you did not need much of it to do a lot of damage. It could be easily stowed in the truck boxes and the pick-up could be parked without drawing too much attention. After Oklahoma, the authorities had been looking for Ryder-type trucks that were big enough to pack a ton of fertiliser. Still, Jewel was nervous, more nervous than he had ever been. He had usually done the short runs with tiny amounts of gear brought to him, so he could dump it in the dead drop under the drainage cover on the Virginia side of the Appalachians. This was a long trip, but Reece figured he needed a major player and that had appealed to Jewel's sense of self-importance. He and Ricky were going to pick up the consignment, then drive to the other side of the mountains and leave the truck in the usual place. From there, they would be collected and somebody else would come for the truck. All he had to do was shove the keys up the tailpipe.

The dirt road to the rendezvous point was pitted and small hills climbed amid the thick covering of trees. Still, Jewel thought, as he wrestled with the steering wheel, it was nice and secluded at least. The changeover would take no more than a few minutes, then they would be away again. If all went to plan, he would be home around midnight. Next to him, Tomlinson had his handgun out of the concealed shoulder holster he liked to wear and was playing with the chamber: talon-coated bullets, the kind that would pierce body armour. Cop-killers.

They crested the short rise and the truck swayed like a roller coaster. Jewel had been told to drive until he came to a stand of cedar trees, on the right-hand side of the road, with a massive split boulder between two of them.

'There.' Tomlinson spotted it first and pointed. 'Right there, Vern. We must be early.'

Five hundred yards behind them, two agents from the special operations group were tailing them in another truck. They drove with no lights – the driver wearing night-vision glasses to penetrate the deepening gloom. The passenger had a flat, metallic box open on his knees and was preparing the 'sticky' electronic homing device. Up ahead, Jewel's truck slowed, then came to a stop, and the FBI driver killed his engine. Beside him, his colleague took the homing device and slipped into the trees.

Harrison saw the truck parked as they came up the trail. It was sitting with its lights on, just to the right of the dirt road, under a stand of trees. He shook his head. Why not broadcast where you're at? He thought of Penny and Jean and whoever else might be following, and his heart began to pump. Whatever happened here, it was time to break his cover. He had enough on tape to get Sidetrack the needle. And seeing Jean with Penny had reminded him of the life he did not have, and the life he really wanted. This was definitely his last mission. McCall, Idaho, get your fishing poles ready.

He could feel the sweat forming on the palms of his hands, though: Sidetrack's mood was still to be bargained with. The truck lights went out as soon as Sidetrack signalled to them, and then both doors opened and two men climbed into the back. The five of them set their packs down by the wheels of the truck and Harrison withdrew the twenty pounds of C-4 he was carrying: two-pound rolls wrapped in oiled paper. He passed them up to a grizzled-looking man in his fifties, who placed them very carefully inside the silver-coloured truck box. The others emptied their packs, the whole operation taking less than three minutes. The last of the C-4 was stowed and the truck boxes secured, then the two militia men jumped down.

Harrison stood to one side as they climbed back into the truck, started the engine and headed back the way they had come. The gloom was complete now: a tight mountain road, with tree, rock and shrub on all sides. Harrison watched until the lights of the truck disappeared round the first corner, then he turned back to the others. 'So what now?' he said to Sidetrack.

'We get paid,' Hooch put in.

Sidetrack shook his head. 'We get paid back in Texas.'

Hooch's jaw dropped. 'We gotta go back to Texas?'

Sidetrack showed his tooth. 'Train'll be along in a while.' He nodded to Limpet, then they set out once again, walking back the way they had come.

Sidetrack walked next to Harrison this time, shoulder to shoulder. 'You did a good job, Four-String,' he said. 'Kept your nose clean and held your end up.' He slipped an arm about his shoulders. Harrison tried not to tense, aware that Limpet was right behind them, Carlsbad and Hooch on either side. 'You're a brother now,' Sidetrack said, and let his index finger trail the length of Harrison's spine.

Harrison tried to roll to the side, but Limpet reached forward and whipped the 9mm from his waistband. Carlsbad came at him from the right, and Harrison aimed a kick hard and down on his knee. The big man yelped like a dog. At the same time, Harrison jabbed his elbow into Sidetrack's ribs and he winced. Then Limpet cocked the hammer on the Beretta and Harrison froze. Somebody reached for his boot and snatched out the .38.

He was helpless, limbs trembling, mind working. Sidetrack moved in front of him.

'Big, big mistake,' he said. The others were either side and behind him. Limpet about a yard behind, with the 9mm pointed at the back of his head. Sidetrack stepped out of the line of fire. 'Shoot yourself a Fed, Limpet.'

Limpet started to squeeze the trigger. Then he jerked like a marionette and reeled back, blood spurting in a single cord from the side of his head. Harrison dropped and spin-kicked Sidetrack's legs from under him. He scrabbled in the dirt for the fallen 9mm and, at the same moment, a dozen torches shone and a dozen MP5 carbines were aimed at the rest of the group.

Harrison heard Gerry Mackon's voice from behind the lights. 'FBI. Stand still.'

Nobody moved. Sidetrack lay on the ground where Harrison had the 9mm pointed at his head. Hooch and Carlsbad just stood like two impotent giants, blinking in the ferocity of the torchlight. Then black shapes gained definition as the SWAT team came forward to disarm the prisoners. Harrison sat where he was, his gun on Sidetrack, and reaching up under his shirt he ripped away the recorder. He looked at the tape heads by the light of one of the torches. They were still turning.

Sidetrack and the others were marched to the vehicles, which were waiting further down the trail, completely sealed off now by the FBI and state police. Harrison walked behind them with his guns intact.

Gerry Mackon, the SWAT team leader, came alongside him. 'You OK, Johnny Buck? Boy, but you led us a merry dance.'

'I'm glad you were there, Gerry.'

Penny suddenly materialised beside him. 'You can thank me later.'

'Hey, bubba.' Harrison slapped him across the shoulders. 'I saw you down in Texas. How the fuck did that happen?'

Penny told him what had been going on. 'I guess some of it was luck.'

'Well, we were due a little, huh?'

Penny looked sideways at him then. 'What's in the pick-up?'

'You tailing it?'

'D.C. is.'

'About a hundred pounds of C-4.'

Harrison got a ride with the SWAT team back to the highway and a rest area they had used to land the chopper. He saw Jean standing by his Chevy and could see the fear in her eyes as her gaze jumped from face to face. Then she saw him and broke from the truck at a run. His knees went weak. In all the years he had been alive, nobody had made such an overt demonstration of affection. He took her in his arms and held her close, kissing her face, neck and hair.

'Oh thank God,' she said. 'Thank God. Thank God. Thank God.'

The prisoners were moved from the cars to the twin vans that were waiting.

Sidetrack came alongside and looked at Harrison, then leaned and spat on the ground. 'Hey, Four-String,' he said. 'You're dead meat,'

Harrison turned then, one arm about Jean's shoulders, and held the tape up in his free hand. 'Just keep talking.'

'Every FTRA member in the country will be looking for you.'

Harrison stepped closer to him. 'Sidetrack, by the time we're done, there ain't gonna be an FTRA.'

He turned on his heel then and guided Jean over to his truck. 'Who was that?' she asked him.

Harrison looked back as Sidetrack was manhandled into the back of a van. Turning, he gently cupped her face in

539

both his hands. 'Jean,' he said very softly. 'That's the man who killed your son.'

For a moment, Jean stared at him, her mouth open, tongue drying. Then she looked to where the van doors were being slammed and back into Harrison's weary eyes. Penny walked over to where they stood and Harrison held up a palm to keep him away. Gently, he lifted Jean into his truck and held her in the darkness while she cried and cried.

The two special ops agents followed the stolen pick-up truck at a good distance, leaving the hard work to the overhead surveillance crew. The driver took the road into the Appalachians, climbed through the highest pass and then descended towards Virginia. He parked the truck in another deserted rest area and left it. A second truck picked him and the passenger up and they drove off into the mountains. Halfway along the road, they were stopped by SWAT team members fast-roping from a helicopter.

Harrison drove his own truck, with Jean next to him on the bench seat and Penny pressed up against the window. They were heading for Washington D.C. Jean was no longer crying and she sat close to Harrison, one hand resting on his thigh and her head against his shoulder. After a while, she slept. Harrison glanced over at Penny, who was on the cellphone. 'What's happening?' he asked, when Penny came off the phone.

'SWAT team just picked up three members of the Mountaineer Militia. They dumped the truck at another dead drop. D.C.'s got it staked out now. They think Harada's gonna collect it.'

'The explosives were for him, then. I didn't think there was a connection.'

'Neither did anyone else until London found out that a European Nazi group, called the Shield Society, have been paying US servicemen to steal military ordnance. Harada used the Shield Society in one of his messages.'

Harrison nodded. 'So who's been killing the militia men, then?'

'We still don't know.' Penny shrugged. 'That's the bit that makes no sense at all.'

They drove for half an hour, Harrison leaning back in the seat. 'Matthew, just remind me will you, that's the last time I ever go undercover.'

'Did you get much?'

'I got everything we needed.'

'How did they figure you?'

Harrison shook his head. 'I don't know. But my ugly mug was plastered over the militia websites for a while, a year or so back. Maybe somebody recognised me.'

'They shoulda pulled you out as soon as there was a militia connection.'

'Maybe.' Harrison made a face. 'Anyways, I got it all on tape, Matt. I've got the whole organisation implicated. We can pick up every bandana-wearing sonofabitch we find, make the skids safe for the real hobos again.' He looked down at Jean, then kissed her lightly on the hair. 'I've also got Southern Sidetrack telling me how he played Russian roulette with her boy.'

Penny looked at Jean where she slept. 'You're kidding me.'

'Nope.'

'Man, that is good news. Perhaps she can get some of her life back now.' Penny paused for a moment. 'Are you coming back to New Orleans?'

Harrison shook his head. 'I'll give you the tape, but I'm staying in D.C. for a few days.' He paused then. 'Besides, this ain't over yet.'

'It's not?'

'Not by a long way.' Harrison squinted at him. 'I think I know who Whiskey Six is.'

Penny was staring at him, and Harrison rolled the sleeve up on his jacket and twisted round so his tattoo was showing. 'This is what endeared me to Sidetrack and the crew in the first place. Their overall leader – Whiskey Six – has got one just like it. Makes sense now. A whiskey bottle and a six-gun. A Tunnel Rat tattoo.' He reached for a Marlboro and popped a match on his belt buckle, then looked at Penny once more. 'Matthew, I think Whiskey Six is an ex-Tunnel Rat called Ray Martinez.'

Harada parked the pick-up truck in the garage of his house in Falls Church, having made three separate circuits of the area to ensure it was clean. It was 2 a.m. and he rolled back the tarpaulin and checked his cargo. One baseplate, one Lockheed Martin bipod and firing system, and one box of 120mm mortars with a range of four kilometres. He knew how to launch them and he knew exactly where to launch them, having calculated the distance and trajectory many times. There was a District of Columbia law that ensured no building between the White House and Capitol Hill was more than seven storeys high. He would not even have to use the guidance system. Noncombatants would be killed, but as far as he was concerned now, every person working in the federal area was a legitimate target.

Back inside the house, he took a cold shower and dressed in his silk kimono. He washed the dye from his hair and then sat in the lotus position before the Shinto shrine; and his mind rolled back to the past and the face of Tetsuya Shikomoto. Would that his friend and lover could be there in the final moments. Would that there were someone to aid him should his courage fail, or the ordeal prove too much. But it had fallen to him to do this alone. He knew that this was what was ordained, that the only way to regain all that was lost was to finish it with a courage that had failed him throughout his life. He completed his meditation and then he sat in front of his computer, encrypted his e-mail and began to type his message.

Harrison parked his truck under the 4th Street field office in the early hours of the morning. Jean was awake and rubbing her eyes. Penny got out and stretched. Upstairs, Harrison saw Swann and they shook hands and then hugged one another.

'How you doing, duchess?'

'I'm doing OK.'

'Still here, though, huh?'

Swann nodded. 'It beats teaching a class in Baton Rouge.'

'Where's the lovely Logan?'

'With Kovalski.'

'They working on the stake-out in Virginia?'

'They're up in the command post, yeah. This is our chance to get Harada. We've been watching a self-storage unit we know he's been using, but he's not come back.'

Harrison poured a large cup of coffee and passed it to Jean. She looked very tired, but smiled at Swann and went to sit at a desk. Harrison poured more coffee. 'I found her son's killer, Jack.' Swann stared at him and he nodded. 'He's the leader of the southern crew.'

'Does she know?'

Harrison nodded. 'Yeah. I told her when we popped him. Or rather, when the boys from New Orleans did. I was about to get one in the back of the head.' He rubbed his neck under his hair.

Swann was looking at Jean. 'I suppose she'll be going back to London now.'

'Yeah, I guess she will.'

The Cub ate dinner with Sinil Kapoor. Across the road, the halal butcher's shop was very busy. Earlier, he had walked up one side of the street and then down the other, hand in hand with his date, and browsed through the racks of clothing that cluttered the pavement. He had picked up al-Bakhtar's spotters relatively easily and that disturbed him. If he could do it, then undoubtedly al-Bakhtar could too. Bin Laden's intelligence-gathering capability would make some countries look silly and he felt sure he would be aware of this sudden interest.

The Cub had seen al-Bakhtar arrive an hour earlier and disappear into the back of the shop. There was another exit at the rear, but the British had it covered. And yet, Bin Laden went to the mosque on a Friday. The Cub ate a piece of chicken and sipped his glass of beer. Sinil sat quietly opposite him and smiled appreciatively now and again. The Cub was half watching his plate and half watching the street. His gaze was drawn to the pitched roofs of some of the buildings opposite. They left the restaurant and walked hand in hand down the street, The Cub deep in thought. He had a bad feeling about this.

The sun rose early in Washington D.C.; nobody in the field office had been to bed. Kovalski and Logan had spent much of the night in the command post, monitoring the surveillance teams at the dead drop in Virginia and the self-storage unit off North Capitol Street. Nobody had collected the pick-up truck and it still stood in its parking spot, the ignition keys up the exhaust pipe and the cargo of C-4 intact in the truck boxes. The watchers were placed in the woods, agents in gilly suits, as well as further up the mountain. All access routes to the rest area from the highway and the dirt road were being watched. The same went for the self-storage units: teams from the task force were *in situ* both across the street and in the units opposite. Nothing happened. Nobody came. No movement whatsoever.

Swann left Harrison and Jean in the squad room and went upstairs to find Logan. Kovalski sat at a desk with his tie undone and bags billowing under his eyes.

'Harada won't leave a truck-load of C-4 for very long,' Swann said.

Kovalski looked at his watch and nodded.

'How many men have you got out there?'

'Enough. There's no way anyone can slip through the net, Jack. Believe me.'

Swann sat down on the edge of the desk. 'Has anyone got any clue what he's got planned? You can do a lot of damage with that much C-4.'

Kovalski shrugged. 'No idea. How's Harrison?'

'Fine.'

'He did a real good job.' Kovalski looked at Logan. 'I know you think he's just another old school buddy of mine, Cheyenne. But he's the best UCA the Bureau ever had.'

Logan looked at him and smiled.

'I think he's worried that Jean Carey's going to go home now,' Swann said. 'It seems there was something going on between them.'

'That lady doctor and Harrison?' Logan arched her eyebrows.

'He seems pretty keen on her.' Swann swung himself off the desk and moved back to the door. 'If nobody minds, I'm going out for a stroll.'

He went out on to the street and found Harrison sitting on the wall of the Federal Museum building opposite, smoking a cigarette. Pennsylvania Avenue was getting back to normal, the government determined not to be undermined. The damaged buildings were being made safe with scaffolding. Harrison flipped away his cigarette and rubbed his eyes with the heel of his palm.

'Why don't you find somewhere to crash,' Swann said. 'You've been up for days.'

Harrison made a face and reached for another cigarette. 'What's England like?' he asked.

Swann cocked his head to one side. 'It's all right. Why?'

'Is it like here?'

'In some respects, I suppose. It's more expensive. Petrol, beer, that kind of thing.'

Harrison cupped his hands to the match.

'Oh, I see,' Swann said. 'Jean.'

Harrison blew a stream of smoke and Swann stole a Marlboro from his shirt pocket.

'You really like her, don't you?'

'We got kinda close, bubba. Yeah.'

'She's a special woman.'

'You're not kidding me.' Harrison sucked hard on the cigarette. 'Her kind don't come along very often.'

'How is she now?'

Harrison made a face. 'Relieved, I figure. She's real tired, but I can see a bit of the weight has lifted. She knows who murdered her boy. Knows the sonofabitch is in custody. It's gonna help her a lot. She can mourn properly now.'

Swann nodded. 'Will she come back here for the trial?'

'There may not be one. We've got taped evidence against Sidetrack. He may go for a plea bargain to save him from the needle.' He leaned one foot flat against the wall. 'I guess she'll wanna see him sentenced, though.'

'When're you going back to New Orleans?'

'I don't know.' Harrison looked beyond him then to the grey walls of the field office. 'I'm going after Whiskey Six, Jack. I'm gonna give myself a coupla days. Spend some time with Jean, then I'm going back on the skids.' Harrison pushed himself away from the wall. 'I'm gonna try and do a deal with Sidetrack, get him to give up Whiskey Six instead of taking the needle.' He pushed out his lips. 'It might work. It might not. If not, the bastard can die.'

Swann nodded. 'And after that?'

Harrison laid a hand on his shoulder. 'Who knows, duchess? Who the hell knows?'

Harada woke with the dawn and prepared himself one last time before the Shinto shrine. He showered, dressed and checked the house before wrapping his silk kimono in brown paper and sliding the half-length sword into the same bundle. He stowed it in the truck, took two handguns and placed them under the seat, then he checked the map which was laid out on the floor of the garage. He knew everything would depend on the parks police. Finally, he took a registered disability permit from the drawer in the worktop and dangled it from the rearview mirror. For a moment he sat there, looking at himself. No make-up, no disguise. He was Fachida Harada, the warrior, and he was no longer *ninja*.

28

Carl Smylie read his e-mail, with the hairs lifting on the back of his neck. He looked at his watch, stared at the phone and, for the first time in all of this, considered calling the FBI. But then he looked again at the message and the Pulitzer prize beckoned.

Picking up the telephone, he dialled. 'Jim Morris, please.' He waited until Morris came on the phone. 'Jim,' he said. 'This is Carl. Look, I need a cameraman with a radio link to a van.'

'What for?' Morris was a producer on the *Live Tonight* news programme that was beamed all over the country.

'Trust me, Jim. I guarantee you it'll be the biggest broadcast coup of the century.'

Harada drove the pick-up truck into the city and headed for the Lincoln Memorial. Cops were everywhere. He saw Federal Defense Service cars, the parks police and uniformed secret service agents all over the place. There were no roadblocks, however, the traffic already being snarled to breaking point by the mayhem he had caused off Pennsylvania Avenue. He eased his way towards Constitution Avenue and Memorial Drive Bridge. He had waited until the rush hour was over and everyone he wanted to target would be at their desks. He drove with both hands on the wheel, skin moist, and a hollow sensation in his gut that he knew was brought on by fear. Every now and then, he would catch his reflection in the rearview mirror, where the disabled sticker was hanging. A parks police car was parked on a patch of rough grass at the head of Memorial Drive. Crossing the bridge, Harada eased the pick-up round the roundabout and pulled off to the right of the Lincoln Memorial. He watched in the wing mirror, but the police car remained where it was, and then he looked ahead to the nine parking bays set aside for the disabled. The last one, the one nearest to the white stone flower vases that formed the block in the road, was empty. He slowed. The other cars were all parked nose in. He hauled hard on the wheel and backed up the truck so the flatbed was facing the city.

Harrison sat in Kovalski's office on the phone to New Orleans. The task force had raided the rogue base at Wichita Falls and recovered a massive amount of weapons. Paulie Caulfield had been arrested, along with seventeen other US service personnel named by Patterson and Stoval in London. The FTRA members, who Harrison could identify, were being hunted at that very moment. In the north, Detective Spinelli was co-ordinating the search for The Voyageur, and the San Francisco field office had trapped Ghost Town just outside of Oakland, in the early hours of the morning. Harrison put down the phone and rubbed his jaw with a calloused palm. Swann was sitting across from him with Logan, who was talking on the radio to the agents at the Virginia stake-out. There was still no sign of Harada, or anyone else, coming for the C-4.

'He must have got wind and given it up,' Swann said.

Harrison nodded.

Swann looked at him then. 'So why don't I feel any relief?'

Harrison got up and paced to the window, where he pressed his face against the glass. Penny had flown with the SWAT team back to New Orleans, where Sidetrack would be extradited to stand trial for Tom Carey's murder. Harrison and Jean were staying at the Hyatt with Swann and Logan, and Harrison had taken her there that morning. He pushed himself away from the glass and he and Swann went outside for a smoke.

'So you're going after Whiskey Six?' Swann said.

Harrison nodded. 'Then I'm outta here. I'll give evidence at whatever trials I need to, but after that, it's over.'

Swann cocked his head to one side. 'You really mean it, don't you?'

'Yeah.' Harrison rubbed his arm with a palm. 'Duchess, I'm too old for this shit any more.' There was a distance in his eyes that Swann had never seen before.

'What will you do?'

'That depends.'

'On Jean?'

Harrison sighed. 'I don't know, Jack. We got kinda close, but now this thing is over. She's got a life back in England, and it's always struck me as funny how emotions change when the moment of tension is gone. You understand what I'm saying?'

Swann nodded. 'What're her plans?'

'I figure she's gonna go back to New Orleans and then on home. We'll let her know when the trial's at and she can fly back.'

'Is that what she told you she was going to do?'

'Not in so many words, but it don't take a genius to figure it out.' Harrison pushed himself off the wall and flipped away the cigarette butt. 'I gotta get my shit together, duchess, go see that long-toothed sonofabitch.'

Harada had the truck backed in, and he sat and counted ten seconds, taking in the movement all around him. To his right were the park-information huts, and ahead, the old Vietnam veteran who kept a candle burning for those GIs still missing in action. Tourists were everywhere: on the steps of the Lincoln Memorial immediately to his left; down by the black-glassed waters of the reflecting pool; and crowding the Vietnam War Memorial through the trees. Harada opened the truck door and climbed up into the back, his kimono and sword bundled in one hand. With one movement, he whipped off the tarpaulin. The mortar-firing system lay flat against the bolted-down baseplate. Twelve in the first minute, then it would be so hot that he could only fire four. But a minute was all he needed. Kneeling, he ignored all that was around him, and laid a 9mm pistol beside the baseplate. Then he lifted the bipod and secured the legs so that the mortar faced right across Constitution Avenue. He looked up: people everywhere, but no cops and nobody taking a blind bit of notice of what he was doing. He set the angle of trajectory and calculated the distance. Then he primed the firing pin and picked up the first 120mm shell.

The Fugitive Publicity unit faced the street at the front of FBI headquarters. They had moved from across the quadrangle only three weeks previously, as theirs was not a secret information facility like some of the other departments. Jenny Yates was on the phone to her boyfriend, while her boss was at a meeting down the hall. The office was quiet this morning, only two other support staff at their desks. The rest were involved in the hunt for Fachida Harada. Jenny twirled the telephone cord round her fingers and pressed the receiver against her ear. They had had a fight last night and she was trying to get hold of Bobby to apologise. She was not sure it was actually her fault, but she knew there was no way that Bobby would apologise for anything.

She heard the sudden whine in the air outside just as Bobby came on the line.

'Bobby, it's . . .'

And then the mortar hit the FBI building facing Pennsylvania Avenue. The windows shattered right by Jenny's desk. Glass flew, masonry crumbled and the whole building seemed to shake. She went down with a pain in her eyes that made her scream and scream. The door to the corridor was blown off its hinges and people outside were sent reeling by shuddering masonry. Jenny was on her hands and knees, unable to see, and when she lifted one hand to her face, she could feel the shards of glass sticking out of her eyes. She screamed again, fear rising in her throat, and, as she screamed, she heard that same whining sound for the second time.

Harada had already pumped in his second mortar when the first one impacted and the explosion resonated through the entire city. He stood now, hefting fresh mortars and dropping them into the firing tube. People on the steps of the Lincoln Memorial were watching him, puzzled initially, and then one man began to shout. Thirty seconds later, there was pandemonium, people running into each other like ants.

The noise was incredible: the shuddering bang as the mortar was lobbed into the air over Constitution Avenue; the smell of cordite and the smoke; and then the massive explosion a matter of seconds later. Harada worked feverishly. At any moment, a wannabe hero might storm the truck. Sweat poured from his brow as the third mortar went in.

On Pennsylvania Avenue, the FBI building was hit again and again. The corridors were filled with smoke and the sprinklers came on, soaking the mass of agents and support staff trying to get out of the building. There were assembly points and designated controllers, some of whom were already dead. On the second floor, doors were blown off and some of the interior walls had collapsed. Shrapnel damage had one man desperately trying to flee, hopping like a broken insect, dragging a mutilated leg behind him.

The mortars kept coming; every few seconds that terrible whining and then the building would shudder all over again. Downstairs, the police were being scrambled, but they had no idea where the attack was coming from.

At the field office, Harrison stared out the window as the first explosions shredded the stillness of the day. Logan was on the phone and when she put it down, her face was as grey as he had ever seen it. 'The puzzle palace is under mortar attack,' she said.

Harrison ran for the stairs, Logan and Swann behind him.

Pennsylvania Avenue was panicking, cars smashing into one another as bits of the Hoover building tumbled to the asphalt below. The police were powerless and still the sky rained mortars.

Harada could hear the scream of the sirens. The police would not know where to go initially, but as he looked up from firing the eighth mortar, his eyes fixed on the man talking on a cellular phone and looking at him from the steps of the Lincoln Memorial. Harada wiped the sweat from his brow and picked up the 9mm. The man's eyes balled and he dived for cover in the bushes. Harada looked up and down the road: still no police officer.

The final four mortars landed close to the FBI building. The Old Post Office building across the street took a direct hit and the diners in the Pavilion were showered with flying glass and rubble. One bomb landed right in the middle of the road, tearing up great chunks of asphalt and hurling them into the air.

Swann, Harrison and Logan got as far as the Canadian Embassy, but could get no further. Logan was on the cellphone. 'He's at the Lincoln Memorial. Let's go.'

Harrison was driving and he had the strobe lights flashing and the siren wailing. He headed straight down Constitution Avenue, weaving in and out of the traffic, following the great gaggle of police cars that were racing for Memorial Bridge. Coming the other way, the emergency services vehicles were ploughing their own furrow into the heart of the city.

Harada fired the last mortar as the first parks police car drew up and the driver leapt out to take cover behind his door. Harada emptied the entire 9mm clip into the door and the driver slumped on to the pavement, with blood gushing from wounds in his chest. Picking up his bundle, Harada walked calmly over to the police car, kicked the body out of the way and jumped behind the wheel. He swung in an arc, siren howling, lights flashing; and drove the wrong way towards the Memorial Bridge. He bumped on to the roundabout and took it the wrong way. Behind him, police car after police car converged on the truck he had abandoned.

Harada passed between the twin bronze statues of Sacrifice and Valour, given to the city by the Italians. He crossed the bridge, hitting eighty miles an hour, and went straight over the far roundabout and up Memorial Drive. He pulled over on the right and got out of the car. Then he looked back the way he had come and saw a trail of police cars following him. Calmly now, he straightened his jacket and walked down the escalators to the Blue line metro platform at Arlington Cemetery station. A train heading for Franconia-Springfield was just pulling in.

Carl Smylie waited with his cameraman at the Howard Johnson Plaza, directly across the road from the Hyatt and National Airport. They waited on the third floor, which was in the throes of renovation, with dust and bits of wood shavings everywhere. The long corridor was lined with new mattresses, shrink-wrapped in polythene and propped against the walls. Smylie had looked in one room and thought it reminiscent of a bonfire: every piece of furniture piled on the floor as if awaiting only a match. He looked at his watch and heard the explosions in the city. Quickly, he pulled out his cellphone and spoke to Morris. 'What's going on?' he demanded.

He watched the cameraman watching him, as Morris told him that the FBI building had just been attacked by what were thought to be mortar bombs. Smylie shut off the phone and slipped it into his pocket.

'You sure this is gonna happen?' the cameraman said.

'Positive.' Smylie went into room 306 and looked across Jefferson Davis Highway to the parking lot next to the Hyatt. The radio van was parked there and he could bounce his signal off the satellite dish on the roof.

Harada rode the Blue line three stops to Crystal City, where he went up the escalators, his package under his arm and the freshly loaded 9mm in his waistband. He walked through the underpass and saw a man getting into his car outside the post office. Calmly, Harada walked up to him, drew the pistol and forced him on to his knees. The man begged for his life, and Harada snatched the keys from his hand and got behind the wheel. It was a matter of a few blocks along South Eades Street and he pulled into the parking lot of the Howard Johnson hotel. He left the car, keys in the ignition, and went into the lobby. He had been here before of course, and, ignoring reception, he went straight to the elevators and climbed to the third floor.

Smylie paced the corridor, looking at his watch and wiping the perspiration from his face. He went back to the elevators, where the cameraman was looking bored, and waited. The bell tinkled and the doors slid back, and Fachida Harada crooked a finger at them, the muzzle of a 9mm pointed at Smylie's stomach.

Smylie blanched and the cameraman nearly dropped his equipment, and again Harada beckoned. The two men got into the elevator with him and, for the second time, Smylie wondered if he should have phoned the FBI.

The doors closed with a hiss, and Harada pressed for the eleventh floor and the elevator began to rise. 'I am Fachida Harada,' he said. 'Samurai warrior. Thank you for coming.'

'Pleasure,' Smylie uttered. 'In your e-mail, you said something about an interview.'

Harada smiled a thin and mirthless smile. 'After a fashion, yes.'

When they got to the eleventh floor, he ushered them out ahead of him. Directly to the right was an unmarked door, which Harada gestured for Smylie to open. It led to a grey-walled staircase that rose two flights to another door. Smylie paused at this one and looked through the glass panel to an asphalted roof. Harada kicked the lock and the door flew open, and the heat of the day hit them.

Harada motioned for them to go out on the roof, while he waited at the head of the stairs. 'You may start filming,' he said. 'I would suggest you make it clear that you are being held at gunpoint.' He smiled. 'For your own protection, later.' Then he began to get undressed.

Smylie stood on the roof, nodded to the cameraman, who spoke over the radio to the van downstairs. 'Get it rolling,' he said. 'Live to the network.'

Smylie held his microphone and, pushing his hair away from his eyes, he looked into the camera. 'This is Carl Smylie and I'm broadcasting to you live from the rooftop of the Howard Johnson on Jefferson Davis Highway, where myself and a colleague are being held at gunpoint by the Japanese Red Army terrorist, Fachida Harada.'

The camera panned to Harada, who was naked now, pointing the pistol at them as he unrolled his bundle and stepped into his silk kimono.

In the command post on 4th Street, Tom Kovalski stared in disbelief at the naked image of Harada pointing his gun at the camera. He snatched up the radio. 'All units. All units. SWAT roll. Channel six. Suspect is on the roof of the Howard Johnson hotel on Jefferson Davis Highway. I want eyes on target. Repeat, I want eyes on target.'

Two Blackhawk helicopters took to the air as Kovalski ordered a no-fly zone round the hotel. It was a problem because National Airport was only a few blocks across the railroad lines and he told them to close down and reroute aircraft until further notice. Every phone in the command post was ringing off the hook, and Kovalski knew it would be the politicians demanding an update. He ignored them, kept the radio channels open and watched the macabre scene unfold live on national television.

Harrison dropped Swann and Logan at the door of the Howard Johnson. They were first on the scene, and as

Harrison idled the car, he tugged the Beretta from his waistband and tossed it to Swann. 'All yours, duchess. Point the sharp end away from you.' Then he slammed the car door and was off across the highway to the Hyatt.

Swann weighed the gun in his hand and grinned. At last, he no longer felt impotent.

Logan was already through the doors. She flashed her shield at reception. 'How do I get to the roof?'

Harada could feel the wind in his face and he walked solemnly away from the staircase to the far end of the roof. He knew that FBI agents would storm the stairs and he knew they would mount snipers on the rooftops opposite. The Hyatt was taller than the Howard Johnson and, in a way, he knew he had made this choice deliberately because of that. Smylie and the cameraman followed him, and he kept the gun on them, but walked barefoot over the sizzling asphalt, with the robes of his ceremonial costume flowing. In his free hand he carried the half-length sword. At the far end of the roof, he stopped and faced the camera. In the distance, he could hear the whump whump of helicopters.

'My name is Fachida Harada,' he said to the camera. 'I am a warrior. The life of the warrior is one of sacrifice and honour. It is but a passing thing, like the breath of wind in winter, the spark of the firefly in the night. As each day passes, the shadows lengthen into darkness.' He paused then, and, momentarily laying down the gun, he drew the sword and tossed away the scabbard. He bent for the gun once more, pointed it at Smylie and slowly sank to his knees.

Swann and Logan hit the eleventh floor and burst into the stairwell, then they slowed, one on either rail, and carefully made their way up, gun arms extended.

Logan got to the doorway, peeked out and saw Harada at the far end on his knees. 'What the hell?'

Swann followed her gaze. They could not see him

clearly, because he had placed Smylie and the cameraman between himself and the door.

Harrison was already on the roof of the Hyatt opposite, when the first of the SWAT team fast-roped from the chopper. He was at the parapet, armed only with his snub-nosed .38 and was staring across at Harada. He wore white and Harrison could not see him properly, just the top of his head. Clearly, Harada was kneeling, and the two reporters, one of them filming, were standing between him and the exit at the stairwell.

A sniper came alongside him. 'Who the fuck are you?' he demanded.

Harrison looked into his face and flapped open his shield. 'I'm your back-up, buddy.'

The sniper took up his position and two others, backed up by their observers, set up at other points on the roof.

Across Jefferson Davis Highway, Harada held his sword in one hand and looked again into the camera. 'Life flees the warrior like cherry blossom in the winds of April,' he said softly. Then he laid down the gun, bent his head so he could not be shot from the roof opposite and took the sword in both hands. The cameraman rolled his film and Smylie looked on in horror. And then Harada thrust the sword into the right side of his abdomen. He gasped and looked up, blood spilling over his hands and sweat standing out on his brow. He looked into the camera. 'The centre of man,' he whispered. 'Passion, ambition, the spirit home.' With that, he dragged the blade right across his middle and thick ribbons of blood sprayed Carl Smylie's shoes.

In the command post, all were silent. Kovalski watched, frowning. Next to him, Carmen McKensie's eyes popped out on stalks.

Harada pressed the short sword four inches into his gut. He

gasped and blood flew in bubbles from his mouth. Smylie was rooted, the blood sucking at his feet and spreading in a darkened pool behind him.

At the steps, Swann and Logan saw the blood and Swann let go a breath. '*Sepukko*. Like Mishima on the balcony.'

'We gotta shoot the sonofabitch, Jack. This is live television.'

With one final effort, Harada ripped the sword up to his sternum and flopped forward to rest on both hands, hilt against the asphalt. Smylie turned and vomited, and the cameraman gagged. Harada lifted his head, eyes balled and staring as his blood and guts spilled out before them. With one bloodied hand, he picked up the 9mm and pointed it at the camera. 'Keep filming or I'll kill you,' he whispered.

He lifted his head higher now and pointed the gun, arm extended, hand trembling, while the flow of blood slowed and his innards hung from the wound in his belly. The sword was still embedded and he made no attempt to pull it out. He looked into the camera, and his face was set and cold, and his arm no longer wavered.

Swann stood in the doorway and looked at Logan. 'This could take hours. I mean literally hours and hours. He'll sit like that till he dies.' He sucked breath. 'When Mishima did it, he had another guy there with a sword to cut off his head.' He steeled himself, looked at Logan once more and stepped out on to the roof.

'Jack.'

Swann waved a hand at her and, gun arm down, he walked slowly towards Harada.

Across on the roof of the Hyatt, Harrison was staring as Swann emerged from the stairwell. 'What's the limey sonofabitch think he's doing?' He looked at the agent in SWAT gear next to him. 'Hey, kid. You got a clear shot?'

'No, sir. His head's too low. I can't see anything.'

Harrison watched as Swann slowly made his way across the rooftop, with Logan covering him from the doorway. Still Harada knelt there, and still he held the gun on Smylie and the cameraman, and the film rolled as the life bled out of him.

'Fachida.' Swann called across the rooftop. Harada looked up and their eyes met, and for a moment Harada swung his gun arm towards him. Swann stood his ground. He did not raise his own gun, but motioned for Smylie and the other man to step back. They eased their way aside and Harada swung the gun again, but his hand wavered and his eyes began to glaze.

'It's over, Fachida.' Swann called. 'Finished. There's no swordsman here.' He paused then, biting down on his lip. 'Lift up your head.'

Harada knelt where he was, his blood drained and the pain was all but unbearable.

'You're samurai,' Swann called to him. 'Lift your head, Fachida.'

Harada was drifting. He saw the master on the rooftop, as he had done as a boy. He saw Shikomoto when they led him away in handcuffs and he saw him naked in their room in Jakarta. He looked at Swann then, who still stood with his gun pointing down, and slowly he raised his head.

Harrison watched Swann from the Hyatt roof, heard him calling, saw the two hostages step back and realised what he was doing. And then Harada slowly lifted his head. The sniper alongside Harrison tensed. 'Clear shot,' he said.

'Take it.'

The single shot echoed across the roof and Harada twisted like a broken puppet.

Swann saw him buckle and a string of blood spurt from his skull. Then he crumpled on to his side, the sword still embedded in his guts. Looking round, Swann saw that the cameraman had stopped filming. They stood in silence, the three of them, and then Swann felt Logan at his side.

Harada lay at their feet, deep in his own blood, head twisted back, his suddenly dull eyes looking up at the sky.

Across on the far rooftop, Harrison laid a hand on the young sniper's shoulder. Downstairs, he went to his room and found Jean watching the television news. Her face was white and she looked up as he came in, then back at the TV once again.

Harrison picked up the remote control and switched off the set. 'Did you see all that?' he asked her.

'Yes,' she said quietly, 'I did.' She sat with her hands in her lap, then looked up at him once more and he could see tears at the back of her eyes. 'John,' she said. 'I want to go home.'

The Cub lay in the back of the van, watching the mosque through the smoked-glass windows. One was rolled down far enough for him to nose through the muzzle of the barrel and get off one clear shot. One was all he needed.

People thronged the pavement as the mullah called the faithful to prayer. The Cub was watching the entrance for the arrival of the man the British did not know for sure was there. The van was hot, although there had been a little bit of rain during the day, and The Cub was less than comfortable. He also had a bad feeling deep in the pit of his stomach that Bin Laden would not show up. The time ticked towards the hour and The Cub watched through the rifle sight and waited.

Cars drew up, pedestrians arrived and still there was no sign. Then, just before seven, a blue car pulled up and The Cub saw the Butcher of Bekaa step out. He was flanked by another man and then between them came a third, and when he stood to his full height, he was over six foot. He wore traditional clothing and sailed up the steps with al-Bakhtar covering his back. The Cub watched, but could not see his face and could not get a clear shot. Within seconds, the car was gone and the mini-entourage had disappeared into the mosque. The Cub rolled on his side, looked at the ceiling and swore softly to himself.

He waited until 10 p.m., watching as all the worshippers left. He waited for al-Bakhtar and his quarry to emerge. But they did not come and when ten became half past, he took the rifle apart, climbed into the front seat of the van and started the engine. He pulled on to Chevening Road and saw a red van watching the doorway of the mosque. Further up the road, a man in a suit and tie waited at the bus stop. The Cub could make out the radio piece in his ear.

He drove to Ealing Road, cruised the length of it and saw that the halal butcher's shop was not only closed for business, but the grilles were down and the windows were empty. He pulled over, looked for the spotters and saw nothing that resembled them. He parked the van in a side road and made his way on foot back behind the shops and again scouted for surveillance. There was none. He shook his head and considered, then looked at his watch and climbed the short fence into the yard at the back of the shop. The basement entrance was down a flight of six steps and The Cub pressed his ear to the door. He looked up again – all was dark and quiet – and took a single-bladed knife from his pocket.

Inside, the small basement smelled of blood and animal entrails. The Cub had no light, save that of the streetlamps outside, but he took in a desk and a chair and marks where some sort of equipment had been. The floor was littered with papers and he bent and fished in his pocket for a match. He lit one and held it up, and gazed at the shreds of paper. Just bits and pieces of headed notepaper with scribblings that meant nothing to him. He went upstairs and checked the shop, and then the rooms above and finally the attic. He had been right: it was connected to the one next door. In the distance, he could hear sirens and his senses sharpened, and he went back to the basement again. He paused at the door for one last look round and struck another match. The sirens were louder now and it was time for him to go, but something by the unused fireplace caught his eye. Sections of paper that had been partially burnt. Quickly, he picked them up and stuffed them into his pocket.

Outside, he closed the door and went up the steps, and walked back to Ealing Road. He crossed to the Indian restaurant and found Haan enjoying a meal. He slid into the chair opposite and ordered a beer, and then he took the scraps of burned paper from his pocket. 'Look what I found,' he said.

Haan laid down his fork and wiped his mouth, then studied the papers.

They looked at one another for a long moment and The Cub arched his eyebrows. Then they sat and ate, and watched as the police broke down the door of the shop across the road.

29

Harrison sat across the table from a manacled and orange-suited Southern Sidetrack.

'It's that or the needle, asshole.' Harrison looked coldly at him. 'I got you on tape admitting to the murder of Tom Carey and the DA's gonna push all the way for the big one, seeing as how we know you killed a whole bunch of other guys.'

Sidetrack sat back, showed his long tooth and looked Harrison right in the eye.

'You figure I'm afraid of dying?'

'I don't know. Are you?'

'Nope.'

Harrison nodded and rested his arms on the back of the chair. 'You ain't bothered by all those years of appeals and then the governor saying: "No way, José." You ain't bothered about the last night, with the minutes ticking away and the clock being all there is. And that last meal, the one you can't eat because your stomach's all in knots. And you're thinking about how there just might be a God. And if there is, you might be going down instead of up when it's over.' He lit a cigarette, flapped out the match and blew smoke in Sidetrack's face. 'And then the guards coming and the preacher man, and that one guy hollering to everybody how there's a dead man walking.' He sat back. 'None of that bothers you, huh?'

'Nope.' Sidetrack looked evenly at him.

'OK.' Harrison stood up and banged on the door of the interview room. He crushed out his cigarette, and then the key turned in the lock.

'Four-String.'

Harrison looked back and saw Sidetrack staring at him. 'Shoshone, Idaho. If he's any place, it's there.'

He had not watched Jean pack, but stayed in his room on Burgundy and Toulouse, having said his goodbyes the night before. In the morning, he gathered his ancient hobo clothes and drove to the field office. Penny met him on the squad-room floor.

'You not going to the airport with Jean?' he asked.

Harrison shook his head. 'I never did do goodbyes.' He laid his bundle on the desk and went up the stairs to where Hammond was in a meeting with Mayer, the special agent in charge. Harrison rapped on the door and went straight in. Mayer looked up at him.

'John, we're in a meeting.'

'I know. But this won't take a minute.' Harrison sat down in the empty chair and looked at Hammond first, then Mayer. 'I know where I can find Whiskey Six,' he said. 'I've sorta done a deal with Sidetrack to try and keep him away from the needle. I don't give a fuck whether the DA keeps to it or not. But I think I can get Whiskey Six.'

'How?'

'I know where he might be at. It's just a small town, but the Union Pacific freight line runs right through it.' He paused and hissed breath through his teeth. 'I'm gonna ride the boxcars to see if I can track him down.'

'You think he's this ex-Tunnel Rat Martinez?' Hammond said quietly.

Harrison nodded. 'The last time I saw him was in a hole in the ground in Vietnam.' He stood up then, took his FBI shield from his back pocket and laid it on Mayer's desk. 'As of now, I quit the Bureau, Charlie. I'm going after Martinez as a private citizen. I'll find him, round him up and deliver him to the nearest sheriff's office. While I'm gone, do me a favour and have the puzzle palace sort the paperwork, so I can get some money.'

Mayer looked at him, eyes thin, then at the shield lying

on his desk. He sat back in his chair, fingers steepled before his mouth. 'You're really gonna do this?'

'Yes, sir. I am.' Harrison shook his hand, then he shook Hammond's and walked out of the office.

In the parking lot on level seven, he fired up his Chevy and pulled to the top of the ramp. Matt Penny was standing in his way. Harrison stopped, grabbed a cigarette from the dashboard and rolled down the window.

'You're outta here, aren't you?' Penny said.

Harrison lit the cigarette. 'Yeah.'

'Where you going?'

'North.'

'You coming back?'

'I've still got my room in the quarter. I figure I've got to leave my stuff somewhere for a while.'

'Call me.' Penny offered his hand.

Harrison took it. 'Say goodbye to Jean for me. Better still, take her to the airport. She's about ready to go.'

Penny nodded. 'Anything I should say to her?'

'Tell her I don't do goodbyes.' Harrison leaned and spat tobacco juice. 'And, Matthew. Tell her that I love her.'

He gunned the engine, spun the wheel under his hand and drove down the ramp to the street.

Swann and Logan watched Washington D.C. slowly get back to normal, though the Federal Triangle had been badly damaged by the mortars, especially the front of the Hoover building. The FBI was rehoused in the contingency facility within hours of the evacuation, and was up and running the following morning. It would be some time before they could return to the puzzle palace.

Harada was dead and his public suicide was on everybody's lips. There were pictures in every newspaper, and the video footage was being run and rerun. Smylie was on every talk show, talking about his 'ordeal'. He claimed he had been contacted and asked to show up at the Howard Johnson for an exclusive, and thought it would be with one of the militia leaders. He had no idea it would be Harada, or that when he showed up he would be held at gunpoint.

The cameraman had not caught the moment of death on film, and all of the networks had wanted to interview Swann. But he declined to talk to any of them. He sat in the bar at the Hyatt with Logan and Kovalski, who was on his way home to Springfield. They shared a bottle of wine.

'There's one good thing about what Smylie did,' Kovalski was saying. 'It showed the militia, more importantly the regular American people, that Harada was nothing to do with us.'

Logan sipped wine. 'The unrest hasn't gone away, though, Tom. It won't till we find out who's behind the killings.'

Kovalski sighed. 'One step at a time, Chey.' He looked at Swann, who sat deep in thought. 'You took a chance up there, Jack. Walking out like that.'

Swann shook his head. 'I don't think so. Harada wanted to finish it.'

'It's a good job you didn't shoot him yourself, then I *would* have a bunch of explaining to do.'

They were quiet for a moment, then Swann laid his hand on Logan's knee and squeezed. 'I'm going back to London,' he said. 'The Louisiana course seemed to get by without me and I miss the kids.' He looked at Kovalski. 'Is your new terrorism response co-ordinator broken in yet?'

Kovalski smiled. 'I guess so.' He glanced at Logan then. 'You can get yourself to the leg-att any time you want.'

She kissed him on the cheek.

'Can't say I'm not gonna miss you.' Kovalski stood up. 'You're a lucky man, Jack Swann. A very lucky man.'

They shook hands and Kovalski went out to his car.

Swann sat down again and summoned the waiter for another bottle of wine. Logan looked thoughtful. 'Jean Carey's gone back to England,' she said.

'At least she now knows who killed her son.'

'Harrison quit the Bureau. He's gone after the leader of the FTRA on his own.'

'And the Bureau is happy about that?'

Logan made a face. 'The Bureau doesn't have a choice. We've rounded up a whole bunch of FTRA members and Harrison will give evidence against them. But if he wants to quit, what can anyone do about it?'

Swann finished his wine and stood up. 'Cheyenne, I'm going to go and phone my kids. I'll see you in the restaurant.'

He walked over to the bay of public telephone booths. Logan watched him, then looked up at the glass-fronted elevator. Smylie was coming down. He had spotted her and had a massive grin on his face.

Logan sat where she was as he appeared at the arm of her chair. 'Agent Logan,' he said. 'Is this seat taken?'

'Does it matter?'

Smylie sat down. 'Incredible television, wasn't it?'

'It was appalling.'

He nodded. 'You think so? You know, I had no idea that's what he intended when he showed up. Pity the cameraman got sick to his stomach, though, huh? The finale would've been good.'

'So why didn't you call us when he arranged to meet you, Carl? If you had, we might've been able to stop the mortar attack.'

'I didn't know it was him.'

Logan leaned close to him then and her eyes were chill. 'Save the bullshit for the talk shows, asshole.' She stood up. 'You're a piece of shit, Smylie. Not even fit to step on. Keep away from me. Understand? Come nowhere near me, or so help me, I'll find a way to indict you.'

The Cub flew into D.C., and called Cyrus Birch from Dulles Airport. They met at the same Leesburg restaurant as the last time and Birch was there by five. The Cub was sipping cold beer at a table in the corner of the room. Birch slid into the seat opposite and, for a long moment, they just looked at one another without saying anything.

'So, is the mission aborted?' The Cub asked finally.

'For the time being. We really have lost him this time. Even the Israelis don't know where he is.'

'And the Butcher?'

'The same.'

The Cub nodded slowly. 'I watched them go into the mosque, but they didn't come out again.'

'He has many allies. He was probably already out of the country by the time evening prayer was over.'

The Cub sat for a moment, and then he fished in his pocket and brought out the slips of charred paper he had found in the West London basement. He looked at them briefly and then handed them to Birch. 'I found these at his premises, just before the British raided it.' He stood up and walked out of the restaurant.

Birch watched him go, sighed and glanced at the scraps of paper. Goose flesh broke out on his cheeks.

Kovalski met Swann and Logan in his office, on the morning of their departure to London. Logan's promotion had been finalised and she was due at Grosvenor Square the following day. Swann was as happy as he had been in a while. He was going home. His children were at home and the woman he loved was going home with him.

Swann and Kovalski shook hands and Kovalski looked at Logan. 'I might catch up with you two in London at some point. Now this Balkan thing is over, we'll be sending a whole bunch of agents to look at the war crimes issue.'

Just then, his assistant buzzed through to him. 'I've got Mr Birch in the outer office, sir,' she said.

Kovalski lifted an eyebrow. 'OK. Send him in, Mary.'

'We better go,' Logan said.

'Hell, no. Stick around. See what other little surprises the CIA has got for us.'

Birch appeared at the door and Kovalski came round

from behind the desk. 'Cyrus. What a surprise.' He made no attempt to keep the sarcasm from his voice. 'Pity you didn't tell us about Harada earlier, wasn't it?'

Birch coloured below the ears. He glanced briefly at Swann and Logan. 'I need a few words in private, Tom. It's why I called by, instead of phoning.'

'This facility's a SCIF, Cyrus. Shoot.'

'Private, Tom. Please.'

'We've got to go, anyways. We got a plane to catch.' Logan kissed Kovalski and then she and Swann left the office. They went downstairs to where an agent with a car was waiting to drive them to Dulles. 'Whatever it is,' she said to Swann, 'it's not my problem any more.'

Up in Kovalski's office, the two men sat on the leather couch, with the door closed. Birch fished in his pocket for the small polythene envelope. He looked at it briefly, then passed it to Kovalski. 'These were found in West London,' he said. 'We were working on some covert action and . . .'

Kovalski was staring at the papers, his eyes bunched in his head. On one was the transcript of an interview. Halfway down the page a section had been marked with an asterix: 'Listen to us you people of America, if you hold worth in your lives, in the lives of your children and your children's children, then change your way in the world. Find a government for your own people, not one which struts the stage of the world pandering to the interests of Jews. If you do not, the fight will come to America and you will mourn the loss of your sons.'

Kovalski looked at Birch, his mouth suddenly dry. He had read those words before. He looked at the two other pieces of paper, sections of headed notepaper with some unintelligible scribble on them. One had a PO box in Germany as the address, with 'American Militia Abroad' printed at the top. The other was less clear, the page badly charred. Kovalski made out part of two words – 'hield Soci'.

'I think that should read Shield Society,' Birch said quietly. 'Again, registered in Germany.'

'These are the groups behind the military ordnance theft.'

'I know.'

Kovalski looked at the section of interview transcript. 'But this . . .'

'I know.'

'Where did you find them?'

Birch took a deep breath. 'In the basement of a halal butcher's store in West London.'

'A butcher's store?'

'Yes.' Birch sat forward. 'You see, we were watching Mujah al-Bakhtar, better known as the Butcher of Bekaa, bodyguard to Osama Bin Laden.'

Kovalski felt the chill rush through him, the prickling of his scalp as the implications hit him.

Birch's face was the colour of slate. 'He's behind it all, Tom. He got hold of Harada and funded his grudge. He used Harada's yakuza contacts to pose as Hong Kong troops and kill the militia leaders, to incite the people against us. Then he funded the weapons for them to fight us with.' He shook his head slowly. 'He knows he can't beat us by conventional terrorism, so he's fomenting revolution.'

Harrison drove his truck for three days, north and west from New Orleans. As he passed the airport at Kenner, he heard a jet taking off and he thought of Jean, and for just one moment his eyes glassed. He knew he would see her again; she would come back for the trial, but it would not be the same. The emergency was over, the circumstances that had thrown them together had passed, and now lives had to be looked at in detail. He could sense the need in her to get back to London, to return to the sick children she cared so much about. And who could blame her? Before her son died, they had been pretty much her whole life. Equally, he needed to get on with his, make something of it, yet his direction was much less sure.

They had spent one last night together in her room at the Hotel Provincial. They made love for hours, but talked little, as if there was nothing more to say. When she was asleep, Harrison had got up and smoked a cigarette at the open window, listening to the hiss of the rainstorm on the pavement below. By the time she had awoken he was back in his room on Burgundy and Toulouse.

Harrison left the truck in a lock-up garage in Laramie, Wyoming, slipped the snub-nosed .38 into his boot and the Beretta into his waistband. He had his bowie knife and his FBI-issue Sig-Sauer in his pack. In the pocket of his army jacket, he found the black bandana he had earned by initiation at the Saratoga freight yard.

For a month, he rode the northern railroads and was surprised to find a lot of regular hobos on his travels. He ate with them, talked with them, stayed out of the cold with them, and huddled round camp fires at night. And he sensed an ease about the way they talked and carried themselves. He saw barely a handful of blue bandana-wearers, the Highrollers of the FTRA. The Voyageur was now in custody and the word was out that the FBI had smashed the membership.

He lost himself in the journeys, allowing his mind to beat time with the rhythm of the wheels as they rode the iron tracks. He wondered at his past and he wondered at his future, and then one day he jumped the Union Pacific at Cokeville, Wyoming, and headed into Idaho.

Harrison had been to Shoshone a few times before, when he was on an undercover mission a couple of years previously. It was a small, wind-blown town with the freight line dominating it. Once upon a time, Amtrak had run its passenger service through here, but not any more. He jumped off the train as it slowed on its westbound journey and listened to the bell ringing as it rumbled across the junction. He stood with his pack on his back, rolled a cigarette and cupped his hands to the wind. One or two of the old-timers he had met since leaving the truck had told him whispers of the man they called Whiskey Six, a name that for years had struck terror into seasoned men of the skids. Harrison could have come straight here, given what Sidetrack had said, but he figured that Six would be lying as low as the rest of the FTRA membership.

He stood in the road, listening to another long whistle blast from the locomotive, and then he crossed the street to the Columbia bar. The interior was dark and empty: a couple of pool tables, and one long bar to the right as he entered. He ordered a Coors Light and shot of Blackjack, and sat and nursed his drinks. The bartender cleaned glasses and wiped down the counter. Harrison ordered another shot and asked her if the haunted McFall hotel, a couple of blocks along, was still empty.

'Oh, yeah,' the girl said. 'Nobody ever bought that place.'

'Still got that big old yard?'

'Oh, yeah.'

'Still got all the rattlesnakes?'

'I guess. Nobody ever did anything about them.'

Harrison knew that the run-down hotel had been subject to a rattlesnake infestation problem, largely due to the plentiful supply of rats.

He sipped beer and was suddenly aware of a weird sensation across his shoulders. He swivelled round on his stool and looked through the window. Across the train tracks, a hunched figure in a battered cowboy hat paused at the door of the Manhattan Café to put out a cigarette. Something about the set of his shoulders, the stoop, the skinny frame in profile, sent Harrison's mind spiralling into the past. He sat for a long moment staring at the half-empty bottle of beer, aware of a tingling sensation running through his veins. He took a ten-dollar bill from his money clip and laid it on the counter. Then he went outside and looked across the street as the sun beat down on his head. He hesitated, considering for a moment, then walked the two blocks to the hotel and vaulted the fence at the back.

From his pack, he took the small hessian sack he had procured for just this purpose, and then he stood absolutely still in the shadow of the cedar tree that rose beside the fence. The hotel was still, dark and malevolent. Harrison could feel the menace in the place and he figured it was an excellent home for Idaho's largest population of diamond-back rattlesnakes. He stood for maybe fifteen minutes, and then he saw movement to his left and caught sight of the tail of a snake as it disappeared under a rock. In a split second he was across the yard, had grabbed the tail and hauled the snake into the air. It was about six feet long, and Harrison cracked it like a whip and its head flew off. He stood for a moment, as it jerked, the rattle like a maraca under his fist. He could not see the head anywhere, but that did not matter. He laid the snake on the ground and squatted, the hotel brooding behind him. Carefully, he coiled the snake and placed it inside the hessian bag. When he was done, he vaulted the fence, checked his guns and crossed the street to the Manhattan Café.

He paused for a fraction of a second outside the door and then pushed it open. There were not many diners, just a couple in a booth and a trucker on his own drinking coffee. And there at the counter, slicing a piece of pie, sat a man in a T-shirt and jeans. He had a multicoloured kerchief tied at his throat: red, blue and black. On his right forearm was the tattoo of a grinning rat standing upright, a whiskey bottle in one hand and a six-gun in the other. Thirty long years had passed since Harrison had seen him – Ray 'the Probe' Martinez.

Harrison stood a moment, then stripped off his own jacket. He was wearing only a singlet underneath. He took a stool three down from Martinez. His own tattoo was exposed now and he felt the sudden weight of Martinez's glance. He kept looking ahead, and the waitress served him iced water and some coffee. Martinez spooned pie into his mouth and chewed very deliberately.

Neither of them spoke. Martinez did not look at him again and, for a moment, Harrison wondered if he even recognised him. Mentally, he checked his weapons, aware of just how hard his heart was beating after thirty long years. He needed all his senses working together in unison. Martinez was one of the most dangerous men he had ever met in his life. And then the irony struck him: the last time they had seen one another, Martinez had saved his life.

Martinez finished his pie, sipped coffee and dabbed at his mouth. Harrison heard the whistle of the approaching train, and Martinez tugged dollars from his pocket, tossed them on the counter and slipped off the stool. Picking up his coat and his pack, he stepped out into the sunshine. In the mirror behind the counter, Harrison saw him shuffle off up the sidewalk. He sat for a while longer, listening to the train and attempting to still his heart. Then the bell rang at the crossing and Harrison paid for the coffee, and the train thundered through Shoshone behind him. He knew it would slow and slow, until eventually it stopped for the drivers to swap over. Outside, he could see Martinez walking the length of the tracks.

The day was dying now, the sun sinking in the west and the shadows long. Harrison had to shade his eyes to see. Up ahead, Martinez disappeared from view. This was dangerous: Martinez out of sight and with his back to the sun. Harrison kept one hand on the butt of his 9mm. He walked on, with the train on his right, until he was a quarter of a mile outside town. He passed tanker cars and open-topped coal cars, and cars carrying lumber and potatoes. He passed enclosed metal containers in yellow, rust and blue. Then he came to the first wooden boxcar and saw that the door was open.

He slowed and, as he did so, the train started to lurch forward. Up ahead, the whistle blew across the empty Idaho landscape. Harrison grabbed hold of the rail and hauled himself into the semi-cool of the darkness.

He rolled on his side and for a moment thought he was alone. But then he saw the hunched figure, back to the far wall, knees drawn up to his chest and his hands hidden in his lap. Harrison shuffled backwards until he squatted against the other wall and there were eighteen feet between them, broken by the light from outside. Martinez did not move. Harrison did not move, but he had his pack, with the hessian sack inside, open and the .38 was loose in his boot.

The train gathered speed and the wheels rattled and clanked underneath them. Harrison watched Martinez, unable to see his eyes, and he figured Martinez was watching him. The train rolled on through Bliss, following the line of the Snake River towards Glenns Ferry. Harrison could see flashes of the river through the open door on his left, the sun sheeting across the surface in bands of silver.

'Johnny Buck.' The voice was quiet, almost a whisper, and it came at him out of the darkness. Harrison felt the hairs rise on the back of his hands and all his senses were tingling. 'Hello, Ray.'

'Last time I clapped eyes on you was in the Iron Triangle. You remember, Johnny, when that VC fucked with your head?'

'I remember.'

'You blew it, man. That was your last time in the hole. Guess you didn't have the stomach for it, after all.'

'Guess not, Ray.'

And silence between them, thirty years of it, laid out in grey like a ghost. Harrison eased his hand inside the hessian bag and gripped the snake.

'You ruined a good business, Johnny.'

'Did I?'

'Oh, yeah. I never woulda figured the Feds to bother enough to get wise.'

'Who'd give a fuck about a buncha hobos?'

'Who indeed?'

'You made a mistake, though, Ray. Sidetrack killed an English kid on his way to New Orleans. He was the son of a friend of mine.'

Martinez did not say anything for a moment and then he hissed breath. 'Well, there you go. You of all people. You come up here to arrest me, Johnny?'

'Something like that.'

'Got yourself a SWAT team backing you up?'

'Just me, Ray. I figured after thirty years, this was personal.'

Silence again and Harrison tensed. He could see Martinez draw one foot up a fraction further, and he gripped the body of the rattlesnake. Martinez had been more adept with a handgun than any other Rat in the platoon and Harrison knew he was still no match for him in a straight fight. He heard him sniff and cough, and the rays of the sun pierced the shadows across his face. His eyes were as wild as they had been thirty years previously.

Harrison hurled the snake. The rattle sounded and Martinez screamed like a child. He threw up his hands, as the snake thwacked against him and curled round his neck.

Harrison was across the floor in a flash. He hit him full in the face and Martinez's gun went spinning. Harrison knelt on his chest then, and pointed the 9mm at his face. Under him, Martinez was stiff as a board, back arched to breaking point, the weight of the snake still on him. His eyes bulged and saliva bubbled at his lips like a rabid dog. Harrison eased the snake's body from his throat and then showed him the decapitated end. He pressed the barrel of the 9mm against the flesh between his eyes.

'I quit the FBI, Ray. I'm a private citizen now, so I got no rules and I've a mind to pop you right here.'

Martinez's twitching was slowly subsiding.

'You wanna give me one good reason why I shouldn't? You know, gut-shoot you and drag your pants down to your ankles. Toss you over the side.'

Martinez looked him in the eye. 'A hole in the ground in Cu-Chi.'

Harrison stared at him – the hammer cocked on the 9mm, the barrel pressing into the skin of his forehead. He thought of Jean and all he had found and then lost. He thought of the other killings; the sedition, treason and murder. And then he heard the voice of that VC underground, calling out his name, and this man taking over as he fired six rounds in panic.

Reaching to his back pocket, he pulled out a set of handcuffs, then rocked back on his heels. 'Buckle up,' he said, and dropped the cuffs on to Martinez's chest.

They jumped off the train at Glenns Ferry, and Harrison called the FBI computer center at Pocatello, told them who he was and that he had Whiskey Six in his custody. He sat by the banks of the Snake River, watching the sun go down in the distance. Martinez sat with the cuffs on, a safe distance from the gun.

Three agents came down from Boise and took him away. As he was being led to the car, he looked back over his shoulder. 'You never forgot about the snakes, then, Johnny.'

Harrison had a cigarette burning and he let smoke bleed from his nostrils. 'Some kinda purgatory, huh?'

He took a flight to Wyoming and went back to Laramie for his truck. She fired up first time and he sat behind the wheel not knowing where he should go. He could go back to Idaho and check on that cabin by Payette Lake, but for some reason his instincts told him south. He did not hurry: there was much to think about and no special place to go. But a week after he left Wyoming, he parked his truck in the French Quarter and climbed the stairs to his apartment. Mrs Abbeyville, the old black lady who rented across the corridor, must have heard him because she opened her door and handed him his mail. He thanked her and went into his apartment, threw the windows open and lay down on the bed. The city sweated and he could hear music drifting from Bourbon Street.

He dozed, then woke and sat up, rubbing his eyes. He picked up the bundle of envelopes and shuffled through them. They were mostly bills, but then he saw a blue airmail envelope. It was postmarked London and his heart leapt against his ribs. He tore it open and found a plane ticket written in his name. The smile twitched at his lips and he opened the single sheet of paper accompanying it. There was Jean's handwriting and the words: *I love you. I miss you.* And her phone number. Harrison closed his eyes for a moment, then dialled the number and waited. Finally, it connected, rang in that peculiar English way, and then a voice drenched in sleep sounded in his ear.

'Hello, Jean Carey speaking.'

Harrison lay back on the bed, the heat on his face through the window. 'Hey, Miss Lady Mam,' he said. 'I'm sorry if I woke you.'